BENEATH THE
BURNING GROUND

D1253178

X

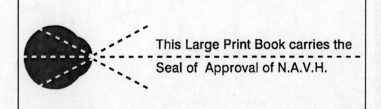

This Large Print Book carries the
Seal of Approval of N.A.V.H.

BENEATH THE BURNING GROUND

A FRONTIER STORY

JEANNE WILLIAMS

WHEELER PUBLISHING
A part of Gale, Cengage Learning

GALE
CENGAGE Learning

Detroit • New York • San Francisco • New Haven, Conn • Waterville, Maine • London

Wheeler Publishing Large Print Western.
The text of this Large Print edition is unabridged.
Other aspects of the book may vary from the original edition.
Set in 16 pt. Plantin.

LIBRARY OF CONGRESS CATALOGING-IN-PUBLICATION DATA

Williams, Jeanne, 1930–
    Beneath the burning ground : a frontier story / by Jeanne Williams.
        pages ; cm. — (Wheeler Publishing large print western)
        ISBN 978-1-4104-5577-2 (softcover) — ISBN 1-4104-5577-7 (softcover)
1. Farm life—Fiction. 2. Rural families—Fiction. 3. Fugitive slaves—Fiction. 4. Children of clergy—Fiction. 5. Antislavery movements—Fiction. 6. Frontier and pioneer life—Fiction. 7. Kansas—History—Civil War, 1861–1865—Fiction. 8. Domestic fiction. 9. Large type books. I. Title.
PS3573.I44933U55 2013
813'.54—dc23   2012043181

Published in 2013 by arrangement with Golden West Literary Agency.

Printed in the United States of America
1 2 3 4 5   17 16 15 14 13

For Francis and Albert Billings who were with me all the way on this story, and to June Wylie, who may have seen more remote parts of the Border than ever she had planned!

■ ■ ■ ■

PART ONE: THE UNDERGROUND RIVER

■ ■ ■ ■

CHAPTER ONE

It was the day! The day the Wares' new home would be built. Christy Ware's heart sang like the orioles flashing among the limbs of the great walnut as she climbed it and clambered from limb to limb, tying the ropes fastened to the corners of the wooden quilting frame till Ellen Ware, her mother, judged it to be at the right level. Neighbors were coming from miles around to help, most of them strangers. The women had sent word that, if Ellen had enough blocks pieced, they'd help her make a quilt while the men raised the house.

The giant walnut sheltered the Ware family that spring while they camped in the wagon after the long journey from Illinois. Spreading branches, feathery with new leaves and catkins, shielded them and nesting birds — the orioles, scarlet tanagers, and yellow-throated vireos — from rain and sun and caught the brunt of early April winds. If winter never came, thirteen-year-old Christy would have been happy to live under the tree forever — no floors to sweep or scrub, no windows to wash, and no furniture to polish except for her mother's piano which stood under the thickest cover of the tree and was protected by a piece of canvas except when her mother played nearly every night before her father read to them, more often from Marcus Aurelius or Plato than from the Bible, even though he was a Universalist minister.

"Isn't it strange," Jonathan Ware said, looking up at their leafy roof, "that black walnut's favored for cradles, but it's also the wood the Army, and everybody else, likes for gunstocks?"

Christy didn't much mind doing dishes after supper to the chorus of chuck-wills-widows, their smaller cousins the whip-poor-wills, and the whistling plaint of screech owls quavering amongst the hoots of great horned and barred owls. A fox watched the humans inquisitively now and then; Robbie barked raccoons away; a mother bear with her cub, small in the spring but growing fast with summer's bounty, often paused close enough to be seen outside the campfire's circle of light.

"That's a musical bear," Jonathan Ware teased his wife Ellen. "Or maybe she's exposing her cub to culture."

To avoid the jeers of her older brothers, Christy didn't say that the bear looked almost like a person when she stood erect on her back legs and reached for something. Christy believed the bear was the spirit of the forest and thrilled when it appeared, a moving shadow against the trees.

Sleeping under the sky was delightful, waking to the whole wide world, but winter would come, however hard it was to believe that in this heat of early August. The pigs, chickens, and sheep had pens and sheds where they could be shut at night to protect them from foxes, timber wolves, and panthers. Zigzagged rail fences, secured near the corners by upright posts, surrounded the cornfield and garden and discouraged wild hogs and the Wares' cattle and horses, if not the deer. Now it was time to build the humans' house.

Christy helped her father and brothers carry big flattish rocks for the foundations of what would be two cabins connected by a roofed breezeway or dogtrot. Piled in stacks perhaps eighteen inches high about six feet apart, foundations discouraged insects that could bore into the logs and destroy them. Jonathan and the boys had cut oak trees tall enough to make logs twenty and sixteen feet long. Piles of these ranged around the foundations, trimmed and hewn on two sides as smooth as broad-axe and foot adze could make them.

The Ware men folk rived out what Jonathan

reckoned were close to five thousand oak shingles to roof the cabins and the ten-foot space between. Everything was ready.

As Christy scrambled back and forth, adjusting the ropes, she thought of the neighbors she knew best, Ethan Hayes and Hester Ballard, and how she'd met them.

As soon as Ellen's pride, her Silver Laced Wyandottes, the most vulnerable of the Wares' creatures, had a log house, Christy's father and brothers, fourteen year-old Thos and sixteen-year-old Charlie, cleared and plowed several acres of bottom land. Stumps of black walnut, hackberry, oak, and hickory jutted from the broken earth to be grubbed or burned out as time allowed. Logs that could be used for fences or buildings were snaked by the oxen or horses to wherever they'd be handiest.

Christy and Thos had planted that first field to corn, following rough furrows that were little more than big clumps of sod bound by interlaced roots, ancient, undisturbed by the fires that swept through prairie and woodland after the first frost when sere high grass would explode from lightning or a chance spark. The family had sold their harrow, so Jonathan had made one by attaching four stout-limbed branches to an oak bar the horses could drag across the plowed land to break up the clumps.

Brother and sister carried hatchets. Where they found no cleft in the earth, they chopped niches in clods and covered the seed corn. They also planted pumpkin seeds to be protected by the growing corn, and string beans to grow up along the stalk. In Illinois, Jonathan and the boys had done all the planting, but, here, Christy had to help and she was glad.

Planting was much more to her taste than carding, spinning, and weaving. The earth smelled rich and moist and, where it was crumbly, felt good to her bare feet. And it was magic that seeds would grow into green bladed corn taller than her head, leafy vines with plump orange globes, and other vines weighted with flavorful green beans.

Nor had it all been work. As summer came on and the creek warmed, Christy and her brothers had swum in a limestone-bottomed hole near the house, and often there'd be a free hour or two when they could explore up and down the creek and in the woods around their clearing. Their best discovery had been a cave in the bluffs to the south. A low entrance opened into a chamber large enough for a score of people, and fantastic shapes formed by drips from the ceiling glittered in the muted light. It must have been used by Indians because a limestone slab near the opening had been hollowed out for grinding. A stone pestle rested at the edge. Who had used it last and when?

These pleasures, though, had been surrounded by all that had to be done. The shorthorn oxen, Moses and Pharaoh, brass knobs gleaming from the tips of their curving horns, broke an acre for sorghum cane, and a small plot for a garden. The sleek white animals, each weighing about twenty-seven hundred pounds, worked best for Thos. He praised and rubbed them down after their labor and put dollops of sorghum molasses in their grain.

While the men folk had planted the cane that would produce the family's sweetening once the big barrel in the wagon was gone, Christy and her mother had attacked the clods of the garden with spade, pitchfork, and hoe, but the sod roots had to decay before the earth could nourish tame seeds. Still, they had planted chunks of potato, each with two eyes, and were planting peas when a plump woman with light brown hair escaping her sunbonnet had jogged up on a little white mule with a couple of big sacks tied behind the saddle.

"I'm Hester Ballard, and please don't 'Miz Ballard' me." She had slid off the mule and given it a soft word and a pat. She had an open kind of face, eager and waiting, like a flower turned toward what the heavens sent, rain or sun. "I'm your nearest neighbor. Live a mile up the creek with my boy Lafe. Reckoned you'd be putting in a garden. Thought maybe you could use some watermelon, cucumber, turnip, and cabbage seeds, some rhubarb that was getting so big I had to divide the roots, onion buttons, and some cabbages I've had buried all winter. Plant them now and they'll grow seeds for next year."

She was about the age of Ellen, likely in her middle thirties. They had smiled, seeming to take to one another on sight. Christy could read her mother's mind, that it wouldn't be as lonesome here as she'd feared.

"Thank you kindly," Christy's mother had said. "I'm Ellen Ware and this is Christy. We'd be grateful for whatever you can spare, especially the onion buttons."

"Guess you know to plant them in the same row with cabbage. The onions' stink keeps away those pesky moths that lay eggs on the leaves to hatch into worms that'll just gobble up your cabbage."

As she spoke, Hester had dug in her apron pocket and handed Ellen three small cotton bags before she untied the lumpy sack from the saddle, lowered it to the ground, and carefully lifted out a dozen big cabbages. You could tell they'd been buried from the dirt that stuck to the leaves.

"Now, of course, you know to plant onions and turnips and 'taters, all the things that grow underground, in the dark of the moon, like you plant peas and such plants as grow above ground on the new moon."

"I'm afraid I don't know much about that, or planting by signs, Hester." Ellen had sounded apologetic. "I was brought up in town and my husband . . . well, he thinks all you need to do is plant when the ground's warm enough."

Hester had chuckled, a deep mellowness rising from her full bosom. "Lige Morrow does that when he leaves off hunting long enough to scratch out a little corn plot. Sits on the ground, bare-bottomed. When it don't chill him, he reckons the ground's ready for seeds. 'Course, you need to plant 'taters and onions a lot earlier. Maybe in March." Her eyebrows had puckered together over a snub nose that gave her somewhat the aspect of an opulent cat. "Once you plant by signs, you'll never do it any other way."

That sounded like more magic. "How does it work?" Christy had ventured.

Hester had puffed out her cheeks. "As well as paying attention to the moon, you keep track of the twelve signs of the zodiac. I use Doctor Jaynes's almanac . . . be glad to lend it to you. Each sign comes around twice a month and rules for two or three days. Plant cabbage when the signs are in the head, potatoes when they're in the feet. Mostly, you plant from head to heart, then from the thighs on down." She had given her head a decided shake. "Never plant in the bowels. Even when seeds sprout, they'll rot."

It *was* magic. Ellen had made a polite murmur, but Christy had said: "I'd truly like to read your almanac, Missus Ballard." She loved to read anything, and, although they'd each brought some of their favorite books, many had been given to the academy where Jonathan Ware used to teach.

After the planting was done, Jonathan had wanted to start on their home, but Ellen had said: "What's the use of planting if wild hogs and deer get at the sprouts? And I saw a big wolf slinking up to the sheep yesterday. It was all Robbie could do to run him off. Build fences first, Jonathan, and shelters for the pigs and sheep. We can wait."

That was when big, yellow-haired Ethan Hayes, long legs and moccasined feet dangling from his white mule, first had come to help. "I run a tannery a couple of miles downstream." The fringes of his supple buckskin shirt had swayed as he slid off the mule and hobbled her. "Been too busy finishing hides for some Cherokees up from Indian Territory to be a good neighbor, but my woman and boys can look after things today while I help you split rails, since that's what you're doing." He handed Ellen a plump cotton sack and a small covered tin pail. "Butter my woman churned last night and some walnut meats."

"Please thank her for me, Mister Hayes," Ellen had said. "I hope to meet her soon."

"Maybe when we raise your house," the young giant had said. "Allie stays right busy with the three boys and our baby girl, not to mention the tannery, but she's glad to have close neighbors."

Without being bossy, Hayes had soon led the work as they chose the straightest and longest of the previously felled black walnuts. Jonathan and the boys had split rails before, but Hayes had used his axe with deft ease, trimming off boughs before measuring off lengths and chopping his log in two with such accuracy that one side of each cut looked as if it had been sawed. He had taken Thos for his partner while Jonathan and Charlie worked on another log.

Hayes had made four oak wedges, tossed two to Jonathan, and made two mauls from oak limbs about six inches thick and the length of an axe, trimming handles with his pocket knife. Hoisting his well-sharpened axe, he had brought it down in the middle of the larger end of the log. Thos had set the iron wedge in the cut. Three blows from Hayes's maul had driven it in and split the log halfway open. As directed, Thos had thrust the wood wedges in to hold the crack open while Hayes set the iron wedge farther down the log. A few more swings of the maul and the log had cracked in half. The halves and resulting quarters had been split in the same way.

By dinner, there were piles of rails ranged around the field and all the best felled walnut trees were used. Hayes had started to pile into the food, but stopped, blushing, and bowed his head as Jonathan asked a blessing. As he had heaped his plate with cornbread, ham with gravy and wild greens, Hayes had said: "Mister Ware. . . ."

"Jonathan, please." Jonathan grinned. "We're neighbors."

"Jonathan." Hayes's sun-bleached eyebrows met above his clear blue eyes. "Mind a straight question?"

"Not if you don't mind a straight answer."

"When you prayed just now you said something about all men being brothers. Did you mean Negroes?"

"Why, yes." Jonathan smiled at Ellen. "I mean women, too, though the language could be clearer. If what you want to know is whether we think slavery is right, the answer is no."

"Kind of figgered that. I don't favor it myself, though I'm sure no Abolitionist." He sighed, chewed a few bites, and put down his fork. "Something awful's happened, Jonathan, Missus Ware. I didn't want to tell you till I got a notion of what kind of folks you are. Andy McHugh, the blacksmith near Trading Post just a mile or so west of the Kansas line, Andy brought some hides for

tanning yesterday. And some real bad news."
He glanced at Christy.

"Our children live in the world and have to know about it," Ellen said, although she was pale.

Hayes took a deep breath. "You'll likely know that Missourians who want Kansas to enter the Union as a slave state crossed the border in droves at the territorial election last year, threatened Free Staters away from the polls with guns and Bowie knives, and voted in a proslavery territorial legislature that still runs things. So the Free Staters elected their own legislature and governor. Early this month, a grand jury indicted the Free State leaders on charges of treason, so last week, May Twenty-First, proslave bigwigs like used-to-be Senator Atchison and George Clarke, the Indian agent down at Fort Scott, led what was well nigh an army into Lawrence and helped proslave lawmen arrest the Free State leaders for treason."

Ellen's hand went to her throat. "Lawmen took part in this?"

Hayes gave a harsh laugh. "Bless you, ma'am, Sheriff Jones hollered it was the happiest day of his life when the Free State Hotel was blown up. Two newspaper offices were wrecked to smithereens, and the proslavers looted stores and houses before they rode home."

"But. . . ."

"There's worse." Hayes shook his bright head. "When word spread about Atchison bringing in his Platte County Rifles from Missouri, Free Staters from all around hurried to defend Lawrence, but it was sacked before they got there. Naturally they were mad enough to kill . . . and old John Brown and his boys did just that."

Into the silence, Jonathan asked: "Who's John Brown?"

"A devil or prophet right out of the Old Testament, accordin' to your lights." Ethan frowned. "For sure, he's a red-hot Abolitionist. Five of his sons settled over on Pottawatomie Creek in the winter of Eighteen Fifty-Five. He joined them last fall. They got up a militia, the Pottawatomie Rifles, that went to help Lawrence."

"So when they knew the town was ravaged. . . ."

"Old Brown had his men kneel while he prayed. Andy McHugh says he called long and loud to Jehovah, Lord God of Moses and Gideon and Joshua, the Liberators. Then he told his men he was going to do something that had to be done, that they all knew how proslavers on the Pottawatomie had warned Free Staters to get out or be killed. Old Brown said he wanted only those men with him who would obey him without question."

Ethan paused, swallowed, and went on in a strained voice. "His son, John, Junior, must have had an idea of what was coming. He wouldn't go. But four of Brown's sons did, and several more of the militia. That night they camped a mile from Dutch Henry's Crossing, sharpened their short swords, and decided who to call on. Next morning they went to Patrick Doyle's place. The Doyles were dirt poor and had no slaves, but they were strong proslavers, and the sons, one of them only eighteen, had run Free Staters away from the polls at the last election.

"Brown's party took them outside. Patrick tried to run. Old Brown shot him." Hayes shuddered. "That was the only pistol fired. Brown's sons hacked the young men to death with swords. They did the same for Allen Wilkinson, who was elected to the proslave legislature . . . when Missourians were allowed to vote and Free State men run off. Dutch Henry Sherman, a loud proslaver, wasn't home, but the Browns took his brother to the river, killed him, and threw him in."

"God have mercy on them," Ellen whispered.

"All of them, the Browns, too." Jonathan's lips were pale. "What horrors in the name of God! They must be insane."

"It's said a streak of it runs in old Brown's family."

Little Beth was fussing. Ellen picked her up and cradled her closely. "What will happen now?"

"Why, ma'am, the proslavers will try to get Brown, but I have a notion we'll hear a lot more about him before he's done. Free Staters like Andy McHugh hate what happened, but they've got to defend themselves or be run out of the country."

Jonathan looked grave. "I'm afraid it won't be settled till Kansas, slave or free, enters the Union."

"Maybe not then. But there's not much we can do about it except be glad we live in Missouri." Hayes stowed away his last few bites of food and got to his feet. "Let's go chop trees and make rails."

That afternoon, two to a tree, the boys and men chopped from either side. Fist-size chips flew till the trees wavered, groaned as the heartwood wrenched apart, and fell.

"That Ethan's a master with the axe," Jonathan Ware said after the young man had vanished into twilight and the woods. Christy was sure her father was trying to make things seem normal and right after Ethan's terrible news. Jonathan gave his wife a hug. "Two hundred rails! We'll start building fences in the morning. When we get tired of that, we'll split more rails, and, when we're tired of that, we'll rive white oak to cure for our floors."

The boys looked glum. They hadn't had a chance yet to swim or fish or just explore. Jonathan caught their look and grinned, gripping them by their shoulders. "Cheer up,

23

lads. There's so much work on a new place that you've always got a choice of it."

"I'm glad we have lots of the same birds we did at home . . . in Illinois, I mean." Ellen smiled at the bluebird braving the Wyandottes to pursue a bug near the chicken house. She poured cornbread batter into the Dutch oven setting among the embers of their cook fire. "It makes this place seem friendlier. Like Cavalier, the Silver Laced Wyandotte rooster, crowing and showing off to his wives."

"No wonder he crows." Jonathan chuckled. "He has a house while we're still roosting under this tree."

Ellen sighed and pinned dark braids tighter on top of her head before she sat down in the rocking chair to nurse Beth who was not quite a year old. The chair and rosewood piano looked strange beneath the tree, but Christy understood that they gave her mother a lot of comfort. She'd need it after hearing about old John Brown. Christy shivered and pushed away the imagined glint of those whetted swords, escaped to memories of their journey.

The Wares' possessions had been winnowed down to what would fit in the big covered wagon pulled by Moses and Pharaoh, and the Dearborn wagon drawn by Queenie and Jed, bays of Morgan blood, who could plow all week and race on Sunday. Queenie's chestnut colt, Lass, in spite of her mother's anxious whickers, skittered ahead, around, and behind while she was fresh of a morning, but, after a few hours, the little filly trudged closely as she could to the mare.

Of humans and creatures, only the chickens, Ellen, and the baby Beth rode all the time in the Dearborn wagon, the cages roped securely on top of Ellen's piano. After the space between the piano's legs was packed tightly with dishes wrapped in bedding, panes of glass for windows in their new home, and other fragile things, it was swathed in featherbeds and quilts which in turn were protected by heavy canvas. Except for the carved maple rocking chair that had soothed four generations of Jonathan's family as they spread west from Rhode Island, the family brought no other furniture. The wardrobe, table, and chairs Ellen's mother had brought from Kentucky were needed less than the John Deere walking plow with its steel-share Jonathan bought from the nearby factory at Moline, Illinois, or scythes, hoes, spades, axes, and other tools.

"I helped my uncle in his carpenter's shop," Jonathan consoled Ellen when she wept to see their four-poster bed and his treasured desk hauled away by the neighbor who'd bought them. "I can make everything you want, love."

Their marriage bed? The cradle she and her children had slept in? The great oak chest her great-grandparents had brought over from England? She turned against him and sobbed. "Oh, Jonathan!"

He stroked her soft dark hair. "Remember why we're going, Ellen. This small farm can only support one family. The boys are growing up. With what we've got from selling this place . . . and, yes, our treasures . . . we can take up one hundred and sixty acres in western Missouri for a dollar twenty-five an acre, enough land for Thos and Charlie, if it came to that, but, when they're twenty-one, each can buy his own quarter section."

"Yes, but. . . ."

"Otherwise, in four or five years, my dear, they'll head West and we'd be lucky to ever see them again." He looked at her with that coaxing supplication in his blue eyes that his wife could never resist.

"But where will you find a school to teach at or Universalists to preach to?" she asked. "From all we hear, Missourians outside of Saint Louis are hardshell Baptists and Methodists with a sprinkle of Presbyterians."

He laughed fondly. "Folks will come to services just to hear you play your piano."

Her eyes were troubled. "Slavery's strong there."

"Only along the Missouri and Mississippi Rivers where big planters grow tobacco and hemp. We'll settle in the southwest where there's plenty of the kind of land not wanted for plantations, but where a family can make a living."

"I suppose I have to be grateful that you don't want to go to Kansas!" Remembering that conversation, Christy shivered again. All they'd known about Kansas Territory, then, was that it was a forlorn place where settlers fought tooth and nail over whether it would join the Union as a slave state or free one.

Ellen wiped her eyes and went back to packing.

They'd brought milk buckets, candle molds, a churn, spinning wheel, loom, tubs, sad irons, the big iron kettle for washing clothes and making soap, smaller ones and a Dutch oven and skillets for cooking, all with feet so they could stand in coals and ashes in the fireplace. The iron tea kettle had feet, too, but the griddle hung from a crane.

The new kitchen, at least, would soon seem familiar with the wooden spice box with six drawers, coffee grinder, crocks, and wooden bowls and spoons. Besides Ellen's cherished silver and china, for everyday there was glazed blue earthenware delft, and iron forks, spoons, and case knives.

Speeded by traveling by steamboat down the Mississippi to Hannibal, then overland to pick up the Boone's Lick Trail west, they'd jounced along the roads and taken ferries across the rivers. Cavalier, the arrogant Silver-Laced Wyandotte rooster, frequently squawked with indignation and glared at the people who dared coop him up, flaunting his rose comb above the demure ones of his two dozen wives. They had, with difficulty, been chosen by Ellen as the best of her more than a hundred hens. For them, Jonathan contrived three long cages with perforated false bottoms that let droppings fall below into a drawer that could be pulled out and dumped as necessary. In spite of this consideration and plenty of grain, Cavalier pecked if a hand came near, and crowed any time he felt like it, which was often in the night.

Jonathan, Thos, and Charlie took turns driving the oxen while walking at their side, driving the team, or herding along the fawn-colored Jerseys — Lady Jane, Guinevere, Bess, and Goldie — who were all heavy with calves, and Mildred, Cleo, and Nosey, the Suffolk ewes, who lambed on the journey. Most laggard and apt to stray after last fall's acorns or a succulent mushroom were the Poland China sows, Patches and Evalina, whose white-spotted black bodies were swollen with piglets. Robbie, the little border collie, kept them moving with firm patience till he got a thorn in his paw. For a day, he rode across Jed's withers. They were the best of friends. When Jed was grazing, Robbie often jumped to his back and had as much of a ride as good-natured Jed was inclined to give him.

They had traveled so long that it was still hard to believe that this was where they'd live always, on the knoll above Clear Creek that flowed into the Marais des Cygnes River. Very near the Kansas border they were, only two miles. So close that five of the ten women now working on all four sides of the quilt lived across the boundary and hadn't been known to the Wares, except by name, till they came with their men folk to help that morning.

As if by common consent, no one brought up old John Brown's slaughter on Pottawatomie Creek or the turbulent events that had followed, news Ethan Hayes had passed along from his customers. A company of Missouri sharpshooters had gone to take Brown, but been defeated. Federal troops kept the Free-State legislature from convening in Topeka. James Lane, a Free-State firebrand, brought six hundred like-minded settlers in through Iowa and Nebraska to make up for those stopped by Border Ruffians at the Missouri border, and Free Staters were besieging four proslavery strongholds.

On this neighborly day, though, no one spoke of the fury raging in Kansas Territory. Tall, fine-boned Lydia Parks, eldest daughter of widower Simeon Parks, a Quaker, who had a grist mill just across in Kansas on the Marais des Cygnes, took tiny stitches to finish off a corner. She made such a neat job of that critical task that Lucinda Maddux decreed: "Best you finish all the corners, Lydia. You've a rare knack for it."

Lucinda, graying and ample, took authority as the oldest woman there. She lived with her husband Arly and their youngest son Tom across the creek from the Hayeses on the road to Butler, the Bates county seat. Their oldest son, she'd explained, was still hunting gold in California, the two middle ones and their families had settled in Oregon, and two married daughters remained in Tennessee.

Lydia Parks's pale skin warmed with a blush at Lucinda's compliment. That turned her almost pretty, although she made her thin face even more so by combing her black hair into a knot as tight as any of the older women's. She must have grown up mothering twelve-year-old David whose birth caused their mother's death. Their brother Owen was married to Harriet, the young woman with braids plump and golden-brown as ripe wheat, who kept leaving the quilt to nurse her fretful baby.

"The mite's teething." Harriet's mother, Mildred Morrison, was buxom where her daughter was pleasantly rounded, but they had the same bright blue eyes. "Don't hurt a baby to cry. Oh, well, that'll come with the next one."

Harriet flushed and tightened her lips, taking up her needle with a jerk. Apparently Mrs. Morrison shared the young couple's cabin, but, from several overheard remarks, Christy surmised that the widow would be glad to relieve Lydia of keeping house for Simeon.

Smoothing the rumpled moment, Susie Parks, black hair escaping a French knot to wave softly about her face, smiled at her hostess. "Let's embroider our names on the back of the quilt so you'll never forget us."

"Not much chance of that." Ellen smiled around at her neighbors. "You've all been so kind. . . ."

"Lord, child, what are neighbors for?" Lucinda, to Christy's fascinated horror, took a pinch of snuff. "Wish we'd had help when we came here. We lived in the wagon, under and around it, till Arly and Tom got a round-log house built. That was just to do us till there was time to make a good hewn log cabin, but we're in it to this day." She looked admonishingly at the younger women. "Don't ever let your man entice you into a round-log hut, my dears, or there you may stay the rest of your days."

"Then there's them as thinks they're too good for logs, and freight in lumber from a sawmill." Nora Caxton was as withered as her husband Watt was sleek and dapper. They lived on the other side of the Hayeses. Watt

31

raised mules and traded in them, cows, and horses. Nora's scraggly rust-hued hair was knotted on top of her skull. Wisps of it jounced as she gave her head a sharp nod and stared accusingly at Lottie Franz. "Both my grandads fought the British in Eighteen Twelve. I had a great-grandaddy at Valley Forge. Don't seem right that some come in from foreign lands and, right off, have things better than us who been born in this country four generations or more."

Lottie regarded the other woman with wide, calm eyes. "But, Missus Caxton, Emil fought in the War of Eighteen Twelve. He had just come to this country, a boy of sixteen. He limps because a musket ball shattered his leg. His only son, my husband, was killed in the war with Mexico seven years ago."

"You're sure not foreigners," Hester said. "Anyway, except for Indians, everybody's family came from somewhere else. Not that long ago, either."

Christy wandered over to watch her father, Ethan Hayes, Simeon Parks, and Owen Parks split out two-inch thick puncheons or floor-boards. Sill beams the length of the cabin had been positioned on the foundation; floor beams hewed off at the ends rested snugly on the sills about four feet apart. Emil Franz, Andy McHugh, and Watt Caxton trimmed off the underside of the ends of the pun-cheons to fit tight over the sleepers.

The boys had the task of smoothing the boards with adzes and knives. Besides Thos and Charlie, the oldest Hayes boys, tow-headed Matthew and Mark, there was a flame-haired skinny Irish orphan who lived with the Parkses, David Parks, and Lafe Ballard. Christy liked Hester so much that she'd expected to like her son, but, on the occasions he'd stopped by, he'd watched her with his pale eyes till she felt handled, and once he'd trod hard on Robbie's tail and pretended it was an accident.

Barrel-chested Arly Maddux, shaggy gray hair and beard framing his red face, moved from group to group with suggestions. Ethan said weeds grew higher than corn in his fields. That didn't matter much since his fences were so poorly kept that hogs and cattle were in the field more than they were out. He was of vaguely Baptist persuasion and his favorite theme was infant damnation.

"A hair more this way, boys!" he called to Andy McHugh, the gaunt red-haired blacksmith from across the border, and Owen Parks, as they placed the first end log in the space left before the first sleeper and lap-jointed the edges to fit over the sill.

After the second end log was in place, Ethan, the acknowledged master at notching, hewed two sides of the end of a log and hewed the top at an angle. The end of a second log, hewn at the ends by Andy, was placed crosswise on top of the first. Using a straight board to measure the angle of the bottom log, Ethan notched the top one to fit perfectly across the first, then did the same to the other end.

The men and big boys settled into a rough rhythm, some laying the sills and sleepers of the second cabin, others splitting puncheons, and Jonathan and Andy hewing log ends and placing them for Ethan's notching, so accurately that he seldom had to lift up a log to trim it more. The resulting dovetails locked the logs so tightly that the cabin would stand solidly as long as the logs were sound, and they were oak, so that should be till long after Christy had grandchildren, hard as it was to believe she ever would.

Cabin-raising was much more absorbing than quilting. When Beth first roused and whimpered from her quilt beneath the tree, Christy hoped she'd quit fussing, at least till Ethan finished this notch. Alternating sides, the logs were now waist high.

Beth's fretting changed to a howl. Sighing, Christy turned from watching Ethan and started for the baby. She stopped with a gasp. That Irish boy of the Parkses — Dan O'Brien. He was cuddling Beth.

He'd trimmed puncheons so smoothly that Ethan had praised him, and the Parks sisters said he was a rare fiddler, but what could he know about babies, American ones, anyway?

What if he dropped her?

Avoiding playing children and the sprawl of Watt Caxton's hounds, Christy sped to the rail-thin lad and reached for Beth, who treacherously gurgled. The baby patted a broken nose that was brown enough to almost hide the freckles that spilled over high-angled cheek bones.

He grinned at Beth but ignored Christy, even turned a bit away. "Here, I'll take her," Christy said. She hoped their mother hadn't heard Beth wail or seen this Irisher get to her before Christy did.

"Indeed, you were in no hurry before."

Stung, Christy snapped: "I came as soon as I heard her."

"That you did not." A foreign lilt flavored his words, but he spoke with precision that must have come from living some years with well-educated Quakers. "You cocked your head this way when the little one fretted, but then you went back to watching Ethan Hayes."

"If you've nothing better to do than spy on a person. . . ."

"I do. This." He smiled at the baby and said something soft in his own tongue. That widened his narrow face, brought a shine to smoke-gray eyes, and made him almost nice to look at.

"She needs changing," Christy snapped. "Are you going to do that?"

It was a chore Thos and Charlie avoided like the plague although her father often did it. "Bring me a diaper," said this unbelievable boy.

"No!" she hissed. "Give her to me. Right now!"

He shrugged and handed her over, but, before he moved away, he pierced Christy with a cool smoke-gray stare that expressed his opinion of her care-giving.

Hateful thing! Christy lugged Beth to the wagon and changed her, cleaning Beth's petal-soft skin. Ellen Ware was particular about keeping the baby dry and fresh so she wouldn't get a rash. Thank goodness for the safety pins that made the task easier. A supply of them, regular pins, and needles were in her mother's sewing basket.

"Do you know you're almost a year old?" Christy asked. Beth laughed and made an assortment of sounds. "You won't remember Illinois at all, or camping under the tree, or how the house was built. But I'll tell you. . . ."

"Christina!" called Ellen. "Grind the coffee, fill the water buckets, and then bring butter and milk and cottage cheese . . . buttermilk, too . . . from the cold-box."

Ellen didn't like to get their drinking water from the creek, and it was a chore to fetch all they needed from a quarter mile away, so Jonathan and the boys had dug for water in a dozen places, but still hadn't struck water for a well. They'd try again when they weren't so busy, but, till then, they'd dug a hole to fit a deep trough made of oak. This was kept full of water in which to place crocks of the rich milk, butter, buttermilk, and cream that came from Lady Jane, Guinevere, Goldie, and Bess after their calves had all the milk they needed. Rived clapboards fastened together with pegs made a cover.

As she ground the roasted coffee beans, Christy reflected that the oldest girl in a family should be twins to help with all the woman work. Charlie and Thos put in long hard hours, but they got to sit and eat while she jumped up for more corndodgers or gravy, and they settled back in comfort while she did the dishes. They wore the knees and elbows out of the clothes she helped her mother sew, and that *after* carding, spinning, dyeing, and weaving the cloth.

After she filled the water buckets, Christy brought the butter she'd churned yesterday, the cream she'd skimmed that morning from last night's milk, the cottage cheese drained out last night from simmered curds, and crockery pitchers of fresh milk and buttermilk. She put these on the beautifully grained walnut table her father had made as soon as the wood had cured enough.

As the women on each side finished an arm-length of quilt, they rolled it up and hurried to put out their contributions to the feast. When there wasn't an uncovered inch on the walnut table, a long table improvised from floorboards for the loft laid across sawhorses was soon crowded to the edges. Christy used tongs to fill a basket with roasting ears pulled from the ashes, steam-cooked to juicy tenderness in their husks. From the Wares' garden came bowls of green beans, creamed peas, beets, and sweet potatoes mashed and sweetened with molasses, and, of course, Ellen had made lots of cornbread and pones.

Hester swung a kettle of hominy up beside her crock of corn pudding. Yellow-haired Allie Hayes was a robust match for her big husband, but it was all she could do to carry a wood platter holding two roasted wild ducks stuffed with nuts, herbs, and sweet potatoes. The Caxtons brought fried squirrel, and the Madduxes contributed stewed doves.

Boys carried up watermelons and musk melons put in the creek to chill. It was hard to say whether the greatest treat was light bread made from wheat ground at the Parks' mill, or the apple and blackberry pies Lottie Franz brought from their wagon while Emil set a basket of grapes on the table and stowed a tub of fragrant apples underneath.

"This old rooster pecked me one time too often," Catriona McHugh said, as she nudged a Dutch oven of chicken and dumplings a safe distance from the table edge. "Onery as he was, he ought to have plenty of flavor!"

Jonathan Ware was a Universalist minister, but, of course, he invited Arly Maddux, as a guest and Baptist parson, to ask the blessing. Arly was in high flight when Watt Caxton's slumbering hounds roused and set up clamorous barking.

"Call off your dogs, Watt!" boomed a voice from the creek.

"I'll bid mine stay here and we'll have no ruckus."

"Willin' to bet mine can't whup yours?" Watt bellowed.

"You want a fight, Watt, I'll give you one."

"Treat your dogs like they was human," Watt grumbled, but he yelled and swore at his hounds that cowered to their bellies and hushed.

The man ambling up from the creek was tall and lank. With summer, Ethan had quit wearing his leather shirt, but the stranger wore one and pants as well, with beads worked along the fringed seams. His sunstreaked sandy hair was tied back with a thong. He carried a rifle under one arm, and the other hand gripped the legs of a big turkey slung over his shoulder.

Beside him like a whisper moved a dark, slender girl in red calico, the only dress that hadn't been made from homespun material. Like the man, she wore beaded moccasins. Her black hair was braided with red ribbon into a single plait that hung below her waist. She carried a covered wooden bucket.

"Sorry I didn't get this turkey to you in time for dinner, but we were getting you some honey." The stranger dropped the handsomely feathered bird on the grass near the trunk of the walnut. He thrust out a hand to Jonathan. "I'm Lige Morrow. This is my wife Sarah. We live across the creek and up a ways."

Ellen came to greet the Morrows, accepting the bucket of honey with delight. "We can't take all of this," she demurred. "Let me pour some for us into a pail and. . . ."

"It's all for you." Sarah spoke better English than most of the gathering except for the Wares and Quakers. Her eyes tilted upward, golden green. Her skin was creamy rose and gold, so rich and smooth you wanted to touch her. "My bees send it willingly."

"Well, then," said Ellen with a smile, "thank them for us, very kindly."

Sarah nodded. "There are many flowers this year. They make much honey. So I ask six hives if they will spare honey for you."

"You didn't smoke them into the top of the hive?" Emil Franz's shrewd gray eyes studied the hunter's woman.

"No."

"You had to stun 'em some way," Nora Caxton argued.

Lige stepped closer to his wife. "The bees

don't sting Sarah. She moves around the bee-gums with no trouble at all." He grimaced. "They'll sure take after me, though."

"Ain't natural." Nora squinted at Sarah and curled her lip.

"Must be redskins have a kind of wild smell."

Lige's yellow eyes had the sheen of a great cat's, but his tone was genial. "Miz Caxton, I'll bet you venison for the winter that, if folks was to shut their eyes and sniff at you and Sarah, they'd say you're the one smells wild. Like a polecat that's been dead a week."

CHAPTER TWO

Lige Morrow spoke with a smile, so gently that no one could believe their ears for a minute. Watt Caxton went red to the roots of his greasy black hair. "Why, you shiftless, woods-runnin' squawman! I'll. . . ."

Morrow raised an eyebrow. "Take a pot shot at me from the brush?"

Arly Maddux puffed forward. "Now, neighbors! Put by your wrath. The Good Book says . . . 'Be kindly affectioned one to another with brotherly love.' "

Jonathan, too, had moved between them and looked from one man to the other. "I'll be grateful if you'll both forget the hard words and join in the feast. Indeed, we'd be grieved, my family and I, if our cabin-raising was marred with neighbors falling out."

Nora Caxton sniffled. "No need for you to jump on your high horse and gallop, Lige Morrow. All I said was. . . ."

"Sarah's half Osage and half French." Tautness flowed out of Morrow and he grinned at his wife. "Sweet as her honey most of the time but stings like her bees when she's mad."

"Otherwise, you wouldn't notice," Sarah Morrow retorted. She, a brilliant poppy beside a withered nettle, smiled at Nora. "I don't mind to be called a redskin, Missus Caxton. At the Osage mission, our priest used to say . . . 'An Indian scalps his enemies, but a white man skins his friends.' "

"Watt, she nailed your hide to the wall," chortled Arly, clapping the trader on the shoulder. "Gather 'round and let me finish the blessing before the food gets cold."

As the crowd drifted back to the tables, Christy heard Lafe Ballard whisper to Matthew, the eldest Hayes boy: "Wonder what color that squaw is . . . you know, in her woman parts?"

Matthew, tow-headed like Mark and Luke — their folks had just started with the books of the New Testament in naming their boys — reddened up to his big ears. "You hadn't ought to talk like that! If Lige hears you, *you'll* be colored black and blue!"

Lafe Ballard giggled. He had delicate features, girl-pretty, with a deep-cleft chin, eyes so pale a blue they had almost no tint, and waving silvery hair. "Bet you don't even know what women look like under their drawers. Sometime you ought to watch your mama. . . ."

Matthew knocked him flat. Lafe was up like

43

a cat, but he didn't strike back although he and Matthew were fairly matched enough — Lafe taller by a few inches, Matthew heavier and broader. They were at the back of the gathering. Only Christy saw and heard them.

"I'll get you for this, Matt Hayes!" Lafe's snarl was muffled by the shirt tail he pressed to a bleeding lip.

"Hey," growled Matthew, clenching brown fists, "come down in the trees where no one'll stop us and I'll give you more'n you want!"

Lafe's eyes glittered like moonlit ice, but he turned and swaggered toward the feast Arly had finally blessed to his satisfaction. People here certainly seemed quick to fight, Christy thought. And Beth was fussing again. Christy sighed and picked her up, joining the older children who'd eat after the younger ones had been helped by their mothers. The men ate first, of course, as they did on any occasion where everyone couldn't sit down at the same time.

After dinner, Harriet Parks and Christy did the stacks of dishes while Ellen Ware put together a stew from leftovers and more vegetables. Lige dug a pit and built a fire in it while he cleaned and dressed the turkey, stuffed it with peppergrass, wild onions, and nuts, molded clay around it, and put the fowl among the coals in the pit, raking some on around the sides and top. He covered the bird with earth and built another fire on top.

"Keep the fire going till the middle of the afternoon, will you, sis?" he asked Christy. "By supper that ole gobbler will taste plumb scrumptious!"

So she kept an eye on that fire, but, when she wasn't adding wood or minding Beth or running errands for the women, she watched the men lap joint ceiling beams to the lengthwise logs paralleling the sills, wall and floor the lofts, secure steeply slanted rafters to the ridgepoles, and split out lathing.

For the first time, nails forged by Andy McHugh were used — his gift along with hinges for the doors and shutters and a rod and kettle hooks for the fireplace. The ring of hammers reverberated as lathing was nailed to the rafters and shingling began with the bottom row. Two shingles were nailed side-by-side to the lathing, and a third nailed across the crack. The next row overlapped the first by about three inches, and, at the peak, the top shingle on one side overlapped the other by three or four inches so rain wouldn't find its way into the joining.

Meanwhile, Emil Franz and Ethan Hayes, the best craftsmen with wood, used axes and Emil's saw to cut out a door, fireplace, and two windows in each cabin. They then used cured walnut to make doors, shutters, and frames, pegging them into the cut logs. Christy held the panes in place inside the frames of one window in each cabin while

Emil pressed gray clay found near the spring around the edges on both sides. The other windows would be open in fine weather and, in foul, closed with shutters.

Much as she liked watching the men, Christy hurried to tend to Beth when she whimpered, not wishing that aggravating Irish boy to have another chance to fault her. As arm-length after arm-length of the quilt was rolled up, Sarah took tiny stitches that rivaled those of Lydia Parks.

"The nuns taught us," she explained. "We had lessons in reading, arithmetic, penmanship, history, and geography at the mission, but we learned cooking, spinning, weaving, and housekeeping, too."

Lucinda Maddux primmed her lips and yanked a recalcitrant thread. "You had to worship statues, I'll be bound . . . idolaters, that's what Catholics are!"

"We don't worship idols." Sarah Morrow gazed calmly at the minister's wife. "We ask the Holy Mother and the saints to intercede for us, but that's because they were human once. God is beyond our finite minds."

"Fi- . . . what?" demanded Lucinda. "They taught you to sew, I'll have to admit, but what's the use of a . . . woman . . ." — she amended hastily — "learning all that stuff? I only got to go to school a few winter terms. I was needed to help at home, but I can read my Bible, write my mother back in Tennessee, and cipher a little. That's all a body needs. Arly can't read at all, but God called him to preach."

"If you can read your Bible, ma'am, you read very well, indeed." Sarah's tone was all respect, but Christy thought she detected a hint of a smile.

"Your dress is beautiful." Susie Parks, whose homespun linsey-woolsey, probably dyed brown with walnut bark, cast wistful eyes at the crimson that would so become her fair skin and black hair. "The skirt's so full you could wear a crinoline under it."

Lydia frowned at her younger sister. "It's vanity to puff out one's skirts with a connivance of horsehair, and costly to boot."

"But it takes the place of at least three petticoats," Susie argued.

"I used to wear ten in Ohio," put in Mildred Morrison, "except in winter when some were quilted. It's so inconvenient to wash here, though, that I make do with five. I think I'll ask my son Barney to fetch me a crinoline from Saint Louis next time he's there. He freights on the Santa Fé Trail, you know." The buxom widow, whose taffy hair frizzed oddly at the temples, preened a moment before she sent a disparaging glance at her daughter Harriet, young Owen Parks's wife. "Barney's a fine son. Nothing's too much trouble for that lad if he reckons it'll please his mother."

"Maybe he thinks that can be done." Harriet, yellow-brown head bowed, stabbed her needle through the quilt.

Mildred sucked in her breath. Before she could blast her daughter, Lydia Parks said: "Father said only yesterday that he hopes ladies here won't feel obliged to keep up with the frivolities of fashion."

Mrs. Morrison looked annoyed. She had made quite a fuss of forcing seconds of her blackberry cobbler on widower Simeon. Appearing not to notice, Lydia finished the last corner and got to her feet, flexing her fingers and sighing with pleasure in a task well done.

"There you are, Missus Ware. It's a beautiful quilt."

Lottie Franz nodded and her blue eyes glowed. "Always you'll remember, when you look at it, this happy day your home was built."

"It will be a happy house." Sarah Morrow's laughter trilled with the tanager's hoarser song, flashing above them, his scarlet brilliant as her gown. "I will ask the Holy Mother to ask her Son that this quilt warm and comfort all who rest beneath it." She said it as matter-of-factly as Mildred Morrison had announced her intention of asking her son for a crinoline.

Before Lucinda Maddux could say something to match her scowl, Ellen said: "Thank you, Sarah dear. It will pleasure me every time I see the quilt to remember all of you.

Christy, you can't climb the tree with the men folk around, so go ask Luke Hayes if he'll shinny up and untie the frame on the near end. We'll leave the curtain hanging on the frame to show the men we've accomplished something, too."

Thousands and thousands of tiny stitches must have gone to make the quilt. It was the Tree of Paradise pattern Ellen had copied from one of her grandmother's before moving to Illinois. Every good piece of cloth was carefully saved from any worn-out garment and cut and pieced into the patterned blocks, but Ellen had dyed newly woven linsey-woolsey a lovely heaven blue for the border and spaces between the blocks.

It hung, bright and beautiful, from the great tree. Christy decided sewing wasn't completely dreadful if something that wonderful could be made, something that would last a lot longer than Thos and Charlie's trouser knees and shirt sleeves.

"Look!" Sarah pointed. "Your doors are on their hinges, Missus Ware!"

"Real glass in the windows!" Lucinda Maddux shook her gray head. "Ten years we've lived here, and all I've got is oiled hides to let in a little light." She turned accusingly to Sarah. "Thought I saw sun sparkin' off window panes at your place as we passed by."

"Lige brought back panes when he went to Independence last fall. My bees gave me

49

enough honey to trade for them."

Jonathan came, smiling, to Ellen, chestnut hair tousled, blue eyes shining. He took her hand and said to the others: "Won't you come, ladies, while I ask a blessing on our home and all our neighbors?"

He had deferred to Arly at dinner, but Christy knew he wouldn't want anyone else to preside at this moment. Bowing his head, he prayed: "Oh, Lord, we thank Thee for the bounty of Thy forests that have yielded the means to build our home. We thank Thee for these friends and neighbors who have been kind and strong and skilled to help us. May we live here in a manner pleasing to You. Ever mindful of Thy gifts, may we share them with others. May this roof shelter those who have none. May these walls protect any caught in a storm. May there ever be food and warmth and welcome for the hungry or the weary, for this is not our house only, dearest Lord, it is Thine." He opened the heavy door with the long wrought-iron hinges. "Lord, we pray Thou wilt bless the coming in and the going out of all who pass this door and let Thy peace reign within."

There was a chorus of "Amens". Lines formed at the tables, Arly gave thanks at considerable length as if to compensate for not being asked to say grace over the house.

Lige had broken the clay off his turkey and carved it on a wooden platter. Christy got a

50

few scraps and bent to fill her plate with stew from the iron kettle sitting on coals at the edge of the fire.

Someone bumped her arm, knocking her wrist against the kettle. She cried out, dropping the ladle, and turned to meet Lafe's gaze. Only a pale rim of iris glowed around the enlarged pupils of his eyes. His lips were parted, as if to taste. She saw his teeth were small and white.

" 'Scuse me," he said, as his mother hurried up. "Didn't go to bump you."

She knew he had. Knew he enjoyed her pain. But she was one of the host family and, anyway, she couldn't accuse him with Hester looking so sorry and so worried. "Come, hold that wrist in cold water, honey. That'll ease it more than anything. Lafe, Son, watch what you're doing, 'specially around a fire."

"I will, Ma." He spoke meekly, but his eyes glittered. "I'm sorry."

Liar! Christy wanted to shout. But Hester, poor Hester, to have her only child like to hurt people and think dirty about women! The cool water did relieve the sting. "Just keep it under water for a while," Hester bade. "I'll bring your stew and you can eat."

"We'll put sweet butter and a bandage on it later," Ellen said, touching Christy's cheek. "Where the veins are so close to the skin, we don't want it to make a bad sore."

Sarah brought her a chunk of cornbread

51

covered with amber honey. "Honey's good for burns," she said. "Trouble is, it's sticky and draws flies."

"*Mmm.* It tastes so good!"

"Yes, and there's still plenty from my bees through the winter."

"How do you get them to stay at your place?"

"They can sip from the log Lige hollowed out for the birds to bathe and drink. Whenever I see a pretty flower or vine, I wait till it goes to seed and try to grow it, so there are blooms from early spring till frost. Bees love the wild plum tree by the cabin, and there's a blackberry thicket big enough to get lost in. I did once." Sarah laughed. It was charming to hear, she was enchanting to watch, and Christy tumbled worshipfully in love.

"Oh, may I come see you?"

"Of course. You'll meet the bees. In a few years, if they like you and are willing to stay with you, I'll give you some bee-gums."

"Gum trees?" Christy puzzled.

"No, pieces of hollowed log with roofs. You'll see." She went off with a swirl of crimson skirts, her kindness sweet as the honey in Christy's mouth.

By the time she had eaten, Christy could hold her wrist out of water without much pain. Her mother gently applied unsalted fresh butter to the red weal that ran almost the width of Christy's wrist, and secured the bandage by running the strip torn from old pantaloons between thumb and index finger before looping it again around the burn.

"No dishes for you till it heals," Ellen said. "What a shame, dear."

"It doesn't hurt much now." Christy wanted to tell her mother that Lafe had jostled her on purpose but, with great effort, held her tongue. That would worry and upset her mother, and supposing she decided she should tell Hester? Whatever it was with Lafe, Christy sensed deeply in her bones that it wasn't anything to be cured by whipping, shaming, or grieved entreaties. What she had seen in his eyes was evil, what her father called the lack of the presence of God; only Christy thought the devil had rooted himself where God was not. She would tell her brothers, though. They needed to be on the watch for him. Besides, she wouldn't care a bit if they waylaid him sometime and thrashed him till he'd never try his tricks at the Wares' again.

The women cleared the tables in the last glow of sunset. The Franzes had cows to milk and took their leave, Emil promising to bring them some Catawba grapevines and Maiden Blush saplings once they went dormant and could be safely transplanted. Matthew and Mark Hayes raced off home to do chores and return. The rest of the assemblage either had no animals requiring care or had arranged with neighbors to take over that evening. Charlie and Thos slipped off to milk, and pen the hogs and sheep. Christy held the egg basket in her bandaged right hand and collected them with her left. Located where it was, this burn was going to be an aggravation, but worse, even after it healed, it would remind her of Lafe's meanness, the devil twisted deeply inside his comely flesh and bone.

"Now we'll get to hear your piano, Missus Ware," bubbled Susie Parks as the men carried it inside the cabin that would serve for everything but sleeping.

It was placed to get light from the glass window, but although the moon was almost full, it was dark enough inside now for candles. Ellen extravagantly placed six in the silver candelabra that had been her grandmother's. The mellow light reflected from the polished rosewood, but the sheen in Ellen's eyes was that of tears.

Was she happy that her piano and candelabra made at least that spot like her old home? Or was she thinking how strange they looked in that cabin, log walls still unchinked, fireplace opening agape?

Whatever she felt, when Jonathan brought the walnut bench he'd made to replace the brocaded one she'd had to give to a friend in Illinois, Ellen seated herself with a graceful sway of skirts and played "Praise God from

Whom All Blessings Flow" with such spirit that those who didn't know the doxology hummed it. Next was Jonathan's favorite "To be a Pilgrim".

Then Ellen smiled at Dan O'Brien whose hair caught the light even from his far corner. "Won't you play your fiddle, Dan? The ladies say you can bring the birds down from the trees."

"Maybe a screech owl, ma'am."

"Come, lad!" called Andy McHugh. "Give us the dance I taught you from the Isle of Skye, the one called 'America'."

"Aye, laddie," old Catriona urged. "Even I'll prance my best to that one! It was the last dance I ever stepped on that dear soil before we took ship and came so far, so far." Her voice caught. "This land's been good to us. No landlord to drive us from our croft, no laird raising regiments for the wars of the English queen. But, och! Never to see the shining lochs or the mists on the mountains. . . ."

"Or the laird's deer destroying our fields," her son reminded her. "His sheep devouring the grass, his agent and the constables tearing down our houses, firing our roofs. . . ."

He turned to the Irish boy who must have seen things as bad or worse, for he was old enough to remember the famine years. "Play the song, Dan." The broad-chested, red-haired blacksmith held out his hands to Susie

Parks who reached about to his heart. "Will you dance, lass, and show our friends the steps?"

Whatever the McHughs had lost or left in Skye, that Western Isle of Scotland with its magic name, it was clear Andy had found his love here on this frontier border, old to the Indians, new to the whites. And whatever the powers in Ireland had done to the flame-haired orphan boy, it left him music.

Thin face bent to the satiny instrument, he played joy and hope out of sorrow and longing. Christy's heart softened, although she assured herself he'd had no right to accuse her of neglecting Beth. Ethan drew Sarah into the dance, and Lige made a surprisingly courtly bow to Allie Hayes. Their baby girl slept in the other cabin so Owen and Harriet Parks joined in, as did the Caxtons. Jonathan claimed Ellen. Hester, in spite of Mildred Morrison's scowl, smiled invitingly at Simeon Parks who grinned back and met her at the edge of the reel.

"We don't hold with dancing," Arly Maddux said, pushing Lucinda toward the door. "And I'm purely astonished, Mister Parks, that Quakers do."

Simeon chuckled. "We heed our inner light. Mine tells me it is not wrong to move nimbly with one's neighbors so long as there be no drunkenness or wanton behavior."

"How about wantin' behavior, Sim?" hollered Watt Caxton in a way that hinted that he, at least, might have imbibed something stronger than buttermilk.

"We'll be on our way," snapped Arly.

Jonathan and Ellen thanked the Madduxes, and Jonathan went out to help Arly hitch up his team. Ellen sat down by Lydia Parks, the only young woman who hadn't been asked to dance. Catriona clapped and called encouragement. Mildred Morrison glowered at Hester.

When Jonathan came back in, one of their silent messages passed between him and Ellen. Approaching the ladies' bench, he drew Lydia up with laughing gallantry.

After a few numbers, Watt Caxton and Nora were panting. "Time we went home," Watt said loudly, pushing back his greased hair. "I've tricked me a big old sow bear into my pen along with her cub. Goin' to have a bear-baiting tomorrow. Men with good bear dogs are comin' from all over. Usually you just turn six, seven dogs at a time in on the bear, but this 'un's so big and mean, 'specially with her cub to protect, that I'm bound she can handle a dozen at a time . . . till she's hurt bad. That should take a while. Quite a while, if the cub shows fight."

"Mother!" Christy gasped. "That must be *our* bears!"

Sarah's hand went to her throat. Lige said: "What'll you take for that bear, Caxton?"

57

"More'n any buckskin hunter's got. Bring your dogs over, though, and prove they're some account."

"I don't hold with bear-baitin'."

"No," sneered Watt, "and you don't like the way I train my dogs, do you?"

"I kill wolves, but I'd never hamstring one's back legs so's all he can do is sit there while a pack tears into him."

Ellen made a muffled sound. Again a look passed between her and Jonathan, who said: "If you'll let the bears go, Mister Caxton, we'll keep you in milk, butter, and eggs all winter."

"You will?" screeched Nora. She caught her husband's arm. "Watt, think how nice that'd be!"

He shoved her hand away. "I've sent word around. The best dogs in the county'll be there. Unless God or the devil turns them bears loose, they'll be there tomorrow, and there they'll die when we've had our fun!"

With a defiant smirk, he swaggered out, trailed by his wife. Jonathan didn't go help harness their gaunt team. The neighbors looked at each other, most of them distressed and shamed that one of their kind could be so wicked.

Simeon Parks shook his white head. "Shall we seek God in silence, trusting him to change the heart of our brother?"

"He's not my brother!" vowed Lige.

"I don't know why you're all carrying on so," sniffed Mildred Morrison. "Goodness' sakes! They're only wild beasts. You'd think they had Christian souls!"

"They have spirits," Sarah declared. "All living creatures do."

"If those nuns taught you that. . . ."

"They didn't. My grandmother did, before she died." Sarah's tawny eyes smoldered. "No one will ever unteach the things she told me."

"Missus Ware," Dan O'Brien said, "will you play? I . . . I hurt my fingers this afternoon. It's hard to fiddle."

"Why don't we settle down and just listen to the music?" suggested Lige.

Susie Parks nodded gratefully. "I don't think any of us feel like dancing now. That dreadful man!"

"Pray for him," her father urged.

Christy saw white light spill through the square cut for the fireplace. The trapped bear and cub must see the moon they had known for all their lives, but did they sense this was their last time to watch it? To die torn apart by hounds after hours of fear and torment?

No! It wasn't going to happen! Not if God, Sarah's wise old god of the spirits, if not the Christian one, would help. Christy had never been to the Caxtons, but she knew their place lay across the creek a little beyond the Hayeses. The Caxtons' shambling old team wouldn't travel faster than she could if she ran a lot.

But that pack of dogs.

She'd just have to get there ahead of them. All eyes were on Ellen, who was playing one of Jonathan's favorites — a sonata by the young German composer, Johannes Brahms. Would the bears ever again hear the strange human music that had seemed to enthrall them so?

Christy slipped out the dogtrot and ran.

CHAPTER THREE

A burning stitch in her side made Christy press her fist against it. She panted when she came level with the whining creak of the wagon and rumble of wheels. She could make out the Caxtons in the pale light, although she couldn't see their faces. The hounds had scented something and bayed along the creek till Watt profanely called them off. He had no time to hunt that night with the bear-baiting next day.

The hounds must smell Christy but had doubtless grown accustomed to her scent during the day and recognized it as one they needn't herald. If only that tolerance would remain on Caxtons' territory! Better yet if she could find the pen and free the bears before the Caxtons arrived.

They must be heading for the ford Ethan maintained upstream from the tannery. That would make their way home easier but longer. Hoofs and wheels of settlers had worn this rough track that was still far from a road but less difficult than driving across this brushy, rocky, wooded region. For closeness to water, the Caxtons' house would be as near the creek as flooding would allow. If Christy crossed now, she was bound to find the cabin as long as she stayed near the creek, and she should get there before the wagon did.

Where pebbles and sand were scoured away from the limestone bottom, the creek was over a tall man's head, but at other stretches it flowed no more than a foot or so deep. She and her brothers hadn't explored this far, so Christy, not wishing to get her clothes wet or swim, hurried along watching for a likely place.

A sandbar with willows reached far into the creek. The current had carved a sharp angle around it and gnawed earth away from the roots of a huge tree on the other bank. From the sound of the water, it ran deeply here, but Christy thought she could leap to the gnarled roots that resembled a contorted giant serpent.

Although she and her brothers ordinarily went barefoot, they had put on shoes for the evening's festivities. Christy took hers off, as well as stockings and pantaloons that reached below her knee, made a bundle, and threw it across. Kilting skirts and petticoat to free her legs, she took a deep breath and jumped, struck the lowest root, caught a grapevine, and sprang upward, scrambling up the bank.

There! She wasn't wet at all. Resuming her pantaloons, she decided her shoes' protection was worth their pinch and the time it would take to put them on. She mustn't lame herself on a stob or rock or briar.

The groaning wagon rattled a little ahead of her now, but she ran in the spangled moonlight, holding her skirts to keep them from catching. A whippoorwill's lament sent a chill through her. She was grateful when several barred owls called to each other: *"Who cooks for you? Who cooks for you all?"* She soon outdistanced the ill-cared-for team. You'd think a man who traded in animals would know the importance of looking after them, but, from the sound of it, Caxton depended on cursing and the whip.

Slowing now and then to catch her breath and ease the pain in her side, Christy hoped she wouldn't be missed at home. She and the boys had permission to go on sleeping beneath the tree till the weather chilled, and, if her mother noticed her absence, she'd probably think Christy had gone to rest outside, too.

A clearing, jagged with rotting stumps, was strewn with logs that hadn't been used or burned. Winded, Christy paused at the edge. Weeds grew high as the tallest stalks of corn in a small patch given little protection by a half-hearted rail fence. A single cabin of round logs squatted near what was probably a smokehouse.

Despair gripped Christy. Where was the bear pen? She had expected it to be near the house. Above the pounding blood in her ears, she heard the distant clatter of the wagon.

Oh, bears! she wailed silently. *Where are you?*

What was that peculiar noise, a sort of muffled, gentle grunting? Scanning the edge of the clearing on the far side of the cabin, Christy could now make out a square log structure with a pole roof.

Let it be the pen, and not a crude barn. Let the gate be one she could open quickly. With silent entreaties, she ran toward the building. The screech of wheels groaned nearer at every second.

No gate on this side . . . or this. . . . Turning the corner, she smothered a scream as she almost ran into someone. Someone who started and whirled on her.

"You!" She and Dan O'Brien spoke in the same breath. And then, again in chorus: "What are *you* doing here?"

"Never mind," growled Dan. "Push in on this spavined gate so I can work the rawhides off the posts. Quick!"

She shoved with all her might, smothering a cry when she bumped her burned wrist. The shift gave Dan the bit of an inch he needed to work off the wide, tough leather loops that held the heavy gate to the upright pole forming the end of one wall.

A strong smell came from inside, but there was utter stillness. "Now," panted the strange Irish boy, "run around the pen to the far end! I'll open the gate. If the bears won't come out, you make some racket down there to send them this direction. Get along with you now!"

No time for speeches of independence, or asking why he'd come. She couldn't have opened that gate alone — and neither could he, unless he had a knife to cut the leathers.

The gate scraped back. No sound from the captives, but their smell was strong through the unchinked logs. The wagon was close enough that Christy could faintly hear Watt's complaining voice. Locating a chunk of wood, she struck the wall.

No response. Good grief! What if they wouldn't come out, what if they stayed frozen till the wagon came? Christy banged harder on the wall, trembled with relief as there was a scuffling. She looked around the corner in time to see the bear and cub lunge into the trees.

Dan forced the gate shut, grabbed her hand. "Hurry!"

The wagon was almost upon them. No time to dash across the clearing toward the creek. Dan and Christy plunged after the bears. Thank goodness, instead of climbing trees where the hounds might trap them, the crunch of twigs testified that they were running.

Since the mother had to find places she could get through, the boy and girl could follow through the trees, now and then catching a glimpse of the cub.

"Can't . . . can't we double back to the creek now?" Christy puffed.

The dogs began to yip, and then to bay. Caxton's distant swearing exploded into a howl of outrage. The hounds' behavior must have caused him to check the pen. Dan hadn't had time to replace the leathers. Caxton probably couldn't recapture the bears, but killing them would be some satisfaction, and with great luck, if he baited the pen again, he might still have a quarry dangerous enough to content the men who were bringing their dogs, maybe a wolf or panther, if not a bear.

Would the excited hounds attack people? Christy didn't want to find out. *Oh, Lordy, Lord!* A bluff loomed before them, pale gray rock bleached by the moon, seventy or eighty feet high, stretching out of sight on either hand.

For an instant, the bears showed dark against the cliff. Then they were gone. "Must be a cave!" Dan gripped her tighter. "Come on!"

Lungs burning, sobbing for breath, Christy dragged Dan up when he tripped on a vine.

He steadied her when she stepped into an old root hole. But there was no cavity, no hiding place in the side of the cliff.

"Go on!" Releasing Christy, Dan gave her a push and picked up a limb. "I'll keep the dogs busy as long as I can."

"No!" In turning back to him, Christy saw a hole in the rocky ground. "Look! Down there! That must be where the bears went!"

"We've got to try it." Dan gripped the rock edge of the opening. "I'll go first."

He dropped the limb through the opening and let himself down. There was a thud. Christy prayed hard. In a few seconds, his voice echoed upward. "Hang onto the edge and drop! I'll catch you!"

As she let herself down, she saw the dogs racing toward her, bellies low to the ground, caught a glimpse of Watt swearing his way through the trees. She closed her eyes, let loose of the rim, and plunged.

Not far. Dan's arms closed around her. They went down in a heap in the moonlight spilling through the hole. "Let's go," Dan ordered in a whisper. "I don't know if those dogs'll jump into a sinkhole, but we don't want to find out."

"But we can't see. We might run into the bears."

Indeed, beyond the halo circling the bold splash of full moonlight, it was pitch black.

"I'll test the way with this limb," Dan

promised. "Hang onto the back of my shirt."

The dogs bayed at the hole, but none, so far, had ventured to leap. In a few minutes, Watt's curses streamed downward. He was telling the bears what he'd do to them if he ever caught them, but he must not have been eager to jump down and meet the bears by himself. Apparently he hadn't seen Christy and Dan. He knew, of course, that human hands had worked off the rawhide loops, but wouldn't know who to blame it on.

"Shall we wait till Mister Caxton takes the dogs away?" Christy asked beneath her breath.

"He may stay up there a good long time, hoping the bears'll come out." Dan sounded worried. "Sinkholes like this can be where the top caved in over an underground river. There's one not far from Whistling Point, close to where we live on the Marais des Cygnes. Sometimes the hidden river's dried up and leaves long tunnels like this. Sometimes the river's still running. You can toss a log in a sinkhole and it may tumble out miles and miles away where the river breaks out from underground."

"So you're saying this cave or old river, or whatever it is, may reach a long way off? But what if there's no way out?"

"I'd like to find out . . . when I have some candles."

Christy shivered. "*I* wouldn't!"

"Caxton won't want to give up on the bears and lose all that money and fun he was counting on. He may stay up there quite a spell."

"The bears are somewhere ahead."

"Or behind. The cavern runs both ways." His hand on her shoulder made the dark less scary. She'd always been afraid of the dark. When they were younger, Thos and Charlie had gotten most of their rare whippings for jumping out of dark corners and sending her into shrieking fits. She found she was getting to like the lilt of the Irish boy's voice.

What would she have done if he hadn't been at the pen? She couldn't have loosed the bears. If she had somehow managed to hack or break the loops, would she have dared follow the bears down the sinkhole? Thankfulness melted away the last bit of her aggravation at him for chiding her care of Beth.

"What do you want to do?" she asked.

"Go ahead as far as we can without passing any side caves that could mix us up if we have to come back. If we come to another sinkhole, we can climb out and try to figure about where we are."

"What if this cavern just goes on and on and on?"

"*We* won't," he said positively. "If we don't find a way out in an hour or so, we'll come back here and hope Caxton's gone."

"Won't your folks miss you?"

"I told Susie I was walking home and asked her to bring my fiddle." There was a smile in his tone. "They know I like wandering in the moonlight, like a cat or an owl, they say."

She clutched his shirt again — the Parks sisters wove excellent homespun — and followed gingerly. The limb he held scratched on rock.

"Down there, be ye, you mangy devils?" Caxton's bellow resounded distantly, but the explosion echoed along the rocky walls. A flying chip hit Christy in the back as shattered rock crashed from where the shot had struck.

At Christy's flinch, Dan turned. "Are you all right?"

"Just a little sting from a rock piece," she whispered. "Let's hurry. He might lean down and shoot our direction."

This was the deepest night she had ever known. A density to the blackness made it stifling and almost palpable. "I don't smell even a whiff of bear," murmured Dan. "I think they went the other way."

"I hope so . . . and I hope they get out."

"Why do you care? Why did you come?"

Christy hesitated, then decided he deserved to know the truth even if he made fun of her. "The bears used to listen to my mother play the piano. At least they seemed to. They stayed at the edge of our firelight for the longest times."

"Probably smelled your food."

"*I* think they liked the music."

He laughed with soft but not unkind derision. "Oh, aye. For sure, it was the music."

Vexed, but not enough to let go of him, Christy demanded: "Why did you come?"

He was silent.

She tugged at his shirt. "Why? It's not fair not to tell when I told and you . . . you laughed."

After a moment, he said: "You have the right of it, Christy Ware. But . . . you'll not be telling this to a soul?"

"Cross my heart and hope to die. . . ."

"Don't say that!" He kept his tone muted, but it was fierce. "Don't ever hope to die, my girl. 'Tis a sin against life and God."

"It's just a verse."

"A brainless yammering."

"Never mind. Why did you want to set the bears free?"

Each word came as if pulled by force from a hidden, hurting place inside. "Killing a beast is one thing. But tormenting it, making sport of any creature's fear and pain, laughing at it . . . that I cannot bide."

"I'm glad you can't . . . Danny."

He stopped moving.

Christy faltered: "Is something wrong?"

Starting out again, he spoke so softly she could scarcely hear. "The gentry, they drove by in their carriages while I rocked Bridget in my arms, trying to get her to sleep. When she'd starved to her wee bones, she didn't cry any more. . . ."

"Oh, Danny, Danny!"

"You would have it."

"Bridget . . . what . . . ?"

"She died a week before her second birthday."

Christy burst into tears. Through her sobbing, matter-of-fact rather than bitter, Dan said: "I know now the gentry didn't laugh at us. They didn't even see us."

"Your parents . . . ?"

"They died of chills and fever in Eighteen Forty-Seven, but it was starving killed them, and being turned out of the farm where Da had worked. I was six. Old enough to try to steal a bite for Bridget when I couldn't beg it."

No wonder he'd gone savage when Christy ignored Beth's crying. What wouldn't he have given to have his sister back — and there was no way he could, not on this earth, ever.

"That's how my nose was broken." Once he remembered the past, he seemed to want to talk. "A woman fetched me a clout with a great iron spoon when I made off with a few of her 'taties." He chuckled at the memory with a certain amount of pride. "Blood poured like I was butchered, but I pelted on. Bridget and I ate that night, though I doubt raw potatoes were the best food for a baby. But she laughed and reached for the pieces. Aye. She laughed."

"Why didn't someone help you?" Such misery, with people all around, was beyond anything she could imagine.

"The schoolmaster did. Shared his hut and the little food he had. Till he died." Dan's voice quickened. "Do you know any Choctaws?"

"Choctaws? Aren't they Indians?"

"I should say so. And they're the reason I'm alive . . . them and the Quakers."

"How . . . ?" Christy broke off in puzzlement.

"The Quakers gave out food and clothing and tried to find shelter for those without a roof. The government of England didn't care if we starved, but good people there and around the world sent help." His voice hardened. "Did you know there was plenty of food in Ireland, Christy? It was only 'taties failed those famine years, the crop that kept life in poor folk. Beef cattle, sheep, wagons loaded with grain . . . all that was shipped to England."

There was nothing to say. But how, with his parents dead and he and his sister starving, he must have hated the gentry and the owners of the food he saw driven past while he and his sister starved.

"I got a fever after Bridgie died," he went

on. "Woke up in a kind of hospital the Quakers ran. One of the ladies is a second cousin to Simeon Parks who had written her he'd undertake to raise some Irish orphans. Three of us traveled to America on Choctaw relief money."

"I think they're one of the Five Civilized Tribes that have reservations in Indian Territory. That's south of Kansas Territory and west of Arkansas."

"Don't you think I found out where they live? When I'm older, I'll go to see them and find a way to thank them. They pitied the Irish, I believe, because they could well remember being hungry and sick when they were driven out of their lands in the East."

Christy was too young to remember that although her father had preached sermons on the wickedness of exiling Indians to make room for whites. "At least, let white settlement cease at the Missouri border," he had urged. "True, California and Oregon are settling up, there are old Spanish towns in New Mexico and Arizona, and the Mormons are established in Utah, but the vast region between should be reserved to Indians already living there and tribes forced out of the East."

That had been government policy for a time, as much as there was a policy. For one thing, the plains and deserts and mountains were considered poor farm land. But the

Colorado gold rush sprouted towns, and there was growing clamor for a transcontinental railroad. Jonathan Ware was increasingly gloomy about the Indians' hope of keeping the spacious interior.

"What happened to the other orphans?" Christy asked

"Peggy O'Donnell was twelve when we came to the Parkses in Ohio nine years ago. She married a young farmer, Harry Shepherd, before the Parkses moved here, two years since. Her brother Tim . . . he must be almost twenty now . . . stayed to work on his brother-in-law's farm." Dan halted. "Is that fresh air?"

Christy sniffed, drew in a longer breath, and gripped his arm. "It must be. Dan, doesn't that sound like water running?"

"That it is," he said after a hushed moment. "Now wouldn't it be a fine kettle of stinking fish if there's a way out but we can't get to it?"

"Maybe the water won't be very deep." Christy spoke hopefully although her heart sank at the prospect of retracing their steps to the sinkhole and risking Caxton and his hounds being there when they tried to climb out.

"We'll just be careful and go as far as we can," Dan said.

The muffled flow grew louder. Then it gushed free. "Must still be a river beneath where we've been walking," Dan guessed. "Here's where it's worn through rock." He tapped with the limb. "A ledge runs along this way. Let's see how far."

Christy took care not to crowd him, although she tightened her hold on his shirt. How strange it was down here in this hidden world with no one knowing where they were. Dan had told her things he might not have in an ordinary time and place. She didn't think she could ever get really angry with him again. Not after hearing about small Bridget.

"Light ahead," exulted Dan. "Did you ever smell such sweet good air? If this ledge just holds out. . . ."

Christy hoped the river would break out of some hillside as a fine spring so that they could easily get through the opening, but, as they neared the glow, it came from the top like the one near the Caxtons'. At least, if the ledge continued that far, they might be able to scramble to the top. Wherever that might be.

Almost anywhere was better than the Caxtons'. How good it was to reach light again. It seemed brilliant after the total dark. As Dan turned to her, she scanned the thin face with its broken nose and cleft chin, memorized his features.

He'd told her things in the tortuous cavern that she was sure he hadn't talked about in a long time. He was like no one she'd ever known, and she knew him in a deep and special way. Beside him, her brothers were children — and so was she.

He smiled. What a marvel people could heal, could be happy again after the grief he'd lived through. "Now then, Christy girl, let's see if there's a way up. The river runs on, but we'd better get out now if we can at all."

Moonlight splashed rock and rippling silvered water, but the aperture was discouragingly far above them. Dan appraised her and shook his head. "Even if I boosted you up on my shoulders, you couldn't get a good hold on the rim."

"Maybe we can find some rocks."

He shrugged. "It's worth a look, though we sure haven't been tripping over any."

"The top had to cave in," she pointed out.

"For sure it did." He struck his forehead in mock shame. "Some chunks should be here, if the water hasn't swept them all away. I'll look here and you feel around over there. Don't fall in the water, mind! It could carry you out some place in God's good time likely, but in a state you might not fancy."

Christy groped along the wall, explored cautiously with her feet, keeping one planted firmly while stretching the other out as far as she could. "Here's a rock!" she cried. Bending to trace it with her hands, she said in disappointment: "It's all jaggedy and doesn't reach to my knee."

"Here's a whole jumble right at the edge of the river. Must be where the roof fell in. If we can heap them up. . . ."

Christy scurried to help. Some rocks were too heavy to shift, but the largest of these was close enough to the hole to serve as a firm base for smaller stones. Together, they dragged over the one Christy had found and banked other rocks around it till the crude platform reached Christy's waist. Dan cocked his head to study the rim. "Reckon I can scramble on top, then lean over and haul you up."

The rocks shifted beneath his weight, but his head and shoulders were above the edge. "Here's luck. There's a ridge I can get a hold on."

"Be careful, Danny!"

He pushed from tiptoe, hefted himself up. "Now for you, Christy!"

"What if I'm too heavy and drag you in?"

"There's a kind of dip where I can anchor myself. Don't fret about me. Just hold up your hands and hang on to my wrists while I grab yours."

She yelped at the very thought. "Don't you dare touch my burned wrist!"

"I'll take your hands, then," he said patiently.

It seemed a long way yet to the top when she stood on the rocks, but she sighed with relief when she saw that she could indeed reach Dan's hands. They closed, warm and strong, around hers, locking with her fingers.

"Up, up, up and away-y-y!"

He was laughing. That gave her heart to trust his hands. In no time, he had her on the rim. As soon as he released her arms, she threw them around him, buried her face against his chest. "Oh, Danny, I'm so glad we're out of that hole!"

"Me, too, but we were mighty lucky the bears showed us how to get into it."

He patted her on the shoulder — as if she were a baby. Attempting to regain some dignity, she pulled away and scrubbed her eyes with her sleeve. "I hope the bears found a way out."

"I expect that smart old mama will. Shucks, she may even have known where she was going. She must have been in every cave and hidey-hole in this neck of the woods."

Cheered, Christy looked around. The sound of water came through the ragged hole but, otherwise, there was no hint of that dark world beneath. "I do hope Mother thinks I went to bed and doesn't look. Do you know where we are?"

He, too, glanced around and gave a soft whistle. "I think. . . . Just a minute!" Springing up, he ran to the crest of the ridge above them. "Whistling Point's just down from here. I can see the mill and our cabin."

"But. . . ."

Chuckling, he trotted back, helped her to her feet. "Remember, I told you there was a sinkhole not far from Whistling Point? This is it!"

"But it must be four miles to the Caxtons from Trading Post!"

"The underground way's a short cut." He looked at the moon that had traveled considerably since she had slipped away from home. "It seems a lot longer, Christy, but I reckon we were in the cavern less than an hour."

"It seemed like forever!" It had changed her life. Their journey through the dark, what he had told her, and the way she had trusted him, made her in a curious way closer to Dan O'Brien than to anyone in the world.

"Well" — he grinned — "now forever's over, we've got to get you home."

"Just show me the way to go." She tried to sound brave.

"Don't be a goose! Come along. There's a foot log across the river and a fairly good track wagons have made coming to the mill or going to the tannery."

"A . . . a *foot* log?"

"Haven't you ever used one?"

She shook her head. Her new sense of having suddenly grown up dissolved in a need to justify herself. "Back home we have proper bridges."

"To be sure." He spoke politely although that frequent smile lurked in his voice that was deepening to a man's. "But you'll find this quite a proper foot log. It's smoothed flat on top, and Uncle Simeon and Owen and I strung a cable from trees on either side." He tweaked the end of her braid. "You can hang onto the rope and prance along with no fear of slipping even when the water's high."

"Is it high?"

"No. There's places we could wade it, but why get wet?" He tossed over his shoulder: "You can hang onto my shirt with one hand and the cable with the other."

"Thanks very much. I'll hold onto the cable."

He only laughed.

Yes, they were back in the real world, on solid earth — but would either ever seem as real or solid now she knew what flowed beneath?

CHAPTER FOUR

Davie Parks stirred sleepily as Dan O'Brien settled beside him on the shuck mattress. Rubbing his eyes, he mumbled: "You sure must have come a long way 'round in the moonlight."

"Uncle Simeon's not worried?" Dan asked, recalling that as they'd driven home from the steamboat landing that fine autumn day nine years ago, Dan and Peggy and Tim O'Donnell, their new guardian, Simeon Parks, had said: "You can hardly dwell with us and call me Mister Parks, youngsters. I know you remember your fathers and you should give that name to no other man. Would Uncle Simeon be agreeable to you?"

The schoolmaster Dan and Bridget had lived with for a blessed space had taught Dan some English, and he'd picked up more on his journey, but he was glad this graying, keen-eyed man spoke slowly enough for him to get the gist of it.

Peggy and Tim understood more English

than they spoke. They implored Dan with their eyes to answer for them. "Entirely agreeable, sir, and we are thanking you."

He had slept with Davie that night, too, while Tim had piled in with Owen, and, although at first Dan kept well to his side of the four-poster, by morning they were snuggled together for warmth, warmth that had melted some of the ice that formed inside Dan since he'd watched his parents die. Lots of that ice was still there. He thought it always would be. But he had been lucky, oh, so lucky, to come to America and live with the Parkses.

He looked up to Owen, would have instantly died for Lydia or Susie, and Davie — well, in spite of their occasional huffs, the younger boy was the one person in the world Dan might have admitted he loved.

Slanting moonlight from the loft's one window now showed Davie's indignant face. "Well, you don't think I went down and told Pa you weren't here, do you?"

Dan tousled his hair. "Thank you kindly, young 'un." He was tempted to tell about freeing the bears and his escape with Christy Ware, but decided the fewer people who knew about that, the better. Davie wouldn't give him away on purpose, but something might slip.

He did tell Davie about the sinkholes and the underground river, though. "Slithering snakes!" Davie breathed. "Let's see how far it goes. Can't we, Danny? Can't we?"

"When the fall work's over. We'll take rope and candles and be real careful." Dan gave his foster brother a playful cuff. "Go to sleep. It's worn out I am, if you are not."

"I'm too excited about that cavern," Davie protested. But he rolled over and was asleep before Dan finished peeling off his clothes.

A few days later, Dan and Davie pulled fodder, stripping green blades from the stalks of hardening corn. After the blades cured a few days, they'd be bound and carried to the end of the rows to be hauled to the barn. Dan wasn't fond of hoeing weeds out of the corn, a constant battle till the stalks got shoulder high, but he never minded working by the harvest moon to tie blades together after dew had softened them enough for one to be twisted around the others and tucked under. The stalks gave out a sweet, clean smell that put him in mind of Christy. He grinned to imagine how indignantly her gray eyes would flash if he told her she smelled like fresh-dried fodder.

"What's the joke?" demanded Davie.

"I was thinking how sweet new fodder smells."

"In a pig's eye! You've been acting peculiar ever since that cabin raising." Davie's green eyes were both worried and reproachful. "A bat with hydrophobia must've bit you in that cave."

"I'll tell you when you're old enough," Dan teased. He dodged a fist.

The sound of hoofs made them whirl. "What's Andy McHugh in such a rush about? And why's his mother hanging on behind him?" Davie wondered. "I didn't know that old sorrel mare of his could go faster than a trot."

"Let's go find out. It's time for a drink, anyway." Simeon never grouched at them to stay on the job. He simply expected them to get it done in reasonable time, so they did, instead of finding ways to thwart him.

Simeon and Owen Parks came out of the mill house to greet their neighbors. Andy McHugh dismounted and swung old Catriona down. "Will you look after Mother while I go help James Montgomery run off Clarke's raiders?" The young blacksmith's glance swept the Parkses. "I know Quakers don't hold with fighting, Simeon, but George Clarke, the Land Office man at Fort Scott, crossed from Westpoint, Missouri, northeast of here, with hundreds of rascally proslavers."

Simeon and Owen exchanged dismayed looks. "Are you sure, Andy?" pressed Simeon.

"You bet I'm sure. They're burning out Free Staters, trampling crops, stealing . . . telling us to leave or be killed!"

Simeon drew himself together. " 'Tis against my belief to fight," he said quietly. "However, I'll protect your mother and my womenfolk with my life."

"Let me go, Father," Owen urged. His Harriet was chalk-faced, and, from her hip, small Letty whimpered.

Lydia, Susie, and Mildred Morrison were trying to help Catriona, but she waved them off, red hair spiking out from beneath her ill-tied bonnet.

"All I need's a cup of tea, if you have it, and to get off that knife-spined old nag. Told Andy I could handle any Border Ruffian that's ever been born . . . what be they compared to constables and scoundrel lairds? But he would have me up behind him, rattling my few poor teeth from my jaws."

The white-haired miller seemed to pray silently before he turned to his tall young son. "Owen, you must decide according to your inner light."

"I'll take Zephyr?"

Simeon Parks nodded. Zephyr and Breeze were fine bay geldings, strong enough to plow, clean-footed enough to pull a carriage or ride.

Harriet's full lips trembled, but she said: "I'll put food in a sack for you." Then she froze. "You don't have a pistol or rifle, Owen."

"He can use one of my Colts." Andy McHugh had a Sharps in a saddle scabbard and carried two bone-handled revolvers in leather cases attached to his belt.

Dan said: "Might I have the use of the other, Andy?"

"You, laddie?"

"I'm fifteen."

Simeon's white brows knitted. "If harm befell you, Daniel, I'd feel to blame."

"Please, Uncle Simeon! I have to help chase that gang away from here. They might burn the mill and cabins, scare the womenfolk and little Letty."

After a pained moment, Simeon met Dan's eyes. "I won't forbid you, son, but take all the care you may. Ride Breeze."

Dan and Owen hurried to fetch the horses from the near pasture. Davie had the saddles, bridles, and saddle blankets ready when they led their mounts to the log stable by the barn. Harriet tied her husband's food sack and a blanket behind his saddle. Lydia did the same for Dan, and Susie added apples, gingerbread, and smoked dried beef to the corn pones that were all the provisioning McHugh had bothered with.

He caught her hand to thank her. She looked up at him, hazel eyes wide with fear and admiration. "Oh, Andy, do be careful. And watch out for my brothers."

It warmed Dan to hear her call him that so naturally. He'd be chopped to pieces before that bunch of cut-throats could come near his . . . family. Yes, they were that. He could claim them wholly now that he had a chance to protect them, pay back a little of all they'd done for him.

McHugh allowed himself to smooth back a tendril that had escaped Susie's braided crown of black hair. "I have you to come back to, Miss Susie. You know I'll be careful. And be sure I'll watch out for Owen and Dan."

He turned to them, taking off his belt and slipping off the holsters. "Each of you put a holster on your belt. Best show you how to use these revolvers."

The six-inch barrel of the weapon in his hand sent a chill down Dan's spine. This was real. He would carry this revolver and shoot it at men, kill or wound them if he could — he, Dan O'Brien, who'd seen so much misery he couldn't stand to let a bear be tortured.

Christy's eyes watched him in her imagination. *I have to do this,* Dan told her. *Have to or the devils might hurt my family, burn them out or worse.*

"These Navy Colts hold six rounds," Andy explained. "Susie, could we have a couple of little bags so I can divide up the cartridges?" She hurried off. "Now, then," he demonstrated, "press the hammer back with your thumb, aim along the sights, pull the trigger . . . and don't expect to hit anything that's more than fifty yards away. When the cylinder's empty, you knock out this wedge just in front of it and the cylinder comes out to reload."

Six shots without reloading! Such power! Fascinated and repelled, Dan stared at the revolver in his hands, the naval battle engraved on the cylinder, the seven-and-half inch octagonal barrel, the polished walnut stock. "Where'd you get such choice revolvers, Andy?"

"A man heading for Oregon with his family traded them for a plow and my shoeing his oxen. After all the trouble in early summer, I laid in a supply of cartridges when I went to Independence for supplies, but I've got powder, bullets, paper and percussion caps if we need them."

Owen looked as blank as Dan felt. Andy raised a rusty eyebrow at them. "You lads have never rammed a charge home, never fired anything? Don't you hunt?"

Owen crimsoned. "Pa won't have firearms on the place."

Andy shook his head. "Then maybe he shouldn't have come out here. I'm mightily afraid it'll be many cruel years before anyone along this border can be safe without weapons."

Simeon approached in time to hear the last statement. "Is anyone safe with them?"

"I'd rather die making a fight. . . ." At the pained look in his prospective father-in-law's eyes, Andy broke off. He swallowed and turned to mount.

"Kiss your old mother good bye, lad!" shrilled Catriona.

He did, but the way he looked at Susie made it plain he longed to kiss her, too. Blushing, she hugged Owen and Dan. Lydia's cool lips brushed Dan's forehead, then her brother's. "We'll pray for your safe return . . . and that you do no murders."

"Fine with me so long as we run them out of Kansas," Andy retorted.

Davie looked up wistfully as Dan climbed into the saddle. "I wish I could go."

Susie put a protective arm around him. "You're much too young."

"I'm only three years younger than Dan."

"Three years is a lot at your age," Lydia chided.

He caught Dan's knee. "Mind now, don't get yourself hurt."

Dan leaned over to squeeze Davie's shoulder. "Scared you'll have to pull all the fodder yourself?"

"God be with you!" Simeon called.

Dan wished he hadn't. How could God be with you when you meant to kill somebody?

A long, high, forested hill with a ledge of stone around its crest rose north of the little hamlet of Trading Post. The Marais des Cygnes flowed against the west end of the great hill and ran south for a quarter mile

90

before sparkling eastward. The rapids at the turn formed a good crossing for the Military Road that ran south from Fort Leavenworth, staying near the Missouri border down to Fort Scott from whence it wound all the way to Fort Gibson in Indian Territory and Fort Smith over in Arkansas.

Here by the crossing was the trading post started by a French trapper twenty years or so ago. In the early 1840s, General Winfield Scott had started a log fort there but moved his dragoons south to establish the outpost named after him — to his considerable disgust. After his victories in the Mexican War, he thought he deserved a better name-sake than such an isolated, unimportant place.

Apart from the abandoned fort at Trading Post, there were only a few cabins — or had been. Blackened ruins were all that remained. Not a person or animal was in sight. Dan's backbone went cold and his scalp prickled. In Ireland, his family and countless others had been driven from their homes, but he'd never before seen homes destroyed on purpose.

Were these the first of many? Would there be a real war? One of grief and terror that would wreck the Parkses' cabins and mill, ruin what he thought of as the Wares' happy house, and all their lives? If Christy couldn't stand the thought of bear-baiting, how would she endure war?

Why did he feel as much worry for her as he did for Susie and Lydia? He'd only known her a little while. But they had worked together, freeing the bears, and then they'd made their blind journey underground. Even if they never met again, Christy would always be special to him.

He patted Breeze's gleaming neck as they followed the road over the pass between the rock-crested hill and a large smooth hill on the east. From the top of the pass, prairie stretched north and east with mounds of every shape rising against the sky. Some were cones, others flat-topped oblongs, but they were all grassy and treeless.

Dan's gaze was drawn from this wide expanse by Andy's cry. "They've burned out Sam Nickel!" Tall, husky Sam Nickel brought his grain to the mill, of course. He was memorable for his golden hair and one blinded eye, but Dan didn't know his family.

Smoke still curled from the heavy sill logs of a cabin east of the road at the bottom of the pass. Four fair-haired stair-step boys, the oldest maybe Dan's age, and a slender woman poked among the ashes. At one side was a straggle of blackened rescued items. A gold-haired baby lay on its back, kicking for pleasure, cooing to a feather it gripped in one chubby fist.

Beyond the cabin were charred outbuildings. A heap of headless white chickens was piled beside what must have been a chicken coop. When the horsemen came in sight, the woman snatched up the baby and a butcher knife. The biggest boy gripped a broken hoe. The others poised the sticks they'd been dragging through burned rubble.

"It's me, Missus Nickel!" called the smith. "Andy McHugh, and Owen Parks and Dan O'Brien from the mill. Where's Sam?"

"He left some hides at the tannery while he went on to Osceola to trade butter and cheese for salt and gunpowder." The sunbonnet hid all but a few wisps of light brown hair. Mrs. Nickel was a pretty woman in spite of dark circles beneath her eyes. "I'm glad he was gone . . . and the team was, too. Clarke was looking for him. Sam doesn't care who knows he's a Free-State man."

"Speaks his mind." Andy frowned, looking at her closely. "Are you all right, ma'am?" He jerked his head toward the charred wreckage. "They didn't . . . do anything but this?"

"Isn't it enough? Thank goodness, the cows were resting under the trees when we heard the gang coming." She nodded toward the taller boys. "I sent William to take the cows deeper into the woods, and told John to run warn the folks at Trading Post and then find his brother and hide out till the rascals left." A wry smile twitched her lips. "Figured men who brag on being Southern gentlemen wouldn't hurt little boys and a woman."

"Looks like they didn't." Andy's voice was deep with relief.

The woman shrugged, nuzzling her baby's curls. He squealed and patted her face. "They held a pistol to my head to make me tell where Sam was hiding, and they cuffed the boys for sassing them." She gave the smaller lads a prideful glance. They puffed out their scrawny chests. "Those varmints ate the mush and side meat we were having for supper and ransacked everything, but, of course, we didn't have any cash money or fancy stuff. When Sam hadn't come by sundown, they reckoned I was telling the truth about him being gone to Osceola, and they went over the pass."

"But your place is burned. . . ."

"They came back after dark, maybe fifty of them." Mrs. Nickel held her baby closer. "They still hoped they could catch Sam. Made them mad as fire when he wasn't here. They tossed the oldest quilts at us and told us to get out while we could."

She broke off, tears filling her eyes. Her biggest son, taller than she was, put his arm around her and went on with the story. "They had a wagon and team they stole at Trading Post half full of things they thieved before they burned the cabins. They snatched the brass candlesticks our great-granny brought from England, and her little inlaid sewing

94

box. One wanted the maple rocking chair Pa made, when I was born, so Mama could rock me to sleep." He clenched his fists and his blue eyes smoldered. "William and me wanted to try to stop them, but Mama hung onto us and cried."

"Things are things, Billy," she soothed, touching his cheek.

"They carried out the cedar chest Grandpa made Mama for her wedding," he growled.

She sighed. "I purely loved that chest. It smelled so good I kept my best quilts in it." Sadness gave way to outrage as she glanced toward the dead chickens. "The worst thing, what I can't understand at all, is they went in the chicken house and cut the feet off my poor hens! There'd be some sense to stealing them, but to do that. We killed the poor things out of pity."

"We'll give you some hens and a young cockerel who was headed for the frying pan," promised Owen.

"Maybe they won't raid you," she said hopefully. "They were likkered up last night, but, from what I could hear, they meant to burn out Free Staters at Sugar Mound, southwest of Trading Post, and then march . . . or carouse . . . north to Osawatomie to get old John Brown." A shudder went through her in spite of the sultry day. "They said two hundred and fifty militia with a cannon were headed for Osawatomie. Dave

Atchison's leading a bigger mob . . . over two thousand men . . . toward Lawrence to finish what he started in May. One of his officers said he was bound to kill an Abolitionist. If he couldn't shoot a man, he'd kill a woman. If he couldn't find a woman, he'd get a child."

Dan gasped. Apparently shocked speechless, Andy recovered after a moment and said confidently: "Jim Lane'll stop them, or the U.S. Army will. James Montgomery and fifty men with Sharps rifles are after Clarke and his hooligans. We're trying to catch up with Montgomery."

"That little Campbellite preacher who lives northwest of Sugar Mound?" Mrs. Nickel shook her head. "They've been burned out once. Friends helped him build a hewn-log cabin with walls eight inches thick and portholes in the loft to shoot from. Sam says, when Montgomery doesn't sleep out in the fields, he and the family have pallets on the floor to be under the line of fire."

"Maybe they won't have to do that much longer," McHugh said, and lifted his reins, but hesitated. It was hard to leave the family sifting the ashes of their home.

"You're welcome to go stay at the mill with my family," Owen said.

"It'd scare Sam into fits to find this mess and us gone. Thank you kindly, but we'll stay here. Might as well start cutting trees for a new cabin. I hid the axe under the cabin. The handle burned some, but we can use it."

"You don't have any food," Dan protested, wincing at the trampled stalks in the corn-field, the garden where horses had been galloped up and down till not a plant or vine stood. He began untying the sack from his saddle. "This isn't a lot, but. . . ."

"Keep it," she ordered. "Are you forgetting that pile of chickens . . . nineteen good hens and a rooster? The boys will help me pluck and clean them. We'll have our fill of stewed, fried, and roast chicken. What we can't eat before it spoils, we'll smoke." She gave a bitter chuckle. "There'll be plenty of feathers to make new pillows and comforters. And we've got cows to milk. The rapscallions didn't ruin all the potatoes, and there's wild plums. We'll do fine." She looked up fiercely. "You just hurry after Preacher Montgomery and teach that bunch a lesson."

Andy nodded at a spider in the sooty array of salvaged things, a three-legged skillet to set over the coals. One leg was broken off. "I can fix that for you, Missus Nickel. Just have Sam bring it to my place."

"You'll have a sight of worse-broken stuff to mend," she said. "Don't fret about us. Get after Clarke!"

They rode.

It wouldn't do to exhaust their horses. As the day burned hotter, they never urged them faster than a trot. Osawatomie was northwest where Pottawatomie Creek joined the Marais des Cygnes, so they left the Military Road and struck across country.

Dan couldn't get the Nickles family out of his mind. His gorge rose at thought of the chickens, their senseless mutilation. It was the kind of trick bullying schoolboys might pull if they dared.

"When you've helped build a cabin and know how much work it takes . . . how every log's cut and hewn and notched, puncheons smoothed, shingles split out, that makes it seem more wicked than ever to burn one down."

Owen nodded, wiping sweat from his forehead and eyebrows. "Yes. And when you've plowed and harrowed and sowed corn, hoed weeds all summer, it fair looks like murder to see the crop ruined."

"If anyone maimed my mother's hens like that, she'd scream like a banshee." Andy grimaced. He drew up, adding the shield of his hand to that of his hat brim. "There's Middle Creek ahead. Can you make out that swarmin' of horses and cattle and men?"

"It has to be Clarke!" Owen's voice rose. "Looks like they stole every wagon they came across!"

"And everything worth carrying off, you may be sure." Andy frowned as his eyes swept the horizon. "Where's Montgomery? This is the time to hit Clarke, while he's having his noon rest."

"Horsemen southward!" Dan pointed.

Andy veered his horse. "Let's make for them and hope they're not stragglers from Clarke's gang. The timber along the creek should hide us till we're almost into camp." He threw back his head and laughed exultantly. "Och, the whelps of Satan! Won't they be surprised?"

CHAPTER FIVE

Fifty Sharps carbines greeted the newcomers. They lowered only when the smallest man of the avengers laughed and raised his hand. "Welcome, Andy McHugh! You're just in time!"

"Glad of it." Andy swept his arm toward his companions. "Captain Montgomery, here's Owen Parks and Dan O'Brien from the mill. Reckon you don't know them since you use the mill on Mine Creek."

Dan felt as if Montgomery's gray eyes penetrated his inmost self. "You're young, lad, for this kind of outing." The leader's voice was deep and pleasant.

"Not too young," Dan said.

Montgomery looked at Owen. "Are you not a Quaker?"

Owen colored. "I am, but Pa let me follow my conscience."

"I'm no man to go against conscience." James Montgomery had a smile of amazing sweetness. His neatly trimmed beard and moustache were a few shades lighter than his black hair that waved softly back from a long face ruled by a straight, thin nose. He turned in his saddle and called to his men.

"Friends, neighbors, you have your Beecher's Bibles and testaments. Let's preach these scalawags a sermon they'll never forget. Spread out as we near the camp but keep to this side so we won't shoot each other. When I wave my hat, fire."

"Testaments are what they call cartridge boxes," Andy said with a grim laugh.

Dan's heart seemed to rise to his throat and pound there as the horsemen advanced across the prairie toward the trees. From the roistering jollity carried on the wind along with the smell of cooking meat, the raiders had found whiskey along the way.

Apparently they had no suspicion of pursuit. A sentry would have warned them a good while ago. Dan fumbled as he took a dozen cartridges from the bag and stuffed them in the holster after he worked the Colt out of it.

Montgomery's force was almost into the timber, Sharps glinting, fanning out to cover the sprawl of the camp Dan could glimpse through the trees — loaded wagons, cattle, horses, men lounging around several fires. Dan took a deep breath, thumb ready on the hammer, and watched Montgomery.

Slowly, deliberately, the gray hat lifted, then

swung down as Montgomery sighted and fired. In the same instant, fifty other Sharps spewed cartridges. The carbines had to be reloaded, but most of the Free-State men had pistols or revolvers and fired these as they rode into the shouting, howling chaos.

Taken unawares, a few of Clarke's men returned fire, but most made for their horses and spurred away, some bootless, some hatless, some without coats or vests.

They hadn't the slightest notion that they'd been routed by a third of their number — they doubtless thought Jim Lane was upon them — but, if Montgomery pursued them, they'd discover their mistake, rally, and attack.

"They're headed for Missouri, boys!" called Montgomery. "Let them run. We'll take their plunder back to where it belongs . . . and share out their belongings with folks they burned out." He scanned his men. "Praise God, none of you was hurt, but look, here's two of them."

One dark young man held his hands to his thigh. Blood seeped through his fingers. An older whiskery raider bled from shoulder and leg as he tried to crawl to a rifle that had been left behind.

A slim, short man, who could have been taken for a boy except for his scruffy dark beard and moustache, sprang down from his horse and kicked the wounded man away from the weapon, aiming a revolver.

"No, Doctor Jennison!" Montgomery reined between the Missourian and the small man who seemed to be all high boots and hat, a peculiar brimless tall hat that reared from his narrow forehead like a grotesquely elongated furry skull.

"Best kill these two, Captain." Jennison didn't lower his revolver. "That'll make a pair who'll burn no more Free-State cabins!"

There was a chorus of approval. Montgomery quelled it with a glance. "I will exact an eye for an eye, according to God's law, but no one was killed in this marauding."

"They beat an old man at Linnville senseless when he tried to defend his ailing son," grated Jennison.

"He'll recover before these two do."

Jennison spat near the man he had kicked.

Montgomery spoke softly: "Will you honor the ideals of your profession, Doctor? Will you attend these men?"

"I'd attend *to* them if you weren't so. . . ."

A warning growl came from the other Free Staters. Jennison shrugged and swaggered to a pile of abandoned gear. "Who needs some Forty-Four Dragoon Colts?" He held them up with a flourish. "Who needs cartridge boxes? Who'd fancy a spotted calfskin vest? And look at these fancy boots with fancier spurs? I'll have the spurs, but someone else can take the boots."

While Jennison doled out booty and others joined in appropriating the raiders' effects, a spry gray-haired man came to kneel by the dark young Missourian. Glancing up at Montgomery, the older man spoke in an Irish accent that gladdened Dan's heart: "Now, didn't I help surgeons patch up many a poor lad in the Mexican War, Captain? Sure, if someone'll rustle me up some clean cloth and water, I'll do what I can."

" 'Blessed are the merciful, for they shall obtain mercy,' " said Montgomery. "You're a good man, Hughie Huston. I'll take these men home, and my wife will nurse them." He turned to the others. "Now, friends, distributing arms is sensible, since we're the protectors of the region, but whatever else was left behind must go to the raiders' victims, including these kettles that have already cooked our dinner."

"What about Osawatomie and old John Brown?" demanded Jennison.

Montgomery shook his head regretfully. "Whatever was fated to happen is over by now, but who'll ride there and find out how the Free Staters fared?"

Andy McHugh had never dismounted. Now he volunteered to make for Osawatomie, and rode northwest. There was only subdued muttering as the other men dismounted and gathered variously around plunder and cook fires.

Dan and Owen hunted through the raiders' baggage and found some clean socks and a clean shirt. There was no water in the camp, although there were emptied jugs testifying to a drink stronger than water.

Dan took a pail and dipped it in the swiftest flow of the creek, hoping that would be the purest. Admiration and gratitude for Montgomery welled up in him. He'd fired the Navy Colt, and, if he'd killed someone, he thought he could live with it after what he'd seen at the Nickles' place, but he couldn't have watched Jennison murder wounded men — and that probably meant Jennison would have shot him, too.

Old Hughie Huston had cut away the white-faced invader's bloodied trousers and said to Dan: "Will ye pour the water over his hurt easy-like?"

Dan obeyed. His stomach roiled at the dark blood that oozed across the pale skin as fast as he rinsed it away. "You're in grand luck, boy." Hughie's tone was brisk and not unkindly. "Yon bullet didn't nick your artery or you'd have bled out by now. It passed clean through, so I won't be digging around for it." He reached toward Owen. "A pair of those socks, if you please, and tear or cut me the longest piece you may of the shirt."

Hughie deftly packed the heavy socks over the wounds front and back, bade Dan hold the dressings in place, wrapped the strip of shirt around the thigh, and knotted it securely.

The young man's eyes opened. "I'm obliged," he gasped.

"Enough to keep on your side of the border, I hope." Placing a lost hat over the sweating pallid face to shield it from the sun, the old man rose somewhat creakily and surveyed the older, ginger-whiskered marauder who glared at him from bloodshot eyes.

"Mind how you handle me, you damned Irisher!"

Hughie grinned at his helpers. "Now isn't it the fine, courteous tongue he has hid by that filthy beard?"

"I'm an Irisher, too," said Dan, but he went to fetch more water.

The bewhiskered one-eyed Owen shrugged and said: "I'm a Quaker."

"Oh, my God!"

"Ye may well pray, spalpeen," said Hughie severely. "Thank your Creator for sending ye help, instead of Jennison's bullet. Now shut your gob so we won't swoon away from that skull-varnish on your breath."

Hughie hunkered down. None too gently, he used his pocket knife to cut blood-soaked clothing from the shoulder and leg. The man howled and cursed as Dan tipped the bucket on the wounds. "Had I good lye soap, wouldn't I scrub out your mouth for ye!" scolded Hughie. "Stop your blaspheming or

I'll let Doc Jennison at ye."

The profane one glowered but held his peace except for an occasional yelp as Hughie probed out the bullets and, with Owen's aid, dressed and bandaged the hurts.

Neither injured man wanted food, but both drank thirstily from the cup Dan held to their lips. Then, for it had been a long time since breakfast, Dan filled a stolen crockery plate with hominy and ham looted from someone's smokehouse.

When Montgomery's men had eaten and loaded the invaders' belongings into the wagons, Dan helped the captain, Hughie, and Owen hoist the wounded on top of purloined Free-State featherbeds and quilts. Tersely Montgomery detailed men from around Trading Post to return livestock and goods plundered from there, some of which was their own, and take a share of things left by the fleeing pillagers.

Dan and Owen exchanged elated glances when they saw a cedar chest, some brass candlesticks, and a rocking chair. "Those are Missus Nickle's," Owen said. "Let's follow along to see her face."

Dan nodded. Montgomery shook hands with them and thanked them as did Hughie, who asked where Dan was from, and than explained that he himself left County Cork in the starving years and joined the U.S. Army straightaway since work was far scarcer than penniless Irish folk.

"It's better here, lad," said the older man, nodding. "Or will be once slavery's gone from the land. I be a preacher of the United Brethren, but I'll soldier again, if need be, and call it God's work." He glanced at the party breaking up to head for their respective homes. "There'll be quite some jollification at Sugar Mound when we turn up with these critters and all this plunder. Looks like we got back just about everything they robbed from Ebenezer Barnes's store before they burned it."

"We'll raise him a new one," said Montgomery. He glanced pridefully at his men. "We'll build back for everybody who lost a cabin. And in a few days I want some of you to ride along with me to call on proslavery men . . . not quiet ones who mind their own business, but the sort who spy for Border Ruffians and help them against us."

Jennison's eyes flamed. "I'll help you hang or shoot them all!"

Montgomery frowned. "There'll be no killing yet. We'll tell them plain that the shoe's on the other foot. They must leave Kansas or be driven out. . . ."

Lusty cheering interrupted him and shouts of: "We're with you, Captain!"

"We'll dose the devil spawn with their own physic!" cried Hughie. He shielded his eyes. "Yonder comes that young Scotsman, isn't it,

108

Captain? Looks like his sorrel nag."

It was indeed Andy McHugh who'd encountered Free Staters returning home after being scattered by invaders who outnumbered them more than five to one and had a cannon as well.

"When old John Brown heard the Missourians were coming, he got together forty men," Andy said, slumping wearily in the saddle. "They posted themselves behind a stone fence near the river and held off the mob till the cannon blasted too many holes in the wall. Brown . . . and everyone else lit out."

"Was anyone killed?"

"Not in the fight. But Frederick Brown, old John's son, was going down the road alone when he met the raiders. They shot him down."

Montgomery bowed his head. "God rest his soul, and pardon him. He was one of the Brown sons who hacked to death the Doyle boys and other proslavery men at Dutch Henry's Crossing in May." He threw up his head. "Where are the marauders?"

Andy shrugged. "They burned four or five Free-State houses at Osawatomie, broke out their whiskey, and headed back to Missouri."

Plainly torn, Montgomery considered a moment. "We can't catch up to them, and, if we did, we can't tackle five times our number and a cannon." His jaw set. "But I'm not through with these malefactors. I'm a teacher and I'm going to teach them to stay on their side of the border."

A young, red-headed Irishman raised a carroty eyebrow. "Now, how will you be doing that, Captain? Preach them a sermon?"

"Why, Pat Devlin" — Montgomery smiled — "I think I'll find a teaching position around West Point and find out who Clarke's main supporters are."

"And then?" pressed Devlin.

"Then we'll raid *them*. Relieve them of enough to make up for what they destroyed over here."

"I'm your man," vowed Devlin, and was echoed by the others.

"I won't need all of you," Montgomery said. "But those who can take the time from your crops meet at Sugar Mound tomorrow morning."

Devlin's green eyes shone. "Will we be calling on the proslavers?"

"We will."

"And maybe lessening the loads and livestock they'll have to take across the line?"

"No robbing." Montgomery's eyes and voice were stern. "I say it now for all to hear . . . if we are raided, we'll raid back. From those who despoil us . . . those only . . . we'll exact compensation. If a Missourian kills one of us in less than a fair fight, we will take him, if we can, try him, and hang him."

He paused, giving weight to each word. "We must be our own law since this territory is in the power of proslavers elected by Border Ruffians. But we *must* have law lest we sink to their level."

Jennison shrugged. "You're too much the parson, Captain Montgomery." He squinted a challenge. "What will you say if a proslaver captures a slave in Kansas . . . as federal law declares that he can . . . and then sells him or collects a reward for returning him. What then?"

"If we catch the man stealer, he shall be tried by a jury of twelve."

"And?"

Montgomery sighed, but his words rang clear. "If he is guilty, we will deal with him according to Exodus Twenty-One, Sixteen. 'And he that stealeth a man, and selleth him, or if he be found in his hand, he shall surely be put to death.' "

"Amen," said Hughie.

"Amen," echoed the others.

Dan's scalp prickled. This wasn't the end of border trouble. It would get worse before it got better. What if someone like Jennison burned the happy house just because it was in Missouri? Or if proslavers burned it because the Wares were from Illinois and almost certain to oppose slavery?

"I'll ride with you tomorrow, Captain," promised Andy.

Owen looked sheepish. "I'll fight if we're invaded, but I don't feel right about forcing neighbors out of the country even if they are proslavery."

Jennison hooted. Montgomery checked him with a glance. "Abide by your conscience, young man. I would not for the world have you go against it. God speaks to us in different ways." Dismounting, he hitched his horse to the back of the wagon with the wounded men, and drove away with the main cavalcade and most of the rescued cattle and horses.

Dan and his friends soon outdistanced the Trading Post wagon that carried Mrs. Nickel's treasures. As the three came in sight of the farm below Prairie Mound, Andy whistled. "It looks like an Indian camp when they're smoking meat."

"Except Indian camps don't have burned cabins," said Owen. "Or cows being milked. Look, that woman and the youngsters have already made a shelter with branches trimmed off trees they've cut for logs."

The family swarmed out to meet the horsemen. When Mrs. Nickel heard the Missourians had been sent scuttling for the border and that her valued belongings would shortly be returned, a joyful smile turned her weary face young and pretty.

"Thank the Lord . . . and James Montgomery! That riff-raff won't be so eager to try driving us away when they know we're going to fight back. Light down, young men, and have some roast chicken. You can see there's plenty."

"We helped ourselves to the raiders' dinner, ma'am," said Andy, chuckling. "Anyway, we need to get home so our folks won't be worrying about us any longer than they have to."

"My sisters will come over tomorrow and bring you some hens and a rooster," Owen promised. "You're sure you'll be all right here tonight?"

"We'll be fine now that thieving gang's run across the border. Besides, Sam might drop dead of apoplexy if he found this mess and none of us." Her smile broadened. "Anyway, won't I soon have my rocking chair to rest in?"

"That's a brave woman," Andy said after he'd collected the spider to repair and they waved and rode on. "She needs to be for what's coming."

Dan thought with a pang of his foster sisters and Christy Ware, of her gentle mother and baby sister. Christy was brave, he knew that, but would they, could they, endure what everyone seemed to believe lay ahead?

CHAPTER SIX

The livid burn scar above the pulse of Christy's wrist throbbed as if probed with red-hot wire. She glanced catty-corner across the table. Lafe Ballard stared fixedly at the scar, then met her look with eyes so pale they were like ice under a winter sky. He smiled, lips parting over narrow teeth.

Christy forced herself to meet his gaze, but broke out in cold sweat when he went back to his ciphering. Her father hadn't seen — he was listening to Matthew Hayes and Tressie Barclay read from *McGuffey's Second Reader.*

Anyway, what had happened? Lafe had only looked at her. She had never told anyone that he'd burned her on purpose because she liked Hester so much. Sometimes Christy even wondered if she'd been mistaken, but the look she'd caught just now made her know it was no accident.

If he got the chance, he'd hurt her again. She'd do her best to see he didn't have that chance. It was a good thing the Hayes boys' way home ran a mile beyond the Ballard place so they saw the Barclay girls safe that far.

Christy tried to concentrate on Henry Thoreau's *Walden* that her father much admired and had assigned as her reading since she and Thos had already finished *McGuffey's Readers.* Her spelling and composition lesson was to look up words she didn't know, learn them, and use them in an essay. Her eyes caught the swirl of golden leaves drifting from the great walnut, and she thought back to that cold wind from the north that brought the first frost shortly after Christy's thirteenth birthday on the 10th of October, two weeks ago.

Overnight, the freeze shriveled sweet potato and pumpkin vines flat and black. Trees began to glow flame, russet, gold, and yellow and skies filled with the high-pitched call of snow geese flying south in long, wavering lines, honking wedges of Canada geese, and the bugling of sandhill cranes. Great blue herons winged silently, usually alone, necks drawn back in elegant S curves, and all manner of ducks landed to feed in the corn stubble where quail, chickens, and wild turkeys devoured both insects and fallen grain.

The great marvel was sky-darkening flocks of passenger pigeons settling like heavy clouds in the forest to gorge on the acorns so relished by Patches, Evalina, and their seventeen lusty white-spotted black offspring. The pigs were shut up in the evening but five of the younglings had fallen prey to wolves, foxes, bobcats, or panthers.

"The pigeons will stay till it freezes," Hester Ballard said as she stopped to visit, and they all looked up at a vast flight of birds. "In spring, they'll be back to gobble fallen acorns. The flock splits up then into pairs that go off to nest deep in the woods. The squabs are mighty tasty."

Jonathan Ware studied the teeming mass of feathers. Unlike ducks, geese, and cranes, the pigeons had no leader or formation. They simply swarmed forward. "From beak to tail, a pigeon's about sixteen inches long and its wingspread would be close to that," he mused. "So let's take a mile-wide, two hundred yard long cross-section of the flock and figure it twenty-five yards in depth, one pigeon above another. Allowing a cubic yard for each, that would make eight million eight hundred thousand birds per minute passing the cross-section." When Hester looked perplexed, he added: "Men who've watched flights for hours on end reckon there may be over two billion in some of them. Those who study such things think the pigeons make up a quarter to nearly half of all the birds in this country."

"There's aplenty." Hester gazed in awe at

Jonathan. "Can you teach Lafe to calculate like that in his head?"

"If he has the knack."

"I hope he'll have a knack for something besides shooting. He brought home a deer the other day that'll help feed us this winter, but I wish he hadn't got it the way he did."

"How was that?" asked Jonathan.

"That no-account Watt Caxton hit on the notion of salting the ground and building a platform to shoot from. Deer watch for trouble at their own level, you know, not upwards. He invited some of his cock-fighting, bear-baiting friends." Her lips tightened. "They killed fifty deer in a few hours. That's not hunting. It's pure slaughter."

"Lafe's young," Jonathan said at last.

Hester shook her head. "There's a streak in him that worries me. I sure don't want him hanging out with the likes of Watt. I'm glad you'll have him in school soon, Jonathan. That should straighten him out."

Christy glanced at the scar on her wrist, the burn Lafe had caused. *Nothing will straighten Lafe out till he's laid in his coffin.* Startled and chilled by the certainty, she wished he weren't coming to school.

"You've got your walls all chinked against bitter weather," Hester approved. With a glint in her hazel eyes, she added: "Looks like your new chimney's not going to topple over like

117

the first one."

Christy had thought they'd never finish chinking the walls inside and out, but at least the pure clay they found in the side of a gully didn't have to be mixed with lime. Thinned with a little water, it dried hard and almost white. After the chimney her father and the boys had made had crashed to the ground, Ethan Hayes had supervised the building of the next one, setting the rock foundation, deep and firm, in the ground, making sure the space above and behind the chimney throat was bigger than it was, and that the chimney narrowed down at the top to the size of the throat so that it would draw properly.

Once corn was in the cribs and fall wheat was sowed and harrowed, Charlie Ware had left to drive a wagon on the Santa Fé Trail for a well-to-do planter named Jardine, who he'd met at Simeon Parks's mill when he took their corn to be ground. Jardine had a controlling interest in the freight company and was one of the few landowners in the region who owned more than one or two slaves. Jonathan and Ellen couldn't have liked Charlie's working for a slave owner, especially one with a pretty daughter that Charlie blushed about, but they left the decision to him. The family all missed Charlie. It didn't seem right that he wasn't there for meals or when Ellen played the piano of an evening.

With farm work pretty much done till spring plowing and planting, school could begin. The study space was chosen to get the best light from one window and warmth from the fire once winter came. Ellen's loom was set up by the other window, close to Beth's crib. Jonathan and Thos made an oblong table of beautifully grained walnut long enough to fit over two benches that each seated four students.

Classes began at nine the first Monday in October. Maps of the world and the United States brightened the wall. Jonathan had a good supply of chalk and enough slates to supply the Hayes boys, whose only book to bring from home was a tattered hymnal.

Lafe brought his mother's old slate and Dr. Jaynes's almanac. The serious little brown-haired twins, ten-year-old Tressie and Phyllis Barclay, who lived beyond the Franzes, had slates, tablets, and *Webster's Blue Back Speller.* Jonathan had several copies of the speller, *McGuffey's Readers,* and texts of history, geography, and arithmetic. Allie Hayes had taught her boys the alphabet and to read a little, so Matthew and Mark went into the second reader with Tressie. Lafe simmered at being in primer with Luke Hayes and Phyllis Barclay, especially when he saw that Christy and Thos were through the readers and studied from their father's library, working mostly at composition and advanced mathematics.

Which, a few weeks later, brought Christy back to Thoreau. Taking care not to glance toward Lafe, she dipped the goose quill pen in the ink well and prayed not to blot her work with a disastrous drop. Mr. Thoreau says he has lived thirty years without hearing a syllable of valuable advice from his seniors. It may be as well that he prefers to live alone.

Jonathan rang the hand bell to signal morning recess. These respites were just long enough for the pupils to get drinks, visit the log privy, and race around a few minutes to work off the effects of sitting on a hard bench. At noon though, after lunches were consumed, they spilled out to play crack-the-whip, red rover, hide-and-seek, fox-and-geese, and drop-the-handkerchief. On rainy days, inside, they played old mother gobble wobble, do-as-I-do, forfeits, and London Bridge.

The older children took turns bringing pails of drinking water from the creek. This morning was Christy's time. In spite of digging in various places, Jonathan, much to his and Ellen's vexation, always struck solid rock that kept him from reaching water near the house.

Watching for cottonmouths, although it was time for any sensible snake to den up for the winter, Christy filled the bucket. Leaning to one side from its weight, she toiled up the bank as Robbie barkingly announced a stranger on horseback.

Tall and gaunt, he wore a dark military coat with a red-lined cape. A slouch hat was pulled down to shaggy eyebrows jutting above dark gray eyes. He was clean-shaven and his face was deeply lined.

Jonathan and Ellen came out to greet him. If he gave his name, Christy was too far away to hear it, but she reached the house as Ellen was saying: "Won't you rest a bit, sir, and have some corndodgers and buttermilk?"

"Why, lady," he said in a voice that had the wild wind in it, "I'd welcome a bite, but I'll have it out here because, unless I'm much mistaken, you have a school and will be calling your scholars in."

He dismounted, towering over Jonathan, who was close to six feet tall, and with a soft word, tied his chestnut gelding to one of the stumps left for that purpose. He frowned at Christy's bucket as Ellen brought his refreshment.

"Wouldn't you like to have a well, lady?"

"My husband's started half a dozen wells, sir. We seem to have solid rock under us."

The stranger's smile used some of the wrinkles in his face and made him less forbidding. "Well, lady, when I've finished this excellent buttermilk, with your leave, I'll cut a willow branch and find a place for your good husband to dig."

"You can witch water?" Jonathan asked.

The cadaverous man's smile vanished. "No witch about it, sir. Does not God command that thou shalt not suffer a witch to live? It's enough that a forked willow branch points down for me where water flows beneath."

"There must be some law of physics operating," Jonathan mused.

"Rather," said the stranger, "call it the grace of God in aiding his children." He looked piercingly at Jonathan. "Before I find your well, I have one question."

"What?"

"If a fugitive slave stopped here for help, would you give it or turn him in for the reward?"

Ellen and Jonathan exchanged glances. Ellen put her hand on her husband's arm as he answered: "With God's help, we will aid anyone who comes to our door."

"If you're going to help a runaway, you'd better devise a good hiding place in case his master's hot on his heels." The stranger peered even more intently at the Wares. "Supposing that master . . . or a proslavery man . . . craved shelter and food?"

Ellen said firmly: "We'd give it, sir. Just as we did to you."

"I fear, lady, that helping all will get you the help of none when the shooting starts. Even the Son of God said he came not to bring peace, but a sword."

The Wares stood close together. They were not touching but it was clear they were joined, soul and mind. After a moment, the tall man shrugged. "I'll find your well."

Jonathan nodded. "We're much obliged for your efforts, sir. It's time I called my students in, but let me know if I can assist you."

Christy carried the bucket inside and set it on the small table that held the wash basin. As Jonathan rang his hand bell and Christy's schoolmates came in, rushing or loitering according to their interest in lessons, she saw the visitor cutting a forked willow branch. Coming up the slope, he gripped one fork in each hand, bending over, with the base of the limb pointing down. She wanted to watch but another ring of the bell called her to her seat.

To settle his pupils down after their racing about, Jonathan usually read to them, or talked a while in a way that interested even the youngest.

"You all know Missouri mules are famous," he began, smiling at shy little Phyllis while keeping a quizzical eye on squirming Luke. "But did you know most of them descend from jacks and jennets brought from New Mexico in Eighteen Twenty-Three? Trading with Mexico and steamboating that began a few years earlier made Missouri prosper. She's still the gateway to the West and that makes her very important."

"Did Missouri belong to Mexico once?" puzzled Matthew Hayes. "Or was it Spain? Or maybe France?"

"France gave Spain New Orleans and all her lands west of the Mississippi in Seventeen Sixty-Two, but when Napoléon came to power after the French Revolution, he made Spain give back Louisiana. He needed money for wars against England, so he sold what was known as Louisiana to the United States in Eighteen Oh-Three. There had been French and Spanish settlers around Saint Louis, but, after the War of Eighteen Twelve, Americans like Daniel Boone swarmed into the eastern part of the territory."

"Weren't there lots of Indians?" breathed Mark Hayes.

"Yes. Some, like the Osages, Kansas, and Missouris, had been here a long time. Others, like the Sac and Fox, had been forced down from the north by the powerful Iroquois. Others, like the Shawnees and Delawares, moved into Missouri toward the end of the last century because American settlers were crowding them. All these Indians have villages and farms. They hunt a lot, but they also grow corn, beans, melons, and pumpkins, and many keep livestock."

"Did they fight each other?" asked Lafe.

"Of course, just like the English, French, and American colonists battled. As white folk poured into this region . . . they'd heard the ground was so rich that if you planted a ninepenny nail at night, by morning it would've sprouted crowbars . . . the government kept making treaties with the tribes to trade their Missouri lands for holdings in Kansas and what's now Indian Territory. By Eighteen Thirty-Six, there were no tribal lands left in Missouri."

"Our grampa fought in the Black Hawk War on the upper Mississippi in the summer of Eighteen Thirty-Two," said Matthew. "He saw Chief Black Hawk when he was a prisoner at Jefferson Barracks. Said he was a fine-looking man, proud as a king."

Jonathan nodded. "Black Hawk claimed the treaty ceding Sac and Fox land in Wisconsin and Illinois was signed by chiefs who had no authority. That's also what the Cherokees maintained twenty years ago when they were driven from the East on the Trail of Tears that led to Indian Territory. At any rate, the Indians who once lived in Missouri are now our neighbors across the line in Kansas and down in Indian Territory."

"Where, more shame to them, Cherokees and others of the Five Civilized Tribes hold slaves." Everyone whirled at the harsh voice from the door. "I've found your water, sir. Let me show you where to dig and I'll be on my way."

"Study your spelling while I'm outside," Jonathan told his pupils.

"I bet that's old John Brown," Lafe whispered. "I've heard he wears a caped coat like that and has eyes like a cold storm."

Matthew's blue eyes widened. "Wonder what he's doing over here?"

"Stealing slaves, of course," Lafe sneered.

"No one around here has any."

"It's not far to some who do, like Doctor Hamelton and Bishop Jardine." This last was the planter Charlie worked for. Apparently it wasn't against his religion to own slaves. Lafe chuckled in sudden inspiration. "I'll tell Watt Caxton on my way home. He says Brown ought to be tarred and feathered. Maybe Watt can attend to that."

"Watt's great for baiting bears, fighting cocks, and shooting treed panthers," Matthew said. "I don't see him getting in range of that Sharps."

Jonathan came in, the boys hushed, and Christy craned her neck to watch through the window as the stranger rode away. She thought about him all day. He, with his sons and a few other men, had murdered five men, two of them not much older than Charlie. That he had prayed first to the stern Old Testament God of Moses, Gideon, and Joshua only made the slaughter more terrible.

Still, if he rescued slaves. . . . Christy shuddered to remember how she'd overheard her father telling her mother about two slaves who had just lately been burned alive in

Carthage for killing their master.

How tangled it all was, right and wrong. Yet Christy knew one thing. She'd help hide any slave who came this way, trying not to get her parents mixed up in it. That meant she needed to find a hiding place better than the corncrib or barn or loft.

What of the underground river?

Her heart raced as she remembered her escape with Dan O'Brien. The cavern, as best she could judge, ran under the ridge that reared gray palisades on the other side of the creek. There must not be any open sinkholes or she and Dan would have noticed the glow of moonlight as they groped their way, but there might be the beginnings of one, a crack that could be pried or hammered at to make an opening.

It was time to gather hickory and hazel nuts. If her mother let her do that Saturday, she'd look hard for a way into the hidden passage.

Saturday, as it turned out, she helped her mother wash in the morning while her father and Thos started the well with a pick and shovels. By afternoon, they had dug too deep to toss out the earth with shovels and handed up buckets of earth that Christy dumped for them. As the hole deepened, Jonathan rigged a log windlass to raise and lower the buckets. Christy stayed busy till time for evening chores.

Sunday morning was given over to simple church services. When neighbors learned that Jonathan Ware was a minister, although a Universalist one, they asked if he wouldn't preach for them. Arly Maddux's fire-and-brimstone Baptist sermons were too much for any of them, except the Caxtons.

"I'll speak of God's goodness and human duty," Jonathan had said, smiling. "It won't be what you're used to, but you'll get a blessing from the way my wife plays the piano."

So Hester, the Hayeses, Lige and Sarah Morrow, and Emil and Lottie Franz filled the cabin they'd helped to build and sang fervently, if not in tune. They listened attentively as Jonathan spoke on some parable, saying, or act of Jesus. After more hymns and a closing prayer, the women set out the food they'd brought to share, and it was mid-afternoon when they took their leave. The Caxtons had come once, the Sunday Jonathan had talked about Jesus's calling the children to him and saying that of such was the kingdom of heaven.

"Are you sayin' babies that aren't baptized still go to heaven, Ware?" Caxton demanded after the service.

"You can't believe God is wicked enough to send babies to hell, neighbor."

"God's ways ain't for us to question."

"He gave us reason. He must intend for us to use it. More, he gave us hearts. Who of us would throw a baby into an everlasting lake of fire? Does God have less compassion than his creatures?"

Caxton choked, muttered something about blaspheming, and hustled his wife outside.

Whatever the other neighbors thought of Jonathan Ware's trust that God was too good to send anyone to hell, most of them gathered at the Ware home Sunday mornings. It being the Sabbath, helping with the well after dinner was prohibited, but Ethan Hayes and Lige Morrow said they'd come next day and dig.

"Better get it done before the ground freezes or the weather turns nasty," Hayes pointed out. "It'll take you and Thos a mighty long time, Jonathan, if you just dig Saturdays and an hour or so after school."

"But you've already helped us so much!"

"What are neighbors for?" Morrow grinned. Clad in buckskins even for church, he shifted his tobacco to the other cheek. "Fact is, the meetin's and the good food, shared after, sure make us feel lots more like neighbors, don't they, Sarah?"

Her dark eyes shone. The store-bought yellow calico, exquisitely sewed with a pointed basque, was bright amongst the muted grays and browns of homespun. Lottie Franz's dark gray serge also came from a store, but the color and style were so somber that Hester whispered to Allie Hayes that it put her in mind of what a nun might wear.

"I love singing again," Sarah Morrow confided. "Anyway, since you hold school here and the children need water, it's only fair for the rest of us to help with the well."

"But you don't have any children . . . ," Ellen began, and broke off.

If that was a sensitive spot, Sarah didn't show it. "Children are everybody's, aren't they?" She laughed. "We'll certainly be better off if neighborhood youngsters grow up to be good people."

She passed her big wood bowl of honey-nut cakes. When they were gone and the dishes washed, the guests went home. Eager to start her search for a way into the cavern, Christy changed Beth's diaper without being asked.

When she looked up, her mother was smiling at her, which made it easy to say: "Could I go look for nuts if I watch the sun and get home in time to feed the chickens and gather the eggs?"

Ellen and Jonathan exchanged glances. Apparently they decided nut gathering was too uncertain an effort to be ranked as work that would violate the Sabbath. "Yes, but take Robbie with you," Ellen said, "and mind you're home well before sundown. Thos, do you want to go with your sister?"

He looked up from *Moby Dick,* a thick novel that Christy hadn't attempted to read. "Not if I don't have to," he said pleadingly.

"I'd liefer have Robbie," Christy retorted. She got an oak-split basket Lige had given them and ran out into the rich autumnal air.

The blaze of reds of golds along the creek made her catch her breath in wonder that was almost pain. The air filling her lungs was so rich that it seemed full of the glorious colors and afternoon sun.

Robbie alongside, Christy ran past the grapevines and maiden blush apple trees Emil Franz had given them, but had to slow down for the rough clods of the cornfield. Jonathan and the boys had plowed and harrowed about an acre early in September and planted it to wheat, but the broken sod of the rest would rot during the winter and, by spring, be much easier to plow. Stumps would be grubbed out or burned as time permitted.

Passing the thicket of papaw trees where she had gathered delicious fruit when its green-yellow turned brown, Christy slipped through the towering brilliance of sycamores, oaks, and walnuts and picked her way through the willows on the sandbar that reached so close to the other bank that she could leap it.

That plunge and her scramble up the snaky roots of a white-trunked sycamore caused an explosion of luminous green parakeets that winged off in a shimmering cloud. Christy watched them out of sight. Then, trying to keep her basket clear of luxuriant tangles of spicebush, sassafras, and young hickory, she found a dense thicket of hazelnuts and picked busily while Robbie lunged about after exciting smells.

Leaving plenty of nuts for the squirrels, she moved toward the ridge she believed must run above the secret passage. Hester had shown Christy several kinds of hickory and told her all had good nuts, except for the bitternut that had tighter, smoother bark than its relatives. "Squirrels like them," Hester explained, "but if you bite into one by mistake, you'll spit it out in a hurry."

As Christy picked from shagbark, kingnut, and mockernut hickories, the four-sectioned husks sometimes finished splitting from the shells. By shaking boughs she could reach, Christy soon filled the basket. Feeling virtuous at fulfilling her alleged purpose for the outing, she hung the basket over a snag on a dead tree and began to explore the ridge.

Falling leaves hid much of the lichen-crusted rock spine rearing above the forested creek bottom. Christy walked along, scuffing leaves and débris away from depressions and crevices.

If Dan O'Brien were searching with her, it would be more fun. Surely he could find a way into what had been their refuge. She frowned to remember the news her father had brought back from the mill, that Dan and

Owen Parks had ridden with Andy McHugh to drive out the proslave invaders.

Dan was too young for that, only a year older than Thos! She shivered at the idea of her brother firing a gun or being shot at. Dan could have been killed. Somehow she knew his answer to that. He'd laugh and say he was lucky not to have died in Ireland.

A distant sound roused her from these thoughts. Dogs? Their baying, far off as it was, sent a chill through her. Even if they were Lige's hounds instead of Watt Caxton's, she didn't want to meet them in full cry, especially not with Robbie who was brash enough to take on a pack.

She called the dog, but he set up a furious barking at something under a ledge. Whatever lured him, fox, bobcat, wolf, or bear, she only wanted to get the little collie safely home.

"Robbie!" She hurried toward the ledge and grasped the ruff of his neck. "Robbie, come on! Don't you hear those hounds?"

"I hear 'em, missy," came a husky voice.

A man rose from his crouch beneath the overhang. His skin was dark as the shadows. He was tall. Big. Black. Christy smothered a cry and shrank away.

"For the love of Jesus Savior, little girl," whispered the man, "you know where I can hide?"

CHAPTER SEVEN

Should she take the runaway to her parents?
She couldn't think of anything else to do.
Frightened as she was, she knew his scent
had to be lost in the water or the hounds
would trail him.

"We'll hide you," she breathed, whirling,
hushing Robbie. "But, first, you've got to follow along in the creek, then run to the cabin.
I'll go tell my parents. Hurry!"

He plunged down the slope. Christy pelted
after him, grabbing her basket as she passed
the snag. It wouldn't do for the pursuers to
find the abandoned harvest near the fugitive's
spoor.

Heedless of scratches, she reached the creek
in time to see the hunted man vanish around
the curve that bounded the cornfield and
thanked heaven for the uncleared woods that
stretched on that side within fifty yards of the
house. The hounds might pick up his trail
again, but no one should glimpse him making for refuge.

Robbie barked toward the increasing racket of the hounds, but Christy called him and he came reluctantly, growling when he looked backward.

Bursting into the cabin, Christy gasped: "A man . . . a slave! Hounds are after him! I sent him down the creek and told him to come here."

Ellen's hand flew to her throat. She glanced around the room and toward the loft.

"The first place they'd look," Jonathan said. "Think of somewhere else. Thos, let's get some burning sticks in a pail. We're going to burn off the weeds and leaves to cover the man's trail on this side."

"Won't the men after him think that's strange?" worried Ellen.

"Most farmers do burn off dry grass and weeds in the fall," Jonathan assured her. "It helps new grass come up and keeps wildfires from being so dangerous. Ethan's been telling me I should do it."

The Ware men folk rushed out with their small torches. Christy stared at her mother. "The barn? Smokehouse?"

Ellen shook her head before a little smile eased the alarm on her face. "The well! We'll give him a quilt to wrap up in and then toss in enough dirt to cover him. If we have time!"

"Maybe the hounds will run up and down the creek a while," Christy hoped. "Oh, I wish he'd get here!"

"Maybe you'd better feed the chickens and gather the eggs. I'll start the milking. Whoever's after the poor man won't know that's Thos's chore."

The hounds! From across the creek, a good half mile away, their clamor froze her blood. What if her attempt to rescue the man got her father killed or their home burned, the happy house their neighbors had helped raise on that day that now seemed so long ago?

Outside, smoke rose from the cornfield and adjoining forest. Although her knees quivered, Christy took a pan and went to where cracked corn was stored in a covered barrel in the granary built onto the smokehouse. As she stepped out with grain for the chickens, she saw the colored man break from the trees. She set the pan on a stump and gestured him toward the well. The hole was perhaps ten feet deep. If the manhunters came this way, Christy hoped they wouldn't wonder why the diggers hadn't cleaned all the loose dirt from the bottom.

Christy got the shovels from the dogtrot as Ellen ran out with a quilt. She explained the plan as she wound the quilt around the panting, exhausted fugitive. "I'm sorry we'll have to cover you with earth," she said, "but it's the best thing we can think of."

The man actually chuckled. Christy saw he was young. A prime hand, a planter would say, with many years of hard work left in him.

"Just so I'm not covered up permanent, ma'am." He leaped down without hesitation, tenting the quilt over his head so he could breathe. "Maybe," came his muffled voice, "your men folk will plumb burn up my trail and the hounds won't come here."

Even if they didn't, the pursuers would almost certainly stop to question the Wares. Heart pounding as the baying sounded just across the creek, Christy helped her mother shovel dirt from the pile beside the hole, trying to spread it evenly over man and quilt rather than dump it in a mass. When none of the quilt showed through, they put up their shovels and went about their chores with the din of the hounds approaching.

Christy's hands shook so much that she dropped an egg, which was too bad since the hens' laying declined with the shortening days. As she barred the door to keep them and haughty Cavalier safe from wild creatures that would fancy a chicken dinner, four horsemen at the edge of the cornfield were silhouetted in the dusk against the burning leaves and brush. They were talking to Jonathan and Thos, but it was too far away to hear what they said.

Hounds milled around the riders or lay as if exhausted. Robbie whined from inside where he'd been left to keep him out of trouble. Nape prickling at sight of the pack, Christy hoped they stayed where scorched soil and weeds should hide the scent of the fleeing slave. She liked dogs but she was deathly afraid of these.

Cold sweat formed beads and trickled between her small breasts as she went inside and put the eggs on the shelf. Beth was still asleep, thank goodness. It would take Ellen a while to finish milking, so, with dry mouth and blood drumming in her ears, Christy built up the fire, lit a candle, washed her hands, and poured cornmeal into a kettle of water. After a hearty dinner such as they'd had at noon, mush and milk was usually their supper.

Outside, voices neared. One was her father's. Thos called that he was going to help Ellen with the milking. Jonathan came in, followed by a well-dressed stout man with thick graying reddish hair, Watt Caxton, and Lafe Ballard, who, from behind the men, and with no warmth in his pale eyes, showed his teeth to Christy in a smile more frightening than a scowl.

"Christy, will you pour buttermilk for our guests?" Jonathan requested. "Bishop Jardine, this is my oldest daughter, Christina."

Charlie's employer. The one with the pretty daughter. Christy mumbled something and started dipping buttermilk from a crock into delft mugs. Jardine continued to appraise her from cider-colored eyes.

"You favor your brother, young lady," he

138

said in a genial tone as she handed him his drink. "You must come visit my daughter for a month or so when your parents can spare you. Melissa gets lonesome, especially with her brother gone with yours to be a teamster."

This wasn't the time to say her parents would never let her visit a household supported by slaves. Christy thanked him and handed a mug to Watt Caxton. His acknowledgement was a jerk of the head that made his pointed black beard seem to stab his chest. Did he have any notion, Christy wondered, who had turned the bears loose?

It was certain that under the guise of needing refreshment Jardine was scrutinizing every niche of the cabin. Short of an outright confrontation, he couldn't let hounds search the property.

As he accepted his milk, Lafe grinned. Perhaps only to her did his — "Much obliged." — sound mocking, but there was no doubt that, as he sometimes did in school, he now stared at the scar on her wrist as if it gave him pleasure.

"Are you sure you won't have supper?" Jonathan asked.

"Obliged, but nothing's going to set well on my stomach till I catch that rascally Justus," growled Jardine. His glance fleered to Christy. "You didn't see my slave, Christina, while your father and brother were burning off the field?"

She hoped she answered swiftly enough and that her face didn't flush as hotly as she felt it was. "I didn't see your slave, Bishop Jardine." *I saw a man in trouble. I don't believe in slaves.*

Watt Caxton said in his braying voice: "Could be the nigger hid in the loft or outbuildings and no one saw him. You won't mind, will you, Mister Ware, if we have a look around?"

Jonathan said with perfect courtesy, meeting Jardine's gaze: "I'm sure you'll understand, gentlemen, that as an American citizen I must oppose the searching of my home by anyone but an officer of the law with a proper warrant." He didn't, of course, know where Justus was hidden.

Jardine sighed. From beneath his well-cut coat, he drew an ivory-handled pistol. At the same instant, Watt Caxton pulled a revolver. Lafe had nothing but his smile.

"I'm sorry for this necessity, Mister Ware." Jardine did sound regretful. "However, views you've been heard to express prove you no friend of owner's rights and you're known to be unorthodox, even denying the existence of hell."

"Brother, I affirm rather the goodness of God."

Jardine shook his head. "I paid a Cherokee planter twelve hundred dollars for Justus only a month ago, sir. I mean to have him back, even if it costs me more than that. I'll make him an example my other slaves will think about if they're tempted to head north."

Jonathan must have remembered what happened at Carthage, the awful thing he'd whispered to Ellen. "Bishop, you wouldn't burn him?"

"No, but my overseer, Blake, down there, who's watching the hounds, will open his back with a lash and fill the wounds with salt before he cuts off Justus's toes. Justus will be able to work, but, I assure you, sir, he won't run again."

Jonathan caught in his breath. "You should beg my daughter's pardon, Bishop, for speaking such wickedness in front of her. Even more, you should be ashamed before the God we both aspire to serve."

Jardine's ruddy face crimsoned darkly. For a moment, he almost raised the pistol before he controlled himself. "There were slaves in Jesus's day, Mister Ware. In Colossians Three, Twenty-Three does not Paul command them to obey their masters in all things?"

"Paul, not Jesus."

It was Jardine's time to gasp. "Will you dispute with the apostle, sir?"

"That I dispute often with Paul is one reason I'm a Universalist."

"God will judge you though man may do so first." Jardine turned to his companions. "I'll keep the Wares company while you check

141

the loft and rest of the cabin and outbuildings." As Lafe got the ladder to the loft and
cast a taunting grin at Christy, the bishop
warned: "Don't damage anything, mind you,
and keep an eye out for Missus Ware and the
boy. I don't want anyone hurt."

Caxton took the candle and went out
through the dogtrot to the other room. The
ceiling creaked under Lafe's tread. He
wouldn't find anything up there but Thos's
pallet and clothes.

"The mush needs stirring," Christy said.
She moved toward the fireplace with a half-
formed thought to throw the steaming mix-
ture on the bishop.

"I'll stir it for you." He did so, rather
awkwardly, without lowering the pistol.

"Nothing up here, Bishop." Lafe dropped
disgustedly down the ladder. "Shall I look in
the barn?"

"Yes, but wait for Mister Caxton. He can
hold the candle while you search."

"Does your mother know what you're doing, Lafe?" asked Jonathan.

"I was at Watt's when the bishop came
along and asked Watt to use his hounds. But
what Ma thinks don't matter, Mister Ware."
Lafe's eyes glittered and he laughed. "I'm
not coming back to your stupid little school."

"Lafe seems a lad of promise and I can use
him," Jardine said. "Our freighting company
has a contract to haul supplies to Fort Ri-

ley . . . that's located between the Oregon and Santa Fé Trails . . . to protect travelers on both routes. And there's more hauling than we can handle from Independence to serve merchants in towns not reached by steamboats."

"I'll wish you luck then, Lafe," said Jonathan.

"Thanks kindly, Mister Ware." Lafe's tone was civil but there was a curl to his lip. Christy longed to slap it off.

"I hope, Mister Ware," said Jardine, "that this necessity won't cause your Charlie to turn against me. I've taken quite a liking to him and he's a steadying influence on my son Travis, who sadly needs it."

"Charlie's doing a man's work. He must make a man's decisions."

"If you didn't tell him. . . ."

"Look, Bishop! You can hardly expect us not to tell our son about this outrage when he comes home. But you'll probably see him before we do. You can make your case first."

With the help of the prettiest girl Charlie's ever seen, Christy thought with a rush of anger and desolation. Could Charlie, *would* he, overlook this trespass? How could he go on working for a man who'd drawn a pistol on his father? An even more wretched question arose in Christy's mind. *Had Charlie been at the Jardines' when the slave escaped, would he have joined the hunt? No! He couldn't! It*

143

would break Mother's and Father's hearts . . . mine, too! Yet to her horror and sense of guilt in doubting her brother, Christy wasn't absolutely sure. He fancied Melissa Jardine, was friends with Travis Jardine, and had been made much of by the wealthy planter. Swept along in the heat of excitement, yes, alas, she could imagine Charlie taking part.

But she *wouldn't* believe he'd approve of lashing Justus, packing the wounds with salt. Charlie had a kind heart, whatever else. Would that be enough?

She thought of Dan O'Brien. He'd never chase a slave. On that she'd wager her life. That certainty for the first time made her think beyond hiding Justus for the moment.

If only she'd found a way into the underground river! She could take Justus to that other sinkhole above the Marais des Cygnes and ask help from Dan or the Parkses, maybe even John Brown. He'd know how to get a runaway safely to Canada.

All these things churned through her head before Watt thrust his head in.

"Nobody there or along the wood stacked in the dogtrot, Bishop."

"Kindly go to the barn and outbuildings with Lafe," said Jardine. "Mind that you don't set a fire with the candle."

"Oh, these folks seem fond of fire, burning off their fields so late of an evening."

"I'm paying you well, Caxton. No fire. And

don't discharge that revolver unless you find Justus and can't stop him short of a bullet in the leg. He's my property, remember. I don't want him damaged."

Caxton gave a disgusted shrug as Lafe joined him. Jonathan said to Jardine: "Would you care to have Watt Caxton approach your wife out of the night with a gun in his hand?"

"He'll obey or lose the money I've promised."

Jonathan's eyes smoldered. "What good is that if he hurts or insults my wife? Keep your pistol in my back if you wish, but let's make sure Caxton behaves."

After a moment, Jardine nodded. "I have no desire to alarm women. But my pistol's ready, sir. Christina, take your mush off the fire and come with us. Don't do anything foolish or, reluctantly, I will have to shoot your father."

Hating the unctuous planter with all her being, Christy set the bubbling kettle off the coals and followed her father outside. The moon had not risen.

Down at the barn, the candle wavered. Her mother and Thos must have had to finish milking in the dark, but they should be through by now. Well, let Watt and Lafe snoop around the barn.

Christy's heart stopped when her father warned: "Take care not to fall into the well we're digging." He didn't know where Justus

145

was. In fact, he wouldn't know that Justus wasn't in the barn. Beneath his calm, he must be agonized.

"Bring the candle here, Caxton!" Jardine called. "Let's have a look down this well."

What if Justus had moved so the quilt shifted from beneath the dirt? What if they tossed rocks down or stabbed with a pitchfork? Sick with fear, Christy squeezed her eyes shut as Caxton bent over with a grunt and held the candle as low as his potbelly would allow.

"Only the bottom of the hole," said Jardine. "Hurry with the barn, man. If that stiff-necked devil isn't here, he'll be almost to Kansas. Not that we'll turn back at the border if we're on his track."

"Can't search if you keep callin' me back," Caxton grumbled, but he hurried ahead of them to the barn where Lafe's silvery hair caught the light of the candle as they passed inside.

There was a yelp, no light, and a string of oaths.

"Who are you?" Ellen shrieked. "Why are you sneaking around our barn?" Her voice rose. "Jonathan! Jonathan! Help!"

"What's got into you, woman?" bellowed Caxton. "Why'd you throw milk over us? Bishop. . . ."

"Missus Ware?" called Jardine.

"Who else would it be, in my own barn?"

146

Ellen had never sounded so — so shrewish. "Who, pray, are you?"

"Mordecai Jardine, your son's employer, madam. I regret the annoyance, but it's possible a runaway slave has hidden here without your knowledge."

"Well, he hasn't, sir! He's certainly not in the barn! I must tell you that I don't appreciate finding a man with a gun nosing into our barn!"

"I humbly apologize, ma'am, but your husband's views on slavery cannot but rouse suspicion. . . ."

"Suspicion's one thing," Ellen cut in. "Searching our buildings with guns is another!" For the first time, fear sounded in her voice. "My husband? Where . . . ?"

"I'm here and fine, Ellen," Jonathan reassured her. "Too bad you wasted our milk."

"I don't grudge it." Was that a hint of laughter in her tone?

Jardine cleared his throat. "Do I understand you to assert, Missus Ware, that my slave is not concealed in your barn or outbuildings?"

"I would swear it before a judge, sir. Indeed, I do swear it before the one who will judge us all."

"Then we'll take our leave."

"Bishop!" protested Caxton.

"We'll take our leave," Jardine repeated sternly. "Again, madam, my apologies."

Some demon prompted Christy to suggest

sweetly: "Perhaps you'd like to take your overseer a drink of buttermilk, Bishop Jardine."

After a moment's astonishment, Jardine laughed. "He'll drink from the creek, young lady. Remember, you're invited to visit my daughter."

"Or," interposed Ellen, "your daughter may visit us."

Once more taken aback, Jardine stammered: "Though deeply obliged at the invitation, Missus Ware, I fear our opinions are too different for an impressionable girl to . . . to. . . ."

"Exactly," said Ellen serenely. "Good night, Bishop Jardine. Mister Caxton, I must say I'm astonished! And Lafe. . . ."

"Thos!" called Jonathan. "Is your bucket of milk safe? I hope so, for I'm hungry. Good night, sirs."

"Isn't it dangerous for them to go crashing around in the dark?" Christy asked as the Wares went inside and Ellen lit another candle.

"I expect they're all used to hunting at night," said Jonathan dryly. "Now where in the world did you hide the man?" He nodded approval at Ellen's explanation. "Whew! And to think I called their attention to the well. We'd better leave our guest down there till we can be sure Jardine's crew is gone, but, Thos, go out and tell him we'll have him up soon and think of what must be done. If we can help him into Kansas. . . ."

Christy looked up from dishing out the mush, including a bowl for Justus. "There may be a way." While her family stared at her in amazement, she told them about how she and Dan had freed the bears and found the passage.

"Christina!" Ellen choked. "How will I ever rest easy now I know you may be wandering around in some awful cavern? If Caxton didn't kill you, the bear might have!"

"But aren't you glad the bears turned up again to listen to the piano?" Christy asked. It was only during the last week or so that the pair hadn't been glimpsed among the trees at dusk.

"I'm glad they weren't killed in that frightful way," Ellen admitted. "But Christy. . . ."

"You must try hard not to worry your mother." Jonathan's stern voice was betrayed a little by the pride in his eyes. "So, while you gathered nuts, you looked for but didn't find an opening to the underground?"

Christy nodded. Thos's eyes sparkled. "Wouldn't it be handy to find a way in? 'Specially if more slaves run our direction."

Jonathan pondered. "To be prepared, I suppose we'd better look for an entry, but I'm responsible for protecting this family. We're not going to become a regular station on the Underground Railroad, though, of course, we'll help fugitives who come to us."

Thos finished his second mug of milk. "Shall I get Justus now?"

"We'll take him some food," decided Jonathan, "but let's wait a little longer to bring him up."

Before Jonathan and Thos brought the young man in, Christy blew out the candle as an extra precaution so the room was lit by the fire only. Ellen, rocking Beth, spoke a soft greeting and asked him to sit down. He seemed to be favoring one foot.

"Lady," he said in a husky voice, "you look to me just like Mary holdin' Lord Jesus. And the rest of you shine bright as angels. I thank Jesus and all of you for helpin' me and I pray God to put it in my life to pay you back some happy day."

"We'll be paid if you get to freedom," Ellen said. "Have you hurt your foot?"

"Ran a stob into it. Paid it no mind with them hounds behind me."

Jonathan pressed him to a bench. "Thos, fill the wash basin with warm water. Put some of Hester's soft soap in it. We'll soak your foot while you eat, Justus, and then have a look."

Hungrily, but taking care not to cram his mouth or make a mess, Justus finished the mush, four eggs Christy fried for him in butter in the three-legged spider, and a chunk of leftover cornbread.

Smiling from his third mug of buttermilk, Justus said: "Nothin's ever tasted so good. First bite I've had since I run off night before last outside of some papaws and nuts."

"Looks like you'd have brought some food," said Thos, and got a reproving glance from Jonathan.

"Young master, I've been watchin' a chance to run ever since Master Richard Frazer sold me away from my folks and the girl I married in the big house, with a preacher and all. Master Mordecai put me in a cabin with five other hands. Seemed like, nights, at least one of them was forever gettin' up or sneakin' in after sparkin' his sweetheart . . . or I'd fall asleep. So when they was finally all snorin' at once, I hightailed it out of there."

"Bishop Jardine didn't beat you?" Thos asked.

"Thomas!" It was seldom Thos got his full name.

" 'Scuse me," he muttered. "None of my beeswax."

Justus shrugged. "Master Mordecai fed us good and kept us in decent clothes the slave women spun and wove the cloth for. His wife's crippled and don't care for nothin' but her childs and roses, but the woman cookin' for us slaves knew a powerful lot of herbs and cures. Everybody gets new clothes Christmas, and the hands hired or bought from other masters have a week off to go visit

151

at home." His jaw set. "Master Richard and Master Jardine thought that ought to make me real grateful . . . that I could go see my folks and Hildy for a couple days a year with the trip takin' most of my week."

"But you can't go back to your old place," said Jonathan.

"No, but I can get up north or plumb to Canada, work and save money. Maybe enough to buy Hildy and my ma and pa, usin' a go-between." Justus considered. "My folks'd be cheap 'cause they can't work enough to earn their living."

Even at that, Christy wondered if the old slave parents might not die before their son claimed them. "After Hildy's mama died, she was raised up alongside Miss Lou, Master Richard's wife, so her white folks might not sell her for anything. If they won't, I'm goin' to steal her away."

Jonathan sighed. "Some day, Justus, no human being will be able to own another. I hope that day comes soon. Now let me see that foot."

After picking out splinters of rotting cornstalk, Jonathan swabbed the puncture with soft soap and packed it with a salve of marsh mallow, chamomile, and yarrow Hester had given them.

Ellen gave Beth to Christy, located a bit of homespun so threadbare it couldn't be salvaged, and bandaged the soft pad in place with a strip cut from an old hucking towel.

"Shamed to put you to all this fuss. No way to thank you." Justus looked at Christy. "You got a hold on me, missy, that no master could. If you hadn't brought me here, I'd be chewed by the hounds most likely 'cause I wasn't goin' back tame to Mister Blake's blacksnake. He don't whip often, but, when he do, it ain't forgot."

"Bishop Jardine doesn't have hounds?" asked Thos.

"Mistress can't abide 'em. They dug up some of her fancy roses a few years ago. She carried on till Master Mordecai gave the hounds to his brother who's got a plantation up by Independence."

Jonathan shook his head. "So if Watt Caxton hadn't joined in with his pack, you'd have had a good chance of getting across the border."

"Reckon I still do . . . a pretty fair chance." Justus stood, head almost brushing the ceiling. "They'll likely keep the hounds along the creek to pick up my scent when I leave the water. If I head west on the high ground. . . ."

"You're not going anywhere tonight," Ellen decreed. "You'll sleep in the loft, rest, and let your foot start healing."

"I've already taken our corn to the mill over in Kansas or I could do that and hide you in the wagon," Jonathan pondered.

"I don't have enough wool to cover you up

or we could send it and you to the carding mill," Ellen regretted.

Christy made a rueful sound. "If I'd just been able to find a way into the cavern! But I heard the hounds, and then Justus. . . ."

He looked up in sudden hope. "There's a cave somewheres around where I was hidin'?"

Again, Christy explained the secret river. "It's likely as dangerous to go back to Caxton's sinkhole as it'd be to go through the woods," she said. "But if there was some way into the underground just across the creek. . . ."

Justus laughed for the first time, looking too young to want to marry, much too young to die by hounds or a beating. "Maybe there is, missy."

"You saw one?"

"That rock I was hiding under . . . well, there was a fox ducked in ahead of me and it sure disappeared! When I heard you, though, somethin' told me to take my chance."

"A fox can squeeze through a little hole," Thos said. "They're mostly fur and tail."

Justus nodded. "Yeah, and any hole I could crawl in easy, so could the hounds."

"If there *is* a cave that leads into the main passage, maybe we could make the opening big enough for a human." Jonathan looked hopeful. "We'll see about it tomorrow. But while the bishop's hunting around, the best place for you, young man, is in the loft."

"If Master Mordecai came back here . . . ," Justus groaned. "No way I could forgive myself if I brought you good folks grief."

"I think the bishop believed my wife." Jonathan laughed softly and gave her a glance so admiring that she blushed. "What she said was true enough."

"And when I told him I hadn't seen a slave, that was true," Christy maintained. "Because you'd run away to freedom, Justus. You decided you *weren't* his slave." Christy hugged herself with excitement. "Please, Mother, may I go across the creek before school tomorrow and hunt for where the fox ran?"

"I think you'd burst otherwise." Ellen laughed. "Yes, Thos, you may go, too . . . after your chores."

"Let us thank God for mercifully protecting us tonight," said Jonathan. "Let us pray He will guide Justus safely to freedom and one day reunite him with his loved ones."

They all bowed their heads.

"Let justice flow down like a mighty river," Jonathan ended.

They all said "Amen."

CHAPTER EIGHT

Next morning, Christy's mind fled her lessons, leaping from the man in the loft above them to the opening beneath the ledge that she and Thos had found before school. It was too small for her to crawl through, but surrounding cracks in the limestone made them hope the entry could be enlarged. What luck it would be if it led to the passage! Seeing Thos fidget, she knew that he, too, was itching to get to work with a pick and crowbar.

She thought school would never end, although, at noon, Hester Ballard tearfully appeared to say Bishop Jardine and Lafe had come to her house that morning after spending the night at Charles Hamelton's, Jardine's proslavery friend.

"They couldn't find hide nor hair of the runaway," Hester told Ellen Ware. "I'm so mortified Lafe came bothering you that I'm ashamed to show you my face. Can you forgive me?"

"Goodness, Hester, you didn't do anything!" said Ellen, hugging her. "You've always been wonderful to us." She fumbled for words of consolation. "Boys . . . well, they get wild sometimes. . . ."

"I couldn't stop him hanging around Watt Caxton," Hester lamented. She drew a tremulous breath. "That's why I decided to let him go with Bishop Jardine. I'm hoping being away from home . . . driving a team and being with a lot of men . . . will straighten him out."

How good it would be not to look up to find him staring at her scar. Christy swallowed a glad exclamation, relief tempered with sympathy for Hester.

Ellen pressed the other woman's hand. "Work, earning some wages, may be just what he needs, dear. You'll miss him, but, at that age, it's hard to keep them at home. Look at our Charlie."

Somewhat comforted, Hester went out with the rest of them to admire the progress Ethan Ware and Lige Morrow had made on the well. "Ground's getting damp," Ethan said. "With luck, we'll hit water tomorrow. That was a mighty fine water witch, to locate this place that goes down between the rocks. Where'd you say he was from?"

"North of Trading Post," said Jonathan vaguely. The Hayeses had never given their views on slavery but only the most fanatical Free Staters approved of Brown's slaughter of unarmed men.

Watching Ethan swing the pick made Christy wish he could be enlisted to help clear a way into the hidden river, but that would be too risky. Most people who didn't hold with slavery still wouldn't break the Fugitive Slave Law that made it a crime to aid runaways or not return them to a master. Christy was sure her parents wouldn't burden a friend with any part in Justus's escape unless they knew that friend shared their horror of bondage.

The afternoon dragged. After school was out and Morrow sauntered off with Ethan and his boys, Jonathan got the pick, Christy lugged a crowbar, and Thos brought a shovel.

"Why, it's like that rock was already cracked inside!" Thos cried as Jonathan swung the pick into a fissure and it lengthened and split into shards of crumbling stone. "Here, Christy, give me the crowbar. You clear away the rubble."

Since Thos could put more strength into plying the iron bar, Christy accepted the lowly chore of clearing away the results of her father's and brother's exertions. They chipped and pried and delved till at last a whole slab fell under Jonathan's assault.

The fox's narrow entry broadened enough to accommodate a man and dimly reveal a larger grotto. Moving into it, Jonathan only had to duck his head a little. As their eyes adjusted to the faint light, Thos and Christy exclaimed and pointed at the same instant: "Look!"

Guarded by fantastically shaped stalagmites and stalactites was a narrow opening. Thos squeezed through it.

"Careful, Son," Jonathan warned. "Don't take a step you don't test first and don't go far! Someone will have to go back for a lit candle if it seems we really have something to explore."

Thos's voice floated back, resounding eerily. "It got wider after just a little way, but I'm crawling now. . . ."

"Mind you don't crawl into a pit!" Jonathan called. "Thos, Son, you'd better come back. Christy, run for a candle."

She was on her way when Thos's shout stopped her. "I'm in a *big* place and I hear water!"

Christy's heart leaped high, pounded with relief. That had to be the secret passage! A hiding place, and a safe way for Justus to cross into Kansas.

"Come out," Jonathan commanded Thos. "You and Christy will bring Justus here when it's dark. He can sleep tonight in this chamber. I'll ride over to the mill and ask Simeon Parks if he knows where John Brown is or who else might help a fugitive go north."

Thos rejoined them, and, although he squirmed, Christy couldn't keep from giving

159

him a hug of congratulation.

"Let me bring a candle in the morning and take Justus to the sinkhole by Whistling Point," she begged.

"I found the tunnel," Thos reminded. "Please, Father, don't you want me to take Justus across the line?"

"But *I* found the underground river!" Christy wailed.

"Maybe your mother will think you should both go," Jonathan said, dropping an arm on a shoulder of each. "Now get the spade and crowbar and we'll tell her and Justus the good news."

Justus was for going to the cave immediately to lessen the Wares' danger, but they insisted he stay till night would hide him from any inquisitive eyes. When it was dark, Justus, equipped with quilts, a coat, and socks and shoes of Jonathan's, set out with Christy and Thos who carried food and a candle in a tin lantern.

"Will you be all right?" Christy asked when a pallet was made. The lantern winked in the shifting, wavering shadows, turning the growths from ceiling and floor into grotesque creatures that might at any moment engulf a trespassing mortal.

Fortunately Justus wasn't cursed with her imagination. "Bless you, missy. Soon's you're gone, I'll kneel and thank Jesus and then I'll go to sleep." He smiled his trust. "Nothin' bad's goin' to happen now. I feels it in my bones."

"I'll stay if you want," Thos offered. From the glint in his eyes, he hoped for more adventure.

Justus gave him the gentlest push. "Get on with you, missy, young master! I declare, I slept fine today, but I'm tired again. Don't that beat all when I ain't done a lick of work?"

"Have a good night," said Christy, picking up the lantern.

"We'll come in the morning," added Thos.

Back in the cabin, Christy and her mother knitted while Thos mended a bridle. The baby slept in the little box bed Jonathan had made for her to nap in since her crib was in the other cabin and Ellen wouldn't leave her alone there. It seemed a long time before Jed's whicker and Queenie's answering neigh proclaimed Jonathan's return.

Thos ran out to take charge of Jed. Jonathan came in and bent to kiss Ellen exultantly. "Simeon Parks will hide Justus till John Brown can spirit him north. Christy, young Dan O'Brien will meet you and Thos and Justus near Whistling Point in the morning and take him to the mill. That is, if you still want to take him through the cavern. Thos could do it."

"Father! It's *my* cave. And Justus . . . in a way, he's sort of mine, too."

"You feel responsible for him, dear." Ellen touched her cheek and smiled. "You and Thos will both go, then, but you'll hurry back so we won't have our hearts in our mouths. And now, Jonathan, it's time we had our prayers and got to bed."

Eating buttered corn pones and carrying some for Justus, Christy and Thos made their way to the fox cave in the first gray light. They had an extra candle as well as the one in the lantern, lit from the fireplace.

Christy smothered a cry as a shadow moved from beneath the ledge. Once again, it was Justus. "You look like angels, you do for sure." He smiled lop-sidedly. "I slept sound after you left last night but an ole hootie-owl woke me up. Been in a cold sweat ever since."

Christy gave him the warm corn pones. "It's all taken care of, Justus. A Quaker family that has a mill over in Kansas will keep you till someone can take you north." She lit the spare candle off the one in the lantern. That way, if one flickered out, they'd have the other. She handed the lantern to Justus and flourished her candle. "Let's go."

The river was a flow of dark melted sky, narrowing between stalagmites spearing into stalactites, sometimes eddying almost to the feet of the intruders in this secret world. The atmosphere was warmer than outside, but Christy shivered to remember how Dan had

162

tested and picked their way in utter blackness, that desperate underground journey when it had been far from certain they'd find a way out.

He'd be waiting for them. That made the blood dance happily through her veins. She hoped he'd think she was a little bit brave even though she'd been nervous of his foot log across the Marais des Cygnes, and she couldn't ride after Border Ruffians the way he had. If that sort of trouble kept on. . . .

Don't let there be a war, she prayed silently. *Not a war with Dan and Thos and Charlie and Matthew fighting, maybe even Ethan and Father and Andy McHugh and Owen Parks. . . . Please, not a war! Let the slaves go free without that.*

"I was this way before!" she called back to Justus. "It's not much farther."

"Christy?"

The voice reverberated through the passage, but even sepulchrally magnified she knew it. Her heart seemed to burst right out of her and fly to him. "Dan!"

Rounding a rose-streaked pinnacle, she saw him, hair aflame with light spilled from the sky above, the blessed, shining, blue sky that lit his smile as he came forward.

He looked taller, not so thin, although it was only two months since she'd seen him. "You . . . you've piled rocks right up close to the top," she said.

He chuckled. "As I remember, you didn't

favor being pulled up by the wrists."

Christy's face heated. If he remembered that, did he recall how she'd thrown her arms around him? Turning from his grin, she said: "Justus, this is Dan O'Brien. He'll take you to the mill."

"That I will not." Dan put out his hand. After a moment's hesitation, a dark one accepted it and brown eyes looked into gray ones. "It's to John Brown himself I'm taking you, Mister Justus. He's waiting at Andy McHugh's with a wagon. They'll take you to Reverend Corder, who's part of the Underground Railroad in Lawrence."

Justus took a sighing breath. "It's too good . . . too good to believe! You . . . both of you young masters, and you, missy, you're all too good. . . ."

"You've got to get out of the habit of calling white men 'master'," Dan growled. He glanced up through the glory of rust sycamore leaves and the golden ones of oak. "Sooner we go, the sooner you'll be out of Kansas, Justus, and into the free states."

"Amen to that, young mas-. . . ." Justus checked himself. A smile widened his face. "Dan, point me the way to go. Now I'm out of Missouri, I reckon there's not a hound or slave hunter can catch me." He gripped Thos's and Christy's hands between his big ones, squeezed them hard and long. "Bless you, young 'uns, and your mama and daddy and little baby sister. Bless you all. I'll pray every day for you the rest of my natural born life."

He climbed up the pile of stones that shifted here and there beneath his weight. Dan followed lightly. "You can walk back outside," he suggested to Christy and Thos. "Save your candles."

So, after all, he did give Christy a hand up and squeezed hers hard before he let her go and started briskly toward Whistling Point and the blacksmith's.

Seth Cooley, Mordecai Jardine's partner, squinted over his ledger as he figured out Charlie's pay. "Can't keep you busy all the time," he drawled, scanning Charlie with keen gray eyes, "but, if you'd like to winter at my farm outside of town and do some short hauls with mules, you'd get room and board and a dollar a day when you're freighting. Jim Mabry's a tough wagon master, but he speaks well of you. Hopes you'll freight with him next year."

"That's real good of Mister Mabry." Charlie hesitated. During the winter, he couldn't be much use at home. That dollar a day even part of the time sounded pretty good. But although Bishop Jardine hadn't spelled it out, Charlie knew he was expected to see Travis Jardine safely home and, while on night guard he'd watched the Big Dipper, he'd dreamed of Melissa Jardine's shining eyes, the fleeting, just one-time brush of her fingers on his arm.

He wanted to see his own family, too. He'd thought of them often, especially his mother and Christy, as he walked beside his oxen or rolled up in his blankets to keep the mosquitoes off or wished he had cool buttermilk to drink instead of brackish water.

"I'd sure like the job, sir. But could I go home first?"

Cooley studied him. "Will you undertake to be back by the middle of December?"

"Sure as I'm alive, I'll be back, Mister Cooley."

"I'll count on you then." The wiry grayhaired man, leather-skinned from years on the trails, opened his safe and counted out more money — gold pieces — than Charlie had ever seen at one time. "Don't flash that around, son. There's plenty of rascals, some of 'em female, who'd cut your throat for just one ten-dollar gold piece." He sighed. "Sorry to say one of the worst is a neighbor of yours. Lafe Ballard."

Charlie frowned. "Lafe? What's he doing here?"

"Seems he helped the bishop chase a slave . . . who got away . . . but Mordecai felt obliged to the kid and hired him, sent him to me." Cooley's mouth tightened. "It's the crack of the whip moves oxen along. No need generally to give one more'n a flick. First day

166

out, Lafe opened a slash down his lead ox's flank. Wagon master fired him then and there."

"Who's he working for now?"

"The devil, mostly, and at that no more than he has to."

"I'm sure not going to tell his mother that. She's a real nice lady."

"Then I pity her. The way that cub hells around, he won't live to grow up."

Charlie dropped the coins in the buckskin pouch that held a few copper cents and some small silver. The gold, he thought, banishing Lafe from his mind, had a special ring, mellow and — well, *golden.*

"The bishop asked me to watch out for a couple of good horses that you and Travis could ride to his place," Cooley said. "They're in the stable at the wagon yard and your saddles are in the shed." He cleared his throat. "Might be a good notion to hunt Travis up and start right now. About the only thing young sprouts your age can do around Independence when they're not working is get into trouble."

Travis could do that without any help. During the freighting trip, Charlie had kept him from shooting at some Indians, who'd come to camp to visit, and smoothed over several arguments that were heating towards fights. Freighters were an independent lot and wouldn't put up with a high-handed pup even if his father paid their wages.

"I want to buy my mother and sister something nice," said Charlie. "If Travis comes in here, sir, will you tell him I'll meet him at the wagon yard in an hour?"

Cooley snorted. "I won't see him again. He drew his wages as soon as the oxen were unyoked yesterday evening. Didn't even help drive them out to my farm for the winter."

Not only that, Travis hadn't helped tote the six, heavy wooden yokes to the warehouse. Leaving them where he'd taken them off the oxen, he'd simply vanished. Charlie lugged them to the warehouse, but that was a bone he meant to pick with Travis no matter how he tried to laugh his way out of it.

None of this was for Mr. Cooley's ears, of course, or Bishop Jardine's. *I'm the steady horse they've harnessed the wild colt to,* Charlie thought with a wry grin. *I've dragged him along the best I could, but, if he won't start pulling his share of the load, I'm breaking out of harness.*

"Thank you kindly, sir. I'll be back as soon as I can."

"Good." Cooley offered his hand, just like Charlie was grown up. Charlie shook it, proud and happy, and stepped outside with the soft clink of his first earned money like music in his ears.

Independence, the seat of Jackson County,

was four miles from the Missouri River and boasted about three thousand inhabitants, a number of two-storied brick buildings, a log courthouse, a ferry, and a teeming dock where steamships unloaded, but its real fame lay in vying with St. Joseph and Council Bluffs as the jumping-off point for the West where travelers and wagon trains outfitted for the Oregon and Santa Fé Trails. A weekly mail stagecoach ran from here to Santa Fé, and there was a monthly mail stage to Salt Lake City. Blacksmiths shod mules and molded iron braces for ox yokes; Weston's factory built wagons to endure the rutted tracks and hazardous river crossings; wheelwrights made and repaired wheels, and merchants stocked everything westbound settlers needed to get there and make a start.

The town was much less crowded now than when Charlie left it in late August. The last emigrant trains had rolled out months ago, of course, and long-distance freighting was winding up for the winter as wagon masters brought in their outfits. Still, the streets were filled with a prosperous bustle. A new brick bank building was going up and Charlie heard one onlooker brag that it would have three stories.

What would his mother and Christy like best? Keeping an eye out for Travis as he went in and out of shops, Charlie regretfully decided against an ornate gilded soup tureen and a porcelain angel with unfurled wings. Neither would be safe behind his saddle. The biggest mercantile solved his problem with a grand array of fabrics but impaled him on the thorn of deciding which cloth to buy.

"You fancy that velvet, sonny?" A plump, gray-haired woman bore down on him as he reached out to touch a beautiful material that reminded him of moss, except that it was dark red.

He jerked back, but stood his ground, emboldened by his earnings. "I . . . I'm looking for some nice cloth for my mother and sister, ma'am. Can you wash this velvet stuff with lye soap and creek water?"

She flinched. "Gracious no, dearie!" She looked him over and drew conclusions which Charlie was sure flattered neither him nor his home. "What most ladies like," she said kindly, "is something pretty for church and parties but that won't be ruined if you spill something on it and won't show every little spot and smudge."

The woman pulled half a dozen bolts out where he could see them. "Calico and gingham cost the least and wear well. Can't go wrong with either." Sarah Morrow had looked like a brilliant flower in her red calico, but Charlie sensed it wouldn't be that becoming for his mother. "This poplin wears well, but I can tell by your face you don't want brown."

"They wear brown homespun mostly."

The woman nodded. "This Scotch plaid flannel is warm. The chambray's nice for summer, but you probably want something for all year round."

"Yes'm. I . . . I guess so." Charlie's head was spinning.

"What color are your ladies' eyes and hair?"

"Mother's are dark. Christy . . . um . . . her hair's black, but I think her eyes are blue or maybe gray or. . . ."

"Complexion?" Charlie stared. The woman elaborated. "Are they fair or rosy or a bit sallow or olive?"

"I don't think they're exactly rosy." How was he so sure that Melissa Jardine was, that her brown hair sparkled with reddish lights, and her eyes were the color of wild gentians? "Christy forgets her sunbonnet so she's sort of brown in the summer. They have nice skin, though," he added defensively. "Smooth and no lumps or spots."

"I may have just the thing . . . if there's enough of it." The woman bent to produce the remains of a bolt from beneath the counter. "This azure foulard should look well on both of them."

The glowing twilight blue was patterned with small scrolls and flowers. Charlie thought it marvelous. But it was so shiny and soft. "Will it wash all right, ma'am?"

"Yes, taking care, of course, for it's silk. No hot water and just a little soft soap. How big are the ladies?"

"Christy's no lady, ma'am, she's . . . well, I guess she just turned thirteen. She's skinny and comes about to here." He measured below his collarbone. "Mother has to look up at me a little."

"She's taller than me?"

"Maybe a tad. But she's . . . ," he broke off.

"Not as fat," finished the woman merrily. "There should be enough material. When you're cutting out two dresses, you can use cloth that would be scraps, otherwise, and can piece where it won't show. I can give you a bargain since it's the end of the bolt. And you'll want thread and buttons, and perhaps braid or ruching for trim."

"Whatever you think, ma'am. I'm mightily obliged."

"A pleasure, dear. Your mother and sister are lucky. Tell them that for me. Anything else?"

Boots, a leather coat, and a blue flannel shirt took a second gold piece. He couldn't flaunt his new things without getting Thos and his father flannel for shirts. Beth would love that cuddly lamb, and he should get some candy. A final yearning pushed then to the front of his mind.

Would Melissa Jardine think him presumptuous if he brought her a present? Would her parents object? She didn't need anything, he knew that, yet somehow he burned to get her something with his first earned money.

As he studied ribbons, artificial flowers, and trinkets, the store lady asked: "Do you need a nice gift for a special young lady?"

He blushed and jerked his head first yes, then no. "I . . . I mean, if there's the kind of thing that wouldn't give offence, ma'am."

"Well, there's these lovely embroidered hankies."

Maybe he should get them for Mrs. Jardine so it wouldn't seem peculiar he had a gift for Melissa. Then he saw just the thing, a translucent gold-brown stone with a reddish hue to its depths, the color of her hair. The polished oval was rimmed with plain gold and had a simple gold chain. He pointed at it. "Would that be all right, ma'am?"

"Jewelry gifts shouldn't be expensive unless you're engaged, but the amber isn't costly." She laughed. "I wouldn't look down my nose at you if you gave it to *my* daughter."

He took it and the hankies. When he left the store, arms full of parcels, cheek swelled with peppermints thrown in for a good customer, he'd spent $22 and couldn't have said whether he was more horrified or delighted. He did know one thing. It was a thrill to be able to buy things without worrying over every cent, and it was mightily gratifying to hear even the diminished jingle of his two remaining gold pieces among the copper and silver.

"Well, look at the big spender!"

Something tripped Charlie. He went sprawling, frantically trying not to let his purchases fall in the mud. The one with the azure material squeezed out of his arms and bounced in front of a carriage.

Still on his knees, Charlie lunged forward and grabbed for the bundle. The carriage splattered mud on it and him in his new coat, but the front wheel rolled over just the edge of the parcel.

The driver called back — "Sorry!" — but didn't stop. In a torment to see if the material was much hurt, Charlie peered inside the torn, muddied wrapping and rejoiced.

Bless the store lady. She'd wrapped several layers of newspapers around the cloth before tying it up in brown paper. The wheel had destroyed some of the paper but hadn't reached the fabric.

Then he saw Lafe Ballard. The eager light in those cold eyes, the twist of the girlish lips, told Charlie the tripping had not been accidental. He took off his coat, spread it on a pile of crates, placed his packages carefully on top of it, and smashed Lafe's grinning mouth.

"Hey!" Backing away, Lafe spat blood. More poured from his nose. "Can't you take a joke?"

"Here's one for you!" Charlie hit him again.

Lafe staggered, reached inside his coat. A knife flashed, a Bowie with both edges honed. People were gathering, including the store lady who held open the door and cried: "Run in here, son! Your mother. . . ."

Charlie would have obeyed. The knife froze him to the marrow. But he remembered a trick he'd seen in a fight between two teamsters. Swerving out of Lafe's way, he kicked up. There was a cracking sound as his new boot struck Lafe's wrist. At the same instant that shoulder was seized from behind and Lafe, howling, was swung around to meet Travis Jardine's fist to the jaw as the knife dropped to the street.

Charlie picked it up and wiped it off. "Guess this makes us even for the mess you made of my things."

"You . . . you broke my wrist!" screeched Lafe. "I'll get even! I'll. . . ."

A man in a dark coat with a gold watch fob across an ample front stepped up and took Lafe by the arm. "I'm a doctor and my office is next door. Come in and I'll see what I can do."

"Can you pay the doctor, Lafe?" asked Charlie.

"What's it to you?" snarled the other.

"I'll pay if you can't."

"Damned goody-good!"

The doctor gave Charlie a gentle push. "Go

175

along, lad. I'll work things out with this young polecat. Maybe break his other wrist."

Refusing offers to buy him a drink from several rough-looking men who looked like they'd had too many, Charlie caught his breath and looked at Travis. "I'm glad you came along."

Travis laughed joyously, brown eyes sparkling. "So am I. Paid you back some for being such a good mama hen."

He exuded a smell that was a little like flowers and more like sweat. Charlie frowned. "Did you stay at your aunt's last night?"

Travis's surprised stare gave him away, although he recovered with a chuckle and affectionate smack on Charlie's shoulder. "She's someone's aunt, I'm bound, Charles."

Charlie frowned harder, remembering his night in the barn at the wagon yard and the way Travis had left his yokes on the ground. Travis gave him a playful cuff on the ear. "Well, old fellow, what was I to tell you without getting a sermon?"

Keeping low company was supposed to make a person get sick and look awful, but Travis was bursting with vim, and somehow, although he was a few months younger than Charlie, he suddenly seemed older, closer to being a man. What had he done last night?

"You didn't put your yokes away," Charlie began. "You told me a flat out lie. You. . . ."

"Oh, come along!" Gaily Travis took some

of the packages and set off at an easy lope. "You can preach on the way. Since it'll take us four days to get home, that ought to give you all the time you need."

CHAPTER NINE

Except for timber-fringed swollen creeks across which they often had to swim their horses, Charlie and Travis rode mostly across lonesome prairie except for a chain of small settlements between Harrisonville and West Point where they crossed into Kansas to pick up the Military Road and were soon in wooded country.

They crossed the Marais des Cygnes at Trading Post. A few new cabins had been built on old foundations but others lay in charred ruins. At the Little Osage, they left the road for the ruts that led through the wintry forest to the Jardines.

Fallen leaves, some still scarlet, orange, and yellow, muffled the horses' hoofs. Trees were bare except for cedars, clumps of glossy mistletoe high in the tops of elm trees, and the black-barked black jack oak that would keep most of its fading red-brown leaves till spring, providing shelter for birds and the squirrel tribe. The colors of the timber came from trunks and limbs, a different beauty from summer's lushness or autumn's glory, but strong like bones stripped of flesh. Oaks were many hues from the pale gray of white oak to the black or dark brown of post oak. The red brown bark of young river birches stood out against the silvery white young sycamores, the white branches and yellow-brown trunks of old ones, the deep gray of hickories and dark brown of walnut.

"Did you get your mother and sister anything?" Charlie asked

Travis's eyes widened. "Why? Father takes them to Saint Louis every year to shop and visit my sister. Anything they need in between trips, he'll get in Osceola or Nevada, the Vernon county seat." He opened his coat to show a revolver in a new holster. "At least I've got this to show for my wages. Good thing I bought it before I got into that poker game . . . and other things."

Charlie well knew the Jardine ladies didn't need anything. Travis's attitude made him feel like a fool for daring to hope they'd appreciate his modest gifts. "You've been away," he floundered. "Some little thing would show you'd thought about them."

Travis sighed. "Preaching Charlie! I guess you bought something for your mother and sister."

"Yes," said Charlie, riling. "And my brother and father, too."

After a bemused stare, Travis laughed. "If I brought Pa something, he'd think I'd done something awful and was trying to put him in good temper before he heard about it."

They rode a few minutes in silence when a buzzing sound swelled gradually into a roar.

"Wild pigeons!" yipped Travis. "I'll try out my Colt. Take a bunch home for supper." He gave Charlie a triumphant grin. "That'll be my present!"

Drawing his revolver, he urged his horse forward. Amidst squeaking and tittering, a vast cloud of shimmering wings rose from the ground, then swooped low. Thousands of slate-blue heads ducked to catch up acorns in slender black bills while light played on crimson eyes and feet and glimmers of gold, violet, and rosy purple on the sides and back of necks. As far through the trees as Charlie could see surged a feathered ocean, gray and blue on their backs as the birds swept down, russet or wine throat to belly as they winged up, flashing white from belly to tail.

Migrating flights had passed over their farm in Illinois but Charlie had never seen pigeons feeding, or up close. How Christy would love this. Father would have called it one of the wonders of God. So enthralled was Charlie that the crash of the gun startled him almost as much as it did the birds.

They rose in a swirling whir through the roof of great oaks, but not before the revolver downed four more. Travis swung down and tossed his reins to Charlie.

"Good shooting if I do say so." He stroked the revolver before he holstered it. "Look! Blew the heads off two of them."

What Charlie saw were two birds flopping helplessly with shattered wings. He hitched both horses' reins over a dead tree, took the smallish heads, one at a time, and wrung the glistening necks. He could barely see through blinked-back mist in his eyes. Going back to his horse, he mounted and rode on.

Why was he so upset? He'd killed chickens, helped slaughter hogs. But to see the dazzle and radiant power of wings changed to bloody gobs of feathers — it was like fragmenting a joyous anthem into obscene curses.

"These won't be as tasty as spring squabs, but they'll go down well, fried in butter." Travis came abreast with Charlie in the silenced woods. He'd tied the pigeons' crimson legs with the rawhide strings behind his saddle.

Two on one side. Three on the other. Spread out, those drooping wings had spanned two feet of boundless air. Charlie counted twelve tapering feathers in each graceful tail. These had white edging, as if an artist had spared no pains to perfect the pattern.

Too full of the merits of his new gun to notice Charlie's mood, Travis chattered till they rode out of the forest into the cleared fields of what he proudly declared the Jardine plantation.

"When the hands don't have something else to do, Pa puts them to clearing land." Travis waved an arm around the vista that included fields on both sides of the river, a large, rambling, white, two-story house with a verandah and lots of glass windows, numerous outbuildings, and about a dozen log cabins, each with a good-size garden patch. "We grow hemp, tobacco, and a little cotton," Travis went on. "Of course, we raise nearly all our food and sell corn, hogs, and the best mules in Missouri."

Charlie gulped. "It's sure a big place."

"Oh, not as plantations go." Travis shrugged with the worldly wise smile that so irritated Charlie. "The big ones in this state are along the Mississippi and Missouri. But when Melissa and I marry and take up land, Rose Haven will be right considerable."

"Rose Haven?"

"That's what Mama named it. Before she'd move out here, Pa had to promise she'd have a prettier rose garden than she did near Saint Louis . . . and she does."

Charlie thought of his own mother who'd nursed the climbing rose at their Illinois home till it ran all along the front porch. She'd be thrilled now with just one rose bush. And how crazy he'd been even to think of offering gifts to the women of Rose Haven. At least, he could give the presents to his mother. He wished he'd asked Travis to lead his mount here — that he himself had struck off afoot from Trading Post. Then he could have gone on hoping that Melissa Jardine might like him a little.

"Is your house built with milled lumber?" he asked, deciding he might as well swallow the worst.

"Lordy, no! When we first got here six years ago, we lived in a couple of log cabins with a breezeway between. More were added on and the slaves rived out clapboards to nail inside and out." He chuckled. "In spite of the verandah, Mama says that underneath it's still a plain old log cabin."

"Not very plain." Charlie decided he couldn't much like Mrs. Jardine. Sounded like she was spoiled rotten.

"Our trees bore fruit for the first time summer before last," Travis said as they rode past scores of young trees. "We've got apples, peaches, pears, plums, and cherries. Grapes, too, and the biggest, juiciest strawberries you ever ate. Too bad they're out of season or we'd have them with shortcake and cream."

As they neared the stables, a spraddle of hounds rose up and eyed them although they didn't bark. "Now whose could they be?" Travis frowned. "Mama can't abide dogs, so we don't have any."

"Those black and tans look like Watt Cax-

183

ton's pack." Charlie remembered the way they'd piled into Lige Morrow's hounds at the cabin raising. "But what would Mister Caxton be doing over here?"

At that instant, a scream came from beyond the stables. The hounds erupted. They raced after a streak of gray that could only be a cat, closing in from several directions.

"Emmie! Emmie-e-e!" In a flurry of skirts, Melissa Jardine pelted toward the dogs and the cat that, caught in the open, arched its back and hissed balefully.

It had no chance at all, but it would rip some noses before it was torn apart. Melissa snatched up a fallen branch and flailed at the dogs, shrieking. They shifted out of her way but poised to rush at the cat.

Charlie sprang from the saddle and dived through the hounds, sweeping the cat high in his arms. The snarling, barking dogs leaped for it, tearing his sleeves and gashing his arms. He kicked through them and ran toward the stable with the cat clawing him.

A gun barked louder than the pack. Charlie stumbled over an animal that fell with the top of its head blasted. There was another shot, a dog weltering in spilled intestines. Then Watt Caxton was panting from the direction of the house, the bishop in his wake.

Cursing and kicking the hounds, Caxton subdued them. Melissa came up to take the spitting, scratching cat from Charlie. It had bit him repeatedly on the hands, and the dogs had gashed his arms.

"You damn' fool!" Travis was pale. "The dogs could have killed you!"

Caxton glowered at his dead hound and the one twitching its last. "No cat's worth two good hounds!"

"My cat's worth your whole pack!" Melissa blazed. Her deep blue eyes widened as she saw Charlie's hurts. "You're bleeding! Your coat's all torn! Oh, you were brave!"

The look in her eyes paid him a hundred times for his pain and the ruination of his sleeves. She caught his upper arm and tugged. "Come to the house, boy. Aunt Phronie will fix you up. She's got some wonderful salve!"

"Travis," said the bishop, "go with Charles. Now then, Caxton, you had no business bringing your pack to Rose Haven."

"You've been glad of 'em in the past, Bishop," Caxton whined.

The bishop's voice dropped but Charlie could still hear, although Melissa's closeness and the scent of her curling mass of auburn hair drove even the aching sting of the bites and scratches from his mind. "It's true I may need your hounds again since I keep none, Caxton. For that reason, I'll pay to replace these two. But never bring them on my property again unless you're told to and they're on chains."

Why would the bishop hire Caxton and his

dogs? Not for 'coon hunting, that was sure. Unwillingly Charlie remembered the runaway Lafe Ballard had helped chase. Lafe hung around Watt Caxton. Had Caxton's pack trailed the fugitive?

With his flesh torn by the hounds' teeth, Charlie felt sick at the notion of a man chased by a pack as if he were a 'coon or fox, and he'd never liked that, either. His revulsion faded, though, with the warmth of Melissa's hand on his shoulder, the scent of her clothing and hair.

"In here." Travis steered him into a clapboarded cabin behind the big house. "We have the kitchen out here so that if there's a fire the main house won't burn."

Melissa ran in first, putting the gray cat on the sunny windowsill with a final caress. "What do you have for dog bites and cat scratches, Aunt Phronie? That nasty Watt Caxton's dogs would have killed Emmie if Charlie hadn't saved her."

"Well, child," snapped a tiny, yellow-skinned woman in a starched white apron, "don't let him bleed all over my floor. Here, honey boy, drip over this bucket while I fix some soft soap with warm water."

Charlie! Melissa had called him by name, not "Charles" or "boy" or "young man". He felt he could float right through the roof, but Aunt Phronie had him sit on a footstool and lower his arms into a tub of soapy water that was hot enough to make him yelp.

"Never mind, honey," adjured Aunt Phronie. "The heat helps draw out poison. Miss M'liss, fetch me some clean rags. You get yourself in to see your mama, Master Trav. She's been missin' you, Lord knows why, and you're just in my way."

Having disposed of her young master and mistress, the spry little woman held a sweetened mug of coffee with cream to Charlie's lips. "Gettin' chewed on's a shock to the system," she told him. Her hazel eyes were red-rimmed, probably from the constant smoke of the kitchen's great fireplace. "This'll perk you up." She glanced severely at Emmie, lying still and soaking up sun as if she hadn't ten minutes ago been in peril of at least her first life. "Miss M'liss is plumb foolish about that silly cat, but why you should be . . . ?"

"Miss Melissa ran to help the cat. I was afraid she'd be hurt." He didn't want to admit that he couldn't watch the cat be torn apart.

"Mmph." Aunt Phronie lifted his arm, lowered it gently, and nodded. "Still bleeding. That's good. What's bad with animal bites, or human either, is li'l bittie punctures that breed pus and corruption and maybe blood poisoning. You'll take these scars to your grave, but at least they won't *be* your grave."

"Sorry to make you so much trouble,

ma'am."

She looked startled, almost scared. "Lord, honey, don't call me that! I'm Aunt Phronie. Anyhow, this ain't a patch on the mess we'd have with my missie if the hounds got her blamed kitty."

Melissa hurried in with an armful of snowy cloth that looked like it'd been cut or torn from good sheets or such. Charlie had watched his mother and sister card and spin and weave too much not to be aghast at such waste.

"Oh, don't use that good cloth!" he protested. "There's an old shirt in my things. . . ."

Aunt Phronie ignored him. "Make a pad for each arm," she instructed Melissa as she herself selected a cloth bag from a number hanging in the darkest corner. "I'll grind this inside bark of slippery elm and mix it with water till it's all soft and spongy. That'll sop up blood and help the wounds heal. Hold up your right arm, honey boy. We'll fix it first."

"Your poor arm!" cried Melissa as blood trickled down to drip into the water.

"Aw, it's not bad," Charlie scoffed, although in spite of the coffee he felt sort of weak and dizzy.

"Missie, put the pad on soon as I have the bark in place," said Aunt Phronie. She wiped Charlie's arm and molded the pulpy mass of wet bark over the gashes. Melissa held the pad while the old woman wound a cotton strip around the arm.

"Your arms'll feel better with slings holdin' 'em," Aunt Phronie said, and grinned a little. "You'll be a sight, though, both arms tied up."

Charlie grinned back. "Well, I just hope I don't meet a bear while I'm walking home."

"You're not walking home!" Melissa decreed. "Trav will take you, but you're not going till we're sure you're all right. Is he, Mama?" She turned to the slender woman who came in supported by a cane and Travis's arm.

"Charles is surely welcome as long as he'll stay." Mrs. Jardine's voice was surprisingly resonant for such a frail woman. Her eyes were not the brilliant blue of Melissa's but a softer shade, and her hair was silver with the faintest hint of brown. Dimples showed in both cheeks. "I fear neither of us can shake hands easily, Charles, but I am delighted to meet you."

He was already on his feet, arms awkward in front of him even though Aunt Phronie had tied one sling a bit higher than the other. His uninjured hands rested at the sling edges.

He inclined his head and groped for something fitting to say to her. He could see why she had her roses and anything else. When he'd been here overnight before, he and Travis had left for Independence, and he'd only known she was ailing. No one had said she

189

was crippled.

"The pleasure is mine, Missus Jardine." He hoped that sounded proper. "I'm fine, though. No need for a fuss. Please. . . ." He didn't want her on her feet because of him, but he didn't know how to say it.

"Come into the house, then," she invited, turning with a slight limp. "Phronie, will you have Lilah bring cheese biscuits, or something tasty, to the conservatory?"

She was leaning heavily on her son and the cane by the time she entered the door Melissa held open, and sank down in a wicker chair on wheels. She smiled, though, as she gestured at a rustic bench and other chairs.

"Sit down, Charles. Travis, ask your father to bring our guest a medicinal brandy. No, none for you, dear. *You* weren't bitten."

Settling on the bench — funny how a person's balance was affected by having both arms secured in front — Charlie gazed about in wonder. Clapboarded log walls rose waist high on the south side, but panels like long, glass windows stretched from there to the roof that covered the other half of the sunny room. Two large windows were cut in the north wall. Roses climbed trellises to the roof, flourished in half barrels, and rioted in a wide log planter built along the southern wall to catch the sun.

"It's . . . it's like fairyland, Missus Jardine," blurted Charlie.

Indeed, except for the aching sting of his arms, he felt as if he had been magicked into another world, one whose queen was this woman with moon-bright hair, one where Melissa was a princess who smiled on him.

The roses were every hue from ivory and yellow to bronze and crimson. Their odor fuddled the senses. One end of the roofed section was latticed into a cage for two green-glistening birds that turned yellow heads with orange cheeks toward the humans and chattered grumpily. Charlie had chased flocks like them out of the corn that summer and knew they were Carolina parakeets.

They raised a din when a green-eyed, honey-skinned girl of perhaps Melissa's age brought in a tray of tiny golden biscuits, salted nuts, cubes of cheese, and slices of pickle. Charlie filled the small plate she offered and tried not to make a pig of himself.

Lilah had to have more white blood than black. How white did you have to be before it would seem strange for you to be a slave? There'd been plenty of white-skinned slaves in Greece and Rome. Why had American slaveholders decided only black people should be slaves?

His hostess' pleasant voice snapped this train of thought. "Soon now a roof that shelters the glass from snow will be fitted to the permanent one and reach out to those posts. The posts *are* there, four of them, though they're covered with honeysuckle and jasmine. Except on cloudy, bitter days, the glass still gets enough sun to warm this room nicely." She smiled at the birds that were attacking apples with their pale yellow beaks. "If it gets cold, Hither and Yon squawk till someone fetches braziers of coals."

"I found that pair in the bottom of a hollow tree after . . . well, after I cleared out a swarm that was tearing up our apples and pears," said Travis.

The bishop appeared in the doorway, holding two glasses. He strode to his wife and put one of the glasses in her hand. The atmosphere of the rose room changed. It was as if the flowers dimmed and their scent faded. The parakeets hushed and the sunlight altered.

"That Caxton rascal! Naturally those hounds you shot, Travis, became blue-bloods, the pride of his pack. If I didn't need him for certain things. . . ."

Mrs. Jardine drew her shawl more closely around her. "I don't trust that man, my dear."

"Lige Morrow has hounds," Charlie said, and then wished he hadn't. He couldn't imagine Lige tracking slaves, but there was no use tempting him.

The bishop shook his head. "Morrow and I can't agree." Jardine's gaze swept over Charlie's bandages. The glimmer of a smile touched his lips. "I see Phronie's been at you.

Hurt much?" Before Charlie could answer, the bishop offered him a glass. "Brandy and water, lad. It'll help. Another stiff one at bedtime and you should feel pretty fair by morning."

"Oh, I can't stay over, sir, thank you," Charlie stammered. "I need to get home."

"Stay at least the night," Mrs. Jardine urged. "We want to be sure the bites won't cause serious trouble. Besides" — here she smiled at her husband and children — "tomorrow's our twenty-fifth anniversary. Please stay and help us celebrate."

"Please!" importuned Melissa.

"I have to help get in the winter wood and shuck corn before I go back to work for Mister Cooley."

"So Seth wants you to go on short hauls?" inquired Jardine. "That's as a good recommendation as there is."

"You can't cut or chop wood till your arms heal a little," argued Travis. "Listen, Charlie, if you miss Aunt Phronie's special cake and syllabub . . . well, I pity you."

A day or two wouldn't hurt. Charlie looked at Mrs. Jardine.

"If you're sure, ma'am. . . . But I don't have any good clothes."

"You can wear some of mine," said Travis. "No fear of your busting out the seams."

"Take Charles to Miles's room," Mrs. Jardine told her son. "That'll be the quietest after Yvonne and Henry arrive with their little ones. That's my daughter from Saint Louis," she explained. "I expected them before now, but it's quite a journey, especially with the children."

"Especially with *those* children," Travis muttered once they were out of earshot. "Vonne lets them rampage through the house like a tribe of monkeys, and Henry pays them no mind unless they tread on his toes."

"Maybe they'll have tamed down since you saw them," Charlie suggested.

"I wouldn't bet on it," Travis growled before he flashed a grin. "And I sure do like to bet."

There was no missing the arrival of the St. Louis family. Racketing footfalls and shrill voices filled the wide hall. After considerable banging of doors, the uproar moved outside and faded with distance except for an occasional extra loud shriek or bellow.

Charlie was amazed, when Travis called him for supper, to be seated near four seraphic blond children who smiled on him benignly while translucent eyelids drooped over sky blue eyes.

Mrs. Jardine presented Charlie to Yvonne and Henry Benton. Slender Yvonne's high-piled auburn curls were striking with her creamy skin and sapphire eyes. Her fair-haired husband was large, slow-moving, and frequently emitted a rumbling laugh.

"Starting with the big girl at the end, the grandchildren are Rebecca, Annette, James, and Tod," said their grandmother, beaming.

Charlie tried not to stare as he murmured his — "Pleased to meet yous." How could these well-behaved if sleepy children, ranging from Rebecca's perhaps six to toddler James, be the same ones clambering through the hall?

"It's belladonna," Travis whispered in Charlie's ear. "Without it, they won't settle down to eat. Aunt Phronie thought of it when Vonne's doctor couldn't figure something out."

So peace reigned through soup, vegetables, ham, chicken, and a special dish of Travis's pigeons. Charlie passed them on. He still felt a pang to remember the sheen of thousands of wings dipping and lifting.

"So you never got back that hand you bought out of Indian Territory?" Henry Benton said to his father-in-law.

"He may wish he was back when he finds out Yankee hearts are cold as their weather," shrugged the bishop. He frowned. "I still can't see how he gave us the slip, unless someone hid him." He examined Charlie with piercing russet eyes. "Your folks likely don't hold with slavery."

"No, sir, they don't."

"Mordecai," began Mrs. Jardine,

"please. . . ."

"Don't fret, Vinnie," her husband soothed. To Charlie he said: "You'd oblige me, lad, by taking a good look at how our people live and telling your parents about it."

Relieved at such a reasonable request, Charlie nodded. "I can surely do that, sir."

Melissa smiled at him. His heart swelled till he thought it would carry him right through the roof and into the sky.

The cabins had hard-packed dirt floors like many settlers' houses, but these were cozy with braided rag rugs or sheepskins and the beds were spread with good quilts. There was a chest at the foot of each bed and pegs held clothing. Several chairs and a bench faced the fireplace.

"Single hands sleep four to a cabin," the bishop explained. "They can cook for themselves or eat at the cook house. Couples have cabins to themselves, of course. Phronie lives in the double cabin near the kitchen with her granddaughter, Lilah, four unmarried older women who work in the house, and my wife's bedridden old nurse, Aunt Zillah."

"I don't see any children around, sir."

"No. I don't keep brood mares and I don't keep breeding women. Only consider, lad. Children are a total loss, eating their heads off and wearing out clothes, till they're at least nine or ten. They don't pay their keep till they're thirteen or fourteen. A hand's in his prime from full growth at seventeen or eighteen till about thirty. With luck, he'll do a full day's work for another twenty years, and can perhaps be useful another ten years, but, after that, he has to be fed and housed till he dies."

"I suppose it is a problem," Charlie admitted.

"One Northern factory owners don't have," Jardine snorted. "If their workers don't have enough to eat, and sicken or die, they're replaced by other poor people, and God help them when they're too old to work. Of the three men now living on my bounty, one was ever stiff-necked and rebellious. The others were good hands. Sam gave me a full thirty years labor and ten of half time. He's earned his pork and corndodgers. But poor Titus was gored by a bull when he was forty-five and hasn't been fit for anything since but mending harness and making shoes." The bishop blew out his cheeks. "Instead of buying new hands, I think I'll hire them. There are always planters with more men than they need who'll let them work somewhere else for about a hundred dollars a year and board." He grimaced. "Where there's plenty of cheap Irish and German help to be had, they do the dangerous work. No one wants to lose an expensive slave."

"You might try what my father says a North

Carolina planter found good," suggested Charlie. "He discharged his overseer and told his people, if they worked well, he'd split the overseer's salary amongst them at the end of the year. They worked better than they ever had, cheerfully, too. Some saved up to buy their freedom."

Jardine frowned. "They must have been older ones who were going to start costing the owner in a few years. I hope those darkies went North. It's not right to have free Negroes living where they'll give slaves rebellious notions. Nat Turner. . . ." He shuddered.

Charlie went cold at the very mention of that slave uprising twenty-five years ago in Virginia. Nat Turner's God led him to gather about seventy other slaves and murder fifty-five white men, women, and children as they swept through the county. Turner was hanged, of course, with eighteen other rebels.

"I think it waste and aggravation to raise pickaninnies," went on the bishop. "The boys in whom carnal nature burns have found wives at nearby farms." He laughed at Charles's unspoken question. "Bless you, the wenches' owners think it a fine thing to increase their work force so the arrangement suits everybody."

Except the married couples who couldn't live together. The voices floating from the gin house were joking and light-hearted, though, and three men in the carpenter shop whistled as they sawed and hammered. An old man in a cabin smelling of leather hummed over a sole he was shaping to a last. The blacksmith hammered out some kind of tool while his helper pumped the bellows. Delicious odors permeated the air around the cook house, and women's bantering voices drifted out.

Bishop Jardine surveyed his kingdom and smiled. "I hope you'll tell your father what you see here, Charles. All my servants are well fed, well clothed, and housed as snugly as most whites. They're nursed through sickness and cared for when they age. All are baptized and attend the services I hold every Sunday." He gave a wry laugh. "Perhaps you know that in the 'Forties, the Baptists, Presbyterians, and my own Methodist church split North and South over slavery, but I'll defend the institution against any blue-nosed Northern preacher." He gestured at the peaceful scene. "Tell me true, son. Aren't these darkies happier and better off under my care than they would be if they were freed and left to shift for themselves?"

Charlie didn't want to anger Jardine but he knew what his father would say. It was on his lips before he knew it. "But if they could choose, sir, how many would rather be free?"

The bishop's jaw clamped tight. " 'Free' echoes finely in the ears. I've no doubt pernicious whispers of Abolitionist rubbish have reached Rose Haven. But you might as well ask ten-year-old children if they want to be free. It would be cruel folly to take them at their word."

"What about Lilah?"

Jardine reddened. "You can see that Phronie is a mulatto," he said after a moment. "Her father was the overseer on my father's plantation and her daughter, Lilah's mother, was the result of a guest's inebriation, the only slave ever born on my property." The bishop sighed. "Her beauty would have tempted even Saint Paul. To avoid . . . problems, I sold her to a neighbor."

"He didn't avoid the problems?"

"No. Lilah's mother died in childbirth. I had let Phronie go help her, of course. Phronie brought home the infant and appealed to my wife, so we had to keep her. To give my neighbor his due, he made my wife a gift of the baby."

"His own daughter!" Charlie gasped.

The bishop turned even redder and made some inarticulate mumble. Charlie thought the neighbor might rather have given his daughter to her grandmother or possibly freed her and sent her to be raised and educated in a convent. It was stirring up a hornet's nest, but Charlie had to speak.

"It doesn't seem fair, sir. Lilah's only one-eighth Negro. Looks like the other seven-eighths would count most." His imagination flashed ahead. "If she has a child by a white man, it'll only be a sixteenth black. If a white fathers a baby on that child, it'll be a thirty-second. Are you claiming a drop of Negro blood has more power than quarts of white?"

"The child of a slave mother is a slave, Charles. Any other system would be pandemonium."

"Sounds like this one is."

The bishop glared a moment, then laid a paternal hand on Charlie's shoulder. "You argue from ignorance and your Universalist upbringing. As a Methodist, I have to give Baptists this much . . . they know slavery is sanctioned by God and is the best means of saving heathen souls. Servitude in this life is a small payment for eternal bliss."

"If slaves go to the same heaven as whites, will they be servants there?"

Jardine blinked, then chuckled. "You've a subtle mind, lad. To be sure, God's mysteries are beyond us, but His word tells us that in heaven there will be no marriage and neither bond nor free. So leave it to Him, and let's get ready for the celebration."

Charlie couldn't wear a coat with his slings, but Travis helped him into a handsome maroon velvet waistcoat and fine wool trousers made by a St. Louis tailor.

"They sag a bit," Travis admitted. "These suspenders will hold them up, though, and won't show under the waistcoat. You should keep these shoes. They pinch my toes and raise blisters on my heels."

"They're just like new. . . ."

"They don't fit. And they sure won't fit Pa or Henry." Travis appraised him. "Your hair looks better now it's washed, but you're shaggy as a shedding buffalo. Aunt Phronie can trim your hair good as any barber."

She did, although in a swivet with preparations for the feast. "Don't you look fine as new paint?" she enthused when she'd finished snipping a bit here and a tad there. "If your arms get to smartin', honey, drink more of the syllabub. For sure and certain, it's more whiskey than cream and eggs. Now take yourselves out of my kitchen, Master Trav. I got rolls to make and the cake to frost and. . . ."

"What kind of cake, Auntie?" Travis peered hungrily at round layers cooling on the table. Charlie thought that, stacked on top of each other, they'd make a cake big enough to feed the whole plantation. Would the slaves get a piece?

"It's Queen Cake, honey, just like my mama made for your mama's wedding. Plenty of wine, brandy, cream, currants, and spices, with six eggs and well nigh a pound of fresh butter to each pound of sugar and flour. I'll use just a tinch of cochineal to make the frosting a real pale pink." She handed each boy several ginger cookies. "Now go along and get in somebody else's way!"

The way they found to get into was Melissa's. While her sister visited with their mother in the conservatory and the Benton children whooped and ambushed each other amongst the arbors and walks of the rose garden, Melissa and Lilah arranged flowers on every available surface in the dining room. Leaves had been added to the table and silver, crystal, and china reflected light from lace-curtained windows.

Fussing with a few bronze roses till they perfectly graced the table's centerpiece, Melissa paused to scrutinize her brother and his friend. "Charlie, you *do* look nice."

He felt his chest expand at her praise. When would he have a chance to give her the amber necklace? If he had a chance would he dare?

"Trav," she went on in a sisterly chide, "do something with that ridiculous cowlick! Aunt Phronie made Pa some excellent hair grease out of lard and oil of jessamine. Ask him for some. And I hope you remembered to get an anniversary present in Independence . . . at least something for Mama."

Travis squirmed. "I . . . uh. . . . Fellows don't keep things like that in their heads the way you females do."

"Trav!" she wailed. "You forgot!"

He hung his head. Charlie's inner struggle was brief. It would never do for him, an outsider, to have a gift for Lavinia Jardine when her son didn't. "Travis, I've got some nice embroidered handkerchiefs. They aren't much, but if you'd like to give them to your mother. . . ."

Travis looked as if a weight had been lifted off him, but Melissa fiercely demanded: "Were the handkerchiefs for your mother or sister, Charlie?"

He was glad to say truthfully: "No, Miss Melissa. I got them other things. . . ." He halted, realizing that must sink Travis even lower in his younger sister's regard.

"See?" She withered her brother with a dark blue glance. "I declare, Travis Forsyth Jardine. . . ."

"Let's get the hankies," Travis said hastily.

Gentleman farmers from miles around shared the festive dinner — suckling pig, saddle of mutton, wild turkey stuffed with rice and nuts, sirloin of beef, rolls of wheat flour, fluffy whipped potatoes and other vegetables, pickled eggs and onions, and a bewildering array of sauces and relishes, the whole followed by puddings, pies, and the rich, moist Queen Cake.

Aunt Phronie's poultices had drawn much of the soreness from Charlie's wounds. He slipped his right arm out of the sling to use his fork, but Travis cut his meat and Melissa, on his other side, buttered his rolls.

The house servants joined in toasts made with syllabub Jardine ladled from a crystal bowl. Charles recognized the genial heat of brandy and smoothness of cream. His head buzzed as he sipped. It was delicious but he declined a second helping. He'd rather die than slip under Melissa's table in a drunken stupor.

She nodded approvingly at his decision and wrinkled her nose at Travis who gave Lilah his glass to be refilled. "A helping of this is plenty for anyone, Trav."

Travis gave her a superior glance. "My dear little sister, you've never even caught a whiff of the skull varnish freighters drink. I could have half a dozen of these glasses and never show it."

"That's because you act wild all the time!"

"Me? I'll have you know I'm the one who rescued our sober-sided Charlie when he was about to get carved up by a no-account Pa hired and Seth Cooley fired."

To Charlie's embarrassment, she had to hear the story, and by then guests were leaving the table and chatting as they made leisurely farewells. The sun set early this time of year. It was prudent to get home before night, especially if creeks or the river had to be forded.

When the last carriage rolled away, Mrs. Jardine's old nurse, Aunt Zillah, was brought in to recline on a sofa, while Aunt Phronie and the household gathered around. Mrs. Jardine opened gifts that Melissa and Yvonne handed her and passed them on to the bishop to admire.

The distant sons sent presents from Oregon and California: a crate of smoked salmon from Miles, dried figs and pickled olives from Sherrod. Henry puffed out his chest as Yvonne presented their gift, a splendid silver-framed mirror. The three older Benton children, escorted from their playing by Lilah, offered their gifts with angelic demeanors. Rebecca, holding Annette's hand, put a gilt box of bon-bons into her grandmother's lap. James strode manfully to his grandfather and handed him a box of cigars.

"May I have one, Grandpa?" he besought.

"If your mama allows, you may have a puff," said Jardine gravely. "That could be all you want."

James stuck his tongue out at Rebecca. "I get a puff but you don't 'cause you're just a girl!"

Lilah, catching Rebecca as she screeched and started to kick her brother, quickly hustled the youngest members of the family away. Yvonne brushed a kiss across the bishop's knitted brow. "Aren't they wonderfully high-spirited, Papa? Oh, look, Mama! Auntie Zillah made you this lovely soft shawl! It just matches your eyes."

The frail white-haired woman, face

wrinkled as an old potato, raised on an elbow to peer through filmed eyes at her nurseling. "Took Phronie a mort of time to get the dye right." Her proud voice was a wisp of hard-breathed air. "It becomes you, Miss Vinnie, darlin'. It'll warm you in the chill winds."

"She's blind as a bat," Travis whispered.

Charlie knew she saw with the eyes of love, and his own misted. Mrs. Jardine, supported by her husband and son, limped over to embrace and thank her nurse. Melissa's gifts were an embroidered nightgown and nightshirt. Aunt Phronie gave an afghan knitted in soft shadings of rose. The other house servants spread a quilt over their mistress' lap, each square an appliquéd bird or flower.

"How beautiful!" Mrs. Jardine's gaze went from one woman to another. "Much time and care is in this. I promise you that I cherish every stitch."

The women smiled joyfully. It was clear they adored Lavinia. Probably Phronie saw to scolding, if any was needed. Lavinia apparently supervised the work of the household, but her actual work was limited to tending her roses as much as she could and working with her women to make the cotton, wool, and linsey-woolsey clothes of the slaves and sew sheets and other such needs for the whole plantation.

Melissa had shown Charlie the room given over to this work. "The married women have spinning wheels in their cabins," she said, "but they do their weaving here. This is Mama's special loom. Her cloth is so fine that our everyday dresses and Papa's and Charlie's shirts are made from it."

There were three other looms, four spinning wheels, and a long, plank table. "That's where Mama and Aunt Phronie cut out clothes. The cloth's too dearly made to let just anyone whack away at it."

"Can you weave and spin?" Charlie asked, hopeful of finding some way where this rich girl's life was like his mother's and sister's.

"I can, but I hate it when the weather's fine and I'd rather be riding or outside." She glanced at the fireplace where the makings of a fire were laid. "It's all right on cold or stormy days. We keep the kettle on for hot chocolate or tea and sing and talk and tell stories."

Rising now, the bishop fastened a diamond pendant around his wife's neck and kissed her cheek. "I pray the Lord, dearest, to give us twenty-five more years."

"I pray that, too, my love." She handed him a slender book. "Yvonne bought this in Saint Louis at my request. It's by a Harvard professor who uses the meter of an ancient Finnish epic in the story of a young Indian who grew up knowing the speech of birds and animals and became a wise and good chief."

" 'The Song of Hiawatha'," mused the

bishop. "We'll read it together, Vinnie. You know how much I like to read about Indians before they became debased, thieving lovers of firewater."

Charlie knew his father would say that a legendary Northern Indian was easier to deal with than the Osages and Shawnees treatied out of this region eighteen years ago. Travis stepped forward and bent to kiss his mother, slipping a tissue-wrapped parcel into her hand.

"Not much, Mama, but they come with lots of love."

She shook out each of the half-dozen handkerchiefs and exclaimed over the embroidery. "Lovely!" She looked up at him with shining eyes. "These will be useful, but pretty, too. Thank you, darling."

Charlie wished he'd had a gift, but it was far better that Travis hadn't disappointed his mother. That made Charlie think of his own. He vowed to leave next morning. Walking fast, he'd be there by noon.

It had been a tiring day for Mrs. Jardine. She graciously thanked everyone and wished them a good night before the bishop and Travis helped her to her room. The Bentons withdrew, and the servants were clearing up.

Melissa spoke softly: "It was truly good of you to give Travis those handkerchiefs." Her hand closed on Charlie's wrist below the bandages. More warming than brandy, her touch sang through him, sweet dizzying fire. "Thank you, Charlie, ever so much."

Scarcely able to breathe, he said: "I have something for you, Miss Melissa." He'd put the necklace in the waistcoat pocket in case he had enough chance and courage at the same time to give it to her. Now, clumsily, he fished it out. Firelight turned the amber into golden flame. "I . . . I sure hope you'll accept it."

She caught in her breath. Dark lashes swept up from those deep blue eyes. "Amber! How gorgeous! Oh, Charlie, I'll keep it always!"

Either she was pleased or a mighty good actress, and, if she was acting, it was to gratify him. That, Charlie figured, was fine either way. Then her face fell. "I wish I had something for you."

"You do."

Her eyebrows arched. "What?"

The perfume of her hair reached deeply into his senses, rousing feelings he'd had only in those troublesome dreams that had started plaguing him a few years ago, feelings it made him ashamed to have near Melissa.

"You've got plenty of it." He tried to joke a little to ease the tightness around his heart. "Could I . . . could I have a lock of your hair?"

"My hair? This old red stuff?"

"It's the prettiest auburn in the world." He searched for words. "Like a . . . a blood bay horse."

"Hmph!" She tossed her head like a mettlesome filly.

"I . . . I'm sorry! I mean. . . ."

She smiled at his confusion. "It's all right, Charlie. Horses are better-looking than most people." She crossed to a graceful writing desk and opened a drawer. "Here." She produced a pair of scissors and handed them to him. "Take any curl you like . . . so long as it doesn't show."

He chose a piece that curved against her ear and back of her neck. One careful snip and it was his. "Thank you, Melissa." He choked on the words. "I'll keep it always."

"Will you?" she teased.

He was solemn. "Yes." *I'll always love you, Melissa Jardine.*

She rose on tiptoe. Before he knew what she intended, her lips brushed his cheek and she fled.

Chapter Ten

Christy didn't know whether she liked Travis Jardine or not. He had kept Lafe from knifing Charlie, no getting around that. The way he laughed, so carefree and rollicking, made you want to laugh with him, but sometimes she felt he was laughing at them. He was charming to her mother, complimenting her almost too much on their simple fare. To her father, he was always respectful. He played peek-a-boo and "this little pig" with Beth till she squealed gleefully, and he treated Thos like a younger brother. Christy he mostly ignored.

Maybe that was the trouble. Christy frowned as she stepped backward three or four steps, turning the spinning wheel with her right hand, drawing out the thread with her left. Her mother, working the foot treadles of the loom, threw the shuttle carrying the weft thread through the warp with expert speed. She could weave two and a half yards in a long day if her husband or one of the boys filled the bobbins, but usually carding wool or cotton into fluffy rolls, spinning these into thread, and weaving were done at night or when an hour or two was found between daily tasks.

It was Saturday. There was no school so Ellen Ware hoped to spin at least a yard today. Jonathan Ware and the boys, including Travis, were using wedges, mauls, and axes to split cleared trees. The muffled sound of their labor reached inside the house. Travis was helping because Charlie had to content himself with trimming branches off the logs. His arms were still sore from the dog bites.

Christy shivered to think what those fangs could have done to Justus. Because Travis was there, the Wares hadn't told Charlie about helping the runaway. All too soon now Charlie would have to leave for his winter job with Seth Cooley. It was grand that he'd be earning cash money — Christy thrilled all over again to remember the excitement of his producing parcel after parcel from his canvas bag — but how they'd miss him at Christmas! She hoped Travis would take himself off in time to let them have Charlie to themselves for at least a day or two.

Soon the men would come in for dinner. Stew simmered, smelling of onions and herbs. The butter Christy had churned last night would soak deliciously into corndodgers, and as a treat, because Travis was company, there was Indian pudding — cornmeal and milk cooked with butter, eggs, and honey from Sarah's bees.

It was some comfort to hear that Travis's mother and sister spun and wove and sewed. Fifty slaves! Just keeping them clothed would be a major task. It would be interesting arithmetic to figure out how many slaves it took just to clothe the others. Seven yards for a dress, two for a shirt, three or four for trousers. Then there were sheets, towels, counterpanes. . . . Christy's head whirled at the thought.

More resigned to her chore, she held the end of a new roll of wool, clipped from the Suffolk ewes and already dyed blue with wild indigo, to a thread attached to the spindle, turned the wheel till the fiber joined with the thread, and walked forward to run up the thread.

Dyeing the cloth was an adventure, sometimes a disappointing one when wild plum roots produced, instead of purple, a muddy shade that couldn't be dyed over, or when hickory bark yielded a dirty sulphur hue instead of pretty yellow. This at least could be rescued by dyeing the cloth brown with walnut roots. It just took *more* work, and meant you wore somber brown instead of happy yellow.

Christy dreamed a moment of the beautiful dresses she and her mother would have from the azure foulard Charlie had brought them. Imagine. Real silk! She hoped she'd stop growing so she could wear it a long time. It seemed like magic to have cloth you hadn't worked for hours and hours to make. Sewing Christmas shirts for her father and Thos from Charlie's gift of plaid flannel was going to be a pleasure.

Beth toddled about the room clutching the fleecy lamb Charlie had brought her, murmuring in her private language as she investigated everything but the fire. At sixteen months, she often dropped to her knees and crawled till frustration with getting her skirt caught under her provoked her into pulling herself upright. Stooping to collect a bit of mud fallen from someone's shoe, she started to taste it.

"No, Bethie!" Christy warned. "Nasty!"

"Nas-ee," the dark-haired child echoed. *"Phu-ee!"* Wrinkling her snub nose, she dropped the mud that crumbled into grainy bits. The mud didn't smell, but suddenly Beth did.

"Will you change her, Christy?" Ellen stood up, flexing her fingers. "I have to make the corndodgers."

Christy changed her sister quickly. She didn't want Travis to catch her at the task. Unfortunately the little homespun gown was wet. Christy changed it, too, put Beth down with a pat, and carried the pail of accumulated baby things out to what they all thought of as John Brown's well. Drawing up a bucket of water, she poured it over the garments and went a safe distance to rinse them before filling the pail.

Back in the cabin, she added soft soap, and put the pail on the dogtrot to soak, although ordinarily it would have set in a corner. She had to grin ruefully at herself, going to such trouble not offend His Majesty Jardine's delicate nose.

Before warm weather, her father would build a well house with big water troughs to cool foods that might spoil, but for now it was cold enough that milk kept sweet on a shelf at the far end of the cabin from the fireplace. Christy brought pitchers of sweet and buttermilk to the table and fetched a crock of butter and smaller pitcher of cream for the Indian pudding.

Her brothers trooped in with her father and Travis, washed in the basin by the door, smeared a clean towel dirty, and eagerly pulled up chairs and benches. Her mother ladled out stew and passed corndodgers while Christy filled mugs according to the drinker's request.

"Milk . . . sweet, please." Sun through the window struck gold from Travis's laughing brown eyes. Had he meant that "sweet" the way it sounded to her?

Deliberately she filled his mug with buttermilk. His eyebrows shot up, but he didn't protest. She gave him a small, grim smile. He was only teasing, of course, but she wanted him to know he couldn't score off her without getting jabbed back.

Her father had just said grace when Robbie set up the jubilant barking with which he greeted Lige and Sarah Morrow, any of the Hayeses, and Hester Ballard. Poor Hester! She'd brought a special balm for Charlie's wounds. No one had the heart to tell her that Lafe had lost his job and attacked Charlie with a knife.

"The kindest thing for Hester may be for Lafe to just disappear," Jonathan said as she rode away.

"Jonathan!" cried Ellen. "That would be terrible, not to hear now and then where he is and what he's doing."

Jonathan shook his head. "Knowing, my dear, might be more terrible."

He went now to the door and called in pleased surprise: "Why, hello, Dan! Get off that horse and have a bite with us."

Dan O'Brien! Christy's face heated. She hadn't seen him since he'd helped her out of the sinkhole near Whistling Point and taken charge of Justus, but he was often in her thoughts.

Strange, but it wouldn't have occurred to her to set the baby clothes outside because he was coming. Hadn't he taken care of his own little sister? There wouldn't be much he didn't know about babies — or being hungry. After the dread and hope he and she had shared the night they turned the bears loose and groped their way along the underground river, Christy felt their lives were bound together — for better or for worse.

He followed Jonathan in, smoky blue eyes settling at once on Christy. Then he saw Travis and his smile faded. They spoke since apparently they'd met at Parkses' mill the day Charlie and Jonathan had taken corn to be ground.

With his flame of hair and thin face, Dan put Christy in mind of a fox, wary and shy. Beside him, Travis seemed an overgrown, ebullient puppy. As he ate, Dan answered Ellen Ware's questions. The Parkses all were well and sent greetings. Andy McHugh and Susie Parks were engaged but hadn't set a wedding date. To replace the cabin burned by proslavers, James Montgomery's friends had helped him build a veritable fort house of upright logs eight inches thick squared out of the heart of big oaks, grooved and pegged together so tightly no bullet could enter.

"There's only one small window set above the level of a man's head to light the whole downstairs," Dan said. "The loft has portholes. A few people shooting through them can defend 'Fort Montgomery' against dozens of raiders. There's a tunnel dug from beneath a trap door in the floor that comes out near the hill rising above the colonel's house."

"You seem to put a lot of stock in Montgomery." Travis spoke in a disdainful tone. "Pa says he's a mad-dog Abolitionist who ought to be strung up beside John Brown and all his sons."

Dan gave a hard, angry laugh. "I was with Colonel Montgomery when he chased Major George Clarke's gang of cut-throats back into Missouri. They didn't make much of their chance to hang him . . . or John Brown, either, though another gang shot one of his sons while he was just walking along the road."

Travis half rose, eyes stormy, but Jonathan raised a hand. "Political discussion is one thing, but there'll be no wrangling at this table."

"But, sir . . . !" Travis cried.

Jonathan quelled him with a look. Jaws clenching, Travis stared at his food. Dan buttered a dodger, praised it and the stew, and asked Charlie how he'd liked freighting. That carried them through dinner, although Travis didn't join in the conversation.

"So it's back on the trails you'll be next summer, Charlie?" There was a wistful note in Dan's voice.

Charlie nodded. "Why don't you come, Dan?" At Travis's scowl, he added: "There's lots of freight contractors. If you can't hire on at Independence or Westport, for sure you can at Leavenworth."

"I'd admire to see those far prairies and mountains," sighed Dan. "Maybe there'll come a time when I won't be needed where I am."

"And you, Travis," Jonathan asked, "will you go freighting, too?"

"My parents are determined that I must go to school, sir." Travis made a grimace. "Pa wants me to attend a theological seminary. Mama prefers the University of Missouri, but we've finally agreed on Kemper Military School at Boonville." He looked at Dan with a gleam in his eye. "That way, it won't be a complete waste of time if war breaks out."

War might settle Travis, perhaps six feet underground, but Christy doubted that the strictest military academy could.

Dan said: "We're doing a little drilling ourselves."

"That bunch of Quakers and Northern farmers?" Travis derided. At Jonathan's glance, he muttered: "Sorry, sir." He didn't look it.

"I delivered your parcel, Missus Ware," Dan said to Ellen.

He must mean Justus was safe. Christy's heart swelled with thankfulness as Dan turned to her. "Remember that cave I told you about? I went back in it a long way, last week. No telling where it comes out." A way of telling her he'd explored onward from the Whistling Point sinkhole. He got to his feet. "Thank you kindly for dinner, Missus Ware. It's to Mister Hayes's tannery I'm bound, so I must be riding."

"Oh, first you'll have Indian pudding!" Christy urged. She didn't want him to leave, didn't want to him to go till they'd had a few private words.

"Indian pudding, is it?" He sat down quickly like the boy he still was.

Around the table, pudding and cream vanished with avid plying of spoons.

Making his farewells again, Dan went out. Christy followed, trying to manufacture some message to Susie and Lydia. She babbled as Dan tightened the saddle girth on Breeze or Zephyr — she couldn't tell the Parkses' bay geldings apart.

Dan gazed at her in a way that made her breath catch and silenced her. Looking stern, eager, and questioning all at once, he seemed about to speak when Travis came out and made a great bustle of getting wood from the dogtrot. When he'd carried in two loads, he came out swinging the water bucket.

With a sound of disgust, Dan mounted. Desperately, for Travis wouldn't be long out of earshot, Christy blurted: "Dan, I'd like to see where the cavern goes. . . ."

"Seems like Travis Jardine keeps too tight a

watch on you for that."

"Dan!"

He was already riding away.

Wrathier than he knew he had any right to be, Dan reminded himself that Travis was Charlie's friend and had to be credited for helping with the chores Charlie wanted to be done so he could go to his winter work with a clear conscience. It wasn't Christy's fault that Travis was there.

Yes, but what had given the hulking spalpeen the notion that he had a right to clutter up their parting? Dan gritted his teeth, as furious with himself as he was with the planter's lordly son.

Why had he snapped Christy's plea off like that when he had offered to run the errand to the tannery for no other reason than to stop at the Wares' and ask Christy if she could investigate the farther reaches of the underground river with him? Her parents might have insisted that Thos come, too, but Dan thought they'd allow the excursion in order better to prepare for more runaways.

John Brown might not always be around to take fugitives North. It would be useful to know how far the passage reached and where it ended. With luck, it might open into a secluded valley or wilderness where it was possible to live in hiding for a time.

Dan decided he'd make up his harshness to

Christy later — if, indeed, she wasn't taken in by young Jardine — but he wouldn't stop by the Wares' again today. He'd take a short cut across the ridge above their farm. The Hayeses' cabin and tan yard were in a gradually sloping hollow that ended at the creek. The clearing was in a forest of blackjack oaks that yielded the bark used for tanning, and a lively spring burst out of serried limestone in between the double cabin and the tanbark house next to four large wooden vats buried in the ground, tops level to the surface.

Ethan Hayes was making the most of having his yellow-headed boys home from school. Luke, the youngest, urged on Ethan's white mule, the halter of which was attached to a bar fastened to a tall post that revolved on a pivot as the mule drew a roller over large pieces of tanbark spread around the post.

Twelve-year-old Mark dumped a bucket of small bits of tanbark into one vat. Matthew and Ethan had stretched out hides lifted from the vat of strong limewater that loosened hair and flesh so they could scrape them off with knives. Only after this could the hides go into one of the tanning vats.

The acrid smell of the vats stung Dan's nostrils, eyes, and lungs. Tanners earned the hide they kept from every two that people brought them. At a safe distance from the tanbark house were ashy remains of the log pyre built to heat limestone rocks till they were white hot and could be put in a vat with water to leach out the lime.

Ethan greeted Dan and bade him get down from his horse. As Dan complied, Ethan removed a last bit of flesh from a hide that looked like it came from a deer and lowered it into the middle vat of brown ooze.

"Mister Parks ready to make shoes for all of you?" Ethan said, and smiled. With his lithe body and bright hair, he looked young enough to be the elder brother of his stair-step sons. Simeon Parks ground his grain and got leather in return.

"We have to make some new harness," Dan said. "And repair the old stuff."

"Come up to the shed," invited Ethan, "and we'll get you just what you need . . . heavy leather for harness and soles, softer and thinner for shoe uppers."

Ethan bundled the tanned hides together and tied them with rawhide strips to fasten behind Dan's saddle. "You happen to know the Wattles folks who've taken up land north of Sugar Mound?"

"Heard of them." Mill gossip had it that the Wattles families were Presbyterian, vegetarian, and the women and girls wearers of bloomers that reached to the ankle beneath skirts that dipped a few inches below the knee.

"The brother called Augustus brought cash money for leather a couple of weeks ago, but

I didn't have any on hand. He asked me to keep the money and send the leather when I could. It bothers me to have a man's money when he doesn't have what it paid for."

"I can take the leather to the mill," Dan offered. "Unless someone heading that way comes by in the next few days, I'm sure Mister Parks will let me or Davie deliver it."

So Ethan added two more hides to the bundle, and Dan went his way. Fretting at Travis's presence at the Wares' and, even more, at the way he'd snapped at Christy, he didn't enjoy the outing anything as much as he'd expected to and was heartily glad when the mill came in sight.

As it turned out, Lydia and Susie Parks took over his errand. "From what I hear of the Wattles, we have much in common," Lydia said. "Augustus Wattles and his older brother John, with their wives, ran schools for freed slaves in Ohio. Amongst them they have several daughters close to our age, Susie."

"The most remarkable thing about those Ohio schools is how they came to be," put in Simeon Parks. "Back in Eighteen Thirty-Two or so, a young Kentuckian named Thom attended Lane Seminary at Cincinnati which was headed by Doctor Lyman Beecher, father of Henry Ward Beecher who's preached so powerfully against slavery and Harriet Beecher Stowe who wrote *Uncle Tom's Cabin.*

Remember the uproar when it was published in Eighteen Fifty-Two?"

Lydia nodded. "For Christmas, Papa, I hope you'll give Susie and me her new book. I think it's called *Dred, A Story of the Great Dismal Swamp*."

"I've already ordered it, my dear." Simeon looked perhaps even more fondly at Lydia, the plain daughter, than at Susie, the pretty one. "At any rate, young Thom was so turned against slavery that he converted his father who freed all his four hundred slaves."

"Four hundred!" echoed Dan, dazed to think of one man having power of life and death over that many souls. Even slaveholders agreed Negroes had souls. The English had never been sure about the Irish.

"Some planters own a thousand or more workers." Simeon shook his head. "Most Southerners, though, have no slaves at all or only five or so who pretty much live and work like the master's family."

"What happened to Thom's slaves?" Davie asked.

"Freed Negroes aren't allowed to live in Kentucky. Ohio wouldn't admit them unless they had a promised livelihood, so the elder Thom gave money to buy tracts of good Ohio farmland for his former slaves. They've lived there peacefully for twenty years. After the children attend local schools, they can attend Oberlin College if they wish."

Dan's head spun. College-educated Negroes! "So some masters free their slaves?" he pondered.

"Yes, out of conscience or affection," Simeon added grudgingly. "A number free their own children born to slave women . . . often educate and give them a start in life. Not only Thom's emancipated slaves, but many others live in the Ohio settlements. The Wattles brothers and their wives taught until the men's health forced them to take up less demanding work."

"They chose to come here and help make Kansas a free state," Lydia finished. "Papa, may we take some wheat flour to them? You know how tiresome cornmeal gets, especially if you're not used to it."

"David, tomorrow morning you and Dan hitch up the team and load a bushel of wheat flour into the wagon," Simeon instructed. "A bag of oats as well."

Lydia and Susie Parks added pickles, relish, wild plum preserves, a jug of Sarah Morrow's honey, a loaf of wheat bread, and a pound cake. They set off in high spirits and returned, tired but happy, about sundown.

"We had dinner with both Wattles families." The sparkle of Lydia's dark eyes brightened her thin face till no one would have called her plain.

"And don't forget those two handsome

young Morse brothers, Orlin and John," teased Susie. "They set up a store at Wattles' crossroads, but they let people take away so much of their stock on credit that they gave up the store and started making furniture. Which one did you like best, Lydia?"

"They're too young for me." Lydia's blush belied the austerity of her tone. "Though they'd be eligible for you, Susie, were you not pledged to Andy McHugh." Dismissing flirtations, Lydia went on enthusiastically. "John Wattles graduated from Yale and is a close friend of William Lloyd Garrison. The daughters are young, but accomplished."

"Celestia played the piano so beautifully I almost wept," added Susie. "The Augustus Wattles have four children. The son, Theodore, is about your age, Dan. Emma's fourteen and a bit rackety. Mary Ann's so smart she terrifies me, though she's only ten. The oldest, Sarah Grimke, is eighteen. We had a grand visit while we cleared up from dinner and washed dishes."

"She's named for the daughter of a South Carolina judge who owned a thousand slaves," explained Lydia to Dan who was the only one who didn't understand the Grimke name. "She and her sister, Angelina, came to loathe slavery so much that they've devoted their lives to fighting to free the slave . . . and women."

"Sarah Wattles told us something her namesake wrote," added Susie, and quoted, " 'All I ask of our brothers is that they will take their feet off our necks, and permit us to stand upright on the ground which God has designed us to occupy.' "

Owen rolled his eyes. "Good grief, Suse! I don't have my foot on your neck!"

"Not physically." Lydia skewered her brother with a stare. "But you can vote. So can any drunken, filthy, tobacco-spitting lout, but Susie and I cannot, nor can your own Harriet."

Perhaps to head off an argument, Owen's young wife asked: "Do the Wattles ladies truly wear bloomers?"

Lydia and Susie exchanged bemused glances. "Why, yes, they do." Susie giggled. "At first, it was all we could notice, but, you know, as the day passed, we forgot all about it. I must say it's perfectly modest. The bloomers fit loosely till they fasten at the ankle. It's a great saving to skirt hems."

"I suppose," sniffed Lydia, "bloomers shock prudes with the evidence that women have legs. So do men, but no one seems to find that scandalous."

Simeon looked so uneasy that Susie laughed and hugged him. "Don't worry, Papa! We've already decided not to outfit ourselves in bloomers."

"We've no wish to embarrass some of the crude men who come to the mill," said Lydia, looking down her nose. She hesitated as if torn between opposing feelings. "Owen," she said to her younger brother, "the Morse brothers are drilling regularly near Sugar Mound with Colonel Montgomery and his men. The colonel told the Morses how much he hopes you and Dan and Andy will join the drill when you can."

Susie lost her smile. "The colonel says it's not a question of if the proslavers will raid across the border again, only of when. He wants to be ready."

Dan glanced at Owen. Almost in the same breath, they said: "So do we."

CHAPTER ELEVEN

May 19, 1858, dawned to a bright sky. The excited bustle that had filled the Parks home for days rose to fevered intensity. "You've picked a grand day for your wedding," Dan told Susie at the breakfast she scarcely perched to eat. "Now if Andy doesn't forget. . . ."

Susie kicked Dan under the table. "Don't even tease about it. We've already had to put off the wedding twice because of rumors that Clarke's bushwhackers were coming."

"Thank goodness they were just rumors," murmured Lydia. "We've been expecting a bushwhacker raid ever since Colonel Montgomery smashed the whiskey barrels at the Trading Post store and told the proslave men who hung around there that they weren't welcome in Kansas."

Dan laughed to remember how the sod-corn whiskey sloshed for a hundred yards down the Military Road. "Yes, and back in January the colonel smashed the ballot box at Sugar Mound and stomped the ballots to pieces to protest the Lecompton Constitution drawn up by the proslave legislature."

"Even without Sugar Mound's ballots, the proslave constitution was voted down ten to one," said Owen. "At this rate, Kansas may never enter the Union."

"Minnesota just did." Simeon brightened. "That makes seventeen free states to fifteen slave." Then he grew somber. "As the slave states lose power in Congress, I fear they'll shatter the Union. These border troubles are just a hint of what's ahead."

"We've drilled with as many guns as we could get nearly every day this spring," said Dan. "But day before yesterday we decided the scare was all talk and we had to get back to work."

"We'll dance at your wedding today, Suse," teased Owen, "but tomorrow we must dance behind the plows."

"Well, right now, you can dance outside and lay planks on sawhorses for tables," decreed Lydia. "The Wattleses and Morse brothers are coming, and Colonel Montgomery and his family and. . . ."

"And the Wares." Susie shot a roguish glance at Dan. "Christy's what . . . almost fifteen now?"

Dan was only too aware of how Christy seemed more a young woman each time he saw her, which wasn't often since that early

December day a year and a half ago when he'd found Travis Jardine behaving like a member of her family.

He probably would be, one way or another. Charlie, when he wasn't freighting, spent about as much time at the Jardines as at his own home, and the bishop spoke of him approvingly. He needed an honest, hardworking son-in-law more than a rich one, a young man who could gradually take over the running of the plantation. Travis, who had been expelled from two military academies and the University of Missouri in less than a year, was now attending a military school in Arkansas and had accepted the discipline to the extent that he'd declared his intention of seeking a commission in the cavalry.

No, not for a long time would Travis care to manage the plantation. By then, if war clouds burst into full storm, there might not be a plantation to run.

Here on the border a sort of off-and-on war had gone on for years although it was more threats and fear than actual killing. Dan and Owen had several times ridden with Montgomery's Sharps-armed volunteers to recover stolen livestock or scare off bushwhackers. This made life safer for Free Staters, but there was no true peace — and couldn't be till the quarrel between North and South was over.

In the last year or so, many new settlers had taken up land in this eastern part of Kansas. Most of them wanted to ensure Kansas' entering the Union as a free state, but some were just as interested in profiting from a railroad proposed to run from Leavenworth to Fort Scott and Fort Smith.

Dan had still not shown Christy the passage he'd explored by entering the Whistling Point sinkhole and going the other direction, instead of making for the concealed opening they now called the Fox Hole. Twice, though, she had sent word by Thos to meet her and an escaped slave at Whistling Point at night and arrange a way to spirit the fugitive northward.

The first time it had been a young woman with a baby, fleeing to her husband who had previously escaped. The second runaway was a young hand like Justus, his bare back lashed into scabbing ridges because he'd tried to keep the overseer from forcing his sister who was barely of an age to menstruate.

"My little sister, she in his cabin now, that fat old white man's." Tears ran from the man's eyes. He swallowed hard. "I kill him if I stay, or he kill me, more likely. Better I run. Maybe save up enough to buy my sister."

Christy had struggled not to cry as she wished the man a safe journey and thanked Dan for taking charge in a polite but cool way that told him she hadn't forgotten the jealous way he'd thrown Travis Jardine in her face.

Those meetings at Whistling Point were truces. Dan wanted peace. More than he could have dreamed, he wanted Christy to be his friend again — yes, even if she had fallen for Travis's easy charm. If only today she'd smile at him, Dan vowed to keep a curb bit on his tongue.

Hughie Huston, the Irish veteran of the Mexican War Dan had met after the defeat of Clarke's bushwhackers, had taken Christy's fugitives to Lawrence since John Brown had been away. Hughie, a minister of the Church of United Brethren, would perform a service today to satisfy guests who might not think the simple self-pledging of Quakers a binding enough marriage. The Parkses esteemed Colonel Montgomery, who was a Campbellite preacher, but Susie didn't want her wedding to be the occasion for one of Montgomery's impassioned sermons against slavery.

Even on a wedding day, it was important not to waste the four or so hours before time to clean up and greet guests arriving for the noon ceremony. Oats and potatoes had been planted in late March and corn was being planted as the fields were plowed. That put in several weeks ago showed bright green blades struggling with lustily growing weeds. Dan and David attacked the weeds with hoes, while, in the next field, Owen and Simeon

Parks used Zephyr and Breeze to haul at stumps and roots.

It was late morning when Simeon peered under his hand toward the rumbling of a wagon. "Hurry, boys!" he called loudly enough to reach Dan and David. "Here comes the bridegroom!"

Working had heated all of them. Rather than get in the harried women's way to wash up, they pulled off their shirts and splashed on chill water from the river, then dried in the sun as they pelted for the cabin. In their loft, Dan and David scrambled into clean clothes, including socks knitted by Lydia and Susie and shoes made by Simeon.

Remembering Travis's unpatched garments, Dan sighed a little at his hand-me-downs from Owen, patched neatly on elbows and knees. He appreciated his foster sisters keeping his clothes from falling apart. Besides, there'd be more grown-up men and women with patches than not at the wedding, but someday Dan was bound he'd have a whole brand new outfit, store-bought top to bottom.

He instantly chastised himself. He was lucky not be under the Irish turf alongside his parents and baby sister. What would they say to his hankerings when he hadn't gone hungry a day since Uncle Simeon had taken him in, or lacked clothes to cover his ungrateful bones? He scowled in the little tin mirror at his broken nose and slicked his wet, fiery hair as flat as it would go.

Uncannily David turned green eyes on him. "How much longer do you aim to stay here, Dan, getting just your keep? You could hire on as a freighter like Charlie Ware and make good money."

"Your pa fed me a good many years when I couldn't earn my keep." Dan shrugged. "Reckon it's only fair to make it up a little." He grinned and cuffed the younger boy. "You trying to get shut of me?"

David cuffed back. "You know better than that! But Pa wouldn't fault you. . . ."

"I know. One more reason I need to pay back what I can. No way to pay it all." For a split second, Dan was six years old again, begging his tiny sister to rouse. *Wake up, Colleen! Dannie has a nice bite for you. . . .*

She couldn't wake, never again, and the bite had been a moldy bit of turnip he'd snatched from a pig trough. Mother of God! Here he was, full-bellied, craving new clothes!

Blinking at the sting in his eyes, Dan swallowed. "Anyhow, even if the militia's quit drilling for now, there's no telling when the bushwhackers may ride back. I want to be here when they do."

"It's not fair, you and Owen drilling while I have to plow and plant," David groused.

"Your time'll come, lad." Dan, by way of consoling David, tousled his just combed curly black hair and got in response an indignant punch in the ribs. "Your time'll come."

A chill fingered Dan's spine, the sensation old Catriona McHugh said was someone walking on your grave. His grave or Davie's? *Holy Mother!* In spite of his Quaker upbringing, Dan still reverted, in distress, to words learned in his mother's arms, the Virgin hazily assuming his mother's sweet face and tender voice. *Holy Mother, if one of us must die in what's coming, let it be me, not Davie. Please let it be me.*

"Don't stand there like a moon calf!" David called from the ladder. "Here come a whole tribe of ladies in . . . in . . . I guess they're bloomers. The Wares are unhitching. Preacher Hughie's just come. Oh, Dan, hurry!"

Dan did, forcing away his fit of dread. Between helping guests take care of their teams and saddle horses and improvising more benches as the crowd multiplied, Dan had no chance to do more than greet Christy along with the rest of her family, but when he didn't have to look somewhere else, his eyes found her as a magnet needle finds north.

That dress! The scoop-necked bodice accentuated Christy's blossoming shape and the full, full skirt flowed like melted sky. The sleeves fitted close to the elbows where they were caught with velvet ribbon to fall in gathered flounces. Only Susie's cream satin and lace gown, inherited from a grandmother, was anything as beautiful. No, wait! Mrs. Ware wore a dress of the same heaven blue cut in a different style.

Relief overwhelmed Dan. For a crazy flash, he'd thought that Travis — but, of course, the Wares wouldn't have permitted such a gift. The costly material must be a gift from Charlie.

Rejoicing, Dan had to snatch a few more words with Christy. Skirting the crowd, he caught up with her as she added plates and utensils to the Parkses'.

"That's a dress to suit the Lord's angels, Christy."

She turned cool gray eyes on him. Dan groaned inwardly. Could she be mad at him after all this time, after they'd twice met at Whistling Point to help runaways? But that was in the dark, hidden as the underground river. Here in full daylight, her face was unreadable, although intentionally or not her lips were invitingly parted.

She'd kissed him when they were children. Would she ever do it again? The hope that she might compelled Dan to brave her aloof stare. "Charlie must have got you that dress in Saint Louis," he said desperately. "Looks like it came from . . . from London or Paris."

"Independence." She laughed, warming suddenly. "Charlie brought the material

239

home that first autumn he freighted. I pestered Mother to help me sew it up as soon as we could. She told me I was growing so fast that I'd be out of it in six months, but I could decide." Had that dimple always been in her cheek? "I'm glad I waited."

"So am I!"

Soft color glowed from her throat to black curls swept up with velvet bows, and she glanced away. "Isn't Susie lovely?"

"So are you."

"It's the dress."

"No, it isn't." She had the clean fresh scent of lilacs. His heart pounded in his ears. He said huskily: "We still need to see where the cavern leads, Christy. When . . . ?"

"We'll talk later. See, Lydia's calling everyone inside." Christy rushed away.

At least, praise be, she was ready to talk to him. And how she shone, prettier by far than the other girls, even the bride. Dan stood with the other men at the door of the cabin. The end opposite the fireplace was banked in lilacs and plum and apple blossoms. Taking their places in the bower, faces flower-like in spite of their gray and brown homespun and those distracting bloomers, the three oldest Wattles girls sang, accompanied by brown-haired little Celestia on the violin. From the sweetness of their voices, no one would guess they had founded The Moneka Women's Rights Society in February to work for rights equal to men's and prohibit alcohol. Lydia and Susie were members, of course, and came home from meetings full of excitement over petitions they'd sent the legislature and the constitutional convention.

The sisters concluded with "My Love is Like a Red, Red Rose". Andy fidgeted at being the center of attention, but the way he looked at Susie showed that he agreed with every word of the song.

Hughie Huston lengthily blessed and admonished the young couple. They then placed rings on each other's fingers and promised in the Quaker way to help and cherish each other all their lives.

Few eyes were dry, but Lydia made everyone laugh when she announced in a stern tone: "There'll be no kissing of the bride. You may shake Susanna's hand as you do Andrew's. Then kindly make room for others by stepping outside." She raised her voice above the commencing hubbub of jokes and congratulations. "As soon as we're assembled at the tables, will you ask a blessing, Colonel Montgomery? After that, all of you please take plates and help yourselves."

Those first in line obeyed Lydia although they pumped Susie's small hand with such energetic good will that Dan reckoned she'd had preferred kisses even from the whiskered gents. When Lige Morrow, however, uncoiled his lanky form from the doorway, he strode forward, beaded fringes swishing, took Susie in his arms, and kissed her soundly.

"No offense, Miss Parks," he drawled to Lydia. He swept a courtly bow to Susie who was blushing but not displeased. "And sure none to you, Missus McHugh, but I didn't come all the way over here to shake the bride's hand."

"Lige!" Sarah scolded, but she was laughing, and so was everyone except Lydia. The fact that she remained a spinster at twenty-four was hurtfully emphasized by her sister's marriage. Not that Lydia lacked proposals. A number of widowers with children and an urgent need for a woman to do the work of the household had frequented the mill till they got it through their heads that Lydia preferred keeping her father's house to any of theirs.

As soon as the remaining guests wished the couple happiness, everyone trooped out to the sheet-draped tables laden with good things that gave out tantalizing smells. Most of the guests had contributed a special dish, from the Morrows' golden honeycomb to Mrs. Ware's richly creamed marble-size new potatoes. Most relished of all, perhaps, were crusty rolls and loaves made of the Parkses' fine-ground wheat, lavished with butter.

Mrs. Ware and the Wattleses had brought plates, cups, spoons, and forks to fill out the Parkses' supply which included one of Susie's gifts from her family, a set of blue and white ironstone dishes. With filled plates, people sat down wherever they could. Dan, one of the last in line, perched on a stump next to the Morrows and their lazing hounds.

Sarah Morrow, in her yellow calico, looked like a tiger lily among the prevalent grays, browns, and blues. She handled her eating utensils gracefully, but Lige Morrow, wielding his skinning knife, was having troubles.

"Give me a good hickory trencher any day," he grumbled. "No chasin' your food all over it like you do on these dog-gone' slippery plates. A body can't stick his knife in 'em, either."

"Well, honey, we'll bring your trencher next time." Sarah's tone was soothing but she had a wicked grin.

"Now, Sarah. . . ."

The sound of horse hoofs rose above the talk and laughter. Lige was on his feet in an instant, knife in hand.

"It's just someone late for the wedding," Sarah guessed.

"No!" gasped Dan. "That man in the middle's being held in the saddle by his friends." Dan hurried forward with Lige. They were joined by most of the men.

"Why, it's Reverend Reed!" cried Hughie Huston when the face of the man sagging on the middle horse could be made out. "He came last year to work among the Indians.

Brought fifty Sharps rifles to help Free-State men defend their families. God have mercy! His bowels are sticking out of him."

Lydia Parks was the first to reach the wounded man. "Owen! Dan! Bring a wide plank from a table and carry him to my bed."

"Bless you, ma'am." Husky Eli Snider, who had a blacksmith shop near the Nickels' farm, supported Reed on one side while his brother, Simon, held him on the other. "We knew it was bad for the reverend to bring him like this, but we couldn't leave him. Them murderin' devils might come back!"

James Montgomery laid a steadying hand on the blacksmith's trembling arm. "Who, Eli? Who did this?"

"Charles Hamelton and a gang of bushwhackers . . . maybe thirty of 'em. Lined up eleven men in a ravine, shot 'em, and skedaddled."

"Where?"

"Back to Missouri, most likely. Hamelton's been living over there since he cleared out of Kansas last year."

"Maybe we can catch them." Montgomery was the smallest man in the crowd, but all eyes fixed on him. "Any man who has a horse and gun and is willing to chase the killers, get ready to ride with me. If you have to go home for a gun or horse, do that, and try to catch up." He swung back to Eli. "Did the bushwhackers kill the other ten prisoners?"

"Five certain dead." Eli shuddered. "Austin Hall played dead even when they kicked him, but wasn't hit at all. One bushwhacker put a pistol to Amos Hall's cheek and the bullet nearly tore off his tongue. He's alive, though. The others may pull through."

"Is someone helping them?" called Jonathan Ware.

"We met Missus Colpetzer with her boy, Frank, and Missus Hairgrove driving a wagon with bedding and water, following the bushwhacker's tracks. They were scared something awful would happen when their husbands were prisoner." The brawny smith choked up. "We . . . we had to tell them. Colpetzer's dead. Hairgrove's so bad hurt, he seems sure to die."

"The ladies drove on to pick up the wounded," said Simon. "Brave they are, and so is young Frank. Only twelve years old and his father murdered."

"I'll go help them," Jonathan Ware said.

"I'll come with you." Ellen Ware was heedless of her fine silk gown. "Christy, do as Lydia bids you and take care of Beth."

Dan held one side end of the plank, Owen, Andy, and Jonathan Ware the others, as careful hands eased the ash-faced minister onto the board. Each struggling breath pushed blood and intestines through the bloody hole in his clothes and abdomen.

"Can someone lend me a horse and gun?"

cried Thos.

"Come home with me," said Andy, yielding his side of the litter to Simeon Parks. "We'll switch the wagon and harness for saddles. You can borrow my shotgun." Andy swept his weeping bride into his arms. "Sweetheart, stay here till I come for you. You know I have to go."

She nodded mutely, then promised between sobs: "I . . . I'll look after your mother."

"Belike I'll look after you!" Old Catriona hobbled swiftly toward the house, clearing a path for the plank litter. "Gabbling whilst this poor man's entrails dry entirely! Fetch your scissors, Susie, so we can cut away the dirty cloth and get at the wound. And then be changing that bonnie gown so the granddaughter you're going to give me can be a-wearing it for her wedding!"

Lydia ran to fetch a clean wet cloth and placed it over the protruding loops of intestine. "Tincture of yarrow," she told Catriona. "After we've cleaned the wound with more yarrow water and sewn it up, we'll put on a slippery elm poultice."

"*Och,* and it's a wise woman you be." Catriona looked with respect at this sister of her new daughter-in-law. "I know the cures from Skye, but you'll ken best what to use here." She called to the litter-bearers: "Leave the reverend on the board, laddies. He can bear its hardness better than being jarred about."

The minister was gently lowered to Lydia's counterpaned bed. As Dan hurried out, he caught a glimpse of Christy, trying to comfort Beth who wailed at the uproar and screamed for her parents. They'd be back, but some fathers wouldn't ever again hold their children.

The Wattles brothers, not joining the pursuit because of poor health, took charge of sorting out what horses could be spared and how families could be gotten home. As Dan and Owen saddled Zephyr and Breeze, Simeon and David hauled out of the barn three old but sturdy saddles that had been left as payment for cornmeal.

"Please, Papa, let me go!" David begged.

"You're too young. Besides, Son, Quakers don't hold with violence."

"Owen's going!"

"Owen's a man who must choose his path. So can you . . . in seven more years."

"Dan's not that old!" yelped David.

"Dan's dear to me as a son," replied Simeon. "God has lent him to us for a time, but I don't have the same rights over him as I do with you."

"Davie, you keep an eye peeled for bushwhackers!" Dan called over his shoulder. "They could swing back this way."

"Our Theo will ride with Colonel Montgomery," Samuel Wattles said. "He can take one of the three Sharps we have in our wagons. John and I will keep the other two and stand guard here till we know the killers are gone."

Snider brothers in the lead with Colonel Montgomery, the party jogged along, soon joined by Andy McHugh and Thos Ware. "Hamelton's gang came through Trading Post and took John Campbell who was keeping the store," Eli explained more fully. "They stopped for Sam Nickel, but he's off acting as a county judge. The raiders held a gun to Missus Nickel's head, but, since she wasn't hiding Sam, there wasn't anything she could tell them. Reverend Reed was marched along with two men he'd met along the road. Hamelton dragged young Amos Hall out of his sick bed and caught his brother, Austin, as he was coming home from getting a scythe sharpened at my forge. . . ."

Eli Snider was unable to go on. His brother Simon took up the story. "The gang took William Colpetzer away from his wife. She saw the raiders coming and begged him to hide, but he wouldn't because he said he hadn't done anything wrong."

"Hamelton found William Hairgrove and his son Asa," said Eli. "Also Michael Robertson and a friend visiting him from Illinois. Herded them along like cattle. When one poor man asked to drink from a stream, they told him he could drink in hell.''

Dan was thankful that he didn't know the Hall brothers or Michael Robertson, and that his acquaintance with the other victims was slight since they had all moved recently into the area. It was horrible to think of the terrified men on that cruel march and the helpless dread of their wives. It was just luck that Simeon hadn't been taken, or Andy, or Owen. Or himself, for that matter.

"When Hamelton had the prisoners lined up in the ravine about a quarter mile from our forge, he and four of his Bloody Reds tried to get us, but three of us had guns so. . . ." Simon's voice frayed. "So they rode back and shot down those poor fellows.''

"The marvel is they didn't kill them all," grated Eli. "They went around kicking bodies and putting bullets into anyone who didn't seem completely gone. Cold-blooded murder of unarmed men!"

Dan's own blood chilled but he couldn't help thinking the same was said of John Brown's slaughter of proslave men — and the Doyle brothers, still in their teens. He also thought of Mrs. Nickel with a bushwhacker's pistol to her head, after being burned out of her cabin less than two years ago. Could anything heal this border before everyone on both sides was killed off?

As the riders neared Timbered Mound, Montgomery called: "Here come the ladies with the wounded!"

One sunbonneted woman cradled a bandage-swathed man on the plank seat, supporting his head and shoulders. The woman in back, beside a body that didn't move, spoke reassuringly to the four men lying on featherbeds, some groaning, all crudely bandaged to stanch blood that still soaked through.

The tow-headed boy, walking beside the yoked oxen, halted the team at the horsemen's approach. He moved stiffly, as if he might break. His freckled face was blanched. Young Frank Colpetzer would never forget this day.

"We're taking the wounded to that cabin over there, just north of Timbered Mound," explained the woman on the seat. Her garments were stained with her husband's blood. She must be Mrs. Hairgrove. "Austin Hall wasn't hurt. He's gone for Doctor Ayres."

"Can we help you in any way?" asked Montgomery, doffing his hat.

The woman's dazed look changed to one of fierceness. "Catch Hamelton and his murdering bunch."

"We'll do our best, madam. Do you have any notion of where they went?"

From the back, Mrs. Colpetzer called: "Austin Hall crawled up the slope and saw the gang looking back from Spy Mound yonder! Then they tore off north and east in twos and threes. I expect by now they've crossed the border."

"We can cross the border, too." Montgomery bowed to the women, raised his hand, and the pursuers rode on.

CHAPTER TWELVE

Where various fresh tracks sheared off from Spy Mound, Montgomery halted. "We'll split up here, boys, and follow each bunch of tracks. If you run into any suspicious-looking fellows who draw guns on you, shoot to kill, but take prisoners if you can. We'll give them a fair trial."

"I bet we sight neither hide nor hair of 'em," said Eli Snider gloomily.

"That's as Jehovah wills." Montgomery's piercing gray eyes traveled over his men. "Let's meet before nightfall at Jerry Jackson's store. Jerry's good-hearted and as upright as a slave-holding man can be and has always let Free-State settlers buy on credit. I think he'll have a shrewd idea of who was with Hamelton. If we can't catch them now, we'll come back later."

Dan rode with Owen Parks and brown-haired Theo Wattles, who looked to be about Dan's age. Tracks slicing up bits of turf in damp spots led east from Spy Mound, north of the dense woods along the Marais des Cygnes. After a few miles, the hoof prints veered toward the river.

"They figure on losing us by riding in the water," Owen growled.

"They'll have to get up one bank or the other sometime," Dan reasoned. "When we find a place to cross, I'll ride along the other side while you and Theo stay over here."

"Don't forget we're in Missouri, or soon will be," warned Owen. "We may run into plenty of men who'd have been with Hamelton if they'd had the nerve."

"Doesn't take much nerve to shoot unarmed men," argued Theo.

"Hamelton gave up on the Sniders pretty fast when he saw they had guns."

Dan glanced at the sun, now halfway down the sky. Was it only a few hours ago when they'd been at a wedding feast? Poor Susie! What a memory to link with her marriage, even if Andy rode home unscathed.

"We're supposed to meet at Jerry Jackson's by nightfall," he reminded the others. "These fellows we're after could hole up at almost any cabin or barn." *Or cave,* he thought, remembering Christy's Fox Hole. "If we don't find them in a couple more hours, we'd better head back. The river doesn't look real deep here. I'll go across."

The current never topped Zephyr's knees. On the other side, Dan led the horse to keep from dodging boughs in the dense timber. How long could those bushwhackers stay in the river? It was bound to get deep sometime and force them out.

Tracks at last. Scarring the bank, kicking up rotting leaves and twigs. They threaded out of the timber, across a stretch of partly cleared bottomland with a cabin and out-buildings, and vanished at an expanse of plowed fields that must have covered fifty acres.

At the far end, a half-grown boy urged along a yoke of oxen hitched to a breaking plow. On the side near Dan, a man drove a team dragging a triangular harrow. The killers wouldn't have to cross the river again. They had disappeared into the woods somewhere beyond the broken ground.

"Mister!" called Dan, cupping his hands. "Mister!"

The man with the harrow stopped his team and wiped his brow. "Yeah? What do you want?"

"Three horsemen must have passed by a couple of hours ago. Did you see which way they went?"

"Youngster, I make it a practice to see nothin' that don't concern me."

No telling where his sympathies lay, if he had any, but Dan had to try. "They were with a gang that just shot down eleven unarmed men a few miles east of Trading Post. Five died. Several of the others may not live."

The man spat out a blob of tobacco. "Dang' Free-State Abolitionists should've stayed up north."

"Charles Hamelton, who led the bush-whackers, came from Georgia."

The farmer shrugged. "I got a field to harrow, boy. Iffen I was you, I'd scoot back to Kansas. And stay there." He grinned at something behind Dan. "Don't get wrought up, Hallie. The young sprout's ridin' on."

Dan looked over his shoulder. A woman with gray hair straggled into a knot had a double-barreled shotgun pointed at his mid-section. From twenty paces, there was no way she could miss. From the look of her nar-rowed eyes, she wouldn't be offering him a glass of cool buttermilk.

"Good afternoon to you, ma'am," he said.

When he glanced back from the timber, she still held the shotgun.

It was twilight when the empty-handed searchers rode wearily up to Jerry Jackson's store on Mulberry Creek. A few slaves were still unhitching teams near the barn behind the slave cabins and clapboarded house. As Dan, Owen, and Thos arrived, Colonel Mont-gomery had evidently just told Jackson of the massacre because the big, ruddy-faced store-keeper was shaking his graying blond head.

"William Colpetzer killed?" There was no

255

mistaking the horror and pity in Jackson's voice. "He had the best mind of any man I ever knew, and was civil and honest like you'd expect from Pennsylvania Dutch. Never worried me a bit that his bill climbed to over a hundred dollars. If his poor wife doesn't know that, I sure won't tell her! Why, Hairgrove was from the same part of Georgia as Hamelton and tried to be neighborly, but Hamelton turned him away. And Reverend Reed, a real saint for sure. The Indians he teaches brought him furs and venison last Christmas and all of them kissed him on both cheeks." The storekeeper went to his shelves. "Let me send some brandy for him and Hairgrove and the other wounded. I'm glad the Hall brothers weren't killed . . . mighty fine young men."

"You haven't seen Hamelton?" demanded the colonel.

"He and his brother and a few other men reined up while I was sweeping out the store. . . ."

"When?"

"Early afternoon. We'd finished dinner a little while before. I had a snooze on the verandah, like always in nice weather, and had just walked over here to the store."

"Did Hamelton say anything?"

"Just that he was going to Westport. They took off north in a big hurry. I suspicioned then they'd been up to something, 'specially

256

after a neighbor stopped by and said there'd been a big meeting of proslavery men up near West Point yesterday, maybe four hundred of them. He said they worked themselves up to cross into Kansas and kill a bunch of snakes."

"Indeed?" murmured James Montgomery.

Jackson nodded. "Judge Barlow tried to talk them out of it. He followed to where they camped on the border that night and told them the truth . . . that their squirrel rifles and shotguns would be up again' Sharps rifles and Colt revolvers. According to my neighbor, most of the mob plumb melted away."

"Except for Hamelton and his worst cut-throats." Eli Snider's tone was bitter.

Jackson looked sorrowful. "Let me fetch that brandy. And some vittles for the widows and orphans."

"Maybe we could still catch at least the Hameltons!" cried Eli Snider.

Plainly warring with himself, Montgomery shook his head. "We're not prepared for a three- or four-day chase, and the Hameltons can hide out at any number of places."

"Then what are we going to do?" blurted Andy, although he, of all of them, must have wanted to go home.

"Right now I propose that we ride back, care for the wounded, bury the dead, comfort their families, and plow and plant their fields."

Someone swore. Unruffled, Montgomery continued. "We'll make a list of the bushwhackers if the survivors recognized them. It's likely lots of them live around West Point . . . remember that's where Clarke's rabble crossed over when they raided us summer before last. When the planting's done . . . we all have to eat, and so do the murdered and wounded men's families . . . we'll ride over to West Point, collect as many bushwhackers as we can and. . . ."

"Hang them to the nearest tree!" yelled Doc Jennison who had just galloped up with a few other men.

"We'll turn them over to Sheriff Colby at the county seat in Paris." Montgomery's voice didn't rise but it cut like the flash of a blade. "Friends, in God's name, let it never be said that we're no better than bushwhackers."

"I say they deserve their own medicine!" howled Jennison. Even his tall, comical hat and slight build couldn't detract from his blood-stirring urgency. "I say let's not waste this jaunt across the border! Jerry Jackson may not be a bushwhacker, but he lets them hang out around his store. He owns slaves! Let's burn him out and teach these Missouri pukes a lesson!"

"No burning, Doctor." With thanks, Montgomery accepted a bag from Jackson and helped him tie it on behind the saddle before he turned to face the younger man and said firmly: "We'll be glad of your company on the way home, sir."

Jennison glared around, found no support, and spurred angrily ahead. The storekeeper brought out two more bags that were lashed on behind Andy and Owen. "Tell the ladies I'm purely sorry," the big man sighed. "Tell them they can have credit at my store for anything they need. I'll deliver their supplies if they don't have any way of sending for them."

"Thanks, Jerry," said Andy. "But we neighbors aim to look after the families." He paused. "Did you hear Doc Jennison?"

"I heard." Jackson's head drooped before he lifted it. "But what can I do, Andy? I live here. Everything I have is tied up in my farm and store."

Two weeks later, after the corn was planted, Dan O'Brien, Owen Parks, and Andy McHugh rode with Montgomery's band as they followed the Military Road to West Point. North of Timbered Mound, earth had been broken, but not for seed. It was a common grave for William Colpetzer, John Campbell, Patrick Ross, and Michael Robertson. Andy had made a wrought-iron marker with their names and date of their murder. It would be a long time before more than that was needed to explain what had happened. William Stillwell had been buried at Mound City.

Montgomery called a halt. The men took off their hats and bowed their heads as he prayed for the victims' families and for God's help in bringing the killers to justice. Montgomery had a list of the bushwhackers. Some, like the Hameltons, had fled beyond reach. The name of Fort Scott Brockett was crossed out because survivors testified he'd wheeled his horse away from the ravine when he realized Hamelton intended to kill the men. "I'll shoot in a fair fight," he had cried, "but I'll have nothing to do with such a thing as this!" Some of other bushwhackers started to ride off with him, but Hamelton cursed and exhorted them back into line and gave the order to fire.

The slaughter outraged Free-State sympathizers throughout the nation. James Lane, the fanatical Abolitionist known as the Grim Chieftain, gathered militia and scoured the border. Old John Brown started building a fort not far from where the blood of the massacre stained the grass and earth. Strangers were brought to him to explain what they were doing in the area.

In spite of all this, none of the assassins had been caught, and Montgomery's band found none in three days of peering into lofts and smokehouses, poking pitchforks into hay, and even looking in privies.

"They're gone, boys," admitted Montgomery that night as they ate roasted prairie hens and rabbits. "We have to get back to our work. But I'll keep the list. If any of them come back, be it ten years from now or twenty, they'll answer for their crime."

They were breaking camp next morning when a singular person rode up on a clay-bank horse. Even in this mild weather, he wore a shabby bearskin coat over a calfskin vest and overalls that could not disguise his thin, bony frame. Lank dark hair stuck out in every direction. He scanned the party with quick black eyes before his lips parted in a grin that revealed tobacco-stained teeth.

"Colonel Montgomery? General Jim Lane, Commander of the Army of the North and Kansas Militia, at your service, sir."

Montgomery inclined his head. "We may not agree on methods, General, but I believe we both serve freedom. As you see, we've found none of the killers."

"No more have I, sir, though we searched Westport top to bottom, and hunted along the border." Lane had a peculiar voice, husky and rasping, of the timbre Dan would expect to hear at a camp meeting. "My men have gone back to their farms and businesses, but I jogged south in hope of encountering you."

To Montgomery's lifted eyebrows, Lane placed his hand on his heart. "You are a preacher, Colonel Montgomery. You see before you a repentant sinner who craves baptism. The water in this stream looks deep enough. Will you do it?"

Montgomery's features softened. "I am bound to, General, if you're in earnest."

"Never more in my entire life, sir."

Divested of coat and vest, Lane was quickly dunked under. Once back in his malodorous outer garments, he thanked Montgomery and shook his hand before he climbed on the claybank and rode north.

As Dan led Zephyr to water, Andy warned: "Don't water that horse downstream from where Jim Lane got baptized."

"Why not?"

"Because whatever the man's got, we don't want to give it to an unsuspecting beastie!"

They had thought Montgomery too far away to hear, but he reined his horse in beside them. "Do you hold it against Lane that he was a proslave Democrat back in Indiana where he was lieutenant governor?"

Andy scowled. "I hold that against him less than the way he sold his wife's property, spent the whole ten thousand dollars to run away from her to start new in Kansas, and is now suing her for divorce."

"Andrew," admonished their leader, "if Lane has repented, he'll atone for his errors. If he lies, God will judge him. Let's go home now and fight weeds out of the corn so our families can eat."

This busy season kept men and boys in the

fields from dawn to dusk, but, as they rode, the men shared out the work of the dead men so their families could survive. Dan wondered if God was responsible for the five dead men, the widows, and orphans? The bloom of Dan's baby sister, crushed so soon? Had God just made the world and turned it loose? Was there any use to pray?

Yet Dan couldn't stop the worship welling through him at the scores of shadings of fresh green from grass to stately oaks, at drifts of fragrant hawthorn, pink blossoms of wild crab-apple, carpets of prairie roses, dogwood's creamy blooms and pink-veined snowy flowers against the dark green leaves of wild plum. His heart sang with the meadowlarks that flashed yellow breasts to the sun, beating their wings, then gliding as if for joy.

This beauty was as real as the blood-soaked earth in the ravine draining down to the Marais des Cygnes. He would hold fast to that. As they neared the common grave by Timbered Mound, Montgomery turned to his little army. "We've had no luck this time, men, unless baptizing General Lane counts, but remember what I say . . . deeds like this massacre will arouse the nation and free the slaves. We who hate slavery are called 'disunionists' by proslavers, but it will be they, not we, who shatter the Union."

A chill shot through Dan as Montgomery raised a hand in the air and his voice rang like a bell. "You may count on the fingers of this hand the years that slavery has to live! By then, there'll be no slaves in Kansas, or Missouri, or anywhere throughout this country. When we dug a grave for these brave men, we also began to dig the grave of slavery." He paused and gave that smile that touched Dan's heart. "Thank you for going with me. Next time we ride, may it be with better results."

James Denver, the territorial governor, traveled to Fort Scott in June to make peace between the proslavery men who controlled the Bourbon County government, and the Free Staters. On his way back, he promised Montgomery to station sixty militia along the border for the rest of the summer.

The truce was further helped along by rumors of gold in the Rockies of western Kansas where a town named for Governor Denver was already being platted. The lure of gold drained off some of the wilder, unrooted adventurers on both sides. Dan was never tempted. What he intended was to work his own farm someday, something no ordinary person in Ireland could dream of. After starvation, he prized corn and wheat more than gold.

To support Governor Denver's peace, when William Hairgrove recovered enough from his wounds, he went with Sam Nickel to visit

Jerry Jackson. Representing people from both sides of the Missouri line, they promised to warn and aid those threatened by either Kansas jayhawkers or Missouri bushwhackers.

Meanwhile, farmers, whatever their politics, waged another kind of war, attacking weeds to keep them from choking out the crops. As rain washed the blood of the massacre into the soil of the ravine and grass healed the broken earth of the grave by Timbered Mound, Dan took turns with Andy, Owen, and David in helping cultivate the Colpetzers' fields and helping young Frank keep fences and buildings in repair. As Dan followed the plow through rows of corn that cut off any cooling breeze as it grew higher, hoed weeds around potato plants, or scythed the golden wheat, he often called Christy to mind, lived over the few moments they'd had together at the wedding.

He dreamed of her in the gown of twilight blue, but more often he saw her in moonlight as she'd looked when they freed the bears, or blurred in the darkness by Whistling Point where he was keenly aware of her voice and scent and presence because he couldn't study her face and try to figure out whether her eyes were deep gray or hazel.

In the middle of August, the men were still at work in the fields when twilight revealed a heavenly body halfway down the northwestern sky. Simeon Parks declared it was a comet with a tail. "Whatever directs them in their celestial journeys, I believe they have no message for us except to declare the wonder of God's handiwork," the miller said reassuringly. "I well remember the autumn of 'Thirty-Three, when meteors fell like snowflakes and many people thought it was the end of the world."

Autumn was a blaze of gold and scarlet with wild geese flying on the first gusts of winter. Corn was cribbed, oats and wheat plowed under, and, when the stubble rotted, next year's wheat was harrowed in. The Parkses' barn was full of wild grass hay and so was Mrs. Colpetzer's. Dan and David filled her lean-to with firewood, including a good supply of oak backlogs small enough for her and Frank to handle.

The time had come for neighborly visiting when the weather was mild enough. Although John Brown chided Simeon for his Quakerish beliefs when the sword of the Lord and of Gideon was needed, the gaunt old man sometimes came to the Parkses, usually with a few of what could only be termed disciples.

The two Dan liked best were only a few years older than he. John Kagi was the son of Austrian emigrants. His dark eyes burned when he blasted slavery, but they softened when three-year-old Letty sidled up to cast flirtatious glances through her long brown lashes. When sweet hickory sap bubbled out of the end of a burning, green hickory log, Kagi would scrape it off with his knife and give it to her.

Sometimes Brown did that, a smile bending his craggy features. After her first stranger-shyness, Letty didn't fear him and clambered freely into his lap as he discoursed on the methods and ethics of war while his young followers hung on every word. Kagi's close friend, Richard Realf, looked like a blond angel. Newly arrived from England, he was a poet like his relative, Lord Byron, and would recite at length from "Mazeppa" or "Childe Harold".

"Byron died for Greek freedom," Richard said one night as they sat around the orange-tongued fire, savoring spiced cider. Owen was mending harness, but the other men folk cracked hickory nuts and ate all they wanted while filling a crock to be used in cooking. Lydia carded wool and Harriet and her mother knitted.

The two Parks households, Owen's and his father's, had supper together and usually spent the long winter evenings in Simeon's house. It saved firewood, but also made company. They all missed Susie's smile and happy nature, and it must be especially hard for Lydia who had mothered Susie. Andy brought her and Catriona over every Sunday when weather allowed, but they had to be home in time for chores.

"Had Byron lived," went on Realf, "he'd be too old to fight in this battle except with his pen, but you may be sure he'd have done that." He drew a folded page from his pocket. "Have you seen Whittier's poem about the Marais des Cygnes? A friend clipped it from the September *Atlantic Monthly.*"

"Oh, read it, please!" exclaimed Lydia. "Mister Whittier is my favorite living poet. He's not tedious like most Abolitionist writers."

"He's a Quaker, too," approved Simeon.

"Oh, Papa! That wouldn't signify were he a bad poet!" She turned back to Realf, sparkling with eagerness. If she always looked that way, thought Dan, she wouldn't be an old maid.

"I have it almost by heart." The young Englishman smoothed out the page and turned it over to catch the lines:

From the hearths of their cabins
The fields of their corn,
Unarmed and unweaponed,
The victims were torn.

When the passionate voice fell silent, Simeon repeated: " 'The crown of this harvest is life out of death.' God grant it."

"Amen." After a moment, John Brown raised his gray head and looked at Dan.

"Could we have your fiddle tonight, lad, some of the dear old hymns?" Nearly always, he asked Dan to play.

Dan played all the hymns he knew. The bitter grooves at Brown's mouth seemed to smooth. He helped Letty onto his lap where she soon fell asleep, soft curls stroked by a hand that had sabered men down.

When Dan stopped, Brown thanked him. "Your music flows through my soul like cleansing waters. Would there was a way I could hear it always." Rising, the haggard old man put Letty in her mother's arms, bade them good night, and went out with his companions.

CHAPTER THIRTEEN

Early in December, volunteers from Lawrence, Osawatomie, and Emporia joined Montgomery's men camped at the head of the Little Osage River in the north part of Bourbon County. In spite of Governor Denver's truce, Fiddlin' Judge Williams kept sending out warrants for the arrest of Free-State men. He had two of them chained to the floor of an old building in Fort Scott with winter coming on and their only bedding a few quilts. The federal judge wouldn't give Ben Rice and John Hudlow a trial or set bail, so Dan, Owen, and Andy were riding with Montgomery to break the prisoners out of jail.

Eli Snider grumbled: "We ought to burn that vipers' nest of proslavers to the ground and roast Judge Williams and his officers in the coals! I'll bet my forge and anvil that the Marais des Cygnes massacre was hatched up down here, just like George Washington Clarke's raid in 'Fifty-Six."

Colonel Montgomery moved into the flickering light, a slight, dark shadow against the blaze. "Now that we're all together, gentlemen, we need to elect a leader. I don't seek that responsibility, but I must make one thing clear. As either leader or follower, I'll have nothing to do with needless bloodshed or destruction. Our aim is to free the prisoners and show Judge Williams and his marshals that we won't tolerate such treatment of Free-State men."

Sam Wood, the young, brisk leader of the Lawrence squad, came to stand by Montgomery. "I'm a Quaker, sir. None of us want killing, only justice. My men and I respectfully urge you to take charge of this expedition. I've spoken to our friends from Osawatomie and Emporia. We are all agreed."

In the chancy glow of the firelight, Montgomery's face showed pleased surprise. "Then I humbly accept, gentlemen, and will do my utmost to see that this enterprise is one you'll be proud, not shamed, to tell your grandchildren about. Now we'd all better rest."

"What's your plan, Colonel?" asked Wood.

"We'll leave our horses with some guards where the military bridge crosses the Marmaton. When it's light enough to see but still so early that most folks will still be in their warm beds, we'll go straight to the old government building at the north corner of the square and bring out Rice and Hudlow."

"How about Fiddlin' Williams?" demanded Eli Snider.

A smile flitted over Montgomery's grim features. "We may burn his law books since he pays no attention to what they say about speedy trials and setting bail. Sleep well, men. We'll need clear eyes and steady nerves tomorrow."

The prairie grass, dried stems still smelling of summer, made a passable mattress and Dan slept close to Owen, but he had the great outdoors on his other side except for where his saddle gave some protection. Whether he turned his back to the wind or his front, he was soon chilled through his blanket and quilt. From trees along the little creek below, an owl hooted and the shrill *yip-yip* of coyotes seemed to answer. Dan snatched catnaps in the intervals before his warmed parts got cold again.

He was cold inside, too. Montgomery didn't want killing, but what if Fort Scott people started it? Riding into a sleeping town where women and children might be caught in crossfire was a far cry from chasing Clarke's bushwhackers or hunting Hamelton's bloody gang after the massacre. Still, two men lay chained to the floor of their prison, had been there for months, simply for being against slavery in Kansas. Dan was glad when Montgomery called: "Up, boys! Eat whatever you have for breakfast, and let's be on our way. We'll drink our coffee in Fort Scott."

Dan munched on cornbread and a hunk of Lydia's excellent cheese, saving a bite of bread for Zephyr who dearly loved it. He whistled and the hobbled horse came to him out of the darkness, daintily lipped the bread. Dan was saddling up by feel more than sight when he heard the muffled sound of hoofs on grass.

"Who is it?" called Montgomery.

"John Brown with two of my sons and Bondi, Kagi, and Realf."

August Bondi, a Viennese, was another of Brown's most ardent disciples. Foreigners often became fiery Abolitionists when they saw the promise of liberty that had drawn them here was tainted with slavery.

"We've come to join you."

"You're welcome," Montgomery said. "So long as you agree that our aim is to free Rice and Hudlow and teach Judge Williams that he must leave off fiddling his proslave tune."

"I say we burn the den of bushwhackers to the ground and kill any who resist!" thundered Brown.

"We want none of that, Captain Brown." Sam Wood, the Lawrence Quaker, spoke with soft force. "We've chosen Colonel Montgomery as our leader. You are, indeed, welcome, but only if you obey his orders."

"I had expected to assume command," said Brown.

There was embarrassed silence. At last a man from the Osage said: "Captain Brown, I and thirty or so of this band trade in Fort Scott and have friends there. Not all pro-slavery men are bushwhackers."

"Then they shouldn't keep such company." Brown's voice rose.

"Remember our slaughtered at Marais des Cygnes!"

"Remember Osawatomie," someone muttered.

"We must ride, Captain Brown." Montgomery spoke from his saddle, he and his horse only a little darker than the night. "Come with us if you will, but keep to what we've agreed on."

Leather creaked and metal jingled as the small army mounted. "I'll go my own way!" Brown cried. Dan was glad the group had rejected Brown's proposal, but he couldn't help feeling pity for the fierce old man's humiliation. This changed to dread as Brown cried: "I'm going to cross into Missouri and bring out slaves! Will none of you ride with me?"

There was no answer but the sound of seventy-five horsemen trotting southeast.

Three hours later, Dan's nose wrinkled at the smell of burning leather-bound law books and the furnishings of Judge Williams's court. Dan's rifle formed part of the pen of Sharps surrounding Judge Williams, Judge Ransom, and several marshals and deputies.

Ben Rice stood next to Dan, a wide grin on his face as he pointed a Sharps toward the officials who'd put him in jail. John Hudlow, on Dan's other side, called to Williams: "Keepin' warm, Judge?"

The portly man chuckled. He'd retained his dignity and good humor even though he'd had to dress in haste with rifle muzzles leveled at him. "It's good of you to care, Mister Hudlow. So long as you don't burn my fiddle or that old wardrobe that's been in my family for generations, I'm well content."

A big, mean-mouthed man from the Little Osage sauntered up with a beautiful violin that sent a thrill of admiration and yearning through Dan. His own fiddle had been left him by a crippled-up old man back in Pennsylvania for whom Dan had done chores, the old man who'd taught him to play.

"Reckon your fiddle will jig a merry tune in the fire, Judge," taunted the big man.

Dan, moving instinctively, caught the fiddle and bow as the other man started to hurl them into the blaze. Giving the fiddle and bow into the judge's hands, Dan's mouth went dry as he met the angry glare of the man with the cruel mouth.

"Who pulled your chain, boy?" the man rasped.

"No need to ruin a fiddle that can be making music long after we're all dead." Dan was surprised he sounded calm when his innards felt like a bunch of wasps swarmed inside them.

"We won't wrangle amongst ourselves," decreed Montgomery. He gave Dan a half smile. "The world needs all the music it can get."

"Music, my foot!" Judge Ransom was red with fury as he glanced around at his captors. "You'll all go to prison for treating officers of the United States in this scurvy fashion! And someone will hang for shooting Deputy Marshal John Little!"

"He used his shotgun on us first, and wounded two of our men," said Montgomery. "Most courts, perhaps even yours, sir, would scarcely find it strange to shoot back. Still, I regret it."

Judge Williams squinted over his shoulder. "Can it be?" he asked in tones of disbelief. "Colonel Montgomery, can some of your high-minded followers be looting that store yonder?"

It was the store from which Deputy Little had fired into Montgomery's men, but the colonel whirled and shouted in a voice that carried: "Men! Get out of that store and board it up!"

They obeyed, but some had suspicious bulges in their clothing. Several came out chewing tobacco they hadn't had when they reached Fort Scott.

"We'll bid you good day, gentlemen," said Montgomery. "I hope you understand, Judge Ransom and Judge Williams, that we won't allow you to harass Free-State men. In fact, you might find the climate of Missouri more salubrious." Montgomery's gray eyes went over the marshals and deputies. "I earnestly advise you not to pursue us."

"Colonel Montgomery" — bowed Judge Williams — "I'll gladly fiddle you out of town." He tucked the mellow wood under his chin and broke into "Old Dan Tucker".

Montgomery's men withdrew, supporting their wounded, rifles in hand, watching behind. At the bridge, they mounted, Rice and Hudlow on horses brought by the Osage men. They rode off to the lilt of the fiddle.

Heart pounding with relief and triumph, Dan grinned at Owen. "You've got to like a man like that."

"Not if he kept you chained to the floor," Ben Rice said.

Early in January, John Brown, Richard Realf, and John Kagi stopped at the Parkses and had dinner with the family. "My work here is finished," the gruff old zealot said. "We brought eleven slaves out of Missouri and now we must see them on their way to freedom. My good friend, Augustus Wattles, has upbraided me for breaking the so-called border truce, but I cannot think I did wrong though one master was killed when he tried to stop us from freeing his slaves. His blood is on his own head."

"That's not the way the governor of Missouri sees it," remarked Simeon Parks dryly. "He's asked the governor of Kansas to arrest not only you, but Colonel Montgomery."

Brown smiled. "What did the good governors do after the massacre at Marais des Cygnes?"

"Denver did his best to make a peace," said Owen.

"They say peace, peace, but there is no peace!" Brown's eyes blazed in the light. "There can be no peace while there is slavery." With visible effort, he controlled himself. "I came to bid you farewell, not to wrangle. Dan, my boy, would you play some of the old hymns?"

Dan could not deny him, this man so terrible yet so bent on what he saw as right. As Dan played, Brown closed his eyes and his breathing grew deep and steady. When Dan played "To Be a Pilgrim", Lydia sang.

Who would true valor see, let him come
    hither,
One who will faithful be, come wind, come

weather. . . .

Brown opened his eyes and rose with a sigh. "Bless you for the songs." Reaching into his pocket, he brought out a tattered little leather-bound book. "Have this to remember me by."

"It's your New Testament," Dan protested.

"I have much of it by heart. Keep it, lad. In the times to come, you'll need it more than I will." Brown offered his hand. Its bony roughness penetrated Dan's nerves and fiber. He wondered if the others with whom the old man shook hands felt branded by his touch.

CHAPTER FOURTEEN

Christy listened to five-year-old Mary Hayes chant the alphabet and felt sisterly pride that Beth, a year younger, knew it perfectly. The little girls were a delightful contrast, Mary with the Hayes' gold hair and blue eyes, Beth with glossy dark curls and hazel eyes. On the wall map of the United States, Christy's father was showing Luke Hayes and Tressie and Phyllis Barclay the location of the first silver strike in the country, out in Nevada Territory.

That was where Hester Ballard thought Lafe was. Christy hoped he'd stay there, although she felt sorry for Hester who still hoped Lafe would grow out of his wildness. It wasn't wildness. He was plain mean.

The little school had shrunk. At fifteen, Mark Hayes, never a keen scholar, chose to stay home and help at the tannery. He was needed more now that his older brother, Matt, had started freighting that summer.

So had Thos, as soon as the corn grew tall

enough to hold its own against the weeds. Christy took over his milking. She did the older, gentler cows while her father milked the young, more fractious, ones. She was also now the principal carrier of wood and water. What the family needed, Christy thought, was a boy in between her and Beth who could grow into the chores of his older brothers. Beth, bless her usually willing little heart, perched on a high stool to dry dishes, set the table, made beds, and brought in kindling, but Christy still felt stretched between inside and outside tasks.

At least, unlike Charlie who made short hauls out of Independence, Thos would be home through the winter and help with plowing, planting, and cultivating till the corn was well up. Christy often hugged her small sister tighter to warm the chill of loneliness that came from feeling that Charlie was more the Jardines' now than his family's.

He still came home in late autumn from his last trip to Denver or Salt Lake City. He brought lovely dress material for his mother and Christy, flannel shirts for Thos and his father, and dolls for Beth, although she loved her battered Lambie best. Before he left, he helped cut and split the winter's wood. But he went to see the Jardines before he came home.

Christy sighed, absently prompting Mary as she sounded out: "Kuh-a-t. Cat." Charlie would turn twenty in December. Even if he couldn't have Melissa, he'd marry someone. Then he really wouldn't be theirs any more. It was a comfort to look across the room at her mother who hummed softly as she worked the treadles and sent the shuttle through the warp threads.

Ellen Ware never seemed to change although her husband teased her a little about the few gray hairs showing at her forehead. Christy knew that she herself was changing, and not just because the blue foulard needed gussets under the arms that spring in order not to fit painfully tight across her breasts. She had changed in the way she felt when Dan O'Brien's smoky blue-gray eyes touched her, then veered away as if he'd been burned. All his growing had gone into height. He was still so thin that he was only muscle and bone beneath his skin. The flame of his hair had darkened a little, but it was as unruly as ever although he apparently tried to slick it down with some concoction before he came to Sunday morning service at the Wares'. He'd been doing that since the border troubles quieted down after the uproar over John Brown's carrying those slaves out of Missouri. In reprisal, proslavers raided Kansas, and, to get even for that, last Christmas Eve Doc Jennison and his jayhawkers looted and burned Jerry Jackson's house and store. Enough reckless Free-State men had come into southeast Kansas to give Jennison his own following. He no longer deferred to Montgomery who was stern but just.

Now that fraudulently elected proslavers no longer ruled the territorial legislature, a fourth convention had framed a Free-State constitution in July. Overwhelmingly ratified by the voters, it would soon be presented to Congress. Thank goodness, the bitter struggle over whether Kansas would be slave or free was all but over.

Dan came to worship, carrying his Sharps rifle, but he also had John Brown's New Testament in his pocket. Ellen always invited him to stay for dinner, but he and Christy were never alone. Christy somehow knew he'd never again ask her to explore the underground river beyond Whistling Point, that they could no longer share that kind of childish adventure.

Did she want him to come courting? Christy blushed at the thought. How could she be mysterious and interesting when they'd met while she was still a child? They knew each other too well, yet Christy often felt she didn't know him at all. When he rode off toward the border, she felt cheated, as if something hadn't happened that should have.

One of the horses neighed, to be answered by a whinny and the sound of hoofs. "Why, it's Dan," said Ellen.

Christy's heart leaped into her throat. Why

was he here on a weekday? Let it be nothing wrong. "Mary, help Beth with the primer," Christy directed, and reached the door as Dan was looping Zephyr's reins around the sapling trunk that served as a hitching post.

This wasn't an ordinary visit, although hides lashed behind the saddle indicated that he was on his way to the tannery. His face told her a bad thing had happened. "Come in, Dan," said Jonathan from behind her. "Is something amiss?"

"It's John Brown, sir." Dan's voice was through changing, but it broke now.

"What's he done?" Jonathan demanded.

Dan gulped. "He and twenty-one men seized the federal arsenal at Harper's Ferry in Virginia."

"What?" cried Ellen, rising from the loom.

"That was on October Sixteenth. They held it for two days. Brown was counting on slaves to rebel and join him."

"A slave insurrection," Jonathan groaned. "The thing Southerners dread above all things."

"There wasn't any uprising," Dan said. "Marines under a Captain Robert E. Lee overwhelmed Brown's party. Killed a number of them, including two of his sons."

"Brown lives?"

"For now. He was beaten to the ground with bayonets and sabers. By now his trial should be under way. He'll be tried for treason against the State of Virginia and criminal conspiracy to incite a slave rebellion."

Jonathan bowed his head. "God have mercy on him. He has done terrible deeds but against a terrible evil."

"Do you think he's crazy, sir?"

"Sometimes we call men crazy to convince ourselves that we are sane. How did you get the news?"

"Some stage passengers from Leavenworth heard it after it came in by telegraph, and told the people at Trading Post. Uncle Simeon heard about it when he went to the post office yesterday."

Christy's breath caught. These awful things! Was war coming? How could it? Yet how could it not? Dan would fight. Her brothers would — Charlie at least. Being a Quaker hadn't kept Owen Parks from fighting bushwhackers. She couldn't imagine Andy McHugh staying at his forge. Matt Hayes and Mark. . . .

Surely it wouldn't happen. The President and Congress knew how frightful it would be to have the country torn with the kind of struggle, many times magnified, that had gone on for years along this border.

"You'd better have a bite with us, Dan," said Ellen.

Dan shook his head. "I'm taking some hides to the tannery. Have to hustle to get home in time for chores."

Christy was already filling a mug from the buttermilk jar. "You'll have this."

He raised an eyebrow, almost grinned. "Yes, ma'am."

Their hands brushed. Warmth curled up her arm, jolting her heart. If only she could take both his hands — no, throw her arms around him and hold him close till the storms passed.

"Thank you kindly." He gave back the mug. Was he careful not to touch her this time?

After Dan was gone, Jonathan went to the map. "Here's Harper's Ferry," he told his students after a moment. "It's a name that'll be in any history books written after this."

Luke and Phyllis were eleven, Tressie a shyly budding thirteen. By the time they were Christy's age, what would have happened to them? Or the little girls bent earnestly over their primer? Kneeling beside them, Christy hugged Mary and Beth so hard they wriggled and looked at her in surprise.

"I see a c-c-cat," labored Mary.

A lump swelled in Christy's throat. The children would be caught in whatever was coming. This was like seeing one of the autumn fires sweep toward them, but having no place to hide, no place to run, as everything caught fire.

On a Sunday in mid-December, a haunted-looking Dan brought word that John Brown was hanged on December 2nd. Six of his men would die later. "I went with Colonel Montgomery, Augustus Wattles, and men from Lawrence, to try to rescue old John."

"You did?" gasped Christy. "Oh, Dan, how?"

"We went separately by train from Saint Joseph to Pennsylvania and met in Maryland, across the river from Virginia. Only one of our people was allowed to see Brown, and then only under strict guard, but there was someone friendly to him who managed to get messages back and forth." Dan turned up his hands and let out a long breath. "Brown wouldn't try to escape."

"Why not?" breathed Ellen Ware.

"He said his jailer and his wife had been kind to him and he had been given special privileges in return for his promise not to try to escape. He didn't want to be the cause of more bloodshed." Dan paused. "Most of all, he hoped his death would rouse the nation against slavery. He said . . . 'I am worth more to die than to live.' On the way to the gallows he passed his jailer a note. It said he had once hoped the nation could be purged of its crimes with little loss of life, but now he was convinced it would only be with blood."

Jonathan Ware put a hand on Dan's shoulder. "Still, it must have strengthened him to know friends came all the way from Kansas to try to save him."

"I wasn't his friend." Dan shook his head as he looked at Jonathan. "I don't know what I was. I played my fiddle for him and he gave me his New Testament."

"God rest him," said Jonathan. "And his men who must die, and those they killed."

Dan pulled out the well-worn little Testament. "Here's what the chaplain read when Brown's body was lowered into the grave . . . 'I have fought the good fight; I have finished my course; I have kept the faith; henceforth there is laid up for me a crown of righteousness. . . .' " Dan's voice wavered.

Blinded by tears, as much for Dan as the God-or-devil-ridden old man, Christy put her arms around Dan's thin body. His face pressed against her hair. She felt the damp warmth of tears. Then he straightened.

"We heard plenty of talk on our journey and back East. Did you know Abraham Lincoln back in Illinois, Mister Ware?"

"No," said Jonathan, "but I voted to send him to the House of Representatives, and, of course, I followed his debates with Stephen Douglas."

"He's made talks this month in Leavenworth, Atchison, and other Kansas towns. He says slavery is wrong, but he's willing to leave it alone where it already exists. That won't be good enough for the South if he's nominated next summer and wins the November election."

"Only a strong proslavery President can satisfy slave owners." Jonathan's tone was rueful. "Oregon came into the Union free early this year. If Kansas is admitted under its Free-State constitution, that will make nineteen free states to fifteen proslavery. The pity is that most Southerners don't own slaves, never will, and may wind up dying for the interests of the planters."

Dan looked from Christy and the little girls to Ellen Ware. "It's been bad enough along the border, but if war really comes. . . ."

"Maybe the President and Congress will just let the Southern states go their own way." Christy almost wished for this, although she knew it was cowardly. Then she thought of Justus and the other slaves she'd helped get away and knew that couldn't go on.

"No person should own another," Ellen said, eyes meeting her husband's. "No one has the right to separate families, to whip, and even kill."

"Charlie and Thos may have to fight!" Christy protested.

Ellen winced. "If I could, I would go in their place."

"Maybe there'll be a way out of it short of war." Dan put John Brown's Testament back in his pocket. "I have to get on to the tannery, folks. Thanks for the drink, Christy."

She watched him and Zephyr fade into the leafless trees before she sat down again with Mary, Beth, and the primer. After school was out, she went to draw a bucket of water from the well John Brown had witched, and whispered a prayer for him in all his blood and terror — whispered a prayer for them all.

Thos got home that night, seeming a foot taller, hair streaked from sun. Charlie, having stopped at the Jardines', came home a few days later, in time for his twentieth birthday. Bronzed and strong from months on the trail, he looked a man grown.

"Good thing they hung that maniac, old Brown." Charlie snorted. "He claimed he never planned a slave rebellion, but, if he didn't, how come he ordered lots of heavy pikes? How come he armed the slaves who were with him when he took the arsenal?"

His views surely echoed Bishop Jardine's. Jonathan said peaceably: "Let's leave him to God, my son. Is it as dry on the prairies as it is here?"

"It's dry. Creeks and rivers are down. But we ought to get rain or some good snows that'll put moisture in the ground for spring planting."

"I hope you're right." Jonathan gazed at the bright, cloudless sky. "We had a good harvest, thank the Lord, but we needed those fall rains."

"We can't do much about that," said Thos, "but we can sure help get in the wood."

Charlie worked hard, but his mind seemed far away.

Hurt that he didn't pay more attention to her, Christy teased: "What's the matter, Charlie? Mooning over Melissa Jardine?"

"Miss Jardine will marry some highfalutin' gent from Saint Louis," he snapped. "When she visits her sister there, Trav says the young bloods cluster so thick you can't stir them with a paddle."

Amazingly Travis was still at the military academy. When Charlie was home over Christmas last year, Travis visited the Wares for a few days. He did look handsome in his uniform, but he positively strutted. He'd waylaid Christy on the dogtrot one night. She scrubbed at her lips even now at remembering the rough, hot taste of his mouth. She'd wrenched loose and slapped him so resoundingly that, although he waited half an hour to follow her in, his cheek still showed the mark of her palm. He pointedly ignored her and left right after breakfast next morning.

To Christy's relief, he didn't come this year. Charlie was grown up now, and Thos almost so. There was no telling if they'd be home next Christmas. *Please, please, let there not be a war they'd have to go to . . . that Dan would fight in!* The worst dread, the one so awful that Christy pushed it away the instant

291

it shadowed her mind, was that Charlie might be so influenced by the Jardines that he'd fight for slavery.

This Christmas Eve, though, before the Wares had their own dinner, they lit a lantern and trooped, escorted by Robbie, to give the animals their Christmas treats. For the geese and Silver-Laced Wyandottes, Cavalier and his many wives, Ellen had cracked corn soaked in buttermilk. Patches, Evalina, and their spotted progeny wrinkled their snouts appreciatively at a soup of potato peels, turnips, and cabbage.

Jonathan had never been able to bring himself to butcher either of the original Poland Chinas, but each fall one of their offspring was slaughtered, skinned, and cut into hams, bacon, and side meat. On that day, Christy wished her family was vegetarian like the Wattleses, although, at least, as Lige Morrow teased, nothing was wasted but the squeal. Ellen made sausage or deviled ham of scraps, pickled the trotters, and made head-cheese of the head, ears, and tongue.

The dark-faced Suffolk ewe matriarchs, Mildred, Cleo, and Nosey, *baa*ed their approval of the oats Thos tipped into their trough before filling those of their score of descendants who furnished wool for blankets and winter clothing. The old ewes had supplied the Hayeses, Parkses, Hester Ballard, and other neighbors with the start of flocks.

No sheep had been killed for meat, but they discovered ways of killing or maiming themselves so mutton or lamb occasionally appeared on the table. Over the years, in spite of Robbie and the fence, five sheep had crawled under or through the fence and fallen prey to wolves or panthers. Jonathan called it their tax paid to wilderness. Ellen was less philosophical.

Now, in the barn, Beth dipped fodder into molasses to feed Moses and Pharaoh, crooning to the gentle white oxen who snuffled their delight and rubbed against Thos, brass knobs on their horns gleaming, glad their favorite human was home. The same treat went to the soft-eyed but temperamental Jerseys, Lady Jane, Guinevere, Bess, Goldie, and the now grown calves they had produced on the way from Illinois — Clover, Hettie, Maud, and Shadow. Yearlings were sold off or traded. Jonathan didn't keep a bull so Ethan Hayes brought over what Ellen called his "male brute" when the cows needed his attentions.

Beth stroked and crooned her way along the cows. As she rubbed the whorl of hair between Shadow's gentle eyes, she looked up at her father. "Can they really talk at midnight, Daddy? Hester says they can! It's a gift from Baby Jesus because the animals let him sleep in their manger."

"Maybe we should let that be their secret,

Bethie." Jonathan smiled at his youngest and picked her up to shield her from the chill wind as they walked to the stable.

Jed nickered as the family entered. Golden lantern light mellowed the rich bay of him and Queenie and burnished the haunches and head of Lass, the chestnut four-year-old. Charlie poured oats in their mangers while Beth offered molasses-dipped fodder.

"Merry Christmas," she murmured to each horse in turn, caressing soft muzzles. Her eyes shone as she gave her mother an exuberant hug around her legs. "We're their Saint Nicholas, aren't we?"

"Where's your pipe, then?" teased Charlie, swinging her to his shoulder as they stepped outside and barred the door. "Where's your round little belly that shakes like a bowl full of jelly? Where's your reindeer?"

"Char-lie!" She giggled and drubbed him about head and shoulders. "You're my reindeer. On, Prancer! On, Dancer! On Donner and Blitzen!"

He capered and bucked with her all the way to the house, set her down, breathless and laughing, by the fire. When dishes were done after supper, Jonathan read "A Visit from St. Nicholas" as he did every year, from Clement Clarke Moore's *Poems*. Only Charlie and Thos could remember before it was part of the Wares' Christmas ritual. Then they gathered around Ellen at the piano and sang all the carols they knew, Charlie's tenor reinforcing his father's.

" 'Joy to the world!' " exulted Christy, loving her family as she looked from one to the other, so grateful for them that she felt her heart would burst.

So good to have Charlie home. And Thos was there till summer. Those were the best gifts. The only other thing Christy wished was that Dan was part of their circle, cheek bent to his fiddle while the candle made a blaze of his hair.

■ ■ ■ ■

PART TWO:
THE HIDDEN VALLEY

■ ■ ■ ■

CHAPTER FIFTEEN

A dry winter and bone-dry spring. Swift rain in April roused grateful pungency from plowed fields, encouraged people, fingerling corn, and greened the grass, but the moisture vanished at once in the thirsting earth.

The hungry grass, Dan O'Brien thought. That's what they called grass in Ireland where some poor soul had died, mouth stained from trying to feed on it. If you stepped on such sod, unknowing, weakness melted your knees, and, if someone didn't quick pop a bite of food in your mouth so you could break free to untainted ground, you'd perish like one famished.

Dan still cringed to remember his baby sister on her knees, trying to eat grass at the door of the schoolmaster's hovel the day that kind man found them, took them in, and shared the little he had.

A swell of longing made Dan's throat ache till he thought he would strangle. Bridgie, little Bridget, who couldn't grow up like Beth

Ware and Letty Parks! Any wee bone left of her rested lonely beneath the sod an ocean away, not even near their parents who'd been tumbled into a ditch with dozens of others who lacked kin able to see their burial.

Homesick? No. Dan never yearned for Ireland even when the sun beat down day after glaring day. Heartsick was what he was when he thought of Bridgie. He doubted anything could ease the pain he felt when he had to face the fact that no matter how fine the crop, she could not eat of it, that all she had known in this world was hunger.

No one was that hungry yet in Kansas this droughty summer of 1860, but, as corn and wheat shriveled and potato vines and gardens burned, wagons began to roll along the Military Road, mostly folks who'd come in the last few years, heading back to Ohio, Iowa, Illinois, or even farther East.

"There won't be much grain to grind this year," Simeon Parks said, looking around the supper table. Instead of succulent new potatoes with peas, Lydia had concocted a stew of shriveled turnips and the tender inner part of cat-tail stalks and root shoots.

Still, the fare was sumptuous compared to that of many households. There was cheese, milk, butter, and eggs, although cornbread, hominy, or mush was only served once a day. The family had agreed to cut back on this main staple in order to give cornmeal to near-starving folk. The Parkses also probably gave away more dairy products than they used.

"I've been studying and praying on it." Simeon's voice was weary but determined. "Seems our best chance is to turn the cows in on all but three acres of corn . . . let them get some good of it rather than just have it burn up."

Cows grazing over seventeen acres that had been so laboriously cleared? Seven years after the first sod-corn crop, men and oxen and horses had wrestled out the last stumps just that February, then plowed, harrowed, planted, and ceaselessly cultivated in that yearly race with weeds.

"We'll starve!" Mildred Morrison cried, clutching at her full bosom. "I knew we should never have come to this awful place! My poor daughter. . . ."

That daughter said roundly: "You could have stayed in Ohio, Mother. Uncle Bart would be glad to have you go back and keep house for him."

"And leave you expecting after two miscarriages?" Mildred gasped. "What kind of mother could do that?"

"Lydia's right here, and Catriona's a fine midwife. Don't stay on my account."

In spite of Simeon's polite indifference, Mildred had still not given up hope of him. She cast him an appealing look. He paid close attention to spooning up the last of his stew.

Lips thinning, the widow turned to her daughter.

"I know my duty. You need a mother's support and comfort."

"I do," retorted Harriet. "So if you're going to stay, please don't gloom and doom."

"Pa," Owen argued, "it could rain! And there'd be all that corn wasted!"

"Not as wasted as it'll be if it doesn't rain and the cows have no use of it, either." Simeon let that penetrate. "We'll have to let the acre of sorghum cane go, but we'll try to save our acre of potatoes, haul water from the river and run it along furrows to reach the roots, mulch with dry leaves and grass to keep the ground cooler around the plants and hold the moisture. If it rains, we'll give thanks. If it doesn't, we'll have a decent chance of lasting till next summer."

"What if it doesn't rain before then?" Owen demanded. He put his hand protectively over Harriet's. After the miscarriages since almost-five-year-old Letty's birth, they were happy that Harriet was expecting a baby that fall, about the time Susie and Andy McHugh would have their first child.

Letty scrambled onto Owen's lap. She was a leggy child with Harriet's yellow-brown hair and blue eyes. She gripped her father's shoulders, and peered at him. "Daddy, we won't dry up and blow away like Gran says, will we?"

He smoothed her hair and laughed, although he shot his mother-in-law a stern glance. "No, honey, we surely won't!" He caught and held his father's gaze. "All right, Pa. We'll do what you say. But if we don't get enough rain to make a crop next summer, I'm taking Harriet back to where it rains enough to make a living."

"You're a man grown," allowed Simeon. "You have to do what you judge best for your family." He leaned over to smooth his granddaughter's hair. "Don't worry, Letty girl. We won't go hungry while our good cows give us milk. Tomorrow you can help bring them to the corn. They'll be happy, if we aren't."

The cows, Jerseys traded for with the Wares, indeed thought the foot-high corn and sorghum cane was paradise. Joanna was dry but Honey, Lucinda, and Bridie had calved in March. After suckling their big-eared, knobby-kneed young, they still gave plenty of rich milk for the household.

The corn in the lower field promised best. Simeon plowed a furrow along each row as close to the stalks as he could get without hurting the roots. Sweating and swatting at pesky insects, Dan, Owen, and David hoed up wells around the potato vines. Small Letty, sunbonneted like her mother and Aunt Lydia, helped them fill the wheelbarrow and baskets with dried leaves and grass and spread them around the vines.

"Always the 'taties!" Dan said, resting on his hoe a moment, flexing his cramped shoulders. "In Ireland, there was water aplenty but they rotted in the ground, a stench like the dead, and thousands died for lack of 'taties whilst the landlords shipped off grain and swine and sheep to England." He swung the hoe deep. "It was the same in the Highlands and Western Isles, Andy and Catriona say, but most lived near enough the sea to live by gathering seaweed and shellfish."

"Those who hardened their heart against the poor will answer at the Judgment," Simeon returned.

"I'd liefer they answered for it now," Dan growled. "Uncle Simeon, it must be as desperate at the Wares' as it is with us. I want to let Mister Ware know what we're doing to try to grow at least some food. Being more of a teacher and preacher than farmer before they came here, he may not have thought of it."

"He only has Thos to help, and of course the womenfolk," Simeon pondered. "We'll start hauling water this afternoon. Owen and I can keep on with it tomorrow, but you'd best head on over to the Wares, Dan. Stay and help them get set to irrigate if they decide to try. Davie, you'll go help Andy if he wants to water some of their crop. Generally he gets paid for his blacksmithing in grain or such, but it looks like he'll have to wait till next year for that and had best grow what he can himself."

Zephyr and Breeze were needed to haul water, so Dan struck out on foot, fiddle in its homemade case under his arm. The trees any distance from the river were sparse-leaved. Some were yellowing as if it were autumn. The river ran, sparkling and cool, but was down at least eight feet from the usual level marked on the limestone through which it had worn its way. A doe and fawn raced away from drinking and a belted kingfisher dived, showing the rusty breast band of the male.

Whether humans came or went, so long as there was some water, wild creatures would live here. Birds would sing. And what had people brought here anyway, but fighting and trouble? We cleared the trees for fields, crowded the Indians out, tried to make the country fit the way we live, instead of fitting ourselves to it. Maybe white folks were never meant to spread away out here. If you're merciless in what you want from the land, won't it be merciless in turn, like the wearied soil of Ireland, like a bitch suckled too hard, too long?

Plaguey, uncomfortable notions. Dan felt almost a traitor for having them, but hadn't God told Cain: "Now thou art cursed from the earth, which hath opened her mouth to receive thy brother's blood from thy hand. When thou tillest the ground, it shall not henceforth yield unto thee her strength."

Brother's blood. Osawatomie. Marais des Cygnes. Scores of other killings, and what was yet to come? It seemed to Dan the outraged earth cried out: "You have given me blood, not water. Now see if you can eat the harvest!"

The heavy sense of doom mingled with his bittersweet belief that whatever became of people, fawns and bear cubs, wolf pups and panther kits would be born in season. Parakeets would flock, chattering, and passenger pigeons would darken the skies in autumn and feast upon the acorns.

He wished he could tell these thoughts to Christy, but, during the two days he stayed to help, they never were alone. He found Jonathan Ware plowing a deep furrow along the corn rows while Christy hoed wells around the most promising potato vines. Thos had left a few weeks ago to sign on with the Pony Express, the exciting mail service from St. Joseph to Sacramento that the freighting kings, Alexander Majors and William R. Russell, had started in April.

"Thos is skinny," Jonathan laughed, "not quite eighteen, and, though he's not an orphan, the kind of rider the company prefers, they hired him when they saw how well he rides. Can you believe the pony boys cover two thousand miles in as little as eleven days, the route that takes mail wagons eight weeks?"

Dan shook his head. "Sounds like greased lightning!"

It was thirteen thousand miles, a four-month steamship journey, from New York around the Horn to San Francisco, and three to six weeks to cover the well over five thousand miles if you took the jungle railroad across the Isthmus of Panama. The overland telegraph was being laid from both directions, racing to meet and span the nation, but it would be at least a year before that happened. There was river travel up the Missouri after it thawed in spring till it froze, but from where the railroad had reached St. Joseph last year on Missouri's western border, mail, goods, and people had to reach the West Coast by wagon, stage, horseback, or on foot.

There was the joke of the five-mile railroad from Elwood to Wathena, the first in Kansas, that opened in April with great fanfare after the locomotive was ferried across the river. Railroad financiers planned great things, but the bill to admit Kansas to the Union had not carried and Lincoln's May nomination as the Republican candidate fanned the embers of Secession talk into open flame. If war came, railroads would be blown up instead of built.

"When the drought made it look like fool's work to fight weeds, Thos reckoned he'd better earn some cash money to help out," explained Jonathan. "We're trying to rescue enough to get by."

"That's what we're doing." Dan nodded. "Uncle Simeon can spare me a couple of days. Shall I plow or start hauling water?"

"I'd sure appreciate your hitching up one of the oxen and getting water to the potatoes," Jonathan said.

"Danny!" Beth Ware came out, hurrying as fast as she could without spilling the contents of a crockery mug. "Mama says you have to drink this buttermilk!"

"It'll be my pleasure, sweetheart." Dan grinned into the long-lashed hazel eyes. "Thank you kindly and thank your mama, too."

"Can you stay to supper? If you can, Mama says she'll make Indian pudding!"

"Well, I'd have to stay for that, wouldn't I? You tell your mama I'll be around a few days if she doesn't run me off."

"She won't!" Beth rejoiced. "She likes you, Danny! All of us do, especially when Thos and Charlie are both gone and we don't have any great big boys." She regarded him with a furrowed brow. "Are you a big boy, Danny, or are you a man yet? Charlie says he'll be a grown-up man when he turns twenty-one 'cause he can vote then. He says he'll never vote for that black Republican, Abe Lincoln. He says. . . ."

"Beth," said her father, "we don't call Mister Lincoln a black Republican."

"Charlie does."

"I've asked him not to at his mother's table." Jonathan Ware, who must be in his early forties, had very little gray in his thick red-brown hair, and was as handsome as his wife was pretty. To Dan, they had always seemed the way he'd have dreamed his parents to be, just as he thought of the cabin he'd helped to raise as the happy house. Jonathan waggled a finger at his youngest daughter. "Anyway, Elizabeth Ellen Ware, you aren't almost twenty-one, so for a few more years I trust you will graciously follow the customs of your ancient fuddy-duddy parents."

She laughed so hard she hiccoughed. "Papa! You aren't an-shunt!"

"Fuddy-duddy?"

She gazed at him thoughtfully. "Luke Hayes says that's 'cause you're a parson, and a Uni-univers-a-list at that."

"Mmm." Jonathan quirked a wry grin over her head to Dan. "Always refreshing to know what your neighbors think. Go help your mother, Beth. You can pester Dan tonight. Take his fiddle to the house, please."

She took the mug, gave Dan's knees an ecstatic hug, and gripped the fiddle carefully, moving to the cabin with Robbie at her bare heels. Dan's eyes met Christy's. In the sunlight, the deep gray looked brighter. The

309

sunbonnet hid her hair except for a few vagrant ringlets. She smiled, like sun edging out from under a cloud. His heart stopped, lurched, and began to pound till it hammered in his ears. Dirt smudged her face and rolled-up sleeves. The skirt of her gray homespun was stained from hoeing and the sweaty bodice clung to her, but he'd never seen her so real and — and beautiful. Not even in the blue silk dress.

Jerking his head toward Beth, he teased to cover his feelings and give him an excuse to speak to her. "Were you like that when you were little?"

"Thos and Charlie say I was worse." Her laugh was a silver rippling like small bells. "I don't believe it! She's had all of us to spoil her." Sobering, she went back to work. "It's good of you to come. Good of the Parkses to spare you when they have twice as many to feed."

Maybe it was best for her brothers to be off earning wages, but Dan couldn't keep from feeling one of them should have been home so Christy wouldn't be doing men's heavy work. He said gruffly: "If it gets to be more than you and your dad can manage, promise you'll let me know. Uncle Simeon's got Owen and Davie besides me."

She paused and looked at him. Again his heart stopped, caught, and began to thump. What would it be like, to take her in his arms, feel the promise of her wind-molded body against him? Would the beaded moisture on her upper lips taste of some private essence as well as salt? She was at once the girl-child he'd refuged with in the cavern and the sweetest mystery in all the world, in some ways known like the beat of his pulse, in others secret as the underground river.

"Thank you, Dan. I'll remember. I'm glad you brought your fiddle."

Full of pride and delight, he laughed as he started for the pasture where Noah and Pharaoh grazed with sun dazzling off the knobs on their horns. "Sure, and we'll have earned some music by nightfall, Christy."

He loved saying her name. He loved her. Suddenly he could admit that. It wouldn't change however far he ranged, however many women he came to know. It wouldn't change, no matter if they both lay under the hungry grass of this starving earth so far away from Ireland.

They had Indian pudding that night, sweet with Sarah Morrow's honey, pungent with cinnamon, one of Charlie's gifts. Ellen Ware knew how to make the best of plain fare — sweet potatoes were whipped with butter and cream, cottage cheese sprinkled with finely-chopped green onions, and the turnips Dan was sick of tasted different with cream and watercress. Maybe, too, because Christy was across the table.

When those rain-cloud eyes touched him, he couldn't have said what he was tasting, except the closeness of her, sweeter than Sarah's honey, headier than a nip of hard cider. After supper, he offered to dry dishes while she washed them, but Beth got the dish towel and hopped on a stool.

"I'll dry, Danny! You play 'Froggie Went A-Courting'." That was her favorite.

Christy groaned. "Go ahead and get it over with," she urged.

Beth made a face at her sister, but her lip quivered. Jonathan scooped her into his lap, chuckled, and sang lustily while Dan bowed his liveliest. Ellen lent her crystalline soprano. Well before the last verse, Christy shrugged, grinned at her sister, and joined in.

They finished, laughing, and it was one tune after another, with Ellen playing the piano, and Christy, Jonathan, and Beth singing. "Oh, Susanna!", "Sweet Betsey from Pike", "Comin' Through the Rye", "The Lowlands Low", "Gypsy Davy", "Sourwood Mountain", and more.

"Here's one you'll like," Dan said, after a rest of his fingers. "For all that an Irishman wrote it last year for a New York minstrel show, it's a mighty good tune. Folks coming in from the East say you hear it all over the country. I'll sing what words I remember, but I'll have to hum a lot."

In Dixie land where I was born
Early on a frosty morning. . . .

On the second chorus, the Wares joined in, and, at the end, Beth cried: "Again, Danny! Play it again!"

He did, wishing he knew the words better. They wound up laughing and clapping. "I never heard the South called Dixie before," said Jonathan. "But with a song like that, it will be."

"Do you know some Irish tunes?" Christy asked.

"Not real ones," Dan regretted. He decided to share his private song with her, although he'd never played it for anyone; it came from so deep within. "I've made up something, though, from what I remember." Christy was sewing quilt pieces together. He pointed his bow at her work, and smiled. "Sort of like that."

His mother's faintly remembered Gælic lullabies and nonsense chants, snatches of a haunting lament for a baby stolen away by fairies, airs gay or lonely Da played on his tin whistle — these Dan had put together in what he thought of as "My Song". It changed every time he played it, but always it began soft like his mother's voice, jigged and flourished with Da, mourned them, but lullabied small Bridgie, mourned her, too, and shrieked of loss and anger. But these at

313

the end resolved into hope, the hope of America, and this time he added his feeling for Christy, the sad-sweet promise he turned in his mind from Gælic to English: *I would go between you and the rocks, I would go between you and the wind, I would go between you and death.*

He finished, drained, as if he had wept again all the tears of his life, as if he had played his dreams and offered them to Christy. Had she understood? Almost in dread, he looked at her.

Tears sparkled on the homespun patchwork in her lap. She had stopped sewing to listen. "Dan." With only the light of the fire and the candle on the piano, her eyes were dark as night. "Oh, Dan! That was the loveliest song I've ever heard."

Ellen watched him as if he had sprouted horns or wings. "Why, Dan, you're a composer!"

He raised a hand in denial. "A little scrap of this, a little bit of that. Nothing grand."

She laughed. "What do you think composers do? Franz Liszt is creating his wonderful rhapsodies out of Hungarian folk music. Where do you think Chopin got his mazurkas and polonaises? Schubert drew from folk music." She smiled on Dan with such kind encouragement that he wished she was his mother, and immediately felt shame for disloyalty to that shadowy sweet-voiced woman of the lullabies.

No. He wanted no other mother. But his heart swelled when Ellen said: "It's wondrous, your weaving a pattern from your memories. Don't apologize, my dear. You're in exalted company."

Beth was almost asleep, hugging Lambie. Jonathan rose with her in his arms. "That music will be a heritage for your children, Dan, a song out of Ireland. We thank you for it." He glanced toward the loft. "It's probably hot up there for sleeping. Maybe. . . ."

"I already made his pallet on the dogtrot." Christy put aside her work. "Good night, Dan. Thank you."

She had understood. Somehow that was more important than whether she'd someday let him kiss her.

There was music again the next night, although Dan was sure Jonathan and Christy must ache from their labors as much he did. Christy, of course, couldn't heft barrels of water, but she had carried buckets of it to fill the potato wells.

By noon of the third day, the remnant crops were watered. After dinner, Jonathan shook Dan's hand. "Much obliged, son. We'd have gotten it done in time, but that time could have cost us corn and spuds that will make it now, by the grace of God." He chuckled. "Tell Simeon we hope to have some corn for him to grind, but he won't get fat off his share!"

"He won't keep a share if you need it," Dan said. "You can make it up next year."

Their eyes met in the knowledge that another year like this would drive them out. Ellen Ware caressed the crude fiddle case. "Thank you for the music, Dan. Thanks for your song."

Beth hugged him and gave him a moist smacking kiss. "Come back, Danny! Soon as you can!"

Christy gave him a wax-sealed crock. "Take care with it, Dan. It's honeycomb. Sarah says her bees won't make much over what they need themselves this year because flowers are scarce."

Their fingers brushed as he took the jar. A warmth golden as honey, slow-moving and sweet, glowed deeply inside him. He wished he could tell her the Parkses could have the honeycomb. He only needed her smile.

"Thanks," he mumbled. "Thank you kindly."

"We're the ones to thank you." Her gray eyes borrowed the blue of the sky. "Thank you, Dan. For everything."

He went off, floating on air, heedless of blisters on his heels, the ache of his shoulders. He whistled his song, his own song. For the first time, in spite of the drought, there was more joy in the song than sorrow.

CHAPTER SIXTEEN

Her mother smiled thanks as Christy drew water from John Brown's well to pour around the rose bushes Charlie had brought two years ago, a gift from Lavinia Jardine. "I hate for you to work so hard, dear. We can do without roses."

"No, we can't!" said Christy.

As if she hadn't seen how her mother loved the velvety crimson flowers, the pink-tipped ivory ones. It wasn't fair that Lavinia Jardine had so many roses, a hundred different kinds, when her mother might lose these cherished two. As long as she could crawl, Christy intended to keep them alive. They'd stopped blooming in this dry heat, but the leaves stayed green. They'd bloom again when it cooled off. The roses usually got the water from the wash basin and dish rinsing, but that now went to the onions and carrots.

Rinse water from laundry went to the maiden blush apple trees and grape vines, but, when the leaves began to curl, Christy drew extra water for them, too, even when she was so tired she could barely make her feet move or her arms pull the rope.

The cows, oxen, and horses feasted on abandoned corn and sorghum cane. "Bless them," her father said as he and Christy paused from filling buckets from the barrels and watched the animals feeding blissfully. "They deserve a treat, but I wish it didn't cost so much in work and hope." His ruefulness deepened. "Are you through pulling up the beans and peas for the sheep and pigs?"

"Not quite." Christy wanted to roll her shoulders, loosen the knotted muscles, but that would make her father feel badly. He hated for her to do heavy outside work. "And there's still the potatoes we can't water."

"Why don't you pull them up while there's good nourishment in them?" Jonathan asked. "I can finish here."

It was his way of sparing her part of their arduous daily chore, but it was also true that each unrelenting hour baked moisture from the dying plants, so she nodded and walked up the slope to the garden where three hunger-emboldened deer had jumped the fence and were enjoying the fare. They sailed over the fence at Robbie's barking. Christy was dismayed at the vines they'd ravaged, but she couldn't grudge the food.

The pods that should have been plump with juicy peas encased tiny nubs, and the green beans were scrawny and tough. Christy winced as she pulled up a vine, shook earth — dry earth — from the roots, and tossed it in the wheelbarrow. If it rained tomorrow, how they'd regret this, the waste of all their labor! But they'd hoped and waited, waited and hoped.

Mildred, Cleo, and Nosey snuffled greedily as Christy scattered the vines from the wheelbarrow so all the sheep would get a mouthful. She had to smile at the lambs playing king of the hill, butting their little heads, although this was one year it would have been better not to have them. Apart from their appetites, if the natural prey of panthers, wolves, and bobcats dwindled enough, the hunters wouldn't all be kept off by Robbie's brave efforts.

Patches' and Evalina's family had increased again, too. Jonathan had traded off all the pigs he could, but more than one would have to be slaughtered that fall. As the black and white animals grunted their pleasure at this surprise, Christy hoped this wouldn't be the year her father decided that Patches' and Evalina's ages doomed them. The Wares had a special affection for the creatures that had traveled the long road with them to this new home.

When I grow up, Christy thought as she trundled the wheelbarrow back to the garden, *I'll try to live from the garden and fields, orchard, vineyard, and dairy. There could be eggs, too. I wouldn't kill the hens when they got past laying age. Even when they didn't calve any more, the cows could go on grazing.*

What if there's a year like this when grazing's pitiful and the chickens can't scratch up enough to live? Would you scant your producing animals to save the worn-out ones? The voice of what-everybody-else-thinks grew jeering. *Even if you're such a fool, what man would put up with that? Your father's so kind he can't believe anyone will go to hell, but even he has to give in to the plain hard facts of living.*

Dan's thin face, nose ridged to one side by old brutality, rose before her. Out of all the people at the cabin-raising, he'd been the other one who couldn't endure that the bear and her cub should be torn apart by hounds — and the bear hadn't even hung around his home, listening to music, as she had at the Wares'. He, unlike most folks, didn't joke about the Wattleses' vegetarian ways, although he'd looked dazed when the women wore bloomers to Andy's and Susie's wedding.

Christy giggled. Probably she'd looked a little dazed herself. Then she sobered as she pulled up vines. Strange how they came up in seconds when each one represented hours of labor. It wasn't only sweat that stung her eyes. To console herself and fret less over this task, she relived every moment of Dan's visit, imagined that he smiled at her, that those eyes the color of autumn haze on the hills had rested on her.

Humming, she tried to remember the melody of his song. She'd capture some of it before what followed eluded her. Her mother had been right. Dan had made something beautiful out of his pain and loss. That set him a world apart from her brothers, not to mention snooty, spoiled Travis Jardine or cruel-smiling Lafe Ballard.

She hadn't thought of Lafe in weeks and shivered now as she did so. Lafe would make pain out of beauty just as he'd scarred her flesh. Always, like an obscene brand, she'd carry his livid white mark above the pulse of her wrist. To banish that ugliness, she fixed her mind on Dan's song and tried to call it back.

As if drought wasn't enough, bugs erupted overnight on the potato vines. Her mother had hit on the notion of turning the chickens into the patch. It was Beth's chore to shoo Cavalier and his wives along if they started pecking leaves instead of bugs, but there were enough of the pests to keep the chickens occupied till the bugs were vanquished.

There was never much visiting among neighbors during summer. This year, there was even less, although the Hayeses, Barclays, Hester Ballard, and Emil and Lottie Franz usually came to Sunday services and stayed to share a meal with whatever they had brought. Being together raised spirits and hopes.

Dan O'Brien came when he wasn't too tired to walk. "The horses need their day of rest," he said. "If I took it, I'd be a hypocrite to sing hymns."

Ethan, Mark, and Luke Hayes were so busy with the tannery that Ethan had to let the crops go. "So many animals are dying or being slaughtered and divvied up fast before the meat spoils that we can't keep up," he said with a shrug. "Allie and Mary tote water to some spuds and garden. Other than that. . . . I'll swap tanned hides for food in Osceola. As long as the Osage River doesn't get too low, steamboats bring supplies that far."

Other neighbors watered some crops from the creek except for the Madduxes and Watt Caxton. The Madduxes expected their congregation to feed them, and borrowed from family back East to eke out the contributions. Caxton let his few acres wither. He'd made his usual rounds that spring to buy up mules and slaves and sell them at a profit. After that, rather than battle the drought, he organized cockfights for a share of the winnings and located runaway slaves and brought them back for the reward.

It was the longest summer Christy could remember. When she and her father weren't watering, they walked the creekbanks, cutting young willow and cottonwood limbs for the sheep and cows. The oxen and horses ranged outside the fences, feeding on grass that had already cured like hay.

The potatoes yielded well, but the family ate sparingly of them, carrots, sweet potatoes, and turnips. Most would be stored in the root cellar for winter. They did feast for days on roasting ears. The buttered tender corn tasted more delicious to Christy than anything she'd ever tasted. She and her father stripped the blades from the ears, let them dry, bound the sweet-smelling fodder, and hauled it to the barn. Only a fraction of what had been stored in previous years, it would be doled out to the milk cows and animals that needed it most.

Christy and her father were cutting willow limbs one searing late August afternoon when she heard Beth give a whoop. Glancing up, she saw her little sister run to hurl herself at Dan who picked her up and whirled her around before he set her down and started for the creek, Beth on his heels.

He stepped into the shade as Ellen Ware came out with a jug and cups. He took the sassafras tea with thanks as Ellen poured more for her husband and older daughter.

"Churches and folks from the East are fixing to send food and other supplies to Kansas," Dan said, beaming around at the Wares.

"Each township is forming a committee to be in charge of what comes in and split it up as fair as they can."

"Well, that's a mercy," Ellen said. "Without help, it'll be a cruel winter for some poor souls."

"You folks around here are hit as bad as those in Kansas." Dan hesitated. "Uncle Simeon's on the committee for our township. He's got the others, Sam Nickel and Andy McHugh, to agree to share with people across the border."

Jonathan Ware straightened. It was only then Christy noticed he was bending so much with the watering that his shoulders were getting a forward slant. "We thank Simeon . . . and you . . . for thinking of us, Dan, but we'll manage."

"Well, if it gets bad later on, let Simeon know. I guess wagons will be hauling grain and such in till summer, but it won't be regular." He handed his cup back to Ellen. "I'm supposed to leave word at the tannery so Mister Hayes can spread the news. The committee needs to know as soon as possible how many families will need help."

"Stop for supper on your way home," Ellen invited.

Beth seized his hands. "Yes, Danny! Stop! If you do, we'll have potatoes! Won't we, Mama?"

"Indeed, we will." Ellen laughed. "And you,

Elizabeth, may peel them."

Looking forward to Dan's company seemed to make the work go faster and easier for Christy. "Why don't you have a swim and freshen up?" Jonathan asked as he started to haul a last load of browse to the sheep. He added with a chuckle: "It might startle Dan speechless to see you in a clean dress, but why not try it?"

The beloved blue foulard had grown too tight for any artifice so it had yielded a shirtwaist for Christy and best dress for Beth, with material left over to make the dress "grow" with Beth till it was worn into quilt scraps. Christy's Sunday dress was now a green-gray plaid Charlie had brought last winter. To wash her hair later, she drew water from the well and left it in a tub and bucket to grow warm while she took her dress, clean underwear, and a towel to the swimming hole.

She couldn't swim more than a few strokes in any direction without hitting the limestone bottom, but even that was refreshing. Rubbing with the towel till her skin tingled, she tried not to think of what would happen if the creek ran dry. They'd have to haul water for themselves and for all the livestock from the Marais des Cygnes a mile away, or take the animals to the river morning and evening.

Would it never rain? The last blazing of the sun gave a pitiless answer, darkening Christy's pleasure at Dan's visit. She hurried to wash her hair and towel it as dry as she could before gathering eggs, feeding the chickens and pigs, and fetching in water and wood. Only then did she change from homemade work shoes into slippers, another of Charlie's gifts.

She sighed as she did so. It was sweet of him to bring the family presents when he finished long distance freighting in late autumn, but Christy would give all the luxuries for him still to belong to them, not the Jardines. She combed the tangles out of her hair and hurried to help with supper that would be special because of Dan.

Robbie escorted him in with joyful barks. He'd splashed water over his face at the creek, and his damp, unruly hair showed the efforts of a comb. He must be tired from working all morning and walking seven miles that afternoon, but his eyes lit at the sight of Christy like deep water struck by sun.

They sat down to potatoes whipped fluffy with butter and cream, crisp carrot sticks, and a dish Ellen had devised — tiny dumplings of cottage cheese, eggs, and a sprinkling of cornmeal boiled first in water, then scrambled with eggs and watercress.

As soon as Jonathan said grace, Dan said appreciatively: "This sure smells and looks good, Missus Ware. We're still getting milk, but the hens have about quit laying."

"We'll send some eggs home with you," Ellen promised, although some of her hens weren't laying and those that were didn't produce as regularly in the hot weather. "How are the Hayeses getting along?"

"Hanging on. Lige Morrow and Watt Caxton brought in some hides while I was there. Lige says he took some fish to the Barclays and found them packing up."

"To go East?"

Dan nodded. "Lige tried to encourage them, but Mister Barclay said what settled his mind was when he went to dig up some potatoes. Instead of potatoes in the hill, there was a great big rattler."

"Good heavens!" Ellen gasped.

"He tried three more hills. Each one had a snake. He told Lige that, even if it wasn't a sign his land was cursed, he sure wasn't trying to farm where you raised rattlers instead of spuds."

Christy would miss her quiet brown-eyed schoolmates but she hoped they'd find a better place. "The Barclays asked Lige to tell their neighbors . . . especially all of you . . . good bye for them," Dan explained. "The snakes were the last straw. They just wanted to be on their way as soon as they could. Lige went home and brought them some jerked venison and smoked turkey for their trip."

"Lige is a good man," Jonathan said.

"Caxton isn't. He was hanging around Westport with Lafe Ballard . . . yes, that's where he is now. They caught a couple of runaways and turned them in for the rewards. Then they happened onto a Negro whose master had freed him and given him a new coat and a hundred dollars. They beat him up, stole his coat and money, and burned his free papers. Then they sold him to a planter."

"That awful, awful man!" Christy choked. "Oh, I hope there's some way the first owner finds out and gets his man free."

"Ethan picked up Caxton's hides and slung them at him. Knocked him down in some fresh cow pies." Dan grinned at the memory. "Ethan told Caxton never to set foot on his land again. Lige said that went for him, too. He helped Caxton fly up in his wagon by shooting around his feet."

"Hester thinks Lafe's mining in the Rockies," Ellen said. "It would grieve her to know her son had a hand in such evil."

Christy's scar throbbed. "I hope he never comes back!"

Jonathan shook his head. "It's a hard thing to say, but the kindest thing for Hester may be if she never sees or hears tell of Lafe again."

"But it's terrible not to know," Ellen sighed. "I worry about Charlie and Thos all the time they're out on those dangerous trails." Meeting her husband's concerned eyes, she added with a little smile: "I start to worry, dear. Then I pray for them, instead."

Beth jumped up to help Christy clear the table. "We've got de-sert! I picked wild plums, didn't I, Mama? A whole pan full! And there's cream to pour on them." Since the ripening of dewberries and golden currants in mid-June, followed into July by raspberries and blackberries, Beth, guarded by Robbie, brought home sweet wild fruit whenever she could find it.

"These are a de-licious de-sert," Dan complimented Beth as he raised a spoonful of the reddish-orange fruit to his lips. "I'll tell Letty she needs to find a good thicket and bring some home."

He didn't have his fiddle, but he stayed to sing along with the piano after dishes were done. How Christy wished she could see him every day, that he could sing with them every night.

When he left in the shallow light of a crescent moon, Jonathan cautioned: "Watch out for wolves. Ordinarily they're shy of humans, but, with prey scarce, they're getting bold. Two came up and watched us cutting willow limbs today."

A chill crawled down Christy's spine. "I didn't know that."

"They were on that bluff across the creek, still as could be. Didn't see any use spooking you, honey. I don't intend for you to be by yourself very far from the house. There's panthers out there, too."

"I've got my Sharps," said Dan. "But I'll find me a club, too, a good shillelagh."

He went off whistling that sad happy song of his own. Christy watched him fade into the trees. Then she did what her mother said. Instead of worrying, she prayed that he would get home safe this night, and all the nights of his life.

Now it was time to plow under the roots of the sacrificed wheat and oats. There wasn't any stubble. The animals had eaten the stalks into the ground. "I hate to put seed into such dry earth," Jonathan regretted, "but, if we don't get rain and make a crop next summer, I'll have to go freighting to get us through."

Ellen smiled at him across the supper table. "We'll do what we have to, Jon."

"Ethan traded some of his hides for seed in Osceola," Jonathan went on. "He'll swap us some for what corn and potatoes we can spare, and for teaching Luke and Mary. The boys'll come over soon with their corn knives and a wagon. I thought we could let them have the stalks they cut for fodder."

"Sharing's the only way any of us will get by," Ellen said.

To be freed of watering crops was like a holiday, although Christy put on one of her father's old shirts, and gloves Charlie had left behind before she used a sharp, murderous-looking corn knife for the first time. She cut the stalks close to the ground, broke off the stripped ears, and tossed them in the wheelbarrow. The family was almost out of cornmeal. As soon as the kernels were hard enough to grind, they'd have to shell a bushel to get to the mill.

A chance to see Dan. Christy hoped her father would let her take the corn. Apart from seeing Dan, it would be fun to visit with Lydia and Harriet. Wiping away sweat and itching chaff, Christy hummed as much of Dan's song as she could remember. In spite of dreaming of him, though, she was so hot and weary when she went to the house for dinner that her parents looked at her in concern. Even before grace, Ellen got a jar of Hester's ointment and smoothed it on Christy's blistering hands.

"I hate for you to do such work." Jonathan scowled. "But I have to finish plowing so the roots will pretty well decay before I plant wheat in a month or so. . . ."

"There's too much for you to do alone, Father," Christy argued.

"There is, but we don't want you worn to a nub, either." Her mother brightened. "Listen, dear. This afternoon, you can take Beth and gather wild fruit."

Now that would be a holiday. Then Christy sighed. "There won't be a lot this year."

"Anything helps. The more wild fruit you girls find, the more of our apples we can dry

331

for winter. Then, in the morning, you can be out in the corn early and work till it starts getting really hot."

"I'll finish plowing this week." Jonathan grinned. "Then, my girl, I'll get a corn knife and race you!"

Christy laughed. "I don't care if you win." She already felt better at the prospect of spending the sweltering afternoon wandering after fruit, instead of bending to hack away with the vicious blade. John Brown and his sons had killed those men at Osawatomie with short swords that must not have looked much different.

"Leave some for the birds and wild creatures!" Ellen called as the girls departed with oak split baskets and a jubilant Robbie. If anything made him prouder than protecting Beth, it was guarding two of his humans. For a dog, he was approaching old age. Christy didn't want to think of the time when he wouldn't dash along ahead, behind, and on all sides of them.

Beth giggled and caught Christy's hand, swinging it so joyfully that Christy realized with a stab of compunction that she hadn't paid much attention lately to her little sister. Giving Beth's hand an answering squeeze, Christy laughed down at her. "You must already know where the best trees and bushes are."

Beth's sunbonnet bobbed denial. "I don't

go 'way far away. I'm scared of bears and panthers and water moccasins and copperheads." She shivered. "I saw a wolf watching me yesterday. He was on a bluff across the creek. Could he eat me, Christy?"

"Maybe he could, but I don't think he would," Christy teased. "You're much too tough and skinny to interest any self-respecting wolf."

When Beth didn't laugh, Christy knelt and looked into solemn eyes that were more green now than brown or gold. "Honey, Father says he's never heard of wolves killing a person in this country. They may have a long time ago in France, during a famine, and perhaps in Russia when they're starving, but. . . ."

"S'pose they get to starving here?" Beth shuddered.

"Then we won't go out in the woods. But they're not starved, Bethie, or they wouldn't let Robbie run them off from the sheep."

"I don't want them to eat Nosey or Cleo or Mildred or any of their lambs." Beth sniffled and rubbed her face on Christy's shoulder.

"Gracious, it's way past time we had a talk, sweetheart. Here I thought you were having a grand time in the timber!"

Beth cast her a searching look. "I . . . I took Lambie. Do you think I'm a scaredy-cat?"

"I think you're brave as a lion." Christy held the thin child tightly and tucked some dark curls under the shabby sunbonnet. "To hunt berries when you're scared is heaps braver than if you were never afraid to start with. What other peculiar notions have you got in that funny little head of yours?"

"Oh, I make believe Charlie and Thos are back!"

"They're growing up, Bethie."

"I wish they weren't!"

"So do I, but we can't change it."

Beth grabbed Christy around the waist. "You're almost grown-up, too, Christy! You . . . you won't go away, will you?"

"Not for a long time." Christy thought of Dan with a wrench of longing, but she couldn't imagine leaving home even to be with him. Not yet. Maybe she wasn't as grown-up as she thought she was. "Anyway, honey, I hope to always live where I can see you and our folks real often. So you just be sure you don't move to California or Oregon!"

Beth chortled at that and they were soon picking purple gooseberries from a big bush that concealed an old nest, possibly a cardinal's. Those scarlet birds favored the dense bushes for nesting.

"When Danny comes, it's almost as good as having Thos or Charlie . . . and some ways it's better 'cause he plays the fiddle and sings so pretty." Beth slanted a hopeful glance at Christy. "When you're grown-up, why don't you marry him? Then we'd have you both!"

"Don't you say anything like that to him!" Christy warned, but it was good to have someone to confide in, even a small sister. "I don't mind his broken nose. It shows he's been through a lot. Do you know, Bethie, the first time he ever spoke to me was to bawl me out because I hadn't jumped up fast enough to change your diaper?"

"Christy!" shrieked Beth. Curiosity triumphed over chagrin. "Did Danny have a sister over the sea?"

"He did." Christy told what she knew of Dan's childhood as they moved on to a beautiful black cherry tree on the creekbank. A squirrel finished gnawing open a cherry stone to get to the kernel and feasting blue jays scolded as the girls began to pick.

"Don't fret," Beth promised the birds. "We'll leave you all the cherries we can't reach." She looked gravely at Christy. "If you marry Danny, I'll try to be like his sister and make up a little for Bridget."

They talked as they roamed, shunning the raccoon grapes that even the animals wouldn't eat, squealing at the discovery of elderberries, a black haw tree — although it had precious little fruit — and wild plum thickets. Well before sunset, their baskets were filled.

"Let's take some spicebush home for tea," Christy suggested as she brushed against the dark green leaves. Fragrance filled the air as they broke off a handful of twigs.

They went home well content in a close-ness they had lost as Beth grew out of baby-hood. Brave, funny little Beth, hiding all those fears as she tried to help feed the family! Christy resolved to be a better sister, especially since it was clear that Beth didn't tell her parents her deepest worries.

Beth joined her in the cornfield next morning, planting her foot on the stalks beneath the ears and twisting them off. Although Christy tried to send her to the house after a few hours, Beth persisted till their mother called them in to help pit the fruits that were large enough for drying, cut them in half, and spread them to dry on a clean sheet in the loft. The plums went into a big crock filled with water. Scum would form after a while and the fruit would keep for months.

Now that the corn was too hard for roasting ears, Christy helped her mother make sweet cornmeal by rubbing the ears over a piece of tin pierced with nail holes. This grating, or "gritting" as Hester called it, made delicious bread and tasty grits and some was dried for later use.

After Jonathan finished plowing, it only took a few days to finish cutting the stalks, haul them to the barn, and crib the ears. At night, the family gathered around a tub and shelled corn by rubbing ears against each other or scraping them against the rim of the tub. Beth put four or five ears in a sack and tromped up and down on them till most of the kernels came loose and she could easily rub off the remainder.

"Wouldn't it be grand if the mill could take out the hulls?" Christy asked. The unbolted meal had to be sifted to get rid of the tough bits.

"Goodness, dear," twinkled her mother, "I'm grateful not to have to grind the corn in a hand mill! And we're mightily lucky to have corn at all."

There wasn't much luck to losing most of the growing crops and hauling water for the rest, but Christy refrained from saying so. Her cheeks grew warm as she summoned up courage to make her request.

"When . . . when we have enough corn shelled, may I take it to the mill?"

Her parents exchanged startled glances. "I'd like to see Lydia and Harriet," she said truthfully enough, but blushed even before her father grinned.

"And Dan O'Brien, perhaps?"

"We . . . e . . . ell . . . yes!"

"I was wondering if you'd mind going," her father said. "Some shingles blew off the barn and smokehouse in that last high wind. I'd like to repair the roofs before I plant wheat."

"I saved some of Beth's baby things," Ellen said. "I'll send them for Harriet and Susie to share. That'll be nice to have cousins the same age."

"I wish I did," Beth said.

"You do, on your father's side, but they're in Ohio," explained Ellen. "I was born late to my parents, an only child. They were carried off with scarlet fever the year Charlie was born. I cried for weeks because they never got to see him." She sighed. "Unless families move together as the Wattleses did, once some move West it's likely they'll never see each other again."

Jonathan took her hand and pressed it to his cheek. "Yes, Ellen, but, when our children marry and have little ones, we'll be a big family again." He gave one of Beth's curls a playful tug. "You can be an aunt. That might be more fun than being a cousin."

The child bounced with excitement. "Who do you think'll get married first? Charlie or Thos or Christy?"

Ellen smiled at Christy with tenderness and a hint of sadness. "We'll just have to wait and see, won't we?"

"I won't move away!" Sudden moisture blurred Christy's eyes. "Not so far that we can't visit often and be together for holidays." She laughed to clear the lump in her throat. "Maybe I'll be an old maid."

"No," said Beth. "You've got to marry Danny."

CHAPTER SEVENTEEN

To Christy's disappointment, Dan had taken a plowshare to Andy McHugh's forge for sharpening, but she did enjoy hearing about the doings of the Moneka Women's Rights Society as she sipped sassafras tea and worked on the socks she was knitting for her father. Harriet was so unwieldy that she moved with effort, but she glowed with happiness. She, her mother, Mildred Morrison, and Lydia were all sewing or knitting baby things.

"I think I'm going to be able to carry this baby." Harriet's blue eyes shone. "If it's a boy, we'll call him Owen Daniel David Simeon."

"A lot of names for a tyke!" Mrs. Morrison snorted.

"There are four men we want to name a son after, Mama. As hard as it is for me to have a baby, we'd better give this one all the names."

Tossing a head that was still as much yellow as gray, Harriet's mother gave her daughter a reproachful look. "It hurts me that you'd pass over your own two dear brothers to name your child for an Irish orphan."

"Mama, how long is it since you've heard from either of my own dear brothers?"

Mrs. Morrison reddened. "Young men who're freighting don't write letters."

"Maybe not, but they can visit their families like Christy's brother does. Dan's a brother to Owen and he's been like one to me." Harriet smiled at Christy. "It was sweet of your mother to send those nice baby things. Between Susie and me, we'll need them all."

"I suppose," said Mrs. Morrison, tight-lipped, "that you have a name ready for a girl, too."

"Lydia Susan."

"Well! What's wrong with *my* name?"

"Mama! We gave Letty your middle name, Leticia, and used Owen's mother's name, Mary, for the middle one."

"No one calls me Letty. To outsiders, it looks like a slight."

"Outsiders can mind their own business!"

Lydia stepped between two pairs of angry blue eyes. "Would anyone like more tea?" Pouring from a treasured china pot, she said to Christy: "You may not have heard, but Eli Bradley and a friend have opened a saloon over at Trading Post. It's a hang-out for riff-raff from both sides of the border, and the

Women's Rights Society is upset about it."

"You mean those bloomer-wearing Wattles girls are sticking in their noses where they don't belong," sneered Mildred.

"I mean I went with them to reason with Mister Bradley and his partner."

"I'd have gone, too," Harriet assured her mother, "except I was afraid of losing the baby."

"Praise be you have a pinch of sense!" Mildred Morrison frowned. "If women don't keep their place, they can't expect to be treated like ladies."

Lydia grinned. Her thin, high-browed face grew almost pretty. "That's more or less what Mister Bradley told us in a nicer way. He and his customers said that's why they'd never vote for giving the women the ballot. 'The minute you could vote, you'd outlaw whiskey, wouldn't you?' he asked." Lydia chuckled.

"Emma Wattles said . . . 'That's exactly what we'll do, sir, and then there won't be so many beaten, abused, hungry, and neglected wives and children!' "

"What did he say to that?" asked Christy. Her mother would relish hearing of the women's courage. It was a shame the Wares lived too far from Moneka to attend the society's meetings.

"Mister Bradley vowed that, if he heard of a customer beating his wife, he'd personally horsewhip the man." Lydia really was quite attractive when she laughed. "Then, most politely, Mister Bradley bowed us out the door."

"Which you should never have darkened!" scolded Mildred.

"Even without rain, our sorghum cane made a fair crop." Lydia was obviously experienced in evading Mrs. Morrison's onslaughts. "I'll send a jug home with you, Christy."

"You may need it." Not guessing that the cane would make a crop, the Wares had turned their livestock in on the field.

"We have enough to last till spring when we can get sap from the maples. Besides, you brought that good butter and cheese. What do you hear from Thos?"

"Just one letter with a few lines." Christy pulled a face. "He says he's too busy carrying mail to write, but he'll try to come home at Christmas."

Everyone laughed except Mildred whose sons neither wrote nor visited. At dinner, conversation centered on whether Congress would ever admit Kansas to the Union. "If it does," mused Simeon bleakly, "I fear it will herald the exodus of Southern states. They won't tolerate being outvoted in the Senate."

"Let 'em go and good riddance," growled Owen.

Simeon shook his white head. "With the Democratic party split, Lincoln's almost sure to win. He won't let Secession wreck this country."

"A war won't wreck it?" Owen asked.

"It could heal back together."

"In a hundred years?"

"That's as God wills."

David's green eyes caught fire. "If there's war, I'm going!"

"David, we're Quakers," chided Lydia. "Besides, you're barely sixteen."

David didn't answer, but the mutinous set of his smooth young jaw spoke louder than words. Simeon studied him in troubled silence before he turned to Christy. "I have to finish grinding for Hughie Huston and Sam Nickel, but I'll have yours ready well before dark. Or, if you'd rather get on home, I can give you meal that's already ground and keep yours."

"Oh, do stay if you can," urged Harriet. "It's lovely to have company! Mostly men bring the grain, so Papa and the boys get to visit, but we don't."

Christy's parents didn't expect her back till dusk. She was enjoying the little holiday, and, besides, Dan might return before she left.

"I'll wait," she told the miller.

The afternoon passed pleasantly. When David came to say the meal was ready and that he'd caught and saddled Lass and fastened the meal sack behind the cantle, the women said their good byes and Lydia tied a jug of molasses into a bag.

"You can fasten this to the saddle horn," she suggested. "Thank your mother for the butter and cheese, and do come any time you can."

"Thank her for the baby clothes and blankets!" Harriet called.

"I will." Christy nodded. "We'll be waiting to hear you have your new baby, and we'll pray that all goes well."

"Your little mare ran into something sharp and cut her shoulder while she was frolicking with Zephyr and Breeze," David told Christy. "Didn't much more than pierce the hide, but it bled some. I washed it with soft soap. You might want to do that again after you're home."

"Oh, poor Lass!" Christy stroked the chestnut's soft nose and moved around to the shoulder. A seep of blood marked a long scratch.

"She probably ran against a snag sticking out from one of those dead trees we haven't cleared off yet," David said. "I'm sorry."

"It wasn't your fault." Christy rubbed her cheek against the mare's as David secured the jug to the saddle horn. "We'll put some of Hester's coneflower salve on it and it'll heal with just a thin line. Thanks, Davie." She hesitated. "Tell Dan hello for me."

David grinned and looked with understanding. "Dan'll be sorry he missed you."

At sixteen, David was losing the angelic look of his boyhood, changing along with his voice into a strikingly handsome young man with dark-lashed green eyes and a mass of curly black hair.

Let there not be war, God. Don't let Davie go to fight, or Dan, or Charlie or Thos . . . or Owen or Andy or . . . or anybody.

She led Lass to a stump and mounted astride, pulling down her skirts as much as possible. The Wares had no side-saddle, and Christy didn't want one. They looked dangerously uncomfortable and off-balance to her, but she did wish for the Wattles girls' ugly but practical bloomers.

Would her mother let her make a pair for excursions like this? She was going to have to dismount to pick some of those ripe red haws yonder, and then climb again into the saddle. Oh, for free-swinging, unencumbered legs!

She popped a few of the small tartly sweet scarlet fruits in her mouth and savored them while she filled part of one deep pocket of her knitted cape. A little farther along, she was tempted off Lass again by a nice clump of elderberries. As she struggled back into the saddle, her delight at having filled both pockets was chilled when she noticed that twilight was hazing the timber.

"We won't stop again for the best fruit in Missouri," she promised Lass. "Let's move along, girl."

Her parents would be worried. That was a poor way to make them think she could be trusted with errands. Something moved at the edge of her vision. When she turned, it wasn't there, but, in a moment, a shadow took form on the other side.

This one didn't vanish. She saw the glow of eyes. Lass snorted and broke into a gallop. Christy hung on to the jug to keep it from banging against the mare. The color of dusk, four wolves broke from the woods and raced after them. Two were bigger than the others. The biggest one of all hurled itself at Lass' throat as a scream ripped from Christy.

Lass rose up in the air, squealing, and struck at the wolf with her front hoofs. It was all Christy could do to cling to the saddle horn. Lass missed, but the big wolf fell back. The mare galloped on. Wolves weren't supposed to attack people! But maybe they were drawn by the smell of Lass' blood. They'd have less prey because of the drought. That could make them desperate. Or — perhaps the big wolf had hydrophobia. Any creature with that dread, foam-mouthed plague, even a normally timid squirrel, would attack anything or anyone.

The big wolf leaped again at Lass' neck. If he brought her down, the other wolves would finish her. Lass reared again and struck down as her wild ancestors must have done. The wolf fell. Lass whirled to kick him with both

346

hind hoofs before she lowered her head and plunged on.

She'd gotten rid of the biggest wolf. There was no more jumping at her throat, but the other wolves pursued. Christy didn't use the reins. Lass knew better than she did what to do. Gripping the saddle horn, hugging the molasses, Christy prayed more fervently than she ever had in her life.

There was the crash of a shot. One wolf yelped, faded into the brush. Another shot. Christy ventured to glance around. All the wolves were gone.

"Christy!"

Dan! His shout sent such a flood of relief through her that her bones went weak and wavery. "Christy!" he called. "Are you all right?"

"Yes! We're fine." Christy leaned over, caressing Lass' neck, drawing gently on the reins. "They're gone, sweetheart. You can slow down now. What a brave girl!"

Dan rode out of the gloaming. Christy didn't know how she got down, but in a moment they were in each other's arms, holding tightly, tightly, as if the other might disappear.

"Oh, Dan! How come you to follow?"

He ran his fingers along her face. "I was so disappointed when I heard I'd missed you that I told Uncle Simeon I was going to catch up and see you safely home."

"Thank goodness you did!"

He reached out to pat Lass' sweaty neck. "Oh, I think Lass would've gotten you away. She brained that big wolf . . . just as well for him, because she broke most of his bones." He took his hand away from the mare and stared at it. Even in the heavy dusk, the stain showed on his fingers. "Did the wolf do that?"

She explained.

"Good!" He released Christy to examine the cut. "Even a scratch like this could be the end of her if that critter had hydrophobia. Christy, when Zephyr shied at that dead wolf, I was so scared. . . ." He took her in his arms again, finding her eager lips with his hard, tender ones. This time her bones melted from sweetness, not terror.

"If anything happened to you . . . ," he muttered at last. "I love you, Christy, sweetheart, darling. I guess I've loved you since the night we let those bears go and walked that underground river."

She laughed tremulously. "I guess I've loved you ever since then, too, Dan, in spite of getting mad at you when you scolded me for not changing Beth fast enough."

"Did I do that?"

"You certainly did!"

He cradled her against him. So wonderful to be like that, to hear his heart pound beneath her cheek, feel the muscle and bone and flesh of him, and all that still just the clothing for his soul, his spirit that made songs.

"I'll change the babes myself when we have some," he teased.

"Danny!"

At her happy cry, he shook his head, burying his face in her hair. "Christy, Christy, I pray above all things that you'll marry me, but it can't be till we can see straight ahead for a time."

"We're old enough! I turn seventeen in a few weeks. You're close to twenty!"

"Neither any great age, love." He laughed huskily. "But for sure, were it not for the great troubles roiling up, I'd ask your parents if they were willing."

"War?" He nodded. She held him closer, although in some way, in his being, he moved away from her. What she held was not what she wanted. "Dan, there's been war on the border for years."

"Yes, and men have died on both sides and left widows and orphans." He put her away from him. "I'll not do that to you."

"But Dan, no one can be sure of living."

"Some can be surer than others."

"You weren't born here, Dan." It was an ignoble argument, but she couldn't keep from making it. "No one could blame you if you didn't fight."

Her shame filled the silence before he spoke. "I'll fight, Christy. Isn't it here I have a way to live free of landlords and have a chance to amount to something? How can I take those gifts and not try to deserve them?"

"We can still be married . . . have whatever time we can together."

"And you have a baby while I'm off, God knows where, not able to take care of you?"

"But. . . ."

He gripped her by her upper arms till it pained. "Christy, if I can help it, no child of mine will starve as I and my sister did."

She swallowed and blinked. "So because of a war that may not happen and a baby we might not have, we won't love each other while we can?"

He kissed her quickly and helped her mount. "We'll love each other. At least I'll sure love you. I ache to show you every way there is. I dream. . . ." He broke off, turning away. "Your folks'll be worried. Let's get you home."

What? What do you dream? I dream, too. Only her dreams stopped with embracing, mouths on each other's, breaths mingled, bodies close as they could be with garments in between. Beyond that, she dare not venture.

Lass still snorted now and then, flinging her head up, as if remembering the attack. Christy stroked her sweat-soaked neck. "You're a brave beauty, Lass. A brave, brave girl. You get some corn tonight."

"She's earned it," Dan said. His voice twisted. "If she hadn't fought off that big wolf. . . ."

Christy began to shiver, cold to the bone, although the night was warm. *If Lass had run on till the wolf pulled her down. . . . If the other wolves had grown bolder before Dan's shots scared them off. . . .* She held to the saddle horn as she had during the onslaught when her only hope was Lass.

Dan's voice roused her. "Look, Christy. Yonder shines a lamp in the window. Your mother's put it there to help you home."

Christy had only been gone since morning, but she felt changed entirely. Swift death had run beside her. Then Dan had come — and he'd declared his love in the same breath that he said they must wait to marry. Christy sighed. It was hard to believe life would ever run smoothly on this border.

The light shining from the cabin was like her parents' love, and love and gratitude for them warmed Christy, melting the chill of shock. "Dan?"

"Yes, sweetheart."

It seemed, at least, he'd allow endearments. "If . . . if we were married, and, if . . . something happened, my parents would help me."

"To be sure."

"Then. . . ."

"They'd help if they could." He added

slowly: "Just as my parents would have helped Bridgie and me."

"Oh!" She recoiled. Her mother and father had always been in her life. She couldn't imagine otherwise. Wouldn't. "But Dan, they're young, almost. Father's . . . *mmm* . . . forty-three. Mother's forty."

"Christy, I'd rather be whipped than say this, but my poor young parents weren't all that much older than I am now. Da, I recall, was twenty-five."

She winced but persisted. "That was Ireland. In the starving years!"

"If this drought lasts, folks will starve or leave. And what will a real war bring when, even without one, we've burnings and murders?" His voice turned grim. "Don't try to wear me down on this, girl."

"What if I'm not available when and if you finally come around to thinking we might run the terrible, unheard-of risk of getting married?"

Even in the dark, she could almost see his angry look. Her heart faltered and her mouth dried in the moment before he answered. "If you would marry someone else . . . maybe that rich puffed-up Travis Jardine? . . . then you weren't, in truth, for me. I'd wish you happy from the roots of my heart. I'll always wish you that, God knows. But don't you expect me to dance at your wedding."

"I'll never have one," she retorted. "Not if

you must wait till all the woes of the world are over!"

"Not quite that long." He chuckled and his hand came out to brush her cheek. "How's this? If Lincoln's elected and the Southern states don't secede, and if things calm along this border, then we'll marry as soon as your folks agree and I can claim some land and get a cabin up."

Christy thrilled, remembering the raising of her family's home, such a happy, friendly, neighborly day. Except for Lafe's burning her. Except for Watt Caxton's planned bear-baiting. Well, maybe in life things were never altogether one way or the other, a little bad streaking the good, a flash of good lighting the murk of evil.

"So?" prompted Dan.

"I'm sure Father would like to have you farm with him. It looks like Thos and Charlie won't. There's too much for him to do even with what help I can give him."

Dan considered. "You have to know it's a long dream of mine, Christy, to own a bit of land. But it would be grand to buy land joining or close to your parents', and there's no man living I'd sooner work with than your father."

Robbie dashed to greet them. Jonathan and Ellen appeared in the cabin door, Beth rushing past them.

"Christy! Christy! Daddy was about to go

looking for you!"

"I'm fine!" Christy called. Beneath Robbie's joyful clamor, she asked: "Shall we tell my parents, Dan?"

"Whatever you want."

"Let's keep it a secret for a while." She couldn't explain the way she wanted to hug it to her, let their understanding grow almost like a baby, warmed by her heart, hidden from the world. "Our secret, Danny."

"No harm in that, I reckon." He greeted her family, swung down, looped Zephyr's reins to the post, and helped Christy dismount. "I'll unsaddle Lass and rub her down," he said. "Mister Ware, when you hear what this little mare did, I think you'll say she can have some corn."

"I'll say so now if you think it, Dan." Jonathan untied the cornmeal and hefted it over his shoulder while Christy loosened the molasses jug. "When you finish with Lass, come in and have supper. We've kept soup warm for Christy."

Ellen held out her arms and Christy ran into them. "What happened, child?" her mother smoothed her hair. "What did Lass do?"

They went inside and Christy told them. "If I hadn't picked the haws and elderberries. . . . Gracious!" She reached inside her pockets and brought out handfuls of berries pulped over the firmer red haws. "The haws are all right," she said, crestfallen, and tried to laugh. "Patches and Evalina ought to love the berries."

"Beth," said Ellen, "dip a pone in molasses and give it to Lass." She rummaged on a shelf. "Take Hester's coneflower ointment and rub it on that scratch . . . or have Dan do it." Her face crumpled. "Oh, Christy, if. . . ."

Jonathan put his arms around them both. "Our girl's safe, Ellen, thanks to Lass, Dan, and the grace of God. That wolf had hydrophobia or went crazy at the scent of Lass' blood. We'd all better be careful till the drought breaks."

Drought. It seemed to Christy that's what the threat of war was — a harsh blast shriveling what would otherwise thrive — but she knew her love for Dan would grow even without more nourishment than what she had already in her heart.

She hoped it would be the same for him as he came in, holding Beth's hand, light setting his hair aflame, making his eyes glow as they fell on Christy.

"Sit down, you two," Ellen said. "It's more than time you ate."

Jonathan cleared his throat. "We've always thought a lot of you, Dan, but, after this, you're . . . well, you're dear to us as a son."

Christy almost blurted: *He's going to be.*

But then she met Dan's eyes, smiled, and hugged their secret.

CHAPTER EIGHTEEN

Outside was winter, but Lavinia Jardine's rose room was warm and bright, sun shining through the glass to caress every bloom from buds to full blown and woo from them the sweet odors that permeated the conservatory and wafted into the house.

Emmie napped on the wicker bench, nose tucked into her fluffy tail, but, when Charlie came in with Melissa, the gray cat dropped to the floor and came to rub against his legs. He bent to scratch behind her ears with fingers that would always bear the scars of her frantic clawing when he'd saved her from the hounds. Hither and Yon raised red-cheeked yellow heads from the apples they were devouring and grouched in parakeet.

Charlie's heart thrilled when Melissa took off her shawl and sun lit the amber around her throat, the necklace he'd given her four years ago. Four years? That made her twenty.

How long could it be till she married some gentleman farmer or one of the Bentons' St.

Louis friends that Melissa's sister kept parading past her? Charlie saved all he could. At Jardine's invitation, he'd invested in the freighting company and that should bring returns in time, but here was Melissa past the age when most girls married.

He hadn't been able to save money that year at all. He and Thos met in Independence as they'd earlier agreed and loaded a wagon borrowed from Seth Cooley with expensive wheat and corn, coffee, dried fruit, and other supplies. Thos volunteered to drive the mule-drawn wagon home while Charlie made his usual visit at the Jardines' before joining the family. After Christmas, the brothers had to get back to their work.

"Father'll have saved what he could of the crops," Thos had panted as he wedged in a barrel of molasses. "But since neither of us was there to help, I'm glad we can do this."

"Sure." Charlie had nodded, heaving on a sack of oats. He was glad, but losing a year's savings put him that much further away from the time he'd dare ask the bishop if. . . .

The soft tap of Lavinia Jardine's cane sounded on the polished floor. Charlie hastened to give her his arm. He thought her limp was worse this year, but didn't say so. Her hair was spun silver now, no hint of auburn left. She smiled up at him with soft blue eyes.

"It's dear of you to come see us, Charles.

We're so far from Oregon and California that we can't expect Miles and Sherrod to visit, but that rascal, Travis! We're lucky to get a few scrawled words once or twice a year."

Charlie blushed. "I'm not much of a hand for writing home myself," he admitted, although if it had been acceptable to correspond with Melissa, he reckoned he would have. "Where is Travis, ma'am?"

"Who knows? If young men could just understand how mothers worry! The last we heard, he was at the Comstock in Nevada."

"When he strikes it rich, he'll come prancing up on a fancy horse flashing silver from its saddle and bridle, all loaded down with presents!"

"Seeing him would be better than any present." Lavinia Jardine leaned on Charlie as he helped her into her wheeled chair by a trellis of ivory roses. She smiled over a twist of pain. "I suppose I should be grateful that Yvonne and Henry visit, but I must admit that the four children, dear though they are, are rather like an invading troop."

"They're brats, pure and simple," declared their aunt. "James and Tod can go to a military academy and learn some manners but Becky and Annette! I can't imagine men brave and foolish enough to hazard marriage with either."

"Melissa!"

"They're little beasts, Mama! Becky slapped

359

Lilah last time they were here because Lilah pulled a tangle while brushing Becky's hair. Let me tell you, I grabbed Becky and shook her till her teeth rattled."

"Is that why Yvonne wouldn't speak to you the last day they were here?"

Melissa shrugged. "Don't fret about it, Mama. She gave me a scold for shaking Becky, and I gave her one back for raising such little monsters. Of course, with Henry for a father. . . ."

Lavinia touched her finger to her lips although her smile was sympathetic. "*Shh,* darling. Henry may be a trifle. . . ."

"Dull!"

"Unimaginative, perhaps, but he's good-natured."

"Lazy!"

Lavinia's smile faded. She straightened and gazed at her younger daughter in a way that made Melissa drop her head and mutter: "I'm sorry, Mama. But he is such a. . . ."

"Husband for your sister," Lavinia finished. She softened the rebuke with a pat of Melissa's hand. "Will you take Aunt Zillah her beef tea? Phronie says she spits it out at her and Lilah." Wheeling toward a bush of deep crimson, Lavinia selected the most beautiful flowers and snipped half a dozen. "These are her favorites. I think she still sees a bit of the color, and she loves their smell."

Charlie started to excuse himself and follow Melissa, but Lavinia gestured at the wicker bench. "Won't you keep me company a while, Charles? I know you have to be off soon to your family. Thank goodness, the terrible drought finally broke. We had nothing to sell this year, but at least none of our folk went hungry."

Much as he liked and admired Lavinia Jardine, Charlie couldn't help thinking that, through the drought, black hands fetched water for the roses while his father and sister battled to save a little corn.

Charlie sat down and stroked Emmie who jumped into his lap. "It's a long while yet till harvest, ma'am, even if spring crops are good."

"At least the drought ran a lot of Abolitionist rabble out of Kansas." Bishop Jardine said as he strode in and stood beside his wife, arms behind his back, cider-colored eyes fixed on Charlie as if trying to read his mind and heart.

Charlie groaned inwardly. This was no accident, the bishop happening by when Melissa was sent on an errand. The Jardines were going to tell him their daughter wasn't for him. Kindly, of course, so long as he didn't get obstinate. He'd rather have been whipped than hear such words from Lavinia.

But the bishop didn't get to that message right away. "Glad as I am that plenty of thieving Free State rogues starved out of Kansas, it's sure to be admitted as a free state since that lanky ape, Lincoln, won the election last month. And that mealy-mouthed State of the Union swan song Buchanan made! States have no right to secede, he says! But the government has no legal right to stop them. What kind of wishy-washy drivel is that?"

"The kind he's used his whole term," shrugged Charlie, who had brought the news and suppressed one bit that he knew would enflame the bishop. The same day Buchanan addressed Congress, December 3rd, the bold former slave, Frederick Douglas, organized a rally honoring John Brown that was broken up by a mob. "Buchanan said one good thing, though . . . that the Union cannot be cemented by the blood of its citizens."

Jardine made a throwing-away motion. "Mark my word, Charles. By the time that black Republican takes office, states will be seceding right, left, and center."

"Do you think Missouri will, sir?"

"Who knows? To balance the big plantations along the Missouri and Mississippi, Saint Louis's thick with Germans. The lop-eared Dutch are against slavery almost to a man. Missouri was settled from both the North and South. Rests on a hair, I'd guess, how it swings."

"Mordecai," intervened his wife. "Could politics wait till we've discussed other matters?"

Charlie's guts tightened. Braced for rejection, he wished the bishop would get it over with.

Hands still behind him, Jardine puffed out fleshy red cheeks. "With everything so unstable, Charles, I feel it wise to take all possible measures to assure the future of this plantation and my womenfolk."

So he'd picked a suitable son-in-law, probably a neighbor. The words husked in Charlie's dry mouth. "I understand that, sir."

"Could you run this plantation?"

Charlie gaped. Had he heard aright? "Why," he floundered. "I . . . I never thought about such a thing."

Jardine's lips puckered up a bit at the edges. "Well, think, my boy! You've farmed. You know livestock and crops."

"Not cotton or hemp or tobacco."

"You'd learn."

"Travis. . . ."

"Travis is the main reason I'm asking, Charles. My other sons are doing well out West. They and Yvonne will inherit my shares in the freighting company. Travis and Melissa get this place. But Travis is too flighty to manage it. He's never taken the slightest interest in farming. The only livestock that brightens his eye are fast, mettlesome horses."

"You'll run the place for a long time, sir. Travis is bound to steady a lot in a few years."

"He takes after my younger brother," Jar-

363

dine gloomed. "Knifed in a card game when he was twenty-two." He regarded Charlie as if planning to buy a horse or ox, weighing good points against bad. "Travis won't resent your being put in charge the way he would anyone else. You're a good influence on him. In time, he might even decide to help you."

"You have an overseer."

"Blake's all right, but he must have direction." The bishop spread his hands. "What I need, lad, is a young man to help me, one who can take over when I'm feeble."

"I . . . I'm honored, Bishop. And flabbergasted!"

Jardine smiled. "Think it over, Charles. If you accept, we'll let Seth Cooley know you won't be back."

Charlie swallowed, head awhirl. Live at Rose Haven? See Melissa every day? But there were the slaves. Jardine treated them well, but it didn't seem right to Charlie to own people the way you did livestock. It wouldn't be right to take the position without telling Melissa's folks how he felt about her.

"There are two things, sir, that won't be changed by any amount of thinking."

The bishop lifted his scraggy eyebrows. "What things, lad?"

Heart tripping, throat tight, Charlie blurted: "I love your daughter."

Both Jardines laughed. Lavinia squeezed his hand. "Lord love, you, dear! Don't you think we've seen that?"

"What's more to the purpose," grunted Jardine, "is that she's set her heart on you."

"Oh. . . ." Charlie felt as if his heart were bursting right out of his chest.

"You might as well know we tried to budge her . . . or at least I did." The bishop's voice held an edge of disgust. "The way you've been raised . . . from Illinois, Universalist minister for your father and all . . . is bound to have rubbed off some."

"Mordecai!"

"Yes, yes, Vinnie, but it's best to be honest."

"While we're being honest, sir, I should tell you my parents won't favor my marrying into a slave-holding family . . . but they won't try to talk me out of it. I know they'll welcome Melissa with all the loving kindness in the world."

Jardine turned a deeper crimson. "Then I wasn't as generous as your people, Charles. I tried, I surely did, to match our daughter with young men of the same background and views, but she turned up her nose at them." The bishop smiled at his wife and placed a hand on her shoulder. "Lavinia was the same. Insisted on me, Lord knows why, till her parents finally agreed."

Charlie's feet scarcely seemed to rest on the floor. It was as if he could float right up to the ceiling. But he had to state his other difficulty, the one that might ruin this dream.

"So, Charles?" Jardine crossed his arms again, standing behind his wife. "What's the other thing that can't be changed?"

"I don't . . . I can't . . . believe in slavery."

The bishop swung away. Lavinia looked distressed. Into the silence, the bishop spoke at last. "Well, that does leave us with a problem. I tell you right now that I won't be coaxed or connived into freeing my colored folks. How would the work get done?"

"Free people can work."

"Not freed slaves. They have to leave the state." Jardine swung around. His eyes bored into Charlie's. "Would it be kind, even decent, of me to free Aunt Zillah who has no place to go, no one to take care of her?"

"Not if she can't stay here," Charlie had to admit.

"I have up to a thousand dollars a head invested in my prime hands. They're worth more than all the rest of my property. I can't just turn them lose."

According to the bishop's lights, he couldn't. There was no way of giving him any other lights. Charlie knew he should be high-minded and refuse to live where slaves were worked, but Melissa. . . . And the slaves would be there whether he was or not. He applied salve to his conscience, something to mitigate his parents' horror.

"You have the legal right to own slaves,

Bishop, but you should know that . . . well, if I ever have the say around here, the slaves go free."

Jardine smiled. "By the time I'm dead, you may view things differently, Charles, but that'll be up to you, Melissa, and Travis." His tone hardened. "You do understand that I'll tolerate no encouraging or aiding my people to run off?"

"Of course." Charlie took a deep breath. "But, sir, if someone runs off, I can't let them be hunted down with dogs."

Veins corded and pulsed in Jardine's temples. "You'd interfere?"

"I'd have to."

"Then. . . ."

Lavinia caught her husband's arm. "Dearest!" So softly Charlie barely heard. "You know I've always begged you. . . . Please."

After a long moment, Jardine pondered: "Only one slave's run away . . . that proud-necked Justus. I'll always think he was hid by someone."

Charlie didn't want to encourage that line of thought. "The hounds didn't catch him, sir."

"No, but I think knowing I can get Caxton and his hounds after them keeps some of the restless ones from straying."

"I suppose," ventured Lavinia, "that they could go on thinking that even when we knew hounds wouldn't be used."

Jardine stroked his chin, gave Charlie a side glance. "Can you live with that?"

It was a compromise, but Jardine had already conceded more than Charlie could have imagined — in fact, this whole conversation was past belief. It would never have taken place, Charlie knew, except for Lavinia, and Melissa's defiant love.

She loved him. That was the lucky, unbelievable, amazing thing that made him feel at once humble and unworthy, yet exalted above all men. He couldn't wait to see her.

"Can you live with that?" Jardine repeated.

"Yes," said Charlie. "I can live with that."

He found Melissa wiping Aunt Zillah's mouth as Phronie held a cup with only a scum of pungent beef tea in the bottom. His face must have told her everything. Melissa gave a squeak and turned red.

"Charlie! Did Papa . . . ?"

He nodded. She dropped the washcloth. "Did you . . . ?"

Aunt Zillah raised on an arm like a brown-barked twig. "Who be it, missy? Who make you sound so glad?"

He went down on one knee by the bed and gently cradled in his own hands the pair that were gnarled and dark as ancient roots. "I'm Charlie Ware, Aunt Zillah."

"Who?"

"Charlie Ware," he said as loudly and

distinctly as he could.

She freed a hand and traced his features with spidery lightness. "Don' matter your name, child. My fingers see your face. You the boy my missy love."

"I sure do hope so."

Whether she heard or not, the old, old woman smiled. "You'll be a good man to her, honey. Your face tell me. Run along and let me smell the roses Miz Vinnie sent."

"You put on this shawl, Miss M'liss." Phronie took one from a peg and draped it around the girl's shoulders. Green eyes glinted at Charlie from the withered yellow face. "Won't hurt you to chill a speck, Master Charlie. That way you won't wander off and worry Miz Vinnie."

"Aunt Phronie!" Melissa sputtered. "We're going to be married!"

"All the same, no use stirrin' up them devils stoked away in any man who can totter."

Phronie might have been remembering her own daughter, born of a drunken guest of the Jardines', so beautiful that to avoid "problems" for himself or his sons, Jardine had sold her to a neighbor. She died birthing Lilah, her master's child. Phronie couldn't be blamed for her low opinion of white men. Charlie gave her what he hoped was an honest look.

"I'll never harm Melissa, Aunt Phronie. I'll do my best, always, to take care of her."

Her face softened. "I knows that, honey boy. Don't you still have the scars from savin' her foolish cat?" She patted his cheek. "You'd be out of the wind . . . and away from windows . . . on the back side of this cabin."

So that was where they walked, and where the clasp of hands turned to an embrace, holding each other as closely as they could, so closely they could scarcely breathe. Her lips and breath were sweet as warm honey, headier than the whiskey that had got him so drunk-miserable once that he'd kept away from it ever since.

He'd been with painted women some, mostly during winters in Independence, and he'd been grateful to them for relieving his throbbing hardness. That was there with Melissa, so insistently that he ached, but with it was such adoration and tenderness that he ached with that, too. He'd be careful with her, oh, so careful. He went dizzy at the thought of lying with her in bed, freed of all restraints but those of loving. He had never dared dream of that, never dared hope beyond a kiss.

He was the one who drew back at last with a soft groan that came from the roots of his manhood. "Oh, Melissa!"

She recovered faster than he, smiling up at him. "I hope Papa didn't have to propose for me."

"No, once I figured he wouldn't run me

off, we sort of talked it out."

"You haven't asked *me* yet!"

He blinked. "By grannies, I haven't! If you won't, sweetheart, you'll sure make monkeys of me and your pa."

"I couldn't do that, now could I?" she teased. She offered her lips again. After what was both a long time and a short one, they walked toward the big white house.

Next day, he rode home, nerving himself to break the news. Just think . . . the wedding was set for New Year's Day, January 1st of 1861. Yvonne's family was coming for the holidays, so no special message need be sent to the Bentons. There was no way of reaching Travis, and his brothers were too far away to come. Thos probably wouldn't be fired from the Pony Express for turning up a few days late, and, if he were, they'd likely take him on again at the first chance. There was a lot of coming and going in that breakneck occupation.

After the way Charlie had insisted that his father take part with the bishop in performing the ceremony, he certainly hoped his father would consent. Charlie could live with the compromises he'd made, but he wasn't sure his parents could. One thing comforted him. They might not attend his wedding, but they wouldn't cast him off. He'd always be their son.

He had purposely delayed at the Jardines' till he figured Thos would be home with the mules and wagon, and, sure enough, the borrowed mules grazed in the pasture and the wagon was near the barn. Thank God, the horses, oxen, cows, and sheep feeding on the drought-cured grass seemed in fair shape.

Robbie's ecstatic barking brought the family out, Beth streaking ahead of the others.

"Why don't you ever come see us first?" she demanded as he swung down and scooped her up.

"Because you ask so many questions." He knuckled her hair and laughed. "Hey, I won't be able to do this much longer! You're big as a yearling calf."

"Mooo-oo-oo." She giggled.

"Go on and eat before the corn pone gets cold," said Thos, taking the reins. "I'll see to your horse."

"Thanks, kid." Charlie shook hands with his father and kissed his mother, startled to notice gray in their hair. Even a brother had to notice how Christy had bloomed although she was thin.

They swept him inside, praising the supplies and presents he and Thos had got, telling him how they'd managed through the drought. It shamed him to think of his sister working that hard, but Christy laughed away his remorse. "I'd rather work outside than in. Besides, if you hadn't earned wages, you and

Thos couldn't have brought us that wagon-load of good things."

"We wouldn't starve without it." Fine lines had deepened at the corners of his mother's eyes. Had the wings of gray at her temples been there before? She smiled as she gave him a quick hug. "Still, it's wonderful not to have to calculate every bite and have enough to share. Wash up, dear. I'll ladle you up some stew. We'll let you feed before you tell us about your year."

He was glad of the reprieve. Bursting with his news, he was also nervous about how it would be received. What if his parents refused to attend the wedding? They loved him, yes, but hadn't they helped Jardine's runaway escape? How much would their consciences allow them to have to do with slave owners?

Still, as he relished the stew and buttered a crisp pone, Charlie had that blessedly secure feeling of being home, under his parents' roof, warmed by their fire, enjoying his mother's food. Lavish as the Jardines' table was, he'd grown up on his mother's cooking. He supposed nothing would ever quite satisfy him in the same way. He also knew that was the sort of thing he'd best not breathe to Melissa.

"The stock's wintering pretty well," Jonathan said. "There's no grain for them and not as much fodder as they need, but that sun-cured grass is just like hay. I planted wheat in October and we've had enough moisture to hope for a crop."

"Harriet Parks and Susie McHugh had little baby boys right after the first freeze when the persimmons ripened," Beth said. "I 'member 'cause Christy and I picked baskets of pawpaws and persimmons and took them to the new mamas. Harriet called her baby Daniel Owen, which made her mama mad, and Susie's red-headed little boy is Andrew Owen Simeon. Andy for short."

"I should hope!" Thos came in, washed sketchily, swung long legs over the bench beside Charlie, and covered a pone with butter.

"Now finish telling us about the Express!" commanded Beth.

"We're racing the telegraph wires being laid from both ends." Thos grinned. He was taller, more sunburned, but he hadn't gained any weight. "There's a hundred and nineteen stations spread over almost two thousand miles of mountains, deserts, prairies, and there's Indians, Bethie. My home station's at Fort Kearny. When the Express rider comes, I'm waiting with my horse. He churns up, and tosses off his mochila . . . that's a thing that fits over the saddle and has four pouches for mail. Then he staggers off to rest. . . ."

"What happens to his horse?" Beth demanded.

"The stock tender rubs him down and

waters and feeds him. I'm gone like lightning. Ten to fifteen miles later, my first horse gets to rest at the next station, but I toss the mochila on a new horse and we're off. Depending on how hard the going is, I change horses six to eight times to cover about a hundred miles."

"A hundred? That's far, far!" Beth said.

"You bet it is. So, afterwards, I loaf a day or so. Sleep, eat beans and bacon with the stationmaster and stock tender and any stagecoach drivers or travelers who've stopped by. I read quite a bit, dime novels that get left at the stations." He grinned at Charlie. "You ever read *The Indian Wife of the White Hunter* by Ann Sophia Stevens?"

"Can't say that I have," Charlie admitted.

"I've read it four times. Well, then the rider from the West sails in, and I'm off for the same hundred miles going the other direction." He chuckled. "I know the first names of every prairie dog and rattlesnake along the way."

"Did the Indians ever try to scalp you?" asked Beth.

"I move too fast, honey." He took half a pone at a bite and chewed reflectively. "The Indians are sure going to want to get their hands on some of the new Winchesters the Army's buying to replace muzzleloaders."

"Winchesters load through the breech," Charlie explained. "They shoot a lot faster and farther than muzzleloaders."

Thos cocked an eyebrow at Jonathan. "I suppose our Border Ruffians and jayhawkers are still using Sharpses."

"They do enough with them." Jonathan's tone was dry. "Toward the middle of November, Doc Jennison and his hot-heads rounded up all the proslave settlers around Trading Post and held a sort of trial, the jury being twelve of the posse. They heard the evidence and gave everyone but Russell Hinds seven days to leave Kansas. Hinds was hanged for returning runaways to their masters. A few days later, a well-to-do old man named Sam Scott was tried by the same jury and hanged in his own yard. Jennison offered another proslave man a trial, but he somewhat naturally preferred to die fighting."

Christy said in a troubled voice: "Dan O'Brien and Owen Parks and Andy McHugh won't ride with Jennison. Colonel Montgomery would never have hanged those men, but he told Dan that Hinds was worth a great deal to hang but good for nothing else and was condemned under the sixteenth verse of Exodus, Chapter Twenty-One."

"The hangings were too much for Governor Medary, though," Jonathan said. "He offered a reward of a thousand dollars for Jennison's arrest. Since United States marshals have never been able to catch Jennison or Montgomery, they asked for help from the military.

General Harney came from Fort Leavenworth with cavalry, infantry, and even artillery. He sent two companies of infantry to Mound City under Captain Nathaniel Lyon. They scoured the countryside but never found either Jennison or Montgomery."

"Lyon may not have wanted to very much," Christy put in. "General Harney's proslavery, but Dan says Lyon is a red-headed antislavery atheist who reads political tracts, instead of playing cards. He's even said publicly that Socrates was nobler than Jesus."

"However that may be, he's back at Fort Scott now with his command." Jonathan shrugged. "Sometimes I don't see how a real war could be much worse right around here than what we've got."

"We're likely to find out." Thos slanted a questioning glance at his older brother. "I aim to fight for the Union the first chance I get. What about you, Charlie? Bishop Jardine sure wouldn't let you come calling on his daughter if you were fighting Secessionists."

Charlie gulped. And told them.

CHAPTER NINETEEN

Rays of winter sun shone magnified and golden through the glass panes of the conservatory where the air was sweet with roses. The parakeets' cage was covered to keep them quiet but muted grumbles punctuated Bishop Jardine's lengthy sermon and Jonathan Ware's brief one. Travis had drifted in from Nevada for Christmas, taller, heavier, his grin as ready and bold as ever. When the Wares drove up in their wagon, he'd reached Christy before her brothers could, swung her off the seat so that for a scary, uncomfortable instant he was her only support, and laughed down at her with a glint in his merry brown eyes.

"What a difference a few years make, Miss Christy! I'm glad I came home."

Did he remember ambushing her on the dogtrot the last time he'd seen her and getting his ears boxed?

"Yes, it's fortunate you arrived for your sister's wedding," she told him, and went forward with her family to be greeted by the Jardines and brought into the big white house with its long verandah.

Now Travis and Thos stood up with the couple as best men while Yvonne Benton attended her younger sister. Except for Hester Ballard, the Hayeses, and the Bentons from St. Louis, the guests were neighbors of the Jardines, and, to Christy's astonishment, the Rose Haven slaves were there, too. Dressed in their best, they spilled out into the living room, except for one frail old woman called Aunt Zillah. She was propped up on a cot beside Mrs. Jardine's wheeled chair. Her white-filmed eyes stared blindly toward the voices, but she was smiling, happier than anyone there.

Christy found it hard to smile. *At least he's not marrying someone in Santa Fé or Salt Lake City so we'd never see him.* Melissa was as generously welcoming as any bride could be on her wedding day, the bishop gruffly kind, and, in spite of a jealous pang for her mother's sake, Christy could see why Charlie so admired Mrs. Jardine. She wasn't the least bit puffed up although she was gracious as a queen. Her tenderness to old Aunt Zillah was not what Christy expected from a slave owner, and the behavior of the house servants toward the Jardines was clearly born of affection, not fear.

Yet Justus, had he been caught, would have

been savagely whipped. None of these people could leave at will or choose their work. And there was Lilah, of whom Charlie had spoken, with her bronze hair and creamy skin, every bit as beautiful as the bride. She watched Travis with such longing in her green eyes that Christy made a quick, fervent prayer for her.

The wedding dinner was sumptuous. Youngsters, including Beth and the Benton children, dined in the conservatory under the sharp, if indulgent eye, of Aunt Phronie. At the table for family and close friends, Christy was placed, somewhat to her dismay, between large, slow-moving Henry Benton and Travis. The bridal pair was seated on either hand of the bishop and Jonathan and Ellen Ware were right and left of Mrs. Jardine.

Roses in crystal vases graced ivory damask tablecloths. Silver gleamed beside gold-rimmed china, cut glass sparkled, and Christy had never dreamed there could be so much food of so many kinds.

"We brought the oysters, lobster, figs, and champagne," Henry Benton informed the table at large as platters of carved ham, turkey, quail, mutton, and beef were carried around and served by Lilah and three other young women. After Christy had edged so close to Benton that Travis's arm could no longer brush hers as if by accident, what she enjoyed most was the gold-crusted rolls of fine wheat flour, fresh and hot from the kitchen, the like of which she hadn't tasted since Susie's wedding.

The tables were cleared and the top table-cloths lifted off to reveal another beneath. The bishop, Benton, and Thos went around tipping glistening champagne into glasses.

"Even if you don't drink, have just a sip to toast the young couple," urged the bishop when a Baptist neighbor demurred, as did a few strict Methodists. Resuming his place at the head of the table, the stout, ruddy man lifted his goblet. "To the bride and groom," he offered, beaming. "May you be blessed with health, children, enough of this world's goods for comfort but not sloth, and may you, in fifty years, love each other even better than you do today!"

With a chorus of good wishes, glasses were lifted high and sipped at or drained, according to the imbiber. Christy liked the bubbles although they made her want to sneeze, but thought Emil Franz's cider tasted nicer.

Henry Benton reached for a bottle and brimmed his glass again, throwing back his yellow head. "And here's to South Carolina whose leaders took only twenty-two minutes to secede from the tyrannous Union on December Twentieth! May that brave example inspire her Southern sister states to follow."

Jardine's applauding neighbors raised their glasses, but Jonathan Ware said quietly: "I cannot drink, sir, to the beginning of a tragedy that will fearfully wound, if not destroy, this republic that was birthed with such high hope and fervent prayer less than a hundred years ago."

Henry Benton stared, heavy face turning redder. The bishop crimsoned, too, but his wife's look caused him to swallow and clear his throat. "Henry," he said to his long-time son-in-law, "this is a wedding, not a political meeting. Perhaps you'll be kind enough to frame a toast we can all pledge comfortably."

Benton's eyes fell before Jardine's. "I regret, sir," he said in stiff tone, "that I cannot imagine such a proposal."

Jonathan smiled and raised his glass. "Here's to the gracious and lovely mothers of the bride and groom. May they each gain a child rather than lose one."

Other toasts were drunk with alacrity. A great crystal bowl of something that looked like vanilla pudding was placed before Mrs. Jardine who ladled it into crystal cups that were passed around the tables.

Travis pressed his hand against Christy's as he gave her a cup. "Aunt Phronie's syllabub is famous," he said. "It's far from as innocent as it looks, though it's against my interests to warn you." He flashed a white grin. "I'm hoping when we dance that you'll lose your balance and fall most charmingly into my arms."

His eyes were admiring, his young male

voice full of bantering good humor, and his well-made body so close she could feel its radiated warmth. It took an effort to say austerely: "Are you afraid you'll forget how to flirt, Travis, if you don't practice at every opportunity?"

"That assumption flatters neither of us." Bowls of ice cream were being brought around. "Here, put some brandied peaches on that and see if it won't sweeten your tongue."

She closed her eyes, both to shut him out and savor the delicious creamy melting in her mouth. She'd enjoyed ice cream a few times in Illinois, but the only kind they'd had in Missouri was snow mixed with cream and molasses or honey. She accepted a small piece of the huge white-frosted wedding cake from Melissa, but was compelled by an overfull stomach to refuse plum pudding and all manner of tarts and fruit-filled dumplings.

The second cloth was carried away and almonds, figs, raisins, and mints were placed on the polished walnut table to accompany strong, rich coffee.

Melissa bent to whisper in Christy's ear: "I'll show you the way to the privy. All this drink. . . ."

Christy waited outside the white-washed little building, wondering how her sister-in-law managed with her crinoline. In spite of feeling that Charlie now belonged to his wife's family more than to his own, Christy found it impossible not to like Melissa who took her to her own room to wash and order her hair. Such a pretty room, all ivory and rose, with a velvet-covered armchair, canopied bed, and large gilt-framed mirror above a long marble-topped dresser. Roses with golden leaves twined the doors of the elaborate armoire and vases of real roses perfumed the air.

Would Charlie share this bed, tonight, after the embroidered satin coverlet was folded over its rack by servants who'd build up the fire before they withdrew? Christy put the perfumed soap — a far cry from the strong yellowish lye soap she and her mother made so laboriously — back in its porcelain dish and rinsed her hands in the flowered wash basin.

"Here." Melissa handed her a small, embroidered towel. Her dark-lashed eyes, an indefinable shade between violet and blue, looked directly into Christy's. "Let's be good friends, Christy, even if we can't agree on . . . things. Charlie loves us both."

"You, the most." Christy, to her amaze, found she could say it without bitterness, even add, smiling, as she squeezed the other girl's soft hand: "That's the way it should be."

"It almost has to be, doesn't it?" Melissa made a face. "Papa was set on my marrying . . . well, someone he shared opinions with, but, in the end, he practically proposed for me." Her eyes danced and there was pride in her smile. "I think Papa already likes Charlie more than that suet-pudding-faced Henry Benton, and it's partly because Charlie stood up to him."

"He did?" Christy warmed to hear this. Not that she'd believed Charlie would truckle to Jardine, but he did so love this girl who would in his arms become a woman.

"Yes, and to Travis and me, too, about freeing our darkies after Papa . . . is gone."

"Charlie got all of you to agree to that?" He had told his family something of his intention, but Christy thought he was placating his parents and his conscience.

Melissa's mouth quirked. "Trav says he doesn't care what we do as long as he gets a fair income from the plantation. Papa, of course, counts on Charlie's changing his mind after he's helped manage Rose Haven a while."

"And you?"

"I don't think most of our people would leave if they could." Melissa looked up from washing her hands. "But when the time comes . . . well, after the way Charlie's talked to me, especially about Lilah, if they want to go, I guess I'd rather they did." She put down her towel and took Christy's hand. "Hear Uncle Fred's banjo and Caesar's fiddle? Let's hurry!"

Melissa and Charlie led in the Virginia Reel and Christy couldn't evade Travis by demurring: "I've never danced except at a few corn shuckings."

She had practiced with Thos before Susie's and Andy's wedding, hoping someone else would take Dan's fiddle so she could whirl and dip and circle with him, but there'd been no dancing on that day, only grief and fury over the men slaughtered on the soft spring grass above the Marais des Cygnes.

"Then we'll watch this time and dance the next." Travis drew her to the side where those not dancing watched, standing or from chairs. The temporary table had been taken away and the other set against the end of the room where an ebony-skinned man with a shock of white hair strummed a banjo while a younger, light brown man played the fiddle. *Not as well as Dan, though,* thought Christy, with a surge of longing.

The crowded space gave Travis an excuse to stand so close his breath stirred the curls above her ear. "I do believe some of the ladies have sewn grapevines into their clothes to make their skirts stand out," he whispered.

"I don't see how you can tell that," she said in her coldest tone even though she had heard two of the neighboring young women giggle about their "hoops".

"For one thing, Thisbe Shelton's trailing a vine from her skirt. Whoops! Your brother Thos just stepped on it. Good thing it cracked off clean so the rest of her framework won't be dragged out."

"You . . . you're not supposed to notice such things!"

"I'm not blind." Travis's eyes drifted over her, not insultingly, but in a way that told her he saw the pulse of her throat, the curve of her bodice. He slipped his hand beneath her arm. "The first set's finishing. Do me the honor, Miss Christy. You have full leave to tread on my toes."

She did on purpose a time or two, smiling at him to let him know it was deliberate, but then her body answered the lilting tune and her feet flew. Quadrilles were followed by polkas, schottisches, and the varsouvienne. *Put your little foot, put your little foot, put your little foot right out. . . .*

Every time Christy tried to retire to the wall, someone claimed her, brothers and fathers of the girls with the grapevine hoops, her own brothers and father, and Ethan Hayes, but Travis most of all.

"A pity my father won't allow waltzing. Then I could get my arm around you properly." Travis shrugged. "Oh, well, for a Methodist, he's broad-minded."

"Especially for a bishop, I should think."

"*Because* he's a bishop. Since the church

387

split over slavery in the Eighteen Forties, Southern Methodist bishops depend a lot on their own judgment. You don't think slavery's right, I guess?"

"That white Methodists own black Methodists?" Christy had resolved not to get into such arguments with her new in-laws, but wouldn't dodge a direct question. "I don't see how anyone can think it's right."

They finished the dance in silence. Christy walked off the floor without waiting for his escort, but in a moment he followed. "Miss Christy, if your parents are willing, would you allow me to call on you?"

Her jaw dropped. Probably he just couldn't stand it that she wasn't thrilled breathless at his attentions. "No," she said flatly. "I don't want you calling on me."

"Are your affections engaged?"

"They are." She couldn't resist adding: "But even if they weren't, we never could agree."

"Indeed? Now why is that?"

"You're much too full of yourself, much too high and mighty."

He eyed her with fresh interest. "Ah, but now we're family, I'm sure your parents won't turn me away if I stop to inquire after their health."

"I can't prevent that, but it won't do you any good."

"I think it will."

He bowed, left her, and in the next moment smiled down at Thisbe of the draggled grapevine, inviting her to dance. Her rawboned, red-headed brother engaged Christy, but all she could do was wish he were Dan and feel annoyed with Travis. She was glad when her father signaled that it was time to go.

Collecting Beth, the Wares embraced Charlie and Melissa. Even Jonathan had damp eyes as they wished the young pair happiness. Mrs. Jardine, in her wheeled chair, smiled up and gave her hands to Jonathan and Ellen.

"Thank you for rearing such a splendid son," she told them. "It's a blessing to know he'll cherish our daughter."

She reached up to draw Ellen and Christy down for a kiss on their cheeks, hugged Beth, and asked Lilah to bring the armful of wrapped roses she'd cut for them. "I know we're a half day distant," she said, "but you are most warmly welcome at any time. I regret that I'm unable to repay visits."

"We understand." Ellen pressed the slim white hand between her chapped ones. "Thank you for your kindness and welcome, Missus Jardine."

The bishop walked out with them to where a servant had their wagon ready. "I could wish us in better agreement." The bishop shook hands with Jonathan, bowed over Ellen's, gave Beth a kiss, and Christy a measuring nod. "Still, there is no mistaking where Charles got his integrity and whole-some nature. I thank you for that." He helped Ellen and Christy to the seat, bundled Beth between them, and waved as they drove toward the swiftly setting sun.

As soon as Thos helped his father cut and split enough wood for the rest of the winter, he was off with the borrowed team to resume his hundred mile stints with the Pony Express.

"We carried the news of Lincoln's election," he said as he lifted the reins. "I sure hope we don't have to carry word that war has broken out." He looked from his father to his mother, gave Christy a long, sober look, and bent to ruffle Beth's hair. "If there's a chance, I'll come home to see you before I enlist."

"Oh, Thos!" Ellen cried.

He lifted a shoulder. "Try not to worry, Mama. Maybe it won't happen." He clucked to the mules. Just before he drove into the timber, he turned to wave. They all waved back, even after he'd passed from sight.

Tears formed slowly and ran down Ellen's cheeks. Christy would have thrown her arms around her, but her father did that first.

"My dear, my Ellen, God has protected both our boys thus far."

She nodded mutely, then said in a twisted

broken way: "But, oh, Jon! Have you thought? What if they fight each other?"

CHAPTER TWENTY

Didn't Melissa know how to do anything? That morning, she'd volunteered to make the mush, but hadn't sifted hulls from the meal, so now the family chewed the tough bits if they were small enough or rolled them into the corners of their mouths to dispose of discreetly.

"I'm sorry!" Melissa looked ready to cry as Beth choked and began to cough, probably from trying to swallow too big a scrap. Melissa had won her, body and soul, by giving Beth a porcelain-headed doll with real blonde hair, ivory teeth, a crinoline under an emerald velvet gown, and brocade slippers. Her own childhood favorite, she admitted, adding with a joyous look at Charlie: "Now I'm grown up, Bethie, so you must have Lynette."

After thumps on the back had cleared Beth's throat, Melissa said miserably: "I'm afraid I'm more of a nuisance than a help, Mama Ware."

"We're very glad you came, dear." Ellen's voice was kind. "It gives us a wonderful chance to get acquainted. Besides, you take the tiniest, most even stitches I've ever seen. If we finish the double wedding ring quilt before you leave, you must take it with you as our wedding gift, even though it doesn't seem quite fair that you're working on your own present."

"I'm glad I can do something." Melissa managed a wavery smile. "I spin and weave, of course. Mama says every woman must be able to teach and supervise her s-. . . ." She broke off. Had she started to say slaves or servants?

"Two of womankind's most ancient and valued skills," Jonathan put in, always the teacher, although he'd dismissed his little school — now only Luke and Mary Hayes and Beth — early in March when the ground thawed enough for plowing. "Long before Penelope foiled her unwelcome suitors by unraveling every night what she wove through the day. . . ."

"Anyone home?" called a voice at the door.

Melissa jumped up and ran to the door. "Travis!" She hustled him inside where, after bowing to the elder Wares and grinning cheekily at Christy, he went to warm himself by the fire.

"I can't believe you got up early enough to be over here at this hour!" His sister eyed him narrowly. "Mama's well? There's nothing wrong?"

"Must there be a calamity? I came to take you home, if you were getting in the way, M'liss. If you aren't, I'll stay and help a few days."

"Can you plow?" Christy didn't try to hide her skepticism.

"I can make a tolerably straight furrow, but, after swinging a pickaxe in the Comstock . . . did you hear that Nevada was made a territory in February? Colorado, too, which cuts off a good slice of Kansas . . . why, I reckon I can make pretty fair potato mounds."

Melissa turned to her mother-in-law. "Please, Mama Ware, tell me the truth! Could you manage better if I went home?"

"My dear, we hope you'll stay." Ellen pressed her hand. "It means a lot to have you and Charlie here, even if he weren't such a help with the spring work. Besides, I assure you that having your help with the quilt makes me breathe easier. I want it to keep you warm this first winter of your marriage, but Christy and I can only work on it a few hours at night." She gave Travis a pleasant smile. "Your brother's very welcome. He's been here before, you know, helping get in the winter wood."

Melissa gave her mother-in-law a swift hug and faced her slightly younger but much bigger brother with bright confidence. "That's fine then, Trav. You stay and plant potatoes or whatever Papa Ware trusts you with."

"Yes, your wifeness." He looked at Christy although he implored the room in general: "Do you suppose I could have a bite to eat? I grabbed a couple of cold biscuits when I left, but the chill's made me hungry as a spring-time bear." He sniffed expectantly. "That coffee sure smells good."

One of the most appreciated things Charlie and Thos had brought was a big box of roasted Arbuckles' coffee beans. Christy rose to get Travis a mug, feeling sorry for Melissa whose fair complexion went a scalded crimson.

"I made the mush this morning, Trav, and there's . . . well, there's hulls in it. Not big ones," she added defensively.

"You made the mush?" He shook his curly brown hair while his grin spread ear to ear. "I wouldn't miss tasting it, and telling Aunt Phronie and Lilah, for all the silver I lost in Nevada."

"Lost?" echoed Melissa. "Don't you mean found?"

"Lost. Cards." He swung a long leg across the bench where Charlie had scooted over. "Bring on your mush, Sis! I hope there's plenty of milk and molasses."

The meal finished in hilarity, even Melissa laughing, although Travis must have downed most of the hulls to spare his sister's feelings.

The sun was barely up when the men went out, Charlie and Jonathan hitching up the horses and oxen, Travis taking a shovel to the acre Charlie had plowed yesterday for potatoes.

Ellen watched them for a moment from the window. "Let's pray for good crops," she said. "We'd be pinched tight by now if Thos and Charlie hadn't brought that wagonload of food, and we'd have had little to share with Hester and the Hayeses."

While Beth dried dishes for Melissa, Christy skimmed cream from the covered pans on the shelf where milking things were kept in winter, and poured it into the wooden churn along with cream saved from the last few days. She worked the dasher up and down, the *swish-swash* calming her as she vented her annoyance on the innocent cream.

Travis was linked to their family now. She had to get used to that. If he chose to help his friend and brother-in-law with the planting, that placed no obligation on her. Of course, he'd really come to take Melissa home if she felt too uncomfortable at the Wares'.

Christy glanced at the slender young woman who nodded and asked appropriate questions during Beth's account of Robbie's latest defeat by a skunk. Who could blame Beth for enjoying someone's full attention? Christy was ashamed of her irritation over the hulls in the mush as it dawned on her that Melissa was as nervous about winning the approval of Charlie's family as he must have been about hers.

Melissa tossed the dish water out on the rose bushes and hung up the pan. When she turned, Christy gave her a real smile, warm as she could make it. Melissa responded with a happy laugh. "Shall I lower the quilt, Mama Ware?"

"Yes, please." Ellen finished picking over dried peas and beans, more of her sons' largesse, rinsed and poured them and dried corn into a three-legged kettle she set on the hearth over a bed of raked-out coals. "We can do a lot of stitching before dinner. Beth, crush these chinquapins as fine as you can and put them in the stew." It was an Indian dish Sarah had taught them to make, using the small, flavorsome chinquapins, thin shell and all.

Jonathan had rigged pulleys to raise and lower the quilt frame that was stored against the ceiling when not in use. Only the night before had the women finished sewing all the pieced blocks together. Ellen had started the quilt as soon as Charlie announced his engagement, gleaning her scrap basket for harmonious colors, an easier task now that they had remnants of a number of garments made from cloth Charlie had brought them.

Needles flew as Ellen and Melissa stitched

through the top, the blanket batting, and the blue floral sateen back that Charlie had intended as a Christmas gift for Ellen. She and her daughter-in-law apparently had little in common except their love for Charlie, but that was powerful enough to impel them to begin forming a bond with shared work and threads of words, weft through warp running in and out like their needles, creating the pattern of what they would be to each other.

Butter was forming. Christy poured the buttermilk into crocks and the bits and chunks of butter into a big bowl. Using an oak paddle to force the remaining milk out of the pale yellow mass, she worked till the butter was ready to press into two one-pound wooden molds. It wouldn't last long with three field-hungry men to feed, but it added so much to their plain food that she didn't grudge the work.

The appetizing odor of bubbling stew made the cabin seem warmer than it was. Christy gave it a stir, replenished the coals beneath it after adding split logs to the fire, stretched to ease her shoulders, and threaded a needle.

She pulled up a stool between her mother and Melissa and started at the border, a lovely muted indigo her mother had worked hard to dye just the right color to make Christy a dress. Christy, who had stirred the cloth constantly in the smelly dye pot, not to mention having helped spin and weave it, had summoned considerable effort to bless the material's new use. She felt gratifyingly noble as she sewed it to the backing.

Melissa, to her credit, didn't prattle of her visits to St. Louis, and her only comment on the difference between her home and the Wares' was to look around with lively interest when she arrived and say: "I think I like log houses more without clapboards and white-wash. They fit the country better and look more . . . real."

This sentiment launched her visit auspiciously. Now she regaled them with stories of Charlie and how he had dived into Watt Caxton's hounds to rescue her cat. "I fell in love with him then and there." She chuckled. "That naughty Emmie, though! She still arches her back and hisses at him if he tries to pick her up when she's being cranky."

Melissa's teeth were white and pretty. Neither she nor her mother, thank goodness, used snuff. That would have been harder to endure, day to day, than conflicting political opinions. As the three quilters stitched and chatted, none of them mentioned what must be at back of all their thoughts, the inexorable slide of the nation toward war.

Kansas had been admitted to the Union as a free state late in January after years of bloody, bitter struggle. This sent a tidal wave of dread and anger crashing through the South. Slave state votes were outnumbered in Congress and would lose their Presidential ally when Buchanan stepped down. North Carolina's fiery secession late in December was followed in January by Mississippi, Florida, Alabama, Georgia, and Louisiana. After his state seceded, Jefferson Davis, a West Pointer and former Secretary of War, resigned from the Senate and had been elected President of the Confederacy.

North and South, the eyes of the shattering Union were fixed on the new island stronghold of Fort Sumter off Charleston, South Carolina, an island in more ways than one, a small Union garrison surrounded by hostile ships and militia.

It could well be the torch to set off an inferno that could not even be imagined. Thinking of her brothers, Dan, and the other young men she knew, Christy felt a cold knot form in her stomach. Strange to think that this quilt might well be in use when Fort Sumter was an echo in history books, as distant as Valley Forge was now.

Our work is slow, thought Christy, *the cutting and stitching of small pieces into a covering large enough to warm a man and woman. Slow, but the quilt may last to comfort the children gotten in that marriage bed, and even their children. Will we ever make such a quilt for Dan and me?*

Beth was at her endless chore of bringing in kindling and collecting wood chips near the chopping block when her *whoop* made the women thrust their needles into the quilt and hurry to the door.

Too early for snakes, but a vengeful black widow or rabid creature? The quilters sighed with relief, and some exasperation, as Beth tore past them to hurl herself into Dan's welcoming arms.

"Danny! You haven't been here for ages, not even on Sunday!"

"We've been taking turns with chills and fever." He smoothed her curls and kissed the tip of her snubby nose. Indeed, Dan did look thin and a little pallid. "I put in a week at plowing while Davie and Owen were in bed. Now they've taken over so I could help you folks." He glanced toward the plowmen and wrinkled his brow at Travis who was covering chunks of potato.

"Looks like I'm not needed as much as I reckoned I'd be." His tone was rueful as he straightened to his long-boned height and he looked at Christy with a hurt question in his eyes.

"Don't fear there's not work for you, if you're set on it." Ellen laughed and embraced him with a kiss on the cheek. Ever since Dan had rescued Christy from the wolves, Ellen had treated him like a son. "The old cornstalks have to be cut and burned before that field can be plowed, and there are still a few stumps to wrestle out of the land cleared year

401

before last. Have you met my daughter-in-law? Melissa, this is Daniel O'Brien."

"I've been wanting to congratulate Charlie on his good luck . . . and you on yours, Missus Ware. Pleased to meet you." Dan bowed to Melissa.

She twinkled back, offering her hand. "I've seen you at Parkses' mill, Mister O'Brien, though we've not been introduced. Charlie's spoken of you very fondly. I declare there must be something in the wind! My brother Travis turned up this morning and behold!" She flourished her hand. "He's actually making himself useful!"

"Well, then, so must I." Dan looked more cheerful. He, of all men, would understand having a care for one's sister.

"Melissa's helping with her own wedding present," Ellen said. "I hope we can finish before she and Charlie go . . ." — she hesitated — "go home."

Dan's eyes tangled with Christy's for a moment. Would they ever lie together under such a quilt? Why, *why* not have what they could? Involuntarily she put out her hand, but either he didn't see it, or pretended not to as he took a glass of buttermilk from Beth and gazed admiringly at the quilt.

"A fine gift, cozy and beautiful at the same time. Now I'd better get to work or Mister Ware will think I came to eat his food and loll at his fire."

Beth held up a bowl of nuts and fruit. "Grab it!" she invited.

Laughing, he obeyed. "You do look after me, Bethie." He went out, munching, and the women looked at each other.

"We'll make him a pallet in this room with Travis," said Ellen. Charlie and Melissa slept in the loft on the boys' old bed. "Beth, crack up several more cups of chinquapins for the stew and add more water."

The quilters resumed their places. Ellen gave a soft laugh. "Jonathan's been worried about managing without either of the boys at home, but, look, here he has three strapping young men!"

"Charlie can always come over for planting and harvest, Mama Ware," said Melissa.

"That would greatly help, my dear, and we hope you'll come, too." Ellen didn't mention what they all knew, that Charlie could be spared because slaves did the field work at Rose Haven.

"I can chop weeds out of the corn," said Christy. She scrunched her shoulders up, then let them fall, as she remembered that summer. "I like working outside better than in, but I hope we never have to haul water for our crops again."

"We only saved a little of our tobacco," Melissa said. "Our people had all they could do to haul water for our food crops."

And your mother's roses. Christy gave herself

403

a mental shake. She absolutely must not dwell on the contrast between the Jardines' life and the Wares', especially not with the envy that sprouted up no matter how fiercely she assured herself that even could she afford it, she'd never exist on the labor of slaves.

There was no denying the perverse allure of having someone else do the things you didn't want to, and it was easier to be righteous if you were poor than if you weren't, so long as you weren't pushed to the desperation of robbery. The thought of starving always brought Dan's fearful childhood to mind.

"Mother," she said in inspiration, "could we make Dan a quilt or blanket all of his own?"

"Why . . . yes, dear, but don't you think Lydia and Harriet and Missus Morrison . . . ?"

"I'm sure he's got covers, but probably not anything special, made just for him."

Melissa's creamy brow furrowed as if she couldn't imagine such a thing. "What makes you think that, Christy?"

"The Parkses made him part of their family, but, when you think about it, Lydia wasn't more than twelve and Susie eight when their mother died birthing David. All of a sudden they had an infant to look after as well as cooking and keeping house for their father and Owen, spinning and weaving and sewing, too. They managed, but I don't see how they had time to make anything special for Dan beyond knitting his socks and making whatever of his clothes weren't handed down from Owen."

Ellen gave her daughter a searching look. "I never thought about it, but I'm glad you did. Why don't we make him a blanket? If . . . well, if he starts moving around a lot, a blanket won't hold dirt like a quilt and there's warmth in wool, even when it's wet."

She meant that a blanket was more practical for a soldier. Christy's heart constricted. All the more reason, then, to see that he had one made for him especially, warm, comforting, and as handsome as they could contrive.

"Could we do a striped blanket?" she asked. "We have the wool already spun that came out such a lovely gold, and there's quite a bit of walnut brown."

Ellen joined in Christy's enthusiasm although stripes took more care and work than a plain blanket dyed all one color. "There may even be enough wool spun to make it, and we can dye some to get several shades of yellows and browns." She smiled at her daughter-in-law. "We'll finish your quilt first, though.

"When is Dan's birthday, Christy?"

"No one knows. Lydia just makes a cake for him and David on David's birthday, August Eighth."

"We'll have it done by then," Ellen promised. "Maybe we'll have wheat flour this year to make him his own cake."

Christy turned to give her mother a hug, heedless of acting so excited over the flour that was used every day at Jardines'. "That would be wonderful! Thank you, Mother."

None of them said what they must all have been thinking: that in August, instead of stripping green blades from the corn ears, there was no telling where their young men might be.

When the men came in, it was satisfying to see how their nostrils swelled to draw in the molasses and cinnamon smells of Indian pudding mingled with that of stew and corn pone. A handsome lot the men were as they washed up with the use of a second basin fetched by Beth. Charlie's wavy hair was browner than Jonathan's chestnut, and Travis's wild mop was the darkest. Dan's hair caught all the light there was. Christy felt a rush of happiness at seeing him come in with her father and brother, just like one of the family.

Travis stepped between them, deliberately, she thought, and then they were all sitting down, Travis on one side of her, Dan on the other, bowing heads while her father said grace.

"Makes a world of difference, four men in

the fields instead of one." Jonathan sobered as he gazed at his eldest son. "I never expected help from you, Charlie, once you took to freighting. It's good to see you working our land again." Jonathan grinned at Melissa. "Even if you are just on loan."

Our land? Well, of course, it would be part Charlie's one day, a thought that had never entered Christy's head before. She quickly thrust away the thought of her parents' death. When Christy allowed herself to dream of being married to Dan, she pictured them on a farm adjoining her parents', close enough that she and her mother could run back and forth easily. Wouldn't it be wonderful if Thos and Beth eventually settled on neighboring land? With Charlie only five miles away, the families could visit often and have holidays together? If they each had three to five children, there'd be a whole tribe of cousins. . . .

"Any news of Fort Sumter?" Travis asked Dan. "Or the inauguration of that beanpole of a lawyer from Illinois?"

"President Lincoln," stressed Dan, "according to the stage driver yesterday, said the Union is perpetual, that no state can leave simply of its own will." At Travis's derisive snort, Dan's tone deepened. "The President also said 'though passion might strain the bonds of affection, it must not break them, that the chords of memory running from every patriot grave and battlefield to every heart and hearthstone in this land will swell the chorus of union when touched by our better natures.' "

"The bonds are broken!" Travis cried. "Whatever Lincoln says, six states have seceded!"

"Seven. Much against Sam Houston's will, Texas seceded the day before the inaugural."

Caught breaths and sighs came from around the table. Texas lay southwest of Missouri with Arkansas or Indian Territory between, not far away if war came. There had been Texans along with Clarke in the infamous raid of 1856 that burned out Trading Post and dozens of Free State settlers.

"What about Fort Sumter?" Travis persisted.

Dan shrugged. "The best guess is that the President will send the garrison only food and non-military supplies."

"But Southern ships won't let Federal vessels reach Sumter." Satisfaction glinted in Travis's dark eyes as well as his voice. "The garrison can't live on air."

"If war must come, President Lincoln is probably determined not to order the first assault."

"You mean he's tricking the Confederacy into taking the blame?"

"I'd scarcely call it tricking," said Jonathan dryly. "In the end, the Confederacy will doubtless get Fort Sumter . . . and with it, a war 'the like of which men have not seen' in the words of Jefferson Davis when he resigned from the Senate."

"Hopes for peace certainly aren't helped by having an officer like that red-headed infidel, Nathaniel Lyon, trying to get the government arsenal at Saint Louis fortified."

"Captain Lyon?" Christy tried to avert an argument. "Didn't you say, Dan, that he was a great supporter of the dancing school at Fort Scott?"

"Yes, but he's famed more for other things. When forced into a duel, he named the weapons, as revolvers fired while the officers sat across a table from each other." Dan smiled. "The other officer chose to drop the quarrel."

"Any sane man would," retorted Travis. "Lyon is a maniac! Look at the way he punished a soldier by making him march around in the hot sun with a barrel over his shoulders so he couldn't brush away the flies and pests."

"He's also taken the whip away from a drover who was cruelly lashing a team and used it on the man," Dan said. "When he caught a soldier kicking a dog, he knocked him down and made him kneel to beg the dog's pardon."

"Crazy as a loon!" blurted Travis. "If he takes the part of animals like that, what would he do about a darkie getting a well-deserved lesson? Such a fanatic shouldn't be anywhere near that arsenal!"

"There are enough arms and munitions in that depot to control the state should Governor Jackson seize them." Jonathan's tone was even drier. "When he took office the last day of December, Jackson called a state convention to consider secession." He raised an eyebrow. "Isn't your father a delegate to that convention, Travis?"

"Yes. He's pro-Union like most of the delegates. He's as opposed to secession as you are, sir." He added what they all were thinking. "Provided his property rights are preserved, of course. Father's sure the convention will vote for compromise."

Jonathan said regretfully: "It may be too late for that."

"It certainly may," rejoined Travis, "with that scoundrel Doc Jennison organizing his thieving jayhawks into militia." He challenged Dan with an unspoken question.

"Jennison's been recruiting from Linn and Bourbon counties for his Mound City Rifles," Dan said. "As you say, many of them are thieves and scoundrels, which is why I haven't joined." His gray eyes locked with Travis's dark ones. "If . . . when . . . Colonel Montgomery calls for men, I'll follow him in a heartbeat."

"Montgomery?" choked Travis. "Why, he's

as bad as Jennison! A slave-stealing. . . ."

"He'd call it slave freeing, his duty before God. Montgomery takes an eye for an eye, but he'll shoot a man for looting."

"You seem mightily well acquainted!"

"I rode with him after Clarke's raid, the slaughter at Marais des Cygnes, and to break prisoners out of the Fort Scott jail. Montgomery is a God-fearing man of honor."

"I'd say the same of my father." Somber for the first time, Travis stared into a future he could not predict. "What happens when honorable men can't agree on what God wills?"

"They fight all the harder and more ruthlessly, each claiming God for an ally." Ellen's voice was full of sorrow. She rose to fetch the Indian pudding. As she bent for the kettle, she brushed her eyes with her sleeve.

CHAPTER TWENTY-ONE

Christy and her mother did the washing on a rise above the creek, high enough to be safe from flooding. It was easier to fill tubs and the huge black kettle from the creek than to haul bucket by bucket from the well. Jonathan Ware had built an open stone fireplace to heat water, made wide benches for the vessels, and grooved the yard-long oak board slanted into the tub. This got clothes cleaner faster than scrubbing them out by hand, although it barked Christy's knuckles if she wasn't careful rubbing garments up and down before wringing them as dry as she could and tossing them into the rinse water. Sheets, washed first, of course, now boiled in the kettle. Ellen Ware gave them stirs between dipping things up and down in the first rinsing tub. Beth did the same with socks and smaller things, wringing them as her mother did, putting them in the second rinse where she soused them around, and at last wringing them and hanging them over bushes and fence rails. For sheets and large things, Jonathan had rigged a rope between two hickory stumps far enough away from living trees not to be stained by perching birds.

Christy straightened to rest her aching shoulders and gazed toward the nearby bottom field. She'd never seen anything so beautiful as the fresh green of the finger-length corn planted a few weeks ago at the beginning of April when shimmering cloud oceans of passenger pigeons flew back north, settling like gray-blue waves into the forests to feed on mast. Some, according to Lige Morrow, would pair off and go deeply into the timber to nest instead of flying on. Christy liked to think of them, sheltered in leafy denseness, perhaps only their red feet and eyes showing as they cooed to each other and their young.

Oddly enough, the sheep were always the first of the farm animals to regain their energy on the new grass. The dark-faced Suffolk matriarchs, Nosey, Cleo, and Mildred, *baa*ed at their descendants or benignly watched the knob-kneed lambs butt their heads together. Cavalier, the strutting rooster, had toppled over as he hailed the sun one February dawn. The Wares mourned him, but he made tasty dumpling stew, nevertheless, and his heir stalked among the hens like a new-crowned king, brilliant rose comb bobbing like the plume of a knight.

Fawn-colored heifer calves suckled Goldie, Clover, and Shadow and Maud's sides bulged. In a few more years, the herd would be back to its numbers before the drought. Spotted piglets squealed from the pen, and Heloise had presented her gander, Abelard, with five gray goslings. On the slope above the barn, a blood bay colt nuzzled at Queenie who arched her neck to admire him.

Jed wasn't getting a holiday. He pulled a shovel plow guided by Jonathan through the rows of young corn, casting the soil around the sword-like little blades to smother weeds that were growing with at least equal vigor. Around the 1st of July, the corn should be up to a man's shoulder and able to fend for itself. After last summer's drought, it was ironic to know that, if there should be so much rain that it was too wet to plow or hoe while the corn got its start, it would be choked with weeds and grass that would take arduous labor to root out if and when the field dried enough.

Farmers had to be the boldest and most intrepid of gamblers, but, after all, as Jonathan said, that was why Joseph in long ago Egypt had built granaries to store up good harvests to get the people through seven years of drought.

Seven years! It had been more than some settlers could do to last one year. Soaping one of her father's shirts, Christy gave a silent prayer for the corn, and the oats, too, planted toward the end of March, and showing bravely.

Yes, it was spring, and, along with happy manifestations, Watt Caxton would be making his rounds to buy up mules and slaves to sell to the river plantations. He was the only person Jonathan had ever ordered off the Ware farm. Caxton had actually had the nerve to stop by after he'd brought his hounds on the Ware place when he was chasing Justus.

Christy wondered where Justus was and hoped he had managed to buy his wife or somehow get her free. If war came, what would happen to the slaves? If the Union won, they might eventually be freed, but what would prepare them to build new lives? For that matter, how was anyone going to manage who was close enough to the fighting to feel its brunt?

Trying to banish the dread that was always coiled in the pit of her stomach like a growing serpent, Christy scrubbed at a stubborn spot and was rubbing on more soap when Robbie leaped up from his guardian post between master and womenfolk and raced off with his welcoming bark.

Dan strode, long-legged, into view, bent to roughhouse the dog, and swung Beth in a circle as she ran to meet him. Christy's gladness at seeing him drained away when she could read the trouble on his face.

"It's happened!" He looked from Christy to her parents. Jonathan had left patient Jed among the corn while he came to hear the news. "Fort Sumter fell, April Fourteenth, after the Confederates bombarded it for two days."

Jonathan paled around the lips. "Were many killed?"

"By a miracle, no one. Major Anderson and his garrison were allowed to leave on the Union supply ship that had been trying to reach the fort."

"Thank God!" Ellen breathed.

Dan gave a tight laugh. "Isn't it strange that not a life was lost in an affair that's setting off a war bound to kill thousands?"

"Maybe . . . ," Christy began.

Dan shook his head. "President Lincoln's calling for seventy-five thousand volunteers to serve for three months to put down what he calls an 'insurrection'." Dan appealed to Jonathan. "Do you think it could be finished that quickly, sir?"

"I'm sure the Confederates think any one of them can lick ten Northerners." Jonathan gave a grim chuckle. "If war must come, the sooner it's over the better for everyone, but I fear it's more likely to last three years than three months."

Dan looked at Christy in a way that made her heart stop. "I'll volunteer as soon as

Colonel Montgomery or almost anyone except Doc Jennison starts recruiting. Talk is that General Jim Lane . . . he was elected to the Senate April Fourth . . . will ask the President for a commission so he can raise volunteers to defend Kansas."

"From what one hears of Lane, he's just as likely to ransack Missouri." Jonathan turned back toward his plow. "We appreciate your bringing the news, Dan, even though it's what we've been dreading. Stay for dinner if you can."

"Do," Ellen urged, with a shaky smile. "We'll soon be through here."

"I'll help." Dan rinsed a pair of Jonathan's trousers and wrung them hand's length by hand's length till the last drop was squeezed from them. "Davie and I don't get dinner on wash days till we've wrung out all the sheets."

"Then I'll go make the corn pone," Ellen said, drying her hands on her apron. "Beth, come along and set the table."

"Race you to the middle," Dan teased, taking one end of a coverlet. Christy fished in the tub for her end. They pressed out all the water they could, and then twisted the heavy cloth in sections as fast as they could, draping the wrung parts over their shoulders, till they squeezed out the middle together and their fingers touched.

Dan closed his hand over hers and laughed. "Call it a tie?"

Breathing hard from exertion, Christy laughed back. "I beat you by at least a whisker!" His hair tangled over his forehead, so unruly that she longed to smooth it, feel it cling to her fingers. Gazing into his eyes, the deep blue-gray of smoke or storm, she ached for the feel of his arms, the hard sweetness of his mouth.

"Oh, Dan! Please! Let's. . . ."

His hand tightened on hers, paining it. "I've told you, sweetheart. I can by no means wed you, bed you, and leave you with the worry of a babe."

"We can't stop living because there's a war!"

"Some will. Many will."

She swallowed but it still hurt to talk. "If . . . if anything happened to you, Dan, I'd want your baby more than ever. To remember you. . . ."

"But if something happens to you? God help us, there might be no one to care for the child! It could starve like my poor little sister." He dropped Christy's hand as if it seared him and took the rest of the coverlet from her.

"Dan!"

"Leave it, Christy."

"I never thought you such a coward!" His jaw dropped. She blazed on. "Of course, you'll volunteer! Shoot and be shot at! No doubt you'll die bravely, if that comes. But

418

you're afraid to live, Dan! Afraid to love me!"

She would never forget the stricken look on his face before he turned away. "Indeed, I fear to love you as much as I do, but I can't be helping that. Nor would I, if I could."

"Dan! Please. . . ."

"I'll always love you, Christy Ware, but if my way of showing it offends you, you're in no way bound to me."

Her heart hammered in her throat. "What do you mean?"

He tossed the coverlet over the line and began to peg it up. "If it's marrying itself you're set on, Travis Jardine would oblige."

She gasped. "What a hateful thing to say!"

"Most would think it no worse than your calling me a coward."

She battled angry tears as they finished the washing in silence. He helped her carry the rinse water to the budding apple trees, empty the soapy water into the grate, and carry one of the tubs to hang in the dogtrot so it would be convenient for bathing.

As they entered the cabin, Dan glanced at the blanket forming on the loom, stripes of gold and dark brown with all the shades between. "A blanket?" he inquired. "Rare pretty. Soft as a baby rabbit it looks!"

"Feel it," Ellen invited.

Cautiously he did, long brown fingers lingering on the wool. "Softer than a wee rabbit." He smiled in awe. "The lucky person wrapped in that will have good dreams for sure."

Good dreams, my love, and a safe homecoming! Tenderness surged over Christy's hurt indignation, sweeping it away. Dan was trying to protect her according to what he knew from his own cruel experience. She didn't agree, she'd gladly run the risk, but she mustn't slash at him for following his conscience. Instead, she'd work hard to help finish the gift before Dan went off so that, wherever he was, something of her love would keep him warm, would lie between him and the hard ground.

Charlie and Travis rode in at mid-morning a few days later while Christy and her father were hoeing weeds from around the potato vines. Christy froze to see they each wore two revolvers, had rifles thrust in their saddle scabbards, and Bowie knives sheathed at their belts. Bedrolls and packs were tied behind their saddles.

"We're joining the State Guard!" Travis exulted as they swung from their saddles. "Old Pap Price is recruiting so we can defend Missouri from those infernal jayhawkers and Federal troops!"

Jonathan's hands seemed to freeze on the hoe. "What . . . ?"

"Militia from Clay and Jackson Counties took the Liberty arsenal across from Kansas

City and are passing out weapons," Travis said in glee.

Jonathan's face turned suddenly old. He watched his son with such grief and worry that Christy wondered how Charlie could just stand there and look glum. "Armed rebellion," Jonathan whispered.

Travis's eyes shone. "The governor, Claib Jackson, told Lincoln what he could do with his call for troops from Missouri! Told him it was illegal, unconstitutional, revolutionary, inhuman, and diabolical . . . that it couldn't be complied with!"

"Some would call it illegal for the governor of a state to defy the President of the United States," Jonathan said.

Travis stared. "They're not united any more, sir. Virginia has just seceded. North Carolina surely will, probably Tennessee. And Missouri shouldn't be forced to fight her sister Southern states even if those lop-eared Saint Louis Dutch are willing to fill the Union quota!"

"I thought the Missouri state convention voted for compromise, not secession."

"That was before Lincoln called for troops!"

Seething, Christy tightened her grip on the hoe. "What else could he do, Travis Jardine, after the Confederacy took Fort Sumter?"

"The South has to be able to defend itself. Arms from the arsenal help, but we need to take the big Federal depot at Saint Louis. Wouldn't I love to get a shot at that little banty rooster Lyon's scruffy carrot beard!"

"I hope you won't." Jonathan spoke to Travis, but his eyes never left his son. "Lyon is a brave officer. His like is needed." A faint smile softened Jonathan's lips. "But I'd be sorry, Travis, to see harm come to you."

"We'll ride right through those Germans," Travis said cockily. "I bet I'll get a commission because of my military training."

"I didn't think you graduated from either of those academies," Christy said.

He shrugged. "I still have a sight more military training than most. One thing you can count on is that Charlie and I will stick together. Melissa made us promise."

"What does she think about this?" Christy demanded of her brother.

"She saw we had to go . . . ," Travis began, but Charlie cut him off.

"Since Travis was set on volunteering, she asked me to keep him from being too hot-headed a fool." Charlie met his father's eyes. "I hate to fight the Union, sir, but, in the pinch, I think states have a right to secede."

"That's not how Missouri's voted," Christy argued.

Travis patted a revolver. "We're going to vote like this."

"Yes!" Christy burst out. "That's how it's been along this border for years. Now it'll be that way all over the country! Oh, Charlie. . . ." Her heart sank at his closed face. She bit her tongue on bitter words. *You're the Jardines', not ours! You'll fight for what they believe, not for what you were taught at home.*

Jonathan leaned his hoe against the fence. "Come in and see your mother, Charles. Have dinner before you ride on."

Travis groaned and rubbed his stomach. "Our breakfasts aren't settled yet, sir. Aunt Phronie stuffed us like Christmas geese." His eyes sparkled and he clapped an arm around Charlie. "Anyhow, we have to hurry. No telling what's going to happen at Saint Louis!"

"Some buttermilk would taste mighty good, though," said Charlie.

He wouldn't look at Christy as he loosened his cinch, but, when Beth came pelting up, he knelt to hug her, face buried in her hair. *He doesn't want to do this,* Christy thought in sad triumph. *He still believes what we do, but he's married to a Jardine.*

Eyes blurring, she started for the well house. Adjacent to the well, the small log structure had troughs made from large hollowed logs around three sides. Every other day, water was drained from these by spigots and flowed to the maiden blush apple trees before fresh water from the well was poured in to cool the jugs and crocks.

Selecting a big crockery pitcher of gold-speckled buttermilk, Christy turned. Travis filled the door. He took the pitcher from her and set it in the trough. Before she could guess his intention, he caught her in his arms and kissed her soundly.

Something female in her responded to his strength, the warm ardor of his mouth, but this was overwhelmed by outrage. Planting her hands against his chest, she shoved him away.

"Why, Christy, sister-in-law!" His voice caressed her in mock hurt. "Surely you won't grudge a farewell kiss to a man going to fight for his country!"

"It's not *my* country, Travis, or my brother's, either."

"It is, since he married into us." Travis took her hands so urgently she didn't pull away. He still was smiling, but with an underlying earnestness she'd never known in him. "Christy, if we got married, you and I, we could save our families the aggravation of getting used to a new set of in-laws."

"What?"

"You heard me well enough."

She shook her head in half-amused disbelief. "That's the strangest reason I've ever heard for a marriage. It's not a very good one. I don't love you, and I don't think you love me."

He wasn't laughing now. "I may not love you, but you're the one I can't forget."

"That's because I don't swoon in your arms."

"No. It's because you're you. I think the world of Charlie. Just seems natural to love his sister."

"Travis," she chided, between sympathy and annoyance, "you think you have to ride off with some lady's favor, the way knights trailed a glove or scarf from their lances!"

"Couldn't we be engaged?"

"Of course not, you ridiculous boy! Even if I adored you, I wouldn't be engaged to a Rebel."

"Your own brother's one."

"Only because he married into your family. I'm sorry for him with all my heart . . . and just as sorry for us." She hadn't meant to upbraid Travis, but she couldn't contain her most terrible fear. "What if he has to fight Thos? Maybe be on different sides in the same battle?"

"Now, Christy, that's not likely. . . ."

"All the boys and men on both sides have mothers. Most have sisters. Some even have children. Think how your mother and Melissa will mourn if you don't come back."

He was completely sober now. "They'd suffer more if I failed in honor."

"Honor! That's a man's word. Women care about life."

"This trouble's boiled and bubbled along for years. It's got to be settled once and for all." Travis's buoyant nature erupted in laughter. "Don't look so sad, sweetheart! We'll only have to whip the bluecoats roundly a few times before Lincoln sees he has to let the South go. Why, I bet the Yanks run so fast there won't be many of them killed!"

"Thos won't run. Dan O'Brien and his friends won't." Christy swallowed at tightness in her throat. "If the whole thing could just stop right now. . . ." Ducking her head, she brushed past him.

The young men stood outside to drink two mugs apiece of the tangy buttermilk. No one said much. Charlie gazed at the animals in their pens and pastures, the blooming fruit trees, the greening fields, promising and beautiful after last year's drought. Robbie pressed close to him, worshiping. What could animals think of their beloveds' comings and goings except say with mute devotion, I'd never leave you. Wherever you are is heaven.

"I always hated hoeing corn above everything." Charlie picked up Robbie and cradled him against his shoulder. "You know, I'd like right well to hoe that field. And pull fodder when the ears are grown, carry it to the barn in the light of the harvest moon."

"Oh, we'll be home in time for roasting ears!" Travis bragged. "But first we have to go. Give us a kiss for luck, E-liz-a-*beth.*"

Beth didn't shriek with glee as she usually did when Travis gave her all the syllables of her name. She kissed him solemnly. "Please don't kill Danny or Thos!"

As he stared at her, crimsoning, she threw herself on Charlie, hugging him around the waist, burying her face against his midriff. "Be careful, Charlie! Please . . . please don't get crippled or killed!"

He put down the dog and knelt to embrace his sister. "I'll be careful, Bethie. Listen, I'll tell you a nice secret." His glance swept to his parents and Christy. "About the time pawpaws and wild grapes are ripe this fall, you'll be Aunt Beth." She blinked. "I mean," he said pridefully, "that we're going to have a baby. Melissa is. So will you promise to love and help her?"

"Oh, Charlie, yes!" Her joy faded. She looked beseechingly at her parents. "We will go see the baby, won't we?"

"If we possibly can," Jonathan said, nodding.

Ellen embraced her tall oldest son. "We'll do anything we can for Melissa and the baby, dear. Be sure of that."

"I am." He kissed her and turned to Christy, blue eyes asking a question.

It wasn't the time to say the Jardines might not welcome them to Rose Haven. The only smile she was able to summon felt stiff on her lips. "I hope the baby's a boy and looks exactly like you, Charlie."

"Poor infant!"

Travis kissed Beth and Ellen, swept Christy a teasing bow, and shook hands with Jonathan. "Save some roasting ears for us, sir."

Robbie began to whimper as the young men tightened their cinches and mounted. They paused at the eastern timber edge and waved. The family waved back till the two vanished into the fresh-leafed trees. Beth ran to cuddle Robbie and be consoled in turn.

Jonathan said almost under his breath: "Instead of pulling fodder, I fear they'll be fodder of another kind. Both sides waste seed corn when our best and bravest youngsters go off to fight."

"All we can do is pray . . . that every mother's son comes home, be they for North or South." Ellen scanned Christy. "You were a long time in the well house with Travis."

"Oh, Travis!" Christy grinned and shrugged. "I should have given him my apron to flaunt from his helmet!"

They all laughed. Ellen's voice was relieved. "You . . . you don't love him, then?"

"Not a bit." Christy looked at her parents and tears filled her eyes. "It's Dan I love!" she burst out. "But he won't marry me because he's afraid he'll be killed and . . . and our baby might have as hard a time as he did."

"He's thinking of you, child," Jonathan said. "I respect him for that."

"It'd serve him right if I did marry Travis!"

Ellen looked shocked. "You won't, surely?"

"Of course, I won't! But I don't see why Dan has to be so stubborn."

"Because he's man, not a lad like Travis." Jonathan smiled and touched her cheek. "That's why you love him, Daughter."

They went back to their work. As she chopped weeds away from the growing stalks, Christy prayed for Charlie, for all the boys who would go for soldiers before they were really men.

Why was Travis still a boy while Dan, who had lived the same twenty years, was not? Travis had driven ox teams on Western trails, seen silver camps and wild life, but he hadn't endured the grief and hardship that gave Dan strength and made him so early a man. Most of all, perhaps, Travis didn't have Dan's song.

CHAPTER TWENTY-TWO

Dan's new black Army brogans pinched his left toes, but he was glad to have them. The last vestiges of his old shoes had been cut to shreds by flint rocks, shreds that melted in the sucking mud of summer rains as the hastily mustered 1st and 2nd Kansas Volunteer Infantry Regiments toiled south from Kansas City with Major Sturgis's Regulars, joined General Lyon's Regulars and the 1st Iowa Volunteer Infantry Regiment, and marched some more, building ferries and pontoon bridges to cross the swollen Grand and Osage Rivers.

Lyon was getting no chance to practice the graces he'd learned at dancing school in Fort Scott only last winter. He'd saved the St. Louis arsenal for the Uunion by forcing the surrender of Governor Claib Jackson's militia and chased the governor and his forces commanded by General Sterling Price out of Boonville and the capital of Jefferson City. This gave the Union control of the Missouri

River and East-West travel and supply routes, vital once the Confederacy had declared war May 6th. Bitterly divided, Tennessee completed the Confederated States in June, making the fourth border state to join the seven of the deep South.

When rumors spread like prairie fire that Price was gathering men in southwest Missouri to reclaim the state and invade Kansas, Dan O'Brien, Owen Parks, Andy McHugh, and Theo Wattles left off cultivating the best corn crop they'd ever seen and rode to Leavenworth in early June to join the forming regiment. David Parks and one of the Nickel boys, begging to the last to enlist, had come along to lead back the horses.

"You're only seventeen," Owen admonished his younger brother. "Father needs you."

"Harriet and your young 'uns need *you*!" David retorted, green eyes brilliant with held-back tears of anger and disappointment.

"I'm only enlisting for three months." Owen tousled David's curly black hair. "Cheer up! When I come home, Father's agreed you can volunteer if you're still set on it."

"The war'll be over!" David blinked and added bitterly: "And by then we'll have the fodder in the barn and the corn cribbed . . . probably even have plowed under the stubble!" But he hugged his brother quick and hard as they parted, hugged Dan, too.

There'd been no uniforms and few weapons. In fact only day before yesterday, August 8th, had a wagon train of clothing finally rolled into Springfield, supplying Dan's shoes, forage cap, and dark blue fatigue blouse with yellow buttons. At Leavenworth, Dan and the other recruits were lucky to be issued Springfield rifles, haversacks, canteens, and oilcloths. Dan passed up an Army blanket to keep the soft warm striped one Christy had given him when he had told her good bye. Rolled inside the oilcloth along with his newly issued socks, the blanket comforted Dan so much that he never swore at the bedroll slung in front from left shoulder to right hip. Christy. Christy and the sweetness of her lips.

So now, partly uniformed after two months in service, marching in the darkness of what might be the last morning of his life along the Little York Road from Springfield, Dan at last felt like a soldier. Of course, on the first and second days of that sweltering month, he'd sweated and choked on dust the sixteen miles to Dug Springs where there'd been a skirmish. Price's Missouri troops broke and ran under artillery fire and cavalry pursuit. The Union volunteer companies were held in reserve while better-trained and equipped Regulars fought the Rebels. Dan's sweat had turned icy and the looseness of his bowels wasn't entirely from three weeks of eating nothing much but fresh-slaughtered beef with no salt, but the fracas had been a lot of smoke, racket, and shooting with only four Union soldiers killed and six injured. The Confederates lost a few more.

Light casualties? Total, if you were one who died. Still, the small victory lifted the spirits of Lyon's badly outnumbered army that had shrunk in even this week since Dug Springs. Three-month volunteer enlistments had run out for three thousand of his seven thousand men, including the 1st Iowa.

They had agreed to stay for a battle, and then they were going home, glad to see the last of an army that once passed on to them a beef carcass so putrid the Regulars had turned it down. The Iowans turned their outrage into a joke, burying the beef with full military honors. Now they marched so close behind Dan that he could hear Bill Heustis's ritual lament: "I wish I'd stayed home and sent my big brother."

"How do you want us to bury you, Bill?" joked another Iowan.

"Well, see you make me a good coffin out of sycamore wood and use brass tacks to hammer on my name and. . . ." He considered a moment. "I want it to say . . . 'I am a-going to be a great big he-angel.' "

"We don't have that many tacks. Besides, Billy, you're more likely to wind up in the other place."

"Not me!" Heustis laughed. He launched

into the song to which the Iowans, down through Missouri, trod on the heels of the Regulars or, when put in the lead, left them far behind. Lyon grumbled at the "damned Iowa greyhounds" and predicted that they sang too much to be good fighters.

The time of retribution am a-coming,
For with bayonet and shell
We will give the Rebels hell;
And they'll never see the Happy Land of
    Canaan. . . .

Slowly, then spreading with mounting gusto from back ranks to front, the Kansans joined in. They were still miles and hours out of earshot of the Confederate forces camped along Wilson's Creek where the Rebels could forage for roasting ears in bottom land fields and graze their thousands of horses and mules. Dan sang, too, but it was his mother's lullabies that sounded in his head, and the tune he'd made for Christy.

He'd left his fiddle in her care. Would he ever play for her again? What was she doing just now? He couldn't believe he'd die, but he supposed no one ever did. He was going to sleep on his feet when the order came to halt. He drowsed, leaning on his rifle, till the march resumed. They might plod only a few minutes to stop again. For what seemed hours, companies and regiments shifted around in the darkness. Caissons and artillery groaned by, blankets muting their wheels, but not Company F's commander, Captain James Totten.

"Forward that caisson, God damn you, sir!" he ordered in his soft Virginia drawl. "Mind that gun!" A profane, hard-drinking, card-playing West Point classmate of General Lyon's, the only thing Totten shared with his commander was being a tough soldier.

"Don't he cuss polite?" admired Billy Heustis. "I'd walk five miles just to listen to him."

A dark shape loomed up and paused. "This is what we came for, boys!" softly called Colonel George Washington Deitzler, the brigade commander. "Colonel Sigel and his brigade will attack from the other direction. We'll have the enemy caught between us." His horse faded away with sack-muffled hoofs.

"Caught?" growled an Iowan. "The Rebs have three to five men to our one. Be lucky if they don't just bust out like homebrew popping corks!"

Dan didn't care to think about that, so he mulled over what he knew about Deitzler. During the Border Ruffians' invasions, he'd risked his life to go to New England and bring back Sharps breechloaders for the Free State men around Lawrence. As soon as Lincoln called for volunteers, he'd organized the 1st Kansas, which along with the 2nd Kansas,

1st Iowa, and Captain Wright's Home Guards, made up the 4th Brigade.

The 2nd's own commander, Colonel Mitchell, reined in next. Dan couldn't see his face, but he'd know that genial, booming voice anywhere. "We won't be in reserve this time, lads . . . or not for long. You may not get another crack at the bushwhackers before your enlistment's up, so make it count!"

Robert Mitchell had brought his law books and hollyhock seeds to Linn County from Ohio during the worst of the border troubles. He had defeated Charles Hamelton for a seat in the territorial legislature, and, after Hamelton shot the captives at Marais des Cygnes, Mitchell had pursued with a party of neighbors.

Dan tried to wipe that day from his memory, all except Christy's scent of lilacs and blue dress, but the rest flooded back — the joy of Susie's and Andy's wedding changing to horror as men rode up with Reverend Reed whose bowels thrust out of his bloodied clothing, the ox-drawn wagon driven by a tow-headed twelve-year-old boy whose father lay dead in back while his mother tried to tend and comfort four bleeding men lying on the featherbeds while the other sun-bonneted woman cradled her terribly wounded husband.

Were some of Hamelton's bunch in Price's army? Likely. Even likelier that scores of

Clarke's raiders were, unless the marauders who'd burned out the Nickels and other families were afraid to face men with guns.

What about Osawatomie? whispered a voice like Jonathan Ware's. *What of the men hacked to death with short swords, two little more than boys? What about Charlie Ware?*

Dan prayed he'd never have to fight Christy's brother. He didn't even want to fight Travis Jardine. He didn't want to fight anyone. He just couldn't stand to see his America torn apart and rotted with slavery, his new country where he had grown up with a chance in life, instead of starving.

Tramping on his right, Andy McHugh put Dan's feelings into words. "Looks like there ought to be a better way of settling things than making men kill each other who'd a sight rather not."

Ahead of Andy but close enough to hear, Owen flung over his shoulder: "I'm a Quaker, Andy, but we've got to fight if we want our children to live in a country uncursed by slavery."

"The war's not about slavery, lads," wheezed Bedad Tompkins, the oldest man in the company. Because the grizzled, stubby fifty-year-old had fought in the Mexican War, he'd been made a sergeant and put in charge of drilling the recruits. "It's about saving the Union."

"Whatever it's about," called Bill Heustis

from the Iowans, "I wish I'd stayed at home and sent my big brother!"

It began to drizzle, livening the smell of earth and hay and grain fields. Some corn was shoulder high, blades whispering sibilantly, but much was heaped in shocks. The oats and wheat had been harvested. Dan treasured in his knapsack two biscuits made of flour from wheat a militia captain had bought in a field, cut with his men, and taken to a mill to be ground. How good bread tasted after nothing but tough beef, boiled, charred, or raw!

Of the supplies Lyon had been begging from the renowned Pathfinder, General John Charles Frémont, commander of the newly created Department of Missouri, only the belated issue of clothing and shoes had come. The rest, if there was more, was piled up in Rolla where the railroad ended. According to what trickled down to the soldiers, Frémont had some grand scheme to occupy the whole Mississippi Valley. He faced east, not west, and the higher-ups in the capital weren't going to worry much about what happened in southwestern Missouri after the Union defeat at Bull Run in Virginia on July 21st, when fleeing soldiers ran pell-mell into Congressmen and sight-seers who'd driven out from Washington that fine Sunday to watch their Army whip the Rebels.

"Fall out, boys," called Sergeant Bedad.

"Find as dry a place as you can and sleep with your weapons. You may need 'em in a hurry."

"Here's a haystack, Dan!" called Owen.

As many as could burrowed under the fragrant hay while others sheltered by corn shocks and fence rows or other haystacks. Dan took off his waist belt on which hung his percussion cap box and scabbarded bayonet, and slipped off the cartridge box he wore slung over his left shoulder. He shoved them under the hay and unfolded his oilcloth, careful to keep it under and over his prized blanket.

Sighing with the bliss of being free of his gear, he sipped from his canteen and munched the biscuits before putting his extra socks in the haversack to use as a pillow beneath the blanket. "Still seems peculiar to be marching past fields, instead of working in them."

"Aye." Andy McHugh spoke through whatever he'd saved from his supper. "Likely the Rebels have feasted fine on fresh corn. Wish they'd left us some."

"Andy! How'd you like it if soldiers ate the corn you planted and battled weeds out of, so that Susie and your mother got none?"

"I'd purely hate it," growled Andy. "But it's what'll happen, you can bet, if we don't rearrange General Price's notions. Anyhow, Dan, Sergeant Bedad says when you're fighting across farmland like this, what one side doesn't take, the other will."

"It's stealing, nevertheless," Owen said quietly.

Andy snorted. "Susie's trying hard, Owen, but she hasn't made a Quaker out of me yet."

"I promised Mother not to do anything I'd be ashamed to tell her about," Theo said wistfully. "If I get killed tomorrow. . . ."

"None of us is going to get killed, lad," Andy said with gruff kindness. "Keep close to me and remember what Bedad's cussed into us."

"But the Rebels have almost twenty thousand men," muttered Theo. "We only have about fifty-six hundred."

"Yes, but General McCulloch doesn't have any faith in Pap Price's volunteers," countered Owen. "Calls them the Huckleberry Cavalry! Says they're great roasting ear foragers but poor soldiers. He claims his Confederate commission outranks Price's as commander of Missouri's State Guard and wouldn't help Price till Price agreed to let him run the whole shebang."

"McCulloch's fifty years old and been fighting close to half of them," said Andy. "He was with Sam Houston when the Texans whipped the Mexicans at San Jacinto, and then, same as Price, was in the war with Mexico. Next, he was a Texas Ranger captain, and then, just during the Mormon war three years ago, he managed to talk Brigham Young and the Mormon elders into agreeing to obey the laws of the United States rather than fight an all out war."

Owen shrugged. "He may have a persuasive tongue, but neither he nor Albert Pike could talk the Cherokee chief, John Ross, into allying with the South. Pike did get promises of support from some of the Creeks, Choctaws, Chickasaws, and Seminoles."

"Choctaws!" breathed Dan. "They gave money to help feed the Irish!"

"Did they now?" Andy lifted a reddish eyebrow. "Well, it's natural they'd feel for starving folk after they were driven from the East thirty years ago like the rest of the Five Civilized Tribes."

"They've got no cause, any of them, to love the Union," said Owen. "But they've begun to prosper in the Territory. I'm bound most of them want no part of this white man's war. McCulloch has the ticklish job of keeping the Union out of Indian Territory without invading it himself. That's how come him to be in Fort Smith with his Texans and regiments from Louisiana and Arkansas."

"The Rebs have lots more cavalry than we do," Andy mused, "but we have sixteen guns to their fifteen, so that'll help."

"Bedad says cannon balls aren't so bad." Theo sounded as if he were trying to cheer up himself and his friends. "Balls kill whatever they drop on, but that's seldom more than one or two men. It's canister, grapeshot, and shrapnel shell that can kill a dozen men and wound more all at once."

"They do say," commented Andy, "that Henry Shrapnel invented spherical case shot during the siege of Gibraltar in the Seventeen Nineties. Wanted to get the same results as heavy musket fire but at long range. He filled a hollow cannon ball with musket balls and gunpowder and added a time fuse. Sometimes the shell exploded before it got out of the cannon, so Shrapnel hit on the notion of attaching the musket balls with resin around a tin tube of gunpowder with the fuse on top. He got his musket volley."

"Yes," grunted Owen, "except one of Major Totten's artillerymen told me some of the balls go sideways or upwards and don't hit the target."

"I hope the ones aimed at us all go sideways," Theo said so comically that they all laughed before they lay down with their rifles.

Dan longed to take off the tight new shoes and debated comfort against the extra minutes it would take to put them on if they were hurriedly ordered up. He finally compromised by loosening the laces and holding his legs up in the air for a while to let the blood drain from his swollen feet into his body the way the men often did on hard marches. Then he shifted around till he rested as easy as he was going to, and pulled Christy's blanket against him.

Did a faint trace of her lilac odor linger beneath his own and the smell of campfires and mildew? Dan didn't want to think of the coming battle. Instead, as he did every night, he thought of Christy. She might have helped her father pull fodder, or perhaps she'd churned. At this very moment, she might be spinning wool like that in his blanket, or mending, knitting, or working at the loom while her mother played the piano.

Soon now the Wares would go to bed. He stopped his thoughts there — almost. Some night, some heaven of a night, would he hold Christy instead of his rifle? He huddled as much of the blanket as he could against his face and dropped into sleep.

It only seemed a minute till he roused at Sergeant Bedad's urgent voice. "Up, boys! Fall in! Don't make a sound! We want to catch the Rebs with their breeches down."

Fingers of light streaked the eastern sky, but it was still too dark to see much. Dan took a swig of water to wash down the night smell of his mouth, tightened and tied his shoe laces, and put on his accouterments before shaking hay off his blanket and oilcloth and rolling them up. As always, he tucked John Brown's New Testament into his extra shirt. How Brown would have loved to march with them! But only if he could command.

Breath seemed to thicken and clog Dan's chest. He had to strain hard to get any air. Grasping his Springfield, he took his place beside Andy. It was light enough now to make out the red bands stitched across the front of Company E's blue-gray hunting shirts.

All companies of the 1st Iowa wore different outfits. Few had traded them for Army issue when they'd finally had the chance. With a chill, Dan realized that with so many differently uniformed volunteer outfits on both sides, it might be close to impossible to tell friend from foe.

"Don't be down-hearted, boys, that we're in reserve," admonished Bedad as the troops moved into line of battle. "Before this day is over, you'll get all the fighting you want!"

"Don't the Rebs have pickets out?" Dan whispered to Andy.

A fusillade shattered the hush. The roll of drums reverberated beneath shouted commands. "Look!" Owen jerked his head. "Yonder in the oaks! See the tents?"

Then they were marching down a hollow and couldn't see the Confederates till they reached the level and could look along Wilson's Creek and the Telegraph Road turning under the bluff below. In encampments spread farther than the eye could reach among farms and fields, men scrambled into lines or ran for their horses.

"Didn't know there was that many Rebs in

the world," Bill Heustis muttered. "Oh, I wish I'd stayed at home and. . . ."

"First Kansas, forward!" yelled Colonel George Washington Deitzler. "Second Kansas, First Iowa, you and the Home Guards are in reserve till needed. Guard the wagons and pick up stragglers."

Totten's cannon roared. From across the creek thundered an answering blast. "Sigel got there." Bedad shrugged. "Maybe having his brigade over there will work out after all, 'specially since we took the Rebs by surprise." He spat a brown curl of tobacco juice on the grass. "Why on earth didn't they have pickets out?" He spat again. " 'Nother good thing is a Reb prisoner says a thousand or more of Price's volunteers don't have weapons. They're supposed to get them off dead or wounded, their men or ours. More'n likely they'll get in the way and cause a sight more trouble than they're worth."

"I didn't come all the way from Iowa to be stuck back with the wagons," grumbled Heustis. "Wish we could get the fightin' done while that nice little breeze is a-blowin'."

"Reckon the boys up ahead feel plenty warm right now," said Andy.

There was a farm cabin on their right a little way ahead. A woman stood in the door a moment as if uncertain of what to do. At the next bellow of Totten's guns, she ducked into the house and rushed out with a sack and crying baby. She grabbed a howling toddler by the hand and made for the timber where two older children could be glimpsed leading a cow and a mule.

"Doesn't seem right to be fighting all over these farms, scaring off the women and kids," said Dan.

"Where else are we going to fight?" asked Owen unhappily. He had to be thinking, as was Dan, of Harriet and Lydia, Susie and Christy, of all the women back home. "They don't mark off some big empty place a long ways from anybody and call it a battlefield."

"I still wish. . . ." Dan broke off.

"The Rebel cavalry's retreating!" hissed Andy. "There goes Colonel Deitzler with the First Kansas! Must be the First Missouri with them. Look at them go! They're chasing the Rebs right up that hill!"

"Wish we was there!" shrilled Heustis. "Our boys must be lookin' down at the whole dang' Confederate Army!"

"Their artillery's openin' up! Hark! That's Old Sacramento!" Bedad's voice thrilled with the delight of meeting an old friend, even if it was once again an enemy cannon. "She's made out of melted Mexican church bells. I was at Sacramento when we took her. She sings because silver was mixed in the metal when a crack had to be mended once."

"I've heard songs I liked better." Dan's throat was so dry he couldn't swallow. Banners flew and drums beat as a detachment of Regulars and Home Guards advanced on a cornfield on the other side of the creek where a swarm of Confederates took cover to shoot at Lyon's main force as they marched toward the Rebels who were spread out across two miles of farm land and scrub oak and hazel. Handsome roan horses galloped past, six horse teams hauling each caisson or gun as a Union battery took positions to cover the men plunging across the creek to the high green corn.

Unlimbered guns spewed grapeshot and canister over the heads of the Union soldiers to explode among the Rebels. The 1st Iowa was ordered forward to support the battery. Then Rebel guns opened up.

An unearthly scream ripped through the din of cannon, muskets, and the cries of wounded men and horses. "That caisson's wheel horse!" cried Owen. "A cannon ball tore off his shoulder!"

Someone mercifully shot the animal. It was impossible to see much of what was going on in the high corn, but apparently the Rebels had clustered near a farmhouse. The Union battery sent two shells into the house, but there were too many of the enemy for the detachment to prevail. After what seemed forever but was perhaps an hour, the thinned Union force retreated.

Billy Heustis had no jokes as the 1st Iowa

straggled back to the envious but appalled 2nd Kansas. At least a score of faces Dan had come to recognize were missing. Other men had roughly bandaged wounds. They sank down in the shade of wagons or scrub trees, drank from their canteens, and devoured any food saved from supper since no rations had been issued that morning.

"Well done, lads!" cried Bedad. "You kept the Rebs from blasting away the main army's flank."

"Yeah," drawled Heustis. "They blasted us instead. But I reckon" — some of his old grin came back — "that we're showing Lyon we can fight, even if we do sing more'n he likes."

Up in front someone yelled: "Totten's battery's blowing up a good five acres of supply wagons! Look at 'em burn! Now he's limbering the guns and making for the battle."

"Can you see the lines?" Bedad roared through cupped hands.

"Maybe, if I shinny up that big tree." In a few minutes, the same voice carried faintly to them, along with the black smoke of the burning supply wagons. "Our boys are spread out three deep for a thousand yards along the ridge. There's not more'n a few hundred yards between them and the Rebs who're headed up the hill." In another moment: "Musket smoke's drifting east, away from our line into the Rebs. Can't hardly see 'em."

"Which means they can't see our boys,"

grunted Bedad. " 'Course that don't keep 'em from firing. Lordy Lord! Old Sacramento sings this day! Wish she was ours."

"Aren't we ever going to get to fight?" Andy growled.

"Be sure we will," Bedad promised.

After the tumult, it grew suddenly quiet. The man in the tree shouted: "The Rebs are pulling back down the bluff to Wilson's Creek! Looks like they're reforming along the Telegraph Road."

Colonel Mitchell loomed out of the smoke. "Second Kansas!" he called, already wheeling his bay horse. "Come on! We've got our fight!"

CHAPTER TWENTY-THREE

Dan's legs didn't seem to belong to him as they tramped through the scrub at Bedad's commands. A battery clattered past and stopped to the right of Dan's company. Up the slope, beyond the unlimbering guns, Colonel Deitzler was regrouping the 1st Kansas. What was left of the 1st Iowa was forming to the left. Beyond them, left, faintly droned the cool Virginia voice of Captain Totten, politely damning his artillerymen.

When his legs stopped at Bedad's shout, Dan looked straight at a Rebel battery, long barrels snouting up the hill. Infantry massed on either side of the guns with cavalry on the left flank and more infantry, cavalry, and guns spread out to the right, even beyond Wilson's Creek. Then Dan's bewildered gaze fixed on a rag-tag force boiling up the slope. Some wore uniforms, but more were in homespun like Missouri Home Guards, long knives belted to their sides, squirrel rifles in their hands.

"Whose side are they on?" rumbled Bedad, biting the end off a cartridge. "They're carrying the Union flag, but they've got the Confederate one, too!"

A volley from the advancing throng answered him. The battle erupted all along the line. Mitchell waved his sword and swept the 2nd Kansas over the ridge.

Dan bit the end off the paper cartridge and ordered his hand not to shake as he poured powder down the barrel. With what was left of the paper for patching, he rammed the bullet home with the iron ramrod that was carried in a groove in the stock beneath the barrel. He eared back the hammer and put a tiny copper percussion cap on the nipple opening into the powder chamber.

"Don't aim above their knees!" Bedad shouted.

Blinding white smoke stung Dan's eyes and nostrils. Cannon fire splintered trees and sent branches and slivers flying. Squinting at a shadow dodging through the fog of dust and smoke, Dan squeezed the trigger.

The something screeched and melted into the dust.

Colonel Mitchell pitched from his saddle. Lyon took shape in the smoke. His splendid gray must have been shot from under him for he rode another horse. He swept off his hat in a flourish that revealed a bloody bandage over the wound that had bled downward to mat his wiry red beard.

"Come on, my brave boys! I'll lead you!" Then he jerked high in the saddle.

Except for a glimpse of him being carried to the rear, that was the last Dan saw of the tough little general.

Stunned, unable to believe the fiery will that had inspired and driven them was gone as well as their own colonel, the 2nd faltered in their headlong assault, but, before the Rebels could break their line, Lieutenant Colonel Charles Blair of the 2nd took command and urged them on.

Dan yelled with the others as they fought almost rifle barrel to rifle barrel. The shaggy Rebel in front of Dan raced him to load, showing strong yellow side teeth as he bit the cartridge although there were several gaps in his front teeth. He was fitting his percussion cap on the nipple when Dan pulled the trigger and lunged over the body while it was still settling to the ground.

No time to feel. No time to think. Load and fire. Load and fire. Cannon balls spat from the smoke, canister and grapeshot knocked down swaths of writhing, screaming men as a scythe mows grain. One row of Rebels dropped to their bellies to shoot from the shelter of the scrub while the next rank knelt, and the last stood, each line covering the others as they loaded and aimed.

Shooting from at least a little shelter appealed to Dan. He dropped to the ground behind a thick, dwarfed hazel, poked his Springfield through it, and fired into smoke and commotion. When he tried to reload in that position, he found that he couldn't pour the powder down the muzzle, so he compromised by kneeling. The air was thick and dust laden with bits of grass, twigs, and chipped rock. Dan, with his comrades, battled the Rebels inch by inch down the slope.

From the corner of his eye, he glimpsed Rebel cavalry plunging through heavy growth to the left. Totten waited till they were close and blew them away with a hail of canister.

The Rebel infantry retreated down the hill. Dan stopped shooting, panting as he leaned on his rifle. Blood dripped on his hand.

"You're hit!" cried Owen.

Dan wiped his arm across his temple. "Can't be much."

Owen produced a handkerchief. "Let me bandage it." As he did, he muttered: "Where's Colonel Sigel? If he'd catch the Rebels from behind. . . ."

"He must be done for," said Bedad. "I heard an artilleryman yelling that the Rebs are firing Sigel's cannon balls at us." The graying old sergeant put a bracing hand on Dan's shoulder. "Don't lose heart, boys! Haven't we held this hill against all the Rebs could throw at us?"

"One of their outfits dropped its flag," Andy

noticed. It fluttered among heaps of dead one hundred yards ahead. Andy was starting for it when a horseman rode out of a thicket, trotting forward.

"He wants to surrender," Bedad guessed. "Don't shoot, lads."

"Don't shoot!" Dan called up the line. Others repeated the caution till it was almost a chant.

The rider came on slowly. About twenty yards from the flag, he spurred forward, snatched up the banner, whirled his mount, and dashed for safety. No one fired. Nor did they shoot at the wounded Rebel who caught a riderless horse and hauled himself into the saddle.

As heat and the sense of danger ebbed from him, Dan never wanted to fire again. Blasted bodies were strewn up and down that scrubby hill. He almost wished for the roar of cannon to drown out the moans and pleadings.

A Rebel who looked younger than David lay half under two dead men. "Thirsty . . . ," came his weak voice. "So thirsty. . . ."

Although his own mouth was parched, Dan went to the boy. When he tried to lift him, Dan's hand dug into a pulp of blood and flesh. The yellow-haired lad didn't seem to feel it. Sickened, Dan shifted his fingers till he found a solid shoulder blade and raised the youngster, holding the canteen to his cracked lips.

The lad swallowed. His blue eyes flickered over Dan's face. He swallowed again. With great effort, he grinned. "If I meet you in hell, Yank, I'll give you a swig."

He took one more swallow. Something went out of him. The grin faded. He stared straight into the dirty white sun broiling down from the zenith through a pall of smoke.

Andy shook Dan's arm. "Back in line, Danny! That looks like Sigel's men crossing the creek, but if it isn't. . . . The devil with both sides having uniforms that look near the same!" He peered under his hand. "It must be Sigel! They're carrying the Union flag and our artillery isn't firing."

Dan wiped the boy's blood off on his pants and went back to his place. The cry of a Union skirmisher, downslope from the main force, carried on the thin breeze. "Not Sigel! Rebs!"

The Confederates opened fire all along their advancing line. From their uniforms, these were new troops, fresh and rested.

Colonel Blair shouted: "Down, men, so our guns can fire over your heads! Fire at will!"

The Union artillery withered the Rebels with shells and balls, but the attackers surged forward over the bodies of their dead and wounded. In spite of his awkward position, Dan managed to get enough powder down the muzzle to shoot. He ran out of cartridges and caps, but wormed over to a dead Iowan and got his.

A huge man in a tall black cap and duster rode up and down to encourage the Rebels. "Big as his horse!" gasped Andy. "Must be Pap Price. Look! He's bleeding from his side. Must not be too bad. He's riding on."

The sun blazed down on the sweltering men. Dan's lips cracked and bled as he bit off cartridge tails. How could the Rebels keep coming, uphill, with canister exploding amongst them like scores of muskets fired at close range?

A choked cry came from beside him. Dan looked sideways. Andy's face welled blood. His rifle and ramrod dropped from his fingers.

"Andy!" Dan cried.

No answer. The Rebels were swarming up the slope. Dan wriggled in front of Andy, and for the first time fired with real hatred, reloaded, fired again.

After what seemed eternity, the Rebels broke off the assault and retreated down the hill across the bodies of their many comrades who had fallen in the three attempts to take it.

A little scrub-grown hill in southwest Missouri.

Dan raised to stare at Andy and breathed his name. There was no answer. Andy's chest labored to rise and fall. Dan got his new socks from his bedroll and doubled one over the bleeding jaw.

"Hold that tight as you can," he told Owen who had hurried up and was cradling Andy's head and shoulders.

"There's no wound in back," said Owen. "If there's a ball, it's lodged inside."

Dan wet the other sock with his canteen and cleaned Andy's face as gently as he could. Blood mixed with clear fluid ran from Andy's nose and seeped from his ear. Freckles splotched his pale, clammy skin. He breathed, fast and shallow.

"I'm afraid the ball tore through his jaw and hit his brain," Owen whispered. "Remember that man who fell at the mill and cracked his head? Watery looking stuff ran from his nose and ears. The doctor said it came from around his brain."

"Poor laddie," Bedad sighed. "Nothing you can do for him, boys. Fall in. Major Sturgis is in command now. We're retreating to Springfield."

"But we drove the Rebs off the hill!" Dan gasped.

"Yes, but they'll be back. That flag the Rebs waved on their last charge was Sigel's. One of his sergeants rode up to say the Rebs overran him. They wore gray uniforms. Sigel thought they were the Iowans and didn't open fire till it was too late." Bedad spit tobacco at a shattered oak stump. "We're running out of ammunition."

"Maybe they are, too." Dan couldn't believe they were abandoning this hill that cost so dearly. Cost Andy.

"Maybe. But Sturgis says to march."

"I can't leave Andy." Owen's mouth trembled. "He's my brother-in-law, Sergeant. How could I tell my sister I walked away?"

"He's not got long." Bedad's tone was gruff. "If he's still alive when the surgeon's party comes around, they'll move him in a wagon."

"You go, Owen." Dan moved over to take Andy from Owen's arms. "You've got a wife and children, and now Susie's going to need you, too."

"But. . . ."

"Go on. I'll catch up."

Bedad squinted through the acrid haze. "Did I hear you say, Private O'Brien, that you're too fagged to move, but you'll be after us soon?"

"Yes, sir."

Bedad gave Owen a push. "Fall in, Private."

Owen took a few long swallows from his canteen and tossed it to Dan. "You need it more than I do. Bring it when you come."

Marching feet shuffled away to the beat of drums. Artillery rattled up the slope. Dan watched his shrunken company vanish over the ridge followed by the depleted Iowans. He had never felt so alone.

"Andy?"

Dan wet his friend's mouth and drank himself. Andy, come all the way from misty Skye to die on this hill. Why? At least Susie had his baby. She'd be helped by her family. But. . . .

Drums rolled below. Shouted commands faintly reached Dan's ears. My God! The Rebs were coming again! Up over the human wreckage that littered the hill.

Dan slumped over Andy so as not to seem a living target. The Rebels toiled past several hundred yards to the side. Dan felt the vibrations of their feet. Thousands of them.

How could so many be left? He breathed the mingled scents of grass, dust, excrement, urine, and gunpowder. A loud cheer sounded and resounded from the top of the ridge.

The Rebels had the hill without a struggle this time, the hill so many had died on. What did it matter, now that no one was fighting over it? Neither army lived here. They'd march away, the lucky ones, while the dead mulched the fields. Warily farm families would come back to trampled crops, wasted grain, ruined fences, blasted houses and barns. It wouldn't matter to them which side had done the damage for which they'd suffer through the winter.

It was high noon when the rejoicing Confederates streamed down the hill to what was left of their camps. Andy still breathed. He had never opened his eyes or spoken, but faint hope kindled in Dan. Maybe the brain wasn't affected. Maybe if Dan got him into some shade till an ambulance wagon came, Andy might live. Freeing Andy of his bedroll, haversack, and rifle, Dan left his rifle beside the pile and struggled up with Andy's limp arm gathered around his neck. Andy was lean but so was Dan. He stumbled through bodies and brush toward a blackjack oak that promised shelter although half the trunk and limbs were blown away.

Panting, Dan didn't hear the horsemen till they were almost upon him. "Look, Quantrill!" The laughing voice was disturbingly familiar. "Two Yanks for target practice!"

Dan dropped, shielding Andy beneath him, but a ball thunked into the back of Andy's neck, splattering Dan with blood as they straddled the limp body of a man in homespun. His sheathed knife was so close Dan scarcely had to move to grasp it.

He drew it from the sheath and sprang up in the same instant, ducked under the mounted Rebel's musket, seized his arm, and dragged him from the saddle. Falling on top of his foe, Dan lifted the knife, but a smashing blow from the side stabbed lightning through his head and knocked him sprawling.

Dazed, he blinked up at the smiling face above him, the hand holding the knife. That cleft chin, silver hair, blue eyes so pale they

460

were almost colorless. A man's features now, not the boy's who'd whispered obscenities at the Wares' cabin raising.

"Lafe!" Dan gasped. "Lafe Ballard!"

The puzzlement in those chill eyes was followed by recognition. "Damned if it's not the fiddling Irisher!" Lafe glanced at the sallow young man holding the horses and the rifle he'd swung against Dan's head. A long black plume furled from his slouch black hat. His red hunting shirt was gaudy with beads and embroidery.

"This is a neighbor, Quant." Lafe grinned and narrowed his eyes. "For old times' sake, I'll just carve my initials on his cheek and let him go."

"Hell." The other shrugged. "I'll sit on him so you can do an artistic job."

Knees pinioned Dan's shoulders. Hands clamped his wrists. Groggy from the blow, he felt his head gripped between Lafe's knees who bent over him from above. Steel glinted lazily. Dan closed his eyes and set his teeth. He wouldn't scream. Wouldn't. . . .

The blade was razor sharp. It bit like ice-fire, but the trickle down Dan's cheek was warm.

"L's easy." Lafe chuckled. "It's hard to curve lines for a B, but, if I loop over the cheek bone and come down to the jaw. . . . It's bleeding too much to be sure, but I reckon it'll heal up to show who marked him."

"Bite a cartridge and rub in some gunpowder," the one named Quantrill suggested. "Give it a little color."

Dan held his breath at the sting.

"Stay there till we're good and gone, Irisher." Lafe's knees unlocked from Dan's head. "If you move while we're in firing range, we'll both shoot."

Even if they missed once, he'd be dead before he could locate a rifle and load. Dan lay still as the horses clumped away, hoofs muffled when they struck something soft. He still lay there after the sounds faded into the groans and begging of the wounded. Andy was dead. There wasn't any hurry. In those moments when he couldn't fight while he was marked for life, something had happened to Dan's spirit. He wanted to wash away his own blood with Lafe's. He couldn't hunt him now in the midst of the Rebel Army, but soon or late, even if it was after the war, he had to kill Lafe or go through life feeling violated.

This must be how a woman felt when taken by force. The thought drove him up to his knees. Lafe and Quantrill had vanished among the horde yelling and exulting at the Union retreat. Head throbbing, Dan turned to be sure about Andy, gagged at the ruined head.

Bury him. See if there's anything Susie

would want. Dan drank from Owen's canteen and sloshed a cupped hand against his cheek to wash out some of the gunpowder. He padded it with a clean sock from Andy's haversack and tied it in place with Andy's shoe strings. The wound burned like fire.

A locket with one of Susie's dark curls was around Andy's pulseless throat. Probably she'd want it left with Andy. The haversack held a crumpled letter Andy had started to Susie and half a biscuit. Dan tucked the biscuit into his own haversack. Susie must have the letter, of course. He could find nothing else for a keepsake, so he searched for a lock of unbloodied hair, found it at the nape of Andy's neck, and cut it with his pocket knife. Trimming off a piece of Andy's blouse bottom, Dan wrapped the still sweaty twist of red hair in that, along with the letter, stuffed them in Andy's other sock, and thrust it deeply in his bedroll.

The shattered tree where he'd been dragging Andy had a deep furrow plowed into its roots by a cannon ball. A bayonet might dig the hollow out enough for Andy. Dan left his friend's shoes for someone who needed them. The oilskin around Andy's blanket was bloody. Dan left it, but he put the blanket over his back. Stooping, each hand grasping one of Andy's limp ones, he half dragged Andy to the tree and dropped him on the blanket.

Earth and sky careened. Dan sank down and leaned his forehead against the tree's splintered trunk. The sapwood smelled as if it bled. Maybe everything would smell like that from now on.

When he could move, he got his bayonet from the scabbard and started digging. He wasn't going to tell Susie that Andy's grave was dug out mostly by a cannon ball.

At last there was room to nestle Andy under the roots. Dan did this as gently as he could, covered his face with his cap. Out of his own haversack, Dan took John Brown's Testament. He slipped it inside Andy's shirt, over his heart, and covered his friend with earth full of splinters from the wounded tree.

CHAPTER TWENTY-FOUR

As the bullets of their troops whistled over them, Charlie, Travis, and Clay Harmon rested for a minute, panting on hands and knees behind the wet hemp bale that was only one small part of the two wings of bales that formed this peculiar breastwork protecting the attack of Pap Price's raggle-taggle army on the fortified Masonic College at Lexington which sat on a bluff overlooking the Missouri River. The Yanks were shooting back, of course, but most of their bullets and artillery fire spanged harmlessly into the thick bales.

"Might as well be a billy goat, buttin' these bales ahead of us!" Clay cupped a hand to the side of his mouth to send his voice through the roar of artillery and muskets. Bits of broken hemp, the same dull brown as his hair, stuck to the crown of his forage cap. His round freckled face was fiery red. "Wonder if it'd be easier to lever this durn bale ahead with poles like some fellas are doing?"

Charlie smeared sweat from his brow

against one arm. "You'd be a better target for the Yanks."

"Yeah, and I'm not a beanpole like you!" shouted Clay. "Smart of General Harris to have us wet the bales, so shells or bullets can't set 'em afire . . . but it sure makes 'em heavy."

The bales had been found in a warehouse by the river and someone had suggested forming them into a movable barricade to shelter an advance on the Union garrison. Yesterday evening and into the night, Charlie helped push and drag the bales to the top of the bluff, facing the Union stronghold on the north and west from about four hundred yards away, although in places the shaggy line bristled within one hundred yards of the fortifications. As he got ready to push the bale with his head again, Charlie raised up enough to glimpse the high sod ramparts, ditches, rifle pits, and sharpened stakes that surrounded the white-pillared three-storied brick building. Giant stumps showed where Colonel James Mulligan of the Union Army had felled the splendid oaks shading the seventeen-acre campus to build the fortifications shielding his Irish brigade, a regiment of Illinois cavalry, one German regiment from Kansas City, and some Home Guards. Mulligan had plenty of time to withdraw, but he'd counted on help since several Union forces were close enough to come to his aid. Besides, according to the local citizenry, he'd buried

$900,000 from the Lexington bank and the Great Seal of Missouri in the basement of the college and didn't want to lose these treasures to the Confederates.

So less than four thousand men had been under siege since September 13th by Price's eighteen thousand who camped on the streets, lawns, and in the churches of the town while he waited for his ammunition wagons to catch up. Volunteers swarmed to him, including a neighboring farmer who came every morning with his dinner bucket and flintlock. From behind a big tree, he fired at any Yankee who poked his head above the earthworks, took time out for his lunch and pipe, and fired away till time to go home to his chores. The ammunition wagons creaked into the camp at the fairgrounds on the 17th. Next morning, Price opened fire with sixteen cannons, including Old Sacramento with its silver bell-like ringing.

Union guns roared back. Sniper fire from a Federal hospital building outside their ramparts struck the thin line of Rebel troops along the river. A Confederate rush took the hospital, Federals charged through the open and regained it, and Charlie, Travis, and Clay were in the company that took it back under withering fire, the "hot" fight Travis had longed for.

Now, bracing his head against the bale as Travis called — "Shove!" — Charlie thought of the poor devils inside the fortifications, and was glad that Thos wasn't there, or Dan, or anyone he knew.

Yesterday the smell of dead horses rose from the stifling heat. It was worse this morning. There were only two cisterns inside Union lines, and for a week the Federals with seven hundred horses to water had been cut off from the river and two good springs near the bluff. Water would be their worst need, but they must be running out of food for both men and horses. A Confederate who'd hidden in a wounded Yank's bed when the Federals took back the hospital gagged as he told his rescuers how the Yanks fought each other to drink from buckets of bloody water left from cleaning wounds. And that had been day before yesterday.

"Tree ahead!" yelled the corporal directing their section of the line.

Charlie and his team shoved their bale to the right while the soldiers on the left butted their hemp in that direction. As soon as they cleared a young oak that was badly splintered by artillery and musket fire, the men worked the bales back together and inched forward through weeds, sunflowers, goldenrod, and asters. The crushed plants gave out pungent aromas that covered some of the stench of rotting horses.

A whine, an impact that crashed in Charlie's skull, snapped his teeth together. The bale rocked, but the cannon ball hadn't torn through it.

"Good thing they don't have much canister and grapeshot," Clay muttered.

"I hear they're shooting our own cannon balls back at us."

"How much farther do we have to push these dratted things?" growled Travis.

"Why don't those damn' Yanks give up?"

"Would you?" grunted Charlie, wondering if his neck and shoulders would ever feel right again.

"No, but I'm not a bluebelly."

"That doesn't make them cowards."

"There's a white flag!" yelled the corporal. "By grannies, they've quit firing!"

"Cease fire!" sounded gladly along the ranks behind the bales. The men stood up to stretch their cramped muscles and watch Price's messenger pass through the Union lines.

He returned, looking downcast. He reported to Price and a disbelieving murmur spread through the troops. Mulligan hadn't surrendered. Without his knowing it, some officer had shown the white flag.

The firing started up again. Charlie and the others dropped to their hands and knees, set their heads against the bales, and pushed. It wasn't long, though, till Mulligan sent out a messenger under a flag of truce. Again, the firing stopped. Again, Charlie and the bale-pushers rested. The sun was well past the zenith and they'd been shoving bales since early morning.

The Union messenger hurried back to the college. Bugles and drums sounded. Soon the troops marched out and stacked their muskets, then stood in ranks as Mulligan, wounded in the arm and leg, and his officers, several of them also wounded, came to General Price to offer their swords.

The white-haired general was close enough for Charlie to hear him say: "You gentlemen have fought so bravely that it would be wrong to deprive you of your swords. You may keep your horses, side arms, and personal belongings. Parole will be arranged as soon as possible."

Then Price quirked an eyebrow at the flag still flying from the surrendered headquarters. "May I ask why, Colonel Mulligan, the Union flag is still displayed?"

Mulligan, tall and dark, with a luxuriant moustache and flowing hair, grinned like the Chicago politician he was. "It's my Irishmen, General Price. They nailed the flag to the pole before I knew what the rascals were about."

Stirring music struck up within the battlements. Price returned Mulligan's grin. "I take it, sir, that those are also your Irish marching and counter-marching around that most beautiful green and gold banner with the harp and shamrock?"

"They are, General."

One of Price's staff started to protest, but Price motioned him to silence. "They'll be along directly," he said. "Colonel Mulligan, allow me to invite you and your officers to a champagne dinner. And your charming bride who was compelled to leave the city a few days ago will be informed that you are well and she may come to you."

Accompanied by their regimental band, the Irish brigade marched into the open field and stacked their arms. Through a blur, Charlie looked at the flag they'd defended, the flag he'd revered from childhood for its promise of freedom and justice. With a heart convulsed till he could scarcely breathe, he knew it was for him the only flag. It always would be.

Charlie looked up from grating corn on a piece of tin pierced with nail holes. A farmer had invited the company to help themselves to the corn in one of his cribs, and his pretty daughters had poured cool buttermilk into eagerly proffered cups.

"Didn't think you were going to get here in time for supper, Trav."

Travis laughed and patted his stomach. "You're welcome to the corn pone, boys. I had chicken and dumplings and a hunk of apple pie."

"You . . . you hog!" Clay sputtered. "That's

why you hung around that oldest gal!"

"I hung around 'cause she was pretty. Anyhow, we're all invited to a big social at the church tonight. There'll be cakes and pies and lemonade."

"*Whowee!* I'd better jump in the creek and clean up." Clay started off, then turned. "You got a clean shirt, Charlie?"

"So would you if you weren't too lazy to wash yours."

"Aw, Charlie. . . ."

"You can borrow it. But mind you don't get in a fight and tear it, and you have to wash it."

"Don't you need it yourself?" Travis asked his brother-in-law.

Charlie shook his head. "I'm going to write to Melissa tonight."

"You write her durn' near every night! How does that make me look to my folks?"

"Like what you are. Someone who'd rather play cards and yarn with the boys than write home."

"I'm trying to win us some horses or the money to buy some!"

"Seems like you'd learn something from already losing ours."

Travis sighed. "Charlie, my father's a bishop, but he's a rounder compared to you! No cards, no dice, no whiskey! Why, when those good-looking Yankee ladies came down to that spring we were guarding at Lexington, you didn't even try to swap them a drink for a kiss."

Charlie's stare made Travis blush and squirm. "Wasn't it bad enough we couldn't let them fill their buckets for their wounded?" he demanded. But he remembered with shame how he'd wondered for a second how the softly rounded girl with yellow hair would fit in a man's arms.

"Saint Charles!" derided Travis. "Don't look so fierce about it! We let them drink all they wanted themselves, didn't we?"

"It was the least we could do, when they'd risked getting shot." Charlie mixed meal with water and shaped pones to bake in corn husks in the hot ashes of the fire where their coffee steamed in tin cups that served for brewing and drinking. He looked up at his reckless, teasing brother-in-law. "I hope Melissa and Christy never have to beg soldiers for a drink of water."

The smile died on Travis's mouth. "That's a hell of a thing to think!"

"It could happen."

"Charlie, you croak worse'n any thunder pumper." That was what folks called bitterns, heron-like birds that poked their heads straight up in the air to blend with marsh grass. At breeding time, they gave a kind of hollow croak. Travis shook his curly head. "After being in the army five months, we get our first real fight and all you can do is feel sorry for the Yanks!"

Their military career hadn't been exactly glorious. They'd reached St. Louis after the surrender of Governor Jackson's militia to Lyon. Citizens had been furious over the way Union troops had killed twenty-eight people, including a baby, when they fired into a jeering, rock-throwing crowd that threatened to mob them as they marched their prisoners along the street to be shut up, overnight, in the arsenal. It hadn't helped that most of the Union volunteers were St. Louis Germans.

Joining Price's Missouri Home Guards, Charlie and Travis had toiled north to Boonville where Price had hoped to gather and train enough men to drive the Federals out of the state. Lyon had pounced. His well-equipped Regulars quickly had routed the green militia under Colonel John Marmaduke. Governor Claib Jackson had fled Jefferson City before Lyon took it and had scurried south with the militia to join Price at Wilson's Creek in southwest Missouri.

"What do you call chasing Sigel's bunch out of Carthage?" Charlie demanded. "Wasn't that a fight?"

Travis grunted. "For all the commotion and cannonading, both sides, put together, lost under fifty men. Wilson's Creek now, there was a battle. A quarter of all the fighting men killed, missing, or wounded!" He kicked a rock disgustedly. "Finally a good fracas and where were we? In camp, with trots so bad we could barely drag up our trousers before we had to yank them down."

"I'm just as glad we missed that one," Charlie admitted.

Travis stared. "Why?"

"My kid brother may have been in Lyon's army. Troops from Kansas were. More than likely some of them helped raise our cabin, like Dan O'Brien and the Parks brothers and Andy McHugh."

That silenced Travis for a minute. Then he said: "You can't afford to think like that, Charlie. Whoever they were once, the Feds are enemies! Hasn't that damned Frémont put Missouri under martial law? Ordered the slaves of Confederate sympathizers freed and any civilian bearing arms to be court-martialed and shot?"

Clay's hazel eyes burned. "I'm glad Jeff Thompson swore he'd hang, draw, and quarter a Union man for every Southerner killed under Frémont's order!"

"Lincoln countermanded that fool declaration," Charlie reminded them. "Anyhow, Trav, I can't help how I feel and I sure don't want to fight Thos." Thank goodness Travis's accusing brown eyes weren't a bit like Melissa's.

After another shocked moment, Travis blurted: "Sounds like if you hadn't married my sister, you'd be on the other side!"

"But I did marry your sister." Charlie unrolled his bedding to produce a wrinkled, somewhat mildewed flannel shirt that he tossed to Clay. "Want a corn pone before you get all slicked up?"

"I live in hopes of pie, but I'll take what I can get." Clay munched a pone and glanced toward General Price's tent and the Mulligans' pitched beside it. Colonel Mulligan had refused parole so he and his pretty young bride rode in Price's carriage and camped near him at night. "Wonder what they're eating?"

"Grated cornmeal like the rest of us," said Charlie. "Pap's not just brave, always risking his life to lead his men . . . he's kind and honorable."

Travis shrugged. "Maybe too honorable. He put nearly all that nine hundred thousand dollars back in the Lexington bank when he certainly needs it for this army. He must know damned well McCulloch won't reinforce us."

"McCulloch probably won't even send Pap percussion caps for the muskets we captured at Lexington," Clay gloomed.

"General Snead's persuasive," Charlie said. "Maybe he can at least get a promise of the caps from McCulloch when he stops by Fort Smith on his way to see Jefferson Davis in Richmond."

"Snead!" Travis grinned, although he, like

476

most of the men, liked the former journalist. "Price made him chief of ordnance when he didn't know a howitzer from a siege gun. He just about figured that out when Price made him his adjutant general."

"Looks like he's learning fast," defended Charlie.

Travis brooded. "That Confederate government in Richmond doesn't give a hoot about Missouri! Without help from McCulloch or the east, there's no way Pap could hold Lexington."

"Why, pure-dee hundreds came in wanting to join up!" Clay protested. "I hear tell there were twenty thousand men in camp a few days after we whipped the Yanks."

"Sure," scoffed Travis. "It was fun to bang away with squirrel rifles, what with Pap winning. And some really would've joined up proper, but Pap couldn't arm a lot of them so he sent them home till later."

"He was counting on an all-out uprising against the Federals," Charlie said. "Guess he still is, but I don't think it'll happen."

"Why not?" demanded Travis. "There's lots of Southern sympathizers along the Missouri River, but, after you get away from the big farms and plantations, folks lean more toward the Union till you get close to Arkansas. Even down there I'd reckon half the people favor the Union."

"We captured a power of muskets in Lexington." Clay seemed to be trying to console himself. "Three thousand of 'em! And seven cannon!"

"And over seven hundred horses, saddles, and sabers and what was left of Mulligan's supplies," added Charlie wearily. "We can make our own bullets like we did with lead from the mines at Granby on the way north, but we can't make percussion caps."

They considered this. After a moment, Travis hunched a shoulder. "At least there aren't so many of us to keep supplied. Men've been dropping out to go home ever since we left Lexington. I heard the sergeant say we're down to about seven thousand." He chuckled. "But we still have the Lexington brass band with us, so we've got dandy music."

Charlie said quietly: "Frémont's got forty thousand men in five divisions he's spreading across the state."

Travis whistled a derisive note. "Who's scared of Frémont? He left Lyon dangling at Springfield and didn't help Mulligan when he could have. C'mon, Clay! Let's spruce up and head for the social."

"Pie and pretty girls!" breathed Clay, and trotted off to the creek.

After they were gone, Charlie carefully sharpened his stubby pencil and built up the fire enough to see. Bedroll propped behind him, he wrote Melissa and his family. The Jardines would rejoice at the fall of Lexington, but the Wares wouldn't. And Thos . . . ? If an evil moment found him facing his brother in battle, he'd wait for Thos's bullet or bayonet. Yes, but what if Thos was too far away to recognize or the cover was too thick?

Charlie put the letters in envelopes with previous notes that he'd hand in to the postmaster. When would his regiment be in one place long enough to get letters from home? It helped to write his loved ones, but what wouldn't he give to hear from Melissa and his family!

Over by General Price's tent, the band was playing "Listen to the Mockingbird". The haunting melody made Charlie's throat hurt and his eyes sting. They had crossed the Osage two days ago, taking three days to get the whole army across. Rumor was they were heading for Neosho way down in the southwest corner of the state. Their line of march couldn't be too far from home. He resolved to ask his captain for a few days' furlough. Travis might not want to come since he'd either have to lie or face the bishop's wrath over gambling away their splendid horses.

Charlie took off his shoes and rolled his pants into a pillow. Rolling up in his blanket, he concentrated on making Melissa as real as he could, imagining she was in his arms, summoning up the softness of her, the taste of her mouth and breath, the way her eyes hazed when she lay fulfilled with loving. Oh, Melissa! He ached, but it was sweet. As he drifted into sleep, a dream of her relieved his body but not his yearning. If he couldn't get leave, he'd just take off. He was almost asleep again when the foot of one of his messmates stubbed into him.

"Hey!" he yelped. Sitting up, he sniffed. "Maybe you went to a church social, but you found something stronger'n lemonade on the way home."

"Wouldn't be friendly to turn down good corn liquor." Travis almost fell beside Charlie. "Do you know what that infernal Jim Lane . . . Senator Lane, Brigadier General Lane . . . the damned jayhawking bastard . . . did two days after we took Lexington?"

"Stole some slaves out of Missouri?"

"A bunch of them! Two hundred!"

"What?"

"Lane burned Osceola to the ground except for three houses," Travis rasped. "Since he was fired at when his bunch rode into town, he held a drumhead court and shot nine men. When he marched for Kansas City, three hundred of his men were so drunk they had to be hauled in wagons."

"And he stole wagons for the three thousand sacks of flour they looted from warehouses where Price's supplies were stored," muttered Clay. "And five hundred pounds of sugar and molasses, and fifty sacks of coffee on top of lots of powder, lead, and cartridge paper. . . ."

"And three hundred and fifty horses and mules, four hundred cattle, not to mention the fancy carriage, piano, and silk dresses he took for himself! He told his men to clean out everything 'disloyal from a Shanghai rooster to a Durham cow.' " Travis gripped Charlie's shoulder. In spite of the whiskey on his breath, he sounded stone-cold sober. "Lane looted and burned all the way to Kansas City! It was just luck he didn't go by our place."

Charlie's blood chilled at the thought of Lane's rabble carousing through Rose Haven. He had to realize fully for the first time that Melissa might face something worse than having to ask enemy soldiers for a drink. "Lane's superiors in the regular army won't let him keep on like that!"

Travis snorted. "Have they been able to stop Jennison? He and his militia jayhawked up and down western Missouri all summer! Just got through corraling all the men . . . three or four hundred of them . . . in the courthouse square in Independence along with mules, horses, and heaps of weapons, furniture, jewelry . . . even spinning wheels!"

"Surely Jennison didn't kill the prisoners?"

"Not this time. He found out which were Union men, apologized for the inconvenience, and let them collect their belongings and go home."

"Then," put in Clay morosely, "he preached the Secessionists a half-hour sermon . . . guess they had been pretty hard on Unionists . . . and finished off by saying for every Union man killed from now on, he'd see that ten important Secessionists died."

"Just like Lane at Osceola!" fumed Travis. "His gang loaded jayhawked wagons and carriages with plunder and rollicked back to Kansas City with a bunch of darkies! When they crossed into Kansas, Lane's chaplain . . . the same one who'd robbed a church in Osceola for an altar cloth and other things to decorate his own church . . . declared the slaves forever free in the name of God, the United States, and General Lane! There they are, Lane and Jennison, two of the greatest scoundrels in the country, ready to burn and plunder as soon as Price is gone!"

"Ever since the Feds were licked at Wilson's Creek, Secessionists have been running Union people out of Missouri," Charlie pointed out. "Remember that eighty-year-old man who'd fought in the Revolution? When he said it was murder when two of his neighbors were killed for being Union men, a gang took him away from his poor old wife and shot him. The story about them cutting out his heart to pickle may not be true, but for sure General McBride ordered Union men to take the oath of loyalty to the Confederacy or be arrested or forced to fight for the South."

"Serves them right!" Travis sank his fingers into Charlie's shoulder. "Don't you care that Lane and Jennison and Montgomery can call themselves Union soldiers and jayhawk to their heart's content?"

"The Home Guard. . . ."

"That's us! You know we're hearing that if the Confederacy doesn't put Price in command of forces out here, those of us who want to go on fighting will have to join the Confederate Army and most likely fight outside the state. There won't be any troops to protect our homes and families from the likes of Lane and Jennison!"

"That's why Lafe Ballard asked us to join up with him," Clay burst in. "He's going to stay in Missouri and fight jayhawkers along with his friend, W.C. Quantrill. You must have noticed Quantrill charging on his black horse at Lexington. Wore a red shirt and a long black plume in his hat."

"Lafe Ballard?" Charlie whirled on Travis. "Don't you remember that row we had with him after Seth Cooley fired him for laying open an ox's back?"

"Aw, Charlie, that was a long time ago!"

"He's always been a foul-mouthed sneak. Trav, any bunch Lafe heads'll be worse than the jayhawkers."

"Can't be."

"Do you want your mother and sister to be ashamed of you?"

"Who's going to make sure they're alive to be ashamed?"

"Neither side's low enough to kill women."

"Maybe not shoot them," Travis allowed. "But is it much better to kill their men folk, burn them out, and steal everything they have?"

"The regular Union officers will get the jayhawkers under control." Charlie had to believe that. "Our families will be a lot safer with Union troops firmly in charge than if gangs like Lafe's give them a reason to go after Secessionists. Don't you see that? My God, Missouri's still one of the United States! Her citizens are under Federal protection."

"Sure," derided Clay. "Tell that to the widows in Osceola and the folks who got robbed and corralled by rifles in Independence."

"Clay," warned Charlie, "I've known Lafe Ballard since we were boys. He's poison."

"He's got enough guts to fight the damned jayhawks," Clay retorted. "I got no interest . . . not a speck . . . in fighting Yanks in Tennessee or even Arkansas. I want to fight 'em right here in Missouri! Looks like the only way to do that is to throw in with them that feels likewise." He stood up, dumpy figure silhouetted against the dull glow of the coals. "Coming, Trav?"

Charlie held his breath. He'd fight Travis if he had to, try to beat sense into his head, but he didn't want to.

"Guess I'll tag along with Pap," Travis said slowly. "Maybe Jeff Davis will put him in charge of all the Confederate forces out here."

Clay made a derisive sound.

Travis's tone grew resolute. "Pap loves Missouri as much as anybody can. Whatever he decides is best for her . . . well, I reckon that's what I'll do. How about you, Charlie?"

"I'm with you." Charlie was so relieved his rash brother-in-law wasn't turning bushwhacker that he stifled the unvoiced hope that, when their six-month enlistments ran out in November and if Price disbanded the state guard, Travis might agree to go home.

The messmates shook hands and wished each other luck. After Clay disappeared, Charlie said to Travis: "We can sign up to serve with General Price again, but first I'm going home, with a furlough or without it."

"Fine." Travis yawned, spreading his bedroll. "Listen, if you don't blab to Pa about what happened to our horses, I'll bet he'll give us new ones."

"I won't blab as long as you promise not to gamble any new ones away, but I won't lie, either."

"Saint Charles!" Travis gave him a friendly buffet. "No dancing, no drinking, no apple pie, or pretty girls! What do you let yourself enjoy?"

"Melissa," Charlie said, and hugged his pants-pillow as he settled down again.

Chapter Twenty-Five

Just as Dan had imagined it so many times — the happy house nestled beneath the giant walnut amidst the warm glow of autumn golds and scarlets. The big white oxen and fawn-colored cows browsed in the stubble while four horses, bays and chestnuts, grazed in the pasture with the dark-faced sheep. The geese snaked their necks forward, hissing at the intruder. From down in the bottoms where two men were scything hay, Robbie dashed forward, his defender's bark changing to one of delight as he smelled Dan.

Just as in Dan's dreams, Christy stepped out, and then she was running, throwing her arms around him as he swung down from Breeze. Had she seen his scar? How could she not? What he hoped he could keep her from sensing was the darkness inside him.

"Dan! Dan! Danny!" Tears spilled down her cheeks as she laughed.

He kissed her tears and laughter. They clung together, close as they could, while

Robbie tore around them in frenzied, narrowing circles. Then Christy's lips moved to the ridged mess of Dan's cheek. At least, even rubbed with gunpowder, Lafe's initials couldn't be read. The B Lafe had carved on the L had twisted into two joined, blurred circles. She kissed the scar as if she would make it vanish, then touched it with her hand. "What happened to you, Danny?"

"I'll tell you later."

Would he? Should he let her think it was a random wound? One thing sure, he wouldn't tell her that he'd been dragging Andy to shelter when Lafe or Quantrill used their friend for target practice. He hadn't even told Owen. It would make it more real by letting others know — and they might glimpse the smoldering rage in Dan, the thirst for vengeance.

Beth had hold of him now, hugging his waist, squealing his name. He stooped for a kiss and smoothed her dark curls. "Look who's growing up!"

He grinned past her at Ellen and the men coming up from the meadow, felt happy surprise at seeing Thos — Thos whose blue fatigue blouse was ragged as Dan's.

After an embrace and kiss from Ellen and handshakes with the men, Thos took over the care of Breeze while Dan was brought inside. He insisted on hearing their news before he gave them his. He wished he'd never again have to tell about Andy. Susie paled when he had told her that morning, after he and Owen rode in with a farmer who was bringing corn to the mill. Staggering as if rocked by a blow, Susie turned blindly into her sister's arms.

"My son, my laddie!" old Catriona wailed. "Was it for this you left the green isle of Skye and the hills of Cuillin? Was it for this I carried you under my heart and suckled you with your sweet cheeks dimpling as you drew in my milk? My son, my son! You shone on us . . . warmed us! And now you are gone away forever!" She keened like a banshee then, without any words.

Little Andy, a year old, almost walking, whimpered at his grandmother's weeping. He hauled himself up on his mother's skirts, burrowing his fiery red head into the folds of homespun. Daniel Owen David, also a year old, shy of the father he didn't remember, screwed his blue eyes shut and howled till Harriet picked him up.

Now, delaying the evil moment when he'd have to repeat the grievous tidings, Dan heard how the advance of Price's army had run off eighty government mules from near Fort Scott early in September. Lane's Brigade, five hastily recruited, understrength regiments, skirmished with some of Price's men, but Price marched on toward Lexington and his victory there.

"Price may never have intended to invade

Kansas." Thos's dark head was level with his father's reddish-brown one and he was leaner and tougher looking than when Dan last saw him. "Or, maybe, when he found Lane's Brigade spread out along the border, he decided it wasn't worth the trouble since his real aim was to reach the Missouri River and get control of it."

"He expected the whole state to rise up against the Union." There was more sadness than triumph in Jonathan Ware's voice. "Charlie and Travis Jardine got furloughs and were here week before last. They expected to catch up with Price around Springfield."

"Price abandoned Springfield to Frémont and is down in Neosho," said Dan. "The news got to Leavenworth when Owen and I were mustering out the last of October. Seems the commander of Frémont's Hussar guard was tired of being called a Saint Louis parlor pet and craved to celebrate the anniversary of the charge of the Light Brigade at Balaclava by leading a cavalry attack on Springfield." Dan shook his head in bemusement. "Zagoni's cavalry wound up taking the town while Price withdrew."

"Balaclava was October Twenty-Fifth," reckoned Jonathan Ware. "I doubt if the boys were in Springfield yet. They were stopping to spend a few days at the Jardines'."

"Frémont's generals have joined him at Springfield, including Jim Lane," said Dan.

"Someone traveling north from Fort Scott yesterday told Uncle Simeon that Price fired a hundred gun salute when the Rebel Missouri legislature convened in Neosho. They voted to secede and elected General Rains to the Confederate senate."

"So now Missouri has two legislatures and two governors, the way Kansas Territory used to." Jonathan Ware's smile was wintry. "Of course, now that Price can claim that Missouri's joined the Confederacy, he must hope to get help from McCulloch."

"He'll need it," said Thos. "Frémont has thirty thousand men." He raised an eyebrow at Dan. "Now that you're out, are you staying that way?"

Christy's hand rested in the curve of Dan's arm. He covered her tightening fingers with his own but didn't look at her for fear she'd see the festering ugliness inside him. "Not much of a time to quit, with Price holding southwest Missouri and hoping to get it all. I'm going to enlist in Colonel Montgomery's Third Kansas Regiment."

"Maybe I will, too," said Thos. "The Pony Express closed down when the coast-to-coast telegraph was finished last month. Anyhow, all I did during my enlistment was escort supply wagons. Nearest I got to a fight was when we brought General Lyon uniforms and mail at Springfield."

Dan touched his frayed sleeve. "That's

where I got this, and these brogans that are falling apart. Too bad you didn't bring us some rations."

"You were at Wilson's Creek?" Thos demanded.

There was nothing for it then but to tell them about Andy and the battle, the retreat from what had been victory on the field, and the desperate families, often wives and children of Union soldiers, who trailed the army toward Rolla with whatever animals and belongings they could collect, a sight Dan would never forget.

"It was like Ireland in the starving times." The words were bitter in his mouth, painful as the saltpeter of a bitten cartridge's gunpowder on cracked lips. "That Americans should fight each other, that's terrible, but for women and children to dread men who were neighbors. . . ." He choked off.

"What happened to them?" Christy's voice was balm to his raw feelings although it couldn't reach what he'd come to think of as an inner wound, seeping poison, that could be soothed only in battle. With his brain, he knew Rebels were mostly decent, but, in the few fights he'd been in since Wilson's Creek, he wanted to kill. He wasn't so far gone that he'd shoot Charlie, or even Travis, if he could help it, but the Rebs he didn't know, they were Lafe and Quantrill.

Now, answering Christy's question about

the fleeing Union families, Dan shook his head. "Some were going to relatives in other states or eastern Missouri. Others stayed around Rolla in hopes that the Confederates will be forced out of the state and they can go back to whatever's left of their homes. A few had train fare to Saint Louis where most of our troops went."

Ellen's dark eyes touched him as comfortingly as did her hand. "Dinner's ready. Come along in, Dan."

He did, Christy holding one hand, Beth hanging to the other.

"If only Charlie were here." Christy's voice was so soft he had to bow his head to hear. "If only none of you had to go away . . . if only no one did!"

"I'm here now."

She drew his head down and kissed the scar. He pulled away, cursed himself for the hurt in her eyes. "It's not you, Christy," he muttered. "I . . . I'm sorry."

During dinner — Lige Morrow had swapped a smoked wild turkey for some corn and potatoes and there was a jar of Sarah's honey — Dan told how the 2nd Kansas was in a few skirmishes near Hannibal before arriving by train in St. Joseph in the middle of the night where they took the Rebel garrison by surprise, drove them out, and held the city till relieved by the Union troops that would stay there.

"We went on to Leavenworth by boat," Dan finished. "Mustered out the last day of October . . . and here I am. Tell me, have you had any trouble because you're for the Union?"

Jonathan shrugged. "Watt Caxton and Arly Maddux stopped by after Price took Lexington. They hinted that I might stay healthier if we moved back to Illinois. I told them this is our home."

"It's what you'd expect from Caxton." Ellen's eyes sparkled wrathfully. "But for Mister Maddux, a Baptist minister, to come on such an errand!"

"Have many of your neighbors joined either army?"

"As soon as their corn was cribbed and the wheat planted and harrowed in, Ethan and Matthew Hayes went to join Price." Jonathan sighed. "Mark . . . he's seventeen . . . begged to go, too, but Ethan told him he and Luke had to be the men of the house. I'm not holding school, but little Mary comes over when she can to study with Beth." He frowned at the strangeness of it all. "Ethan, Matt, and I shook hands when we parted. I promised to help Allie and the children any way I could."

"I thought Ethan didn't hold with slavery," puzzled Dan.

"Nor does he. But he couldn't stomach the way Lane and Jennison have rampaged through Missouri." Jonathan's tone was somber. "It's like the worst times of the border troubles, only multiplied. Both jay-hawkers and bushwhackers have got into uniforms to carry out their wickedness."

Dan thought of Lafe and Quantrill and winced to know that plenty of decent but hot-headed men like Clay would throw in with them in order to harry the Union soldiers they saw as an oppressive army of occupation.

"Emil Franz is too old to fight," said Jonathan. "Lige Morrow's got no use for Frémont's dress parade notions so he's signed on as a scout with Colonel Montgomery." He named off the other Missouri men of fighting age that Dan knew from seeing them at the mill.

"Sounds like they're split just about half and half," Dan said. "Over in Kansas, it's pretty much solid Union."

"Jennison saw to that," said Jonathan. "Will Owen stay home now? When I took our corn to the mill, young David was having fits to enlist."

"I don't think there'll be any stopping him now. Owen pretty much promised him he could have his turn after our time ran out." Ruefully Dan met Thos's gaze. "We didn't think the war would last this long."

"It's just getting started," said Thos.

Beth caught Dan's sleeve. "I don't like having wars, Danny! You and Thos and Charlie won't get killed, will you?"

"We'll try not to," he assured her. He tried not to remember children her age and younger, down to babies, trudging behind Lyon's retreating army.

"Mary cries when she comes to study because her daddy and Matt are gone." Beth stood up, gripped his face in her hands, and stared into his eyes. Hers were deep hazel. Dove's eyes. He hoped she couldn't see that abscess of hate within him. Her sweet breath, milky from the glass she'd drunk, mixed with the air he breathed. Her small hands warmed his face. "Danny, you wouldn't ever fight Matt and Mister Hayes, would you?"

"Oh, Beth, sweetheart!" Tears blinded him for a moment. "I hope I never have to." Had it occurred to her, was it too awful to mention, that he, and even Thos, might have to fight Charlie?

Widening eyes filling with tears, she gave a stricken cry and fled outdoors. Dan felt as if he'd crushed a gentle bird, one with a heart loving and valiant for others. "I'm sorry."

"What else could you say?" Christy's voice was fierce.

Face averted, Ellen got to her feet. "Christy, why don't you and Dan see if you can find some winter grapes along the creek? Look for persimmons, too. That frost we had a few nights ago may have been enough to sweeten them."

It was, Dan knew, her way of giving them time alone. He both longed for that and feared it. He wasn't fit to be with Christy when he had such evil in his heart.

"I hope you'll play your fiddle," she said as they walked through the freshly cut meadow grass.

"I've got out of the habit of playing." He had missed it, missed it in a manner akin to the way he missed Christy.

She looked up at him. The sun brought out a hint of gold in her gray eyes, and his heart stopped with loving her. "Well, if you don't feel like playing today, you can tune up your fiddle and play tomorrow. You will come tomorrow, won't you, Dan?" She slipped her arm through his. "I want to hear your song. And maybe . . . maybe you can make one about Andy."

Not that. Oh, Christy, dearest love, you don't want to hear that. Still, a melody had been slowly forming in his head, a kind of lament, not only for Andy, but for all the young men dead in the broken corn or sprawled in the brush and scrub oaks of what was now called Bloody Hill. The song mourned, too, the maimed trees, the trampled earth gashed by caissons and cannon, blasted with iron balls. Then the song exploded into fury, a howling for blood. He couldn't play that for his Quaker foster family.

"Lydia thinks Susie and Catriona . . . well,

everybody . . . will feel better if we hold a service and put up a marker for Andy down by his forge," Dan said. "I'll play then. Something. Will you come?"

"I'm sure we all will. Andy helped raise our cabin, remember? He made the nails, and, for a welcome, he gave us the hinges for the doors and shutters and made the rod and kettle hooks for the fireplace." Her breath caught. "Oh, Dan, the main reason we moved here was so Charlie and Thos could take up land close to the home place . . . so the family could stay together. But here's this awful war with Charlie on one side and Thos on the other!"

"Wars end."

"So do people."

"Christy. . . ."

She stopped and pressed her palm to his cheek. "Tell me how you got this."

When he told her, she made a strangled sound. "So Lafe still loves to hurt others!" She held up her wrist, showing a white scar Dan had noticed before but attributed to an accident while cooking or washing. "He bumped me against a hot kettle rim. Of course, he pretended it was an accident, but I saw his face."

"You never told anyone?"

"I didn't see any use in worrying my parents. Or Hester, who's been so kind." Christy held her hand against Dan's face as if she could take away the weals. "I won't tell her about this, either, unless you think I should. I don't think he's come to see her in years."

It was as if how evil a one-time neighbor could be was a secret they wanted to protect their loved ones against. Owen knew. He'd helped clean and bandage the festering cuts, but Dan had asked him not to tell the Parkses.

"You're right not to tell Lafe's mother," Dan said. "He and his friend, Quantrill, have turned bushwhacker. Maybe they won't get down this far, but I'm afraid they'll do a lot of devilment."

She buried her face against his shoulder. "Oh, Dan! Will it ever be the way it used to be?"

So dear, so troubled, so sweet she was, and he with the darkness on his soul not fit to touch her although he couldn't resist. He clasped the back of her head with one hand, working his fingers through the glossy curls that held just the faintest smell of apple cider vinegar. Like Lydia and Susie, she must use that in the rainwater with which she washed and rinsed her hair. He kissed her lightly, not daring to linger on her mouth.

"If the Union wins, sweetheart, in some ways, it'll be better. Slavery's still legal, but I'm betting it won't be by the time the war's over. Men like Justus won't be chased with dogs or sold away from their families. Watt Caxton won't come around every spring buying up Negroes the way he does mules. And there'll be an end to jayhawking and bush-whacking both."

She stepped back, holding his gaze. "Susie at least has little Andy. . . ."

Dan stepped back, too. "Don't, Christy! Not if you love me."

"That's why!"

"I'm bound no child of mine will ever starve." More, though he couldn't tell her, never would he make love to her with this corruption tainting him. He would come to her only with clean hands and a clean heart — and he thought now he might never have them again.

"Your child will have the milk of my body."

"So long as you have food. No, Christy!" He caught her arm roughly and drew her toward a tangle of vines festooning from a red oak. "Let's see if the birds and foxes have left us any grapes."

Ash lay white and ghostly in Andy's forge beside the anvil where his hammer rested. His begrimed leather apron hung from one of the poles supporting the roof of the three-walled smithy facing Timbered Mound where the victims of Marais des Cygnes were buried. A broken plowshare awaited his attention. Different sizes of horseshoes were sorted on a shelf.

Eli Snyder, the burly smith who'd stood off

Hamelton over three years ago, had fashioned a wrought iron cross with a hammer and anvil at the center intertwined with Andy's initials. At Susie's wish, he pounded the bottom end into the yellowing grass beneath the huge oak that shaded cabin and smithy.

It was not a formal service, but a remembering. Eli praised Andy's skill as a smith and his courage as a man. "Why, on his wedding day, he left his bride to pursue Hamelton's gang, and he left her again, and his baby boy, to defend the Union. God rest his soul and comfort his loved ones."

Hughie Huston stepped beside the cross, gray hair fluffed around the rosy Irish face that twenty years in the West had not been able to tan. "I first laid eyes on Andrew when we were chousing after Clarke's raiders in late summer of 'Fifty-Six." The lilt of Hughie's accent pleasured Dan. He was American, would have it no other way in spite of this war, but his heart's core loved a soft misty morning and an Irish voice. "We sent Clarke's spalpeens across the line," went on Hughie, "but there was fear for John Brown and Free Staters around Osawatomie since another invading rabble had gone there. So didn't Andrew ride alone . . . when he could have met more raiders at any turn . . . to see if help was needed?"

Theo Wattles told how Andy had cheered him before Wilson's Creek. Owen said Andy had given him his only extra shirt when Owen's wore out and always had a joke or droll word to beguile the marching.

"No one . . . begging your pardon, Eli . . . could shoe a horse or mule like Andy," said big, blond Sam Nickel. He and his two oldest sons were in the 6th Kansas Cavalry and wore amazing hodge-podges of homespun and uniforms.

After the tributes, Dan played the tune that had been growing in him, determined to break off before he got to the cry for vengeance. It began shy as a fawn, quickened to a dance, hinted at the ring of blows on an anvil, the scream of artillery. Then it was a dirge, the strings wailing. Dan saw again the bullet hiss into Andy's neck, felt Lafe's blade grate on his own cheek bone. Possessed, Dan started to play a cry for retribution, full of hate and fury. Then a movement caught his almost blinded eyes.

Little red-haired Andrew Owen, stout legs braced to stand free of his mother's skirt, took a toddling step forward. "Och, now, Andy lad," Dan murmured. "Won't your boy be the spit and image of you and farm this land you claimed . . . you, who could never have owned more earth on your island than it took to bury you? Someday this laddie may even heat iron in your forge and shape it with your hammer."

The lament flowed back into the first tentative, questing notes, then swelled again into the dance. Dan stole a glance at Susie and was glad to see a smile touch his foster sister's lips although tears glistened in her eyes. Christy, beside her, was smiling, too.

Simeon called for a silent moment for each to make a private farewell to Andy. Then he led them in the Lord's Prayer. Dan couldn't pray it. He couldn't forgive those who trespassed against him; he wanted to be led into the temptation of killing.

Susie sent her child home with Lydia and Harriet. He went without fuss at his Cousin Letty's command. At six, the chubby flaxen-haired girl bossed her small brother and cousin unmercifully, but took good care of them, too.

"We'll spend the night here, Mother Catriona and I," Susie told Dan. They needed to mourn freely with no one to hear but the sky, the earth, and the river. "Since you're leaving early tomorrow, I'll tell you good bye now." She hugged him closely and kissed him. "Be careful, Danny. We pray for you every day. Bless you for the music. Andy would have loved it."

Thank goodness the sight of her little son had kept Dan from defiling the service. From a dense hawthorn thicket, a mockingbird trilled, drawing out its notes, embellishing and repeating. Dan's jaw dropped. He stared at Susie who smiled and nodded.

"Yes, I do believe, Dan, he's trying to mimic your song. Andy always liked to have him around and put out suet for him in bad weather."

So the bird would sing to its old friend although Andy's body lay under a blasted oak on the side of Bloody Hill. Dan helped Christy into her family's wagon and mounted to follow with Thos. At the edge of the clearing, Dan heard something that tugged at deep roots.

Turning, he saw Catriona embracing the cross, face pressed against it. She was singing, an old Gælic children's song Dan remembered from his mother.

Matthew, Mark, and Luke and John,
Hold the pony till I leap on.
Guide him safe and bring him sure,
While we fare over the misty moor.

That was the English of it, near enough. Fare safe and well and happy, lad. But if ever I get a chance at Lafe or Quantrill who shot you, when you might have lived, I'll kill them with pleasure.

Dan didn't see Christy alone again, but he left his fiddle with her after playing far into the night. "Your blanket holds off twice the wind and rain because you wove it," he told her. Leaving the fiddle was like trusting his soul to her while he went off with murder in his heart. He kissed her good bye in front of her family, aching at the hurt in her eyes. He couldn't even promise they'd be married after the war. They couldn't if the killing lust stayed in him, or if he did things for which he could never forgive himself. Like shooting a wounded man in the back of the head or carving a face.

Uncle Simeon had known something was wrong. "Shall we pray together, thee and me?" he asked gently. "If something burdens thee, Dan. . . ."

What a relief it would be to pour out his affliction! But Dan couldn't, since he couldn't forgive his enemies. The passion for revenge went deeper than will and mind. It rose in a welter of corruption from his heart and guts.

Reading Dan's answer in his silence, Simeon dropped a hand on his shoulder. "I will pray for you, my boy, just as I will for David."

"I'll watch out for Davie as much as I can," Dan assured Simeon, although his foster father hadn't asked it.

Well supplied with apples, lean bacon, and dried corn, Dan and Thos rode Queenie and her five-year-old chestnut daughter, Lass, when they left the Wares. Owen would take the mares home from the mill. Even as they said their farewells at the Parkses, they heard the rattle of a wagon and hurried toward the

Military Road while Lydia called admonitions to her younger brother.

"Should I bundle up in Pa's overcoat so I'll look bigger?" David worried. Although wiry, he only reached Dan's chin and was delicately built.

Dan ruffled his hair. "You don't want to look like a flea in a buffalo robe, Davie. But since you're pretty young, they may make a sheepskin fiddler or straw blower out of you."

"Sheepskin fiddler?" David frowned. "What's that?"

"A drummer. And a straw blower toots a flute."

David wailed. "I don't want to beat a drum or play a silly old flute! I want to have a saber and be in the cavalry."

"So do we" — Thos grinned — "but you're welcome to the saber. Artillery makes daredevil charges plain suicide, although that idiot, Zagoni, got away with it at Springfield."

The three of them reached the Trading Post store about the same time five supply wagons rumbled up, each drawn by six long-eared mules. The escort, commanded by a young lieutenant, was far from consistently clothed but there was enough braid and gilt buttons to bring a sparkle to David's eyes.

Well, thought Dan, *let them sparkle. He'll learn soon enough. Just please, God, don't let me live if he dies.* The baby of the family, David was the light of his old father's life, and to the sisters who had raised him, he was more than a brother.

"Sure, you can ride with us to Fort Scott," the droopy-mustached lieutenant said in answer to their question. "Just pile on top of the bags and boxes."

They camped ten miles down the road and were invited to partake of Lieutenant Colby's beans, beef, coffee, and hardtack. Of course, they had to share their good things with him, which was probably why the officer had deigned to welcome them. As he devoured bacon and two apples, he told them that Lincoln had replaced Frémont with General Hunter on the night before Frémont planned finally to march on Price.

"There were enough of our boys to whip Price, and the brigadiers warned Hunter that, if he pulled out of Springfield, the Rebs would take all southwestern Missouri." Lieutenant Colby's tobacco juice barely cleared his moustache. "It's hard to keep an army supplied that far from a railhead, and Hunter probably figgered McCulloch would join up with Price. Whyever, Hunter pulled his army back to Sedalia and Rolla, except for the troops under General Sturgis and Jim Lane. They're headed for Kansas." Colby spat again. "The Secesh may laugh at Hunter, but they won't grin at Lane. He's burning their farms and plantations and running off their darkies."

"It's hard to believe Sturgis lets him jay-hawk." Dan remembered his first real taste of regular Army discipline shortly after the 2nd Kansas joined Sturgis's brigade on the way to meet General Lyon. "When the Second came through Harrisonville, a couple of our men stole vegetables out of a garden. Sturgis had them court-martialed. We were ordered to form a hollow square and the men were tied to wagon wheels and flogged." Dan grimaced. "Sturgis had cannon trained on us to keep us from cutting the fellows loose."

"Sturgis sends any darkies who try to refuge with him back to their masters and turns the air blue with ordering Lane to stop plundering." Colby chuckled. "Old Jim Lane's a favorite of Lincoln's. He promises to be a good boy but goes right on looting."

"How can he be a senator and general both?" Dan remembered that Jonathan Ware had said the U.S. Constitution prohibited such dual rôles.

"Lane's a caution!" Colby's tone was more approving than censorious. "Governor Robinson hates his guts. Said Lane's accepting a commission put him out of his Senate seat. But wouldn't you know old Jim got around that? Resigned his Kansas commission and got one from Indiana! Now he's a senator and brigadier both." The lieutenant offered David a can of evaporated milk. "Here, young 'un, try this on your hardtack and pass it around." He squinted at Dan and Thos. "You're signing up with Montgomery? Why not Jennison?"

"He's a worse pirate than Lane," said Dan.

The lieutenant laughed. "He sure put on a pious act on his way to Lawrence with the Mound City Rifle Guards last summer. A farmer offered them a pail of whiskey. Jennison thanked him and said his men didn't drink."

"Jennison doesn't drink?" hooted Dan.

"Not that day, I reckon. A lady who heard about it was so thrilled, she stitched the Rifles a flag. Jennison laid it on thick in his thank you letter. Said his boys wouldn't drink from 'the bowl of poison' and how they'd defend with their lives the banner her 'fair hands had wrought' for them. Naturally Doc sent copies to all the newspapers."

"He got someone to fancy the letter up for him," grunted Dan. "He may be a doctor, but, from the letter he wrote Uncle Simeon once when he wanted some meal on credit, he can't spell for shucks."

"He don't need to." The lieutenant shifted his cud. "He writes in blood and fire to the Secesh. They take his meaning."

The three reached Fort Scott next evening too late to be sworn in, but were welcomed by Theo Wattles and his messmates to a kettle of beans and coffee so strong it could fight back. "I was lucky enough to get in Company K of the Seventh Kansas," Theo boasted, dark eyes sparkling. "You know, John Brown's boys! John Brown, Junior's our captain! He's bringing most of the company down from Ohio, but an advance got here this week. Why don't you join us?"

Although they didn't condone the older Brown's slaughter at Osawatomie, the Wattleses had been his friends. Augustus, Theo's father, had, like Dan, been one of the party that had traveled to Virginia to rescue Brown. It was natural for Theo to thrill at the chance to serve under the martyr-monster's son. Jennison commanded the 7th and the men enlisting in the regiment were fervent Abolitionists to a man.

"My first chase after bushwhackers was with Colonel Montgomery," Dan said. "I was with him when he rode here to Fort Scott to rescue the Free-State men who were chained to the floor of the jail. I want to follow him now."

"He's a good man." Theo knelt to stir water-soaked hardtack frying in bacon grease. "Hunker down and help yourself to the skillygalee."

Eaten with beans, it tasted pretty good. If there were weevils, well, that was just part of the meat ration. One of the Ohioans at the next fire, red-haired and freckled, looked familiar to Dan. Laughing at a messmate, he said: "Sure, lads, a body needs only one spur. If one side of a nag moves, won't the other follow?"

The Irish accent had Dan on his feet. "Tim!" He squatted down by the surprised soldier. "Tim O'Donnell! Remember me? How's Peggy?"

"Danny O'Brien, as I breathe!" The brawny redhead clasped Dan in a bear hug. He had to notice the scar but, to Dan's relief, didn't mention it. "Peggy's bright and blooming with two pretty colleens at her skirts. You're looking at her husband, that great black-haired, squinty-eyed, hump-nosed lummox yonder, Harry Shepherd. I married his sister, a lovely lass in spite of his looks. Makes us closer kin than I care to be, but he's handy in a fight."

"You get us in enough of them." Harry grinned.

"How's Uncle Simeon?" Tim ran on. "Wasn't he the grand one, to take in us three Irish orphans? And how're Lydia, Owen, and Susie? I've asked for a furlough to go visit." He drew bleached eyebrows together as David hurried to them and rose to lift the boy off his feet in a swooping embrace.

"Now isn't it our Davie, all grown up? Will ye be a soldier then, boyeen?"

They were still catching up on the doings of both families since the Parkses had left the grown O'Donnells in Ohio — letters were exchanged occasionally but not often — when the fire was poked up, men gathered, voices hushed, and a willowy, long-haired officer opened a Bible.

"That's Lieutenant George Hoyt," Theo whispered. "He's a lawyer from Massachusetts. Volunteered to defend old John Brown in his trial after Harper's Ferry. Couldn't get him off, of course. Nobody could have."

Clearing his throat, Lieutenant Hoyt read in a resonant tone from a passage Dan recognized as the cry of the prophet, Joel. " 'Put ye in the sickle, for the harvest is ripe: come, get you down; for the press is full, the fats overflow; for their wickedness is great. Multitudes, multitudes, in the valley of decision: for the day of the Lord is near in the valley of decision. The sun and the moon shall be darkened, and the stars shall withdraw their shining. The Lord also shall roar out of Zion. . . .' "

When Hoyt finished, he looked around at the forty or so Ohioans. "Perhaps you don't know that men from Kansas traveled east to help John Brown escape. He refused, confident that his hanging would do more to free the slaves than could his living." Hoyt's voice sank. He raised his arms and whispered in a way that made Dan's skin prickle: "Do you swear to avenge the death of John Brown?"

"We will!" Theo's voice swelled the fervent promise. "We will!"

Dan's scalp crawled in earnest then, for, all around him, men began to sing, softly at first, then with mounting ardor.

John Brown's body lies a-mouldering in the grave,
John Brown's body lies a-mouldering in the grave,
John Brown's body lies a-mouldering in the grave,
But his soul goes marching on. . . .

The last verse swung into fast tempo.

Then three cheers for John Brown, Junior,
Then three cheers for John Brown, Junior,
Give three cheers for John Brown, Junior,
As we go marching on!

The conduct of Company K was certainly different from that of neighboring groups who loafed around their fires playing cards, yarning, and telling ribald jokes, except for those who were writing letters, using hardtack boxes for desks.

"Tattoo" sounded. While the soldiers assembled for the final roll call of the day, Dan, Thos, and David spread their bedrolls near Montgomery's 3rd Regiment. By the time "Taps" signaled quiet and candles out — for everyone but officers — Dan was almost asleep, Christy's blanket pulled over his scar.

He jumped when something touched him. "Dan?" came David's whisper. "I . . . I'm cold."

And a little homesick, maybe a little scared? Company K was enough to scare anyone. "Haul your bedroll over here," Dan invited. "When it's really cold, Davie, we'll sleep so tight in a tent that, if one person has to turn over, he'll give the word and everybody'll switch at the same time."

"Think I'll join you," said Thos, although it was really not that chilly.

Snug between them, David was soon breathing deeply. *He's too young for war,* Dan thought with a wave of foreboding. *Raised Quaker, fussed over by his sisters. . . .*

But those sisters and an old father had let him go because they hated slavery. At least he had no brother on the other side the way that Thos did, and Christy.

Christy. He had kissed her good bye only yesterday morning. How long would it be till he saw her again? Making her as real as he could in his imagining, Dan drew her blanket closer around him and sank into sleep.

Being under eighteen, David presented Simeon's letter of permission to the rail-thin, straggly-mustached orderly sergeant who barely glanced at it before telling the three of them to raise their right hands while he administered the oath. They signed the documents pledging to serve three years or for the duration of the war. The sergeant locked the papers in a metal box and put it inside his tent.

"Now, lads," he said, straightening with a grin, "you said you want to be in the cavalry, but what we need is muleskinners to take supplies to an outpost. As soon as you hear 'Boots and Saddles', each of you get six mules from that bunch grazing yonder. Bring 'em in and string 'em out."

"Sir?" David was trying to salvage something from his dreams of glory. "My uniform. . . ."

"Go see what the quartermaster has, Private Parks, but be sure you're back here in time to harness up. Now, let's have a smart salute, if you please."

"Drat him!" muttered Thos as they hurried off. "He didn't tell us they didn't need cavalrymen till he had us sworn, signed, and sealed!"

"That's why he's a sergeant." Dan grinned at David although he himself was sorely disappointed. "Look at it this way, boys. We already know our job."

CHAPTER TWENTY-SIX

It was for hard for Christy to accept the fact that Thos and Dan would be back in the Army, and this time for who could guess how long? This war wasn't ending as quickly as either side had expected. Each night, in their evening prayers, the Wares especially remembered Andy, his wife, his son, and his mother, along with Dan, Charlie, and Thos.

The memory of how Dan had played at the funeral service for Andy filled Christy with wonder that he'd composed such powerful music. But hadn't there been a few seconds of mounting fury, something terrible indeed, before Dan had glanced at Andy's little son and then changed the notes, the tune becoming almost a lullaby? Christy knew something was wrong inside Dan, and it hurt to remember how he'd seemed almost to shun her. Yet she couldn't doubt he loved her. She had a feeling it had to do with Lafe Ballard and the death of Andy. Whatever it was had folded him in shadow.

The shadow of death? She shivered and reasoned with herself. *No, Thos had walked that valley, too, and Owen. They had changed, were older, tougher. But the chilling darkness wasn't in them.* She might have found some relief in talking to her parents about this dread, but, if they hadn't noticed it, she didn't want to trouble them with something none of them could remedy.

Jonathan had gone to see how Allie Hayes and the family were getting along without Ethan and Matt, and he returned looking worried.

"She'll be lucky to hold Mark much longer," Jonathan predicted. "Even Luke is fancying himself a soldier." He paused and his mouth hardened in a way most unusual for him, mostly a laughing man. "Allie's heard from Missus Maddux that, after Lafe and Tom Maddux, the Baptist minister's son, mustered out last month, they decided it was better looting with one of the gangs that joins Quantrill for big raids but just ranges over the country the rest of the time. Watt Caxton joined the bunch, too, having decided apparently that it would be more profitable than selling a few slaves here and there. Missus Maddux sounds sort of proud of Tom, Allie says, but Hester wouldn't approve of Lafe's actions."

"Lafe never writes or comes to see Hester," Ellen said. "A heartache he's always been for her. I hope he keeps his devilment well away from where she'd hear of it."

Christy's spine crawled. Lafe Ballard a guerrilla, freed from any restraints of Army discipline? She looked at the wrist scar he had caused back at the cabin raising. She'd like to think he'd forgotten all about her. All the same. . . .

She voiced a thought that had been forming since Dan's visit and the certainty that this war was going to last longer than anyone had feared. "Father, why don't we see if the underground river passage has a cavern large enough to hold our animals if raiders come this way? You know, the one right across the creek from us . . . the opening we found when Justus was hiding there? We know the passage goes through Watt Caxton's land. We might be able find a big chamber beyond there."

"That could come in handy," he admitted.

"Oh, Jonathan, please do look," Ellen urged. "There might be a place where we could take refuge, too, if need be. Certainly it can't hurt to be prepared."

Right after chores and breakfast the next morning, Christy and her father set off across the creek with torches and candles which they would use once they were beyond the light of the entrance of the cave where Justus had hid in what seemed a lifetime ago. *Where was he now? Had he ever got back for his wife, his Hildy, down in Indian Territory?* Christy wondered. The strife down there between the tribes that had joined the Confederacy and those who had declared for the Union sounded as bad as that along this border.

But soon everything but the magnificence of this expanse fled Christy's mind as she and her father held their flickering torches and gasped at the sculpturings, pinnacles, and draperies of white, yellow, and rose, the beauties hidden till light struck them. Light flashed, too, on the glide of strange pale fish that must wonder what had happened to their eternal dark.

Not far beyond the sinkhole on the Caxton farm, the passage expanded into a glittering palisaded chamber with the river murmuring through it. After awestruck moments, while their torches traced hunched formations that looked like gargoyles and fantastic beasts, her father whispered softly: "This room would hold all the cattle and horses. And there's water."

"The opening is big enough even for Moses and Pharaoh," Christy said. "Single file, the animals could make it in here."

"Yes, but it'd take a while to get them all across the creek and up the passage. Raiders likely won't give that much warning." Her father shrugged. "Still, it's good to know about it. Let's see if there's a way out on this end."

Walking cautiously, they continued on.

After what seemed a long time, sun-drenched blue dazzled ahead. The river narrowed and deepened although they could still walk without stooping. Blowing out the candles that had replaced their burned-out torches, they came out into a grotto. The rock floor rose on either side of the river that glistened and sang as it hurled itself down from the cave and came in sight again, sparkling through a high-grassed valley, steeply walled all around except for a narrow gorge on the other side that, through the centuries, had been cut by the river flowing to the world beyond. This was a world of its own. A hidden one.

"People lived here once," Jonathan said to his daughter, kneeling to touch a basin ground in the limestone. A stone pestle lay on the earth. He stood again, and pointed out: "Look, there are other caves in the cliffs yonder. With the only entrance being this cave . . . unless some of the others have passages to the outside . . . this is a safe, beautiful place." He laughed, admiring the tranquil meadow and many hues of trees. "I'll wager whatever others called it must have meant peace valley."

Enchanted, Christy thought sighing. "What a wonderful place to live!"

"If you didn't want to get in or out very often," her father replied thoughtfully. The sun burnished his hair into a blaze of russet.

His eyes, though, turned serious. "Christy, if things turn upside down, people could live here. There's graze for animals. The silty land along the creek would grow crops. There's bound to be nut and fruit trees . . . berries. But, now, we need to get back."

They made their way out, following the path by which they had discovered this hidden valley.

Once home, they told of their discovery. Ellen was thrilled to hear of the wonderful place. They promised to show her soon.

A few evenings later, they were about to sit down to supper when a distant thunder neared enough to be recognized as galloping horses, more than just a few. Robbie set up a clamorous barking. It was warm, so the door still stood open, and Jonathan started toward it, calling Robbie inside.

Christy peered out the window at a confusion of armed men, most in the gaudy red or yellow shirts she'd heard Southern guerrillas fancied, along with broad-brimmed, plumed hats. Of the score or so, most were strangers to Christy, but in a swift fearful glance she recognized Watt Caxton and then Lafe Ballard, who was to one side of the hulking Tom Maddux, the Baptist minister's son.

"Father!" she cried. "Don't go out. Let me! They won't hurt a woman!"

"I'll see what they want," her father said as he stepped outside, calling out: "Come ahead! We just sat down for supper, but you're welcome. . . ."

Without warning, Watt Caxton charged toward Jonathan, yelling — "This is for that whelp of yours in the Union Army!" — and discharged his gun.

The shot sent Jonathan back across the threshold, arms outstretched as if still in welcome, blood pouring from his blasted chest. He breathed in labored gasps as Christy and her mother raised him up, having both rushed to his side. He tried to speak, coughed blood, and reached for his wife's hand. The life flowed out of him. Heavy he was suddenly, so very heavy in their arms.

"Next time, Watt, don't you go shootin' till I give a sign, hear?" commanded the leader, a dark young man with what looked like scalps hanging on his bridle.

"Miz Ware!" Caxton shouted, ignoring the man in charge. "Where's them Jerseys and the big white oxen?"

"Jayhawked," Christy lied.

"Funny the bays got left," Lafe Ballad put in.

"Father . . . father had driven them to the mill that day."

Reining his horse between the house and Caxton and Ballard, the leader ordered: "Let the ladies be. "Don't bother the house. Leave these folks some corn and bacon and ham!" he shouted to the men who were already hitching Queenie and Jed to the wagon. "And hustle! Quantrill expects us at Black Jack day after tomorrow."

Christy and her mother somehow carried Jonathan inside.

"Hold Robbie, Beth," Christy choked. "We don't want him getting hurt out there."

Could this be happening? It had to be a nightmare. Yet her father's blood soaked the bed where they had placed him.

Ellen fell on her knees beside her husband. Her silence was worse than screams. She stroked his hair and held his hand to her cheek.

From outside came volleys of shots, wild yells and laughter, the squeals of dying pigs and blatting of terrified sheep. Christy started to run out, but Beth caught her around the knees.

"Christy! Don't! Don't go out! They might kill you, too!"

Trembling, weeping at the piteous sounds of the animals she knew like friends, Christy remembered that they had been keeping the cows up in the woods, along with the oxen and Lass and Laddie, too. Had Christy been alone, if her mother and Beth wouldn't suffer for her actions, she'd have run out anyway, grabbed a hoe or anything handy, and attacked the devils shooting Patches' and Evalina's offspring and using the black-faced flock for target practice.

Beth had crept close to her mother but was not touching her, as if she were afraid this wasn't the woman she knew. Christy dropped beside her, huddled against their father's knee that splayed near the edge of the bed. Beth held to her as if scared she might change, too.

Christy had changed. She would never, ever be the same. But she hugged Beth as they murmured the psalms and prayers they knew by heart. " 'Yea, though I walk through the valley of the shadow of death, I will fear no evil. . . .' "

I do, though, Christy thought, *and it's out there. Hear it, oh, God, no, don't hear.*

After what seemed an eternity, the tumult outside was over, although from a distance the creak of the wagon sounded along with gusts of laughter and yells of triumph.

"Bethie," Christy whispered, "I want to see if I can help any . . . any of the animals. You stay here with Mother. Bring her a drink, honey. While I'm out, I'll bring in the cows. It's past time and they'll be needing to let down their milk."

Outside, twilight hazed the barnyard, stable, and pens, thick with the smell of gunpowder. Pale heaps piled inside the sheeps' fence. There wasn't a moving animal inside. At least, none was crying with pain. The marauders had been thorough. From the best count she could make in the growing darkness, all thirty sheep were dead, left where they fell. Poor Nosey and Cleo and Mildred, who had walked the long way from Illinois, their neat-hoofed black-faced family! Through tears, Christy peered at the opulent black and white bodies of Patches and Evalina. Deemed old and tough, they'd been left, but the carcasses of the younger pigs had been taken. Succulent meals they'd make, spitted over a fire.

At first Christy thought all the chickens had been stolen, but nervous *cluck*s came from the trees where some had found refuge. Heloise and Abelard — no telling goose from gander, they were so ripped with bullets — lay by the sheep pen. *Poor creatures, what had they to do with North and South? What kind of men could take pleasure in this?* Christy told herself that Jed and Queenie were valuable horses. That the mounts of the guerrillas looked well cared for.

A plaintive lowing floated from the timber. The Jerseys and oxen couldn't understand why they had to stay in the woods by day. Christy gave herself a shake. Lady Jane, Guinevere, and Maud would have ordinarily been milked before supper, but, in these harrowing times, her father had begun bringing them in as night fell, when no intruders were likely to come. He milked them then and again in the morning before turning them back into the woods.

Christy trudged toward the forest. No use

wasting the meat of the sheep and Patches and Evalina although she didn't think she could eat such old friends. Tomorrow she'd ride Lass to the mill so it could be arranged for the Parkses to come and get the carcasses to butcher. Maybe Lydia Parks could stay with them a few days. . . .

The cows came to meet her, and she stroked the bump on each of their heads, the one between their black-rimmed ears. "I'm glad you don't know what people can do," she told them, hot tears scalding her face. But they seemed to understand, at least to a degree. Although the pig and sheep pens were a little distance from the barn, the cows appeared nervous.

When she was done milking, she carried the buckets to the well house, which she found emptied of butter and cheese. Several jugs lay wantonly smashed. It was as she washed the pails that she noticed the drying blood on her dress. *Now we must somehow bury Father.*

Back in the house, Ellen, as if in a trance, was bathing Jonathan's ghastly wound. Christy helped without a word. What could she say? They brought lifeless hands and arms through the sleeves of a clean shirt, and finally wrapped him in the treasured quilt the neighbor women, including Nora Caxton, had stitched under the great tree the day the house was raised. How long ago that seemed, and not just in years!

"The ground's softest and sweetest in the garden or fields where the rocks have been cleared," Ellen said as if rousing from a dream. "The edge of the cornfield will be easy to dig. Jonathan would like it there, where he worked the most. It was always something with the corn . . . plowing, planting, cultivating, pulling fodder, cribbing, plowing stubble under, but he said young corn was one of the prettiest sights on earth."

"Do . . . do you want a piece of his hair?" Christy asked as she touched her father's head.

Her mother flinched. "No, oh, no. Let it stay on his dear head. But I'll cut off some of mine for him. He did love my hair."

"All of you," Christy said.

"All of us!" Beth cried, pushing in to bury her face against their mother. "Mama, Mama, put on a clean dress! You're all bloody! Christy, you change, too!"

So they washed, put on clean dresses, set the stained ones and the sheets to soak. Cloth was too precious to discard. Then Ellen and Christy dug the grave in the rich-smelling earth while Beth fished rocks from the soil. They lined the hole with yellow stalks of goldenrod that still flourished and then brought Jonathan, wrapped in the beautiful quilt. More goldenrod covered the quilt. They threw in the first handfuls of sod, then gently filled the oblong, heaping the dirt into a mound.

Kneeling, arms around each other, they repeated the Shepherd's Psalm, but then they sobbed and wept before, at last, going back up to the house. Ellen sank into her rocker. Christy lit the lamp on the table by the forgotten supper. She didn't think she'd ever be hungry again, but she knew they must all eat something, and sleep if they could. She poked up the coals and poured the stew back in the kettle to heat while the teakettle nestled at the edge of the hearth.

Ellen managed a few bites at Christy's urging, but mostly she sipped her tea, letting her hand rest on Robbie's head who sat near her. Christy was too exhausted to do their few dishes so put them to soak while she and Beth made their parents' bed. Christy thought she had cleaned up the blood but found a few more spots that left stains no matter how hard she scrubbed. Maybe black walnut in some butter would cover the places.

"I think we should sleep with Mother," she murmured to Beth. "And keep Robbie close to the bed, too."

Beth nodded. "That way it won't . . . won't be so lonesome. But . . . what'll we do, Christy?"

"Right now, you brush Mother's hair and put it in a plait while I take off her shoes and rub her feet with some of her lavender ointment."

When weariness set in, Christy helped her mother into her nightgown and led her to the bed. Once settled, Ellen sighed and pressed her face into the pillow. Beth got in to warm her back, and, as soon as Christy had banked the coals and blown out the lamp, she put on her gown and lay at her mother's other side. Robbie stayed by the side of the bed where she could touch him. He gave her hand a comforting lick, followed by a soft whimper. *How much does he understand about Father's death?* Christy wondered, and scratched behind his ears.

The next thing she knew it was morning although she hadn't believed she would sleep at all. She roused, a weight on her even before she remembered, waiting for the pain as if it were a stalking beast wakefulness could bring upon her. To her surprise, it didn't seize her at once. She lay still, by her mother, like hiding prey, and rested her tired body. But the beast sensed her consciousness. It padded toward her on clawed feet, sank in its fangs. She fought it off by rising from her parents' bed, trying not to wake Beth, who slept curled in a ball around Lambie, thumb in her mouth, eyes red and puffy. Let her sleep as long as she could. If you slept eight hours of twenty-four, that was a third of the time you didn't have to remember.

Christy planned out the day as she got ready. The cows needed milking and hiding, and then she'd go to the Parkses. Maybe seeing them would help bring her mother out of her numbed stillness.

After she had poured the milk into pans for the cream to form and washed and rinsed the buckets, Christy and Robbie escorted the cattle across their old pasture. Pharaoh, Moses, and the dry cows waited at the gate and lowed to welcome their companions. Lad and Lass grazed in plain sight on a grassy slope.

It might be possible to hide a few animals, but with this many it was just a matter of time till all of them would be stolen. Peace Valley would be the safest place, but Guinevere, Maud, and Lady Jane had to be milked twice a day. Their spring calves still suckled, but were almost weaned. Christy caught Lass with an old halter and led her to the barn. The saddles were gone, but the thieves had left an ancient bridle and a few faded saddle blankets. She tied these around Lass with some strips of canvas hoarded from their covered wagon. She left the mare by the house and went to tell her mother and Beth where she was going.

Ellen had changed from her nightgown, but her hair still hung in the single braid. "What, dear?" she asked, turning to Christy.

Christy repeated herself. "I won't be gone

long." She bent to kiss her mother who placed cold fingers on her wrist. "Have you had breakfast?"

"Bread and milk," Christy said. "Beth, will you make new mush for you and Mother? I'll fry what's left of the old to go with supper."

She never passed a soul till she neared the mill, and was glad. She didn't want to talk to anyone, except to trusted friends. After she told them what had happened, Simeon and Lydia Parks wept with her, prayed with her, and then made her join them for corn chowder before they followed her back with the wagon in which they would haul away the dead animals.

Simeon gave Christy a serviceable saddle someone had left at the mill as payment for meal, so the ride back home was more comfortable. The Parkses tried to persuade Ellen to come stay at the comparative safety of the mill, across the border, but she said: "My daughter-in-law's expecting a baby soon. I'd like to be there when he's born."

He? Then Christy understood. Her mother hoped to see in Charlie's son an infant Jonathan, his smile, some of his features and nature living on. Well, that might be the best for now, for her mother and Beth to stay with the Jardines. Lavinia and Melissa would welcome them lovingly, and the bishop knew his duty.

The Parkses, at Ellen's request, would come back to take her piano, the heirloom rocking chair, silver, and china, and keep them till safer times. Lydia, angular and strong as a man, told Christy she and Simeon would load the pigs and sheep. "I know they were your friends," she said, giving Christy a quick hug. "Go fetch your milk cows while we clear away. You say you have a safe place to take them?" At Christy's nod, she held up a hand. "Don't tell us. Better it's a secret, so there'll be no slips."

Christy was on her way back with the cows when Hester Ballard came up from the creek like a shadow. "Yesterday, at nooning, someone who looked like Lafe . . . but wasn't . . . hanged Emil," she said. "Killed Lottie when she got in the way of bullet."

Hester explained how she had been gathering nuts and had heard the uproar. She had hidden, and, when the gang left, she'd cut Emil down, dug out a grave for him and Lottie in the orchard, dragged a log over it so the beasts couldn't get at them. She couldn't remember much after that. She woke this morning where she must have fallen asleep in a shallow cave. When she heard a man groaning, she'd thought she was remembering the raid, but after a while the sound had come again.

"He's down there by the creek. Too heavy for me to carry and burning up with fever," she said in conclusion.

"Do you know him?" Christy asked.

Hester shook her head. "From the stink of the wound in his shoulder, he was shot several days ago. Will you help get him to your house?"

"A gang rode up last evening," Christy told her. "Watt Caxton shot Father down . . . right in the doorway. If that man you found is one of them. . . ."

"Your father?" Hester broke in. "Jonathan?" Christy nodded.

Hester's anguish came out in a frightening way, with no sound, just a contorted face and heaving shoulders. "God rest that lovely man," she choked at last. "I'll come to your mother as soon as I do what I can for this man . . . whoever he is. All I know, honey girl, is that's he's young and hurt bad and will die if he's not seen to." She turned away, seeming very old.

"Wait!" Christy said. "I'll bring Lady Jane down and we'll see if we can get him slung over her." While she got the Jersey, she thought about what Hester had said. If the same group that had attacked her family had attacked the Franzes, and she knew it had to have been, then Lafe had been among the group. Hester had seen her son take part in this horrible act. But she couldn't let herself acknowledge it.

■ ■ ■ ■

"Let's take him in the other cabin, put him on Beth's and my bed," Christy instructed Hester, meaning the cabin connected by the dogtrot to the larger cabin. "Mother wants to go to Jardines', so maybe she won't know he's here."

"I'll see to him," Hester promised. "And then I'll go speak to your poor mother. Oh, Lordy Lord!"

They dragged more than carried the strange man to the bed. His calico shirt was in tatters and his curly black hair was plastered to his comely browned face that had a hawk nose and imperious brows.

Christy led Lady Jane back to the barn, saw to the milking, and went in to find Hester frying the old mush while Beth set the table. With maple syrup and cream, the mush made an easy supper.

As they ate — Ellen with only a bit of an appetite — Christy said: "Mother, if you want to go to Jardines', let's do it tomorrow. Then, unless you can think of a better place to hide them, I'll take all our animals, except the milk cows, along the underground river to the hidden valley."

"Peace Valley, your father called it," Ellen said. "He said it was a beautiful place. Remember, you two were going to take me

534

to see it."

"I'll take you when you come back from Jardines'," Christy assured her, then changed the subject. "I wonder if Melissa's going to have a girl or little boy."

"I wish she'd have one of each!" Beth brightened at the prospect. Her smooth brow furrowed. "You know, Christy, you don't have to hide Lass from any bad men. They don't steal crippled horses."

Had Beth taken leave of her senses? Christy studied her sister with concern. "Lass isn't crippled."

Beth gave her impish grin for the first time since the horror. "She can act that way, though."

"What?"

"Remember when Lad kicked her when they were playing and she limped for so long?" The other three nodded. "Well," Beth triumphed, "to make her feel all better, I took her apples and turnips and roasting ears and corn pone dipped in molasses. She's so funny and smart! After her leg was fine, she'd limp when she saw me coming, 'specially when I held my hand like I had something in it."

"So you kept sneaking goodies to her," Christy chided.

"Didn't have to sneak," retorted a virtuous Beth. "Mostly, everyone's too busy to notice what I do, as long as I don't get in their way."

Christy exchanged guilty looks with her

535

mother. Beth was the baby and often indulged, but she had no playmate, save Robbie, and was often admonished not to pester.

"I trained Lass," Beth went on loftily. "It was fun to have a secret." She sighed at its loss.

"Being able to keep Lass around will be a big help," Christy praised. "She can pull the cultivator, though we'll have to fetch Lad when we need a team for plowing."

"Plowing?" Ellen looked stricken. "Surely this awful war will be over by spring."

"From what Dan and Thos said, it sounds as if the armies will go into winter quarters, and there won't be much fighting till spring." Christy hated to distress her mother, but there was no use in encouraging hopes that were almost sure to prove false. "Beth should go with you, of course, Mother. Hester and I can look after things here."

"But if more guerrillas come. . . ."

"You know how they brag that they never hurt women." What Christy didn't want to say to her mother, for fear of it sounding like reproach, was that she didn't want to abandon their farm, the garden and fields, the orchards just starting to yield bountifully, the well witched by old John Brown, the home by the giant walnut that had held so much love, life, and laughter. Christy needed to believe it would be the happy house again. To show that faith, she felt she had to stay.

Beth jumped up from the table. "Come on, Christy! I'll show you how to get Lass to act lame!"

As the neared the Jardine plantation, Christy first thought the odor of smoke came from the many fireplaces of Rose Haven.

"Unless they really want me to stay, I'll go back with you," her mother said as she stared off into the distance. "We'll just visit and leave the baby things we've knitted."

"They'll want you and Beth to stay," Christy reassured her. "Melissa loves you, and Missus Jardine's a sweet lady, even if they do have slaves."

"Slaves," repeated Ellen, as if she'd forgotten. She looked distraught. "Oh, dear! Your father wouldn't approve. . . ."

"These aren't ordinary times," Christy said to calm her down. "He'd want you to do whatever helps. Being with Melissa will do that."

"I shouldn't leave you. . . ."

"I want to stay at the house. Besides, Hester'll be with me."

"Hester is demented."

"Just about Lafe, Mother. I guess it's the only way she can stand what he did . . . believing it really wasn't him."

"Poor Hester!" Ellen's voice shook. "It's better to mourn a good man than know a little boy you raised and loved has grown into a monster."

He always was a monster, Christy thought to herself, growing cold at the memory of his pale eyes and parted lips when her father was shot. The leader of the guerrillas had kept his men from robbing the house or offending the women, but Lafe could come back alone. Christy glanced at the crescent on her wrist. Dread surged through her, sweeping away her resolve to protect the happy house as much as she could. *If Lafe caught me alone. . . .* She fought off the terror. He was only a man. He could die. But how she wished Dan or Thos or Charlie was home!

As Lad and Lass left the woods for the cleared lands of Rose Haven, Christy thought they had followed the wrong trail until her brain had to recognize what her eyes saw.

The sprawling two-storied white house with its pillared verandah was gone. Blackened chimneys, tumbled fireplaces, rose from heaps of ashes and charred logs. Smoked, shattered glass was all that was left of the rose room, that and the smell of scorched feathers mixed with the odor of burned wood, fabric, and rotting meat. This last came from the remains of several carelessly slaughtered cattle and hogs from which vultures rose sluggishly at the riders' approach. The rest of the livestock and all the fine horses had vanished. The wagons and carriage had either been stolen or burned. Barns, stables, outbuildings had been fired, but the slave cabins were spared, although no one seemed to be there. Apart from the vultures that returned to their feast, no living creature stirred.

Beth gave a strangled sob and buried her face against Christy's back.

"Dear God!" prayed Ellen. "Oh, dear God. . . ."

Then a shriek cleft the air.

Hair rose at the back of Christy's neck. Did ghosts scream? There was another cry, then a murmur of voices. Christy noticed for the first time that smoke curled from the chimneys of Aunt Phronie's double cabin behind the ruins of the big house.

As another scream resounded, Ellen said: "It's not time for Melissa's baby, but *someone's* birthing."

Nudging Lad and Lass forward, Christy and her mother halted outside the cabin. Ellen helped her younger daughter off, before Christy slid down. As they tethered the horses, a double-barreled shotgun poked out the door, and then a wrinkled yellow face showed behind it.

"Land's sakes!" A relieved smile plumped out the lines in Aunt Phronie's face. "Master Charlie's mama and sisters!" The smile faded. "Reckon you hear Miss Melissa. She tried hard not to holler and upset Miss Vinnie, but that baby's givin' her a sight of misery. Maybe it'll be big and strong enough to live, even it be a good month or more early. Terrible doin's, Miz Ware, terrible!" Face crumpling, Phronie blindly leaned the shotgun against the wall by the door, but she didn't forget the proprieties. "Miss Beth, you run along into the other cabin . . . or, no, go down to that first cabin yonder. Some hens got away and been roostin' there. Maybe you can find a couple of nice eggs. Miss Christy, bein' as you're not married. . . ."

Christy moved past Phronie. "Maybe I can help," she said.

What had happened here was clear enough. It didn't seem to matter much at the moment which side had done this.

Holding Melissa's hands, Lilah bent over Charlie's wife as her knees drew up as her sheeted belly heaved. Lilah, too, was big with child. Her dark eyes looked bruised in her pale gold face that was as sweaty as Melissa's even though wind came through the chinks of the wall, chilling the whole cabin except for directly in front of the fire.

Lavinia Jardine, wrapped in the violet shawl her old nurse had made for her, sat in her invalid chair. Emmie, the gray cat Charlie had rescued, curled up at her feet. Seemingly unaware of her daughter's pain, she threw an unseen shuttle, worked an invisible treadle, and crooned an old song.

For I have dreamed a deadly dream,

540

I fear it may bode sorrow.
I dreamed I pulled the rowan green
With my true love on Yarrow. . . .

"She wheel her chair in front of Master Mord when he was tryin' to keep them jayhawks from smashin' her rose room," lamented Phronie.

Ellen threw off her cloak and went to speak kindly, encouragingly, to Melissa as Phronie went on.

"One of 'em . . . hope he fries in hell . . . clubs her alongside her head. She go limp and I get her outside . . . the house already blazin'. Jayhawks shoot Master Mord a whole lot, bang away after his head's nigh shot off. They strangle Miss Vinnie's birds and toss 'em on top of the master."

"When was this?" Christy asked.

"When?" Phronie rubbed a welt on her skinny arm and thought. "Must've been towards sundown day before yesterday. They had a flag. Some wore uniforms . . . claimed they was Union cavalry and needed supplies. Their captain said he'd give the bishop a chit so he could collect from the Union gov'ment, providin' he could prove he was loyal. Wasn't much the bishop and the overseer, Mister Blake, could do, but, when some of the gang started in on the rose room, Master Mord couldn't stand it and he tried to fight them off. Mister Blake, he just disappeared."

"Where are all the other people?"

"That bluecoat captain, he asks don' they want to be free and come along with him to Kansas. Say they can take anything his gang left. I reckon some would rather have stayed and got along the best they could helpin' Miss Vinnie and Miss Melissa, but that captain said, if Confederates came through, they'd think the colored folks was in cahoots with the jayhawks and most likely would kill 'em or at least break up families and maybe sell 'em away down south."

"So there's just you and Lilah left?"

Phronie nodded. "We got Miss Vinnie in here quick as we could. Zillah, she drag herself out of bed and guard the door . . . she call down all kinds of devils on any jayhawks who peek in till their captain, he say leave us alone, they not fightin' old women or them in the family way."

"Where is Zillah now?"

"When the jayhawks leave off pesterin', she creep over and hug Miss Vinnie, then she lay her head against Miss Vinnie and her poor old heart, it stops. We buried her with what was left of Master Mord. By then, Miss Melissa, she starts her pains." Phronie glared suddenly at her granddaughter, the one Charlie had said was only an eighth colored. Christy remembered uneasily how Lilah had watched Travis with such longing — Travis who'd been chagrined when Christy refused his proposal.

"Don't you even think about having your baby till things straighten out a little!" Phronie admonished Lilah before she glanced at her mistress. "Though I declare I don't see how they ever be straight with Miss Vinnie like she is, shut up some place in her mind. Maybe that's a mercy. She don't know Master Mord be dead."

"Aunt Phronie, will you come here?" Ellen called out. She added in a whisper the gasping Melissa couldn't hear: "I'm afraid the baby isn't turned right."

Phronie lifted the sheet. Her jaw clamped till the bone showed through withered skin. "Lord help us . . . its little rump is comin' first!" Her eyes closed. When they opened, she spoke briskly: "Lilah, you fetch more of the blue cohosh tea. It'll urge her along. Poor lamb goin' to need it. Miss Christy, let her keep ahold of your hands. Miz Ware, be ready to help."

Melissa stared up at Christy, her blue eyes glistening as she blinked back her tears. "Oh, Christy, I'm glad you and Mama Ware came! But I wish Charlie were here!"

"He wishes it, too, dear, be sure of that." Christy tried to speak cheeringly even though her lips were stiff. She raised Melissa so she could sip from the cup Lilah held. *Why bring babies into a world where men like Father were shot down on their thresholds, or killed like*

543

Andy, or mutilated like Dan? Christy thought as she bent to kiss her sister-in-law's pretty well-kept hands. "Just think how happy and proud Charlie will be!"

"Yes!" panted Melissa before her eyes squeezed shut. Pain wracked her. She cried out: "Charlie! Charlie!"

Christy's back was to her mother and Phronie, so she couldn't see what they were doing. Her hands ached, the knuckles ground together, as Melissa grasped them with frantic strength. A scream, a spasm, that seemed to last forever. Melissa went limp. Her fingers drooped from Christy's grasp. Christy caught Melissa's shoulders in a shake, but it was a tremulous wail that opened Melissa's eyes.

"He . . . he's here?" she said weakly.

"Indeed he is!" Ellen gave a sobbing laugh. "A beautiful baby boy! He looks just like Charlie did when he was born." She held the baby while Phronie tied the pulsing cord in two places and cut between them. Phronie washed him with warm water Lilah had brought, and she snuggled the small red creature into Melissa's arms while Ellen took care of the liverish-looking afterbirth and directed Christy and Lilah as they eased the bloody cloths and sheets from under Melissa, bathed her swollen, torn parts, and put a clean sheet beneath her.

"He be good-sized and husky, even if he

came early," Phronie praised. "Look, he's already huntin' his dinner."

Melissa turned and helped the tiny questing mouth find her breast. "Will I have milk, Aunt Phronie?"

"Your real milk won't come in for a few days, honey." Phronie smoothed Melissa's damp curls back from her forehead. "But you'll have a sort of thin yellowish juice he'll like real well and get strong on."

Melissa wonderingly touched the eyelash-fine dark hair thatching the skull with its throbbing soft spot. "Oh, I wish Charlie could see him!" Tears filled her eyes. "I wish Charlie were here!"

"Of course you do!" Tears glinted in Ellen's eyes, too, as she kissed her daughter-in-law's forehead. "Of course you do."

"I have to call the baby Charles," Melissa said, and gave her mother-in-law a look of appeal. "I . . . I hope you and Father Ware understand if I give him Daddy's name . . . not Mordecai . . . that's so awful! But his middle name, Joel."

Ellen nodded.

Christy was sure she didn't speak because she couldn't. How, in all this tragedy, were they going to tell of their own? What a bitter trick of fate that they'd come here for solace and found nightmare.

"Soon's Miss Melissa can travel, I reckon we'd ought to come stay with you, Miz Ware,"

545

ventured Phronie. "No men folk here . . . Miss Vinnie fuddled so bad . . . and Lilah havin' her baby soon . . . well, that just leaves me to look after everybody."

"Aunt Phronie," said Ellen, straightening. "Come over here a moment. You, too, Christy."

When Phronie heard the terrible news, she stifled a groan. "Oh, my dear Lord," she whispered. "Oh, sweet Jesus! Mister Ware, he was a good, good man! Best not tell Miss Melissa for a while. Might curdle or stop her milk. She thought an awful lot of her daddy-in-law." Phronie buried her face in her hands and her frail shoulders convulsed. "Ever since this happen, I been thinkin' we'd go to you folks till we could figger a way to get to Saint Louis and Miss Yvonne, or send word to the young masters out in Oregon and California, though Lordy knows how we'd do that! Oh, Miz Ware, what we goin' to do?"

Ellen took Phronie's hands. "Be grateful you helped birth a baby who probably would have died without your skill. Be glad Melissa, thanks to you, should be all right."

"Bless the good Lord for that," wept Phronie. "But . . . but. . . ."

Even if they had a wagon or carriage, it was a long perilous way to St. Louis where Lavinia's daughter, Yvonne, lived with her complacent husband, Henry Benton.

"The Parkses would help if we went to

546

them," Christy suggested.

"There's too many of us." Ellen looked weary to the bone. "If only there were a cabin in your father's Peace Valley!"

Christy closed her eyes and saw again the broad valley, encircled by cliffs, with the river sparkling through. She saw the mortar in the limestone, a glimpse of women grinding corn, or perhaps weaving, calling gaily to each other from cave to cave as their children played.

"There's no cabin," she said. "But, Mother, there are caves where people used to live. If we find a good big dry one and wall up most of the front, it could be warmer than a house."

"Lord have mercy!" Phronie shuddered. "Live in a cave like an old bear? Best stay here in a decent cabin!"

"Do you think the next jayhawks or bush-whackers will let it stand?" Ellen demanded. "Phronie, it's better to be safe than civilized. Peace Valley is the only close place we know of that won't be found by raiders."

Phronie's jaw clenched again. After a moment, she sighed. "Then we better get ourselves there quick as Miss Melissa's able."

"We'll bring our cattle to the valley," said Ellen. "And all the chickens we can catch. Did the jayhawks leave any food?" she asked Phronie.

"Might be a little in the cabins. They

emptied the corncribs and smokehouses and root cellars. What turnips and cabbages their horses didn't eat, they squashed into the ground by ridin' over 'em. What molasses they didn't steal, they poured in the dirt. Stirred it in with a stick so we can't skim any off."

Such waste of food was almost as shocking as murder. They were all glad when Beth edged in with a carefully held-up skirt.

"I found four eggs! And there was some hominy in a box and a little piece of candle . . . and an apple. It was sort of shrivelly, so I ate it!"

"Bless the child!" Phronie took the eggs as if they were gold, then shot Ellen a pleading glance. "Is it all right, Miz Ware, if I scramble these for Miss Vinnie and Miss Melissa?"

"They need them," Ellen agreed. "But Melissa's asleep." She went to look down tenderly at the young mother and the baby, who was sleeping, too. "She needs her rest, poor lamb."

Phronie put another log on the fire. "I'll fix the eggs when she wakes up. Lilah girl, take a basket and start goin' through the cabins for anything we can use."

Lilah slipped on a cloak and went out, moving heavily. Her time could not be far away. It must hurt her, that her child would not be welcomed like Melissa's, and that no matter how white it was, it would be a slave. Still, in the hidden valley, slave would be an empty word. There would just be women and children who'd have to help each other to survive. *We'll love Lilah's baby and look after it like we will little Charlie,* Christy thought.

"Beth," said Ellen, "why don't you help Lilah hunt for food and any useful things? Christy, you'd better go home and tell Hester what's happened."

"I can bring Lady Jane here this afternoon, so there'll be milk," Christy offered. "Then, if Hester's afraid to stay alone, I can be home before dark."

Her mother nodded and embraced her. "Be careful, darling. Oh, I still can't believe. . . ." They clung to each other.

Why, I'm taller than Mother, Christy thought. *And she feels like her bones are light as a bird's. She needs to eat more.* Strange to worry about her mother who always looked out for everybody else, but, as Christy kissed her and went out, she realized that she now would have to do a lot of the looking after, a lot of the watching over and taking care, even though these terrible happenings at the plantation seemed to have roused her mother from her bewildered reveries.

If only Dan were here. . . . If only he's safe, she amended. As she rode away from the ashes of Rose Haven, his song resonated through her as if he played for her and smiled. From this, she took courage for what she must do now, for all the days ahead.

CHAPTER TWENTY-SEVEN

When Hester recovered a little after being told about the destroyed plantation, she wiped her eyes. "There's food at my place. I'll fetch a load of it, if you'll keep an eye on the lad yonder. Give him willow tea, if he wakes up, and try to get a little soup down him."

His wound seemed to be too old to have been inflicted at Emil's or the Wares', but who knew who and what he was? Christy, none to eager to handle him, nodded reluctantly. "All right, but I want to take a cow to Jardines' today. If you'd like for me to be back here by nightfall. . . ."

"No use in that." Hester's hazel eyes were clear. She had combed her curly, light brown hair and looked more like her old self, not the wraith that had come up from the shadows three nights ago. "Why, child, haven't I lived alone these years since Lafe went off?"

"Yes, but that was before the war."

"I saw Emil hung and Lottie die. And

Jonathan's . . ." — Hester swallowed — "reckon nothing worse than that's going to happen." She touched Christy's cheek. "Don't fret about me, honey. You're needed at Jardines' a lot more than here." She lowered her voice even though the man in the other cabin was probably sunk in fevered sleep. "Fancy that hidden valley! Sounds like heaven in the middle of all this woe. Now we'll put everything we can scrape up together, and share and share alike. More than likely there's provender at the Franzes' the guerrillas didn't bother with, and Sarah, I'm bound, would spare us some honey."

"Sarah!" Stabbed with remorse, Christy caught Hester's arm. "How could I forget about her? And Allie Hayes?"

"Sarah's all right," Hester soothed. "Any bad men come along, she'd just fade into the timber."

"But if they took her food . . . ?"

"Bless you, but Sarah can find things to eat in the wilds that even I don't know about."

"Still, maybe she'd like to go to the valley," Christy persisted.

"Maybe she would, since Lige is off being a scout for the Army, but she'd do it more to help the others than for her own sake." Hester laughed; it was good to hear. "That Sarah, she's always been a wild child. Lige never wanted to settle her down." Hester paused at the door. "I'll stop by the tannery and see how Allie and the young 'uns are. Don't forget to eat yourself, dear. I'll be back in plenty of time for you to get the cow to Jardines' before dark."

Hester vanished into the trees, where red-brown leaves of blackjack oak, the green of cedar, and white of sycamore trunks lent color to skeleton trunks and limbs. *If she ever let herself know Lafe had helped hang Emil, would it drive her mad?* Christy shivered at the memory of his eyes, burning like the iron he'd shoved her wrist against. *If he hadn't been under the command of a man who respected women the other day. . . .* The thought was so terrifying that Christy forced it away. Hester wasn't, thank goodness, totally cut off from reality like Lavinia. With her knowledge of plants and healing, Hester would be a powerful help.

Christy wanted to visit her father's grave, but first she looked in on the wounded man. In his hard-angled fashion, he was the handsomest man she'd ever seen, even with dark stubble covering his jaws and chin. He was tall and well made, but so helpless right now a child could plunge a knife into one of the fluttering arteries in his throat and in seconds he'd be as dead as Christy's father, as dead as Emil and Lottie. Horrified at a flash of desire to do exactly that to a helpless person who might well be innocent of any sort of crime, Christy pulled on her cloak and ran to the edge of the cornfield.

It was plowed under and waiting for spring seed, but never again would Jonathan Ware plant and husband the crop. Husband. That meant to take care of. He had done that, not only with his farm and family, but with his students and neighbors, with Justus and other runaways the Wares had helped.

Father! You can't be dead! We'll wake up from this bad dream and you'll be with us. . . . But it wasn't a bad dream. Christy fell to her knees by the patch of raw earth. He'd never again guide Moses and Pharaoh along the furrows, feast on juicy roasting ears, carry sweet-smelling fodder to the barn by the light of the harvest moon. He wouldn't, with strong, gentle hands, help a scared heifer birth her first calf, or smile at the fine sight of the bay and chestnut horses grazing on the slope. He wouldn't finish teaching Beth and Mary Hayes their multiplication tables or get Luke Hayes straightened out on the difference between verbs and adverbs before beguiling them with *Don Quixote, The Song of Roland,* or *Sohrab and Rustum.* He couldn't delight in the brilliant flash orioles and tanagers in the giant chestnut, or the spring serenade of whip-poor-wills and chuck-will's-widows.

Father, if you can hear me, let me know it. Let me feel your spirit. She waited. What came instead of a sense of communion was a powerful image of him coming toward the house, laughing, head thrown back. *Thank God!* she thought even as she wondered if there was one. Thank God, she hadn't seen his face at the moment of the blast outside the doorway, arms outflung in a strange obeisance of welcome. That had to be his gift to her, to remember him happy and strong. *Thank you,* she told him, touching the cold earth, rising. *Help me, Father. Help us all.*

She decided she should look for food that might tempt Lavinia or build Melissa's strength. In the kitchen, Hester had pressed fresh-churned butter into molds. Indian pudding, flavored with dried persimmons, was the best Christy could think of by way of a delicacy. Potato onion soup should please everyone. When these were simmering, she made willow tea and took it and a bowl of soup to the other cabin.

The man moved a little as she entered the room. "Sir? Are you awake?"

His eyes opened slowly. "Josie!"

"I'm Christy Ware," she corrected him. "Let me prop you up so you can sip some tea."

He drank the brew, grimacing, then smiled at Christy as if his conscience was clear as a newborn's. "You sure look like my kid sister. Her name's Josephine." Appraising eyes were made bluer by black lashes and eyebrows. "She's quite a bit younger than you, though. Just turned twelve. I've got two other sisters, but Josie's my pet."

Christy couldn't chat with a man who might be a guerrilla even though she was sure he couldn't have been present at her father's murder. "She'll be glad to see you again, I'm sure. Now try some soup, please. You've been too feverish to eat."

Although Hester's herbs gave it an enticing smell, he curled his lip at the soup. "What I'd relish is a slab of fried ham," he said.

"You'd better have soup and the like for a few more days. I'm making Indian pudding, and you may have a bowl, after you eat your soup."

He made a face but let her feed him. "I don't remember much after I got shot out of my saddle by someone hid in the timber."

"Hester . . . the woman who's been tending you . . . found you by the creek yesterday morning. We brought you to my family's home."

His eyelids drooped before he finished all the soup, and he drowsed half propped on the pillows. She hurried to stir the pudding and collect food to take back to Jardines' — she couldn't call the place Rose Haven any more. The Parkses had insisted on trading a winter's supply of wheat flour and cornmeal for the slaughtered hogs and sheep, and had left it when they had come for her mother's things. Christy put about five pounds of flour and fifteen of meal into pillowcases inside tow sacks. A pound of the fresh butter, a jug of molasses, a hunk of ham and bacon, bags of beans, hominy, and dried fruit, and candles.

Surveying the growing pile, she knew she'd have to rig some kind of panniers to balance the supplies on Lass. How long would it be till Melissa could travel? Christy prayed that Lilah's baby would wait to be born till they were safe in the valley. Their refuge must be a complete secret. Even Lige Morrow had never mentioned it.

Taking the pudding off the heat to cool, Christy ladled some into a bowl for the dark young man to have later. Thought the world of his sister, didn't he? Why was it when men had mothers, sisters, wives, and daughters they loved and wanted to spare grief, they went off to kill the brothers, sons, husbands, and fathers of other women? *Father! Would it ever stop hurting?* The pain, a presence she could almost see, kept its distance till she exposed herself for a second. Then it seized and mauled her till it tired and dropped her like a cat losing interest in a dead thing.

When the spasm of grief eased enough for her to move, Christy put on a shawl and went out to the root cellar. She'd take a bag of potatoes and big sweet onions that came from sets Emil had given them, and some apples gathered from his maiden blush tree. *God rest him,* she thought. *And Lottie. . . .* Emil had come from another country at sixteen. He had limped the rest of his life from a musket ball taken in the War of 1812. He'd lost his only son in the war with Mexico. Who could call him a Dutchman after that? At first it had seemed wrong that the trees and vines he'd cherished could outlive him, but, when Christy remembered Emil's delight in his orchard and vineyard, she had to believe his spirit would rejoice in spring blossoms and ripening fruit, even on the tree where he had been hanged.

A trundling sound brought up Christy from her knees. Why, here came two wheelbarrows, one pushed by Hester, bright as a tiger lily in her store-bought calico, and the other by Sarah Morrow, Lige's hounds streaming around her. Christy ran to meet them, only now admitting that she'd been nervous there, alone, except for the wounded man.

Sarah dropped the handles and held out her arms. Christy flew into her embrace. Some of the strength of Sarah's lithe body passed into her own. "I'm here to help every way I can. Lige dried lots of venison for me before he went off to scout, and I've got bushels of nuts and dried persimmons." Sarah's blue-green eyes were startling against skin the color of sassafras tea with cream and her black hair caught back with a scarlet ribbon. "Of course, I've brought honey and some maple syrup."

"Best thing is you've brought yourself!" Christy turned to Hester. "Is Allie all right?"

Hester nodded. "One of the guerrillas is a friend of theirs, so that gang they didn't bother her."

"But the jayhawkers . . . ?"

"Mark and Luke heard them coming in time to drive the cows and mules into the woods. Not even jayhawks will yank stinking hides out of tanning vats, and I expect they figgered they'd get all the plunder they could carry at the Jardines'. The captain made Allie cook them a big meal, but that was all the bother they were."

"Is she going to stay there?"

"Says so." Hester shrugged. "She thinks the war'll be over soon and Ethan and Matthew will come home. She wants to keep the tannery going. Mark's well nigh man-size and does a lot of work."

"Yes, and he's going to cut loose any day and join the Army." Sarah's tone was sad.

Christy turned to her. "How did the guerrillas happen to miss you?"

"They knew who had anything worth stealing. We don't have livestock or corn or much else worth their time. Watt Caxton must have guided them."

And Lafe, Christy thought but couldn't say it out loud in front of Hester.

"So Rose Haven was cleaned out by jayhawkers?" Sarah went on as she and Hester pushed the wheelbarrows forward. "Never had much use for the bishop, but he died like a man. Fancy you finding that valley, Christy, when, for all his ridge running, Lige didn't know about it! Of course, he was never one for caves."

"The underground river is the only way into the valley, except for a steep, narrow chasm where the river flows out through the cliffs on the other side."

"I want to go to that valley," Sarah declared. "I'll bet I can find a bee tree or two, and next summer I'll fix a bee gum so whoever's living there will have their own honey."

"You probably can tell them more than I can about wild foods and what roots and bark make good tea," said Hester. "But I'll help put in a garden and plant a little corn."

"I hope everyone's out of there by summer!" Christy blurted, unable to imagine this kind of raiding and daily fear going on for long. "I hope the war's over and. . . ." She broke off, realizing that things couldn't, not ever, be the way they were. *Father is dead. So is Andy. So is Bishop Jardine, and Lavinia will probably never regain her right mind.*

"I've got to be getting along to Jardines'," she said with a glance at the westering sun.

"I'll go with you," Sarah volunteered. "The hounds'll keep off anything short of an army. Lige told old Sam and Blue Boy to look after me, and Chita, that young red bone, I hand-fed when her mama died." Then she patted the fullness of her skirt. "There's a sheathed knife in my pocket. I always sew in great big ones that hold all kinds of stuff. Come in handy.

Swiftly they added provisions from the wheelbarrows to Christy's piles, did them up in two sheets, and tied them across Lass' back. The young mare eyed the bundles with suspicion but was mollified with a wrinkled apple. Hester took the wheelbarrows to the house.

Escorted by the hounds, hurrying all they could, the young women reached Jardines' by sundown. Ellen held Christy a long time. "Thank God you're safely here! And how good to see Sarah's all right."

They put together a good meal from the supplies Lass had carried, but Lavinia scarcely ate in spite of Phronie's coaxing. Better received were the old nurse's exhortations to Melissa to eat so she could feed her baby. No one felt like talking. They were all tired. As soon as dishes were done, they wrapped up close to each other for warmth. Christy dropped at once into heavy slumber.

The waiting beast had no chance to savage her next morning for she woke to Phronie's wails.

"Oh, my poor lady! She gone. She gone away."

Death had come gently for Lavinia. She was smiling, with a look of expectation.

Everyone wept, especially Phronie, but Christy's sorrow was mixed with relief. Getting a wheelchair through the cavern would have been near impossible. In fact, Christy and Sarah had been planning to take it apart, for easier carrying, and bringing Lavinia in on an improvised litter. But they would have been moving a shell. When he had been placed in her arms, Lavinia had held Joely — as the women found themselves calling him — but she hadn't seemed to know or care that he was her grandson. That blow on the head had destroyed the essence of a lovely, loving woman. Huddled in old Zillah's shawl, she had sung and woven her invisible patterns, a ghost of Rose Haven, a ghost of what had been.

Melissa insisted that her mother be buried in the violet shawl even though Phronie warned that all their wool and the looms had burned with the house. "The livin' need warm things more'n the dead," Phronie said. "Miss Vinnie would be the first to say so."

"We don't have a single rose for her," said Melissa, pale but determined. "She won't have a coffin. She's going to have the shawl."

The ground wasn't frozen beneath a thin crust. With the shovel and pickaxe, Phronie and Lilah had salvaged to bury the bishop, Sarah and Christy dug a grave between him and Zillah, grateful that the bitter cold kept the corpses from stinking. They lined the narrow place with cedar boughs and, with Phronie's and Lilah's help, eased Lavinia into her resting place.

What's happening to me? thought Christy in horrified contrition as her mother led them in the Shepherd's Psalm. *Here I am glad that we don't have to go to a lot of fuss to get Missus Jardine to the valley.* Christy would have felt differently had Lavinia's mind been clear, but she still felt guilty as her mother praised Lavinia's sweet nature, courage in her invalidism, and the way she had tried to protect her husband.

"He tried to save her rose garden and birds. She tried to save him. Their love was great. Melissa, my dear daughter, you were born of that love. It will be part of you as long as you live, and your parents will live on in your son."

"Let's sing Miss Vinnie's favorite hymn," Phronie suggested as her quavering voice steadied as it soared into "Amazing Grace". After the Lord's Prayer, Melissa dropped the first of the waiting boughs over her mother, then sobbed and let Lilah take her inside while the others finished their sorrowful work and dragged burned rails over the three mounds to keep out scavengers.

"This redbud was a pet of Miss Vinnie's," Phronie said, fingering the leaves of a rose-bush near the graves. "It'll bloom over her this spring, every spring, till this trouble's over and the young folks raise a proper stone over their parents. Zillah deserves one, too."

"She'll get it," Christy vowed. Till then, it was better not to mark the graves. She'd heard of guerrillas and jayhawkers digging up new graves in hopes gold or valuables were concealed inside them.

Five anxious days later, Melissa was able to travel with little Charles Joel Jonathan. If men kept getting killed, every new baby boy would carry a string of memorial names — a heavy load for them, to try to fill the places of two or three men, dead, in their families.

After Lady Jane was milked and wood carried each morning at the Jardines, Christy and Sarah had been going to the Wares'. Then, after checking with Hester to be sure her patient was still in bed, they led an animal apiece through the cavern, across the creek, the gentler ones laden with supplies.

"You don't want to take too many critters through at once," Hester warned. "Too much commotion or noise can play peculiar tricks in caves. I remember hearing about a hunter who followed a bobcat into a cave. He shot at the cat, and the roof caved in on him. Best you keep quiet, step careful, and take your time."

Moses and Pharaoh were so big that, in a few places, they could barely get through, and Lad's head had to be held down so he wouldn't bump the lower-hanging stalactites, but, by the day Melissa was ready to go, all the animals, except the milk cows and Lad and Lass, were in Peace Valley and supplies had been heaped inside the cave entrance from the valley.

As soon as it was light enough to move around that morning, the company set out with Sarah's hounds — Sam, Blue Boy, and Chita — keeping close, while Phronie and Melissa rode the horses. Melissa cradled Joely, and, in front of her, Phronie held Emmie cat, tied up in a pillowcase. Walking beside Lilah, to whom she'd taken a great fancy, Beth carried Lambie and the Lynette doll Melissa had given her, along with her clothes. Lilah balanced her awkward body with the help of a hickory staff.

If the child she carried wouldn't be born to freedom, what was the use of all of the killing and all the pain? Christy thrilled neither to the idea of the Union's supremacy or the Confederacy's states' rights. What she cared about was rights of everyone. If it took war to get them, standing on her father's grave, she'd say it was worth it. Her eyes blurred. The chickens, in the covered basket she carried, squawked at the jounce they got when she tripped on a rock. The surviving Jardine chickens clucked nervously from the willow chest her mother and Sarah held between them. Her mother's remaining Silver Laced Wyandottes would join them as soon as a pen was made. So would the other cows, except for Guinevere. They feared the wounded man was likely to notice a sudden absence of milk and butter.

Hester had been warned to make sure that he didn't look out the door or window that morning. Through the leafless trees and bushes, anyone standing in the doorway could look across the creek in the general direction of the hidden cave entrance. It wouldn't do for a stranger to see this singular caravan disappear into the bluff.

"Are you going to stay in the valley?" Sarah asked Christy over her shoulder.

"I don't know," Christy admitted. The tranquil serenity drew her, yet abandoning the happy house was like abandoning her family's hopes and dreams. "Hester wants to go to the valley to help out, so I don't know how bad I'll be needed."

Ellen glanced back as she and Sarah switched sides on the heavy chest. "Of course, you'll stay in the valley, child! I couldn't draw an easy breath if you were out here alone."

"I'll stay with Christy," Sarah promised Ellen. She jerked her head toward the flow of hounds, blue ticks, and red bones, sniffing and exploring ahead. "What with the dogs, no one can sneak up on us. There's no stock or food left to steal, and you've sent your best things over to Parkses'."

"That could make thieves so angry that they'd burn down the buildings," Ellen worried aloud. "They might even hurt you."

Sarah shrugged. "The devils on both sides claim they don't kill women."

"They killed Lottie Franz."

"Hester said she got in front of a bullet."

"So might you."

"I doubt it." Sarah grinned hardily. "I've already taken my cooking stuff, bedding, and tools to the valley. Guess I'll move my bee gums over to your house, Christy, if you and I stay there."

"But . . . ," Ellen began.

Christy shifted her basket to just one hand long enough to press her mother's shoulder. "It's really not far away, Mother. We can go back and forth. . . ."

"I hate caves!" Ellen blurted out. "Once I get to that valley, I may never come back."

"When Charlie and Thos come home, we'll put a blindfold on you and lead you out," teased Christy.

"Oh, if I could see my boys, I'd walk through hell!"

They didn't speak again until everyone had gotten across the creek by taking turns on the horses. Praying the recovering man would stay in bed, Christy handed candles to everyone except Beth, who she adjured to stay between her mother and Lilah.

"Don't talk," Christy reminded them. "Move quietly as you can and try not to let the animals brush into anything."

Sarah led with Lady Jane. The cow, considerably smaller than the oxen, could pass through with her panniers. Melissa followed with the baby, tagged by Phronie. To keep Lilah's staff from making noise, Christy shredded the bottom of it with a knife. Ellen carried Emmie over her shoulder, still curled in her pillowcase. Christy brought up the rear with Lad. They'd have to make another trip for the chickens. Lad had worn his shoes down, so they barely made a sound except where silty dust gave way to stone. These chinkings, Lady Jane's shuffle, muted feet scuffs, and muffled clinks of tools and cookware were the only sounds except for indrawn breaths when light danced off crystalline rose or gold formations.

The river, sometimes hidden, sometimes murmuring like a fluid mirror, reflecting the glow of candles and sculpturings of roof and walls, now and then yielded glimpses of weird white swimming things. Scorpion-like creatures pursued quarry too small to be seen in the gloom. A pale lizard scuttled from a rock near Lad. Startled, he reared his head into a low-hanging swag before Christy could control him. The end of the swag crashed down, striking Lad's shoulder. The impact brought down a hail of fragments and whole stalactites. Scared, drubbed, and smarting, Christy urged Lad forward. The candles ahead halted at the racket. Fortunately Christy was far enough behind that the mineral downpour hadn't struck anyone else.

"Are you all right?" her mother whispered.

Christy wiped blood out of her eyes, explored the cut on her forehead, and then felt along Lad, searching for any injuries. "I'm fine," she whispered back. "Lad has a gash on the shoulder, but it's not bleeding much."

"I hate caves!" Ellen breathed.

It seemed forever, but, at last, the heaven of blue sky shone ahead. One by one, they blew out candles in the big open chamber. As they waited for their day vision to return, a figure rose from beside the ancient mortar.

"Animals are welcome here." The voice had a husky, unused quality, like the rustle of cornstalks. Beyond her, in the valley, they saw the cattle grazing. "But if humans mean to stay, as it seems you do . . ." — she indicated their belongings with a sweep of a leather-clad arm — "I must ask why you've come and who you are."

■ ■ ■ ■

PART THREE:
THE TRAMPLED
FIELDS

■ ■ ■ ■

Chapter Twenty-Eight

Hildy added a double handful of cracked hickory nuts to the peas, corn, beans, and venison stewing in the pot hung over the fire and gave the Tom-fuller a stir. There was a big washing to do, but dinner would take care of itself now except for making ashcakes. She made them with plenty of molasses. Her husband, Justus, before he had been sold away, used to say they were better than his mama's — not where his mama would hear, of course. Aunt Becky, as Justus's mama was known, already had held grudges aplenty toward her daughter-in-law.

"Puttin' on airs 'cause Miss Lou raised you in the big house after your ma died," Aunt Becky often had sniffed. "Taught you alongside her own young 'uns till they went off to school. While my girls and Justus worked, there you was with your nose in a book, or sewin' with Miss Lou."

After Hildy's mama had died, it had been Miss Lou who had said: "Don't be scared, honey, Master Richard and I will take care of you. You're going to sleep in that little room next to ours." It had been Miss Lou who had come in softly, at night, to make sure Hildy was covered up, and who started her in primer with Master Edmund who was just her age then, five. Miss Alice had been three years older and could write a beautiful hand and cipher in her head fast as lightning. That had made Master Richard chuckle and say that before long she could straighten out his careless records.

Hildy's throat tightened. Master Richard had laughed a lot, gray eyes shining like he found the world so full of joy he was about to bust with it. Except when he flew into one of his rages. No one could do anything with him then, not even Miss Lou.

It had been in a fit like that he had sold Justus off to that Missouri bishop just a few months after he himself and Miss Lou had given them a wedding — a real wedding in the dining room with Parson Douglas, and a fine dinner served on the good china on a damask tablecloth, not just a moving in together with the master's approval and a jollification.

None of that had signified when Master Richard Frazer had taken Justus to task because a favorite mare had gone lame and he had thought Justus hadn't shod her properly. Justus had reminded his master that he'd warned him the mare had thrush in the frog of her hoof that needed to be cleaned and treated every day till it healed.

The veins had swelled in Master Richard's forehead. "Are you talking back, you insolent nigger?"

"No, Master Richard, but. . . ."

That had set Master Richard off, probably because he had known he should have made sure the stable help doctored the hoof. It had wound up with the first whipping Justus had ever got — not enough to break the skin bad but enough to make him swear he'd run away.

"I'm a good smith," he had growled while a sobbing Hildy salved the welts. "I'll save up to buy you, or, if that takes too long, I'll just come back and take you North."

Before he could find a good time to run, that bishop had passed through, needing a smith. Hildy had heard Miss Lou pleading, but Master Richard had told her to say no more. He wouldn't tolerate an insubordinate servant.

White folks at Waverly had never said "slaves". It was hands or servants or "our black people". When Hildy had begged to be sold along with her husband, Master Richard had upbraided her for ingratitude. Then he had tried to console her. "The new smith I'm getting, Hildy, is of amiable temper and fine-looking. He needs a wife."

She hadn't understood for a moment. When

she had, it had hurt worse than a whipping. What Master Richard had meant was a slave's marriage didn't count. She purely had hated him for a heartbeat, although she had grown up worshiping him almost as much as she had Miss Lou.

"I'm married to Justus, Master Richard," she had said when she could speak. "By the parson. You watched with your own eyes."

The pupils of those eyes had swelled like he was going into a fury. Women weren't whipped at Waverly, but she could have been the first. When he had spoken, though, his voice had been controlled and she had known he wouldn't change his mind. "Your marriage is annulled as of this minute. I won't force you to take another husband, Hildy, but you'll stay here because your mistress relies on you."

Miss Lou, at forty-three, had been in the family way. It had happened pretty often when a woman neared the end of her child-bearing years. One more bitterness. Hildy and Justus hadn't started a baby, never would. For Bishop Jardine had written how Justus had run off a few months after he was fetched up to Missouri — asked Master Richard to watch out for him in case he tried to get back to Waverly and see Hildy.

He hadn't. Not in five long years. The way North was dangerous. Hildy feared he might be dead, but refused to have another man.

She had loved Justus ever since they were thirteen, when he'd rescued her from a drunken overseer. Master Richard had horse-whipped the white man and run him off the place.

The recollection softened Hildy, brought back a rush of good memories of Master Richard. He had called in doctors if any of his folks were bad sick; old folks were taken good care of till they died; he gave four full holidays in the summer and a week at Christmas with new clothes and a feast for everyone.

Most of all, there was that light, bright heart in him. How he'd grab Miss Lou off her feet, swing her around, and hug her while she'd blush and laugh and scold! Aunt Becky had grumbled about that, too. "Married twenty years and still carryin' on like they just laid eyes on each other!"

No one would lay eyes on Master Richard again. Killed three months ago at Wilson's Creek up in southwest Missouri on August 10, 1861. Our Cherokees captured all save one of the enemy's artillery pieces, his colonel had written, thus assuring a Confederate victory. Your brave husband, madam, died attempting to take that last Union howitzer. May pride in him and the cause he died for be of solace and know that all here grieve the loss of their gallant captain. I assure you that he is decently buried.

Miss Lou hadn't smiled since then except when little Master Richie climbed into her lap, gripped her face between his palms, and commanded: "Laugh, Mama! Richie wants to hear you!"

She would, a little, then call him her big boy, and gather him close as she buried her face in his hair, curly gold like his father's. Very winning was Master Richie. At first, Hildy had succeeded in hating him, blaming him for her not being sold along with Justus, blaming him because she couldn't have a baby of her own. She'd changed him and bathed him and walked him, when he cried and Miss Lou was too tired to cosset him, but she hadn't crooned to him or cuddled him, had hardened her heart against his tiny perfect fingers, the pulse beat of that soft spot in his skull.

I could drop him. . . .

The wicked thought had scared her into being extra careful, but she still hadn't touched him one bit more than she had to. Then Miss Lou's breasts had caked. She had wept when she tried and failed to nurse the baby, suffering something terrible in spite of the hot poultices Aunt Becky put on her. The doctor had lanced her breasts, and her fever had dropped, but her milk had dried up.

The baby had sucked his sugar tit and wailed high and shrill with hunger. Out of the fifty slaves in the cabins and big house, there had been only two nursing mothers. Each had tried to suckle Master Richie, but Ruby's milk had been too rich — gave him colic — and Amelia's nipple had been so small he kept losing it. Richie hadn't had the strength to howl, had just mewled like a kitten. The nearest plantation was that of the Cherokee chief, John Ross. Master Richard had sent to hire or borrow a wet-nurse, but it would have been hours before one could come, hours that the poor little scrap might not have been able to last.

Had he been Master Richard's by another woman, Hildy might have told herself it was no sin to let nature take its course. The helpless infant might well grow into his father's rages. But the babe was Miss Lou's, had cost her mightily — and he was so hungry.

"Wait, Amelia." Hildy had motioned the young woman back into a chair and got a bowl. "See if you can't squeeze some milk in here."

Once Amelia had gotten the hang of it, she quickly had the bowl half full of thin bluish milk. "Good!" Hildy had praised her. "Let's see if this works."

Cradling Richie, she had soaked the muslin sugar tit in the milk and poked it in his mouth. He had sucked greedily, delving his fingers into her breast. Hildy had felt an odd sensation beneath his hands, as if the veins were engorging. He nearly emptied the bowl

579

before he drowsed off with the first content stomach he'd had in days.

Rising to go, Amelia had gazed at him proudly. "Sure do look like my milk agrees with him." She had been doing only light work till her baby was four months old. Then she'd leave him with the other babies at Aunt Becky's.

"He's sure happy." Hildy had said, smiling. "Belly's round as a drum. Come back when you hear the dinner gong. He'll need his milk every two or three hours."

"When the wet-nurse comes. . . ."

"I'm going to tell Master Richard to send someone to catch up with his messenger and say we don't need a woman. Her milk might not suit him or her nipple mightn't."

Those had been the reasons she had given Master Richard as she held the bright head against her shoulder. They had been true enough. But the deep, main reason had been that Richie had become her baby. He still was.

This day, Amelia was collecting the rest of the laundry as Hildy stripped Miss Lou's bed — much too big now — while her mistress sat in the rocker, dutifully sipping the honey-sweetened tea of St. John's wort and ginseng that Aunt Becky prescribed for spells of the blues. This wasn't a spell of Miss Lou's. She didn't eat much more than she slept. Hildy, from her little room next door, waked through the night to hear her walking up and down, up and down, like someone soothing a cranky child. Only there was nothing in her arms but sorrow.

As she put on sheets woven from flax grown, retted, combed, and spun at the plantation, Hildy talked briskly, trying to win more from Miss Lou than a listless nod or: "Do what you judge best, Hildy."

"The smokehouses are plumb full of hams and bacon. We finished making sausage yesterday, and there's plenty of lard, enough extra that, if we put some butter with it, we can trade it at the store for coffee and white sugar, and there's several barrels of sorghum molasses to swap, too. The corn's all cribbed, and a load taken to the mill. Aunt Becky and the girls who help tend the children are shelling out the dried beans and peas, and the root cellars are filling up with potatoes and turnips and cabbages. The older children are hunting nuts and persimmons. We'll eat good this winter, Miss Lou."

Waverley people always did. They could help themselves to the milk kept cool in the springhouse, even churn butter if they'd a mind to. For extra meat, men hunted 'coons, 'possums, and squirrels. Anyone who chose to could keep chickens and have their own garden patch. The same good smells filled the cabins and the big house: Tom-fuller, hickory nut grot, Tom-budha, and roasting ears, potatoes, ashcakes, and pound cakes baking in the ashes.

Miss Lou set her cup down with a sharpness that made Hildy straighten and turn to her. Those eyes, the color of blue flax flowers, were sunk in dark hollows! Hildy's heart constricted. Never robust, this beloved woman looked so frail and brittle that it was a wonder her bones didn't snap. There was no luster to the once beautiful wheat-yellow hair she hadn't yet combed this morning, and a faintly sour smell came from her nightgown — Miss Lou, who used to be so dainty!

"Hildy," Miss Lou whispered. "I don't know what to do."

Never had Hildy heard those words from a white person. Maybe what they planned to do was wrong but they were sure about it. It was as if the solid oak floor rolled and buckled beneath her feet. She swallowed to get control of her voice. "How . . . how do you mean, Miss Lou?"

"You remember Chief Ross and his wife came calling last week on their way to Tahlequah?"

Hildy did, of course. How could she forget that fancy carriage with the little black boy in uniform perched up behind? The second Mrs. Ross, a Quaker lady from Delaware, was pleasant and gentle-spoken, but Hildy had had a feeling she'd never feel at home in what must seem to her the edge of the world.

The chief, a short, dignified man with red hair faded by his seventy-two years, was only an eighth Cherokee, but, although he owned one hundred slaves and lived in a colonnaded mansion reached by a rose-bordered drive half a mile long, he had the trust and support of the mostly poor full-bloods and "pin" Indians who wore crossed pins on their coats to show they were converts of Northern missionaries who preached Abolition along with Jesus.

Ross's Cherokee wife had died on the horrible Trail of Tears over which, in 1838, the Cherokees had made their forced journey from the East to Indian Territory. They had buried four thousand of their people along the way. Also driven from their ancestral Eastern homes were the Chickasaws, Creeks, and Choctaws. The Seminoles in the Florida swamps put up a long and desperate fight, but at last they came, too — all that could be caught.

There had been treaties, to be sure. The government liked its robberies legal, Master Richard used to say. The master's parents had died on the way West, although like most wealthy mixed-bloods they'd traveled pretty comfortably by steamboat and wagon, along with their slaves. He'd been raised by the aunt and uncle who had built Waverly into a plantation almost as prosperous as the one by the same name in Georgia that they'd been forced to sell for next to nothing. The aunt and uncle were childless except for two daughters the uncle had by a pretty quadroon who had died on the Trail.

Fortunately for Master Richard's uncle, he hadn't been a signer of the treaty which violated tribal law. The signers, well-to-do mixed-bloods, believed removal was inevitable and the only way the Cherokees could live unmolested by the whites, but to the majority of full-bloods they were traitors. Master Richard had said they were condemned to death by their clansmen, who drew lots for the part of executioners. Before dawn on a June morning twenty-two years ago, John Ridge had been stabbed to death by twenty-five men in front of his horrified wife. At the same hour, his cousin, Elias Boudinot, had been killed and slashed with tomahawks. Later that day, Major Ridge, John's father, had been shot and killed from ambush.

The only signer to escape had been Stand Watie, Boudinot's brother, who had been warned by a friend. In spite of the danger, Watie had ridden to Boudinot's home and uncovered the mutilated body. They were full brothers, although out of respect for a white man who'd befriended Stand while he was getting a higher education in Connecticut, he had taken his name. Turning to the crowd that surely included conspirators, Watie had offered $10,000 to anyone who'd tell him who had hacked his brother's face.

No one had spoken. No one had attacked him. He rode away, the only signer of the treaty to live. There were killings back and forth for years, including the murder of Watie's younger brother, but in spite of the bitterness on both sides the Cherokees prospered in their new country. The tribe set up schools, and there were two newspapers. Master Richard had been a member of the Masonic Lodge in Tahlequah. Miss Alice attended the Female Seminary there, and Master Edmund, graduated from the one for boys, went East to medical school, where he was still studying. Miss Alice had married a friend Edmund had brought home for a visit and lived now in Boston, a shame when her mama needed her so badly.

Chief Ross had claimed innocence in the treaty signers' deaths, but from then on Watie had been his implacable enemy — and Watie, leader of most of the mixed-blood slave owners, was now raising men to fight for the Confederacy.

These griefs and murders flashed through Hildy's mind. She poured more tea for her mistress. "Did Chief Ross say something to fret you, Miss Lou?"

"He's fretted himself, poor soul." Miss Lou smiled faintly. "As you know, he's favored the

Union . . . which happens to still owe the Cherokees five million dollars for our lands in the East. He's done his best to stay neutral, although General Ben McCulloch tried to persuade him to join the South. So has the Indian Commissioner, Albert Pike, with his wagonloads of presents."

Hildy nodded, chuckling at the memory of the immense bewhiskered man with his flowing hair who had passed by Waverly on his way to visit Ross. "Reckon he's trying to get the other tribes to go Confederate with his bolts of calico, store clothes, and trinkets."

"He's had good luck," Miss Lou said. "The Choctaw and Chickasaw Nations joined the Confederacy. The Creeks and Seminoles are split. After the Federals were beaten at Wilson's Creek . . . which left the Confederates in control of everything around us except Kansas to the north . . . Chief Ross was afraid Watie would overthrow him unless Ross let the Cherokees vote on whether or not to go with the South. He held a council late in August. As you know, most of the tribesmen there voted to make a treaty with the South and raise a regiment to serve under McCulloch."

Puzzled, Hildy nodded. That had happened a few days before they had learned about Master Richard's death. "Yes, Miss Lou, and Stand Watie, he's heading up his own Cherokee mounted volunteers."

"Yes, but plenty of Cherokees favor the Union. A great many Creeks do, too. Like the Cherokees, they have a feud going back to when their mixed-blood chief, William McIntosh, signed the removal treaty. He was killed for treason, but his sons survived. They can fight for the South and get revenge on the full-bloods who are mostly for the Union."

Miss Lou paused as if her strength had given out. She shivered although the room was comfortable. Hildy put a shawl around her and built up the fire.

"Whatever the rest of this is, Miss Lou, it can wait till you've had your breakfast. Could you relish some milk toast?"

Miss Lou raised a silencing hand. "Chief Ross thinks there's going to be nothing but trouble in Indian Territory till the war's over. All the Nations have blood feuds because of the removals, and now there'll be no outside force, like the Union Army, to keep any sort of peace."

Hildy couldn't get too worked up over the Trail of Tears although her mother and father had traveled it along with the Frazers' other slaves. They hadn't lived to tell her stories, but Aunt Becky, when spiteful, called her a "bone-wicked Coromantee" because her father's parents, captured as children on the Gold Coast, belonged to that fierce people. She doubted the Trail had been worse than crossing the ocean packed in the belly of a slave ship.

"Chief Ross," said Miss Lou, "advises me to move to Fort Smith. Opothleyaholo, the Creek chief, is for the Union, though he owns dozens of slaves. Chief Ross says that about four thousand Union Creeks, at least a thousand of them warriors, have gathered at Opothleyaholo's plantation and are moving north. Daniel McIntosh, an ordained Baptist minister, is after them with his First Creek Regiment, and then there's the Choctaw-Chickasaw regiment, a battalion of Creeks and Seminoles, and the Fourth Texas Cavalry."

"Lord have mercy!"

"Indeed. Ross hears Kansas jayhawkers have come down to help Opothleyaholo . . . what a name! He's eighty years old and still believes in his ancient gods. He's moving along the border of Cherokee lands, but hasn't crossed into them."

"Maybe all he wants is to get his people safe to Kansas."

"The McIntoshes will stop him if they can. It was his followers who murdered their father for signing a removal treaty back in Georgia." Miss Lou pushed distractedly at her tangled hair. "Chief Ross says rascals on both sides are using the war for an excuse to loot and kill."

"But if we go to Fort Smith. . . ."

"The chief has a trustworthy friend who's willing to take charge of Waverly for a share of the crops and increase of livestock."

Including slaves? Hildy thought to herself.

Miss Lou looked at Hildy in appeal. "If we go, I might lose the plantation for Richie. But if we stay, we could lose our lives."

"It's a hard choice, Miss Lou," Hildy said while thinking: *But at least you've got a choice. Slaves don't. Of course, since we're valuable property, no one's likely to kill us.* "Let me bring your breakfast and get some women started on the washing. Then I'll brush your hair and we can talk about all this, and pray."

Miss Lou's hand caught at hers, white and fragile against Hildy's strong brown one. "I don't know what I'd do without you, Hildy." She gave a tremulous laugh. "The best thing I ever did for myself was taking you to raise."

And the worst was letting Master Richard sell Justus . . . though I guess you couldn't stop him. A sudden thrill shot through Hildy. *The war . . . all this upheaval . . . will it somehow make it so Justus can come for me?*

Her heart raced at the thought, but, as she told Miss Lou she'd be right back and left the room, the brief flare of hope wavered and faded. Even if Justus were alive, even if he came, how could she leave Miss Lou in her trouble? And Richie, dear to her as a blood child? She grasped at the only straw she could

589

imagine. *Maybe . . . maybe Justus would stay and help take care of Miss Lou.* That seemed so unlikely that Hildy floundered into an even wilder fancy. *Maybe Miss Lou would come North with us, where we'd be free but could still look after her and Richie.*

Hildy dusted a bit of cinnamon on the milk toast, stirred a tablespoon of molasses into a glass of milk, whipped cream into some persimmon pudding, and sprinkled pecan halves over it. Miss Lou needed all the nourishment she could be coaxed to take, so Hildy used the best china and a silver tray.

Once she had Miss Lou eating, Hildy went down the back steps with the willow laundry basket. Cedar smoke wafted up to tease her nostrils from the wash fires at the creek. The ring of axes resounded from the timber beyond the fields and orchards.

Most of the men were getting in the winter's wood for the cabins and the big house. Others plowed under stubble in the broad fields. Their exhortations to the mules mingled with the battling of the oak paddles on the white things that had been rubbed with soft soap and boiled in the big black kettle before they were spread on the bench to have stains beaten out of them.

Ruby and Jane, Justus's older sisters, like him tall, well-built, and the color of creamed coffee, joked as they wielded the paddles.

Olive and Nell, tawny of skin, eyes, and hair, were actually Master Richard's cousins, daughters of his uncle and the quadroon who'd died on the Trail. The handsome sisters added Hildy's basketful to the clothes they were soaping.

All these women worked in the big house. Ruby's husband had been Tack, Master Richard's body servant, who had died trying to carry his dying master from the field. Marsh, Jane's husband and Master Edmund's servant, was off with him in Boston. Nell was married to the foreman, Harvey, and Olive to Jabez, a fine tailor who used to make his master's clothes and still did Master Edmund's. Their children, of varying ages and hues, clambered with Master Richie on the big, gray rocks along the creek. Younger children played in and out of Aunt Becky's double cabin where she and her girl helpers also looked after several old folks who had no families.

To Hildy's prideful eyes, Richie shone like a gold piece. She knew his sweet, fluting voice from all the others — her lamb, her own lamb. As soon as she helped Miss Lou dress, Hildy would bring Richie up to see his mama.

Miss Lou had drunk the milk, eaten a little of the pudding and toast, and was putting on one of the dyed black gowns that made her look so pale. Hildy buttoned the dress, and, while she brushed the light brown hair, once silky but now dry and lifeless, she told Miss Lou about the work going on outside. Miss Lou showed no flicker of interest. It was a good thing Harvey was honest and smart and kept things going without a master to answer to.

Hildy made as graceful a twist as she could of the limp hair and secured it with pins and jet combs. "Miss Lou," she ventured, "maybe you should ask Master Edmund to come home. He's up there with all those Yankees, and. . . ."

"I won't interrupt his studies." From the firmness of Miss Lou's tone, these days usually vague and hesitant, Hildy knew she had already struggled with this. "With mail so uncertain, I sent Edmund three letters about his father. I won't try to stop him if he decides he has to volunteer for the Army. I've assured him we're managing quite well at Waverly, thanks to our black family, and he need have no concern about us."

"But, Miss Lou! If Chief Ross thinks you'd better leave. . . ."

"I'm praying over it." Miss Lou closed her eyes. "Hildy, it was wrong for Master Richard to part you and Justus. My lawyer is drawing up papers to free you both."

"Free me?" Hildy felt as if gongs echoed in her head.

"Yes. If . . ." — the soft voice faltered but went on — "if you want to try to find Justus,

I'll give you enough cash money for the journey and to keep you till you find employment."

Hildy felt as if her head was full of air and about to float away. "Oh, Miss Lou!"

"It's only right. The way I miss my husband makes me know what a terrible thing we did in separating you. I begged Richard, but perhaps I could have done more."

"Don't see what." Hildy had a sudden illuminating thought. "Why, Miss Lou, bless your heart! When you stop to think about it, white ladies with mean husbands are almost as bad off as slaves."

"Master Richard was never mean to me, but. . . ."

"I know," comforted Hildy. "When he got sot, he was sot for sure."

Her mind churned. How would she find Justus? Many runaways kept going till they were safe across the Canadian border. Hildy had never been off the plantation except for trips to Tahlequah a few times. There were some bad people out in the world beyond Waverly, some who'd destroy your free papers and keep you for a slave or sell you. Still, she had to take this chance. "I'll go, Miss Lou . . . and, if the good God lets me find Justus, we'll come back and help you. Just now, though, I'll fetch Richie to see you."

Passing down the hall past the dining room, Hildy heard the *clink* of silver. What could possess any of the women to polish silver on washday? She opened the door and froze.

Three men, in filthy buckskin and homespun, stuffed silver from the sideboard and cupboard into bags, including the huge claw-footed eggnog bowl, candelabra, and trays and pitchers of every size. Through the window, she saw horsemen gallop through Miss Lou's flowers. Down by the smokehouses, men loaded a wagon with meat. She saw all this in a flash.

The thieves laughed. One put down a shining pitcher and started for her. "Looky here, boys! Did you ever clap eyes on a purtier nigger wench?"

"That's not all we'll clap on her."

They stank of whiskey, tobacco, stale sweat. One looked Indian. *Richie! Miss Lou! Oh, God. . . .* Hildy glanced around for a weapon. She didn't scream because she prayed for a miracle — that Miss Lou, at the back of the house, wouldn't hear, that this trash would finish their stealing and leave. If only she could reach the fireplace and the poker. . . . She edged in that direction while the robbers came around the great table to advance on her.

"Hold off a minute, boys!" A whiskery beanpole who smelled rank as a boar hog came out of Master Richard's adjoining study with a bulging sack. "Bein' a pet house nigger, this 'n' likely knows where the money's kept."

Hildy lunged for the poker. He was on her like a panther, stench so foul it made her gag. "Where's massa keep his gold coin, gal?" Only snags remained of rotting teeth. One hand closed on her breast, fingernails digging.

With all her strength, Hildy jerked free and grabbed the poker. *What is going on outside? Where are the hands?* "There's no gold," she lied. "Master lost it all on slow horses he thought were fast."

"You might recollect better if we heat that poker and decorate you." The lanky man grinned. He seemed to be the leader of this gang who seemed to be plain thieves, not any kind of soldiers. "Tell us nice . . . treat us nice . . . and we might even leave you a dollar."

They had pistols and wicked knives, but they didn't want to kill her. Not yet. Apart from galloping horses, it hadn't been noisy outside, but suddenly firearms roared. Shrieks and howls reverberated.

What is going on out there? Have the robbers started fighting each other over the loot? Miss Lou had to hear.

Ignoring the uproar, the four marauders sidled toward Hildy. They could rush her, but the first one would get the poker across his face. With luck, she'd break one of their ugly jaws, splinter some teeth.

There was the *click* of a hammer thumbed back. Miss Lou stood in the door, holding with both hands the heavy Remington .44 revolver Master Richard had taught her to load and shoot before he went to war. She shot the leader through the middle. "Hit them there and they'll die sometime," Master Richard had instructed.

Hildy crashed the poker down on the closest thief's head. He toppled, but didn't thrash around, yelling, like the gut-shot one. The two remaining had their guns out. Miss Lou blasted one in the face. The other shot her as Hildy swung the poker as hard as she could against the side of his neck.

She heard it snap. Above that sound came firing and yells, a thunder of hoofs, but although Hildy heard, it meant nothing, nor did the groaning curses of the dying looters. She fell on her knees by Miss Lou. Blood pumped from the wound, soaking the black cloth of the bodice.

A linen tablecloth protruded from a robber's bag. Hildy seized it, tore open Miss Lou's bodice and chemise, and stuffed the cloth over the ragged blood-pulsing hole.

"Richie!" gasped Miss Lou. Pink froth bubbled from her mouth. The fingers that had fired the revolver reached blindly and fell. She made a kind of choking noise.

596

"Miss Lou!" Hildy raised her. "Miss Lou, honey!"

The hazel eyes stared, but they weren't seeing anything. Hildy heard feet pounding up the hall. She saw blue legs, fringed buckskins, and plain old butternut homespuns. Lifting her gaze, she saw Justus. *Is he real?*

He shot the tall thief in the head, thumbed back the hammer, and finished off the one with the ruined face. A man in buckskin, accompanying Justus, bent to slice his knife across the throat of the robber she'd stunned with the poker.

Justus dropped to his knees beside her, felt for a pulse at the side of Miss Lou's throat. He shook his head, shook it again as he saw the revolver by her hand. "Miss Lou used that?"

"She . . . she kept them off me. . . ." She stared at one of the dead robbers. "Are you with them?" she asked Justus.

"No, they're just a bunch of no-goods. Where's Master Richard?"

"Dead at Wilson's Creek." *Am I dreaming? Is Justus here? Is Miss Lou dead?* "Master Edmund's studying up in Boston."

Justus took in a sighing breath. He gripped Hildy's hand. "Miss Lou was a good lady. We'll bury her before we leave."

"Leave?"

"Well, sure!" His eyes caught hers. She breathed in the special scent of him. Yearning throbbed between them. "I've come back for you, Hildy. Joined the Army at Fort Scott and volunteered to join one of the detachments that are scouting this north part of the territory to keep Confederate troops from stopping the Union Creeks get safe over the border into Kansas."

Union soldiers? But . . . they aren't acting much different from the out-and-out bandits! Why did part of this dream come true have to be a nightmare?

As if he knew she couldn't think, Justus squeezed her fingers. "Get a quilt, sweetheart."

The buckskin-clad man with Justus stank almost as badly as the thieves. He peered into one of the sacks and chortled: "Look at these candlesticks and pitchers! All bagged and ready to go!"

Hildy scrambled up, started for him. "You can't . . . !"

Justus caught her wrist, gave her a warning look. His companion tied the bag and started out, saying: "Keep your gal in line, Jus. She oughta be glad we're settin' her free." He looked Hildy up and down. "Where's your master's gold?"

"In other men's pockets." Hildy was amazed at how easily she invented another lie. "He liked cards too much."

"You sure about that?"

Hildy looked him in the pale eyes. "Sure as sure."

"That's the gospel truth," said Justus. He gave her a little shove. "Hurry and get that quilt."

These might be Union men, but it looked like to them Justus was still a nigger. Hildy wasn't daft enough to get him killed over the family silver. "I have to go see if Master Richie's safe."

"I'll go with you," Justus said. "I've got to see my mama and sisters."

He steered her past a number of dead men on the way to the cabins. Except for one bearded man with a blue uniform and a hole in his forehead, it was hard to tell to which band the dead belonged — the thieves or the men with Justus. They had one thing in common. They were all dead, some with slit throats or bashed-in heads. Neither side was taking prisoners or letting the wounded crawl away.

The big iron kettle spilled soapy linens that were being trampled into the sodden earth. The kettle was too hot to handle, but men were dousing it with rinse water from the tubs. Some had taken over where the other gang had left off, heaping wagons with corn from the cribs, all the cured meat, butter, and cheese from the springhouse, and kegs of molasses.

"Don't look, Hildy." Justus gripped her arm

and drew her along toward his mother's place. The wails of frightened children came from behind the barred door. "Mama, it's me!" Justus pounded on the heavy oak boards.

The door opened in a twinkling. Aunt Becky stared up at her tall son. The wrinkles of her brown skin seemed to smooth, and her eyes shone. "My Lord, dear God!" She lifted trembling hands to touch his face. "Oh, child! Haven't I prayed . . . every night and day I've prayed . . . to lay eyes on you again?"

They held each other closely, Justus's cheeks as wet as his mother's and sisters' who swarmed to hug him.

"You're real!" Jane laughed as she wept.

Aunt Becky turned to jerk her head toward the rambunctious foragers. "Why you with that white trash, boy?"

"They're mostly jayhawkers, all legal now, rigged out in uniforms" — Justus shrugged — "but I'd have ridden with Old Nick himself to get home."

Small heads began to pop up from behind cots and the chest. Half-grown girls scuttled in from the other cabin with their charges. Master Richie ran to Hildy and buried his face in her lap.

"We . . . we heard the guns, Hildy! I want Mama!"

How to tell him? Should he see her? Poor lamb, no Mama now, or Daddy. . . . Master Ed-

mund and Miss Alice both back East. . . .
Thoughts spinning crazily as a broken mill wheel, unable to speak even if she knew what to say, Hildy hugged the little boy.

Harvey, the tall foreman, and Jabez, the mulatto tailor, rushed in with a mallet and sickle they'd snatched up for weapons. "Bless God, you're all right!" Harvey gasped to his wife Nell as Jabez hugged Olive. They recognized Justus in the same moment.

"Where'd you get that blue coat and a gun, Jus?" demanded Harvey. "You with this gang of thievin' rascals?"

"That thievin' bunch wouldn't have left a solitary egg, let alone a chicken!" Justus gave a short laugh. "Fact is, Harve, if we hadn't turned up, more'n likely all of you'd get hustled off to be sold in Fort Smith." Justus raised his voice to reach the others who came crowding in. "We're Union men. No one'll hurt you, long as you don't get in their way. Miss Lou's dead. . . ."

Wails broke out. Justus held up his hand. "The bandits did it, not us! She'll be buried decent."

"Master Richard, he's dead, too," mumbled Harvey. "What we goin' to do? Oh, Lordy, what we goin' to do?"

"You want to be Lincoln soldiers?" Justus asked.

"Soldiers?" Harvey and Jabez shrank, but some of the younger men whooped and yelled. "Soldiers? Us?"

"General Jim Lane'll take you," Justus explained. "Mark my words, it won't be too long till there's goin' to be whole regiments of black men!"

"Fighting the masters?" Jabez choked. "Sweet Lord Jesus! If they caught us, they'd skin us alive!"

"They'll shoot us if they can, that's certain."

Justus sounded so cheerfully confident that Hildy's heart swelled with pride, even in her grief. He'd always been the man she loved, but now he wasn't anybody's slave! He was a warrior, just like those wild Indians farther West. Now he grinned at his old friends, and held up his revolver. A black man with a gun!

"If you want to join the Army, hurry and get ready to come with us. We're down here to help Union Creeks fight off that whole damn boilin' of Confederate Creeks, Chickasaws, Seminoles, and Cherokees . . . even Texans!"

"You aim to fight with all that plunder in the wagons?" asked Harvey.

"Call it our supply train." Justus laughed, then sobered. "You women and whatever men don't want to be soldiers, you got two choices. Stay here and hide out when one side or the other tears through, or head for Kansas with all you can carry. You'll be free there. No one'll send you back or sell you."

His mother caught his arms. "Lord God,

boy, I've lived here my whole born days! I don't know nothin' about Kansas 'cept it's full and runnin' over with crazy folks."

Harvey pondered, turned to his gold-skinned wife, Nell, Master Richard's cousin. She looked at him above the coppery hair of their three light-skinned children. "Let's go, Harvey, for the children's sake," she pleaded. "If we stay and the South wins, we be slaves for always."

After a second's hesitation, he threw back his head. "We'll go," he said.

"So will we!" echoed a score of others.

"Then fill up the carriage and carts and anything that'll hold stuff," Justus advised. "No use leavin' things for the next raiders. Take any mules and cows the soldiers leave. Everything at Waverly came from your sweat."

Jabez caught Harvey's arm. "Don't be taking everything! Some of us druther stay . . . build cabins way back in the woods."

Olive, his tawny-haired wife, nodded. "Sounds better to me than trying to get North. S'posin' you meet up with more bushwhackers or Confederates than you can fight off? You'll get sold if they don't kill you."

Harvey's shoulders hunched forward but his tone was stubborn. "You that feels like that, come along, and we'll share out whatever the soldiers leave."

"I'm stayin'!" Aunt Becky appealed to her tall, handsome daughters. "Ruby! Jane! Don't be leavin' your old mama, at least not the both of you!"

"I got to stay, Mama." Jane put an arm around the frightened old woman. "Marsh wouldn't know where else to look when he and Master Edmund come back."

"My man died tryin' to haul Master Richard out of the firing," Ruby said. "I love you, Mama, but I'm takin' my children up where they'll never be sold." She added in a wondering tone: "Where they be free! Free! Can't wrap my mind around that yet."

"You'll get used to it," Justus assured her.

"Why can't we follow along with you?" Ruby asked.

"Too dangerous. There's bound to be fighting. On top of that, we can't be slowed down. You go with Harve's bunch, honey." He gave his sister a gentle push. "Go get your things."

She hurried off with the others. At last Justus caught Hildy to him, tight as he could with Master Richie in between, and kissed her long and hard and sweet. Oh, so sweet. . . .

"Thought my heart with break with longin' for you," he whispered. "All the time I was helpin' runaways go North, I tried to figger how to get you loose 'thout gettin' caught my ownself. When the war broke out, I was in Canada . . . come down and drove supply wagons for an Ohio regiment till I heard about Lane's jayhawkers bringin' out slaves from Missouri. Why not Indian Territory? I say to myself. Barely got sworn in at Fort Scott when word came that a lot of Union Creeks, headin' for Kansas, was being chased by all manner of Secesh. When Colonel Jennison called for volunteers to help the Union Creeks, you bet I was first in line."

"Oh, if you could just have got here before Miss Lou. . . ."

His tone hardened a little. "Well, at least you don't have to feel bad about leavin' her. Anything you need, get it fast, sugar. I'll find you a horse or mule."

She blinked. "You . . . want I should come with you?"

"Why else you reckon I'm here?"

"But . . . how'll I bring Master Richie?"

"You can't. And, Hildy, he's not Master Richie. You never goin' to call anyone master again!"

"I can't leave him."

"Sure you can! My mama and sis'll look after him, or someone can take him to Chief Ross's place."

Richie wailed and gripped her around the knees. Hildy knelt to hold him.

"Leave him," Justus ordered.

"I've looked after him since the hour he was born."

"Yes, instead of you and me havin' a child. A leech, that's what he is, a little white leech!" Justus's hands closed on Richie as if to force

605

him away.

Hildy shielded the boy with her body. "You go on with your soldiers. I'll travel with Harvey and the others."

"You daft, woman?"

"Why?"

"What's goin' to happen if Secesh catch a bunch of runaways with a little white brat?"

He was right. Richie's presence could make the difference between being saved alive and sold, or death by flogging or burning. She couldn't put such danger on the rest. Although her heart chilled, she said: "I'll go North with him alone, then."

"You're crazy!" Justus's voice dropped, filled with hurt and pain that stabbed her deeply. "I'm your own married husband. Don't that matter?"

"I love you! I do, Justus!" She kept her arms around the boy. "But. . . ."

"That bleached-out little maggot couldn't suck milk out of you, but he sure sucked out who you are!" Justus's powerful hands flexed, hands she loved but that could snap Richie's neck like a dry twig.

Hildy backed away with the child. Justus gave a laugh that was close to a sob before he swallowed. "Go alone, you're better off without a mule or horse. Won't be so easy seen or tracked, and you won't get killed by some thief. I remember you can wear Miss Lou's shoes. Better find a couple of stout pairs . . . and warm clothes. It's a long walk to Kansas."

Tears filled Hildy's eyes. She tried to speak, couldn't, and mutely stretched out her hand. To see him just these few minutes, then maybe never again! It was too hard, too hard!

"You can pick up the Military Road to Fort Scott, if you follow the creek east about five miles," Justus told her. "Fade into the timber when you hear anyone comin', but try not to get too far from it."

A bugle sounded. "Best place for you to go is to some Quaker folks named Parks, who run a mill close to Trading Post," Justus decided. "They be friends of the Wares, those folks who helped me get away. I'd send you to them, if they didn't live across the Missouri line where you could be picked up for a runaway. The girl, Christy, she'd be a good friend to you. If you meet her and her folks, tell them I pray for them every day of this world."

The bugle called again. Hildy couldn't bear to let him go, clung to him when he kissed her. He had to loosen her hands away. "After the war," he promised. "After the war, I'll find you sure!" He hurried off.

Hildy went light-headed and dizzy as if tight bands holding her skull together were slashed. But this was no time for fainting. "Richie," she said. "We have to go, you and me, honey boy."

"Mama go, too?"

"Your mama. . . ." Hildy couldn't keep from sobbing. That frightened Richie. He tugged at her.

"I want Mama!"

"Honey, you have to tell her good bye. Like you did your daddy. . . ."

"Daddy's dead! He was a brave, brave so'jer!"

"So was your mama, Richie. Just as brave as your daddy. . . ."

"Gracious' sake, Hildy!" Aunt Becky summoned her daughters with a jerk of her head. "Come along, Master Richie. Your mama's gone to be with Jesus. You kiss her and I'll cut off a piece of her hair for you."

The disappearing soldiers had dug the grave. One blue-coated man waited by it and the quilt-wrapped body. "I'm a minister of the United Brethren," he said. "I'll give a service for the lady."

Even the Waverly men who planned to join the soldiers gathered for the brief ceremony, but it was the women who lowered Miss Lou into the grave. Frost had killed the flowers she loved so much, but Harvey and Jabez broke off cedar limbs to put over her and soften the fall of the red earth.

Then, over the grave of their mistress, the folk of Waverly wished each other luck and gave Richie a kiss or pat on the head before those who wanted to join the Army went off after them and Jabez's and Harvey's groups hurried to finish their preparations.

"Where . . . where we going, Hildy?" Richie wasn't letting go of her for an instant. He hadn't wanted to kiss his mother, but he held tightly to the lock of hair Aunt Becky had put in a little tin box for him.

"We're goin' where bad men won't be ridin' through."

"Can . . . can I take my toys?"

"Just a few, darlin'. We have to carry food and blankets and some clothes. You be brave now and help me."

How long would it be before one rampaging bunch or another burned the house after looting whatever the robbers and soldiers had left? She hoped Harvey's and Jabez's bands took a lot of useful things. Nell and Olive had vowed to rescue what they could of family heirlooms and hide them in the woods till Master Edmund or Miss Alice came for them.

"Go to your room, Richie," Hildy said. "Get out three sets of clothes . . . don't forget your socks and drawers! Bring your other shoes, your mittens and wool cap, and a jacket. . . ."

"It's not cold. . . ."

"It will be."

"Can I bring my little men?" He meant his lead soldiers. Hadn't he seen soldiers enough for the rest of his life? But they had been his last birthday gift from his father and were his favorite toys.

"Pick the eight you like best."

"What . . . what'll happen to the rest?"

"Ruby and Jane and Olive will likely hide them away with your other things." *Though if you ever set eyes on them again,* she thought to herself, *you'll likely be too old to play with them.*

His mouth quivered. "I can't go to sleep without Mister Bun."

Knitted from softest blue wool by Miss Lou and stuffed with cotton lint, the flop-eared bunny had been mended till probably no original stitch remained, but, however bold and venturesome Richie was by day, at bedtime he wanted the comfort of his grimy old companion.

"Of course, we'll take Mister Bun."

"Do . . . do we got to go today?"

"As quick as ever we can, child."

He ran to his room like a scared little shadow. Hildy felt like a thief when she got out Miss Lou's sturdiest shoes, but she knew bruising and cutting her feet would slow down their journey. Miss Lou's lined, wool, hooded cape would keep Hildy warm by day and serve as a blanket by night. Although no one had bothered anything else in the room, likely out of respect for a woman who'd died defending her slave, they had cleaned out the

610

crystal bowl where Miss Lou kept a little silver and gold. Most of Waverly's money was invested with trading enterprises.

Hildy took a last look around Miss Lou's room, full of the scent and memories of the woman who had raised her. *Good bye, Miss Lou. Good bye, my sweet lady. . . . I'll do my best for Richie, but I'm afraid, and Justus's gone and . . . and if you can at all, Miss Lou, help me!*

Hildy closed the door and stumbled blindly into her own room. One blanket was all she could carry. She laughed shakily to realize she had her own Mr. Bun, the indigo, wool blanket Miss Lou had woven with her own hands and given her one Christmas. Hildy spread it on the bed, put on it a change of clothes for herself and the shoes, thread, scissors, and needles, then carried the blanket to the kitchen to add a skillet, cook pot, forks and spoons, bacon, venison jerky, beans, hominy, cornmeal, salt, coffee, dried peaches, apples, and pears. They'd be like candy to Richie, but food as well. She got flint and steel, and then remembered Master Richard's box of matches in the study by his chest of Havana cigars. They'd be handy when a fire was needed in a hurry.

The robust odor of the tobacco made her glance around as if Master Richard might stroll into the carpeted, velvet-draped room. She hoped, somehow, the books, footed globe, rosewood furniture, and bronze figures would survive to belong to Master Edmund or Richie, although God only knew what would happen to any of them, much less to things.

Going to Richie's room, she helped him pack Mr. Bun, his little men, and clothing in a pillowcase he could carry, and added the rest to her burden.

So much here they needed, but there was no use starting out with more than they could carry. *The butcher knife . . . useful, and a weapon.* She wrapped the blade with a dish towel and thrust it through an improvised sash made of two towels tied together.

Through the window, she saw the trees bounded by their shadows the way it was at noon. *Had the world ended in just one morning? Miss Lou, Miss Lou, good bye.*

Hildy took Richie's hand and a deep breath. "Come on, honey boy. Tell Mister Bun we're going where there won't be all this trouble." She had a good mind to try to find that Christy Ware that Justus had mentioned, the one who'd helped him get away North. But the first safe place she found for Richie, that's where they'd stay till this was all over.

"My little men'll help us," Richie said. "They're so'jers just like Daddy."

Which got him and Tack buried up there at Wilson's Creek in Missouri.

"Will we ever come back?" the child asked.

"Most likely you will, Richie," she comforted. "After the war. After Master Edmund comes home."

But I won't. Never.

CHAPTER TWENTY-NINE

Ellen Ware, her two daughters, Christy and Beth, Sarah Morrow, and the survivors of the burning of Rose Haven, made their heavily laden way, along with their animals, through the underground passage toward the secret valley that spread below the opening now blocked by a woman whose skin was as brown as her leather garments — a woman who wanted to know who they were and why they had come?

When the Wares had begun to fear they might need to hide from the thieves and the Confederate guerrillas who were raiding the homes of Union sympathizers along the turbulent border of Kansas and Missouri, Christy and her father had discovered this way to the valley. Little more than a week ago, guerrilla raiders had shot Jonathan Ware dead, on his own threshold and killed most of the livestock. Ironically a wounded man, who was probably a guerrilla, lay recovering at this moment in the Ware house.

Jonathan Ware's family had found no refuge at Rose Haven, the grand plantation of the Jardines' whose daughter was the wife of Charlie Ware. Instead the Ware females and their friend, Sarah, had found ruins, a slaughtered Bishop Jardine, his wife Lavinia, already an invalid, demented by his death, and Melissa Jardine Ware near childbirth.

Lavinia Jardine, perhaps mercifully, died before her daughter was fit to travel. Her old nurse, Aunt Phronie, and Phronie's beautiful half-white daughter Lilah had come with Melissa. Now, after their journey from the plantation, the remnants of two very different families, one of wealthy slave owners, one of a Universalist minister who had helped runaway slaves escape, gazed at this woman who barred their way.

Her tunic was pieced together from a number of small hides that had been patched often. Neither dress nor moccasins were ornamented or fringed. Not one of the incomers questioned the woman's authority, although any one of them, even Phronie, could have physically overwhelmed her. She was like the spirit of the valley made flesh. Beyond her, in the shadows, a pretty brown-skinned woman sat with her arms loosely clasping a white child with curly golden hair who looked about five. Beth saw him, too, and gave a bounce of excitement. When her mother didn't speak, Christy stepped forward.

"Perhaps you don't know there's a war outside. . . ."

"There's always a war." The old woman's English was very good, but had a soft Scot's burr. She nodded toward the dark young woman. "Hildy told me about this one. North and South. Union. Confederacy." She gave a lift of her shoulders. "Whichever side wins, they'll steal my people's land."

"Aren't you Osage?" asked Sarah. "I am."

Keen black eyes examined her. "You look like my dear friend, Si-zhe-Wah'i, Shy Deer, who the missionaries called Mary. She married a Frenchman, I recall. You have his eyes. It was a real wedding, according to our customs, not just going off into the bushes."

"Then you went to school at Harmony Mission with my mother?" cried Sarah between joy and disbelief.

"Yes. Like me, Shy Deer was the eldest daughter of an important family and had the sacred spider on both hands . . . see?" She held out the backs of her hands. Black spiders moved when she flexed her fingers. "I remember those," Sarah whispered. "I wanted to have them."

"I don't suppose you do now." The woman's tone was dry. "Shy Deer was of the Deer Clan and I of the Eagle. I hoped she would marry my brother, but once the Frenchman watched

616

her with eyes like the sky . . . well, after all, the Deer clan are Sky People."

"Sky People?" Sarah repeated.

The woman frowned. "Shy Deer never taught you who you are?"

"She died of cholera when I was three. My father was sickening and took me to the mission before he died. That was after the Osages moved to Kansas."

Teeth the color of old ivory showed in the wrinkled face. "I didn't go."

Ellen Ware gasped. "You've lived here since . . . since Eighteen Thirty-Seven?"

"No. I was married to a man of Scotland, a freighter on the Santa Fé Trail. I used to travel with him, and cook. He died defending me from a teamster who thought, because I was Indian, I was for anyone's pleasure." She paused. "I had no wish to live on the Kansas reservation or marry again. The old ones of my people knew about this valley. They said some of the Land or War People lived here when the Sky or Peace People found them, and they united to become the Children of the Middle Waters, the Osage." She thought a moment as if calling back things no longer important. "It was while the whites were fighting the war with Mexico that I came here."

"Eighteen Forty-Six?" murmured Sarah. "That's still a long time."

"At first it was. Not now."

"No one's come here?"

"Just Hildy" — the Osage woman gestured to her side — "and the child. They've run from the white man's war. And winters ago, a hunter came once, after a bear. He shot at it right here. The bear escaped into the valley, but rocks fell on the hunter. His bones are still under them."

"Do animals find their way in very often?" asked an awed Beth.

"Bears. Sometimes a panther."

"I suppose you snare them for food and hides," Sarah ventured.

"No. Whatever enters the valley dies in its own time. Then I take the hides, even the meat if it isn't tainted. There is no killing here."

Sarah protested: "But Osages hunt!"

"The Wa-kon of this valley, its mystery power, gave me a vision. This is a place of life."

"The panthers must have killed to live!" objected Sarah.

The valley's guardian smiled. "That is their Wa-kon. I don't have to kill to live. Besides nuts and fruit and wild foods, I have two bee gums, and grow corn, squash, and pumpkins as my people always have." She seemed to make a decision. "I am One Eagle, but my husband called me Star."

"A lovely name," said Ellen Ware.

"It belongs to Sky People," admitted the

woman. "But my husband Geordie said my eyes were like star shine in the night. Every day, all these years, I've talked with him . . . in his language, for he never could learn mine. Sometimes, now, I hear him answer." She glanced kindly at Melissa and Lilah who seemed dazed by all that had happened. "You are tired. Sit down. Now tell me who you are."

Since no one else spoke, Christy did. She introduced Sarah, Melissa, Lilah, and Phronie, then gave her own, her mother's, and her sister's names.

On hearing them, Hildy sprang up. "Ware? You be the Wares who helped my man, Justus?"

"Justus?" Startled, Christy stared at the other. "You're his wife . . . Hildy?"

"Yes. Married by the preacher and all, but that didn't matter when Master Richard. . . ." Glancing down at the little white child hanging to her skirt, Hildy didn't finish.

"We helped him get over to Kansas, where John Brown took him North," Christy said. "He wanted to save enough money to buy your freedom."

"Not enough money in the world to do that as long as Master Richard was alive." The soft voice was bitter and sad at the same time. "But Master Richard got himself killed at Wilson's Creek. Bandits killed Miss Lou. Then Justus came along with some Union

619

soldiers, but I couldn't go with him. . . ."

"Justus is a soldier?" Christy burst out.

Hildy's smile was wry. "This bunch were down to help the Union Creeks fight off the Confederate ones, but they finished stealing what the bandits had started loading up."

"Trust the heavy eyebrows . . . the whites . . . to break the Indian nations in half." The leather-clad woman's voice was weary.

"Justus told me to ask for you at Parkses' mill," went on Hildy. "Richie and me got off the Military Road when we saw anyone coming, but we were too slow one day and this gang of cut-throats took after us. Ran us through the brush and timber till I nearly fell into a sinkhole hid by a spicebush. We crawled down. Pesky varmints was yelling and tearing around. Reckon they never saw the sinkhole. Long way off, I saw light, so we started toward it, walking real careful. When we were far enough inside that I reckoned the devils couldn't notice, I lit a candle. We came out of that littlest cave on the far side, yonder."

"So Justus doesn't know where you are?"

"No. But he sent me to the Parkses, so, when this war's over, he'll come there . . . if he's alive."

Star sighed, keen eyes looking at each newcomer in turn. "You are welcome to the valley so long as you need refuge. Come, I'll show you several other caves that are easier for living." The valley's guardian grinned. "Caves that don't have a smashed hunter in them."

Lilah and Melissa waited in what they began to call the River Cave while Star showed the others the cave she thought best suited to them, a spacious limestone grotto. "It's close to the river" — she pointed out — "but high enough not to flood. There's this big chamber with a fairly level floor for cooking and work, and two shallow rooms for sleeping. We can wall up the front with rocks and mud mortar, make a fireplace and smoke hole. If you have a saw, you can make a door out of wood." Reading their faces, she explained: "It'll be dark, but a fire will give light. You could make a big door and leave it open when the weather's good. And in summer, you can knock out some of the rocks to let in fresh air and light." Her face lit up. "No! In summer, if you're still here, we'll build a long house of the kind my people live in, one big enough for everyone."

"Of logs?" Christy was dubious, remembering the raising of the Ware's happy house and how much skilled labor it had taken. Rather than try to saw logs to make a door, she and Sarah could bring back the door of one of the corncribs; there certainly wasn't any corn left to protect.

"We can build a house," Star assured her guests. "There are plenty of young hickories for poles and cat-tails and bark for walls and roof. I could have made a small round lodge of the kind my people used when hunting buffalo on the plains, but when I came here, it seemed good to dwell in Mother Earth as our people did in the beginning before the Sky folk came." She smiled at Sarah. "You are of the Sky People, daughter of my friend. Wah'-kon-tah has surely brought you here."

Sarah looked eagerly at the older woman. "I hope you'll tell me more about my parents and my people."

"Winter is a grand time for stories, my husband always said." Star laughed as she watched the fair-haired little boy grasp Beth's hand and tug her off to admire some secret of his. "How fine it is to see children again! You even have a baby, with another coming." For Lilah was heavy with child, quite probably by Melissa's careless, handsome brother who was off fighting for the South. As, to Christy's grief, was her brother, Charlie, who had married Melissa.

"Yes, and we'd better help Melissa and Lilah down here," Ellen said. "The cave's nice and dry. We can leave an overhang outside the wall where we can work on fine days."

"Like a porch," said Phronie, cheering a bit.

"There's two smaller caves across the valley, if you'd rather have separate dwellings."

"Right now," said Ellen, "I think we'd like

to stay together."

With Hildy and Star helping, the supplies were carried to the cave. Star had a long band of leather that she slipped around bundles in order to carry them more easily. By placing the band where hair and forehead met and securing the chicken basket with the other end of the loop, she easily carried the scolding fowl down the hazardous rocks.

These and the other Jardine chickens were turned loose near a makeshift shelter of stripped branches closing all but an entry to a long shallow cave. The door could be closed with more branches at night till some kind of door was fashioned. A fallen tree with plenty of good roosting limbs had been dragged inside. Lilah and Melissa, still exhausted, were persuaded to rest on rush mats Star brought while the others unpacked and put things out of the way on numerous ledges. The willow chest, cleaned of chickens, held sheets and Melissa's baby's clothing. Strange that a cave might be the first home remembered by the child who would have been heir to Rose Haven!

Nooning sunlight shone almost to the back of the stone room, pleasantly warming it, but, in a few more hours, it would be shaded again. They stopped work to go to Star's home, sit out in the sun, and share herb-flavored stew of chopped hickory nuts, dried corn, and squash ladled with a wood spoon into wood bowls. The incomers contributed cold cornbread, butter, and buttermilk.

"I had forgotten how good butter tastes," Star allowed. "Many inventions of the heavy eyebrows are useful. My people traded with the French long before the Americans came, back when they were arguing with the Spaniards over who owned our country." She glanced at the iron kettle and an axe, hoe, and shovel leaning against the rock wall. "I brought as many good things as I could from the cabin where we lived when Geordie wasn't freighting, but I've never wanted anything, even salt, enough to leave the valley."

"My husband swapped molasses and corn for a year's supply of salt at the store in Trading Post," Ellen said. "We have dried red peppers, too, that are good seasoning. We'll share."

Star nodded as if that were only to be expected. "I have much dried fruit and nuts, besides my crops. There will be food enough for everyone." She got to her feet. "We'll begin the wall of your home this afternoon and finish it tomorrow. You're welcome to sleep in my cave, if you wish, but it should be warm enough here if you have a fire."

"Thank you." Ellen's face lightened as she watched her daughter-in-law nurse Charlie's son, Joely. "We'll stay here. I think we'll all want to sleep close together tonight anyway."

■ ■ ■ ■

The good weather held, although it was cool next morning. By mid-afternoon, the mud-mortared rocks, mostly gray but also red, yellow, and white, walled in all but the door space of the cave. A rock chimney rising from above the fireplace jutted out to form part of the wall.

It was dark inside, but a warm, welcoming dark, scented with cedar and oak boughs burned last night. In the wreck of the world they'd known, in the midst of nightmare and disaster, what a blessing to find Star and Hildy in the valley! Beth, nearly two years older than Richie, took charge of him to their mutual enjoyment and their elders' relief.

"If we hurry," said Christy, shielding her eyes toward the sun, "we can bring the Wyandotte hens and all but one cow back before night."

"The cows can carry several mattresses," Ellen said. She rubbed her back. "Your rush mat helped a lot, Star, but I need a little more between me and the ground."

Beth caught Christy's hand. "Bring Robbie! Please!"

They hadn't brought the little border collie yesterday for fear he'd get under Melissa's or Lilah's uncertain feet, or, indeed, those of any of the burdened persons or animals he might have tripped. Christy looked at Star for permission.

"Robbie's a good dog, but he'll chase rabbits and squirrels."

"That's his nature." Star shrugged. "We cannot expect him to live on squash and dried persimmons."

"A dog!" squealed Richie. "Oh, Hildy! We're going to have a dog!" Clearly, with Beth's advent and now a dog, his four-and-a-half-year-old life had brightened tremendously.

With an ache in her throat, Christy hugged Beth. How would these children and countless like them grow up after what they'd seen, after the death of parents, the savage destruction of their worlds?

Once again she blessed the valley. If only Dan O'Brien, her sweetheart, and Charlie were here! But they were men and had to fight their battles. *I'll fight mine, too,* Christy resolved, straightening from her sister. *I'll stay at the happy house. If anyone, jayhawk or bushwhacker, burns it, I'll rig a shelter under the big tree, the way we lived when we first came. And as long as I have food or a roof, I'll share them as Father and Mother did, the way Star shares with us.*

Christy untangled her sister's wild curls. "Take care of Richie and help Mother while I'm gone, Beth."

Beth thrust out her lower lip and shot an

annoyed look at her oblivious sister-in-law. "I'm Joely's aunt! I want to take care of him, but M'lissa won't let me."

Small wonder that Melissa clung to her baby. Within a week, she'd lost mother, father, home, everything familiar excepting Phronie and Lilah. Christy dropped on one knee to gaze into Beth's hazel eyes. "You can help a lot with Joely when he's a little bigger. Right now you can help best by not pestering Melissa and doing good things like gathering wood and kindling for the fires."

Ellen nodded. "You'll have chores here, just as you did at home. And we'll have lessons."

"Lessons?" Beth's lips quivered. "But . . . Father was the teacher. . . ."

"I am now," said Ellen. She included the other women with an encompassing gesture and smiled. "All of us are."

Promising not to forget Robbie, Sarah and Christy made the steep ascent to the river cave. "Powerful lot of teachers for two children," Sarah mused as they passed from the light and lit their candles. "But when you think about it, look at all they know . . . Phronie and Lilah and Hildy have been slaves. Your mother can teach reading and ciphering and such. Star knows how to live in the valley and the old Osage ways I hope she'll teach me."

"Are you going to live in the valley?"

"Aren't you?"

"No. I'll go back and forth, of course, but I'm staying outside," Christy answered.

Sarah didn't speak for a time. Then she asked: "Why?"

"Because . . ." — it was hard to put into words — "I guess I can't stand to turn things over to the Watt Caxtons, Doc Jennisons, Jim Lanes, and especially not to the likes of Lafe Ballard." Lafe who loved pain, who, at the raising of the happy house, had deliberately pushed her wrist against a searing hot kettle. She still wore that brand. Worse, he had carved his initials on Dan's dear face after killing Andy McHugh on the bloody hill above Wilson's Creek. Apparently Lafe had served his brief stint in the Confederate Army and then had gone into the less dangerous and more lucrative career of riding with guerrillas. He'd been with the band that had killed Christy's father.

Sarah nodded slowly. "How can a wonderful lady like Hester have such a varmint for a son? You say she doesn't know he was with the gang when they killed Emil Franz and Lottie?

"When she brought the wounded man to us, she said one man in the group that hung Emil looked like Lafe, but wasn't."

"Well, let's hope she never has to remember." Sarah's smooth jaw hardened. "You'll try to farm?"

"I'll try."

"If you manage to raise a crop, one thieving bunch or another will steal the grain or turn their horses loose on it."

"If it's early enough, I'll plant again. If it's too late, then spring will come."

"And so will they! Union, Secesh, or just plain robbers!"

Christy again saw Caxton blasting her father down, watched that awful crumpling, arms still extended in welcome. If she'd had a shotgun. . . . Yes, glad and gladly she'd have killed Watt Caxton if she could have. The rage in her heart when she thought of him did not belong in Peace Valley.

"Whoever comes, I'll stay."

"Then I'll stay, too, though I want to visit Star and hear all she can tell me about our people." Sarah laughed. "I like belonging to the Sky People, and I don't think Blessed Mary or her Son mind a bit. I'll fetch my bees to your place. Star doesn't need them."

"You don't have to stay with me."

"I've had enough of my own company, what with Lige gone." Sarah hesitated. "I remember your cabin-raising and how we made the quilt while the sill boards were laid on the foundation. While we stitched and talked, the walls went up."

"They only used nails on the roof," Christy remembered. "Andy McHugh made them." She swallowed hard, thinking of Andy's red-haired baby boy who'd never know his father, killed at Wilson's Creek. *Please, please! Let Joely know Charlie!*

"I wonder if that'll ever happen again," Sarah mused. "Neighbor men raising a cabin or barn or trading work at harvest while the women make a quilt and put together a feast?"

Christy thought of her father, how he expected good from people and usually met with it. Till that last day. *Will it always hurt this much? How does Mother stand it?* "We have to believe that someday neighbors will help each other again," Christy said. "Anyway, Star has welcomed us, and you and Hester are helping us. . . ."

"Ourselves, too," Sarah insisted. "One good thing, the hounds will set up such a racket that no one's going to sneak up on us."

The women were growing familiar enough with the sinuous cavern to traverse it more speedily, especially unhampered by burdens. As the azure sky shone from the entrance, they blew out their candles and walked slowly to accustom their eyes to the brightness. Perhaps, too, Sarah, like Christy, needed time to change from the timeless underground, with neither day, night, season, or weather, to the outer world, so different from the valley.

Hester Ballard, across the creek, stood in the winter orchard, her hands on the branches, as if she would warm the buds into life. A cloud of cedar waxwings dropped into their namesake trees edging the cornfield beyond Jonathan Ware's grave, and a brilliant red male cardinal flew from a tree to offer a berry to his demurely hued mate on the fence. A busy, happy, beautiful world, in spite of what had happened here, in spite of the oblong of broken sod at the edge of the stubble.

Christy and Sarah told an amazed and delighted Hester about the valley, Star, and Hildy while they fitted the raucous Wyandottes into covered willow baskets, haltered Lad and the dry cows, and fastened cornshuck mattresses on the animals' backs, holding them down by roped baskets of indignant chickens.

Christy hated not to keep Dan's fiddle near her. At least she could polish it and remember his long skillful fingers holding it and drawing the bow. It was too risky, though, to have it where raiders might break or steal it, so she nestled the fiddle in its battered case into one of the mattresses and secured it firmly.

"I'd admire to see that valley and meet Star," said Hester, adding a bag of turnips to Lad's burden. "And that little fair-haired boy. . . ."

"Why don't you go with Sarah?" Christy asked.

"But that man in there. . . ."

"Isn't he still sleeping most of the time? He

631

doesn't even need to know you're gone. Stay as long as you like."

"I'm mending his shirt."

"I'll finish it. Won't even leave a needle, sticking out, to jab him."

When Hester still hesitated, Sarah touched Christy's arm. "I'll come back tonight. Dark makes no never mind in the cave, and I don't mind it, anyway."

So while the younger women started the animals toward the entrance, Hester got her things together. Robbie wanted to turn back when Christy did, but she gave him a hug and pointed at the procession. "Run along, pup. Beth wants you . . . and so does a little boy!"

He went, glancing back with inquiring whines. Christy watched them vanish except for the candles' flickering. She'd look in on the wounded man before she milked Guinevere, who, not much comforted by the presence of Lass and the wounded man's black horse, lowed unhappily after her companions.

Going to the bedroom cabin, Christy froze at the sight of the empty bed. A soft laugh came from the bench by the window. "You sure have been busy, Christy Ware. Is there a big room in that cave where you're hiding all the critters?"

The stranger they had nursed through violent fever was cleaning his revolver with the care and tenderness of a lover. With an effort, Christy kept from shuddering. Even before her father's life was blasted away by a gun, Christy had a fear of guns.

"You've been spying!"

He quirked a dark eyebrow. "Wouldn't say that, Miss Christy. I just wasn't asleep all the time Miz Ballard thought I was."

She thought of the valley, of her family taking refuge there with Star and Hildy. This man wasn't going to carry his war to that hidden place. If she had to, she'd find a way to kill him.

"There's a cow and mare left here," she said. "Can't you be satisfied with them?"

"Why, Miss Christy, do you think I'd steal from you ladies after you saved my life?"

Almost going limp, she said faintly: "I hope you wouldn't."

"Depend on it." Reading her thoughts, he gave a disarming grin. "I won't tell the boys."

"Thank you."

"Least I can do."

Putting the gun aside, he got to his feet and crossed the space between them. Hester had shaved him or he had done it himself. His salty male odor was not unpleasant, thanks to her mother's soap, and it stirred an awareness in Christy as unwelcome as it was sudden and unexpected. He wore a shirt of her father's, buttoned only part way to accommodate the dressings of his wound. The muscles in his tanned throat and shoulders flexed as he dropped his hands on her shoulders and the blue blaze of his eyes engulfed her.

"You were wondering how to kill me. Weren't you, Christy Ware?"

His amusement stung. Warmth pulsed from his fingers through her body. *Dan! Dan!* It took all her strength to step back. The man didn't try to hold her. He just watched her with those brilliant dark-centered eyes.

"I . . . I'd have to kill you if I didn't believe you'll keep your word."

"I'll keep it. Who knows? I might need to hide in your cave someday."

This man in the valley?

He laughed at her dismay, lifted her chin with a caressing hand. "Have you got a sweetheart, Miss Christy?"

How to answer?

Her face had. He released her. "I reckon he's fighting for the Union?"

"Yes."

His smile was crooked. "Guess the best thing I can wish for you is that he gets hurt enough to get sent home, but not hurt so bad you'll be sorry he was." The dark young man sat down on the bed. "Dog-gone it! Still weak as a kitten."

"You're lucky you're alive!" Christy couldn't keep from saying it. "My father isn't. A gang of guerrillas rode in here, killed my father, killed the sheep and hogs, and stole

634

close to everything."

The blackness in the center of his eyes covered the blue. "Your pa must have been a Union man."

"He was, but that was no excuse to kill him when he stood in his own door and welcomed the riders."

His eyes veiled. "Christy Ware, I'm sorry about your pa," he said at last. "Will you be sorry for my pa, too? A squad of Union soldiers hanged him, along with my uncle for sympathizing with the South."

Christy gave an involuntary cry. She could no longer hold back her tears. "Where does it end? You're here because your father was killed. My brothers are fighting, one on either side. My sister-in-law's family was burned out by Union soldiers. I expect we'll be burned out by men like you. . . ."

"Maybe for you it ends here . . . with you taking care of me in spite of everything." He touched her hand briefly, and let out a sighing breath. "I'll send the word around that anyone who bothers you or this farm answers to me, Bill Anderson. Not many would care to do that, not even Quantrill."

The name meant nothing to her, although he seemed to think it would. "I suppose I have to thank you."

His teeth flashed. "Don't choke on it. I promise you that I'll kill every jayhawk and bluebelly I can."

"My brother. . . ."

"If I knew he was your brother, I wouldn't kill him if I could help it, Miss Ware. But men don't swap calling cards in the middle of a fight. You could tear off the bandage now and let me bleed to death. I'm weaker'n a cat and I don't even have claws." His eyelids drooped, lashes thick on his cheeks.

"Don't be silly. Rest, and, when you wake up, you'll get some pudding."

He grinned faintly. "You sound like Josie, too. My sister loves to spoil me."

Christy looked down at the man, wondering with a pang where her own were, praying they were alive and well and had warm clothing. And Dan. Where was he? And David Parks and Theo Wattles? She was relieved when Sarah returned while she was ladling up the stew, and more relieved when Sarah and Bill took a liking to each other and bantered as if they'd grown up together.

Lighting a candle so she could see to mend his shirt, Christy realized she was almost enjoying his company. They were like survivors of wrecked enemy ships washed up on an island, united by the will to live and their youth. Bill, he admitted, was only twenty, the same age as Thos, her brother, a year younger than Dan. If they lived through the war, would these young men be able to pick up the lives they should have led or would they miss battle and danger?

"Your sister made you a beautiful shirt," she told Bill as she repaired the stem of an embroidered rose.

"Josie's a rare hand with a needle. Maybe someday I'll bring her to see you."

"I hope you can," Christy said.

CHAPTER THIRTY

Christmas came. Bill Anderson had ridden off on his black horse, turning in the saddle to wave a good bye. Lilah had had a baby girl — very fair-skinned — she had named Noelle. All the animals and chickens were now in the valley for safety and so Christy and Sarah could go there for a visit. At noon, everyone, except Lilah, was gathered under the broad overhang of the unwalled front of the newcomers' cave. Delicious odors wafted from three Dutch ovens nestled in the coals of a fire built in a rock oblong that accommodated a large coffee pot at one end.

It was good to sing again, although it hurt to think of how Jonathan Ware would have loved to learn the Osage hymns. Christy could almost see him, throat swelling lustily, auburn head thrown back. How could someone so alive, so joyous in this world, suddenly not exist? His body was returning to the soil at the edge of his cornfield, but where had his spirit gone?

Jonathan's faith had had to do with how to live on this earth with its fellow creatures. He had never talked much about the afterlife beyond maintaining that God was too good to send anyone to hell. Her straying thoughts were caught in his favorite carol as her mother's clear voice led it.

Mary and Joseph walked in an orchard
   good
Where was cherries and berries as red as
   any blood. . . .

Then Joseph's fury at being cuckolded: "If he's a man can get a child, he's a man can climb a tree. Go tell you that man, and tell him speedily, that cherries and berries mean nothing to me." The babe, from his mother's womb, commanding the cherry tree to bow down to her hand. Joseph's awed contrition when he realized his innocent wife was with child by God.

"Every child is born with God in him," Christy's father used to say. "It's men who call some bastards."

Why, you are with us, Father! Christy thought. *As long as we remember how you lived and what you said, you live in us. You'll be in your grandchildren, too, though you'll never know them, because Charlie and Thos and Beth and I will tell them about you. What's more important, we'll live the way you taught us.* Christy wanted to call this out to her mother, but, when she caught her mother's eye, she was sure she already knew it.

Richie settled into Hester's arms. She held him loosely as if he were sunlight, brown head bent to his golden one. Surely she was remembering Lafe at that sweet age before something took over and turned him mean.

From beneath a blanket, Star produced two stick horses. Their heads were cut from chunks of sycamore limb that still had white bark on them, flaps of it peeled up to shape pricked ears. Shredded bark fibers wedged tight in grooves made creditable manes, and the eyes were black pebbles glued into hollows filled with pine resin.

"Now you can ride your ponies all over the valley," she said. "But, mind you, lean them against the wall when you're not galloping so that no one trips over them."

While Beth and Richie charged off toward the river, whooping and hollering, Star raised the blanket from what could only be Joely's cradleboard. She smiled as she brought it to Melissa, brass hawk bells fastened to the hooded top of the board, jingling gaily. "Cedar stands for eternal life. A cradle of it should bless your son with many years. I made the hood with part of my last buffalo robe."

Melissa gazed at the present with a stunned expression. To cover the silence, Christy touched what was probably a cardinal's scarlet feather attached to the head of the board next to the striped wing feather of a woodpecker, and a blue one that could have come from a grosbeak, jay, or bluebird. She couldn't identify the bits of fluff tied to the hawk bells.

"What beautiful feathers!"

"It makes a small star's eyes keen to have something to watch," the guardian said. She didn't seem to notice Melissa's strange behavior.

Ellen took the baby from Phronie's arms and handed him to Star. "Will you show us how to lace him in? I wish I'd had one of these when my children were little!"

Star regarded Joely's flannel gown and diaper with disfavor and tilted the board to show the soft dry moss in the bottom half. "Moss soaks up the child's messes and keeps him comfortable till his mother cleans him and puts in clean moss. With that thing" — she touched the diaper — "he will cry, and his skin will get sore if he's not changed right away."

"He will be!" Melissa almost snapped.

Star said no more but left the moss in place, doubtless hoping it would keep the cedar's fragrance from being overpowered. Taking Joely, she crooned to him softly as she placed him on the board.

Melissa, watching with dilated eyes, suddenly cried: "No!" She snatched up the baby. Startled, he began to yowl as she ran away with him, not to Star's cave, but to the one where Lilah drowsed. With a shake of her grizzled head, Phronie went after her.

"I'm so sorry!" Ellen's face was crimson. "I beg your pardon for my daughter-in-law, Star. Losing her home and parents has made her . . . not herself."

"She is very much herself." There was no censure in Star's tone. "She fears her son will become a savage. That is too bad. He would feel safe and happy laced snug on the board, carried on our backs or hung by the loop to a tree limb. But Lilah will be glad of the gift, I think."

Beth and Richie were trotting back, Beth slowing to let the younger child reach the grown-ups first. "Oh, Star!" she begged, hazel eyes glowing. "Give our ponies some Osage names!"

Star considered. "How about Gleh-mon? That means Arrow Flying Home. And Wind, perhaps? I-ba-tse Ta'dse."

Richie stroked his mount's fibrous mane. "Gleh-mon! He my Arrow. Can't say the Wind name."

"I can!" Beth scratched between her steed's bark ears. "It's like a rhyme! I-ba-tse Ta'dse!" Her eyes widened as Sarah presented her with the elegantly doll-sized, fringed, and beaded buckskin dress and moccasins. "For

Lynette? Oh, Sarah, thank you! She'll love being an Osage princess!" Beth caught Star's hand. "Could we put spiders on her hands, just like yours?"

Star looked quizzical. "Spiders would look strange when your doll wears white lady clothes."

Melissa wouldn't like it one bit, having her favorite doll marked with what she'd think a heathen symbol. "Maybe," Christy suggested, "we can paint spiders on with pokeberry juice . . . something that'll wash off."

Richie, enthralled with Lige's whistle, hooted eerie owl cries till Beth lured him away to play with Thos's marbles and experiment with catching the ball in the small wooden cup and spinning the hickory top. Christy stitched on Lambie's soft new covering with long-lashed embroidered eyes, and the gifting was complete.

Phronie marched her nursling along the path. "I beg your pardon, Star." Melissa was shamefaced but defiant. "It's very kind of you to make Joely such a beautiful gift. But I. . . ."

Star gently cut her off. "The cradleboard is the beginning of the Road of Life. It is your right to decide which road to set him on."

Gathered by the Dutch ovens with their plates, they all bowed their heads while Ellen, in a voice that wavered a few times but then resonated, thanked God for their food, for health, and for this valley.

Then Star raised her arms to the sky and thanked Wah' Kon-Tah for brightening their lives with two little stars on this day of the birth of his own beloved Son. The rest of them raised their arms, too. Christy had to admit that offering herself to the heavens with embracing arms, filling her lungs with the air that nourished all life, made her feel closer to God, Great Mystery, or whatever one called the power, than did closing her eyes and lowering her head.

"Here in winter, we know spring will come," Star finished. "Thank you, Grandfather, for the winter that lets us joy in spring."

Facing the sky, Christy made a silent prayer. *I'm glad we had Father as long as we did. I'm grateful for his life. Thank you for him. Thank you for his grandson. Help me protect the place he loved, plow and plant his fields so he'll hear the rustling corn. Help us make it a happy house again that welcomes everyone.*

By evening, the sky clouded. There was a scurry to bring wood into the caves or store it under overhangs. Christy and Sarah milked the cows that sheltered with the other cattle and horses under a grotto-like overhang where Hildy, Beth, and Richie had cut and piled up quantities of dried grass. Hildy and the children shut the chickens in their roost cave with heaped-up boughs and brush.

"I'm glad we brought Guinevere and Lass," said Christy. "I'm sure they're happier with their friends, and we don't have to worry about getting back to milk."

Snow fell faster, soft and noiseless as an owl's fringed wing. Near the blazing, cedar-pungent fire in the new cave, the remains of the noon feast tasted delicious. Noelle slept soundly, laced into the cradleboard leaning against a rock. Lilah sat up with pillows between her and the wall. Melissa was silent, but at least she was there.

Before she got in bed with Beth that night, Christy got Dan's fiddle out of the safe niche she'd found for it, took it out of its case along with his precious letter, and held them against her. The letter smelled of wood smoke and tobacco although Dan didn't use it.

Dan, oh, Danny, be well . . . come back to us. Come back.

The strings made a sound like a lonesome wind.

The Christmas storm was the beginning of weeks of rain, sleet, and more snow. To lessen the number in the cave, Christy and Sarah went back to the Ware home at the first break in the weather. It was well they did. Owen Parks rode up on Breeze that afternoon, hailing the house. When Christy answered, he put the bay gelding in the barn out of the drizzle, and ran to the house, panting good naturedly as he pelted across the threshold.

"My womenfolk have been hoping for

decent weather so they could visit, but it seemed a shame not to get these letters to you, and this package." With a flourish, he pulled two crumpled letters and a small packet from inside his coat. "Two from Dan and one from Thos. We didn't get a scratch from that rascal, Davie. Maybe Dan will say what he's up to."

"Read your letters," Sarah bade Christy. "Take off your coat, Mister Parks, and warm yourself while I brew some wild rose hip tea." She smiled at the dismay in the handsome young man's brown eyes. "It's quite nice with a little honey and helps ward off colds," she added, and hung his coat on a chair a prudent distance from the fire and swung the cast-iron water kettle over the flames. Two kettles salvaged from Rose Haven were in the valley, so this one could remain at the cabin.

Skipping the parts of Dan's letters that made her blush happily, Christy shared the rest. Captain John Brown, Jr., had arrived from Ohio with the rest of Company K and taken up his command, although greatly plagued by rheumatism. Doc Jennison had no desire to stay in winter camp near West Point with his men, but had turned up with his wife a few days after Christmas to be entertained by stirring music from the twenty-two regimental buglers.

Colonel Dan Anthony, who was in command, had heard several hundred guerrillas were in Dayton, Missouri. They were gone when he got there New Year's Day of 1862 with two hundred men and a howitzer, but, since the town had allowed guerrillas to gather there, Anthony burned forty-five of Dayton's forty-six houses. The spared one belonged to a Union man who had somehow managed to stick it out amongst his Secessionist neighbors.

I have no stomach for such doings, Dan wrote. Rather drive mules and pry wagons out of the mud. Please tell Uncle Simeon and the family that Davie isn't writing because a mule's heel connected with his hand the other day. Didn't break anything, but he can't hold a pencil. He's the best teamster we've got, except for Thos, which is a great marvel to the rest of the boys since neither of them whip their beasts or turn the air purple.

"So Davie's all right." Owen sighed with relief. "I could almost feel sorry for him, skinning mules instead of flourishing a saber, but I hate to think how Pa would worry if the boy was in an outfit facing battle." Sipping the lemon-scented tea and munching on a persimmon sugarplum, he glanced around the room that was much barer without Ellen Ware's piano and the carved family rocker. "Father and the women want you and Missus Ware to know that you're welcome at the mill." He shook his head wonderingly. "It's hard to believe your mother's really living in

647

a cave, Christy. And Melissa Jardine . . . I mean Melissa Ware!"

"Melissa's the only one who seems to hate it, but she'd not be happy anywhere right now. I wish we could get her to her sister in Saint Louis."

Owen considered. "She could take the stage to Leavenworth and get on a steamer there that would take her down the Missouri to the city."

"Yes, but that would be a great deal out of the way . . . a very hard trip with the baby . . . and expensive."

"Most of our customers pay in kind, not cash," Owen said, "but some do buy flour, and so do the Trading Post store and the Army camp close to there. I reckon we have money enough for your sister-in-law's journey."

"You're kind, Owen," Christy responded, "and thank you. But if Melissa still wants to leave, when the weather's fit for travel, we'll take her to Sedalia and the train."

Owen frowned. "Let me drive. It's too dangerous for women to jaunter about alone."

"I think it's much more dangerous for men. So far neither side's killing women on purpose."

When Owen rode away, clearly unhappy about leaving two women by themselves, even though Christy had told him about Bill Anderson's promise of protection, she read

648

again the more personal parts of Dan's letter. Thank you for the splendid handkerchiefs, mittens, and socks. My others were worn to pieces. These will keep me warm, doubly warm because you made them, but, oh, how much I'd rather be warmed by holding you, my darling. You're always in my mind and heart but most especially when I roll up in your blanket. Please do think of me then. We haven't been paid and there's not much I'd like to give you in the Fort Scott stores, anyway, but I did whittle this locket for you out of cedar. I'm afraid it smells nicer than it looks, but I can't tell you how many pieces I ruined trying to make something that looked more like a rose than a cauliflower. The cord's braided out of hairs from Raven's tail. He's a beautiful black artillery horse I hope I get to ride if I ever get out of driving mules.

Christy pressed the wood to her cheek, smiling as she pictured Dan squinting at the design in fierce concentration. Placed around her neck, the horsehair cord chafed a little, but nothing, nothing, had ever been more precious.

CHAPTER THIRTY-ONE

Beth said the valley was magic because of Star, and Star was magic because of the valley. Beth said Richie could be her little brother, and that Robbie was his dog, too, although Robbie might not know that since he still slept beside Beth. It was nice to have a sister although Richie couldn't see why she thought the babies were fun and why she liked to hold them, not when she could be pulling him on the sled Aunt Sarah had made, or playing marbles or make-believe. Still, she was a much more satisfactory sister than Alice who was old, at least as old as Hildy, and his really big, big brother, Edmund.

Richie cried sometimes because his mama couldn't hug him and tuck him in at night, and he got a peculiar hurting inside when he remembered how his papa would pretend to be a bear and wrestle with him or hold him in his lap and read him stories. He missed Aunt Becky and all his playmates, but he loved having his own cozy little sleeping hollow in the wall above the main cave.

Mr. Bun lived in a nook and there were plenty of ledges for treasures, the little box with his mother's hair, his eight favorite soldiers, and now the owl whistle, marbles, and top. Living in the valley was like playing make-believe all the time, especially since Star was a real Indian. Aunt Sarah's mother had been Indian, but she acted pretty much like Aunt Christy and Aunt Ellen.

There certainly were a lot of aunts! Aunt Phronie was the main one since all the others called her that, except for Aunt Lilah who called her Grandma. Star had told him and Beth that she liked to be called just that. Hildy stayed Hildy to him, but was Aunt Hildy to Beth. The good thing, in Richie's view, was that all the women treated him like their own little boy, except for Aunt Melissa who hardly ever smiled except at Joely or her dumb, old cat, Emmy, who hissed at Richie and scratched him hard the time he tried to pick her up.

Aunt Hester hugged him and told him Emmy was a nasty grouch who didn't deserve to be petted. She put good-smelling salve on the scratches that stopped the hurting. When his legs were worn out from trotting after Beth, Aunt Hester held him and sang about how froggie went a-courting, weevily wheat, skipping to my Lou, and the jolly miller boy.

He was too big to nap, but sometimes he went to sleep in Aunt Hester's arms and it was like being in his mama's arms again. Aunt Hester told him her boy was grown up, so she was especially glad to have him to love — and he knew her love was somehow different from the kindness the other aunties had for him.

He could read lots of words in Aunt Ellen's primer, print his name and Beth's and Robbie's, count to twenty, and add or take away from the pebbles he and Beth used to do sums. They had school for what seemed a long time, every morning. Every afternoon, Beth was supposed to write in her journal, so usually he did, too, at least he drew pictures, and Beth and one of the aunts would help him spell the words he needed. Most of his journal was about what Star showed them.

She read the outdoors like Aunt Ellen read the hardest, longest words. She knew whether rabbits or deer had gnawed twigs because rabbits make sharp cuts but deer leave raggedy edges. If tracks in the snow were too blurred to tell what made them — a raccoon or 'possum — Star knew a raccoon never drags its tail although a 'possum often does.

She knew stories about all the creatures, and a dandy one about the great big woodpecker, the one with the bright red topknot. "When the Sky People first traveled west on the plains, they were driven back by fierce, pale-skinned warriors who wore buffalo horn headdresses," Star said. "The Sky People had to run away, and that made them feel bad. While they rested at their fire that evening, the great woodpecker flew up and called to them. They saw he was black as night except for white marks of day and his splendid crest that was the color of Father Fire.

"He had come to be their guardian on the plains. They shot him with a blunted bird arrow and put his skin in a rush bag the leader could carry around his neck. The head they skinned, also, and hung it from the sacred pipe. After that, they were not afraid on the plains, though they sometimes had to fight the pale warriors."

Star took Beth and Richie to watch an otter family play on their slide on a slope above the river at the far end of the valley. Five of the sleek, small-eared creatures, who were longer than Richie, took turns tucking their forepaws close to their bodies, launching themselves, on their bellies, down the icy bank, shooting into the water, then bobbing up and again making their way to the top. They had a snow wallow, too, where you could see the print of their webbed, clawed feet.

"I wish I could slide with them," Richie said once to Beth.

"Silly Billy! You wouldn't like winding up in that cold river! Come on, let's go see what's happening at the hotel."

The hotel was almost as much fun as the otters. It was a giant dead tree, charred down the side by lightning that had set it afire. Rain must have doused the flames quickly along the scarred slash because loosened bark was gradually peeling off the rest of the trunk and, in places, was held only by the gnarled grip of a huge grapevine that twined and looped to the stubbed upper branches. There was perched what Beth called an "e-nor-mous" mass of dry leaves and twigs. It probably belonged to the dark gray squirrels that popped in and out of several hollows, chattering irately at their visitors. They had the most beautiful fluffy white-fringed tails that stretched out behind them when they sailed through the air, curled around them when they dozed, slowed their downward plummet if they fell, and arched handsomely over them when they paused to relish a nut.

Woodpeckers drummed as they pillaged the bark crevices for larvae, the Osages' magic crested one who seemed to live in the tree; the jaunty little white-fronted, black-masked sort with white bars almost like rounded checks on his black wings and a small red band at the back of his head, and his larger but similar-looking relative. Black-capped nuthatches moved jerkily down the bark, headfirst.

A 'possum occupied one cavity halfway up

the trunk. Once, the children glimpsed her sitting on her hind legs and funny bare tail on a nearby limb, licking herself like Emmy did. Star said her babies would be born soon and live in her pouch, hanging onto the nipples on which life depended, till they were big enough to venture out. There often weren't enough nipples for all the babies. Star said the weak ones would never live to grow up, but Richie couldn't see why there should be any weak ones.

There was a mysterious hole burrowed under one snarl of roots with a heap of earth beside it. Richie and Beth hoped it was a fox, but Star thought it was likely *otchek,* the woodchuck, snoozing away the winter in his grassy bed after feeding so fat on greens he could scarcely waddle.

All around were marvels. Flocks of rusty-breasted bluebirds shimmered like patches of the bluest sky as they settled to feed on dried berries in thickets beyond the tree. There were flocks of robins, too, and goldfinches caught any sun there was as they perched to dine on thistles.

Perhaps the most interesting thing of all was the bear log. The day Star took them to see it, she told them to tie Robbie so he couldn't follow. "It's not wise to wake up this mother," she warned as they neared the great log that thrust broken, rotted roots far higher than her head. "Be quiet now. Quiet as falling snow, and step as lightly."

When they stood beside the scarred, peeling trunk, she pressed her ear against it and motioned for them to do the same. From within the wood came a happy, buzzing sound.

"Bees?" Richie started to ask, but Star touched his lips to close them and moved silently away. When they were quite a distance from the log, she said: "That sound was the baby bears nursing. There are probably two of them. Farther north I've heard bears sleep sound all winter, but here they wander around between long naps. The cubs are born tiny and almost naked. Their mother won't bring them out till it's warmer."

"Oh, can we see them then?" cried Beth.

"Probably, but from a safe distance. Don't come here without me. Mother bears take great care of their babies. She might think you mean them harm."

Above these secrets of woods and river was the sky. Bald eagles, white-headed and white-tailed, that roosted at night in trees along the river, soared with flat wings till they were gleaming pinpoints or played and tumbled in currents of air, much as the otters reveled on their slide. Ospreys vied with them for fish, but the red-tailed hawks, that had a big stick nest in an oak not far from the bear log, circled for mice or rabbits, or even smaller birds.

Just as the air kingdom was different from those of water or earth, night brought a different world. When Moon Woman glowed or when her face was hidden, the song of wolves came faintly from above the valley, a panther might scream like a woman, a bobcat or fox crush the dying shriek of a smaller creature. When such sounds came, Richie hugged Mr. Bun tighter and was glad Star, Aunt Hester, Hildy, and the rest of the aunties were near.

As flesh-hunters stalked forest and meadow, the clans of the Owl People ruled the air: the tiny screech owl trilling as darkness fell; the barn owl with its heart-shaped face gliding over the meadow; the great horned owl uttering its hunger cry that sounded much like Emmy's shriek if her tail were trod on. Star said this owl's wings spread as wide as she was tall, and it could sweep up a fox or big turkey in its steel talons. This made Richie afraid to use his owl whistle after twilight. He didn't want the owl to get him.

Living so near wild things was exciting, but Richie was glad of the cattle and horses, even the chickens, because they reminded him of a home that grew hazier each time he tried to remember it but that still mattered deep inside, just as he'd always be his mama's own boy no matter how much he loved his aunts, Star, and Hildy. He helped Beth pull grass for the animals to store for when snow covered the ground, and helped gather the eggs and shut the chickens up before twilight. Three had been killed and eaten, but, when they saw the shadow of a hawk, they squawked an alarm and made for their shelter.

Early in what Aunt Hester's almanac called February, Richie and Beth watched a flutter of small violet-blue butterflies hover around swelling buds on purplish dogwood twigs. The butterflies were a chance delight on a visit to a small pond where a turtle foraged amid fresh green spikes of cat-tail. The pond flickered with tadpoles and from all around rose a sound like the jingling of the hawk bells on Noelle's cradleboard. How spring peepers, brown frogs no longer than his little finger, could make such a racket was beyond Richie.

"Hear the chickadees?" Star was carrying several bark troughs and baskets. "They're building nests and singing for their mates now, not just having conversations. They're also telling other birds not to come near their nests. Cardinals will be the next to set up housekeeping, and then wives will join the red-winged blackbirds who'll be here soon."

Richie tip-toed to peer in the troughs. Star smiled at his disgusted sigh and ruffled his hair. "They won't be empty long, Sun Boy."

That was her name for him. Richie liked it. It made him feel Indian. Of course, he *was* Indian, three-sixteenths. Hildy tried to show him by counting out sixteen twigs. "Your daddy be four of these." She set four to one side. "Your mama be two. You get two parts from him, one from her . . . three parts, see? That's how much Cherokee you are. The rest from your daddy is a kind of white . . . from Scotland long ago . . . and from your mama, there's English and French."

Richie stared at his smooth pale honey-colored hand. "I don't look that mixed up, Hildy."

"Lord, child, you're nothin' compared to some white folks who've got a sprinkle of well nigh everything." She drew herself up proudly. "My daddy, he was pure Coromantee, my mama, Mandingo with likely some Arab."

It was a puzzlement to Richie that Aunt Phronie, Aunt Lilah, and Hildy were all "colored" — they said so themselves — when Lilah's skin was fairer than that of any of his aunts, save Melissa. That was one of the grown-up riddles he supposed he wouldn't understand till he was grown-up, too.

Touching the side of a bark trough, he looked up at Star. "What are you goin' to put in them, Star?"

"Come and see." She left the baskets near the pond and started for the timber. "As we walk, see how the buds on most of the bushes and trees have started to swell."

"Why?" asked Richie.

"It's warm enough that sap's starting to rise through the trunks and branches to the twigs. That makes the leaves open, though the redbud will get its flowers before it has leaves. Now is the time to ask the maples to share their sweet juice. It's one of the best gifts of Wah'-kon-ta."

"Maple syrup!" Beth squealed. "Hayeses used to trade us some for eggs and butter!"

"Oh, look at the deer!" Richie pointed. "They're eating the twigs!"

How beautiful the deer were with their big ears and white tails! Three of them stretched graceful necks to browse the parts of trees they could reach. At Robbie's approach, they bounded away, one with swollen sides behind the others.

"She'll have her fawns soon," Star said. Taking her knife from its sheath, she made two cuts that came together at a sharp downward point. Shaving a stick to a point, she drove this into the bottom of the slashes. "Now put the trough where the sap will drip down in it from the stick," she said.

They did the same to another tree, and then Star took them to the pond and put them to gathering watercress in one basket while she waded into the cat-tails and slipped her hand down along one stalk into the water. "You don't want to pull on just the stalk," she explained. "It'll break off and leave some of the best parts in the mud."

She yanked out a big brownish root and placed it with the stalk at the edge of the pond, pulled up three more rope-like roots, rinsed them, and trimmed off small white shoots that she dropped in her basket. "This lump the stalk grows out of is very good." She cut what looked something like a potato free of stalk and root and added it to her harvest. Next, she cut off the green top of the stalk and tossed it away along with so many layers of the stalk that it seemed nothing would be left. "This part . . . only the inner three or four rings . . . is tender. Beth, Sun Boy, I'll trim the rest of the stalks and you may peel them."

Richie wasn't sure about eating cat-tails that evening, but he was sure he didn't want to aggravate Star. He pretended he was all Indian, not just three-sixteenths, and tasted of the inner stalks, root shoots, and lumps sliced and cooked in butter and a cream soup of watercress and sheep sorrel.

"It's good!" He blinked in surprise. "Let's have this every day! There's lots of cat-tails!"

"Yes, and we want to leave plenty to grow," said Star. "When the spikes are green, we'll boil some and eat them like roasting ears. When the spikes turn brown and are gold with pollen, we'll shake it off and use it like flour. Cat-tails have something good from spring till autumn."

It snowed that night. Star, with Robbie,

kept watch by the sap troughs for many wild creatures would revel in the sweetness. When Richie and Beth plunged knee-deep through snow turned to frosted rose by the dawn, Star was lifting a chunk of ice from one trough.

"The water from the sap freezes. What's left is thicker, sweeter, and stronger flavored. It still needs to be boiled to make syrup or sugar, but freezing saves a lot of time. Here, I'll make you some candy."

She dipped blobs of the sap on the snow. It hardened to wonderful chewiness. Not even Richie's mother's French chocolates had tasted so good!

"Now," Star said as the children licked their fingers, "gather the driest wood you can find and bring it here while I fetch a kettle. We'll start boiling this batch while the troughs fill again."

That night, they had a special treat — pancakes of their hoarded wheat flour, rich with pecans and chunks of dried persimmon, drizzled with hot syrup. It was still thin, but made the pancakes so delicious that Richie ate till he couldn't hold another bite.

Curled up in Aunt Hester's arms, lulled by the sound of her heart and breathing as much as by her songs, he cuddled Mr. Bun, sighed blissfully, and drifted off to sleep.

CHAPTER THIRTY-TWO

It was a good thing that over the past five years Jonathan Ware and the boys had plowed up most of the rocks and cleared away the stumps. Now that the ground had thawed, Christy could hold the plowshare deep enough to cut a respectable furrow as she followed Lad and Lass under the cold moon. Sarah had stayed in the valley to help with the last of the maple sap boiling and the cutting of bark for the lodge they'd build before winter, but the hounds sprawled at the edge of the field, and they were company as well as sentries.

At first the bleached light and weird shadows made Christy nervous, but, as the horses' hoofs clomped on earth that opened to the share with pungent richness and as she watched the team move willingly along in spite of the strange hour, she fell into the age-old rhythm, the reassuring familiarity of carrying out the proper work of the season.

Plowing, planting, cultivating, harvest, storing for the winter. Late freezes, heavy rains, drought, blight, and grasshoppers, or other plagues might damage or ruin a crop, but these themselves came at certain times and were part of nature whose scourges must be accepted as well as her bounty.

War had no season. It destroyed all the others, savaged the pattern of planting and reaping, killed young men rather than old. And these young men, instead of planting and tending it, trampled the young corn, looted the harvest, ravaged in minutes what they knew had taken months of work to grow. It was because of this chaos that Christy had to plow by night and hide the horses in the timber by day.

Still, she was plowing. Hester's potatoes, saved for seed, would be planted by the end of this month of March. So would the oats, with corn shortly after, and then the garden.

At first she wept as she gripped the plow handles worn smooth by her father's hands and those of her brothers who now carried muskets, but, as she walked where they often had, breathing the same ripening earth, she gradually felt as if they were with her, Father, Charlie, Thos — Dan, too, and she was a little comforted although her shoulders ached and her fingers pained.

This was her war, not only for food, but for the peaceful, ordered flow of life the way it had been before. As spring came on, she mourned the sheep and the lambs that should be frisking now on the slopes. No pinkish black-and-white piglets tumbled over Evalina and Patches. Heloise and Abelard would honk no more warnings or deftly pick bugs out of the strawberries.

Still, in the valley, Moses and Pharaoh were safe, and Bess, Goldie, Clover, and Shadow had knobby-legged, big-eared calves at their sides. Her mother's surviving Wyandottes had hatched out adorable little fluff-balls. And there were the human babies, Noelle and Joely.

Christy sighed and confronted the truth. Melissa was not cheered by the lengthening, brighter days, the quickening of new life. She scarcely ate. Her milk seemed to give Joely colic, but she refused to permit Lilah to suckle him.

When Christy and Sarah had gone to the valley for the horses — *Where were Jed and Queenie? Pray God they fared well.* — her mother had taken Christy aside.

"I'm terribly worried about Melissa." Ellen herself was thin, but her color was good. And although there was an underlying sadness in her eyes, she enjoyed the other women's company, mothered Lilah, and often laughed, especially with the children. "Even Joely can't rouse her out of this soul-sickness," she had told Christy.

"She could go to Parkses'."

"That won't serve. She longs for her sister . . . her accustomed life."

Christy's heart sank but, indeed, watching her sister-in-law's prolonged despondency had made her fear the perilous journey to Sedalia would be necessary. "We'll plow and plant the potatoes," she said. "Then I'll borrow a wagon from the Parkses . . . some money, too, I'm afraid . . . and take Melissa to where she can get the train. Phronie will want to go with her, I'm sure."

Melissa had flushed at the news and thrown her arms around her mother-in-law. "Oh, Mama Ware! I can really go?" Then she had drooped and shook her head. "No. It's not fair to make Christy run such a risk." Her mouth quivered and she turned away.

Forcing down her resentment and misgivings, Christy had embraced this girl her brother loved. "Listen, dear, it's not your fault you can't like living in a cave, or even the long house Star's going to build. It's up to us to look after you and Joely since Charlie can't. You just eat and sleep so you'll be ready to travel in a week or so if the weather's decent."

So now Christy finished plowing the field, unharnessed the horses, rubbed them down, and treated them to dried persimmons. "I'm sorry there's no corn, you dear good ponies, but maybe Mister Parks will lend us a little so you won't get too gaunted-up on the way to Sedalia." She stood between the horses, running her fingers through their manes. They whuffed gently and nuzzled her. "I'm scared, ponies," she whispered. Lafe's taunting smile and chill eyes rose before her.

Again she heard the roar of Caxton's revolver, saw her father pitch forward. Trembling, she pressed her face to Lass's sweat-smelling, hard-muscled neck until grief and fear eased a little. "I hope we don't run into guerrillas or jayhawkers or just plain rascals. I hope I don't get you stolen away. Oh, Dan! I need you! I need someone!"

His last letter had said the Kansas regiments were being reorganized. Colonel Montgomery, sick of Lane's and Jennison's methods, had gone to Washington to seek a new command. Dan, Thos, and David would be serving with the 1st Kansas Battery. I'm mighty tired of wrestling wagons through the snow and mud. Hope I can get assigned to a gun crew — and I hope we see some action. General Curtis's Union troops have chased Price out of Springfield and driven Old Pap Price and McCulloch, both, into the Boston Mountains down in Arkansas. Jeff Davis figured out a slick way to handle the trouble between McCulloch and Price. Instead of placing either in top command, he's formed the Trans-Mississippi Department No. 2 — which is them, Jeff Thompson's swamp rats, and Pike's four regiments of Indians. The whole shebang is under the orders of General Earl Van Dorn, who will have about forty-five thousand men to Curtis's less than eleven thousand. The Confederates may not be able or willing to fight for a divided border state like Missouri, but they have to defend Arkansas. The 7th Kansas has been ordered out of Missouri to Humboldt, Kansas, a good forty-five miles west of the border — too far for quick forays across the state line. Anthony's cracked down on them hard — no more stealing pigs and chickens and cider. He's keeping them busy with three hours of company drill every morning and two hours of battalion and regimental drill in the afternoon. As you might suspect, quite a few men deserted who'd rather loot and burn, than learn to be soldiers.

And then there were the dear words, sweet words, that she read till she knew them by heart. She kept Dan's letters in the cherry-wood box her father had made for her. Ten of them, treasured and read over and over. Her mother had saved the two they'd had from Thos. *Would he be angry that they hadn't told him about Father and the raid? Yet what use was it to upset him when the plain truth was he might not live to come home, might never have to know what had happened?*

Her despairing wail to Dan faded as she thought of how lucky she was to be able to get his letters when nothing was heard from her brother Charlie or Travis Jardine. If they lived — how dreadful to always have to add that! — they must have been with Price in the retreat to the Arkansas mountains. God keep them.

The plea turned to driest ashes in her mouth. How many women were imploring God to save sons, brothers, husbands, or sweethearts who fought on different sides and would have to try to kill each other if they met? Still, she prayed.

Simeon Parks cheerfully loaned what should have been more than enough cash for Melissa's fare. "Better to have some extra than need it and not have it," he said. "You really should let Owen drive. . . ."

"We've been over that, Mister Parks. It's safer for me." She had a cup of sassafras tea with the women, and one of Catriona McHugh's scones, while watching red-headed little Andy and fair-haired Danny, both sixteen months old now, play with the wooden train Dan and Davie had carved and sent for Christmas.

"I'll bring the wagon back as soon as I can," she promised, returning the farewell embraces of Simeon's two daughters, Lydia and Susie, and his daughter-in-law, Harriet.

It was noon before Christy reached her home. She hid the wagon near a thicket of serviceberry, not yet leafed out but lovely with clustered white flowers, and turned the horses loose before going to the valley. Along with Robbie, Beth and Richie ran to meet her as she descended the rocks. "Come see Bob White!" called Beth.

"And . . . and Bobble!" shouted Richie.

Christy knelt to halt the hurtling little bodies with hers. They scrambled free after tumultuous hugs and kisses.

In the five days or so since she'd been gone, spring had quickened Peace Valley. Budding leaves were a mist of freshest green against dark cedar, white sycamore trunks, and the grays, browns, and silvers of the tribes of hickories, oaks, and maples. Some dogwoods were in flower, especially beautifully neighbored by blossoming redbuds or the fragrant yellow flowers of spicebush.

Brighter than spicebush blooms were male goldfinches shedding drab winter garb for bright yellow courting suits smartened with black wings, tail, and cap. Over the *jug-a-rum* of bullfrogs, red-winged blackbirds sang from the cat-tails and willows by the pond. Chickadees made two-noted nesting music, the first sound higher than the last, quite different from their usual namesake greetings. From everywhere — pond, river, meadow, cliffs, and woodlands — winged and chorused a celebration of birds while in the pale blue sky a wavey skein of geese called on their journey north.

Among the trees, Star, Hildy, Sarah, Lilah, and Ellen were collecting bark for the winter lodge. The loop of Noelle's cradleboard was hooked over the stob of a broken limb. In her third month now, the baby watched the women with curious brown eyes as the breeze tinkled the bells attached to the hide canopy and swayed the blue and scarlet feathers.

Christy proffered a finger. Creamy gold fingers gripped it; the tiny nose scrunched as the baby gurgled and squealed. *Poor Joely, inside the cave with his brooding mother on a day like this that smelled and glowed and sang! Well, since Melissa hated it here, he'd be better off in Saint Louis. But look at Richie, not missing his big house and fine toys, full of glee as an otter pup, secure with his "aunts".*

When Christy spent a night in the cave, Beth still sometimes cried in her arms for her father, for murdered sheep and pigs, geese and chickens, for stolen Queenie and Jed — for Thos and Charlie and Dan. Yet most of the time, Christy had never seen Beth happier — protector and chief of Richie, with two babies to fuss over.

The mothering group of kind, capable women stopped their work to greet Christy.

She told them she had the wagon and money and wanted to leave as early as possible in the morning. Ellen took her daughter's hands and looked into her eyes in a way that sent Christy's heart thudding.

"My dear," said her mother, "I'm going, too."

"You mean you'll help Melissa and Joely get to Saint Louis?"

"Yes, but when they're safe at her sister's, I'm going to be a nurse."

"A nurse?"

Ellen nodded. "Should my sons, or Dan, or Travis, or young Davie Parks be wounded, I pray they'll be well cared for, but, from what we hear, the wounded lie untended for hours on a battlefield and then are tossed into any kind of wagon and jolted to filthy makeshift hospitals." She paused to get control of her voice. "How can I hope some other woman will give our boys a cool drink, help them eat, wash off blood and dirt, or soothe a fever, if I'm not willing to go and do what I can?"

Christy hadn't even thought of such a course. Now, compelled to, she tightened her hold on her mother's hands. "Mother, you can't do that! I . . . I'll go! Beth needs you."

Ellen freed one hand and smiled as she caressed Christy's cheek. "Bless you, I know you would, but I'm sure the nursing organizations wouldn't accept a young, unmarried woman. Besides, it's your staying that makes it possible for me to leave Beth." She glanced at the circle of women with gratitude. "Of course, I wouldn't go if these kind and caring friends hadn't agreed to look after Beth, but, even so, I couldn't leave her if you weren't here."

"But. . . ."

"Also, I'll probably be in and out of Saint Louis and can see Melissa and Joely often. I'd like to do that for Charlie's sake as well as my own." Ellen took Christy's face between her hands. "Please believe me, love. I need to do this. Just as you need to plow and plant and hold our land."

For the first time in her eighteen years, Christy saw her mother as separate from that identity, a woman with unsuspected depths and feelings, who had lost the husband who had also been her lover, who knew the agony of having sons on different sides in this war. Small wonder she was driven to throw herself into the relief of suffering men.

"Father would be proud of you." Christy spoke through aching tightness in her throat. "So would Thos and Charlie . . . and Dan and Travis." She brought her mother's hand to her lips and wet them with her tears. "So am I."

It was overcast next morning with a dull glitter of frost on the ground. Their chances of making the long journey in March without being rained or snowed on were slight, yet Christy had hoped for fair weather at the start and few uncomfortable nights of soaked featherbeds. The jayhawkers, not to mention guerrillas, had spent the winter pillaging and burning the region the women must travel through, although at least, thank goodness,

Jennison's and Anthony's 7th Kansas was no longer marauding. The travelers couldn't count on the hospitality that had been the rule before the war; indeed, they'd be lucky if the wagon and horses weren't stolen. Christy only hoped, if that happened, it would be after her mother and Melissa were safely on the train.

Ellen hated the thought of Christy's driving back alone, and Sarah had offered to come, but any extra burdening of the horses seemed cruel. "If I don't meet bad people, there won't be any danger," Christy argued. "If I do, there'd be one more person in trouble."

"Your father and brothers would. . . ."

"Not worry half as much as if they knew what you intend to do, Mother!"

That forced a grudging laugh from Ellen. Now, preparing for the journey, Christy spread the wagon bed with the heavy canvas that had covered their wagon on the way from Illinois, left over half of it trailing, and heaped featherbeds, quilts, and blankets to make a resting place. She filled a Dutch oven with coals, covered them with ashes, and set the iron pot in a big cast-iron skillet beneath the wagon seat, securing them with boxes of food. These were buttressed with sacks of oats and corn Simeon Parks had given her for the horses who'd have little time to graze even if the grass were more than a green shadow here and there. She flipped the loose canvas over the bedding. If it stormed, everyone but the driver could shelter under the cloth.

Taking their halters and a pocketful of oats, she went to get Lad and Lass who enjoyed their treat and nuzzled her as she led them toward the hazel thicket. She almost had them harnessed when Melissa came up with Joely in her arms and a grumbling Emmie on her back in a rush basket contrived to leave only her gray head free. Ellen and Phronie followed, cumbered with bundles carried in rawhide slings and fastened to their backs.

The softer belongings served as pillows. The others were stowed wherever they fitted best. Emmie's carrier was cunning, indeed. Set lengthwise, it was a comfortable lodging for the cat. Star had contrived it to close with thongs, and lined it with woven rushes that could be cleaned out as necessary.

"She was nice enough not to remind me that I wouldn't put Joely in the cradleboard," Melissa confessed. A spark of the old playfulness was back in her deep blue eyes. "I wish now I'd used it. Think how amazed my sister's friends would be!"

Christy took her place on the blanket-padded seat while Phronie scrambled up beside her. "Bless God and you, child," she muttered. "I'm almighty thankful to be out of the cave! But it served its turn, it surely did."

Christy hoped Lad and Lass's shoes would

last out the journey. With Andy McHugh gone, they hadn't been shod that spring. Their hoofs needed trimming and the old shoes were wearing thin. If there was money left after train fares, she'd find a blacksmith in Sedalia.

They didn't stop at the Hayeses' tannery, but forded the creek and took the rutted road to Butler, the county seat. Allie Hayes wouldn't willingly cause them trouble, but the less people noticed them, the better.

"How far to that train, Miss Christy?" Nothing would induce Phronie to drop the "Miss" although Lilah and Hildy did now without embarrassment.

"Over a hundred miles. It'll probably take us four or five days."

They passed the turn-off to Lige and Sarah Morrow's and shortly after rumbled past the Franzes' abandoned house. The apple tree where Emil had been hung was budding, but the grapevines were still bare gnarls. The log in the orchard still protected the grave Hester had dug for Emil and Lottie. When there was time, time to do more than just stay alive, Christy resolved to bring Lass over and haul a big stone beside the log, chisel on it the Franzes' names and day of death.

Shingles had blown off the Barclay cabin's roof and it was almost overgrown with vines. "I hope the family's doing well back in Ohio,"

Ellen said. "Tressie and Phyllis were bright, sweet little girls."

How long ago those school days seemed, thought Christy. To think that five years ago Lafe Ballard had studied across the table from her! Now Matthew and Mark Hayes might have to fight Thos, their schoolmate. And the man who had made ancient times and far places seem real to the children, who had taught with laughter and love, was now returning to the earth at the edge of his field.

They stopped at noon near a little creek. Christy unharnessed Lad and Lass, let them go to water, and then put grain in their nosebags. Walking around to stretch their cramped bodies, the women ate sliced raw turnip, cold oat cakes, and finished with nibbles of the dark maple sugar Star had given Melissa as a gift to her sister. When the horses had rested a while, Christy hitched them up, and the party traveled on.

The sky overhead darkened even more. Christy glanced up at the teeming clouds that shadowed the land as far as the eye could reach. Suddenly the mass descended, glimmering giant veils of blue and gray, dropping through distant trees to feed on acorns left from their autumn foraging.

"Passenger pigeons!" Phronie sighed. "Nothing tastier than a mess of squab cooked in butter."

Some would nest deeply in the woods but

most would gorge and fly on northward as they had done time out of mind. To see them pursue their age-old rhythms in spite of human woes strengthened Christy. That was good, for as the road left the trees for rolling prairie, they began to pass what had been farms and was now wasteland — straggles of rail fence that the jayhawkers hadn't used to roast stolen cattle, pigs, and fowl; charred stubs of logs amid toppled foundation stones; heaps of hide and bone from hastily butchered cattle, but not a living farm animal except a blind old horse with skeleton ribs and a white cow that had eluded capture and now wandered with her calf.

Christy stopped, gave Phronie the reins, and put oats and corn in her skirt. Calling softly to the horse, she dropped the grain in easy reach. "Poor creatures!" Ellen said as Christy got back on the seat. "Why do they suffer for our quarrels?"

There was no answer to that, or the ruin brought to families who had once lived in homes marked only by blackened débris and chimneys thrusting up like elongated tombstones. "Jennison's monuments" they were called, although most likely some of the farms had belonged to Union folk driven out by Secessionist neighbors when it seemed Price would reclaim the state.

"Nothing but chimneys," Phronie groaned. "Same as at Rose Haven!"

Dusk was falling when they came in sight of what had to be Butler since there were no other towns anywhere close. The hopeful little town, barely settled, had just been made the county seat when the Wares passed through almost six years ago. Now lamps or fires glowed dimly from a few houses scattered forlornly around the burned courthouse, businesses, and torched dwellings.

"Shall we ask to spend the night with someone?" Christy asked.

"No." Her mother's voice shook. "I . . . I'd rather sleep in the wagon. Even if it rains."

Although dogs barked and raced beside the wagon, not a soul opened a door or appeared in a window. Christy drove past the charcoal shards of the courthouse to halt a mile out of town in a fringe of trees along a stream.

While she hobbled, rubbed down, and grained the horses, Ellen scooped out a hollow for the coals from the Dutch oven. Soon a crackling fire warmed them, heated the skillet of hominy seasoned with butter, and boiled water in the coffee pot to brew spice-wood tea.

Joely whimpered at the strangeness, but Melissa's milk apparently agreed with him now, because, after nursing hungrily, he fell asleep. Phronie took him to bed in the wagon, curling her slight frame at one end to make room for Melissa and Ellen.

After the coals were banked against the

morning, Christy took off her dress, put it under the canvas, and got the oldest blanket and quilt. Mantling these around her, she crawled under the wagon, arranged the bedding as comfortably and warmly as she could, and fell asleep to the "who-cooks-for-you-who-cooks-for-you-all?" of a barred owl.

CHAPTER THIRTY-THREE

Only one house stood in Dayton among over forty burned ones. "I can't imagine anyone could be very glad to have their house spared when all their neighbors' were burned." Her mother's words were Christy's thoughts. This was the town Daniel Anthony had destroyed on New Year's Day two months ago.

"I wonder where everyone's gone?" Melissa held Joely closely as she peered around.

"It'd be no marvel if the men joined the guerrillas." Christy's voice stuck in her throat. "Some families probably moved far enough east to be out of reach of the jayhawkers."

"It's a dirty, dirty war!" Melissa cried. "Lincoln's a long-jawed ape, but I'd think even he wouldn't want robbing murderers in the U.S. uniform!"

"I don't think any of the regular Union officers like the way Jennison and Lane have behaved in Missouri," Ellen said. "They've been ordered far enough into Kansas to stop their looting."

Melissa curled her lip. "After there's not much left!"

"The Seventh Kansas will probably get sent a long way from the border," Christy guessed. "But that'll give the guerrillas a freer hand, and they're certainly no better than the jayhawkers."

With grain and several hours of rest at noon, Lad and Lass were holding up well. Christy and her mother took advantage of the halts to gather young cat-tails, wild greens, and onions, welcome additions to their food. Cloudy skies threatened and thunder reverberated after distant zigzags of lightning, but, to the travelers' relief, the storms spent their fury elsewhere. It rained the second night, but not enough to penetrate the canvas.

There were no towns between Dayton and Sedalia and only sooted chimneys remained of the few farmhouses they passed. Except for the shadows glimpsed through windows in Butler, they had not seen a single human being.

"It's as if we're the only people left," Melissa said in a frightened tone. Ellen touched her hand. "There'll be plenty of folks in Sedalia . . . and Saint Louis must be overflowing with people, from both sides, seeking refuge."

"Oh, I hope the city hasn't turned horrid!"

"There hasn't been any trouble there since

General Lyon took the armory," soothed Ellen. "Gracious, that seems so long ago, but
it's really less than a year!"

"Yes." Melissa's tone was bitter. "Charlie
and Travis rode off like knights of the round
table, and we all thought the war would be
over by autumn."

Thos went, too. Christy thought of her
brother. *And Dan, Owen, and Andy . . . Andy,
who'll never come back to Susie and his little
son . . . Andy, buried with John Brown's testament under the roots of a blasted tree at Wilson's Creek.*

"My mother's dead and my father's murdered," Melissa went on. "Rose Haven's
gone. Papa Ware was such a good man, and
he's killed, too!" Melissa's voice caught on a
sob. She buried her face against Ellen's
shoulder. "Oh, Mama Ware, I can't bear it . . .
I can't . . . if Charlie and Travis don't come
back!"

Ellen held her close. "We have to pray they
will, my dear."

Christy swallowed and rubbed an arm
across her eyes. Then she rubbed them again,
unwilling to believe what she saw. Trees followed a creek perhaps half a mile away.
Christy had just been planning to stop there
for the night. Now, out of the trees rode a
dozen men or more.

Phronie moaned. "Oh, Lord, have mercy!"

Melissa screamed.

"Hush!" warned Ellen. "Melissa, you and Phronie get under the canvas with Joely. I've got the butcher knife. But remember . . . so far, neither side's hurt women on purpose."

No use hoping the riders lazily closing the distance between them could be anything but jayhawks — those were by no means limited to Jennison's uniformed ones — or, more likely, guerrillas or downright thieves. There was little to choose between the species.

"If they try to bother us, Phronie, grab the shovel and hit anyone you can reach." Christy's mouth was dry. "I'll toss the coals at them and hit them with the lid."

None of this would do much good if the men meant serious harm, but chances were they'd ride on when they saw no men were with the women and there was nothing worth stealing — except, oh, my God! The fare money!

"Mother," called Christy softly, "put the money at the bottom of the diaper bucket."

Ellen actually laughed. "What a wonderful notion! If I know men, a sniff of the bucket is all they'll want."

The leader rode a big bay, not Bill Anderson's handsome black, but perhaps he'd be a friend of Bill's — or at least afraid of him. The horsemen moved like part of the gathering dusk, the hoofs of their mounts muffled by new grass and sere tufts of last year's. Christy could now see their plumed hats and bright guerrilla shirts, red and blue, embroidered and beaded, although a few wore fringed buckskins.

Something about the man on the bay. . . . His dark hat with a flowing black plume shadowed his face, but she could tell he wasn't Bill Anderson. Mounted on mettlesome horses that were clean-limbed and deep-chested, the guerrillas ranged in front of Lad and Lass, forcing them to stop. At most of the bridles hung what looked like wigs, some of them long. The band carried rifles or shotguns and each man bristled with revolvers, some carrying half a dozen in holsters or thrust through belts. Clumsy, beef-shouldered Tom Maddux was the only one Christy knew — till the leader swept off his hat.

Lafe Ballard chuckled at her instinctive shrinking. "Miss Christy, Miz Ware, what a delight to meet with neighbors! But I do hope you're not leaving the country."

"We're bound for Sedalia." Ellen tried to keep her tone pleasant. "I'm going to visit my daughter-in-law in Saint Louis."

One bleached eyebrow lifted towards silvery hair. "Miss Jardine . . . beg pardon . . . young Miz Ware's gone to the city? I heard what the confounded jayhawks did to Rose Haven."

"It's natural that she wished to join her sister, though we miss her, of course."

"Of course."

Could he say anything that didn't sound mocking? Christy thought, before she said: "We should move on." She lifted the reins. "We need to make camp before nightfall."

"Allow me to invite you to stop near our camp in the trees across the ford. A lop-eared Dutch farmer compelled us to take a pig and fine turkey that are cooking on spits over our fire. You're welcome to share."

"Thank you. We have our own food." Christy's mind whirred desperately. These men would surely not hurt Melissa and the baby, ardent Southerner that Melissa's father, the bishop, had been, but they might well seize Phronie and sell her. And some man might brave the smell of the diaper bucket.

"At least accept our protection." Lafe's teeth flashed. "I insist!"

"Cap'n!" bawled Tom Maddux. "Somethin' be wigglin' under the tarp!"

"You'll excuse us if we satisfy Tom's curiosity?" Lafe drawled.

"My dear boy . . . ," Ellen began.

He raised a peremptory hand. "I was never your dear boy, madam. Endured with a smile, yes, because of your soft-brained Universalist nonsense, but let's not pretend that had it not been for my mother, your husband would have expelled me long before I took myself off."

"Your mother's well. . . ."

"I supposed she would be." His voice was

indifferent. "All right, Tom. Let's see what's under that canvas. Have your pistols handy, men. These ladies are for the Union. Might have a jayhawk tucked away."

Melissa threw back the cover and sat up with blazing eyes, Joely clasped so tight he howled. She did have the presence of mind to leave Phronie hidden. "I'm no jayhawk, Lafe Ballard! You ought to be ashamed of yourself, skulking around stealing pigs and turkeys and plaguing women, instead of fighting with General Price like my brother and my husband . . . Mama Ware's son, remember!"

"To be sure, Charlie and Travis have doubtless run valiantly with Price all the way to the Boston Mountains. Never mind. They may be fighting this very minute at Pea Ridge, just over the border in Arkansas." Lafe scratched his head in mock puzzlement. "Now how is it your mother-in-law's traveling to visit you in Saint Louis, Miz Ware, when you're right here?" He shook his head and looked sorrowfully at Ellen. "I'm afraid your husband would be disappointed, madam, to hear you lie so glib."

"We are going to Saint Louis!" Melissa's cheeks were furious red. "I'm going to my sister whose husband is in the real Army!"

"Yes," murmured Lafe. "The real Army that cares not a fig for Missouri and abandons it to the likes of Jennison and Lane. These are hard times, yet I can scarce believe, Miz Jardine-Ware, that the young mistress of Rose Haven is traveling without at least one servant."

Phronie rose up, put a protective arm around her nursling. "I be here where I belong, Master Lafe, but you, you sure not where you ought to be!"

"The wagon's full of surprises." Lafe grinned and gestured to his men. "Have a look in the bedding and bundles, but first help the ladies down."

Ignoring the brigands' offered hands, the women got down. Christy, soothing Lad and Lass, didn't try to smother a laugh when Tom Maddux yelped and dropped the hot lid of the Dutch oven. No one, thank goodness, explored the contents of the diaper bucket.

"Nothin' worth havin', Cap'n, 'cept this maple sugar," growled a man with a tangled red beard.

"That's for my sister!" protested Melissa.

"As fine a Confederate lady as she must be, she won't grudge it to defenders of the cause." Lafe's indulgent manner changed. His pale eyes narrowed, reflecting the dying light. "You must have money for train fare. Kindly let us have it."

"I must ask the Union commander in Sedalia to pay our passage."

"For the wife and mother of a Rebel soldier?"

"For the wife of a murdered Union man and the mother of a Union soldier."

"How differently that rings! Yet I trust you won't blame me, Miz Ware, for not quite believing you after the way you've endeavored to deceive me. I'm afraid I must ask you to yield up the money or be searched, shameful and distressing as that will be."

Ellen stiffened but held her tongue. With an effort, so did Christy. What could they do? Resisting would only lead to violent manhandling, possibly even worse.

Tom Maddux, grinning, turned toward Melissa.

"Don't touch me!" she hissed. "The money's in the bottom of the diaper pail. Have a good time finding it!"

"Reckon we won't do that." Lafe stared at Phronie. "I remember how you never let me eat in the kitchen at Rose Haven. Sent me out in the yard. All right, you old yellow hag, fish the coins out for us. Don't try to hold back any. We'll dump the bucket just to make sure."

"You was snot-nosed then, you be snot-nosed now, and that's the way you'll die." Phronie's green eyes shone like a cat's. "I'd sooner wade up to my neck in a baby's mess than touch ary one of you with a ten-foot pole."

"Wonder how much we can get for the old nigger," Lafe said to the red-beard who was munching some of the maple sugar he'd handed around. "Might bring a better price without that sassy tongue."

"White trash you be, Lafe Ballard. Never had the price of a one-eyed gaboon in your pocket! You. . . ."

"Aunt Phronie!" Melissa begged, tugging at her. "Get them the money."

Phronie rolled up her sleeves, reached through the diapers soaking in soft soap and water, and tossed coins out on the turf. They winked silver and gold. "That be all."

"We'll see. Dump the bucket," Lafe instructed one of the men.

Phronie stooped, gripped the handle, straightened, and, as she did so, tossed diapers and sudsy water all over Lafe.

"Oh, Phronie!" wailed Ellen.

One yellow-splotched diaper dangled from Lafe's plumed hat. Another festooned a shoulder. More lay about his boots.

Horrified as she was, Christy couldn't keep from laughing. Nor could Lafe's men.

"Got you right smart, Cap'n!" chortled Red Beard, doubling with hilarity. "Good God A'mighty, when Quantrill hears about this . . . !"

"He better not hear." Lafe shook off the smelly encumbrances and stepped out of the puddle. A revolver flashed in either hand. "Now, gentlemen, if anyone still thinks it's funny, here's his chance to die laughing."

There was instant sobriety. "Aw, Lafe!" whined ungainly Tom Maddux.

Christy put herself in front of Phronie, who did not flinch at the pistols. "Haven't you heard that Bill Anderson . . . who was left at our house . . . will come after anyone who bothers us?"

"Ah, yes, Bill. Gets a trifle above himself sometimes." Lafe moved to where he could pin Phronie with his eyes.

She didn't cringe, but after a moment she shivered.

Lafe smiled. "You want me to kill you, don't you, you old yellow whore?"

Phronie didn't answer, only glared at him like a small, cornered beast. He shoved Christy out of the way and slapped Phronie so hard she staggered against the wagon. Blood oozed from a split lip.

"Don't want to be sold away from your mistress? Answer me, bitch, or I'll cut off that curly hair of hers and tie it to my bridle."

"Rather I die than leave my Miss Melissa."

"You won't get what you want."

"What you mean?"

"If you're alive, when we get through with you, we'll sell you for whatever we can get." Lafe shrugged. "If you're dead, we'll toss you to the first hogs we come across."

Ellen laid her hand on his arm. "Lafe, you don't mean it! You can't hurt an old woman like Phronie!" He didn't step back from her

691

hand, but, at his stare, Ellen drew away her fingers as if they'd touched corruption.

"I can do anything I want to her, Miz Ware." Lafe's tone was soft as his gaze swept over them, stopping at Christy. "*Anything* I want. To *any* of you. As far as you're concerned, I'm the devil and God Almighty rolled into one."

Tom Maddux stirred uncomfortably. "Now, Lafe, Cap'n, do whatever you want with the old nigger, but we ain't hurtin' white ladies, 'less they pull guns or knives on us."

"Still, it may edify them to know what we'll do with the hag," Lafe mused, then chuckled. "Rather wade in baby shit than touch us, would you? Well, we can have some good of you, first. It'll soon be so dark we can't see your ugly face. While the boys wait their turn, they can be filling up a trench with piss and shit. You can have a nice soak in it when we're finished. If you don't drown or choke, we'll souse you in the creek and sell you to the first one who'll have you."

"You can't do that!" Melissa placed Joely in the wagon bed and threw her arms around Phronie. "You'll have to kill me first!"

Ellen took the butcher knife from under her shawl. "You'll have to kill us all."

"Aw, Lafe," muttered Red Beard. "Cain't we jist . . . ?"

Christy said: "Lafe, I want to talk to you. Please."

692

"Now that's a word I thought never to hear from you, Miss Christy." He smiled into her eyes, his own like frost. "Indeed, I like the sound."

"Please."

He offered his arm. "Shall we have a stroll, then?"

"Christy!" called Ellen. "Don't . . . !" Her voice broke off as if she didn't know what to ask Christy not to do.

Christy slipped her hand as loosely as possible through Lafe's bent arm, but he caught her fingers in a grip cold and hard as steel. "So, Christy?"

"Don't hurt Phronie. I'm begging you."

"Beg harder."

"How?"

"Make me an offer."

"You have our money, borrowed, at that. Take the horses."

He shook his head. "That's not enough to save that yellow hide."

Christy's blood chilled, then thundered in her ears. She could barely whisper. "What is?"

"You."

Her heart beat like the wings of a caged hawk. "Now?"

"No. It's not the time or place for what I've dreamed about." He laughed at her start of surprise. "Don't think I love you. It's not that." He lifted her wrist, kissed the scar he'd made there when they were children. "You're the one I think about when I do things to girls. More than being my first woman, you're the first I hurt."

It was like looking into a slimy, stinking pit that crawled with eyeless monsters. Christy tried to take her hand away. He held it in that steel grasp, a thumb splayed on the scar over the pulse of her blood.

"Let me visit you." He laughed as her imprisoned hand convulsed. "It may take only a few days and nights. Usually a single night gives me a disgust of any woman I've wanted."

She was in the pit, fondled by obscene creatures, mired in their filth. *Dan, how can you love me if that happens? How can I stand myself?* "Let Phronie alone, let her stay with us . . . and I'll open the door to you."

"And yourself?"

"Yes."

"I won't burn you again." His voice was husky. "That was the crude work of a boy. I know better ways now, Christy, to put my mark on you."

"How Hester can have a son like you. . . ."

"I had a daddy, too. Used to go at Ma even in daylight. Shut me out of the cabin, but I watched through the chinks." Lafe chuckled at Christy's sound of abhorrence. "Ma thought he stumbled and fell on the scythe, although he'd sure have had to fall at a peculiar angle to get the blade in his neck like that."

"You did it?"

"I wanted to have Ma to myself." A dismissive shrug. "No more locked doors. Guess what? Once I got her attention, I didn't want her."

At Christy's shocked silence, he laughed and let his long cold fingers trail down her face from temple to throat. "What a dirty mind you have! I never wanted Ma that way. I just didn't like her studying to please that man, instead of looking after me."

"Let's go back," Christy suggested.

He turned obligingly. "I know what you're thinking."

"Do you?"

"You think you'll open the door to me, but you'll kill me if you can."

"That shouldn't be too hard."

"You may be surprised." He paused. In a voice like silk, he spoke dreamily: "The best time I ever had with a woman, Christy, was with one I choked to death. She bucked and fought . . . emptied me out clear down to my toes."

Christy refused to allow herself to tremble. "Maybe we'll both be surprised."

"I'm sure of that." Laughter came from so deep in his throat it was almost a growl. "So we have our bargain. The old wench stays with her mistress, and you'll unbar your door.

I'll be delayed, I fear. My band's joining Quantrill for some important action, but I suspect you can control your impatience."

"Will you give us back the train fare?"

"We need it to buy cartridges to protect Missouri." At her derisive laugh, he added: "Doubtless we'll buy some whiskey, too. Be grateful I'll leave you the horses and wagon."

"Oh, I am," she said sarcastically, but with truth. "Very, very grateful."

He released her only after they reached the shadowy group near the wagon, but it was so dark that she didn't think anyone could see her hand had been in his. "Let's get back to camp, boys!" Lafe called.

No one argued. It could be some of them would have vented their lust on Phronie, but probably not even they had any stomach for the whole of Lafe's plan.

"You're still welcome to share our supper," Lafe told the women mockingly.

"I think we'll get a little farther down the road," Christy said, glancing at the fires flickering through the trees across the creek. She wished they were the flames of hell, waiting to embrace Lafe Ballard. One thing sure: she'd never tell Hester about this encounter, much less the pact she'd made, a promise to the devil. To her mother's and Melissa's anxious queries, she only said she'd talked to Lafe of their childhood and of his mother.

"We must pray for him . . . for Hester's

sake," said Ellen.

"I pray for him!" Phronie's words were distorted by her swollen lips. "Pray he burn infernal and eternal!"

Ellen didn't chide her, but said with a surprising twinkle: "You ought to think instead, Phronie, of how droll he looked with a diaper hanging from his plume."

Phronie cackled. "Oh, I'll study on that, Miss Ellen!" She added darkly: "I'll get the shivers to my dyin' day when I remember how he looked at me with those blue-john eyes and said what-all he aimed to do with me! I hoped I could make him mad enough to shoot me in the head."

"Thank God, he didn't!" shuddered Melissa. "Don't you pull such a trick again, Aunt Phronie! If you got sold away, I'd get you back."

"Lord, child, I know you'd try, you and Miss Yvonne. But in this war, where everything's turned topsy-turvy and upside down, who knows what's gonna happen?" She giggled as she took Joely. "Won't it a be story to tell him, how his didies hid gold coins and got tossed all over a fire-breathin', cock-struttin' guerrilla?"

By the time they got to Sedalia, Lad had lost two shoes and Lass one. Since they had to throw themselves on the mercy of the post commander, Christy hoped he might tell a military farrier to shoe the team. Sedalia thrived from the railroad and being one of the major Federal military posts on the eastern boundary of what amounted to a guerrilla-haunted no man's land now that the 7th Kansas had been ordered well over the state line.

Christy halted the team near the railway station to hear what the jubilation was about. It didn't take long to learn that the Union had won a decisive victory at Pea Ridge two days ago, March 8th, after a day and a half of battle.

"They're calling General Price 'Old Skedad'!"

A just-arrived train passenger waved a St. Joseph paper. "Editor says as a racer he's got few equals for his weight . . . he weighs close to three-hundred pounds, you know! Pity the horse that has to tote him!"

Glancing from her mother to Melissa and Phronie, Christy knew they all had the same thought. Had Charlie and Travis lived to skedaddle? That anxiety, along with the certainty that countless men on both sides were dead or maimed for life, blunted Christy's relief that the Union had won. Melissa, of course, looked devastated.

"Pike's Choctaws took scalps," growled a soldier.

"Yes," countered a citizen who looked anything but joyful. He must have been one of the few Secessionists left in town. "And Sigel's lop-eared Dutchmen butchered surrendered Confederates! We know Sigel, damn him, he was in command of a division here after he ran away at Wilson's Creek! Some might call murdering unarmed prisoners worse than scalping dead enemies."

"Who says they were all dead?" bristled the soldier. "Some wounded had their skulls split by Bowie knives before the hair was ripped off."

A blond, young captain stepped casually between the angry men. "You've got to credit Van Dorn for guts," he said. "He was sick and still not recovered from a bad fall from his horse, but he commanded from an ambulance."

"That may be," granted the man with the paper. "But he had between sixteen thousand and twenty-five thousand men against Curtis's ten thousand five hundred. Curtis reports almost fourteen hundred killed, wounded, or missing. There's no telling how many Van Dorn really lost, because they deserted in droves after the battle. He admits to a thousand, with three hundred more taken prisoner."

"He's making for east of the Mississippi where a battle's shaping up at a place called Shiloh," put in the captain. "Van Dorn needs to win back his reputation. Pike and his Indians headed back to Indian Territory, but

Price will follow Van Dorn. Pea Ridge had to prove, even to Pap Price, that he can't regain Missouri without a lot more help than the Confederacy has given him so far. Maybe he hopes, if his Missourians fight hard in the East, other troops will eventually be put under his command for a fresh attempt." He shook his head with considerable sympathy. "Poor old Pap! In spite of the luck he's had, he just can't believe there aren't enough Secesh in Missouri to flock to his banner and run out our Federal troops!"

"At least Ben McCulloch won't give him any more trouble." The soldier grinned. "Killed in battle the first day. Someone stole his weapons and gold watch, but they left him his fancy Wellington boots. Seems that only an hour after a carriage rattled into Fayetteville with his body, another rolled in with General McIntosh."

"Brave generals, both of them," said the captain with respectful sadness. Noticing the women in the farm wagon, he came over, doffing his hat. "Is there any way I could serve you ladies? You seem to be traveling."

"Indeed, sir, we'd be much obliged if you'd escort us to your commanding officer," said Ellen Ware. "Guerrillas robbed us of our train fare. My daughter-in-law and I must go to Saint Louis, so we're hoping for assistance."

"I'm bound you'll get it, ma'am. Just follow me."

On hearing their story, the colonel scowled. "This happened day before yesterday? There'll be no finding them, I'm afraid, but I'll send out a party. Like will-o'-the-wisps, these rascals! Bands of three or four hundred gather for a raid, and then melt into the countryside. After all, that's where they live, which makes this kind of war the very . . . I beg your pardon, ladies!"

He wrote passes for the three women, and insisted on lending them some cash they could repay to the company fund. He assigned the captain to help them on the train, and tried to persuade Christy to go with them.

"You'd be much safer in Saint Louis, my dear young lady." Instead of the fatherly-looking officer wearing his colonel's eagle on his shoulder straps, it was embroidered inside a gold-edged circle of infantry sky blue. "Surely you should remain with your mother."

Amazed that she hadn't considered going, despite the threat of Lafe's visit, Christy did try for a moment to imagine what she'd do in St. Louis, but, even if Beth hadn't been in the valley, she couldn't abandon their home, her father's fields and grave, the ground ready for planting, the hope of harvest.

"Thank you, sir," she told the major, "but I'm going home."

"I can't spare an escort."

701

"Sir, I'd never ask for one. Perhaps, though, my horses could be shod?"

After a regretful stare, he said: "Captain Hunt, after the other ladies are on the train, see that this young woman is provisioned, including grain for her horses, and make sure the horses are shod." He rose and bowed over the women's hands. "May God keep all of you."

The train huffed in from Jefferson City, disgorged passengers, and was hastily unloaded. While it took on wood and water, Christy and Captain Hunt helped Ellen, Melissa, and Phronie aboard. Joely howled at the commotion and strangeness, but the captain diverted him with a chunk of villainous flat bread he extracted from a pocket.

"Hard tack's just the thing to teeth on, ma'am," Hunt assured a dubious Melissa. Joely attacked it with gusto.

Christy kissed them all good bye, urging her mother to be careful, and begging them all to write.

As cinders flew and black smoke curled, they waved to each other till the train dipped out of sight. The captain offered Christy his reasonably clean handkerchief. "Miss Ware, while our farrier sees to your team, allow me to treat you to pie and coffee at the home of a widow who is of estimable character, although she profits madly from selling baked

702

goods to soldiers."

The frank admiration in his merry blue eyes took away some of the dirty feeling Christy had since the encounter with Lafe Ballard. "You're very kind, Captain Hunt, but perhaps you should know that. . . ." She hesitated. It seemed presumptuous to warn him that she was engaged when doubtless he regarded the hospitality as part of his duty.

"Of course, you have a sweetheart, Miss Ware," he said with a wry laugh. "How could it be otherwise? Is he in the Army?"

"With the Third Kansas." Far be it from her to reveal Dan's despised job of driving mules!

"Then he won't grudge a fellow soldier the pleasure of a few hours of your company." Hunt ordered a private to take the horses to the farrier and scrawled a note to the quartermaster for grain and food to be stowed in the wagon. That done, he offered Christy his arm, gilt eagle buttons at the cuff, and helped her across the muddy street.

In her gingham-curtained kitchen, on an oak table polished with beeswax, the Widow McNelly served them big chunks of dried peach pie with thick cream. There was more cream for the coffee, although, as she filled their ironstone cups, the pretty brown-haired woman apologized. "I can't get real coffee beans most of the time. The soldiers sell me their used ones. You'd think they might give

703

them to me."

"I'm sure they would, dear lady, if you ever gave them a free piece of pie. Anyway, you charge them for the coffee they drink here, don't you?"

"Of course I do!" she said indignantly. "I have to earn my living!"

"Just so, ma'am." Captain Hunt smiled. "I'll tell my striker to bring you the part of my coffee ration I'm bound he's selling somewhere."

Christy had never flirted, but the captain was so adept at it that she found it fun and easy. Underneath her laughter and word play, though, she knew that somewhere beyond this protected town Lafe Ballard ranged at will, and many others like him.

Later, when Captain Hunt helped her into the wagon, he dropped his bantering gaiety. "It seems terrible to let you go like this, Miss Ware. I'm sure Missus McNelly would share her home with you if you'd stay on."

Christy took the reins and smiled with more cheer than she felt. "You're very good to care, sir, but I have crops and a garden to plant, a house to keep, and friends who expect me."

He closed his big hand over hers. "Then I can only beg you to be careful. And remember I'll always be very much at your service if . . . ," he floundered. "If you ever need me."

She knew he meant if Dan were killed, and was glad he hadn't said it. She returned the pressure of his fingers. "Thank you for everything, Captain. If you ever pass near my home, you'll be welcome."

"I'll remember." He stepped back.

Her hand, briefly comforted by the warmth of his, felt chilled and lonely. She started the team. The merry *chink* of their new shoes found no echo in her heart. Her mother was gone. That struck now with full force. Until her mother had gone to live in the valley, Christy had rarely been away from her for more than a few hours. Her mother expected her and the other women to look after Beth, but didn't she think Christy needed her, too?

Desolation welled up in Christy along with the angry hurt she'd managed to deny till then. With her father dead, it was too much to lose her mother, too! Tears slid down Christy's face. No matter how fiercely she blinked, she had to keep scrubbing them away.

Gradually she had to listen to an insistent voice. *Your mother didn't try to persuade you to go with her. She could have insisted you and Beth come to stay at Melissa's sister's, which would certainly have relieved her mind, but she knew how you feel about the house and farm. You can't know how she feels about losing her husband . . . having sons on different sides of this awful war. She's not just your mother, you selfish stupid! She's Ellen Ware.*

The sense of loss was still there, but self-pity withered. If only there were some way to know if Charlie and Travis had survived Pea Ridge, know where they were! Charlie didn't even know his baby was a son; he was missing these months when Joely constantly learned and changed. And Travis, how could he resist winsome little Noelle, who had his eyes and hair?

As Christy passed the last farms protected by closeness to the soldiers at Sedalia, Lafe's taunting face rose before her. What devilment would he be up to with Quantrill? She grimaced at the thought of their claiming to be patriots, defending Missouri. They certainly hadn't done much to keep Jennison's jayhawkers from burning towns and farms!

She hoped Lafe wouldn't live to visit her. If he did, at least he knew she'd try to kill him. What would be the price if she succeeded? As always when the quicksand of hate and grief swelled high and threatened to overwhelm her, Christy imagined being with Dan. She kissed his roughly tender mouth, the cruel marks on his cheek, rested her face against his heart. And heard him play his song.

CHAPTER THIRTY-FOUR

While Kansas regiments reorganized that spring of 1862 at Leavenworth, Dan O'Brien and his friends gritted their teeth at delays as news came of distant battles. Charlie Ware and Travis Jardine had probably been with what was left of Pap Price's command, early in April, at the two-day battle of Shiloh in Tennessee where Grant had held fast. Neither side could claim victory, only count their losses, great as many whole armies were here in the West — thirteen thousand Union soldiers, ten thousand Confederates. A week later, Nashville fell, the first Confederate state capital to be vanquished. By the end of that month, Admiral David Glasgow Farragut's fleet had taken New Orleans. Way out in New Mexico Territory, even, Confederates won battles at Val Verde and Tucson while the Union triumphed at Glorieta Pass.

After what seemed forever, Dan's group rolled out of Leavenworth in early June, part of a properly equipped battery. They finally had real uniforms, even if they were made of shoddy — a cheap cloth of reused fibers that must have made the contractors a fortune. Besides six, long-range, ten-pounder Parrotts of three-inch caliber with their caissons, the 1st Kansas Battery owned a forge, water wagon, a wagon with leather and harness repair supplies and tools, six wagons of camp gear, provender for men, mules, and horses, six ammunition wagons, and one ambulance. Dan thanked his stars that this time he rode Raven, instead of perching on the left-hand wheel mule to control one of the six-mule teams with a jerk line.

Soldiers who lived near the route were given brief furloughs, so Thos Ware and Dan were allowed to ride battery horses home. Dan stopped at the Parkses' mill just long enough to embrace Lydia and Susie — Uncle Simeon, too. Lydia fetched the resin for his violin bow, and he and Thos rode on to Wares'.

Is that Christy, Dan asked himself, *face hidden by a sunbonnet, using all her slender strength to hold the plow between the rows of green corn that reach to her knee?*

The bay started limping. The woman stopped the plow and waited in the field, till she recognized the two and ran forward, arms outstretched, bonnet flying from her hair — laughing, crying, calling their names. . . .

Dan's throat ached when Christy showed

him Jonathan Ware's grave at the edge of that field. Thos knelt by the grassy mound and sobbed till Christy hugged him and said they must come with her to see Beth — and something wonderful.

Leading their horses, the men followed her through the cavern, flickering with the dance of her lantern light. Dan gasped at sight of the broad green valley, and, as they stared down, Beth and a golden-haired little boy ran to meet them.

Sarah, Star, and Hildy made them welcome while Lilah smiled at them over her baby's curly head. Dan's heart lurched as he recognized Travis Jardine's imprint on this little girl named Noelle. Please God, she at least would never be a slave.

Star bade the men hobble their horses where the new grass was highest. A feast was prepared, and, besides things Dan had never eaten before like young cat-tails, there were eggs, buttermilk, butter, cheese, and Sarah's honey, but no flesh of any kind.

Dan chilled, then burned, at Christy's account of Lafe's halting the women on the way to Sedalia. "No doubt he looked comical, darlin', with a diaper hanging from his hat, but, if you won't stay at the mill, at least keep to this valley."

"The farm's not worth it," Thos growled, catching his sister's hand. "Father wouldn't want you running such risks! When Charlie and I . . . and Dan . . . come home, we'll rebuild the cabin and fences, if they've been burned, plow the weeds and brush out of the fields, and start over."

"This is my war, Thos." Christy touched her brother's cheek, then hurried to get Dan's fiddle out of the bark-covered long house. "Play your song, Dan," she said when she returned.

He did, but he couldn't finish it because of the hatred for Lafe Ballard that boiled up in him. His cheek burned as if the gunpowder rubbed into the cuts smoldered with invisible flame.

That night, back at the cabin, with Thos tactfully asleep in the loft, Dan held Christy, close to groaning with need and the sweetness of her mouth, her yielding body so soft to him in spite of the muscles in her arms and shoulders. When he couldn't stand it another minute, he kissed her good night and scrambled up the ladder to throw his bedroll down beside Thos.

Dan and Thos caught up with their battery at Fort Scott. The suffering of Union Indians driven from Indian Territory into Kansas had convinced President Lincoln that they should be allowed to form regiments to fight for their homeland, and the 1st Kansas was ordered to join an expedition into the territory. On the Neosho River, they picked up the 1st and

2nd Indian Regiments, which boasted four hundred tall, painted Osage warriors from their southern Kansas reservation. At Baxter Springs, in the southeast corner of Kansas, they were joined by companies from the 9th, 10th, and 2nd Kansas, 2nd Ohio Cavalry, Rabb's 2nd Indiana Battery, and the 9th and 12th Regiments of Wisconsin Infantry. This Army of the Frontier, under command of Colonel William Weer, a jayhawker who had stolen plenty of fine Missouri horses in territorial days, proceeded down the Grand River.

When they had to camp some distance from this running water, Dan and the others scooped up water from slimy, stinking pools in the summer-parched creeks where Indian cattle stood to save at least their legs from buzzing, stinging swarms of green-headed flies. The water was a stew of rotting plants, manure, and sediment, but, boiled with enough coffee to turn it completely black, it had to serve.

Rebel Indians fled their breakfast campfires at Locust Grove. Dan's long-time friend who had lived with the Parkses, Tim O'Donnell, swore because the battery couldn't use its guns for fear of hitting their own troops, but Dan was relieved. What if he killed Choctaws from families that had sent money to buy the food that kept him from starving back in Ireland?

Colonel Weer stayed drunk in his tent at camp on Cabin Creek while the Indians and cavalry took Fort Gibson and, near Tahlequah, captured the Cherokee chief, John Ross, a Union sympathizer, who had signed a treaty with the Confederacy only after Federal troops had abandoned Indian Territory. Dan glimpsed the old chief pass by in a fine carriage, bound for Washington, with his pretty young Quaker wife, their daughters, the Cherokee nation's archives and treasury and wagonloads of prized belongings.

Ross's old enemy, Confederate General Stand Watie, had retreated south of the Arkansas River with his Rebel Cherokees. So had Colonel Douglas Hancock Cooper with his Choctaws, Chickasaws, and Texans. A 3rd Union Indian Regiment was organized — swelled by Cherokees deserting from Confederate commands. The Union Indians had recovered much of their stolen livestock, and now the three Indian regiments decided to organize into a brigade to defend Indian Territory north of the Red River.

The Indian Expedition had done all that could be expected. Weer's disgusted officers placed their drunken commander under arrest. Leaving two Parrott guns with the Indian Brigade, the rest of the Army started back to Fort Scott. Half the horses were so gaunt and broken down they had to be left behind.

"These tough Western horses manage pretty well on grass, but our Ohio animals need corn and oats, poor critters," lamented Tim O'Donnell. "Some of them chewed off each other's manes and tails while they were picketed."

Dan's battery was camped with the rest of the Army of the Frontier on the banks of the Marmaton at Fort Scott when a messenger galloped into camp after supper on August 14th. "Boots and Saddles!" Tents were rolled up and stowed in wagons, cooking gear packed into mess wagons. Dan's crew harnessed the team to their gun. Two thousand infantry piled into mule-drawn wagons, cavalry mounted, Rabb's Battery rumbled up, and they were off on a forced march of four nights and three days, only halting for fifteen minutes three times daily to feed and water the mules and horses.

Confederate forces rampaging through Missouri overwhelmed Union troops at Independence on August 11th and captured twenty wagons of arms, ammunition, and supplies before marching away to join with other Rebels at a village called Lone Jack, twenty-five miles from Independence. They intended to attack Lexington. If they took and held it, they'd break Union control of the Missouri River and shipping of vital supplies to Leavenworth. It was up to this part of the Army of the Frontier, now under the personal command of General James Blunt, to drive the Rebels out of Missouri.

"Where'd all the Rebs come from?" demanded O'Donnell, on one of the brief rests.

"After they got trounced at Pea Ridge in March, there were scads of deserters," explained Harry Shepherd with the all-knowingness of a sergeant who was chief of a gun crew. "Plenty of Old Skedad Price's Missouri State Guard didn't fancy joining the regular Confederate Army to get sent East, so they've come back home. Their officers don't mind throwing in with the guerrillas who're already thick as maggots on a dead hog." He spat disgustedly. "Quantrill helped take Independence. He's got a captain's commission in the Confederate Army now, but he's still a plain old bushwhacker!"

Quantrill! The scar on Dan's face burned at the name. Where Quantrill was, Lafe Ballard wouldn't be far away. If he could kill Lafe, would the burning end?

"There's not much to stop the Rebs," Dan said, surprised that his tone was even. "Most Federal troops have been pulled out of Missouri to fight farther east, just like the real Confederate Armies."

"Didn't Missouri pass a law this year that all men between eighteen and forty-five have to join the state militia?" asked Davie Parks.

"Sure, but most of the best young men have already joined one army or the other," Dan pointed out. "Of course, lots of the militia will fight the best they can, but plenty will use being in it as an excuse to murder and steal."

Drowsing off on Raven. Falling asleep as he fed and watered him. Eighty-four hours after leaving Fort Scott, they neared Lone Jack on the sweltering evening of August 17th to learn that the day before yesterday, less than eight hundred loyal Missouri militia had fought desperately, all morning, against three thousand guerrillas and Rebel militia. What was left of the Union force had retreated to Lexington.

Thunder crashed in the northwest and heavy clouds loomed over victorious Confederates who were camped in and all around Lone Jack half a mile away. Blunt ordered his exhausted men into battle line and sent out skirmishers as the storm broke and the Confederates retreated through heavy timber.

Pursuing in the dark over a route cut up by ditches and gullies, Dan and the other artillerymen sweated in the rain, wrestled gun carriages and caissons through the mud, and battled to keep them from turning over.

Three days' and nights' chase southward, spread out for four or five miles, stopping only twice a day for an hour to rest and feed themselves and hard-pushed animals that had never had a chance to recover from the

Indian Expedition.

"If you and I are still alive when this war's over," Dan said to Raven as he slipped on the nosebag, "I'll buy or steal you, boy, and the rest of your life you'll get corn, oats, and fine grass right up to your belly!"

Blunt's advance cavalry caught up with the Rebels several times and skirmished, but the Rebels slipped away. At Carthage, loyal Missouri cavalry took over the pursuit and drove the Confederates into the southeast corner of Missouri while Blunt's command toiled back to Fort Scott.

They weren't there long. Late in August, General Thomas Hindman was put in command of the Confederate District of Arkansas, which included Missouri and Indian Territory. By sending armed squads around a countryside from which all able-bodied men had supposedly been sent east to fight, he forced twenty thousand unwilling Arkansans into his army — and quite a few into the 1st Arkansas Union Cavalry that was beginning to organize. The Confederacy had passed a law conscripting for three years all able-bodied men between eighteen and thirty-five who owned less than twenty slaves. Naturally those who had no slaves felt they shouldn't have to fight in the place of those who did.

Rebel victories at Independence and Lone Jack fired General Hindman with hope that he could win Missouri. He sent, northward, three regiments of Missouri militia under Colonel Jo Shelby, Stand Watie's Cherokees, and General Cooper's brigade of Chickasaws and Choctaws. Cooper had only been a colonel when chased south of the Arkansas River about seven weeks earlier, but now he had taken the flamboyant and poetic General Pike's place as Indian Commissioner and commander of the Confederate Indians.

Dan's battery, with units of the 1st and 2nd Brigades of Blunt's Army, rolled up after these Rebels had fought with Union soldiers all around the stone fences of a farm outside the little college town of Newtonia, south of Carthage.

Hogs were coming to investigate soldiers of the 9th Wisconsin who lay dead in a little field, stripped of their arms and clothing. Dan joined in the hasty building of enough rail pens to keep the bodies safe from the hogs till they could be buried. Several of the Wisconsin boys looked younger than Davie Parks, whose face was pale and clammy as he helped Dan hoist life-emptied bodies and drop them inside the rails.

Fighting from plum thickets and rail fences, the Union men forced the Rebels to take cover in the town. All that afternoon, the guns loaded and fired. Dan had emptied his canteen hours ago. His arm and shoulder ached from yanking the lanyard, but the cannonading held the enemy at bay till twilight when the order came to withdraw.

Rebel cavalry poured out of the town, shouting their glee, but fresh Union troops came up to stiffen the weary ones and masked a battery behind clumps of post and blackjack oak. Trained on the Confederates spurring after the foe, the guns hurled grape and canister that blasted men and horses into heaps where some struggled and others were deathly still.

The cavalry fled. Union soldiers hurried to Shoal Creek where they could water their animals, splash their own dusty faces, and drink their fill. That was on September 30th. On October 2nd, Blunt marched up with the rest of his army and prepared to take Newtonia.

The Confederates abandoned the town without a fight and made for the Arkansas border. Dan winced at seeing where cannon balls had torn through college buildings and houses, but it wasn't only the *buzz* of flies and stench that sickened him when he saw the ripped and mangled horses, especially an artillery team — all six animals — slaughtered by an exploding shell.

Supplies were short and the hard-used mules and horses needed grain. The Army of the Frontier foraged what the retreating Rebels had left behind. Union farmers were supposed to be given chits of payment, but it made Dan ache to see women, whose men were off fighting on one side or the other, come into camp to plead with an officer for that last side of bacon, the last load of corn or wheat, the pet milk cow so needed by the scrawny children, the horse needed to plow and carry grain to the mill.

More than once, Dan, Davie, Thos, and Tim O'Donnell — for he'd known hunger, too — gave women and children most of their rations of hardtack, bacon, coffee, and sugar, keeping just enough to sustain them along with windfall apples, papaws, and wild grapes.

Shelby and his Missourians took shelter in the Boston Mountains near Fayetteville, but scouts reported that Cooper and Watie had collected between four thousand and seven thousand Indian troops at long abandoned Fort Wayne, just over the Arkansas line in the Cherokee Nation.

After an all night march, Blunt struck on the morning of October 22nd with a flying squadron of cavalry and howitzers while the rest of his army followed, including Dan's battery. They arrived hours after the whole Rebel battery was captured and Cooper's force raced for the Arkansas River covered by Stand Watie's more disciplined men.

To keep Confederates out of Missouri, Union encampments were scattered for one hundred miles along the Wire Road as far as Wilson's Creek, some at Pea Ridge battlefield. Blunt's men were camped southwest of Bentonville, at the southern end of this Union line late in November, when scouts dashed in with word that General John Marmaduke, a soft-spoken West Pointer whose father had been governor of Missouri, was advancing with artillery and seven thousand cavalry — Jo Shelby's Iron Brigade, Missouri militia, assorted bushwhackers, and Quantrill's men.

Would Lafe be with them? Dan rubbed his scar to ease the stinging. Quantrill had gone to Richmond to try to get a higher commission than captain. The South had to be desperate to commission a bushwhacker, but Quantrill could scarcely be worse than Doc Jennison or Jim Lane who had Union commissions.

General Hindman would join Marmaduke with twenty-five thousand men. It was clear that he hoped to win back northwest Arkansas and Indian Territory, and, from that strength, invade Missouri.

At the hamlet of Cane Hill, Blunt struck Marmaduke full blast on the morning of November 28th with five thousand cavalry, howitzers, and light artillery. Dan's battery of heavy Parrotts, positioned with the infantry, caught up after the battle had turned into a race. All Dan's crew could do was send a few shells after Rebels who were a mile away, scrambling into the rocky foothills of the Boston Mountains.

To prepare for Hindman, Blunt telegraphed

for reinforcements, and had all the wheat to be found in the area taken to mills and ground to feed his men. His supplies had to come from Leavenworth two hundred fifty miles away, so the more his army could live off the country, the better for them — and the worse for the farmers in that fertile region renowned for its peach and apple brandy, its grain, potatoes, and fruit.

General Francis Herron, commander of the cantonment at Wilson's Creek, got telegraphed orders to aid Blunt and was on the march in a few hours' time with six thousand men, their knapsacks carried in wagons to speed them. While Hindman came half that distance, they had to cover one hundred twenty-five miles, chewing raw pork and hardtack as they marched thirty-five miles each twenty-four hours, snatching an hour of sleep whenever they could.

On December 7th, this exhausted, footsore Army encountered Hindman's two-mile-long battle line near Prairie Grove church among farms with rail-fenced fields of withered cornstalks and bare orchards. The *boom* of cannon reached Blunt at Cane Hill, eight miles south.

Bugles sounded, drums rolled, and up the Fayetteville road galloped Blunt, cavalry at his heels, batteries and infantry following as fast as they could. This was the first time the 1st Kansas Battery had really been under fire.

Ordered to the right to meet the charge of General Daniel Marsh Frost's entire division, they were raked with rifle fire before they were in position.

Dan crouched low on Raven's outstretched neck. The coarse black mane whipped his face. His lips stung with the salt taste of the wheel horse's sweat. Raven's flared nostrils showed crimson. His eyes were wild. The postilions ahead and all around lashed their horses at each heart-bursting leap. Raven gave all he could without a whip, but at the gunner's shout — "Faster! Faster!" — Dan echoed the cry in Raven's pricked-back ear. Dan's gunner was red-headed Tim O'Donnell and their chief-of-piece was O'Donnell's brother-in-law, big, black-haired Sergeant Harry Shepherd.

Madly spinning wheels of gun carriages and caissons hurtled and clanged from rock to rock through the trees while artillerymen hung on for dear life. Cavalry, bent over saddle horns, spilled out of the woods fringing this Arkansas prairie of withered cornstalks and December-naked orchards. The horsemen spurred past guns and infantry, who, mostly hatless and coatless, held tightly to muskets and ammunition.

The Rebels occupied a wooded ridge to the south. Stocky, black-mustached General Blunt, all alone on the field at first, waved guns and troops into position. Dan almost fell off Raven and helped unlimber the ten-pound Parrott.

Here came the Rebs, trying to overrun Blunt before he formed his battle lines, but men were grouping by regimental banners with the Stars and Stripes floating above them all.

"Load with canister!"

Davie Parks brought the round from the limber chest in his leather haversack, and put the tin can filled with eighty-five one-ounce lead balls in the muzzle. Mac Ford, a skinny, freckled Missourian, rammed it home, and Bob Hendricks, dark eyes blazing, trained the gun according to O'Donnell's orders.

"Ready!" Hendricks pricked the powder bag through the vent near the bottom of the barrel; Dan hooked the lanyard to the primer, stuck it in the vent, and moved to the side and back while Hendricks covered the vent with his mittened hand to prevent an accidental discharge.

"Fire!" Dan pulled the lanyard. The charge exploded, belching the canister with its scattering balls into the Rebels who were firing muskets as they charged.

After two rounds, a thick cloud of the white smoke made from the black powder created a shroud. Through it, Dan glimpsed an officer urging on his men, saw him and those around him fall as if scythed down.

Over and over. "Load!" "Ready!" "Fire!"

And then O'Donnell looked at Dan through the smoke just as a cannon ball carried off his head.

Somehow, they went on. Harry Shepherd yelled at them to load as he took his brother-in-law's place as gunner. After a final twilight artillery duel closed the day, setting straw stacks on fire, the crew buried O'Donnell in his corporal's uniform under a black-jack oak overlooking the creek. Shepherd cut off a lock of curly red hair to send to O'Donnell's sister, Peggy, along with O'Donnell's few personal belongings, before placing the battered forage cap over O'Donnell's face. Tears wet the rocks they heaped on the mound to keep out digging animals. Tim O'Donnell, friend of Dan's childhood, who, like Andy McHugh, had crossed the ocean and half America to die. Dan clung to the grace that at least his friend had lived a number of good years in Ohio, rather than having starved as a lad in some County Clare ditch.

The supply wagons had not caught up and they'd had nothing to eat all day. They filled their bellies with water from the creek. Dan and Thos put Davie between them as they burrowed into a straw stack to escape the cold.

Next morning, they expected the battle to resume, but Hindman had sent a flag of truce, asking for twelve hours to take his dead and wounded off the field. Blunt agreed although most of the Union wounded had already been taken to a field hospital behind the lines.

Stretcher-bearers and burial details went out from both armies. Ladies came in wagons and carriages to help collect the wounded and take them to Fayetteville. Dan and Davie helped bury the dead. Some of Herron's men, who had not a wound, had died in the chilly night, exhausted from their grueling march and the battle.

"Our guns must have got these," Dan said as he and Davie approached bodies that lay close together as reaped grain. He bent to pick up a bullet. "This hasn't been fired."

"Here's more like it," said Davie.

Dan stared at the stiffened bodies in the bloody muck as an infantryman began to scoop bullets up in handfuls. "They bit the bullets off and spat them out. They only fired blank loads." Dan spoke through a lump in his throat. "These'll be Union men Hindman forced into his army . . . men who wouldn't fire on their country's flag."

Davie's eyes widened. "Look over there! The straw stacks that caught fire last night!"

The breeze carried the unmistakable smell of burned flesh from the black remnants of the stacks. Hogs rooted through the ashes, emerged with a leg, an arm, a head, intestines, and fought over these prizes. Wounded and dying soldiers had crawled into the straw for shelter and died in the blaze.

"Look what this lad had in his pocket!" The freckled doughboy picking up bullets flourished a leaflet. "Did you ever hear such a mess of lies?"

Dan read the beginning. "Sounds like good advice, especially to fresh recruits. 'Single out your target, aim as low as the knees, shoot officers when possible, kill artillery horses. . . .' "

"You ain't read far enough!"

Remember that the enemy you engage has no feelings of mercy or kindness toward you. His ranks are made up of Pin Indians, free Negroes, Southern Tories, Kansas jayhawkers, and hired Dutch cut-throats. These bloody ruffians have invaded your country, stolen and destroyed your property, murdered your neighbors, outraged your women, driven your children from their homes, and defiled the graves of your kindred. . . .

"Reckon it's all in your point of view." Dan squinted toward the nearest living Confederates. "Say, they're picking up weapons and ammunition, instead of their dead and wounded!"

Just then one of Blunt's staff rode up. In tones loud enough to reach Dan, he told the Confederates to carry out their proper duty. The message was delivered around the field; most of the Rebels departed, leaving many of their dead to be buried by the enemy, and their wounded to be sent as prisoners to Fayetteville's churches and college buildings that had been turned into hospitals.

A new buzz spread through the Union burial teams. "Hindman sneaked off in the night . . . muffled his wheels with blankets! That flag of truce was a trick to give him a whole day more to get ahead of us . . . and scavenge weapons!"

About then the supply wagons clattered up, rations were shared out, and Dan's crew feasted on water-soaked hardtack fried with bacon, and strong coffee.

Hindman didn't give up easily. Toward the end of December, Blunt's Army was resting near Cane Hill when word came that at Van Buren, on the Arkansas River, Hindman had new supplies and was organizing for yet another campaign.

What a time the batteries had getting their guns and caissons over the mountains! It took double teams and the crews and other soldiers hauling with ropes and pushing the wheels up rocky ledges, but, after twenty hours, Blunt's and Herron's commands struggled out of the mountains.

Encountering the 1st Texas Cavalry, Herron's cavalry chased them through Van Buren and shelled the steam ferry they tried to escape on with howitzers. Hindman's battery opened up from across the river, bombarding the town, but the light cannon were no match for Blunt's two long-range Parrotts.

Cavalry and howitzers forced four supply-laden Confederate steamships to surrender. Great was the joy among the Union troops to have all the molasses they wanted and plenty of sugar! The *Rose Douglas* alone yielded forty-three hundred bushels of corn, so the weary horses had their feast, too. Also, the next day, the steamships could carry the Union men and horses across the river to the Confederate camps.

Once again, Hindman's Army retreated in the night. He abandoned Fort Smith, destroying two steamboats and all the supplies he couldn't take with him. Blunt, having driven the Confederates well south of the Arkansas River, burned the ferry and four captured steamboats along with fifteen thousand bushels of corn and other supplies he couldn't transport.

Once back north of the Boston Mountains, there was a chase after Marmaduke, Jo Shelby, and Quantrill's men who tried to capture Springfield. Fought off by the garrison, they pillaged back into Arkansas and left a song in their wake: "Jo Shelby's at your stable door. Where's your mule, oh, where's your mule?"

Union men shouted it out as they marched along, along with the three most favorite of

728

all — "John Brown's Body", the stirring new "Battle Hymn of the Republic", and their own version of "Dixie".

> Away down South in the land of traitors,
> Rebel hearts and Union haters,
> Look away, look away, look away
> to the traitor's land.

From Springfield, knee deep in February snow, the 1st Kansas Battery moved to Fort Scott, then to Lawrence in April. Dan had to chuckle bitterly as he remembered how a party of important citizens met the battery four miles out of town and suggested they camp on the Wakarusa rather than in Lawrence whose citizens didn't want their peace and quiet disturbed by rowdy soldiers. That didn't matter much to Dan. Didn't he have two weeks' leave? He'd soon be with Christy.

As he roused that morning, he draped Christy's blanket to air over a budding oak limb. He'd taken the best care of it could, but it was frayed in places. Dan craved strong coffee, but the preserve can in which he cooked it had burned through yesterday and he hadn't taken time to replace it. He wanted to spend every minute that he could with Christy. Thos and Davie had diarrhea and had urged him not to wait for them. He put on his coat with its corporal's stripes — he was a gunner now, replacing poor Tim

729

O'Donnell — tugged on his boots, gave Raven a nosebag of corn, and chewed hard-tack dunked in water from the Marais des Cygnes while rolling his blanket. He couldn't wrap it in the oilcloth because that protected the calico he'd bought at Fort Scott. He'd spent all his pay at the sutler's for the cloth and a knapsack full of treats.

He'd thought about wearing his artilleryman's sword to impress Christy, but decided that was more trouble than it was worth, which was about the value of the weapon in battle. As Raven jogged east of Osawatomie across the prairie broken by those peculiar mounds, Dan wondered why Andy McHugh and Tim O'Donnell still called to him from dreams when he'd seen so many men die since Wilson's Creek and Prairie Grove. That battle had killed Tim, but surely crushed all hopes of the Confederacy to possess Missouri.

It was noon when Dan stopped at the Parkses' mill to say that Davie and Thos were plagued with the trots but would be along when they could stay on a horse longer than they were off it. He was embraced, questioned, and fed, but not till Susie assured him that Christy had just, day before yesterday, brought letters to be posted to him and Thos. Relieved, Dan produced his gifts of canned pineapple, salmon, peas from France, and taffy for the children that Susie put up till after the meal.

"Where's Lydia?" Dan asked, when she didn't appear for dinner.

Uncle Simeon shook his white head. "When she heard that Missus Ware had gone to be a nurse, nothing would do her but to go. You were at Prairie Grove. So was Lydia, after the battle . . . Missus Ware, too. They came with a wagon for the wounded. What a waste . . . what a terrible waste of our best young men! Truly we are grinding up our seed corn."

Remembering Tim, Dan swallowed hard. "Yes, between twelve and thirteen hundred were lost on either side." How cold numbers were! Each of those men was mourned by family and friends, would be achingly missed all the days of their lives just as Susie and old Catriona mourned Andy. And his little son would never, ever know him.

Blue-eyed Letty Parks confided that she had just turned eight, and had charge of her sturdy dark-haired brother Danny, and her cousin Andy, red-headed, thin, and quick. The boys, two-and-a-half years old, nodded yes, they would like a ride on Raven when Dan offered.

Owen walked with Dan as he led the horse around. "I feel like a slacker." Owen's brown eyes were troubled. "Here I am, safe at home, while my kid brother and you and Thos Ware dodge cannon balls."

"You were at Wilson's Creek. No one who

was needs to apologize for getting out when his enlistment was up."

"I know. Close to a quarter of all the soldiers were lost. To top that, you've got to look back to the charge of the Light Brigade where over a third died. But I still feel like Davie's taking my place."

"Owen, you have two small children and Susie McHugh's boy to raise, not to mention Catriona and your mother-in-law to provide for. Uncle Simeon needs you or Davie . . . and Davie was busting to go."

"But. . . ."

"With guerrillas swarming over the western half of Missouri, there's no telling when they'll raid across the border. There'll be precious few regular troops to stop them." Dan looked ruefully at his foster-brother. "*I* feel guilty for racketing off and leaving Christy alone."

"Scarcely alone. Not with Sarah Morrow and those women in the valley. We've begged her to come here, Dan, but she won't." Owen reached up his arms to scoop all three children off Raven. "Uncle Dan has to go, youngsters. Give him a hug and thank him."

Letty not only hugged him, she touched his scar and kissed it. The deadened tissue couldn't feel the moth-like brush of her lips, but a painful tingling shot through Dan like that caused by stirring a leg or arm that has gone to sleep. He couldn't repulse her sweetness, yet he wished, as if it might contaminate her, that she hadn't kissed Lafe Ballard's mark. It couldn't quench the brimstone smoldering there. Only Lafe's blood could do that.

It was twilight when he came in sight of the happy house. A curl of smoke rose from the chimney. *Intruders? Or might it be Christy?* One part of his mind hoped it was, while the saner part knew it was risky for her to be there. He didn't want to scare her, nor did he wish to give some bushwhacker a chance to shoot him down. He compromised by reining Raven in near the cover of some trees.

"Hello! Anybody home?"

Christy ran out and toward him.

He came out of the saddle to meet her. "You . . . you shouldn't have rushed out here like this!" he chided, when at last he made himself draw back. "What if it hadn't been me?"

Her eyes sparkled even in the dim light. "Do you think I don't know your voice?" she scoffed. "Let's turn Raven into the pasture and have supper. Sarah and I are staying here while we plow weeds out of the corn." Her voice rose. "Where's Thos?"

"He'll be along," Dan assured her. "Has a little stomach complaint, is all."

Lad and Lass came over to greet Raven. Dan put his saddle over the edge of a manger in the barn, and dropped his knapsack to give Sarah a hearty embrace as she hurried out to greet him. War stripped away conventions and Dan was mightily grateful that she was Christy's friend.

"How long can you stay?" Christy asked as they walked to the house.

"Ten days here. Took me two to come, and I'll need that to get back."

There was no bread, but the stew was thick and good. Dan had two bowls while briefly relating where the battery had traveled these past ten months. He didn't tell them about Tim O'Donnell.

The spring night brought a chill. Sarah built up a fire and brewed sassafras tea. He didn't want to talk about where he'd been and what he'd done since he saw them last. Christy already knew that her mother and Lydia Parks had gone to the battlefield at Prairie Grove and carried away the wounded, but Dan had to admit he hadn't seen them.

He briefly sketched the battery's travels and told them all the funny tales he could, including the many ways to vary hardtack. They told him that baby Noelle was taking her first teetering steps, Beth had almost complete charge of Richie and was teaching him to read and write, and that corn promised well, both in the valley and here in the field Jonathan had broken from wilderness.

"Tomorrow we'll go the valley so you can

see Beth and the others and bring back your fiddle," Christy said.

Sarah yawned and stretched. "I'm pretty tired, folks. Good night and happy dreams." She disappeared into the bedroom part of the double cabin.

Into a deep, pulsing silence, when Dan could scarcely breathe, Christy stretched out her hand and rested it on his. "Danny. . . ."

He turned her hand over and kissed the calloused palm. "I'm mighty tired, too, sweetheart. Got some quilts I can spread in the loft or shall I get the blanket you made me?"

After a moment, her jaw set. "There's an extra cornshuck mattress and a quilt . . . even a pillow. I'll make up a bed for you."

"No need you climbing up there. Just give me the things."

He was surprised that she didn't argue further. In a few minutes she was back, heaped with bedding. Lordy, how could he stand ten days — and nights — of this when she didn't understand, couldn't help him? He'd have to take himself off to the woods at night or stay in the valley.

He spread the rustling mattress by the lamp light from below and folded a quilt so it was both beneath and over him. The pillow smelled of Christy. He started to toss it down to her, but stopped. He couldn't have her, but he could have the comfort of something she had used. He undressed as the lamp below was extinguished, and, although he'd thought he couldn't get to sleep easily, he huddled into Christy's pillow and seemed to fall into sleep.

He dreamed of her, as he often had, but this was so real. She was in his arms, bending over him so that her hair veiled his face, and then she brought him into her. There was a gasp as his hardness met resistance. Then that was gone and there was only softness, moist satin that yielded and clung at the same time. He groaned with release and woke.

Slowly, as she stroked his back and shoulders, he realized it was not a dream. Horrified, he tried to pull away, but she held him. "We have ten nights, Danny."

After a moment, he drew her close. "All right. But tomorrow we'll go to the mill and get Uncle Simeon to marry us." He sighed and buried his head on her breast. "Oh, Christy, I tried. . . ."

"Well, now you just need to stay alive and come back," she whispered.

He yearned to take her again, awake and knowing everything, but he was sure she was tender, and so he held her and they slept.

Sarah plowed weeds from the rows of young corn next morning while Dan and Christy went to the valley and invited the women to their wedding. Hildy couldn't take the chance of being caught by guerrillas and Star said she would rather not leave the valley, but Lilah and Hester came, along with Beth and Richie.

If the Parkses were startled to see Dan again so quickly, and with such a mission, they didn't betray it. Letty and Beth chattered while looking after small Danny, Andy, and Richie. Susie made a bouquet of daffodils and lent her ring to Christy. It was a bright day, so they gathered outside under the fresh-leafed trees. Christy wore her least faded dress and Dan had brushed his uniform.

Simeon read from the Song of Solomon. Set me as a seal upon thine heart, as a seal upon thine arm: for love is strong as death. . . . Many waters cannot quench love; neither can the floods drown it.

They pledged each other in the Quaker manner, kissed sweetly, and then were surrounded and embraced by happily weeping friends, including old Catriona McHugh. Even Owen had to blink as he shook Dan's hand and clasped his shoulder.

Susie insisted they have dinner. She had baked that morning, and there was a pound cake as well as fresh bread and butter to enjoy with a chowder of onions, potatoes, peas, and dried corn. Catriona set out jars of pickles and preserves, and there was real coffee as well as buttermilk.

As they traveled home, Dan, with Christy

holding onto his waist, saw that Lilah, mounted on Lad with Noelle in front of her, was shaken with smothered sobs. Hester, who rode with Sarah on Lass, nudged the mare close and put her arm around the young woman. "You've got beautiful little Noelle, dear. After the war. . . ."

"After the war, I'll still look black to Master Travis."

"He won't be your master," Dan cut in. "And who knows? It'll be a whole new world, Lilah."

She straightened and managed a wobbly smile. "Bad of me to cry on your wedding day. I . . . I do for sure and always wish you happy."

Sarah said bracingly: "Listen, my girl, if that Travis doesn't know how lucky he is, there'll be plenty of other men."

Lilah didn't answer.

At the Ware cabin, Sarah grinned. "You honeymooners can have the place to yourselves. I'll go on with Lilah and Hester, but, mind, I'll be back in the morning to plow those weeds!"

"I'll plow, too," Dan promised. "I want to do all I can while I'm here."

"Oh, you will," laughed Sarah, and left them, blushing, suddenly shy, although that didn't last for long.

Chapter Thirty-Five

It was late August, four months since Dan had ridden away. The corn, so young and green then, was now stripped of blades fodder and today Christy would start cutting the plump, hardening corn ears off the bare stalks. Sarah had taken Lass, laden with fodder, to the valley so late that she'd spent the night, but she'd be back by noon.

It seemed strange that Hildy was no longer in the valley, but last month Justus had sent word to the Parkses that should his wife come to them, they could tell her that he, being a good blacksmith, had been put on more or less permanent duty at Leavenworth and had quarters next to the smithy. If Hildy could come to him, he'd send money for the journey. Simeon and Susie had taken her to Leavenworth in their wagon, Hildy posing as Susie's maid the few times they were questioned. Hildy had wept to leave Richie but knew he'd be fine with the other women and Beth to care for him.

Smiling to think of that reunion, Christy yearned for the next time she'd be with Dan — and prayed that time would come. At least her morning sickness was over. Christy finished her mush and sassafras tea. When clothed, she didn't show, but, when she undressed, she could see just the slightest rounding. Four months now. The baby should come near the middle of January. She hadn't written this news to her mother in the hospital in Louisville, Kentucky. Much as Christy wanted to have her mother with her during the birth, sick and wounded soldiers needed her more.

Maybe the war would be over by then. Christy drew in a long breath and closed her eyes. *Oh Dan! Danny!* If he could be with her, too — but she didn't dare hope for that. The war showed no sign of ending quickly, even though on July 4th Grant had taken Vicksburg.

This gives the Union control of the Mississippi and cuts the South in half, Dan had written jubilantly. No supplies or troops from Texas and Louisiana can get through, which hits the Rebels hard. We were camped at Rolla when the news of Vicksburg came. Our battery officers bought six kegs of beer and set them on cracker boxes scattered around camp. You can bet we celebrated!

On July 3rd, the Union won the hard-fought three-day battle of Gettysburg in

Pennsylvania. Instead of pursuing General Lee, five regiments with Gatling guns, a terrible new invention, were ordered from Gettysburg to New York City to quell an ugly draft riot in New York, four days of terror in which one thousand people were killed.

Dan's next letter told about the battery getting off the train at St. Louis. We felt like we'd been dropped in the middle of another world. Close to two hundred thousand people live here and it looked like all of them were in the streets that were lit up almost plain as day. We didn't like it much when the lieutenant told us we had to pull over to let civilian wagons pass, but we finally got to an old stockyard where we were supposed to camp. I wasn't about to spread your blanket in that mess, so I climbed over a board fence and landed in the nicest thick grass you can imagine. Got the finest rest I've ever had in the Army and woke up at "Reveille" to stare up at a marble tombstone! I'd spent the night in the Wesleyan cemetery!

The battery was sent by train to Cincinnati, in case General John Morgan besieged the city on his dare-devil raid through Indiana and Ohio. We saw neither hide nor whisker of him. His little band was being chased by fifty thousand men. When he was finally surrounded and had to give up, he had only three hundred and thirty-six left of his two thousand four hundred cavalry he'd brought from Kentucky.

Dan was back in St. Louis now, at Camp Jackson. Thos and I did as you asked, sweetheart, and visited Charlie's wife at her sister's mansion. The colored maid didn't want to let us in, but Melissa heard us and welcomed us graciously. I can't say the same for her sister, whose husband is in a Union prison. Joel is a handsome, sturdy, happy, little lad with a strong look of Charlie. Melissa can't write to Charlie, but once in a great while he gets a letter to her by using tobacco to bribe a Union picket to send it. He and Travis are with Price's command at Little Rock.

It was good to hear Joely was thriving, and have some news of Charlie. Melissa seldom wrote. Trying not to be hurt by that, Christy told herself that Melissa couldn't be blamed for avoiding reminders of that terrible winter when she'd lost her parents and Rose Haven and had to shelter in a cave.

Resting her hand over the baby, Christy wished it would quicken so that she could be sure he was really there, almost halfway through the time before she could hold him in her arms. *Him?* She laughed softly at herself.

Of course she wanted a son, with Dan's flaming hair and smoke-gray eyes, but when he'd responded to her news with proud excitement, he'd hoped for a daughter. Could we call her Bridget Ellen or Ellen Bridget for my sister and your mother?

Boy or girl, she prayed the baby wouldn't be two or three years old before it got to know its father, but she vowed to be eternally grateful if Dan came home at all.

Tying on her sunbonnet, she got a corn knife from the barn — Dan said that bayonets would make splendid corn knives after the war — and trundled the wheelbarrow to the field. It was a laborious way of moving the corn to the crib, but she didn't risk the horses, even Lass with her feigned crippling, more than absolutely necessary.

Christy knelt beside her father's stone. In December, it would be two years since he had been shot in the act of welcoming the guerrillas. She hoped he knew she was holding the farm, but hoped he didn't know how bad things were along the border.

Most Union troops had been ordered east of the Mississippi to fight battles where, as at Gettysburg, the North lost twenty thousand men. General Thomas Ewing, commander of the recently created District of the Border, had less than three thousand men to garrison and protect eastern Kansas, western Missouri, and guard the supply line from Leavenworth to Fort Scott and General Blunt's District of the Frontier. In May, guerrillas had attacked Diamond Springs on the Santa Fé Trail, one hundred miles into Kansas on the western fringe of settlement. They held up a stage, robbed, killed, and slipped back into Missouri with considerable plunder. At the same time, on the Osage reservation in southern Kansas, sixteen Confederates, carrying orders to recruit Southern sympathizers in Colorado and New Mexico, were killed by the Osages. A month later, guerrillas dashed over the border to raid Shawnee. No small Union force in Missouri was safe from ambush.

Lacking enough troops to hunt down the guerrillas who scattered to their homes or the woods after a foray, Ewing set up stations along the border about twelve miles apart, one at Trading Post. The distances between were patrolled every hour. Invading guerrillas were to be instantly pursued, help sent for if the band outnumbered the soldiers, and threatened settlements warned.

Meanwhile, George Hoyt's Red Legs terrorized Missouri, burning homes, stealing horses and mules, and killing men in front of their families. Hoyt, the Massachusetts lawyer who had headed John Brown's defense, had become captain of John Brown, Jr.'s Company K of the 7th Kansas when ill health forced Brown to resign in May of 1862, about the time Jennison resigned command of the regiment. After the 7th was ordered east, partly to stop its jayhawking in Missouri, Hoyt convinced his superiors that the climate of Mississippi had him at death's door. He resigned his commission in the summer of 1862, and came back to Kansas to lead the Red Legs, so called from their red leather leggings. Jennison, now recruiting for the 15th Kansas Volunteer Cavalry to be used only in protecting Kansas, was suspected of being in cahoots with the Red Legs.

This border war was waged by devils on both sides. Yet as Christy cut off the ears of corn, her spirit calmed to see the cardinal bring seeds to his fourth brood of the summer and glimpse the yellow-billed cuckoo or rain crow nesting for the first time.

As the day warmed, she unbuttoned the top of her dress. Before long she'd put inserts in the sides to accommodate her swelling breasts. It was good luck Danny — or Bridget Ellen! — would be able to inherit Noelle's outgrown things, since there was no wool. Next spring, if the war dragged on, Christy had better plant cotton or flax, if she could get some seed. Even Sarah was getting ragged, for she'd shared the dresses made from the gay materials lavished on her by Lige, her husband.

One of the hounds rose, lifted his nose to catch the breeze, and bayed. In an instant, all the pack was up. Above the pounding blood in her ears, Christy heard the *jingle* of spurs and bits, the *thud* of hoofs, the *creak* of saddles.

Could she hide? Get to the cavern across

the creek? She caught up her skirts to run. A volley of shots froze her. All but two hounds fell, most of them yelping and writhing. Calling the dogs that lived, she ran toward them and hauled them close against her while keeping her grip on the knife.

The wounded dogs tried to crawl to her. She dragged the two unhurt blue ticks to where she could shield them, along with three others, and straightened to face the oncoming horsemen, a score of them.

Fine mounts, brightly embroidered shirts, braces of pistols, and plumed hats proclaimed them guerrillas. Some led pack animals loaded with plunder and most led a horse or mule. If Bill Anderson was in command — but he wouldn't have let them shoot the hounds. A redbone that had crept under her skirts whimpered, twitched, and went still.

The man in the lead swept off his hat, flourishing the black plume. The sun turned his fair hair to spun silver. "Step away from those curs," Lafe Ballard said in a pleasant voice. "I don't like to be barked at."

Christy spread her skirts around as many animals as she could. Lafe raised an eyebrow, shrugged, and said to his men: "Finish the dogs you can hit without hurting my old schoolmate."

The men used the hounds for targets, riddling them.

"Not as much fun as killing the damned

Lawrence Abolitionists," laughed a bulky young man Christy dazedly recognized as Tom Maddux.

"Lawrence?" Christy echoed.

Lafe smiled. "We hit that nest of Red Legs and nigger-loving psalm singers at dawn three days ago. Oh, not just my boys, Christy. Colonel Quantrill had four hundred and fifty men."

Tom Maddux chuckled. "Burned the town. Killed every man we found, 'cept some old friends of Colonel Quantrill. A hundred and fifty or more! You should have seen 'em crawl and beg for their lives!" He added virtuously: "We never killed a single woman, but I was hard put to it several times to reach around one who was hanging onto her man, so I could blast him."

"We roasted some of 'em, too," added a barrel-chested redhead. He spat at a dead hound. "Ole Jim Lane got away, though . . . damn his eyes."

Even in her horror, Christy wondered how many of the slaughtered men had been in the delegation that had visited Dan's battery only four months ago and asked them to camp beyond the town that didn't want soldiers roistering through the streets.

"Too bad some of them nigger recruits got away across the river," Maddux said, sighing. "They need a lesson, what with that Harriet Tubman leadin' nigger troops into South

Carolina, burnin' plantations, and freein' slaves. They do say she brought out eight hunnerd of 'em."

"Don't forget them Massachusetts nigs that attacked Fort Wagner close to Charleston," put in the redhead, who spat again. "Hell, some black sergeant's up for the Medal of Honor. Makes me want to puke!"

"Honey Springs down in Indian Territory last month was worse," growled a man with a bushy black beard. "Blunt's niggers and Union Injuns whupped the tar out of twice as many of Cooper's Texans and Southern Injuns!"

"Cooper claimed his powder was wet," said Maddux. "Stand Watie wasn't there to lead the Cherokees, and, anyhow, Blunt had white troops, too . . . even some of that bunch from Colorado."

The redhead spat a third time. "Hey, when has Cooper ever won anything like an even fight? He had three or four hundred pairs of handcuffs. He reckoned them niggers would jest walk into 'em, so's he could give 'em back to their masters! Well, the niggers and Pin Injuns sashayed north with the hand-cuffs . . . and Cooper's supplies!"

Maddux wrinkled his brow, then thought of something cheerful. "At least up at Lawrence we killed some of the niggers Jim Lane stole out of Missouri. Maybe it'll be a lesson to 'em."

Lafe listened to his men with one leg cocked across the saddle horn. Now he grinned at Christy as if reading her one forlorn hope. "You'd better not count on any favors from Bill Anderson, my dear. You probably know Ewing's been exiling or imprisoning the womenfolk of guerrillas. Three of Bill's sisters and some other females were jailed on the second floor of an old brick building in Kansas City. It caved in August Thirteenth. Damn' Yanks may've tunneled under it on purpose. Killed five of the girls."

"Not . . . not Josie?" choked Christy.

"Yes. Josephine Anderson, all of fourteen years old, died in the wreckage. Her sister Mary is likely crippled for life."

Maddux's eyes bulged. "Did you see that silk cord Bill carries? He started tying knots in it when he heard about his sisters." Maddux giggled. "Bill tied a bunch of knots before we rode out of Lawrence."

Sparring for time, although she didn't want Sarah to walk into this, Christy asked: "How did you get through Ewing's border patrols?"

"Colonel Quantrill's scouts watched," said Lafe. "When the patrol passed, we knew there wouldn't be another one along for an hour. That was long enough to get across."

"You must have all the troops in central Kansas after you!"

"They were on our trail in a hurry, but we broke up after we crossed the border above

Westport." Even in her terror, Christy gave thanks they hadn't struck Trading Post or the mill. "We know the country and Ewing's men don't," Lafe boasted. "They'll never catch us." Lafe turned to his men. "Ride along with Maddux to his folks' place. His ma'll be glad to cook up some of the fancy vittles you got in Lawrence." His smile chilled Christy to the bone. "I'll have dinner with my old neighbor. Catch up with you at Madduxes tonight."

Would she be dead by then? Or just wish she were?

Lafe waved an expansive hand. "Take all the corn you can carry for your horses, boys. We won't find many fields between here and Arkansas."

Plowing, planting, weeding — all the months of care, the main winter food for herself and her friends. "Tom . . . ," Christy began. She broke off as she sensed Lafe's pleasure. He wanted her to beg. Trying not to show that she felt a pang at the sound of each breaking stalk, Christy said: "Let me take care of the dogs, Lafe. Then I'll fix your dinner."

He leveled a revolver at one of the bristling hounds. Christy knelt, embracing the animals so that he could scarcely kill them without hitting her. After a moment he lowered the gun, but rested it on the saddle horn.

"I expect you'll be more . . . hospitable, if

you don't want me to kill the brutes. Throw the knife here on the ground and see to them quickly then."

Of the three wounded dogs sheltered by her skirts, an old blue tick, Sam, bleeding profusely from several bullets, licked her hand, feebly moved his tail, and put his head against her foot as if very, very tired. By the time Christy could see through her tears, Sam's eyes were starting to glaze.

Chita, a young redbone, heavy with her first litter, was grazed along one flank. Sarah's favorite hound, Blue Boy, had a shattered right forepaw. It might have to be cut off, but, for now, Christy decided to put on Hester's salve and a bandage.

Lafe didn't let her out of his sight as she got ointment and clean rags from the house. After tossing the corn knife far into the field, he unsaddled his horse and hobbled it in the corn. The moment she'd finished tending Blue Boy, Lafe slipped his hand under her arm, drawing her toward the house.

"All right, Christy. Time to keep your bargain."

"I'm married," she told him.

Lafe's eyes dilated, black covering the crystalline iris. "To the Irisher? He deserted?"

"No! He was home on furlough in April."

Lafe smiled enough to show small teeth. "I like to imagine a husband's face as I enjoy his wife. Dan's face is far from handsome

751

now, but it would be beautiful to me if I could see it while he watched us."

Then they were in the house. He turned her hand to look at the livid scar on her wrist, brought it to his lips. "I was a boy when I marked you, Christy, but even then I dreamed about the things I'd do with you when I got the chance."

The odor of smoke clung to him — was that hint of burned flesh her imagination? His mouth seared her throat. She caught his hands as he began to undo the rest of the buttons.

"I . . . I'm going to have a baby."

He drew back as if she were suddenly filthy. Then his eyes narrowed. "You're not showing."

"I've missed. . . ."

He made a gesture of repulsion. "All that makes me sick. I'm not sure I believe you, either." He pondered, watching her.

Her heartbeat slowed. She felt like a hunted animal feigning death.

His pale eyes glinted as he laughed. "Perhaps I can make you lose it. Yes, if I can remember that's Dan's thing growing in you. A mare aborts if she's ridden too hard and long. Don't see why that shouldn't be true for a woman. Get me a drink first. Is there any coffee?"

"Only sassafras tea."

He made a face and turned to the water bucket.

As if offering a drink, Christy raised the dipper and sloshed it in his face, grabbing at the same time for one of his guns. With any other man, she thought she could survive rape like a maiming but not fatal accident. With Lafe, she'd rather die.

He bent her wrist till she had to drop the revolver. She fastened her teeth in his hand, tasted the salt of blood before he struck her so hard lights exploded in her head. Then, through a dizzy whirling, she heard the dogs and the sound of horses.

Catching up the gun from the floor, Lafe peered from the edge of the window. "Bill Anderson! Now we'll see, Christy, how he feels about you with his sister dead. If he still has a kindness for you and you have some for him, don't cry-baby. He's got a bunch with him, but I can certainly blast him before he finishes me."

"Miss Christy!"

It was Anderson's voice. She should hope they would kill each other, Lafe and Bill Anderson, who was now implacable, but she remembered the handsome young man she'd helped nurse back to health, the one whose hawk face softened as he spoke of Josie. She buttoned her dress, smoothed her hair, and stepped outside.

While his wild band kept their saddles,

Anderson trailed his reins in front of his black horse and strode toward the house. He motioned toward the dead hounds sprawled at the edge of the trampled, broken stalks.

"Had some trouble, Miss Christy?"

Lafe stepped around her. "My boys got a little out of hand, Bill. Didn't like the hounds baying at them."

"Looks like your horse hobbled out in what's left of the corn."

"Hell, Bill! This is war."

Anderson's face twisted. "Yeah. Yeah, it is." A red silk cord with many knots was looped around the crown of his black hat. What looked like human hair decorated either side of the headstall at the brow band of his bridle. "Where are your men, Lafe?"

"Headed for Tom Maddux's folks a few miles away."

"You can show us. Quantrill's orders are to gather all the men we can, and meet him down in Texas, paying our respects along the way to any bluebellies or Union militia we're strong enough to tackle."

Lafe stiffened. Then he looked at the fifty or sixty guerrillas and gave a short laugh. "Fine. Texas ought to be a warmer place to spend the winter." He bowed to Christy. "Thanks for the drink. Sorry we can't visit longer about old times." He strolled toward his horse.

Anderson's blue gaze searched Christy.

"Are you . . . hurt?"

"Not really. If you'll take him with you. . . ."

"You bet I will." Anderson hitched a shoulder. "I'd kill him for what he did to your corn and hounds, but we need him. He's the devil in a fight, and smart. Helped Quantrill plan the Lawrence raid."

This guerrilla had shot down helpless men, some in their doorways like her father, yet something in his eyes made her ache for him. "Mister Anderson, I . . . I'm sorry about Josie."

A muscle jerked in his cheek. "You're lucky you look like her, and that you saved my life." He swallowed. "Good bye, Christy Ware. I doubt we'll see each other again in this world."

"Good bye, Bill Anderson." She rose on tiptoe and kissed him for his dead sister.

He gave her a startled look — half of a wry smile — caught up the reins, and mounted. Lafe fell in beside him. In minutes they passed out of sight along the creek.

CHAPTER THIRTY-SIX

Christy began to shake. Her knees gave way. She sank down on the step, burying her face in her arms and wept for Lawrence, the widows and orphans there, wept for Josie and the dead young girls, for Mary Anderson who might never walk, wept with fresh pain for her father.

Blue Boy limped up with the other dogs that made soft mourning sounds as they pressed against her. She was caressing them, thankful that at least they were alive, when Sarah arrived.

Digging a grave deep and wide enough for ten animals in the rocky soil was such a formidable task that, instead, they pushed and pulled the wheelbarrow, laden with several hounds at a time, to a gully in the pasture, lowered them gently, and shoveled in earth from the banks.

"I want to tell Lige they weren't torn up and eaten," Sarah muttered through her tears. She and Christy rolled big rocks over the burial, held each other a while and sobbed. "Do you think your father would mind . . . would you . . . if I buried old Sam beside him?" Sarah asked. "Lige thought a lot of your father. It'd make him feel better about Sam when he comes homes . . . if he does."

"Father liked dogs. He'd be glad to have Sam close to him."

When the old hound was curled for his long sleep in the rich earth by Jonathan Ware's stone, Christy and Sarah bowed their heads. After a time, they studied the field.

Here and there, an ear of corn stood on an unbroken stalk. There were probably more, hidden by the shattered plants, but most of the crop had been stolen or wasted. Outrage smoldered in Christy as they washed blood from the wheelbarrow, tilted it to dry, and began the pitiful harvest. Nearly all guerrillas — most soldiers, for that matter — were farm boys, who had stumbled to bed worn out from plowing or chopping weeds away from the corn. Yet, in ten minutes, they had destroyed the reward of months of work. But considering the bloody harvest they'd reaped in Lawrence, it was lucky they hadn't fired the house. And Christy was lucky, so lucky, Bill Anderson had come to say good bye.

"Seed corn and a little to eat. We'll get quite a bit of fodder from the stalks," Sarah said, rubbing her back as she appraised the good corn in the wheelbarrow and the heap of ears beside it that had been smashed into the earth or partly crushed by hoofs or boots. Seed could be gleaned from them. "At least we grew some corn in the valley, but we'll have to gather all the nuts and wild fruit we can. With Hildy gone to Justus, there's one less mouth to feed, but one less woman to help, and Hildy was good help." Sarah looked straight at Christy. "Are you going to tell Hester about Lafe?"

"No, nor the others, either. They'll have to know guerrillas came and took the corn, but there's no use grieving Hester."

Sarah nodded. "Maybe we should dig the potatoes and get them to the valley before someone steals them." She frowned. "What with bushwhackers and soldiers after Quantrill, we might better stay in the valley."

It made sense. Christy didn't think there could be anyone as cruel as Lafe Ballard, but there might be. Yet glancing from her father's grave to the house, she felt that abandoning them was giving up all he had stood for, all she believed in, all she wanted to save for Dan, and surrendering to the evil of men like Lafe and Quantrill, Jennison, and the Red Legs.

"I can't leave, Sarah. But you don't have to stay."

"Of course I do!" Sarah gave her an exasperated hug. "I guess I know what you mean.

The house stands for when neighbors helped each other, instead of killing them. It stands for the good ways we hope there'll be again . . . school and Sunday meetings, quilting, trading work, opening your door to strangers and giving them your best because that's how it should be, not because there's a gun at your head."

"Sarah. . . ."

Frowning at the row of bee gums ranged on stumps between the small orchard and the garden, Sarah turned with an exultant laugh. "There's bound to be some thieves want our honey. I just thought of a way to fix them good! We'll loop a rope around the bottom of each bee gum, so they're all connected. Then we'll tie on pieces of rope, hiding it in the grass, till the end reaches the dogtrot. . . ."

"And a yank on it will turn over the bee gums!" Christy finished for her.

"Yes. When my bees get after them, they'll skedaddle, whether they're bushwhackers, jayhawks, or soldiers. I hate to upset my bees, but it's better than the rascals making off with all their honey so they'd starve this winter."

Sarah could work around the bees without getting stung, so she tied the rope around the bee gums. Christy ran it behind the woodpile on the dogtrot and left the knotted end where it could be jerked without the perpetrator being seen.

The rest of the day, they dug potatoes, wheelbarrowed the sacks to the creek, and carried them to store inside the cave till Lad and Lass could take them through the passage. No more than a week's supply of potatoes would go in the root cellar, with a similar amount of turnips.

Next morning they were shaking plump brown potatoes loose from earth and plants when a wagon clattered out of the woods on the west. Relieved at the sunbonnets of driver and passenger, and recognizing Zephyr and Breeze stepping smartly along, Christy and Sarah went forward to meet Susie McHugh and Harriet Parks.

Their somber faces were not due entirely to the butchery at Lawrence. "That dreadful Jim Lane's been tearing around, working people up to cross into Missouri and serve the border counties as Lawrence was . . . burn, kill, get back stolen property and a lot more, besides." Susie shook her head. "Lawrence is in all the Northern papers, New York, Boston, Chicago . . . everywhere. You know, Lawrence was settled almost ten years ago by the New England Emigrant Aid Society, which was determined to make Kansas a free state. Most of the murdered men have friends and family back East. Money's pouring in to rebuild Lawrence, and the North's calling for vengeance, especially since Quantrill holds a Confederate commission and the raid's being praised in Southern papers."

"They're remembering the Red Legs and jayhawkers." Not much else could have been expected, but Christy's heart sank. "Is Jim Lane in Missouri?"

"General Ewing stopped him," Harriet said. "But he had to promise Lane that the Army would clear everybody out of the Missouri border counties so the guerrillas can't find shelter and support."

"Everybody?" Christy repeated.

"Everybody." Susie fumbled for a paper, then she handed it to Christy. "I made a copy of Order Number Eleven for you from the one sent Captain Wright, who's in command of the soldiers at Trading Post."

The words danced crazily as Christy tried to understand, reading snatches aloud: " 'August Twenty-Third, Eighteen Sixty-Three . . . All persons living in Jackson, Cass, and Bates County, Missouri and that part of Vernon County included in this district, except those living within one mile of the limits of Independence, Hickman's Mills, Pleasant Hill, and Harrisonville, and except those in Kaw township . . . embracing Kansas City and Westport, are hereby ordered to remove from their places of residence within fifteen days. . . .' "

Skimming ahead, Christy summed it up for Sarah before giving her the paper. "People who can convince the commanding officer of the nearest station that they're loyal to the Union will get a certificate allowing them to move to any military station in the district or anywhere in Kansas except the border counties. Everyone else must leave the district."

Sarah read angrily: " 'All hay or grain in the field or under shelter . . . within reach of the military stations . . . will be taken to such stations . . . specifying the names of all loyal owners and the amount of such produce taken from them. All grain and hay . . . not convenient to such stations will be destroyed."

She and Christy looked toward the ravaged corn. "I don't know if it's better or worse to have your corn taken by the Army instead of bushwhackers," Christy said. "Lafe Ballard and Tom Maddux were through here with a gang yesterday. Killed most of the hounds and stole the corn."

The visitors' eyes widened as they looked more closely at the field. "Papa will give you some corn," Susie assured them.

"We have a little, and enough for seed," demurred Christy. "There are going to be people who need it a lot worse than we do when Missouri Unionists start crossing the line. As if a government voucher's going to feed them when their crops are lost! I'm glad Thos and Dan and Davie aren't stationed where they'd have to do such rotten work."

"Captain Wright's a decent man," Susie comforted. "He's from Mound City and met your father at the mill. He knows Dan from riding with Montgomery."

"He has his orders." Christy gazed at the house, the giant walnut, so dear, and dearer still because of her father's death and these years she'd struggled to protect it. "Are , . . are they supposed to burn the buildings?"

Susie brightened a little. "General Schofield, who commands the Department of Missouri, won't approve the burning of property, and he and Ewing have issued strict orders that neither Kansas nor Missouri militia can cross the border without direct command from Ewing. Neither can groups of armed civilians on any pretext whatever."

"Order Eleven's hard and cruel," said Harriet. "But everyone says it's merciful compared to what Lane's thousands and the Red Legs would have done."

"That's not much comfort, but at least, thanks to you, we know what to expect." Christy wiped her hands on her apron. "Come in and have some tea."

"We'd better get back," Harriet said. "Mama gets cranky with the children, if she has to look after them very long." She sighed. "I wish she'd go live with one of her darling sons. She and Catriona are always bickering."

"Papa's certainly never going to marry her," Susie declared. "Christy, Sarah, we brought the wagon to help you move, in case any of you want to come stay with us. I'm sure we can persuade Captain Wright to look the other way."

"Unless Trav . . . I mean, the father of little Noelle . . . comes to get Lilah, I wouldn't be surprised if she stays with Star even after the war. Hester seems happy as long as she has Richie." A lump rose in Christy's throat as she looked at the house. "If . . . if I can't stay here, I'll go to the valley."

"So will I," said Sarah.

They waved the two women out of sight, looked at each wordlessly, and went back to digging potatoes.

Two days later, a squad of mounted men behind him, Captain Wright explained Order Number 11, looking as unhappy as if he were being exiled. His mild brown eyes avoided the women's. "I've already signed your certificates, Missus O'Brien, Missus Morrow. Since the order requires signatures of people affirming your loyalty, Missus Nickel and the Parkses gave theirs." He tugged ferociously at his flowing moustache. "I regret this, ladies, especially since your husbands are both Union soldiers. To some degree, it's for your own safety. General Ewing fears when the guerrillas' families are forced to leave, the devils will take vengeance on any Union folks left in the district."

Sarah thinned her shapely nose. "This feels

like vengeance!" She stalked toward the house.

"There's no corn for you to take," said Christy. "The guerrillas helped themselves."

"You don't seem to have any animals except the dogs."

"We don't have as many as we did before the guerrillas hit four days ago."

Captain Wright blushed. "I'm sorry . . . they dodged our patrol."

Christy showed him a little mercy. "They crossed farther north."

"Good. I mean . . . it's not good they crossed, but. . . ." He floundered. "I hope it'll cheer you to know that Fort Smith fell to the Union again. This time, we'll keep it. All Stand Watie and his Indians can hope to do now is raid supply wagons along the Military Road. We will win, Missus O'Brien, and then. . . ."

There was sudden commotion, crashing, and shrieks. Christy and Wright whirled to see three of his men bolting for the creek, covering their faces, slapping wildly at bees swarming out of overturned beehives.

Two of the soldiers dived in the creek, but the third tripped on a log and went sprawling. A fresh scream burst from him. He sat up, swatting at the bees, but he couldn't get to his feet.

Sarah, coming out from behind the wood-pile, ran till she began to encounter angry bees and slowed to a walk. She wafted her skirts carefully around the soldier who had buried his face in his arms. The bees hovered. Then their buzzing numbers, including those that had pursued their molesters to the water, began to drift back to their toppled hives.

By the time Christy and Wright approached, Sarah was slapping mud on the soldier's hands, head, face, and neck.

"My leg!" he moaned.

"Let it be a lesson to you, Hawkins. No foraging except by order." Wright's tone was severe, but he was gentle as he slit the boy's pant leg with his pocket knife.

No bones protruded, but there was a deformity under the skin, and, when Hawkins stirred, there was a sound of bone grinding on bone. "Any of you men know how to set a broken leg?" the captain yelled.

No one did. Sarah bit her lip, peering at the injury. "I helped Lige set his leg when it was broken about like this," she said. "He gripped hard below his knee, and I pulled from just above the ankle till the broken edges separated and could be eased back together. I padded boards and bandaged them on each side to keep the bones straight. Healed just fine."

Young Hawkins's blue eyes fixed on her from a mud plaster, only a few strands of chick-yellow hair escaping. "Would . . . would you help me, ma'am? I was just so hungry for some honeycomb. . . ."

"Will you hold his leg below the knee, Captain?" Sarah asked. "Christy, will you find some boards and something to pad and bandage with?"

Two soldiers squatted at the creekbank, daubing mud on their stings. As Christy ran to the house, a grizzled older man passed her with a flask. "A good slug of whiskey'll help the boy. Maybe the cap'n won't romp me too hard for breakin' rules and havin' a mite along for my rheumatiz."

Cloth was more precious than ever, now there was no wool, and, concentrating on food crops, they hadn't been growing cotton or flax. Christy's dress was patched in a dozen places. She'd make up the beautiful blue gingham Dan had brought this winter, but she'd save it for his next visit — or homecoming! — as long as she could. Good thread was unraveled, to be woven again, but the ragbag held enough worn-out scraps for padding. The middle cut from an old sheet could bind in place shelves she took from the well house.

When the leg was set and held in place by boards well padded and bandaged, one of the squad approached. "Shall we rig a litter, Cap'n?"

Wright scowled. "Four miles of that would jar him plenty. Best thing is for some of you to ride back and fetch a wagon . . . with lots of featherbeds!"

"Why not leave him here?" Christy began. Then she remembered. September 9th, ten days from now, was when she and Sarah were supposed to be gone. The captain turned red, but suddenly his mild features perked up.

"You'd look after him?"

"Of course we would, but. . . ."

"If any of our men are wounded or fall sick while patrolling this region, would you take care of them?"

Christy caught in her breath at the glimmer of hope. "We would. We've nursed a man with an ugly bullet wound and know something of healing herbs."

"I reckon I have some discretion," Wright said. "Sure seems useful to me to have a place this side of the border where our soldiers can be looked after." He glanced at his men. "I'll argue this with General Ewing himself, if I have to, boys, but I don't see why anyone but us needs to know."

There was general nodding and approving murmurs. While Sarah and Christy hurried to fix a bed, four of the men carried Hawkins to the house. Before they brought him in, Sarah cleaned the mud off him and replaced it with dock root ointment that she passed around to the other afflicted soldiers.

Hawkins's bedroll and pack was brought from his saddle, and his blanket spread to protect the sheets. "I'll send over his rations,"

768

said Wright while friends took off Hawkins's boots and outer clothing. "I'm mightily obliged."

He took the certificates and scribbled notes on each. "There. Says you're hereby charged with nursing and sheltering Union soldiers who require such aid. Since my command's responsible for this section, you shouldn't have any trouble with our soldiers, but, if you do, send them to me."

Sarah and Christy said as one: "Thank you, Captain."

He grinned, plainly as relieved as they were. "We'll take Hawkins's horse with us, just in case a thief happens along, but a man'll bring it for him when he's able to ride."

As Wright and his band rode off, Sarah eyed the youthful invader of her hives. "I'm going to set up the bee gums again, and tell my bees it's all right. If they let me take some honeycomb for you, will you promise never to steal from a hive again?"

"But we keep bees at home, ma'am. Mama takes care of them."

"She always leaves them plenty for winter?"

"Oh yes, ma'am. She's real careful about taking honey. Won't let the rest of us come nigh. And she plants all kinds of flowers they like."

"Then I'm surprised you didn't know better."

He squirmed. "Mama'd give me a hiding, if

she'd seen me. But I could just taste honey-comb, ma'am. And . . . oh, I don't know, when you're a soldier, even militia like us, and a bunch of you are out somewhere. . . ."

"You do things you wouldn't if you were home."

"I'm afraid that's about the size of it, ma'am."

He looked very young. The swellings puffed out his round, freckled face even more, and his body hadn't caught up with his gangling arms and legs. "Don't call me 'ma'am'. I'm Sarah and this is Christy. Who are you?"

"Will Hawkins, ma . . . I mean, Miss Sarah. From south of Mound City."

"How old are you?"

He crimsoned. "Fifteen."

"They take boys that young in the militia?"

"Bushwhackers kill us for men," he re-torted. " 'Most all the soldier-age men in Kansas joined the Army a long time ago, so the militia can't be choosy. Anyhow, I said I was eighteen, and Mama signed for me."

"I hope she's got sons at home with better sense."

"Matt's twelve and Billy's fourteen. My big brother Harry lost an arm at Pea Ridge, but he's learned to do most anything."

"Where's your father?"

"He . . . well, he got himself killed at Pea Ridge along with my Uncle Bax."

This was what it meant for just one family

when it said one thousand three hundred eighty-four Union men were lost in that battle. A father and husband and kinsman dead, a son and brother maimed for life. If the war ground on, besides Will, there were two more boys who might be harvested long before their season.

Look at Mrs. Nickel: of her sons who saw their cabin burned by Clarke's marauders seven years ago, six were in the Army as well as her tall, golden-haired husband. Who would be left when it was over?

"I'll get you some honeycomb," Sarah told the boy.

"I'm going to the Hayes tannery," Christy said. "Allie will have to move. I'm afraid she doesn't have anywhere to go."

Sarah raised an eyebrow. "Do you think . . . ?"

"I don't know. I'll ask in the valley before I go see her."

Hester Ballard vouched for Allie as being a good woman, and Christy described all the help Ethan and Allie Hayes had given her family when they first moved here. "Mary and Beth were great friends," she said, and then frowned. "The two older boys are in the Army, but Luke may still be home, helping his mother. He's fifteen."

"He should not come here." Star's tone was positive. "He is of warrior age, and is bound

771

to go soon. Better he not know about the valley. But his mother and sister are welcome."

Lilah nodded. Matured by motherhood, she was so lovely that Christy thought Travis Jardine, if he ever saw them again, would have to want to take care of her and sweet little Noelle.

"I'll see what I can do," Christy promised. "Thank you, Star."

Star chuckled. "I was surely wrong when I thought I would live alone all the rest of my life."

Allie Hayes was thirty-nine, four years younger than Ellen Ware, but she looked the older now, yellow hair streaked with white, sun wrinkles at eyes and mouth, beginning to stoop from labor. Only her brilliant blue eyes were the same. They sparkled with angry tears as she gestured at her cornfield.

"That jumped-up Captain Wright's sending a wagon and men to take my corn on the Ninth, and Mary and me have to be gone by then! Where and how, I'd like to know? Nora Caxton's already gone to live with her sister in Springfield and the Madduxes still have a team and wagon and enough money for the train or steamboat, but how'm I supposed to get back to Kentucky, where we came from when we first got married? I haven't heard from any of our folks since the war began. Luke took our old mule when he headed for

Arkansas to join up with Pap Price and find his brothers and pa. When he came by here last week, Lafe Ballard stole our last critter, a runty hog."

Mary, at nine, leggy and reaching to Allie's breast, hugged her mother around the waist and tried to pat her cheek. "We can walk, Mama. We've fed lots of people and let them sleep in our house or barn. I bet there's plenty of folks'll do the same for us. . . ."

"Won't be anybody left till we get to the south end of Vernon County, and not many after that all the way down through Arkansas, where there's been so much fighting." She brooded, holding Mary close. "What makes it worse is half the men in Wright's bunch, includin' him, have brought hides to the tannery for years. They know us."

Christy remembered Watt Caxton shooting down her father. "That's what makes it so awful."

Allie reached for her hand. "I'm afraid I haven't been much of a neighbor these last years, Christy. Seems like I haven't had time to breathe since Ethan and Matt left, and then Mark. Still, I'd've got over, someway, if I hadn't known Sarah was with you, and Hester." She gave a wan smile. "I heard you married Dan O'Brien. Always liked that lad, and could he fiddle! I hope he'll come home safe to you."

"And I hope Ethan and your boys will."

"It don't seem right that you and Sarah have to leave, too, when your men are in the Union Army. Reckon you'll go to Kansas."

Christy gazed at Allie and tried to gauge if she could be trusted, if she could fit in with Lilah and Star.

"How's little Beth?" Allie asked. "She must miss your mama, who I hear tell has gone to be a nurse. She can be right proud of doing that. Only thing I've got to brag on is how I kept the jayhawks from stealing our lard last year." Allie grinned. "The captain was having it loaded when I said . . . 'Oh, well, it would've been a shame to make it into soap.' He said that would be a terrible waste, and I said . . . 'To be sure, sir, but the hog had cholera.'" Allie laughed hugely. "He thought I might be lying, but he didn't dare chance it. I didn't let you say, though . . . how is Beth?"

"Beth's fine." Allie would never do anything to hurt Beth — any child. "Allie, if . . . if there were a place close by where you could stay, would you do it till the war's over?"

"A place to hide?"

Christy nodded.

"Honey," said Allie with fervor, "I'd live in a cave if I could be around when my men come home."

Christy burst out laughing. "You won't have to live in a cave now," she said, and told them.

CHAPTER THIRTY-SEVEN

A son! He, Daniel Patrick O'Brien, whose birth family had long since returned to the sod of County Clare, had a son in this new world, born of his beloved. Even if he died, part of him would live in the child who'd claim his share of joy, grief, work, and rewards in the country Dan fought for.

Jon's hair is between yours and mine, Christy wrote. I'm sending you a curl. It's much the color of Father's, rich red-brown, and lots of it, but he's going to have your eyes, Danny, hazy gray like autumn mist on the hills. Beth and Mary won't let him whimper for more than a second when we're in the valley, so he keeps Sarah and me hopping when we're at the cabin. How I wish you could see him! How I wish I knew where you are! It's been a month since I had your letter saying you boys were fed up with guarding the road to the harbor there at Johnsonville and that you want to see more action. I can understand that you'd rather get hurt in a real battle, rather than be picked off by guerrillas, but, oh, my darling love, take care of yourself. Little Jon needs a father and you need him. Also, there's that little girl we both want, remember?

I'm going to have all my babies the Osage way. It makes a lot better sense to be upright and hold onto willow posts to work with the baby. Star gave me cherry bark tea to help make the pains powerful enough, and, after Jon came, Hester gave me lots of fennel tea to make sure I had plenty of milk.

Star made him a pine cradleboard. You should see him watch a tail feather from the scarlet tanager that nests in our big tree, and the bright green parakeet feathers Richie found. The board's so convenient. I can carry Jon and have my hands free or can prop him against something or even hang him from a tree. That sounds awful, but you know what I mean!

Dan held his son's bright curl to his cheek. It clung there, soft, finer than down. He wrapped it carefully in the envelope and put it in a lined oiled-silk bag he'd bought in St. Louis to hold such treasures. The letter was dated February 10, 1864. Because of the vagaries of military transport, after weeks of no mail, he'd had four letters from Christy that afternoon of April 13th, including one written the day of Jonathan Daniel's birth. He, Davie Parks, and Thos Ware got boxes, too, that day, but, although they'd existed that winter on the worst rations of Dan's entire time in the Army — hardtack and barreled salt pork with lean streaks turned a villainous green — they read their letters several times over before attacking the boxes with bayonets, purloined because they weren't supplied to artillerymen but made wonderful candle holders with the sharp end stuck in the ground and were generally a useful tool around camp. Soldiers hated to use bayonets for their real purpose and very seldom did, even under orders.

"If they have to dig through our boxes at regimental headquarters to make sure there's no whiskey, you'd think they could at least have a care about how they treat our things," Dan grumbled, using a pick to pry up the last nail from Christy's box. He had two more! One from the Parkses, and one from his mother-in-law who was nursing in Nashville, only eighty miles away. Several times he'd been granted a few days' furlough to ride the train to the city and visit her and Lydia, who was also there, looking almost pretty in spite of her exhausting work.

"It's plain craziness about the whiskey." Thos held up a wool shirt from his mother and admired it before unwrapping some chocolate and savoring it with his eyes closed. "Officers get all the commissary whiskey they can pay for anytime they want it. Plenty of them are drunk when they're giving orders that could get us killed, but an enlisted man can't buy a drop without a written order signed by his captain, and any sutler who sells spirits will lose his license."

"Ah, but look what my clever Peggy contrived, lads!" Harry Shepherd exhibited a big roasted turkey. His dark eyes glinted as he reached inside it and produced a corked bottle. "Peach brandy, bless my girl's heart! And here's spiced nuts, gingerbread, sausage, lean bacon, pickles, cheese!" His black eyebrows knitted. "But why did Peg send six pairs of socks?" He read a note and his grin faded. "She'd made three pair for Tim. Since he's gone, she wants me to give these and some of the goodies to soldiers who haven't got families to send them things."

Since it had been months since the battery got any boxes, most men received at least one as the wagon was unloaded. The half dozen or so who got nothing watched the joyful unpacking wistfully or moped off to their tents.

"We'll all share." Davie put a ham on the lid and unwrapped socks and a warm shirt from around jars of preserves and relish. "Look! Susie's made my favorite black walnut applesauce cake! Catriona sent currant scones . . . Harriet put in gingersnaps and caramels . . . Missus Morrison did nice big handkerchiefs . . . and Papa's sent two books . . . George Borrow's *Wild Wales* and Palgrave's *Golden Treasury!* And there's potatoes, onions, and apples tucked in every place one'll fit, and dried apple and pear slices in any little chink!" A smaller box from his big sister Lydia contained envelopes, writing paper, needles, and thread to share with Dan. Dan got the same delicious edibles from his foster sisters, as well as sewing needs, a shirt, and chocolate from Mrs. Ware who'd asked him to please call her Ellen. But it was Christy's box that made his eyes blur.

She must have unraveled her best shawl to make the soft muffler, mittens, and socks. The picture of her doing that by firelight, big with his child, wrenched his heart. He knew guerrillas had ruined or carried off the corn, but a note explained she had devised the fruit bars with ground nut meal, more nuts, applesauce, currants, and honey. Pear, peach, and grape leathers or dried apple and persimmon slices were wedged into every possible space. Honeycomb from Sarah Morrow filled a jar sealed with beeswax. A large crock was jammed with pickled eggs and a smaller crock held butter. From Star there were cakes of maple sugar and candy of maple syrup boiled with all manner of nuts. Hester sent boneset leaves, ground coneflower root, and black haw bark for colds and flu, and, for enjoyment, a tea of fragrant crumbled sassafras bark and spicebush. Lilah's petticoat must have supplied three finely stitched handkerchiefs with his initials embroidered in a corner. Beth had drawn a creditable likeness of Jon in his cradleboard, and written proudly that she would help him learn to walk. There were notes and pictures from Richie and Mary Hayes. Dan was touched to have them, even if they were "school" assignments. Since Ellen had left, Star, Sarah, and Christy were teaching the children, along with Lilah and Hester, who were learning to read and write.

After the bounty was shared with men who'd got no boxes, Dan's mess — Shepherd, Thos, and Davie — had a banquet.

"I'm glad we got potatoes," Shepherd said as he fried some in butter. "When we're guarding the supply route for the Army of the Cumberland, you'd think the quartermaster could give us some fruit and vegetables, so we won't all come down with scurvy. Five men have it so bad, they've been sent to the Nashville hospital."

Happily replete, the battery boys lounged from tent to tent that night, joking and exchanging choice viands. The commander's sister was visiting with her baby, a winsome lass of less than two years, whose golden hair shone from beneath the red hood of her cloak as her mother sat with her on a box outside their tent. Her name was Annie and she laughed and reached for the faces of the men who crowded around to see her.

We serenaded her with 'Annie Laurie'. She laughed and called us "nice, pretty so-jers," bless her heart. Her father, a captain like her uncle, is stationed in Nashville. Seeing such a darling little colleen made us almost as happy as getting our boxes. Dan wrote by candlelight in the Sibley tent his gun crew shared. These twelve feet high, teepee-like shelters had passed out of official use two years ago because the iron tripods that held them up were heavy and cumbersome to transport, but the quartermaster had located some for the long-encamped battery. Each was supposed to shelter twelve men, so the nine of them almost had enough room. The cone-shaped stove was useless for cooking and not much better for heat till Shepherd thought of building a little oven of bricks and setting the stove on top to serve as part of the chimney. The stove pipe supplied by the quartermaster was too short to reach the top of the tent, so the men chipped in to buy enough pipe to vent the smoke outside.

All our crew got boxes and are writing home tonight before we turn in like spokes on a wheel with our feet to the stove and our heads to the canvas. Usually Davie reads anything he can find, Thos plays checkers with Mac Ford or Harry Shepherd, and the rest play cards or smoke their pipes and tell yarns. Tonight, though, we're all scribbling away to finish our letters before "Taps".

He would read her new bunch of letters till he had them by heart, but now he glanced back through them quickly, reading news he'd skipped the first time in order to find her love words and how she and the baby were doing.

In a letter inexplicably delayed since he'd had several with later dates, she had written: You'll have heard that about three hundred of Quantrill's men, some dressed in Federal uniforms, attacked the little garrison at Baxter Springs, perhaps one hundred black and white soldiers, about noon, October 6th. The soldiers were holding them off when the guerrillas galloped away. They'd learned General Blunt was on his way to Fort Smith with eight wagons, some ladies and civilians in buggies, a brass band — mostly young German boys in brand new uniforms — and an escort of one hundred men. Because of the stolen uniforms, Blunt thought the Union garrison was coming to meet him. When the guerrillas opened fire, Blunt's men were so startled that some ran. The officers rallied them when more Rebels burst out of the timber. Blunt got the ladies to safety, but most of the escort were chased down and shot even after surrendering. The bandwagon tried to get away — the musicians weren't armed — but the youngsters were all shot and the wagon set afire while some were still alive. Quantrill rode on to Texas for the winter. We hope he won't be back.

You remember William Hairgrove who was terribly wounded by Hamelton's gang in that gully above the Marais des Cygnes. He's a soldier at Leavenworth now, though his hair's white and he's old for the Army. Anyway, he found out that William Griffith, one of the murderers, was living across the river in Missouri. Griffith was arrested, tried in Mound City, and hanged. Susie McHugh says everyone thinks he's the only one who'll ever be punished, though surely some of them have been killed in the war.

An early February letter had happier tidings. The Ladies Enterprise Society of Mound City has organized to build a meeting house. They give glorious suppers to raise money and have musical evenings, plays, and lectures that the soldiers stationed there are glad to support. There's a singing school, children's classes, and the United Brethren, Baptists, Methodists, and Presbyterians each have a day to hold services. It would be heaven if you were stationed that close, but surely the war can't last too much longer, can it, Danny?

He had already written her of his high hopes once General Grant was put in command of all Union forces April 4th. What it amounts to, darling, is the Union controls the Mississippi and everywhere west of it except for the Confederate forces left in Arkansas and Indian Territory. Grant can get more men and supplies. The South's running out of both. Grant hopes to break Lee's Army in Virginia and have Sherman and the other Union generals push east to the ocean.

"Taps" sounded, that poignant, most beautiful of all camp melodies. Dan put his letters and writing things in his knapsack, nestled Jon's fiery curl with Christy's black one in the silver snuff box he'd bought to keep the precious lock from getting lost or dirty, and blew out his candle. Except in the bitterest weather, he stripped to his underwear before rolling up in Christy's blanket. He tucked the snuff box beneath the shirt he used for a pillow, imagined her asleep with their son nearby, and was soon asleep in spite of Shepherd's resonant snoring.

Word came next day of the slaughter of two hundred thirty-eight Negro soldiers and many white ones at Fort Pillow, Tennessee. General Nathan Forrest's troops swarmed through, killing men who were trying to surrender. The river ran red with the blood of those shot while trying to escape.

"There won't be any Negroes surrender after this." Shepherd's tone was somber. "Of course, they've known all along that the Rebs'll most likely kill them when it's not possible to capture and sell them as slaves."

"Lincoln tried to put a stop to that," said Dan, "by ordering that a Rebel prisoner would be shot for every Union soldier killed contrary to the rules of war, and for each sold into slavery, a Rebel prisoner would be put at hard labor till the Union man was released. That probably kept the South from executing or selling the Fifty-Fourth Massachusetts men captured after their attack on Fort Wagner."

"Father doesn't believe in war at all." After more than two years, Davie still didn't look old enough to be a soldier. "But he says it's shameful that colored soldiers are paid only ten dollars a month to a white's thirteen, and then three dollars of that's held out for clothing, so they only get seven dollars."

"I'll bet Colonel Montgomery and the other white commanding officers are trying to change that," said Dan. "For that matter, boys, have you heard we may get a pay raise?"

"I'll believe it when I see it!" snorted Shepherd.

At the end of April, Captain Tenney had official business at Waverly, an outpost ten miles from the river. The road wound through thick timber, the sort guerrillas liked, so the captain was escorted by twenty men, including Dan and Davie, mounted on battery horses and armed with Colt revolvers.

It was the kind of spring morning that proclaims with moist earth smells, birdsong, and fresh leaf that winter is over. Raven pranced a bit, although he was getting old for a battery horse. After Dan married, he'd had two-thirds of his pay sent to Christy, in care of Uncle Simeon, but he was saving all he could with the hope of buying Raven when the war ended, or if the horse became unfit for duty. They'd been through a lot since Dan first harnessed the big black horse at Leavenworth two years ago. Two years, and Dan had been in the Army almost a year before that. Close to three years of his twenty-four spent in this war.

The captain and riders in front stopped to let their mounts drink from a stream flowing across the road. Suddenly shots hummed around the escort.

"Up ahead, men!" yelled Captain Tenney. "Take cover behind that ridge!"

Gaining the other side of the rocky spine, Rebels whooping after them, they flung themselves from their horses and knelt where they could steady their pistols and aim at the oncoming band of wild-looking men armed with muskets, squirrel rifles, and shotguns.

By a miracle, no soldier seemed to be seriously hurt, but one horse lay quietly in the stream, and another thrashed on the bank, screaming, till it gave a final convulsion and its head dropped.

"Make your bullets count, boys!" called Tenney. "We're almost as many as they are! They didn't count on a fight. Let's give them one!"

A shot whipped off the hat of a gray-coated man in the lead, baring his golden hair. *The color of Richie's,* Dan thought with a pang. Although his scar smoldered and the man was his best target, Dan aimed at the raggedy knees of a wiry, bearded fellow in the act of firing his musket. Dan missed. Someone else didn't. The man dropped his weapon, threw up his arms, half turned, and fell.

Dan eared back the hammer and fired at a redhead in a greasy vest. He yelped, clapped his hand over his bleeding thigh, and staggered into the brush as the others were doing, except for three sprawled bodies and a man with sunny hair who moaned as he pressed his hands over a wound in his belly. Blood leaked through his fingers to dribble to the ground.

Davie gripped Dan's arm, jerked his head toward the wounded enemy. "I shot him! I . . . I did that!"

"He was after us." Dan dropped a bracing hand on the boy's shoulder. "Look, Davie, you've been on a gun crew for two years. . . ."

"Yes," whispered Davie. "But I was never sure we'd hit anyone."

"If we didn't, lad, we've wasted a great lot of shell and powder," Dan said, and turned to his brother-in-law. "Thos, looks like you'll have a permanent part on the left side. Here, let me bandage it. My handkerchief's cleaner than yours."

When Dan turned back, he saw Davie kneeling by the blond Rebel, offering his canteen.

A swift glance must have assured the captain that his soldiers were all fit to ride. "Mount up, men!" Tenney called. "Take turns riding with the two who lost horses." He wiped his forehead and settled his hat more firmly. "We gave those gentlemen more than they reckoned on. I'll bet we've seen the last of them for today." Tenney scowled at the fallen guerrillas. "Guess we shouldn't leave them for the hogs. Who'll volunteer for burial detail?"

"Davie and I will," Dan said. "Shall we rig a litter for the wounded one?"

Tenney rode over to stare at the Rebel. "Gut-shot. No use jouncing him along."

"Be a mercy to shoot him in the head," Shepherd muttered.

Davie looked up. His face was tear-streaked. "I've told him I'll stay with him."

Tenney considered. He must have sensed that no order would make Davie budge. "All right, then, Parks, O'Brien. Catch up as soon as you can."

It was only then that Dan saw blood trickling from a wound in Raven's shoulder. The dead Rebels wouldn't need their shirts; he'd use some of their clothing to make a dressing and bandage. On his way to the bodies, he paused beside the man in the gray coat. From the intricate knots of tarnished gold braid above the cuffs and the gold star on each lapel, Dan knew he must have once been a major in the regular Army, or had stolen the coat from one.

Davie cradled the golden head, speaking so softly that Dan caught only a few words. " 'Yea, though I walk through the valley of the shadow of death, I will fear no evil . . . for thou art with me. . . .' "

That face! For a horrible moment, Dan went dizzy as Richie's six-year-old features masked the dying Rebel's. He remembered Hildy's saying Richie had an older brother in school, in Boston, when the war broke out.

"Frazer?"

Blue eyes opened. "How'd you . . . know . . . ?"

"If you have a little brother named Richie, he's safe with good people who love him."

Sweat dewed Frazer's pallid forehead. "Thanks, Yank," he panted. He tried to lift a bloody hand, but it dropped again, exposing the top of a gold signet ring. "Give Richie . . . love and . . . ring. . . ."

"We'll take care of him," Dan promised.

He hurried to strip shirts from the nearest dead men and ran back to Raven. Fixing a pad in place with the sleeves and strips of torn shirt tied together to make a bandage, he was making a final knot when the *crack* of a shot was followed by a cry.

He whirled to see Davie collapse over Frazer, the ring glinting as it slipped from his grasp. A colored man dragged himself out of the trees, leaving a trail of blood, dropping a musket in order to crawl more swiftly to the bodies.

"Robbin' the wounded!" he snarled at Davie, and shoved his limp form off Frazer's. "Oh, Lordy, Master Edmund! What they done to you?"

Dan had his revolver cocked, but, when he understood the servant's mistake, he couldn't kill him. There wasn't any need. Pink foam bubbled from the Negro's mouth. He huddled against Frazer's side and didn't speak again.

Dan dropped beside Davie, frantically seeking a faint breath, the dimmest heartbeat. There was none. A bullet had crashed through the back of the head to burst out the left temple. It must have plowed crossways right through Davie's brain.

And Frazer was still alive. Again his face changed, narrowed, developed a cleft in the chin. Gold hair paled to silver, blue eyes faded to mocking crystal.

Dan's cheek throbbed, stung as if gunpowder was again being ground into his raw flesh. He leveled the Colt. Then it was once more Frazer who watched him. Dan shuddered and thrust the revolver into its holster as he took Davie's place, pillowing Frazer's head, holding one gory hand. Frazer had fumbled the other so that it rested on his servant's head.

Through the tightness in his throat, Dan said: "Since Davie can't, friend, I'll stay with you."

Frazer's eyes thanked him. The light was fading from their blue depths when two Rebels came out of the brush and blazed away at Dan.

Dan roused to the *creak* and jolting of a wagon. His leg hurt like fury, his head, bandaged, felt as if it would split, his upper right arm ached, and the forearm was bent and bandaged to his chest. Beside him, blood had soaked through the blanket wrapped around what must be the mortal remnant of Davie.

Two black ears caught the edge of Dan's vision. He looked higher and sighed with relief. Good old Raven, following along, not limping much.

"You back with us?" Harry Shepherd leaned from the driver's place on the board seat. "When we heard a shot, we headed back. Then we heard more shots. Got there just as a bushwhacker was fixing to blow off your head at close range."

"We borrowed the wagon at a farm," explained Thos. "Captain Tenney detailed us and half the escort to get you to camp and send you on to the Nashville hospital on the next train. Your skull's so thick the bullet bounced off the side of it, and the bullet went clear through your arm, so the surgeon won't be probing around with his filthy hands to get the bullet out. Your leg bones are all busted up, though. Damned Miniés. . . ."

Fear twisted Dan's guts worse than he had felt at sight of the bushwhackers aiming at him before he could reach his Colt. He remembered the heaps of arms and legs he'd seen outside field hospitals, and broke out in cold sweat.

"I'm not going to let some damn' sawbones take off my leg!"

After a moment's silence, Thos leaned around to place a hand on Dan's shoulder. "They'll use chloroform. And Mother'll take care of you."

It wasn't the pain of amputation Dan shrank from, but afterward. He might have gotten along without an arm, but how could he plow and work cumbered by a crutch or wooden leg? He'd be a burden to Christy, not a help.

"Listen, boys," he said. "Leave a revolver under my mattress or pallet or whatever they lay me on."

Thos swung around. "Dan! You won't . . . ?"

"Oh, I won't kill myself." He forced a grin. "Just want something to fight off the surgeon, if he tries to chop me up in spite of what I say."

"All right," conceded Thos. "I'll leave you

my Colt and use yours when I get back to camp."

"The things some fellows pull to get out of burial duty!" Shepherd said. "The other boys must still be digging graves for those six Rebs and the colored man." The joshing was meant to cheer him up, Dan knew, but he couldn't summon a chuckle. He hurt too much, and although he still couldn't believe Davie was dead, he knew he was.

If it would bring Davie back, Dan would let them take both legs. But it wouldn't. Nothing could. Uncle Simeon must mourn his youngest son, fruit of his mother's early death. Lydia, Susie, and Owen would weep for the brother they'd helped to raise. And Davie, so fresh and young and beautiful, would never exult in a girl's love, never have a child.

"Since Lydia's nursing in the city," said Thos, "we thought she'd want to get her brother ready to be buried and have the service there, where the grave will always be looked after."

"Yes," Dan managed. "That'll help the family . . . to know Lydia took care of him. . . ."

"There was a signet ring on the ground by the blond Reb," went on Shepherd. "We thought maybe it was something he'd asked you to send his folks, so we put it in your haversack."

Dan wasn't sure if he said — "Good." — or

only tried to before he lapsed into a stupor.

He roused at his own moaning when they lifted him out of the wagon, and again when he was carried to the train on a litter that Thos and Shepherd held by the ends that rested on feed sacks.

"Raven?" he muttered.

"We'll see to him," Shepherd promised. "The rest of our crew'll baby him till Thos and I get back."

The suspended litter swayed and jolted with the train's motion in spite of his friends' steadying hands, but it was a lot more comfortable than the wagon. When Dan next became fully aware, his nostrils tingled at a pungent odor. Someone was working on his wounded arm. Other gentle hands were busy at his leg. He gazed into the kind dark eyes and sweet face of Ellen Ware. She wore a brown dress over brown bloomers of the kind that had startled the neighbors of the Wattleses.

"You . . . you sure look better than any angel, Missus . . . I mean, Ellen." He couldn't keep the hot sting at the back of his eyelids from changing into tears, he was so happy to see her.

"I'm glad I'm here. I've always prayed that none of my boys be wounded, but if they were, that I could be with them."

Her boys? She truly ranked him with Thos and Charlie? Christy was his love, but she was not his mother, lost these many years. His heart expanded at Ellen's tenderness. Then, for the first time, he noticed something was gone.

His scar didn't burn! Not the slightest bit. There had been that moment when Edmund Frazer had turned into Lafe, one moment of furious searing, and then Lafe's mark had tormented him no more. Warily he raised his good arm and ran his fingers over the wealed edges. It was just dead tissue. A scar that was finally healed. He then reached under the thin mattress. Thos hadn't failed him. The Colt was there.

Reassured, he glanced around and saw he had the corner bed in a long room with an aisle running between two rows of cots, ten on each side. The bandaged legs of several men were elevated by pulley affairs. The man next to Dan had a cloth-swathed stump of an arm. Beyond him, a gray-haired nurse changed dressings on one poor soul who had lost both legs at the thigh.

"Danny!" Lydia Parks moved into his range of vision. She bent and kissed him. "I . . . I'm glad you were with David. The shot must have killed him instantly, didn't it?"

"Yes." At least there was that comfort. Any Quaker would be proud of the way Davie had died. Summoning all his strength, Dan told her about the dying Rebel. "The strangest thing of all is that he was little Richie's brother. I've got his ring. Maybe you'd send it to Christy when you write." He glanced ruefully at his wounded arm.

"I'll write for you," Ellen promised.

"Thos brought David's books and things," said Lydia. "I'll send those home, too." Grief contorted her thin face. "Poor Father! He loves us all, but David was the apple of his eye." She turned away, shoulders heaving.

Ellen slipped an arm around her. "It'll help your father and family to know that you got David ready for burial. He'll have a marker. His grave will be tended, not like so many lonely ones grown over with weeds."

"I know." Lydia wiped her eyes. "And I'm thankful my brother died helping a man, rather than in the act of killing." With obvious effort, she composed herself and took Dan's hand. "Surgeon Townsend is extremely skillful, dear. We're not getting new battle victims now, so he's not rushed and can take every precaution. . . ."

"Not with me!" At the women's shocked faces, Dan spoke more calmly. "If I were a teacher or merchant or something where I could earn my family's living with one leg, I guess I'd let the surgeon take the other one." He clamped his teeth till he had control of his voice. "All I know is farming. I'll go home able to take care of Christy or I won't go home at all."

"Dan," entreated Lydia, "Christy wouldn't want that! She'd feel like Colonel Montgomery's wife, who told Susie, if they shot off both her husband's arms and legs, she still wanted him home so she could take care of him."

"I doubt he'd want it!" Dan retorted. "Anyhow, they've been married a long time and have children old enough to do the farm work. If I die of this leg, Christy'll find a good man after a while."

"I doubt she will," said Ellen of her daughter.

"At least," said Dan grimly, "I won't be in her way."

The surgeon came in, a robust graying man in a once-white linen duster. Two soldiers followed him with a litter. "Awake, are we, Corporal?" he boomed. His light brown eyes swept Dan from head to foot. "The arm, nurse?" he asked Ellen.

"The ball passed through, Doctor Townsend. I cleaned the wound and dressed it with lint soaked in turpentine."

"That should do finely." The surgeon drew back the sheet and examined Dan's leg. "Sorry, my boy. We'll have to take it off." He motioned to the stretcher-bearers.

"No," said Dan.

Townsend gave an impatient sigh. "Corporal, the middle third of your left tibia and fibula are fractured and extensively comminuted. Gangrene or pyæmia is almost certain."

"I'll take that chance, sir."

The surgeon chewed his lip. "If you're set on trying to save the leg, I might perform a linear incision along the inner anterior aspect, excise perhaps three inches of fractured bone. . . ."

Dan looked at Townsend's hands, blood and other things crusted beneath the fingernails. "I'm obliged, sir, but no."

"You'll die."

"Then at least I'll go to heaven or hell with both legs."

Townsend turned to the bearers. "Come, lads, take him up gently."

Dan produced the revolver and cocked the hammer. "I'll shoot whoever lays a hand on me."

The bearers froze.

"You damned young fool!" growled the surgeon. "Give me that pistol!"

Dan kept it leveled.

"Keep it and die then!" Townsend dismissed the bearers and glared at Dan. "I should let you lie there and suffer till you get some sense, but I'll let you have opium balls. Nurse, see to it." He stomped on through the ward, attending to other patients.

"Dan," ventured Lydia as he slipped the revolver under the mattress. "You and Christy can live at the mill. There'd be things you could do. . . ."

The leg hurt so much, Dan almost wished it was off. He gritted his teeth. "I'm not going to be a burden, Lydy. Now, you two go look after the other men that need it." He patted her hand. "I'm lucky to have you both here."

"I'll bring your opium and some coffee and soup," Ellen said, and smoothed back his hair.

Dan kept watch on the surgeon and braced himself for another argument when Townsend doubled back toward him, instead of leaving the room.

"You do understand, Corporal," Townsend said, "that your behavior is going to get you reduced to private?"

"That's the least of my worries, sir."

"Even for an Irishman, you've got a thick head."

Dan grinned. "Maybe that's why the bullet just grazed me."

Townsend shrugged. "I've been wanting to try the water cure on a serious wound," he said gruffly. "Will you consent to the treatment?"

"What is it?"

"Suspicious?" There was actually a twinkle in Townsend's eye. "It's simple. Clean lint covers the wound and clean cold water is poured on it three or four times a day. The wound is covered with cloth to keep the water from evaporating and air from getting in. Both North and South have had good results with the treatment. I've used it, but never on a wound like yours." He added disgustedly: "The other patients all had better sense."

"How many of them died?"

The surgeon's ruddy skin went even redder. "About half," he admitted. "It's more for this treatment . . . about sixty percent . . . with excisions of both tibia and fibula."

"Well then, sir, I can't see that I'm being too foolish. If I let you try the cold water, will you promise not to sneak off my leg?"

Townsend sighed. "I promise. But if you change your mind. . . ."

"I won't."

As Townsend explained the treatment in greater detail, Ellen returned with a tray and a pill. Townsend instructed Ellen that Dan could have opium as needed, and gave Dan half a smile, saying: "Good luck, Private O'Brien. I advise you to give that pistol back to the friend who left it with you, before he gets in trouble."

"Thank you, sir," said Dan.

Lydia had written a letter to this patient's mother. She looked up and saw in the dim lamplight of the hospital tent that his lips were trembling. That was how David had looked as a child when he was trying not to cry. But this lad's bowels protruded.

"Ma'am . . . ma'am! I'm scared. . . ." She knelt beside him, gathering his head against her, murmuring that he would soon see those he loved, it would be joyful with no pain or grief forever.

When his last breath escaped, she kissed him, drew the sheet over the face that had the faintest down, and went to the next bed.

"Water," moaned an older man. "Please, give me a drink of water."

She did, and bathed his wounded thigh. On to the curly-headed youngster whose jaw was shot away. All night and day she worked, all the next night till the head nurse commanded her to sleep. As she huddled in a blanket under a wagon, she gave thanks she was able to help, that she, Lydia Parks of the neat quilt corners, could now sew up wounds with her tiny stitches.

In proud humility, she gave thanks, too, that she, plain, raw-boned, an old maid, could be the most important person in the world to the men whose life or comfort depended on her, or when she held them as they crossed over.

If only she could have held her younger brother.

CHAPTER THIRTY-EIGHT

Charlie Ware couldn't believe the change in General Price since he'd ridden up and down the line of his troops at Pea Ridge, encouraging them although he was wounded. Nor did the general, who'd allowed a captured Union officer to be hanged and his men shot at Pilot Knob, resemble the chivalrous victor of Lexington who'd let the defeated commander and his wife ride in Price's carriage.

At six feet two, Price had always been a giant. Now he was a flabby one. He led this expedition into his beloved Missouri in an ambulance drawn by four white mules. Not even his splendid white horse, Bucephalus, could carry his three hundred pounds for long, although the general heaved himself into the saddle near Jefferson City to exhort his troops.

At the sight of the United States flag, flying from the Capitol, Charlie's heart constricted. He could never hate it as the flag of the enemy. It was still his flag, just as Thos was still his brother and Dan his friend. In the end, at Jefferson City, Price decided against attacking the seven thousand troops manning five outlying, palisaded forts linked by connecting rifle pits. The ramshackle horde meandered on along the Missouri River, winning small victories and accumulating more rag-tag followers.

Price's Army, Charlie brooded, was as unwieldy as its general. Twelve thousand cavalrymen divided into three divisions headed by Shelby, Marmaduke, and Fagan, seemed an impressive force. After all, hadn't Jo Shelby led his Iron Brigade clear up to Boonville a year ago on a forty-one day raid, burning bridges, wrecking railroads and Union depots?

In spite of his devotion to old Pap Price, Charlie couldn't help but wish Shelby was commanding this Army. Four thousand had no weapons, one thousand had no horses, and all fourteen cannon were small caliber. Worse yet, the Army spread out for five to six miles, cumbered by five hundred creaky old wagons loaded with plunder, and hundreds of cattle, not all of them taken from Unionists. There were orders against looting, but the Army had to live off the country and it was hard to draw a line between necessity and pillage.

This autumn of 1864 had seemed a good time to enter Missouri what with most Union troops sent to the savage fighting in Virginia, Alabama, Tennessee, and Georgia. After several summer battles, Union forces had retreated to Little Rock, where they were said to be on half rations and unlikely to hinder Price. General Kirby Smith, Confederate commander of the Trans-Mississippi Department, had been ordered to send all the infantry in Arkansas and Louisiana across the Mississippi to do something to divert some Union troops from the ferocious struggles in the East.

What could be better than a strike into Missouri? The Union high command didn't care about the rest of Missouri, but whoever held St. Louis controlled the vital traffic above it on the Mississippi and Missouri Rivers.

Price had crossed into Missouri on September 19th, bound for St. Louis with high hopes of gaining most, if not all of Missouri, and recruiting soldiers for the desperate Confederacy. Charlie's highest hope had been that he and Travis Jardine could see Travis's older sister, Yvonne, in St. Louis and get news of Melissa and all of the Jardines. That was one of the worst things about this war — not being able to get letters back and forth — worse than fighting, maggoty food, worn-out shoes, even the trots.

Three years since he'd seen Melissa or his family! To Charlie's bitter disappointment, Price learned that four thousand five hundred infantry, veterans of Vicksburg bound down the Mississippi for Georgia, had been put off their boats to help defend St. Louis. Over three thousand more men were camped below the city, and regiments from Illinois were on the way. Price had lost one thousand five hundred men in brutal fighting at Pilot Knob, eighty-six miles south of the city. Rather than attack St. Louis, he decided to proceed northeast to take Jefferson City, the capital.

There, once again, Price feared to attack. He easily took Boonville where the Army was welcomed by the mostly pro-Southern citizens on October 11th. And there. . . .

"I still can't believe it," Charlie muttered to Travis as they halted for their noonday meal near a handsome two-story farmhouse surrounded by broad fields. "How could General Price have anything to do with guerrillas who ride in with human scalps tied to their bridles?"

"Pap's got to take whatever help he can get." Travis shrugged. "Anyhow, he wouldn't talk to Bloody Bill Anderson till he and his men got rid of the scalps, and then he just ordered him to blow up bridges on the North Missouri Railroad. Anderson's bunch wiped out one hundred and fifty Federals at Centralia a couple of weeks ago. Maybe that's where the scalps came from."

Charlie shivered. "I don't know, Trav. That

hair on Bloody Bill's bridle looked like women's hair to me." He changed the subject. "All we've done on this jaunter is wreck the country we pass through. I don't suppose we'll even try to tackle Kansas City or Leavenworth."

"We traveled too slow. General Curtis, who whupped us at Pea Ridge, is in front of us with his Army of the Border." Trav, for once, looked sober. "General Pleasanton's on our rear . . . he was the Federal cavalry commander at Gettysburg, remember. Nine thousand of those Vicksburg veterans are marching toward our left. About all Pap can do is retreat south through Kansas." His brown eyes glinted with irrepressible high spirits. "I hope we get a chance at the Red Legs or that damned Doc Jennison!"

Charlie swallowed the last of his water-soaked hardtack and jumped to his feet. "Look! Sergeant Matthias is firing the house!"

"Must have found out it belongs to a Union man."

"I'm going to make sure there's no one in the house, hiding." Charlie broke into a run. He still remembered a charred body he'd found dragged about by hogs near a fired cabin. The man had not quite been dead.

Matthias lit a torch in the fireplace, held it under a stool and bench. One of his squad yanked towels and all manner of ironed linen goods from shelves in a cupboard, shook them out, and tossed them and an embroidered tablecloth over the benches.

"That'll do." Matthias lit another torch. "Get yourself some fire, men. Bedrooms are fun."

Charlie pelted up the stairs ahead of them, ran through the four bedrooms, peering under beds, yanking open chests and wardrobes. In the last room he entered, Matthias pulled back a counterpane, heaped pillows in the middle of the great carved bed, stuck the torch among the pillows, and pulled up the coverlet. Charlie raced back to the first room he'd searched, the one that looked like a girl's, all pink and white. Maybe not too old of a girl. An elegant doll smiled from the ruffled pillows on the canopied bed. A white robe and nightgown hung from pegs behind the door. Charlie leaned out the window and threw the doll as far as he could into some bushes.

"Yank down the drapes and pile 'em on!" called Matthias, dragging a featherbed out of a chest in the next room. "Damn' Union trash won't put this fire out."

Where were they? Charlie thought. *Somewhere close. The cornbread on the table was still warm. Likely hiding out in the trees. Could they see their house burn?*

"No silver and such," grunted Matthias. He had run down the steps in front of Charlie and was ransacking a china cabinet while smoke and flame furled from the kitchen. "Bet they buried it some place. Get out of here, boys! Look around for sign of fresh digging."

Beyond a half dozen slave cabins, each with its garden patch, was a fenced graveyard. Most of the sunken mounds were grown over, but at the far end was a raw red mound with a little wooden cross.

"Bet their silver and jewelry and all's hid there!" yelled the sergeant. He grabbed a pitchfork from beside a shed, thrust it down. There was a dull *thunk*. "Didn't bury it very deep!" he crowed. Moving the fork to one side, he sunk the tines, tossed away clods, dug deeply again. This time he brought up the edge of a box. A colored woman burst out of the cornfield.

"Cap'n, for Lord's sake, leave my baby be!"

"Baby!" Matthias snorted. He set the box on the ground, held it with his foot, and worked a tine under the lid, prying up one edge, then another, shaking off the woman who clung, weeping, to his arm. Forcing the lid back, he grasped the edge of a piece of cloth. It matched the dress the doll wore, the doll Charlie had thrown into the bushes. Something dropped from the swaddling. The woman caught the infant.

Before he turned away, retching at the smell, Charlie glimpsed a small face underground things had been at, and a mass of springy black curls.

"Maybe there's stuff underneath," persisted Matthias. He started to use the pitchfork again, but Charlie caught his arm.

"There's the bugle! Come on, Sarge. There's nothing here but dead folks."

But he hoped the girl was alive, and her family, and that she'd find her doll.

CHAPTER THIRTY-NINE

On that late October morning, the clouds in the east looked like white paving stones crumbling at the edges. A rich harvest had come from the seed corn rescued last fall from Lafe Ballard's gang. Christy gave thanks as she hefted sacks of grain into the wagon. There was so much corn that, rather than take over a few bags at a time on Lass, Christy had decided to take the team to the mill.

With the aching question of whether Charlie and Travis were still with Price, she'd heard about that general's rampage across Missouri from the Parkses and young Will Hawkins, who had recovered and visited whenever his captain would let him. Will scarcely limped on the leg Sarah had set, and he was glad to chop wood or do other chores, if he was asked to dinner. Sarah, with mischief in her eyes, always gave him honey.

Anyway, Price was now fighting his way west along the Missouri. How strange and terrible it was to wonder if her brother and Travis might come as invaders through their homeland! Of course, either or both might have died of wounds or sickness any time these past three years. Christy breathed a prayer for them and tried not to think of their appearing on the border as enemies. If Price came this way, it would be well to have the corn ground and most of it stored in the valley.

Sarah came from the cabin with a crock of honeycomb tucked against her with her good arm. The other had a sprained wrist, which was why she was minding little Jon, instead of going to the mill. Jon clambered down the step and lurched along beside her, grasping her skirt to steady nine-month-old legs. He hadn't seen the wagon before; it had been hidden in the woods ever since Christy had driven it home from Sedalia.

He tried to bite the spokes, and would have toddled under Lad's hoofs if Christy hadn't grabbed him. She sat down on a stump and opened the bodice of her blue dress, the one made of Dan's gingham, her only unpatched garment although faded from many washings. Jon could eat mush and mashed fruit and vegetables, but he still loved his mother's milk. He set his summer-browned fists against her breast and his cheek dimpled as he suckled blissfully.

Watching him, Sarah laughed. "Reminds

me of what Will Hawkins said about that hard-drinking sergeant of his . . . 'If he was as fond of his mother's milk as he is of tangle-foot, he must of been almighty hard to wean.' "

Christy laughed and promised: "I'll leave the corn, wagon, and Lad, and come straight home on Lass. I'll go back for the meal when Mister Parks has it ground. Or if he has meal on hand, I'll swap for it."

"Don't rush. Have a visit with Susie and Harriet." Sarah lodged the crock securely among the sacks. "Jonny likes applesauce, and there's maple syrup for his mush. He won't starve."

"Yes, but. . . ."

"You haven't been out of shouting distance of him since he was born." Sarah's sniff was almost unnoticeable, but it was a sniff. "A change'll do you both good."

Christy didn't argue as she kissed her son's red-brown curls and gave him to Sarah who scooped him up with her sound arm. How could Christy not love him with all her heart when he was so like the men she loved best in the world, Dan and her father, and yet was so much his own new self?

Blue Boy begged to go with her. At her gesture, he jumped into the wagon, nimble in spite of the withered paw that had healed but was almost useless. In spite of that, he lorded it over the remaining hounds. As Christy drove off, she ached that her father would never know his namesake and that her mother and Dan were missing his babyhood. Still, what she'd told Dan was true. Jon adored Noelle, only two years older, and both had Beth, Mary, and Richie for idols and playmates. He had love, training, wisdom, and laughter from Hester, Star, Lilah, and Sarah. But, oh, if only his father were home!

His last letter had been dated mid-August. His leg was still draining and the surgeon wanted to keep him in the hospital, but he was determined to start home on Raven. I could travel faster by train and boat, sweetheart, but then I'd have to get home from Leavenworth or Sedalia or Rolla. Besides, the bullet Raven took from that bushwhacker ruined him for a battery horse. He was turned out to live or die, but Thos and Harry looked after him. So Raven and I will come home together. Don't you fear! After all this, nothing's going to keep me from seeing you and our boy.

The letter before that had told about Davie Parks and, enclosed, had been the signet ring from Richie's brother. After the war, they'd have to find out if the relative in Tahlequah was still alive, in spite of all the raids and fighting in the region. On the same day Price had invaded Missouri, Stand Watie and a Texas brigade had captured a Union train of three hundred wagons bound from Fort Scott to Fort Gibson with food, clothing, medicine, guns, and ammunition for the soldiers and refugee Indians. Those supplies and the seven hundred forty mules were a windfall to the Confederates who hustled them to the southern part of Indian Territory — where Confederate Indian refugees huddled as miserably as Union ones did at Gibson or southern Kansas.

Indian Territory couldn't be in much better shape than the wasteland of western Missouri. The Burnt District, they called it since Order Number 11, had finished the work of Border Ruffians, jayhawkers, Union troops, and guerrillas. Soldiers on both sides would come home to find cabins, barns, and fences burned, livestock stolen, families scattered. How many would or could start over here?

As she neared the mill, she saw plumes of smoke to the north that looked like fires along the Military Road, not just smoke from chimneys. Alarmed, she clucked to the horses. She could see the mill now. The buildings looked as usual, but Zephyr and Breeze weren't in their pasture, no chickens pecked in the barnyard, and there were no pigs in the pen. Surprisingly the cows grazed peacefully along the slope.

Now she could see that many horsemen had been here since it rained three days ago. Hoofs had chewed up the turf. Feathers from luckless chickens fluttered in the brush near ashes of several cook fires. Crows pecked at the heads of Simeon's prized Yorkshires. Flies swarmed on their hides and hoofs.

The sights and smells called up memories of the slaughter of animals at the Ware farm and Rose Haven. Fighting nausea, Christy drove the wagon into the barn. Price's Army, or some of it, must have passed through. They seemed to be gone, but stragglers would be glad of good horses. Anyway, if Union troops were in pursuit, they might need fresh horses, but Christy was not of a mind to supply them.

Susie answered her knock, four year-old Andy peeking from behind at her right while his cousin of the same age, Danny, peered from the left. Harriet clutched a poker. Nine-year-old Letty gripped a club-like limb, doubtless snatched from the kindling box.

"Christy!" Susie drew her in. "If you rode Lass, it's a mercy you didn't come while Price's men were here! They'd have stolen her like they did Breeze."

"Did they hurt anyone?"

"Not really, though Missus Morrison worked herself into hysterics and is in bed with one of those headaches that last for days. Papa and Catriona were in bed with ague, and Owen had ridden Zephyr to join the militia at Sugar Mound. He came home after the battle to tell us he was all right. . . ."

Christy's heart squeezed tight in her chest. *Charlie? Travis?* "There . . . there was a battle?"

Letty rested the poker on the floor. Her blue eyes were big. "We heard the cannons while we were having breakfast. The dishes rattled on the table!"

"Our men caught up with the Rebels by Mine Creek day before yesterday," Susie said, her eyes lit with un-Quaker like pride. "They outnumbered our men three to one and had cannon, but Pleasanton's cavalry charged so hard, the Confederates broke after a mêlée."

"Our boys trounced them so thoroughly, Price had to forget about taking Fort Scott," put in Harriet. "He was whipped at Westport on the Twenty-Third, and skedaddled this way. Folks say there must have been twenty-five thousand Rebels scattered all over the prairies the night of the Twenty-Fourth. Of course, most were just rabble . . . hungry, ragged, stealing everything they could eat, wear, or carry off."

Christy shut her eyes. Bad enough to think of Charlie as one of a regular Army; far worse to imagine him acting like a bushwhacker or the Union soldiers who'd carried out Order Number 11. She really would rather see him dead!

"They dug our potatoes and turnips," Susie enumerated, "roasted the chickens and pigs, and ran the mill all night, grinding our wheat and corn and all the grain people had left with us." Wrathful spots burned in Susie's cheeks. "Over a thousand pounds they carried off in our wagon, hitched to Breeze, but that wasn't enough! They came in the house and would have shaken the last flour out of the barrel, except their captain made them give us about five pounds, and he made them leave half a ham when they raided the smoke-house."

"I'd just churned and made six blocks of butter," Harriet said, glancing at the scrubbed, empty wooden frame. "I couldn't keep from crying when they took it, so they gave me back one block."

"It's a marvel they didn't take the cows or eat them," puzzled Christy.

"Oh, they had lots of beef on the hoof and hundreds of wagons," said Harriet. "Over at Trading Post, they butchered three hundred head, but, when they heard General Curtis was on their heels, they left the carcasses and cleared out . . . not before they burned the store and looted, though. They stole everything the Nickelses had, but Doc Jennison caught one thief and hung him in the Nickelses' barn."

"An officer tucked a bag of grain under a baby's pillow and soldiers let it be," added Susie. "The captain who was here said he was sorry to take our flour and food, but he knew supplies would be sent to us in a week or so while he and his men had a long way to go."

"Owen went back to help bury the dead

from both sides," Harriet explained. "One hundred and fifty Union soldiers are being buried at Mound City. The Rebels will be buried on the battlefield or wherever they fell in the retreat, way over three hundred of them. More were wounded, nine hundred taken prisoner, and Price lost eight cannons and lots of supplies. General Marmaduke surrendered to a young private. If it weren't for Jo Shelby's brigade, Owen says the Rebels would have had it a lot worse. Shelby guarded the fords while the others came across."

"Yes" — Susie nodded — "and those wagons that slowed down their army the whole month of the foray and got stuck at Mine Creek so the men couldn't get across before our cavalry came up . . . well, Price ordered most of those wagons burned as soon as what was left of his men crossed the Marmaton. Except for Shelby's brigade, it's not an Army now, just a mob." Susie paused. Regret deepened her voice. "Price may get some new recruits back to Arkansas, but they're not armed or trained. All he really did in the state he loves so well is lay waste to the countryside for sixty miles along his line of march, and stain his reputation by accepting help from the likes of Bloody Bill Anderson, Quantrill, and George Todd."

Bloody Bill? Christy remembered the scalps on Bill Anderson's bridle, the knotted silk cord. It had to be the same person; yet, to her, he would always be the handsome, blue-eyed, young man whose voice softened when he spoke of his sister Josie. Josie, crushed with three other girls in the collapsed jail in Kansas City. It seemed to Christy that, at least along this border, there was more wrong than right on both sides.

"The meeting house in Mound City was turned into a hospital," Harriet added. "The Wattles women, Amanda Way, and a lot of other women nursed both Rebels and our men. I went over and helped yesterday till ambulances came to take the wounded back to Leavenworth."

"You . . . you didn't see my brother Charlie or Travis Jardine?"

Susie's face stiffened. "Oh, Christy!" She put her arms around her. "Oh, my dear, we weren't thinking. . . . No, I didn't see either Charlie or Travis."

No one said what they were all thinking: that the two could be among the hundreds of Confederate dead shoveled into mass graves along Sugar Creek.

Harriet shook her head. "We're sorry, honey. How dreadful for you to have brothers on both sides."

Christy straightened. "That's happened in a lot of families. It's worse for Mother. We just have to pray they come home safe and can be brothers again." She swallowed hard. "Is there any way I can help you here?"

"Thank you, but we're managing." Susie's smile was faint, but she did smile, and tousled Andy's bright hair. "After all, the Rebels cleaned our cupboards out for us and there's no grain to grind."

"There's my wagonload of corn. You can have all you need."

"I'm sure Papa will appreciate that. We'll pay you back when we can. Harriet, let's help Christy unload."

"I'll drive over to the mill," Christy said.

When the bags were stored inside and Christy was leaving, Susie pressed her hand. "I'll ask Owen about Charlie and Travis," she promised. "If we hear anything, we'll let you know. Owen is sure he can put together a wagon from wrecked ones left on the battle-field. After he gets your corn ground, we'll use the oxen to bring your meal over." She sighed. "Poor Breeze! I hope he breaks away and comes home. Zephyr won't know what to do without him. They've been together since they were colts."

"Don't get your hopes up," Harriet advised. "You know Owen said there were hundreds of wounded horses lying on the field or gal-loping around it in panic. They trampled scores of the dead and wounded."

"Dear God! I wish animals didn't get slaughtered in our wars!" Christy said, think-ing of Jed and Queenie stolen so long ago, and knowing their chances of being alive now were slim. She blinked back tears to think of the dark-faced ewes, and Patches and Evalina, the Poland Chinas who had suckled their piglets with such pleasure. She also remembered Raven, wounded and turned out to die. "I hope Mister Parks and the ladies get well quickly," she told her friends. "Tell Owen there's no hurry with the corn."

Susie hugged the crock of honey. "At least this should finish the war in Missouri and the border. General Curtis and General Blunt are chasing Price. They won't stop till they run him into Southern Arkansas. He won't be back . . . and neither will anyone else." She called after the creaking wagon: "When Dan comes home, let us know right away!"

"I will!" Christy shouted back, and drove past the scattered remains of the pigs without looking.

She intended to drive the team to the woods near the Ware home, unhitch and unharness them there, and leave the wagon, but Sarah ran to meet her at the edge of the clearing.

"Christy! Christy! Dan's home!"

CHAPTER FORTY

Sarah climbed into the wagon and took the reins. "Go on in! I'll hide the team and wagon. Dan's fevered and his leg's ugly. We'd better get him to Star and Hester."

Christy flew into the rear cabin. Dan lay on her bed — their bed. Sarah had cut away his pant leg. Corruption oozed from the inflamed puckered wound. Dark lashes lay against bones that drew the skin taut above cheeks that showed hollows even under a short curly red beard. A cup, bowl, and basin with a towel were on a stool. Jon sat on the rug, examining his father's battered forage hat.

Sinking on her knees, Christy kissed Dan's cracked, dry lips. "Danny! You're home!"

His eyes opened, those eyes he'd given Jon. "Home to stay, darlin'." She could tell the words and smile took effort. He raised a hand to her cheek. "Sorry Raven and me look so rough, but, now we can quit traveling, we'll soon be worth our feed."

"You are anyway!" She hugged him the best

she could. The stench of the leg came through his odor of smoke, sweat, and grime. "Oh Dan! I've prayed and dreamed and hoped . . . I can't believe you're here!"

"Neither can I, sweetheart." His fingers tangled in her hair. "And to finally clap eyes on our boy! He didn't know what to make of me at first, but he quit crying when I let him have my hat."

"He doesn't see many strang. . . ." Christy broke off.

"Well, I am a stranger." Dan chuckled. "We've got all the time in the world for him to get to know me. If I'd been fussed over by so many womenfolk, especially my mama, I don't think I'd much like a big old geezer moving in."

Sarah came in with the teapot, poured him another cup of the honey-sweetened willow tea, and held it to Dan's mouth while Christy raised him. "I think you're better already, Corporal," Sarah told him.

"Seeing Christy's better than any medicine, but I'm just a plain old private again." He held up his arm. His eyes danced with some of their old zest. "See where I lost my bars for telling the surgeon he couldn't saw off my leg? Howsomever, ladies, as of June Twentieth, Congress voted us a magnificent raise of three dollars a month for a grand total of sixteen!"

"You're still in the Army?" Christy couldn't

keep fear out of her voice.

"Not for long," he assured her. "Surgeon Townsend wrote the surgeon at Leavenworth. When I can ride, I'll report there to be mustered out. No hurry. I cut Price's trail on the way here. Just as soon wait till he's long gone."

"He is . . . or will be as fast as he can." Christy told of the havoc inflicted by the retreating Rebels, and their crushing at Mine Creek. "There could be stragglers. As soon as you've rested a little, Dan, we'd better get you and the horses to the valley. Star and Hester can do more for your leg, and for Raven, too, than we can."

Dan sighed. "I'd like to sleep a month, wake up all better, and then. . . ." He grinned wickedly at Christy.

She blushed. Warmth stirred within her, almost like a quickening child. Dan's wound and emaciation filled her with protectiveness, but now his gaze made her aware of him as a man, as her lover. That was like the promise of a feast after years of starvation.

Sarah watched them with amused sympathy and a touch of wistfulness. "You've kept your mush and tea down all right," she said. "How about a bowl of Tom-fuller? While you eat, I'll put a slippery elm poultice on that leg."

"And I'll feed the baby." For Jon had dropped his father's cap to pull at Christy's arm — her breasts were full.

She started to go in the next room.

"Please give our laddie his dinner here," Dan said.

So, feeling oddly shy, she opened her dress and cradled Jonny. She loved the feeling of her milk flowing into him, a link between their bodies, although she no longer carried him under her heart.

"Greedy little cuss!" At Christy's affronted look, Dan gave a tender laugh. "Oh Christy, darlin'! The two of you are the fairest sight to ever bless my eyes! Wait'll I get my hands on my fiddle. I'll make you both a song." His eyes darkened. "I've a song for Davie in my head and must work that out, too."

"The Parkses will like that," Christy said, and thought: *I hope your mother met you, Davie, and you're happy now wherever you are.*

Sarah used a clean, ragged towel to fasten the mass of dampened elm bark over the wound. "Can you keep low against one of the horse's necks so you can ride through the passage?" she asked. "Skinny as you are, you'd be quite a load for Christy and me to manage."

"I'll ride low," Dan said. "I've done it often enough when we hauled our gun into position. I hate to ride Raven. The poor fellow's tired. But if I'm not on him, he might panic in the cavern."

"You ride him. I'll bring Lass, and Christy can carry the baby. One of us can come back for Lad. We'd better plan to hole up for a while."

"I know one guerrilla who won't come through again," Dan said. "Wasn't it Bill Anderson you took care of when he was shot?"

Christy nodded. A wave of dread swept through her.

"Some Union troops caught up with his bunch," said Dan. "Anderson was killed and. . . ." Seeing Christy's face, he broke off. "You had a kindness for him."

"He probably kept us from being burned out. And . . . he told me about his sisters." Dan didn't speak. "What happened to Bill?" she pressed.

"The soldiers cut off his head and stuck it up on a telegraph pole."

"Good God!"

"You've got to remember that on top of plenty of killings, he and his men took twenty-three unarmed Union soldiers . . . some wounded . . . off the train at Centralia and made them strip, then slaughtered them."

"I know, but. . . ."

"We'd better go," Sarah prompted. "I'll bring Raven up to the door and then fetch Lad." She picked up Dan's hat, holstered revolver, and brogans. "Best not leave anything to show a soldier was here." She hesitated. "I'd like to take the hounds. When Lige comes home, he'll be sad enough about Sam

826

and the others without these getting killed."

"Blue Boy's so slowed down by his leg, he can't catch anything," said Christy. "Chita and the others sort of do what he does. If Star worries about the 'coons or 'possums, we can tie the dogs up. Shouldn't be for long. In a week or so, the last of Price's rabble ought to be out of here."

Christy walked ahead with a candle lantern, Jonny settled on one hip. She had cried out with pity when she saw Raven, shoulder leaking foul-smelling pus, once glossy hide scruffy and dull. He lipped an apple from Dan's hand, though, and set out willingly although he shambled. "I wish we could tell him he can rest in the valley," Christy said. For some reason, she thought of her father reading from *Le Mort d' Arthur*. "And heal himself of his grievous wound. Like you, Danny."

"Sure." He reached to touch her hair, then leaned against Raven's mane as they entered the cavern. "Hester and Star will fix us up. But I think I'd get well just from being home with you."

Sarah was behind them with another lantern, bringing Lad, the sound of his hoofs muffled by the soft padding of the dogs.

When they finally reached the broad opening and blew out one candle, Dan slid down from the saddle and steadied himself with the its horn. "Ladies, I'm staying here till whoever fetches Lass comes back."

"But. . . ."

"Star and Hester can begin on me right here," he pointed out. "But I'm watching this passage till everybody's safe."

Christy looked at his revolver that he had belted on. "Don't shoot unless you have to. It could bring down the roof of the cavern."

"I'll go back for Lass," offered Sarah. "But first I'll lead Raven and Lad down."

"I'll take Jon to the women and tell them about Dan," said Christy. She kissed her husband's bearded jaw. "Then I'll come back and wait with you." She helped him settle against a boulder, picked Jonny up again, and turned at a strangled cry.

"Drat and dog-gone it!" gasped Sarah, looking up from where she'd fallen at the bottom of the rocks. Tears glistened in her eyes. "A hundred times I've been down this cliff, but today I have to twist my stupid ankle!" She tested it and grimaced. "I hope I haven't broken it."

"You'd better ride Raven to the house," Christy urged. She slipped the halter off Lad and gave him a slap on the rump before she helped Sarah mount.

"I can take the baby." Sarah reached for him. "You hurry and bring Lass back so we can get your husband to a proper bed."

The women and children had come out of the bark long house. Christy waved and scrambled back to the entrance. "You're soon going to have more help than you'll want," she teased Dan.

They kissed hungrily, with longing, thankfulness, and promise. She picked up the lantern and moved into the eternal night of the cave.

Christy blew out the candle, paused at the opening of the cavern as she always did, and scanned the cabin, outbuildings, harvested fields, and pastures across the creek. Wild geese called from a shimmering wedge high above. Flaming maples, sumac, and russet oaks blazed among cedars and pines. The great walnut by the cabin had lost its nesting summer birds but was a splendor of gold.

Birds and wild creatures had missed some clusters of grapes on the huge grapevine tangling up the white-limbed sycamore at the creek crossing. The papaws beside it looked ripe. Christy decided to take a basket of wild fruit to Dan. She wanted to look over the cabin, anyway, before shutting it up.

She entered the main cabin. Coming in out of the sun made it dark inside. It was a moment before she noticed the man sitting at the table, eating from a bowl. His back was to her. He wore a blue uniform, but many of Price's men did, either for disguise or because their own clothes were in rags. Heart tripping, Christy wondered if she could creep out unseen. Then the man turned, rising in the same instant, sweeping his hat off silver hair.

"Your Tom-fuller would be tastier with meat." Lafe Ballard smiled, showing small white teeth. "I was sure you'd not grudge some to an old neighbor."

"Were you with Price?"

"Till he burned the wagons on the other side of the Marmaton. I've no taste for being chased clear to Arkansas by the damned blue-bellies. Reckoned I'd come home and see if Ma can give me any money before I head West."

"I think she's gone to stay with relations."

"We don't have any." Lafe closed the space between them. He was between her, the poker, the ash shovel, or the iron skillet, anything she could use as a weapon. "Ma, I reckon, is somewhere in that cave you just came out of . . . or on the other side of it."

He'd seen her. Tongue dry as burned cotton in her mouth, Christy said: "We . . . we just store things there. . . ."

"I'll look for myself." He drew something from his pocket. "You see, my dear, I found this under your bed." He held out a yellow button and moved closer. "Since there were no cobwebs to show this has been there a long time, I take it to mean a Union soldier's been here. Recently." With his toe, he nudged a grimy pus-soaked bandage. "From this, also fallen under the bed, I surmise the bluebelly

830

was wounded." He set his hands on her shoulders. "My guess is your Irisher's dragged himself home and you've hidden him in that most interesting cave."

"He has a revolver," Christy warned.

"Bless you, so do I, two of them as you see. And I have two loaded cylinders, a little guerrilla trick. There's also a shotgun in my saddle scabbard . . . my horse is in your barn enjoying your corn . . . but I shouldn't need that."

His brand on her wrist felt seared anew. Her flesh prickled beneath his hands. It was like being toyed with by a giant cat. "Go away, Lafe! Don't grieve your mother more than you already have."

"I want to grieve her. I want to make her sorry she ever had me."

"What made you like you are? How can you be Hester's son?"

"I wonder that myself." He stepped back.

Chill eyes swept her from head to foot. The ice-burn spread from her wrist through her, paralyzed her mind. Somehow she had always known this time would come, just as she knew someday she must die.

Lafe's amused smile changed and his voice thickened. "I wonder why I've never got you out of me." Again he came closer, forcing her head back, and brutally took her mouth. Slow, numbing poison spread through her, but a detached part of her brain whispered: *Don't fight him now. Wait till he's off guard. . . .*

831

She almost fell as he pushed her away from him, mouth twisting.

"You're nursing that damned brat I felt kick in you last time!" He rubbed the fingers that had closed on her breast on his trousers to wipe off the milk. "I wish to hell I'd ridden him out of you!"

She started to drift toward the poker, but he caught her. "I'm not giving up on you. I'll leave you while I go tend to Dan . . . or could it be your brother, Thos? Whichever, when I bring you his head, it should hurt you so much that your pain'll overcome my disgust. If it doesn't. . . ." The pupils of his eyes spread over pallid irises. "Then I'll have to take my pleasure out of doing other things to you. I could start by cutting off your breasts. Seeing how milk looks mixed with blood."

She wrenched free, dodged, almost grasped the poker when his fist crashed into her jaw. Lightning exploded in her head.

Dazed as she regained consciousness, Christy tried to touch her aching jaw and found her hands were tied behind her. She remembered then, tried to sit up, and fell back. Her arms were bound to her sides by strips of sheet that went all the way around her. Her ankles were pinioned. Lafe hadn't bothered with a gag. There was no one to hear.

Thank God, Dan had his revolver. But Lafe was tricky. If Dan used up his six shots, he'd

832

have no chance to load again. If only she could come up behind Lafe with a butcher knife or poker. . . .

Frantically wriggling her ankles and wrists, she found no give in the knots. She swung her legs off the bed, thrusting her upper body erect. After several attempts, she managed to stand, but was too tightly bound to shuffle. In spite of the way her hands were fastened tightly behind her so that she couldn't use her elbows to crawl, perhaps she could snake across the floor to the fireplace and burn some of the knots enough to tear them apart.

She knelt and dropped on her side, rolled on her belly. Thrusting herself along by toes and hips was excruciatingly slow. She rolled. Much better! The door to the dogtrot was open. So was the one across it.

Ah! She'd forgotten about the axe beside the stacked wood. She'd rather get cut than burned. Leaning sideways against the blade, she frayed the sheet between her arm and side, worked back and forth till the cloth split.

Now she could get her wrists on either side of the blade and see-saw. Why hadn't she sharpened the axe when she noticed it was getting dull? This is taking so long!

The knots gave way. Her wrists were scraped and bruised, tingly from hampered blood flow. She was clumsy in using the axe to free her ankles, but at last she was free! Racing through the kitchen, she snatched up butcher knife and poker and ran for the cave.

Lafe had taken the lantern, but she'd been through the underground way so often that she thought she could avoid the drop-offs even without a light. How long had he been gone? How long had she been unconscious? Christy ran in smooth places, slowed where she had to sense her way around the river. She doubted she could catch up before he reached the entrance, but, if she could steal up on him, she'd kill him if she could — drag his body out and bury him so Hester would never know.

After what seemed forever she glimpsed the firefly glow of the lantern. Soon, beyond it, glowed the distant oval of blue, blue sky.

If she shouted now, surely Dan would hear her. It would warn him and startle Lafe. But it might also set off vibrations that would violate the silent world of the cave, bring stalactites or ceilings crashing down. Dan, in the entrance, should be safe, but as for herself and Lafe. . . .

She drew in her breath. "Dan!" she cried. "Lafe's here! La-a-afe!"

The lantern stopped, as if set down. There was no sound as she ran except the pound of her heart in her ears.

Then Hester's voice pealed, echoing through the passage, magnified by every formation. "I remember now, Lafe! *You* hanged Emil Franz. Go! Go away from here. . . ." Like one demented, she began to scream, shrieking like the voice of the long-suffering, outraged earth.

A groaning reverberated in the cave. Christy ran for her life. Bullets crashed. In front of her, to one side, Lafe ducked behind a boulder. He and Dan fired again in the same instant. Before Lafe could shoot again, the cave's muted protest broke into a thunder of plummeting rock.

It buried Lafe. A single cry broke off, echoed and reëchoed, before the rocks settled. Some pelted Christy as she raced for Dan, but nothing large hit her. From the passage behind came rumblings and sounds as if hundreds of windows were shattering. Then she was at Dan's side.

Blood trickled through his fingers as he gripped his shoulder. "It's not much," he assured Christy. "See to Hester."

Hester was trying to wrench the stones away that had buried her son. Christy helped her shoulder several to the side. When they saw Lafe's crushed head, there was little to be done till a horse could be brought to drag off the fallen chunks.

"Did my voice bring it down?" Hester sobbed.

"I'm sure my bullets caused it," Dan told her.

"When I yelled, I heard something begin." Christy tried to put her arms around Hester,

835

but the older woman knelt in silence a moment, and then got to her feet.

"I tried to pretend he wasn't mean when he was little and liked to torment things. I told myself he couldn't have anything to do with my second husband's getting killed. I made myself forget about Emil." Her eerily steady voice broke. "But he was still my little boy once. God forgive him."

"Amen," said Dan and Christy in one breath.

Before Dan let the women dress his shoulder, he kissed Christy long and hard. "As soon as you've plugged me up," he said, "let's go down to our son."

Allie and Sarah, with Lass hitched to a rope, helped Hester clear away enough rocks to free Lafe. It was possible for people on foot to thread their way through fallen rocks and stalactites to the other side of the cavern, so the women carried Lafe home and buried him under a tree he would have loved to play in when he was little.

Hester didn't speak of him after that, but Richie clearly became more than ever her son as he was in the days of his innocence, as well as the grandson she'd never have.

So successful was Star's and Hester's treatment that, in ten days, Dan could get around with a crutch of peeled apple wood. His gaunt face and body were filling out. The children's hero, he told funny stories and sang marching songs with the ribaldry toned down, but what everyone loved was for him to play his fiddle. He managed to do this for short spells in spite of his wounded shoulder.

After Jon's first wide-eyed alarm at this tall scratchy-faced man creature who claimed all too much of his mother's attention, the child decided it was nice to curl up in his father's arms and nap against the thump of his heart. He learned fathers can whistle and trot babies on their good knee. In short, he quickly turned into daddy's boy, except when he was hungry or very tired and cross. His jabberings, accidental or not, began to have a recurring "Da-Da" oftener than his first refrain of "Ma-Ma".

Christy was anxious about Lass. When she announced her intention of bringing the mare through the other passage — the one Hildy had used to enter the valley — Dan insisted on going with her. Sarah wanted to check her bees and Allie was anxious about her cabin and the tannery vats, so they all went.

"I hope there'll be something for Ethan and the boys to come home to," Allie said as they came out of the dark passage.

"There is," Dan said. He grinned at her questioning look. "Oh, Allie, Allie! There's you and Mary!"

"Ethan can use our oxen and horses to plow till you can get some more," Christy said. "And we can give you a cow, calves, and some chickens. Look at all the help you gave us when we settled here."

"And I'll give you some bee gums," Sarah promised.

Allie smiled through tears. "It's going to be good to really be neighbors again!" As soon as they crossed the creek, she started for her home through the splendor of autumn leaves.

Christy froze as the three of them neared the cabin, going slow to accommodate Dan's limp. "Look! Two strange horses in the pasture with Lass!"

Dan drew his revolver. The cabin door opened. A tall, thin man in butternut stood there. He lowered his shotgun.

"Christy!"

They ran to meet each other, brother and sister, but as they met in a laughing, weeping embrace, Charlie held her back and asked: "Where's Melissa? Where's Mother? How did Father die? I found his stone."

"And my folks?" Travis's eyes no longer danced. "We've been to Rose Haven."

First assuring them that Ellen Ware was safe when last heard from and that Melissa and Joely were well and in St. Louis, Christy explained all that had happened, faltering now and then.

"We couldn't imagine what had become of you," Charlie said after a hushed moment. "But the cabin wasn't burned or ransacked and Lass was in the pasture so we thought we'd rest and wait a few days. Figured you'd maybe gone to the Parkses during Price's retreat, but we were nervous about riding there, in case Union soldiers were around."

Travis slanted an oblique look at Dan who'd sat down to ease his leg. "Looks like one is."

"Not for long." Dan shrugged. "I'm mustering out as soon as I can travel to Leavenworth."

"Our war's over, too." Charlie gazed at things Christy couldn't see. "Pap Price furloughed lots of the Missouri boys. He knows we won't be catching up with him."

"No use starving out another winter south in Arkansas." Travis's tone was bitter. "There's still skirmishing in Indian Territory, but the fight's really over west of the Mississippi."

"The South is whipped," said Charlie. "Lee and his generals will fight to the last in Virginia and Georgia, but the Confederacy's out of weapons and supplies . . . everything but spirit."

"I'm out of that," said Travis flatly. "Taking up with the likes of Bloody Bill and Quantrill's more than I can stomach, let alone acting like damned jayhawkers."

He looked at Christy. How long ago it seemed since they had danced at Charlie's wedding! How long ago, a life ago, since he had stolen that kiss! "I'm glad you're well, Christy," he said, "and that your man's come home."

"I'm glad you're home, too, Travis."

He shook his head. "It's not home any more, and it'll be less that once the Union has its foot on our necks." He turned to his brother-in-law. "Charlie, do you want to head West with me, or are you of a mind to stay here? Seeing as how the rest of your family's Union, it should be easier for you."

Christy listened with her heart in her mouth. *Please stay, Charlie, please!* But remembering how Melissa had mourned Rose Haven and the life that could never be again, Christy wasn't surprised when her brother said: "That depends on what Melissa wants."

"Why don't one of you borrow my uniform and go see her?" suggested Dan. "Matter of fact, I've got an extra shirt, and they gave me the first overcoat I was ever issued there at the hospital. Ought to be enough clothes to let you both look like furloughed soldiers."

"I want to see Beth first," said Charlie. "Wish I could see Mother, but, if we do go West, I'll get back to see her . . . all of you."

"There's someone in the valley you need to meet, Travis." Christy told him about Lilah and his little daughter.

The startled look on his face turned to pleasure, then to dismay. "But I can't. . . ."

"Lilah's whiter than I am," Sarah adjured him. "You're lucky, Travis Jardine, to have such a sweet, brave, beautiful lady in love with you! And Noelle! Wait till you see her!"

Charlie nodded. "Melissa and Lilah grew up together. They'd be company for each other, if Melissa wants to move away . . . and I'm pretty sure she will. She's probably had enough of Yvonne's company to last the rest of her life."

"Come along," invited Sarah. "I'll take you to the valley."

Christy sat down beside Dan, watching the others out of sight. "It's going to be different," she sighed. "But I'm glad they're safe. Now if Thos and Mother were home. . . ."

"They will be, sweetheart. So will everyone, I'd bet, before another autumn." He took her in his arms. "I love the valley and everybody there," he murmured against her throat. "But you know, honey, it's good to be alone. Do you think maybe . . . ?"

"I think for sure." She kept her arm around him as they went, together, into the happy house.

EPILOGUE

1871

The meeting house at Trading Post was packed, so Dan stood at the back of the room with seven-year-old Jon and other younger men, including his brother-in-law, Thos. Ellen Ware held her dark-haired, four-year-old namesake, Ellen Bridget, while Christy lulled Thos David. Not quite a year old, he didn't appreciate so many strangers and being kept on his mother's lap, but he was tired and she hoped he'd soon go to sleep.

He'd have plenty of children to frolic with as he grew up. Lydia Parks McRae cradled her youngest, while her husband, a cavalry major she'd nursed back to life, proudly held their three-year-old. He sat, no shame to him, because, although he got around fairly well on his artificial leg and a cane, he couldn't stand for long periods. Harriet and Owen Parks had a two-year-old boy. They looked too young to be the parents of seventeen-year-old Letty, who just a week ago had married the much younger brother of Major McRae, come out from Indiana to assist his brother in his law practice.

Beth Ware was sixteen. How swiftly they grew up! She and Luke Hayes were courting. Matthew had died at Shiloh, but Ethan and Mark came home safely. Mark couldn't settle down and had gone West just like Charlie, Melissa, Travis, and Lilah, and many, many more. Mary Hayes was keeping company with a young blacksmith who had taken over the Franzes' old place. Caxtons and Madduxes had never returned. Lige and Sarah Morrow had moved to the valley, and there Star was helping them rear their three young children.

Daniel Owen Parks and his same-aged cousin, Andy McHugh, stood as quietly as eleven-year-olds could manage, near Owen and Andy's stepfather, Captain Aldridge. This handsome Ohioan, a former Army surgeon now in practice at Mound City, won Susie two years ago after a long, insistent courtship, and Catriona's death, which had perhaps freed Susie of any guilt for taking a new husband. In the full bloom of her early thirties, Susie was expecting the captain's child soon.

Hildy sat next to Hester with Lou, one of the twins born to her and Justus more than a year ago. Hester held Jonathan, who would be the second Jonathan Ware since Hildy and

Justus had asked if they might take Ware for a last name. Justus and several comrades from his regiment had formed a freighting company and were prospering.

Now and then, Hester glanced back to see that Richie, her golden boy, was behaving. He was, of course, under the strict but kindly eye of his adoptive father, Simeon Parks, who, to the approval of family and friends, had wedded Hester a few days before the war ended.

As old Hughie Huston rose to introduce Colonel James Montgomery, Christy's gaze roved over those she knew less well. Sam Nickel stood between the two sons left of the six who'd served with their father in the 6th Kansas. Near the front sat the Hall brothers, Austin and Amos, who'd survived the slaughter of Marais des Cygnes by feigning death. Beside Mrs. Nickel was Mrs. Harvey Smith, once Mrs. Colpetzer, who'd driven a wagon to aid the victims and found her own husband dead. Including Dan and Owen, there must be, at this meeting, a score of those who had ridden with Montgomery after the murderers.

Thank God, those days were done, although Christy wished Jennison had not fared so well from his plundering. He owned an opulent saloon in Leavenworth, and his showplace stock farm, a few miles south of there, boasted the best of cattle, swine, and horses.

As one newspaper said: For some five or six years the Colonel enjoyed unusual facilities for selecting fast horses from numerous stables. He had just been elected to the Kansas State Senate. As for James Lane, depressed and in poor health, the senator killed himself the year after the war ended.

Quantrill got his death wound in one of the last skirmishes of the Civil War, out in Kentucky, and died in a military hospital. Jesse James, Frank James, and their cousins, the Youngers, who had ridden with Quantrill, turned to robbery.

The Burned District was green again with grain, orchards, and pastures. Some blackened chimneys stood like huge gravestones, but many new cabins rose on old foundations. The wounds of the border war might be like Dan's leg, still draining, although he did a man's full work, but Beth's generation was growing up. To her children, the war would seem long ago.

"Let us rise." The war had broken Colonel Montgomery's health. His beard and hair were gray, but his eyes were piercing as ever. "We will sing 'The Battle Hymn of the Republic'."

The room reverberated with Howe's words, but in Christy's mind ran the original song: "John Brown's body lies a-moldering in the grave." When the congregation was seated, Montgomery read the text. Be not deceived.

God is not mocked; for whatsoever a man soweth, that shall he also reap.

He preached that communities and nations are as subject to the laws of God as are individuals. Even small children were held by his voice. No one nodded during that sermon.

At last he paused to search the faces of his neighbors and those who had ridden with him to quell the Border Ruffians. "I call on my old friends to remember what I said at a sorrowful meeting almost fourteen years ago. I prophesied that the remaining years of slavery could be numbered upon the fingers of one hand, and that during that time I would lead a host of Negro soldiers, dressed in the national uniform, in the redemption of our country and the Negro race from the curse of slavery.

"Brothers and sisters, I believe that with us tonight are the spirits of those who died for our country . . . your fathers, brothers, sons, sweethearts, and husbands. They fought a good fight. They finished their course. In our hearts, they can never die.

"Let us give thanks for them, for their courage and devotion. Let us give thanks we had them as long as we did, and let us rededicate ourselves to ever waging their war for freedom."

He held out his arms. That smile of great sweetness touched his mouth. "Dearly beloved, let us pray."

■ ■ ■ ■

When the O'Briens and Wares got home that night, Dan got out his fiddle and played his song, the seasons of his life from Irish lullabies through war, hate, and love. And then, with Jonny leaning against his knee and Christy's eyes on him, he played the seasons of peace.

AUTHOR'S NOTE

Rural settlers in western Missouri, Arkansas, eastern Kansas and Indian Territory lived much as their colonial grandparents had. It was only after the war that harvesting machines, threshers, binders, and the like came into wide use. Women often sheared their sheep and carded, spun, and wove not only wool but flax and cotton, into clothing, towels, and bedding. Soldiers on both sides were overwhelmingly from farms. Those who used fence rails for campfires had split plenty of them and knew the labor involved. When they turned their horses into a cornfield, they knew how the owners had worked to raise it. When they heaped curtains, clothing, and coverlets on a bed and set them afire, they knew from having watched their mothers and sisters how much patient work they destroyed.

Next to Virginia, Missouri had the highest number of Civil War engagements, though most of these were skirmishes. Indians fought on both sides and black soldiers served for the first time in Missouri. Throughout most of the war, Union troops controlled St. Louis and sizeable towns but the countryside was ravaged by regular and irregular forces of both persuasions. I spent my teen years in Missouri ten miles from the battleground of Pea Ridge. My grandfather told me stories his grandfather had told about Quantrill and the war. Like many Missouri families, we had members fighting on both sides. Thus the war was an early part of my consciousness but I hadn't thought of. writing from both sides of that long, cruel struggle between neighbors till I read *Inside War: The Guerrilla Conflict in Missouri During The American Civil War* by Michael Fellman (Oxford University Press, New York, 1989). Fellman brilliantly shows in incident after incident how the world turned upside down, the outrages on both sides, and the twisted honor that boasted of not harming women though sons, brothers, and husbands were slaughtered in their arms.

It was only when I read the true story of a slave woman who loved her white nurseling too much to abandon him when a band of liberators killed his parents and tried to persuade her to go with them that it struck me that such love was the underground river that flowed beneath the killing grounds and burned fields, that love, with hope, faith, and gratitude for the beauty and rhythms of the natural world are the only answer to chaos, destruction, and hatred. There was really one house along the border that was spared because the mistress nursed the wounded of both sides. There really was a soldier who ran to the man he'd mortally wounded, promised to stay and pray with him till he died, and was himself killed.

It is a kind of magic that lets us bring back vanished creatures of a vanished time, and show vast flocks of passenger pigeons darkening the sun for hours, settling in a great cloud to feed on autumn mast or capture the emerald glint of Carolina parakeets gorging on roasting ears after a family has battled weeds out of the corn for months. Who, in 1860, could believe these birds would utterly vanish?

Leland Sonnichsen wrote: "Truth is the sum of many facts. Truth is the forest, and facts are the trees which keep us from seeing it." Still, he would be the first to urge us to have the right trees in our forest — and the right birds in the trees at the right time of year.

Ferocity increased as North and South declared war, and the Indians south of Kansas in Indian Territory were drawn into the struggle, fighting on both sides. The Indian rôle in the war is depicted in Annie Heloise Abel's *The American Indian as Slaveholder and Secessionist; Between Two Fires* by

Laurence M. Hauptman; *Stand Watie* by Kenny A. Franks; and *The Civil War in the Indian Territory* by Donald A. Rampp and Lary C. Rampp. Chronicles of the border war that I used most were William E. Connolly's classic, *Quantrill and the Border Wars;* Carolyn M. Bartels's *The Civil War in Missouri Day by Day 1861–1865* and *Civil War Stories of Missouri;* Joanne Chiles Eakin's *The Little Gods: Union Provost Marshals in Missouri 1861–1865,* and *Order Number 11;* and Thomas Goodrich's *Black Flag. Gray Ghosts of the Confederacy* by Richard S. Brownlee has a list of all known members of Quantrill's, as well as other, guerrillas with notations of their fate. Very few survived the war. *Bushwhackers of the Border* by Patrick Brophy presents a strongly pro-Southern view and has a map showing the dividing line between prairies and the woodlands that created such a haven for guerrillas. *Three Years With Quantrill as told by John McCorkle to O.S. Barton* gives the guerrilla side of things from the standpoint of a man whose sister was killed in the collapse of the women's prison in Kansas City. *General Sterling Price and the Civil War in the West* by Albert Castel shows Price as a kindly, honorable man who valued Missouri above the Confederacy, but who, through vanity or ineptitude, bungled several good chances to expel Union forces from Missouri. The account of Wilson's Creek is mostly gleaned from *Bloody Hill* by William Riley Brooksher.

I found much of value in Henry Steele Commager's monumental *The Blue and the Gray,* which covers every angle of the war from the writings of participants. Other excellent sources were *Soldiers Blue and Gray* by James L. Robertson, Jr.; *Army Life in a Black Regiment* by Thomas Wentworth Higginson; and Bell Irvin Wiley's wonderfully readable *The Life of Billy Yank* and *The Life of Johnny Reb.* These reveal the life of the common soldier. An engaging and detailed memoir of the Union Army is *Hardtack and Coffee or the Unwritten Story of Army Life* by John D. Billings. *Doctors in Gray* by H.H. Cunningham shows some of the terrible difficulties of caring for the wounded or sick. Excellent information on uniforms and equipment are in these volumes of the Osprey Men-at-Arms series: *American Civil War Armies, Union; American Civil War Armies, Confederate;* and *American Civil War Armies, Volunteer Militia,* all written by Philip Katcher and illustrated by Ron Volstad.

An excellent overview of the border troubles is in *The Civil War in the American West* by Alvin M. Josephy, Jr. Jay Monaghan's *Civil War on the Western Border 1854–1865* is lively reading that captures the human essence of the conflict, although events are sometimes telescoped as is inevitable in a work covering so many complicated situations.

Soldiers have always sung, and the war had spirited tunes on both sides. I listened often, with great enjoyment, to Bobby Horton sing *Homespun Songs of the Confederacy, Volumes 1 through 6* and *Homespun Songs of the Union Army, Volumes 1 through 4.* From the humorous "Goober Peas" to the cantering lilt of "Riding a Raid", the fervor of "Maryland, My Maryland" or "The Battle Hymn of the Republic" to the melancholy "Lorena", these evoke the dreams, fears, courage, and laughter of those young men.

Thomas Goodrich's *Bloody Dawn* is a graphic account of the Lawrence massacre. *Early Days of Fort Scott* by C.W. Goodlander is an eyewitness account of the fort, the town, and that strategic corner of Kansas from 1858 to 1870. It was fascinating to visit the fort, and it was in the cannon exhibit that I finally could understand how they were loaded and fired. *The Chronicles of Kansas,* bound volumes of the publications of the Kansas Historical Society, have yielded much enriching material, especially memoirs of the Civil War and pioneer life.

On a misty day of fresh green April, we sought out Marais des Cygnes Kansas State Historical Site. Although it was closed, Curator Brad Wohllhof kindly came up to let us in the small cabin and explain the exhibits that memorialize the murders in that peaceful copse. The fascinating Trading Post Museum was only a few miles away and there Curator Alice Widner explained many of the rare artifacts, photos, and records donated to the museum by the families of some of the people in this book.

At the Linn County Historical Museum at Pleasonton, Oklahoma, May Earnest, curator, answered many questions and pointed out things of special interest. The Baxter Springs Museum in Baxter Springs, also in Kansas, has spirited murals, period rooms, weapons, clothing, and household furnishings of the Civil War times. It is good to find local history preserved in these museums, often staffed by volunteers. I thank them for their graciousness and help in bringing life to the pages of this trilogy.

Special thanks to my cousin Francis Billings and her husband Albert, who has immersed himself in the Civil War. They live in historic Warrensburg and took me to Lexington where we explored that famous battlefield. Al also hunted up elusive details on weapons. He and Fran did Fort Scott, Pea Ridge, and parts of the Old Military Road with me and have been interested in this story since the idea first entered my mind.

My friend, June Wylie of Austin, valiantly undertook driving us through Kansas, Missouri, and Arkansas, tracking down places I needed to see. I am grateful for her help, exemplary patience and humor. Thanks to the great spirit of my old friend Fred Grove, himself part Osage and Sioux, who generously shared his knowledge of bushwhackers' tactics.

I've altered timing in a few places for fictional purposes. Charles Jennison didn't move to the Mound City area till after the Marais des Cygnes massacre. Bill Anderson didn't become a guerrilla till after his father was killed by a Union man in June of 1862. He is known to have ridden with Quantrill that September on the Olathe, Kansas raid, but he wouldn't have been one of the band that killed Jonathan. However, the final scene in December, 1871, happened essentially as related. James Montgomery preached to a congregation including survivors of Marais des Cygnes, and reminded them that he had foretold the end of slavery. A few days later, he was dead, but in the words of the hymn he requested at that last service, his eyes had "seen the glory of the coming of the Lord."

Jeanne Williams
The Chiricahua Mountains
August 2012

ABOUT THE AUTHOR

Jeanne Williams was borne in Elkhart, Kansas, a small town along the Santa Fe Trail. In 1952 she enrolled at the University of Oklahoma where she majored in history and attended Foster-Harris's writing classes. Her writing career began as a contributor to pulp magazines in which she eventually published more than seventy Western, fantasy, and women's stories. Over the same period, she produced thirteen novels set in the West for the young adult audience, including *The Horsetalker* (1961) and *Freedom Trail* (1973), both of which won the Spur Award from the Western Writers of America. Her first Western historical romance, *A Lady bought with Rifles* (1976), was published in 1976 and sold six hundred thousand copies in mass merchandise paperback editions. Her historical novels display a wide variety of settings and solidly researched historical backgrounds such as the proslavery forces in Kansas in *Daughter of the Sword* (1979), or the history of Arizona from the 1840s through contemporary times in her Arizona trilogy — *The Valiant Women* (1980), which won a Spur Award, *Harvest of Fury* (1981), and *The Mating of Hawks* (1982). Her heroines are various: a traveling seamstress in *Lady of No Man's Land* (1988), a schoolteacher in *No Roof but Heaven* (1990), a young girl heading up a family of four orphans in *Home Mountain* (1990) which won the Spur Award for Best Novel of the West for that year. She was also the recipient of the Levi Straus Saddleman Award. The authentic historical level of her writing distinguishes her among her peers, and her works have set standards for those who follow in her path.

The employees of Thorndike Press hope you have enjoyed this Large Print book. All our Thorndike, Wheeler, and Kennebec Large Print titles are designed for easy reading, and all our books are made to last. Other Thorndike Press Large Print books are available at your library, through selected bookstores, or directly from us.

For information about titles, please call:

(800) 223-1244

or visit our Web site at:

http://gale.cengage.com/thorndike

To share your comments, please write:

Publisher
Thorndike Press
10 Water St., Suite 310
Waterville, ME 04901

CPSIA information can be obtained
at www.ICGtesting.com
Printed in the USA
FFOW031445230113